D1439905

DEMON WORLD

Transcendence

Balvir Bhullar

1st Edition, 2021

Book Design by Michael Maloney

ISBN 978-1-913479-83-1 (print)
ISBN 978-1-913479-84-8 (ebook)

Published by That Guy's House
www.ThatGuysHouse.com

ACKNOWLEDGEMENTS

I would like to thank my mother for always believing in me and encouraging me to pursue my dreams.

I would like to thank my brother, Inderjit, for helping me to become a stronger person, and to understand the world in a unique light.

I would like to thank my youngest brother, Suki, for giving me the tools to create my story, and also for patiently listening while I recounted my story to him every day!

I would like to thank my sister, Meena, for her continual support and encouragement. Thank you for helping me to edit my book, I learnt so much from the process. Thank you for your much needed wise counsel, without which I would probably be lost right now.

I want to thank Seán, for taking a chance on me, helping me to pursue my dreams and see them become real. Thank you for your kindness and patience, it has meant so much to me.

Thank you to all those at That Guy's House, who have worked hard to bring the vision of my book to life. I appreciate all of the work that has gone into producing it.

I want to thank the Universe for teaching me wisdom through patience and for showing me how beautiful life can be...

Thank you to my Angels and Demons.

"Dum spiro, spero"

-Marcus Tullius Cicero

CHAPTER 1

As the cold moon rose, its rays briefly illuminated a neo-gothic building, comprised of spires and steepled roofs: an architect's gothic vision. The former government building had shut down for the day, and all the windows were dark except for one, lit with the last remaining soul...

Rowanne put her long, dark hair into a chignon, not bothering to secure it in place as she worked late in the office, finishing off her day's work.

The stars were hidden in the bitterly cold Autumn night as the winds picked up and dark clouds covered the moon. The lightning storm converged above the heart of the city, swollen with fury, unleashing nature's most brilliant light show in flashes of blue and violet.

From one of the towers outside of the office, a man stepped out of the shadows, having concealed himself there for the past half hour. His patience would now be rewarded, and with no more thought he stepped off the edge. He fell like a dark, avenging angel as his long coat flowed out behind him, spread like two black wings. A rush of wind accompanied his descent and, landing easily, he slowly straightened up whilst keeping a firm eye on the two men before him.

A streetlight partially revealed his fierce, sapphire eyes, as his black-gloved hands slowly unsheathed his sword from the scabbard on his back. He brought the sword around, gripping it in both hands. The streetlight briefly glinted off the cold metal revealing cold grey eyes in place of sapphire as his body prepared itself for the anticipated fight.

Alexander waited a heartbeat before rushing towards the men. His sword clashed with theirs as he parried two swords at once, easily deflecting their strikes.

Alexander recognised these two men as Shadows. These demonic creatures were virtually impossible to kill in their shadow form; he needed them to solidify in order to cause them any harm.

The Shadow men stepped back from the melee and began to circle Alexander, trying to divide his attention.

Alexander was in no way daunted by this tactic; on the contrary, some may say he had eyes in the back of his head. The slight displacement of air behind his back let him know exactly where the Shadow men were and he intuitively turned, raised his sword, and again deflected the oncoming attack from the first Shadow man. He immediately followed through with a counter-attack of his own, slashing down the centre of the body of this Shadow man in the blink of an eye. He turned his attention to the remaining demon who stood dumbfounded.

After all, what had they expected? Alexander was here to do his job in the most efficient way possible; he had no intention of wasting his time with these demons.

The remaining Shadow man trembled with fear and rage as he helplessly watched his partner disintegrate into ashes, drifting into the night. After seeing his fate reflected in the cold, merciless eyes of the man before him, the Shadow man made a hasty retreat down the road.

Alexander wiped the red, smoky residue from his blade, leftover from the first dead Shadow man, until it was once again gleaming. With a quick flick of his wrist he sheathed his sword back into the scabbard resting between his shoulder blades. After all, the last thing he needed was to draw attention from the humans. Turning his back, he walked down the road, hell bent on finishing the job.

Rowanne put on her soft, black winter coat, and adjusted her bag so that it sat comfortably on her hip. She took one last look around, making sure that everything was in order before she left. Usually her editor would have been the last to leave, but Eileen had a meeting outside of London and had left early with a few of her colleagues, leaving Rowanne behind to meet her deadline. She switched off the last light, plunging the office into darkness.

She decided to forgo the lift, and practically flew down the curved staircase, descending it in record time. She opened the main doors and stepped out.

Alexander was slightly further down the road having followed the trail of the remaining Shadow man. Sensing something, he paused, turned back and noticed the lights go out from the building he had just left the shelter of. *Damn it*, he thought, and decided to do one last check to make sure there were no more demons lurking around; gut instinct was also urging him back and though he could not ignore it, he just hoped he would not live to regret it. Retracing his steps back down the road, he was in for a nasty surprise.

Rowanne had taken a couple of steps outside before she started to button her coat. The rain had lightened up by this time. *I should still have brought an umbrella*, she thought, grimacing as she got wet.

Her amethyst pendant glinted beneath the street light, attracting the attention of further Shadows who had just portalled in close by. They felt an irresistible pull towards the human, and swiftly took on the form of men before cautiously stalking their prey.

Rowanne instinctively felt uncomfortable, as if she were not alone. Though she was not the type to spook easily and was normally quite comfortable in the dark. Having left work late on numerous occasions, she had never encountered any problems before.

She noticed two men approaching from the rear of the building, but was not unduly worried as she made her way towards the car park. However, the unmistakable sound of running behind her was all the encouragement she needed before deciding to instinctively break into a run herself.

She sprinted towards the giant fountain situated just before the car park in order to hide. Her heart beat fast, and she had a sick feeling in the pit of her stomach. As she turned to glimpse at what was happening from behind, she saw the men continuing to run towards her. *What do they want?* she thought. *What will they do once they're caught up with me...*

The Shadow men increased their speed, not wanting to let the woman out of their sight.

Years of cross country running now came in handy as Rowanne too, sped up. As she neared the fountain, only a couple of yards away now, something whooshed past her. *What the hell was that?* After a careful look, she finally noticed that the objects flying close by her face were in fact weapons of some kind. God only knew how she managed to dodge them, and bizarrely they vanished as soon as they had passed her by.

The street lights glinted off the weapons, and she saw that they were long and tipped at either end by metal spikes. Though the rain had become heavier, it in no way slowed these spears down as they gracefully glided by, cutting out a path for themselves. *That's just great,* thought Rowanne, irked.

Her adrenaline kicked in, keeping her tired legs going. She had no idea who was following her, let alone why. Never in her wildest dreams did she expect to be attacked by spears of all things. This situation did not make any sense to her. *Maybe it's some kind of mix up*, she thought.

Alexander's intuition proved accurate as he spotted more demons. He ran towards them in the hope of catching them before they could transform into people, but he was too late, they were already in pursuit of a human. He picked up his speed as he pursued them, and, getting closer, he withdrew his sword.

Rowanne turned around to face the men. Even with the street lights illuminating the area, she still could not make out any of their features. The car park had always been poorly lit, and no amount of complaining had resolved the issue; there was always some excuse as to why it could not be done.

The rain poured down soaking her to the bone. The occasional flashes of light revealed something that her mind could not, or more likely would not, fathom.

As the men approached, Rowanne was paralyzed with fear. Only the lightning helped to briefly illuminate her otherwise dim surroundings. Her heart was in her mouth, and suddenly the whole area plunged into darkness as the street lights chose to give out that very moment. *Seriously?* thought Rowanne. She did not need this as well, her situation was already dire.

Each pause of darkness and flash of light brought them ever closer until she was face to face with them.

Rowanne noticed that the men appeared to be completely made of smoke, and had to stifle a scream as she finally noticed their faces. They had hollow sockets for where their eyes should have been, and a slit for a gross imitation of a mouth. They appeared to be smiling at her as their mouths curved up simultaneously, moving in a parody of a laugh, though no sound came out.

The Shadow men looked at each other; an unspoken message passed between them, and they unanimously took a step towards her.

Rowanne retreated until she felt the rim of the fountain at her back, hindering her progress. Unable to think about what her next move should be, she faced the inevitable.

Suddenly the sound of approaching footsteps caught her notice, and even the men before her became disturbed by this new addition.

A man ran flat out towards her, and, grabbing her, pushed her roughly behind himself.

'Hey? What do you think you're doing?' Rowanne snapped, affronted with the rudeness of the stranger, her paralysis finally broken.

The man clearly saw no reason to reply to this inane comment, as his sole focus was on the two Shadow men before him.

As soon as the words had come out of her mouth, Rowanne regretted them, knowing how ungrateful she must have sounded. But she could not help it, she was not the type of person to ask for help. *This man is clearly trying to protect me, and at immense risk to himself,* she thought.

The Shadow men looked at the man, the human momentarily forgotten. He was one of their own kind. They knew who he was; he had made quite the name for himself in their world. Here was an opponent to both respect and fear. Still, if one of them could kill this vile man, they thought, so much the better.

The Shadow men worked together, all of their movements perfectly synced. They snaked their spears in a figure of eight above their heads, and a whistling sound could be heard as they cut through the air with deadly precision, before finally angling their spears towards him in invitation.

Alexander's attention was divided between the demons in front of him, and the human behind his back. *I suppose this is what they call being stuck between a rock and a hard place,* he thought disgustedly. *How many more of these demons will I encounter tonight?* he wondered.

He assumed the Fool's guard stance, and as they attacked, he blocked and retaliated. Their spears gave them the advantage of a longer reach, making them a formidable weapon to use against a sword. Was he worried by their advantage? Hell no. It just made it more interesting. He liked a challenge after all.

The Shadow men separated and approached him from either side, hoping to divide his attention. They angled their spears and simultaneously thrust them towards Alexander's head with the intention of blinding him.

However, Alexander anticipated their attack, and dropped to the ground elegantly, taking the human with him. The Shadow men vanished into smoke to dodge their own attack, and stepped back.

The woman gasped as she was knocked towards the ground, but a moment before hitting the cold, damp floor, Alexander caught her. She looked up into Alexander's grey-blue eyes whilst his body protectively leaned over hers like a human shield.

Alexander silently laughed at the stupidity of these creatures. *They actually think they have a chance to beat me?!* he thought, as he glowered at them for having the audacity to approach him. He jumped up, lifted the human, threw her behind him, and stepped out of reach, moving to the side of the fountain.

'Hold on,' whispered Alexander.

'Pardon?' said the human, barely a second before he grabbed her hand and turned to her, spinning her around so that her back leant against his chest. He held her close with his arms enclosing her shoulders as he pulled them into a vortex.

Rowanne saw what appeared to be a glowing sphere in the darkness through which they passed. She turned awkwardly around, not liking the feeling of being out of control, and ended up facing her saviour, as time seemed to slow right down. Out of necessity she held onto him for stability as they began to spin in a circle. She closed her eyes, feeling extremely uncomfortable and nauseated, like she was on a rollercoaster about to plunge over the highest point.

They reappeared behind the Shadow men. *What the hell was that?* wondered Rowanne, disorientated, as she tried to get her equilibrium back.

'Hell's right, my lady,' the man replied coldly, and missed her bewildered expression behind him.

Alexander stepped back and deflected the oncoming attacks. He used his speed to get closer into range than the demons would have expected, and to their surprise, parried both spears at once. Unfortunately his attempted counter-attack met air as the demons again vanished into smoke. His eyes sparkled with a grey light as he eagerly awaited their next move.

The Shadow men simultaneously appeared on either side of the fountain. The one closest to Alexander rushed towards him, intending to cut out his arrogant heart, whereas the other demon preferred a smarter tactic: one that would keep him safe, yet hurt his enemy. This demon pulled back his arm and, after judging the distance, hurled the spear towards Alexander's back.

Rowanne could see this all unfold in slow motion. The man defending her had his attention focused on only one of the men. *By the time he notices, it'll be too late.* Running on pure adrenaline, Rowanne threw herself in the path of the oncoming spear, with no thought of the risk to herself.

8

Alexander smiled arrogantly, caught up in the violence of the moment. He had anticipated their pathetic plan, and as the Shadow man came at him with a spear, he used his supernatural speed to whittle it down to size before repeatedly striking the Shadow man in a series of short sharp attacks which found their mark. The blade briefly glowed red with the smoky residue from the demon as he disintegrated.

The spear flew true from the demon behind Alexander, having been hurled with great force. Unfortunately for the demon, he had not anticipated an intervention, and raged silently as it pierced the human. The demon immediately vanished, giving up the battle for now.

Rowanne gasped as the silver spear head protruded from her chest. Her eyes closing, she succumbed to oblivion as she fell into the bitterly cold water of the fountain.

Alexander froze, as the sound reached him. He slowly turned around to face the disaster the demon had left behind. His eyes locked onto the prone figure of the human in the deep fountain, her hair fanned out, like a halo around a martyr.

The rain continued to lash down, sounding like a thousand needles striking the fountain. A flash of lightning illuminated the fountain's centrepiece, revealing an angel attacking a demon. The angel wept at the loss of life. The irony of this was not lost on Alexander as he turned his attention towards the human.

He reluctantly climbed into the fountain and slowly waded through the water. He scooped the woman up into his arms, and checked for a pulse, even as her pale lips spoke of death. He snapped the protruding spear in half, and carried her lifeless body back towards what he knew to be her office building, having earlier gleaned the information from her mind. Her arms dangled by her side as the wind whipped her hair. Her beautiful amethyst pendant dangled like a dead weight around her neck, but strangely began to vanish, unnoticed by Alexander.

Alexander climbed the stairs to the human's office, supporting her weight. He commanded the double doors to open before him. As he walked through, he gently lay her down on a couch near one of the desks, and her left arm fell lifelessly to the side. He pushed her wet hair away from her face, and took a good look at the woman before him. He took off her coat, gently peeling it back from her arms whilst supporting her head, and discarded it onto the floor. He opened a cupboard beside the couch and found a blanket which he covered her with gently.

Alexander took her wrist and checked again for a pulse; he knew it was stupid, but it categorically confirmed what he already knew... *I was too late to save her because of my rage and arrogance,* he thought bitterly. *I am solely to blame for her death.*

To make matters worse, he noticed her photo on the desk near him. It showed her smiling with a look of determination in her eyes; here was a woman who could have done anything, even conquered the world. In a fit of helpless rage, the glass shattered from the force with which he slammed the frame down.

Alexander was quiet for a moment with his head down and eyes closed, kneeling by her; the very image of an angel seeking absolution. He breathed deeply as he contemplated the situation. He came to a decision he never thought he would have to make, or would make under any condition.

His earlier words came back to haunt him; he was most definitely going to regret this. Whether he would *live* to regret it was a point of contention.

His eyes turned green as he drew upon his power, took on his demonic form. He knew that, were any human to look upon him, they would in all likelihood run a mile.

He rolled up his left sleeve and retrieved a pure silver knife from his coat pocket. The blade was inscribed with an ancient language which no human could decipher, or so he thought... Though occasionally, it had leaked into this world with devastating consequences, spoken by those possessed, but unable to understand what they were saying. He shuddered at the memories, briefly feeling pity for the mortals of this world.

Alexander drew the tip of the blade, smooth on one side and serrated on the other, across his palm. Gently taking the woman's right hand, he made a similar cut on her right palm, before joining their hands together. He spoke in an ancient language, whilst slowly withdrawing the spear from her chest.

He covered her heart with his left hand as he again drew upon his power. After an hour or so of deep concentration, it was done. He removed all traces of blood, restored the woman's clothes to their original state, and modified her memories. *Trust me, my lady. It's in your best interest... or our interests.* His eyes returned back to their natural sapphire, and colour slowly returned to his drained face.

He bent down, and gently brushed her forehead with a kiss; as he looked at her, there was a bleakness to his eyes. Alexander knew that many things had changed on this fateful night, and that he would have to answer for the unbreakable oath shattered by his morality.

The storm outside grew in intensity as lightning lashed the city. Two realms bellowed their horror at what had occurred, and as the winds picked up, a loud unearthly scream tore through the night.

Alexander ignored the turmoil outside. He had turned his back on everything that he had ever known. *My life is no longer my own, it does not solely belong to me,* he thought caustically. A soul was precious in any world and he had put his in jeopardy. He glared at the woman who had taken his life, and slowly bent down until he was level with her face.

Rowanne's body restarted with a slow heartbeat, as blood began to pump around. A reflex action suddenly caused her eyes to open, staring directly into his. Her mind awakened briefly and she felt his strong arms supporting her, as he whispered in her ear.

Only the end was partially audible to her, as Alexander whispered, 'The veil between our worlds lies asunder. Bound we are by the blood of genesis, and before the Trinity in blood I make the ultimate sacrifice...' He lay her gently back down on the couch and turned away from her to leave.

At midnight, Rowanne's body underwent a metamorphosis. Black and white lights started to emanate from the cut in her palm. It moved in two separate directions, completely enveloping her whole body so that it was cocooned: one half in white light, and mirrored on the opposite side by its dark counterpart. A circular tattoo appeared on her left shoulder, near her heart. It was comprised of two angels (one light and the other dark) embracing each other, and between them lay a sphere containing a triskelion.

A supernatural wind blew back Rowanne's hair as she was briefly cocooned in a second layer of radiant light. Slowly the lights receded from around her body, drawn towards her heart until they resided within. The tattoo began to fade, and with each passing moment she appeared more alive as her body healed itself throughout the night.

CHAPTER 2

Rowanne began to stir awake, feeling completely rested after a deep sleep. A dream lingered on the edges of her subconscious, intangible and just out of reach. She stretched her arms and inadvertently caused the green lamp on her desk to shatter as it hit the floor.

She watched as the shards flew in different directions, and for one ephemeral moment they glimmered like emeralds caught in a beam of sunlight. In that instant, a memory of green eyes and strong arms flared to the surface of her mind, but this too was fleeting, and it was ruthlessly buried, never to be unearthed again.

I must have stayed up late last night, thought Rowanne, rubbing her eyes with her forefingers. *I definitely have to stop this overtime, otherwise I'll be heading for a burnout.* She recalled the numerous late nights she had spent at the office since starting this job three years ago. Looking back, she realised disconsolately that she had spent more time at work than at home, or anywhere else for that matter.

She was hit by a wave of dizziness as she got up from the couch too quickly. 'Whoa.' *What the hell happened last night...* she wondered. She sat back down and closed her eyes as she waited for the sickening sensation to pass.

After a couple of moments, Rowanne knelt on the floor and began to clear away the pieces of glass. As she got up, she accidently bumped into the table beside her, and as she tried to restore her balance, her hand closed on a small shard left behind.

'Great. That's just what I needed!' she winced, looking down at her bleeding palm.

She went to the toilet to clean her hand and after inspecting it for glass, rummaged around in her bag until she finally found a plaster. Ripping it open with her teeth, she applied it to her palm.

By the time that Rowanne was ready to leave, sunlight dappled through the trees outside and played across the furniture, signalling the start of a new day. As she walked along the corridor, it occurred to her that she had not seen anybody else in this part of the building this morning, and maybe even since the evening before.

Surely Thomas would have come in last night to check in with me, and then report to the head of security, she thought. In all the time that she had worked at the newspaper, she could not recall a time when Thomas had not checked in, as security at her building was of paramount importance.

It was Thomas's job to check the offices: making sure that they were empty or verifying anybody that was working late. After carrying out the relevant checks, he would have locked up the department, before finally ascertaining that this part of the building was secure. Rowanne assumed there must be a simple explanation for his absence. Shaking her head, she left her office and went down the stairs.

She pushed open the doors to a beautiful crisp autumn day, the sky blue with just a hint of pink above the horizon.

She quickly made her way over to one of her most prized possessions: her 1955 black Pegaso. Reversing her car out of the car park, she headed home.

Her apartment was less than half an hour away. In no time at all, she pulled up outside of a tall building just as the sun reflected harshly off the imposing glass structure. These skyscrapers were the latest addition to London, with people investing considerable amounts of money to be located in the heart of the capital with magnificent views of the famous skyline.

Rowanne had only lived here a couple of years, having bought her apartment through hard work and many late nights. As a result, she was one of a select few who were the big earners, and thus was able to afford a few luxuries.

She drove down into the car park underground, and eventually parked in her reserved spot adjacent to the lift.

The lift doors shut behind her and she pressed the button for the top floor. She watched as the car park disappeared below through the glass floor of the lift as it steadily climbed up. *The architect who designed it had a wicked sense of humour*, she thought; essentially it was a glass box.

Rowanne could see Westminster Bridge and the London Eye in the distance. She would sometimes walk down to the bridge, and spend time looking out across the River Thames; it was a peaceful way to pass the time.

The lift reached the 51st floor and the doors opened to reveal the door to Rowanne's apartment directly opposite. As she rummaged around in her bag looking for her keys, she hissed as she cut her palm a second time.

She opened the door with her left hand, and, dumping her belongings on the floor, she quickly made her way to the bathroom. Her right hand stung as she ripped off the plaster, and fresh blood rose to the surface. She again cleaned her hand and applied a fresh plaster.

She took a paracetamol for the headache that had gradually developed, and seemed to get worse when she had cut her hand a second time, called in sick to work, and headed straight to bed.

She had a peaceful, dreamless sleep and awoke around two in the afternoon. Mercifully the pain in her head had abated. She was amazed to have been asleep for so long and put this down to all those long nights she had spent at the office working towards deadlines. *I have to stop pushing myself too far,* she thought. But deep down, she knew that this was the reason for her promotion to the inner circle. For the past few years, she had worked so hard to have recognition for her dedication to the newspaper. Being at the top required a lot of sacrifice and Rowanne fully intended to stay there, no matter what.

Feeling hungry, she made herself a sandwich having not eaten anything since the night before. She ate in front of the TV and watched the usual uninteresting, mid-afternoon shows. In between switching channels, she came across the news and one story in particular caught her attention and had her sitting upright. There had been a break-in at her workplace.

How could it have happened last night, I would have known, right? wondered Rowanne, thoroughly confused. *I worked there the whole of last night, although, admittedly I fell asleep, but the office was in order, nothing was out of place...* and as she tried to recollect she was hit with a brain fog.

The news reporter went on to state that there had also been an altercation outside the building witnessed by a passerby. The details of what the witness saw were very vague and sketchy. *Maybe they're deliberately leaving details out,* Rowanne mused.

How worse can this situation get? she wondered incredulously. However, she was forced to swallow her words as further details emerged. Not only had her department been wrecked, there were signs of a possible altercation inside the office as well. The police investigation was on-going, but there was no report of anybody being injured. Rowanne's blood ran cold as she looked on at the footage of her department. The camera slowly panned across the scene of destruction. *Oh My God, that's my desk?!* she thought, noticing a dark stain on the floor nearby; it looked suspiciously like blood and lots of it. 'That wasn't there when I left this morning... it would have been hard to miss...' she reasoned aloud unsuccessfully.

Who could have been hurt? she wondered, mentally going through a checklist of her colleagues who had worked the day before. The idea of any of them being injured was unbearable; after all, she had known these people for years.

It had escalated from possibly being a break-in, to something else entirely. Police had cordoned off the department until further notice, and were requesting for anyone with information to come forward. Rowanne wondered what she should do; technically she had been there, but as a witness, she had nothing of value to offer.

She switched off the television, unable to hear any more. The sinking feeling that had crept in had got progressively worse after listening to the news reports. She felt sick with guilt: guilt for having been there yet unable to recall a single thing. Not to mention, it was a miracle that she had survived unscathed when someone else had clearly been hurt.

She tried to picture how the office had looked prior to her leaving it earlier that morning. 'Was it really intact?' she asked herself aloud, now less confident of her answer.

She tried to recall what she had been doing prior to falling asleep at the office, but any attempt to bring the memories of the night before to the surface of her mind caused her head to pound.

Still it played on her mind, refusing to go away. She was first and foremost a journalist. 'What exactly happened last night?' she wondered wearily. She considered the facts at hand, as she checked them off her fingers:

1. *I was there last night working on a deadline, and at some point in time I supposedly fell asleep.*

2. *I woke up today feeling confused, and apparently without some of my memories from last night. What does this have to do with what happened the night before, or possibly in the early hours of this morning?*

The headache reared its ugly head as if it were a ghost lurking in her mind, always on the offensive. It aggressively diverted her mind from the events of the night before. *What the hell is happening to me?* she wondered, but soldiered on painfully through the red haze engulfing her mind.

One thing became very clear: the question she should really be asking herself is why she could not remember. Was it simply a case of being so overworked that she had fallen into a deep sleep, or was there a more disturbing explanation? Could she have been rendered unconscious? *The blood stains were specifically next to my desk... so, am I somehow involved?*

If she went down this line of reasoning, then she had to ask herself whether she had been involved in the alleged altercation inside the office. However, after a thorough check, there was not a single scratch to be found on her, apart from the cut on her palm.

She was left with a further consideration: were any of her colleagues involved in the alleged incident? This only led to more questions, questions that she did not have the answer to.

Suddenly a piece of the puzzle fit into place. A rather obvious piece. 'And I call myself a journalist... uh-huh,' she said sardonically. How could anyone have come undetected into the building without someone spotting them? Surely they would have had to get past security... Then a name sprang to mind, and she slapped her forehead. *Of course, the night watchman.* She could not believe how stupid she had been, only this morning she had been thinking of Thomas and now it seemed there might be more to his absence then she had initially thought.

An unsettling idea occurred to Rowanne: Thomas might have come in and surprised the intruders, and if he had gotten in their way, then perhaps they had panicked and attacked him. She felt sick to the core and clutched her hair, desperately trying to make sense of everything.

She could not seem to stop her morbid train of thought. What could have happened afterwards... had they taken him? *Oh God, what if the worst has happened...* but she refused to let herself finish the thought.

There was a lot to consider, and even as she tried contacting Eileen, all she got was an automatic voice message saying that she would get back to them, and that under no circumstances were any of the employees to go back to the office.

For now, there was nothing useful she could do, and she did not know how plausible any of her scenarios were. All she had at this point was a lot of conjecture with limited facts.

It was five in the evening by this time, and she had spent hours going over possible scenarios, but she couldn't take it anymore. She had to relieve the tension, and decided a run was exactly what she needed. She got changed into her running gear and put in her headphones.

Rowanne felt confused and angry, and rock metal complimented her mood perfectly as it blasted into her ears whilst she pounded down the streets of Westminster. Though the words did not make any sense, they did at least help to drown out the noise in her mind. She was lost in the music, in oblivion, listening to someone else screaming for a change. She ran fast, steadily increasing her speed and paying no attention to her surroundings. The cars went by in a blur, and the people she passed appeared faceless. Her muscles protested against the punishment as her exhausted body worked hard to keep her going.

She ran alongside the river with sweat running down her face, but did not care as a cool autumnal breeze played along her skin. She ran beneath a string of lights strung from lamppost to lamppost, and from the corner of her eye, she could see the twinkling lights reflected in the inky river that acted as an expansive dark mirror.

When she was almost back home, Rowanne suddenly broke out in a cold sweat at the sight of police cars, and quickly took out her headphones, and her heart began to pound as they turned into her road. She skidded to a stop, and changing direction, ran blindly towards a tunnel.

It was late evening and the sky had grown darker as Rowanne ran faster than she had ever run before. The comforting light of the street lamps was extinguished the moment she entered the dark tunnel. Her heart and mind could not stand the shock, and she could hear a roaring sound as the blood pounded in her ears in this soulless place. As she tried to calm her nerves, she heard a sound. It was not that it was particularly loud, but in this dark place, she would even have heard a pin drop. Her nerves were shredded; after all, there was only so much a person could take.

She was not alone - there was someone else in the tunnel with her. Her mind had not yet fully recovered from her earlier trauma, unbeknownst to Rowanne, and combined with the stress of the incident at work, and now this, it was just too much for her to handle, and she lost consciousness.

Alexander decided to check up on the woman whose mind, he could sense, was a raging cacophony. He could sense that she was in the apartment, pacing up and down, clearly agitated about something. He wanted to make certain that he was not the cause of it.

After all, his fall from grace, no pun intended, had placed them both directly in the path of hell. Alexander was at his satirical best tonight.

However, it was short lived. *She had better not remember anything,* was the one thought occupying his narrow world view. His eyes blazed with rage, as he thought, *God alone knows how I have suffered for this...*

Alexander followed her from the apartment, concealing himself in the shadows by blending effortlessly into the night. Years of training meant he could become virtually invisible, if he so desired. Though this was nigh on impossible in twenty first century London: camera's and streetlights had the monopoly of the whole area. *After all, they had been trying to capture the supernatural for centuries, yet how close were they to any so called documented live footage?* he thought contemptuously.

He had been taken aback initially as he had not expected her to run out of the apartment. At one point, she nearly ran towards him, but at the last moment, instinct made her change course. *Too late. One night and a couple of hours too late,* he thought sardonically to her retreating figure. *Run where you want, but you cannot outrun yourself; no more than I can change what I am.*

He watched her with dark amusement; he had never seen a human run so fast, as if the very hounds of hell were at her heels. He kept up an easy pace, curious as to her sudden panic. After all nothing was after her... except himself. He stayed in the shadows, matching her pace for pace. He could feel the adrenaline coursing through her veins as her heart beat fast. Even with her muscles tiring, he watched as she raced into the unknown.

There was a blinding flash of light thrown across her path from a passing police car which seemed to frighten her, he noted, throwing her off course so that she unwisely ran into a tunnel.

Irritated beyond belief, Alexander raced ahead of her, his presence barely registering with the woman. How do you distinguish shadows? He decided to scout out the tunnel, being alert to any dangers it could hold for her.

As far as Alexander was concerned, the only dangerous thing about this tunnel was the damp disgusting smell offending his highly developed senses. He turned around just as he felt the woman's presence behind him.

Caught off guard, he stupidly inhaled sharply. That did it, it was enough, the woman heard him. He pressed himself flat against the tunnel wall hoping she would run straight past him. Instead, she spun on her heel and tripped.

Alexander raced forward at inhuman speed and caught her before she hit the ground. He gently lowered the unconscious woman and checked her pulse rate. It was racing. *She must have fainted,* he thought.

'Stupid. Utterly stupid,' he mouthed in a fierce whisper. 'How many times do I have to save your life?' Truth be told he was angry with himself. 'I should have stayed away.'

Alexander proceeded to gather her in his arms as he started the irksome journey to her home. He continued to speak to her, keeping up his one sided tirade; more to pass the time really, than any considerate gesture.

He carried her using pathways: they were portals, secret roads in the world made of supernatural energy. Demons and others could use them as shortcuts when travelling through the world.

Alexander was briefly outlined in a fiery red light as he sped along the illuminated path. In those brief moments, the river had glowed a demonic blue, and the stars burned fiercely above them. Everything had either passed by in a sickening blur, or at other points time had slowed down, so that every image had burned brightly, and he reached her home in no time at all.

He arrived barely out of breath. He admired the building before him; it was as lofty as his ideals. He carried her through the dark underground car park, heading straight for the lift. As he approached, the lights went out and silently the lift took them up.

The doors silently parted, and he immediately walked towards the apartment directly in front, instantly knowing that this was where she resided. The door opened before him, and he walked through the dark apartment, eventually laying her down on the couch and, grabbing a chair, he sat before her. He was almost her dark guardian angel. Though he felt less than angelic towards her.

'What am I, her bloody babysitter or something?' He scowled at the woman. *This is what you've reduced me to.* He thought of the great warrior he was once considered to be, now reduced to a new low. *And I thought it couldn't get any worse.*

He crossed his long legs and, drawing in his coat, folded his arms as he settled in for the long night ahead, glowering at the woman before him. *I'm damned either way*, he thought as his expression reflected his troubled mind.

He looked out of the window and observed the stars burning fiercely, and the moon that blinded in its intensity. He was blessed with superior senses courtesy of his heritage. Sometimes within a curse were gifts; if only he had looked close enough, he would later learn...

Alexander decided that he had a few hours to kill, so why not spend his time more productively. He left the woman dreaming as he wandered around her apartment, intending to get fully acquainted with his charge.

He admired the ornate black mirror that hung in the hallway. Demons and angels were carved into the ebony frame, with vines and roses binding them intricately into the eternal dance of death. *Danse macabre,* he thought resignedly. Reflected in the mirror was the face of a thirty year old man, who currently had tranquil sapphire eyes. There were no lines etched into his pale face to tell the story of his life. His hair was the colour of midnight, and his features appeared as if they were carved from granite, with high etched cheekbones.

He turned away from the mirror as he continued his exploration of her apartment. 'Who are you, my lady?' he mused aloud, but for now she was an unknown woman.

He wandered into the open plan kitchen that adjoined the living room, and feeling quite hungry, went directly to the fridge. He looked over its contents, *this woman certainly likes to eat,* he thought, admiringly. Alexander loved food, and had an insatiable appetite. He spotted a homemade chocolate fudge cake and, cutting himself a slice, placed it on a white porcelain plate edged with silver. *I think I'll have another one. Strictly speaking, just to keep my energy up.*

He walked over to the kitchen unit and opened a draw at random. *It must be divine intervention,* he thought, amused at the draw full of cutlery. Grabbing an ornate silver dessert fork, he made his way over to the dining table.

His expression lit up at the first mouthful; never had he tried a cake so rich and decadent yet soft at the same time. 'My compliments on your extraordinary culinary skills, my lady.'

Finishing the cake, he switched on the coffee machine, then got back to the task at hand as he made his way over to her bedroom.

Alexander felt awful about going through her private things, thinking it beneath him, but needs must, he reminded himself, as he began his search.

On the bedside table was a photograph with writing beneath it. In it was a woman with long rich brown hair that framed her soft face. Her striking green eyes captured his notice as he looked upon her joyous expression.

Standing on either side of her was a man and a woman. The man had large honey brown eyes with short brown hair framing his face. The woman on the other hand, had the same brunette hair as his charge, and her green eyes were beaming as she too, wore an expression of fierce joy.

The inscription below the photo read: *Miss Rowanne*

Knight and parents on this joyous occasion of her Graduation with First Class Honours in Journalism and Mythology. University College London. They were standing in front of a grand white domed building. *Impressive facade,* he thought absently. 'But more to the point, Ms Rowanne Knight, I have finally made your acquaintance. Even though I lament the fact that we have not as yet, on your part I should say, made a formal introduction.'

Alexander saw no further need to pry and, leaving the bedroom, he returned to the kitchen just as the machine signalled that his coffee was ready. He rummaged in her cupboards, but this time he was not so lucky; but on the fourth attempt he finally found one containing cups. He took his coffee and settled into the chair before her, ready to begin his vigil.

Rowanne was trapped in a nightmare from which she could not seem to awake. She was running away from something... She was in a midnight world where the landscape was deformed, and the darkness infinite, and in every direction she turned, there were shadows. As they moved towards her, she ran blindly down unknown paths heading towards... *There's no light, there's no light!* her mind screamed. The darkness suffocated her as the shadows began to close in.

She screamed, her heart beating wildly. In the midst of her inner turmoil, she reached out for something... anything to keep her sane. Inexplicably she saw a flash of green, and suddenly someone was holding her hand, even though its owner was obscured. It guided her through the nightmare world. The green fire which was blinding in its intensity seemed to keep the shadows at bay.

Alexander felt her panic as her breathing quickened. Putting down his coffee, he leant forward just as Rowanne screamed and grabbed his hand. Caught off guard, his power

25

surged to the surface, his eyes blazing an emerald green.

He hissed, feeling her fear as she squeezed his hand in a death grip. Slowly he encased her hand in both of his own to act as an anchor for her in this world so that she could safely find her way back. Alexander knew the power of dreams: it was so easy to get trapped within them, not knowing what was real and with no palpable way out. *Especially the dreams of my world,* he thought with a shudder.

Gradually Rowanne's heart slowed its frantic beat, returning to its normal rhythm. Still, Alexander could not make himself let go in case she relapsed. His green eyes smouldered as he continued to watch over her, never stirring from his position.

The moon bathed the apartment in a warm light as it passed through the floor to ceiling windows, creating a silhouette that played on the wall, outlining a man sitting beside the prone figure of a woman, with their hands clasped together for dear life.

CHAPTER 3

Rowanne tried opening her eyes but it was a tremendous effort. Still in that transitional state between sleeping and waking, she felt her hand encased in another's. *Is someone holding my hand?* she wondered, smiling.

Alexander slowly removed his hand as her eyes began to open. He vanished just before she woke.

Finally her eyes snapped open, confirming what she already knew, that she had been holding tightly to the blanket. Slowly, reluctantly, she let go.

The cold morning light illuminated her empty room, banishing the last remnants of night. Rowanne felt peace and disquiet in equal measure, not to mention the missing security guard weighing heavily on her mind.

She checked her messages; ten missed calls from work. Eileen wanted to know whether the assignment was completed for the main cover story for the weekend. 'Drat. I should've completed that piece within two days.' It was Saturday morning, and she had until midnight to submit it in for the editorial team, she reassured herself.

She immediately logged onto her laptop and accessed her work account. She emailed her manager to let her know that she would be working from home. Not a minute had passed before she received an instant reply from her head of department, which read: *'Not happy, Rowanne. Your outstanding record seems to be slipping. I'll get David to cover the weekend issue next time. Clearly you have other important matters to attend to that take precedence over your work. FYI, we have a temporary office set up on the top floor, just in case you were under the mistaken belief that we had shut down in the interim.'*

Rowanne counted to ten, slowly exhaling. Eileen had this effect on all who worked for her. Of course they would set up a temporary office whilst the investigation was ongoing; contrary to what her manager had thought, she had actually been expecting it. There was a reason why their paper was successful; Eileen would not let it close under any circumstances.

Rowanne could practically hear the acid drip off each word. *Honestly,* she thought. *Not a week goes by that she doesn't threaten an employee with David taking over their position.* She laughed it off, as she imagined poor David with a look of confusion as to why the rest of the team avoided him most of the time; he was the only one out of the loop.

She definitely needs to work on her staff motivational techniques! However, Rowanne reminded herself, instantly sobering up, she worked for one of the top newspapers in the city; excuses were unacceptable.

She opened the article she had been working on and found that it was not nearly as bad as she had initially thought, in fact it was almost complete. There was some source verification to do, and then it was just a matter of concluding the piece.

Rowanne went to the kitchen and made herself a coffee. She turned the radio onto *Magic,* with all her old favourites beginning to play. The joy was fleeting as she took her coffee directly to the bedroom, and worked away.

Her phone was her background accompaniment, constantly ringing with colleagues checking in to verify last minute information, not to mention the editorial team, who wanted to ascertain whether they were actually going to receive a completed piece. Finally, as the sun set, she was almost finished, her coffee long forgotten, but she forged on working with ruthless precision. It was just before nine when she sent off her final completed copy to the editorial department.

Rowanne got out of bed and stretched her stiff muscles, having barely moved from the same spot all day. She dragged her tired body to the kitchen, and looked in the fridge for something easy to eat - she had no intention of cooking this late. Luck was on her side as she spied leftover pasta which she duly took over to the microwave. She spotted her shop-bought fudge cake, and cut herself a slice. Rolling her eyes heavenward, she sighed as she spotted two slices already finished off. *It's gotten to the point where I've absentmindedly started eating... Well, it's not like I always have the time to cook.* The first mouthful of pasta brought instant gratification, even if it did taste a bit like cardboard.

Rowanne waited anxiously for the team to get back to her as to whether they would be running her piece or not. She decided to run a hot bath to help her wind down. She looked at her tired gaunt reflection in the bathroom mirror; the puffy eyes and dark circles certainly complemented her undead look.

As she was stripping out of her clothes, she froze. 'Why am I wearing my running gear?' then as quickly as the panic had set in, it left as she recalled the events of the evening before. She had been running along the river last night and then... came back home and collapsed on the couch, too tired to change or go for a shower. *I must have just fallen asleep.* Thinking no more of it, she slipped into the bath and closed her eyes, letting the troubles of the last two days melt away.

The editorial team finally got back to her confirming that her piece had been met with approval and would run alongside tomorrow's headline. She realised that the majority of headlines and stories would be centred around the break-in, as well as the altercations. *I want to know what's happened myself,* she thought, having a vested interest in the investigation.

However, she was shattered and let her train of thought go momentarily. The last email she received was positive, reading: '*Congratulations, Rowanne. Knew you could do it, had complete faith in you. I'm sure you know the David thing was just a joke. Enjoy the weekend, but don't forget, bright and early Monday morning.*'

Ha-ha, I'm in stitches, thought Rowanne, irritated and dead tired.

She respected Eileen; no matter how much she got on her nerves, she could still picture her sitting in her office, working well into the night. Eileen was tall and slim with raven hair that was always tightly pulled back into a bun to stop it from distracting her. Her piercing gray eyes could turn glacial if anyone were to get on the wrong side of her. It was a hard business running a newspaper but Eileen did it with a steely determination. She was meticulous; all stories had to meet her high standard before receiving her stamp of approval, only then would she go home after a long day's work.

Rowanne fell into a deep sleep just before midnight and had the same nightmare. She was being chased. *Just run, don't look back,* she thought. To make matters worse, she was constantly being bombarded with sharp objects which she tried to evade as best she could, but her legs were in agony, as she pounded along looking for a way out. Unfortunately, this time there was no hand to guide her, but suddenly her amethyst necklace shone so bright that it was almost too painful to look at, causing her to close her eyes. She cautiously opened them whilst shielding them with her hand. She could see paths that seemed to criss-cross over each other winding away in different directions. Without another thought, she picked the path closest to her and ran blindly down it, hoping that it would take her away from whatever was chasing her...

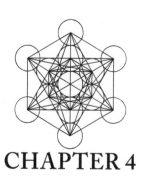

CHAPTER 4

Rowanne's eyes flew open, and, checking her alarm clock, she saw it was ten o' clock. 'Damn, I've overslept.' She got changed, peeling off her clothes that were drenched in sweat as if she really had been running all night.

She looked out of the window at the miserable day; the city was covered by an incessant downpour. *I can't even see as far as St Paul's, it's that bad,* she thought.

After breakfast she set about cleaning the apartment and completing all the tasks she had neglected for a week. By twelve o'clock, she could hear thunder as lightning flashed haphazardly throughout the city, and feeling restless, she decided to go for a run.

Rowanne was completely drenched but she didn't care, and continued to run right across Westminster Bridge, turning in the direction of the London Eye. To her it looked like a giant water wheel, the way the water cascaded off the pods, curtaining each one as it did so.

Poor tourists, not the best day to view the city, thought Rowanne. They were paying to have a bird's eye view of nothing. Some people would not let anything get in the way of what they wanted, even when it was hopeless, and staring them right in the face.

She ran past the Eye, noting that the river Thames was swollen with the amount of rainfall that London had received recently - in just the last few hours alone there had been no break. She turned her face up and watched the gray clouds roll along as lightning continued to pound the city.

She ran along the Southbank, and continued on under the Waterloo Bridge. Across the river she spotted St Paul's. The normally beautiful Cathedral looked cold and foreboding in this weather. She eventually came to the Globe, and stopped to catch her breath.

Rowanne decided to go into the impressive building, took the stairs to the first level, and after getting herself a hot drink, promptly sneaked into the seating area while it was still empty before the next performance. She admired the inside of the structure, with its central stage and curved seating, almost reaching right up into the rafters. Rowanne sat down amongst the empty aisles, and looked in contemplation at the empty stage.

The stage was wet as the roof only partially covered it, but the rest was open to the heavens, not to mention the standing area. The customers would either love the experience of watching *The Tempest* ironically while it poured down - it would give it a certain kind of dramatic atmosphere - or they would be miserably soaking wet! Rowanne smiled sweetly as she thought, *Well, at least it's not me!* and laughed darkly. The show would still go on, rain had never stopped it before. The technicians did last minute sound checks and laid out props on the stage.

Rowanne closed her eyes and smiled, listening to the pitter-patter of the rain, but all too soon she felt the cold seep into her muscles as she finished the last drop of her drink.

Sneaking out of the theatre, she stepped back out into the rain. However, by this time a fog had rolled in, and she could barely see across the Thames, let alone a few paces ahead. *Damn it, I didn't even bring any change for the tube,* she thought dismayed. Pulling on her hood, she ran back in the direction of Westminster Bridge.

The freedom and energy that Rowanne had gained by running in the rain faded quickly, replaced by a panic that slowly spread through her. *This is too much like my dream.* Rationally she knew that nothing was following her, but how could she be certain in this fog?

Her heart beat fast, and her mouth felt dry as every couple of yards she saw a man out of the corner of her eye. When she turned her head to look directly at him, she found that nobody was there. This gave her a sick feeling in the pit of her stomach. Racing through her mind were the stories of stalkers that she had covered in the past. *I wish I didn't have such a good memory,* she thought.

Based on her research, she knew it began with the victim being followed a long time before they even began to suspect what was happening. Now she too had the feeling of being watched... She remembered that in some of the cases, the perpetrator would make himself known to the victim: approaching them, trying to get to know them, and even deliberately standing outside their home to intimidate them. Eventually it would escalate to... *Don't even go there,* Rowanne thought, as she desperately tried to block the images that were trying to form in her mind.

Thunder boomed, and as Rowanne tilted her head back to look up, she could have sworn that there was movement within the clouds. It lasted less than half a second, but it appeared as if there were a battle raging up there... The flashes of lightning reminded her of supernatural battles, like the ones she read of in mythology.

Oh God, I'm seriously losing it! I'm not getting enough sleep, but what can I do when my dreams are plagued by nightmares, she thought. *It's finally all getting to me...* Intellectually she believed that this was the reason for her delusions but her heart thought otherwise.

Rowanne slowed down as she approached the Eye again, noting that it was deserted. The giant wheel had come to a standstill, and fog obscured the top half of it. There was no one around in the immediate area. *Where has everyone gone?*

Rowanne heard faint howling in the distance that gradually grew louder. *It's getting closer, whatever it is.* Immediately, macabre images of beasts and jackals were conjured up in her mind. *Last time I checked, you don't usually find wolves or jackals in London*, thought a desperate Rowanne. She shook her head to clear away the images and ran as quickly as possible towards home.

Rowanne got back to her apartment just after one. Sweating and drenched, she was a sight to behold as she looked at herself in the bathroom mirror. *Where on earth did my morning go?* she wondered, as she stepped into her well deserved hot shower.

She changed into her favourite oversized jumper and comfy jeans then, making herself a tea, she promptly settled onto the sofa. She relaxed as she watched the rain pound the living room windows; it had a soothing rhythm.

However, it was only the brief respite of a few precious moments before her mind wandered back through the events of the past couple of days. *What the hell happened this week? It's like something out of a Victorian 'penny dreadful,'* she thought, trying to make herself laugh, but something stopped her.

In a few short days, she had gone from being a successful journalist rising steadily to the top of her profession, to becoming neurotic. *I'm unravelling*, she thought, *maybe time off will do me some good.*

At around six in the evening, Rowanne got ready to go out. She put on her favourite shade of wine red lipstick paired with a killer floor length, black dress made of rich satin, the slit in the back showing glimpses of her long legs whenever she moved. She put her dark hair up into a French twist. Her mane was so long that it took a lot of bobby pins, and at least half an hour before it was perfectly styled, not forgetting hairspray. *Which is every girl's best friend, especially in this country,* she thought wryly. Finally she encased her feet in her favourite black, Christian Louboutin high heeled stilettos - she loved the contrasting red soles.

Grabbing her oversized black clutch, she headed into the hallway, and took one last look in the antique mirror her grandmother had gifted her. It reflected an attractive thirty year old with dark, smouldering emerald eyes lined with kohl, which gave them an almost striking feline quality. Around her neck rested the amethyst pendant she so frequently wore. It was in the shape of an elongated heart encased in silver Celtic scrollwork. The silver rim at the top of the pendant was engraved with stars and suns, as well as writing that she could not make out, but which her grandmother had said was their true ancestral name, whatever that meant... Maybe she'd ask her about it sometime.

It was special to Rowanne, who wore it close to her heart, especially because it had originally belonged to her grandmother, who had passed it onto her on her eighteenth birthday.

She took the lift down to the car park. And though her heart was racing, she walked sedately, belying the sudden panic that had arisen within her, and it certainly did not help that this section was poorly lit. Fine tremors ran along her hands as she reached for her car door, and she breathed a sigh of relief once she was inside.

She pulled out of the car park and tried to clear her mind as she drove to her favourite restaurant, The Caelum, situated in the heart of the capital. The rain had by this time lightened to a fine mist.

Rowanne pulled into view of the restaurant and stepped out into the misty evening as a valet took the keys to park her car. An usher held an umbrella for her as she approached the front entrance, who then proceeded to personally escort her into the fine establishment.

Her stiletto's struck the marble floor as she walked through the centre of the large hall and reached the golden, 1920's scroll-worked lifts adjacent to the magnificent ebony spiral staircase. The doors swished closed behind her and she was taken to the top floor. Even the interior of the lift was elegant with a mirrored ceiling and walls, all etched with sleek gold horizontal lines running along the top and bottom.

Her tired reflection looked back at her; outwardly she appeared immaculate, but it was the eyes that held the truth. They were tinged with weariness, and she turned away and looked at the floor the whole way up. Rowanne pulled herself together and walked out with her head held high and a smile pasted onto her face. The ushers opened the grand doors to the restaurant.

'Welcome, Ms Knight. What a pleasure and great honour it is for us that you dine here tonight.'

Rowanne was a long standing client, and her reputation preceded her. She inclined her head at both of the ushers and acknowledged their compliments with a warm smile.

'Hello, Richard,' she said, addressing the senior manager.

'Nice to see you again, Ms Knight,' he replied, escorting Rowanne to her favourite spot in the glass-walled main room which had magnificent views of the city.

'I'll be back in a moment to take your order, Ms Knight.'

Rowanne thanked him and proceeded to look through the menu. She could not help but look up in admiration at the beautiful interior. It was a circular room with an unusually high domed ceiling. The floor to ceiling windows created a feeling of spaciousness with an elegant bevelled edge that curved around the back of the room. The mirrors reflected the city outside as well as the room, lending it a hauntingly beautiful atmosphere.

Music from the adjacent room drifted in, a sombre melody being played on the grand piano. Rowanne closed her eyes for a few moments, losing herself in the evocative tune. Sighing, she reluctantly opened her eyes.

A waiter came to take her order, '*Madame* is ready to order?'

'Yes. I'd like a salad to start with, and can you also bring me a non alcoholic, dry white, please.'

'*Très bon*, very good, *madame*.'

'*Merci*,' replied Rowanne.

She looked out across the London skyline. *The city certainly looks eerie tonight*, she thought, shrouded as it was in a fine mist. By the time her order had arrived, Rowanne had a contemplative look on her face as she started on her salad.

Nearby, a waiter served a man seated four tables down from Rowanne. The restaurant was mostly quiet, with the bad weather to blame for keeping people away.

'Good evening, sir. Here is your Romanèe Conti, and may I say what a first-rate choice you have.'

'*Merci*,' replied a highly amused Alexander, as he maintained a stoic persona despite feeling the waiter's heart rate pick up with the effort of trying not to fawn over him. *New guy, no sense of etiquette. A bit of a buffoon really.*

'Will that be all, sir?' The waiter looked expectantly at the gentleman before him.

'Yes,' replied Alexander in a cold bored tone of voice.

'Are you sure?'

'Leave,' said Alexander, his tone leaving no room for arguments; letting the waiter know that he did not suffer fools well.

'Tha-Thank you, sir, ver-very goo-good.' The waiter was no fool; one look into the man's glacial eyes had left him with the promise of violence if he did not leave at that very moment. No wonder he had started stuttering. He smiled crookedly at the gentleman, and forced himself to turn his back on him when all he really wanted was to walk backwards whilst keeping an eye on him. He forced one foot in front of the other, barely able to walk, let alone stand, that was how shaken he was.

Alexander was once more left to his own devices. He observed the woman across from him who seemed to be lost in a world of her own with a vacant expression on her face. He mused as to what she could be thinking about. She was not eating much, just sort of picking at her salad really, he noted.

Her heart rate was normal, and her entire being seemed to be engaged with the view outside the window; although, that was just his supposition. He resisted the temptation to test out his theory. Alexander corrected himself, *No not 'the woman,'* he thought amused. *Now that I have been introduced to you informally, even if it was via searching your apartment,* he thought ruefully. *I shall now refer to you as Rowanne.* He wondered briefly what it would be like to actually walk up to her and introduce himself...

He was abruptly broken out of his reverie by a disturbance. He briefly closed his eyes while scanning the environment. *No, nothing out of the ordinary. Oh great,* he thought, as he observed his waiter exchanging heated words with the manager, all spoken in a whisper, of course.

Alexander suddenly laughed aloud, drawing the attention of the waiter to himself. *If looks could kill,* he thought drily; the waiter was clearly disgruntled with him.

The waiter was in a rage, as he indicated furiously but discreetly in Alexander's direction with the constant inclination of his head.

Come on, who wouldn't laugh at this imbecilic marionette? Time to leave, he thought disgustedly, not wanting to draw any more unwanted attention to himself. With one last malignant look in the direction of the waiter, he left.

Rowanne blinked, broken out of her reverie by the sound of laughter from a nearby table. Her heart rate picked up and her hands began to feel clammy. The sound alone had raised goosebumps on her arms, and left her chilled to the core. The only way she could describe it was as if someone had walked over her grave.

It belonged to a man, and its deep strong tone drew her attention behind her. She knew it was indelicate to stare, but could not help herself. However, glancing back proved futile as the tables were empty. She focused her search on the doors, and just caught a glimpse of a shadow passing through them before they closed behind whoever it had been.

She nearly screamed at the sound of breaking glass, and quickly looked up to find that a young waiter had fainted. *It's probably best to go,* she thought, *my nerves aren't up to any more shocks.* Paying her bill, she left as quickly as possible.

'I hope to see you soon, Ms Knight. I am so very sorry for the disturbance,' the waiter said in a slightly embarrassed tone.

The most Rowanne could manage was a weak smile before finally being able to leave. The last thing she saw was an ashen faced waiter lying almost lifeless on the floor, surrounded by his confused colleagues.

Rowanne took the lift back down and left the restaurant. She waited for the valet to bring her car around just as a black Lamborghini drove by.

To her dismay, she found herself in a traffic jam, forced to wait it out. Any amount of rain brought the city to a standstill. *Honestly!* she huffed. *It's not even snowing.* One of the most frustrating things about living in London was the traffic jams that were a constant source of irritation.

Meanwhile, Alexander had circled back and was now following Rowanne discreetly. He reminisced back to how she had looked at The Caelum. He had admired her dress; *Elegant, yes that's the word that springs to mind*, he smiled. Shaking his head to sober up, he thought, *what's gotten into me?*

Rowanne had in fact noticed the car behind her. It was definitely the same black Lamborghini that she had seen outside of the restaurant. At first, she had thought that it was simply heading in the same direction as her. However, for the last twenty minutes it had matched her every turn. *It could be a coincidence, I suppose. Or it could be something else...*

It paid to be cautious, so instead of driving straight for her home, she decided that a little detour was in order. Driving around aimlessly, she wondered where to go until she spotted The Salisbury pub. *Thank God*, she thought, relieved.

Driving up to it, she noticed the unsmiling faces of the cherubs on the outside; more likely to turn people away, rather than welcome them. She parked her car on a side road, and walked up to the front doors as if she had always intended to go in there. *At least I look calm*, she thought, though her eyes told another story.

Alexander noticed that Rowanne's car was parked outside one of his old haunts. Pulling into a side road he parked his car and headed towards the pub. He smiled as he reminisced of the many good times that he had spent there with friends and humans alike. Being centrally based, it was a good place to pick up information... His train of thought was cut short, as he approached the doors; he could sense her in there, and felt her heart flutter as if something was not quite right with her world. She was nervous.

Taking one last look to confirm that nobody was around, he cloaked his presence. A shield of energy surrounded him that would divert people's attention away from him. He did not intend to become fully invisible, as this would require more of his demonic powers, not to mention the fact that others of his kind would be alerted to his whereabouts; it would not serve Rowanne, or himself.

Was it really about what was best for Rowanne? Or more, if not equally, about that element of danger: that fine line where people could still bump into him. He didn't know why he was behaving so recklessly and truthfully he didn't care as he paused before the doors to the pub, vaguely noticing the angel figurines above his head who looked down upon him with their empty eyes. *What's new there?* he thought resentfully.

Rowanne sat on a red, leather, buttoned seat in a saloon off the narrow walkway adjacent to the bar. Here she had a perfect view of anyone who came in, but had the added advantage of the panels partially concealing her. The mirror panels were etched in an Art Nouveau style, and the long walkway was decadently painted in a rich red with cream wood mouldings giving it a Victorian feel.

She observed the people sitting at the mahogany bar, laughing and generally having a good time. How she wished that she could have spent her time here under different circumstances.

Slowly Rowanne began to relax amongst the people, they seemed to have a calming effect on her. *Nothing can happen to me here, it's completely safe. Am I being paranoid or what?* she wondered, feeling slightly foolish. Still, the reporter side of her could not let it go. *I'll just keep an eye out for anybody that looks out of place. I hope to God, that I'm just being neurotic*, whilst in the back of her mind lurked the idea: 'somebody might actually be following me'. It didn't help that the whole pub had a reddish tinge given off by the Victorian style lights, giving it a spooky Dickensian atmosphere that only served to fuel her fear.

Her time as a journalist had brought her into contact with

many horror stories. Occasionally, it paid to play it safe, even at the risk of looking like a fool. *After all, I've always followed my gut instinct, and it hasn't led me astray so far. I am safe,* she kept repeating the same thing to herself like a mantra, hoping that if she said it enough, it would come true, even when her gut instinct was screaming at her to stay put.

Her eyes were almost glued to the entrance, however the tapestries on the wall could not fail to grab her notice, and she peeled her eyes away to have a quick look. It fascinated her, not just because it was located right next to the door. It was of a hunting scene: wolves on a mountain looked down upon the people passing underneath on the path below. There was something sinister about this picture; the people were smiling, oblivious of what was lying in wait for them as they walked under a twinkling moonlit night, but in the distance there were dark clouds...

The doors swung open, ripping Rowanne's gaze from the scene. Her heart rate sped up, *this is it...* she thought.

Alexander entered the pub, and even through the garish glow, his eyes immediately locked onto Rowanne who was sitting alone in a saloon near the bar. Her soulful green eyes panicked as they looked directly at him, and he began to walk towards her. *She's not even wearing a coat in this weather,* he noted absently.

There's nothing there. Nothing, she kept repeating to herself. She felt a cold breeze blow in from outside, reaching all the way towards the back of the room to where she was seated.

Rowanne looked towards the entrance with a sick feeling in the pit of her stomach, her hands felt clammy as she broke out in a cold sweat. The room that had only moments before been warm, now seemed to grow darker, and the sudden drop in temperature only added to this. She looked around, but everyone else seemed oblivious to what was happening around them. *I'm not crazy!* she thought, her heart racing.

Rowanne watched as the empty chair at her table appeared to jerk back, then forward just once as if it were caught up by a powerful draft. The doors were closed and nobody had entered the pub; she had no explanation for what had just happened.

Alexander knew that he should not have pulled the stunt with the chair, but *c'est fait*, he thought, with a particularly wicked expression on his face. He studied Rowanne - this was the first time that he had actually been this close to her in a reasonably normal setting. Well, normal for her anyway.

Her green eyes seemed to look straight through him, fixated by something behind him. She was very perceptive, noticing things others would just miss, or not acknowledge, and she had an instinct for self preservation. *Journalists,* he thought with disgust, *always in the wrong place, at the wrong time.*

Alexander noticed that her hands were trembling, and there were fine tremors running through her body as she shook. *It's me,* he thought wearily, shaking his head. *I can never be in human company for long without something happening.* He got up, satisfied that she was safe, but appalled with himself for having frightened her so badly. Not to mention his earlier debacle with the waiter, which he now felt ashamed of, and would rectify.

Rowanne had felt something, she could not name it, but it felt close to terror and something else... Rationally, she knew nobody had entered the pub, it was an old building and was bound to have drafts, but even so, she was unable to let the thought go. The way the chair had moved had scared the life out of her. *Almost as if...* She reached out a pale trembling hand, and bit down on a scream. She clamped a hand over her mouth, because for a nano second, it had felt as if her hand had brushed the rough surface of... a coat? *Except,* she thought, smiling maniacally, *there's nothing there.*

Abruptly the doors swung shut, and the room came back to life. The cold oppressive feeling lifted and she could hear people talking and laughing again. Rowanne rose up slowly and kept her gaze fixed on the chair opposite her whilst trying to keep the trembling in her legs to a minimum. The people around her in the pub seemed indifferent, and carried on as if nothing out of the ordinary had just happened. She calmly walked out.

'I should have brought a coat,' laughed Rowanne despondently. She shielded herself from the rain as best she could, and, wrapping her arms around herself as much for comfort as to keep dry, she ran to her car, water running down her face.

Rowanne drove in a quiet mood as the rain pounded the car. Arriving home a little after ten, she walked through the car park quickly. The lift doors closed behind her, and only then could she sag against them. She could not seem to stop shaking. Finally, after what seemed like ages, the doors finally opened and, sliding up the wall, she made herself walk to her front door. She fumbled with her keys for a moment before at long last managing to get them into the target of the lock.

She went through, immediately slid down, and sat with her back to the door. Reaching a shaky hand behind, she turned the lock. *I've never felt the need to use the extra security locks before. Get up Rowanne, this is not like you!* she thought sternly. She wiped her eyes, smudging her mascara in the process, and tried to pull herself together.

She made the effort to get up and headed into the bathroom. Switching on the light, she was shocked as she studied her listless appearance, noting with amusement her panda eyes. Whilst washing her face, she also noticed how frightened her eyes looked. Stepping into the shower, she turned the nozzle on to full blast, sending cascades of hot water running down her body, but she still could not seem to stop shaking, so she sat down and let the water carry her troubles away.

Afterwards, she went into the kitchen and made herself a hot drink. Getting into bed, she held the mug close, inhaling the warmth of the camomile drink. Finally feeling relaxed, she flipped open her laptop to check her emails; thankfully there weren't any work related, and in no time at all she had gone through the whole lot.

However, next week would be quite busy, with events lined up that she would be expected to cover. *Yes, love it,* she thought beaming. There'd be no time to feel sorry for herself, not with this busy schedule. She completed her work just before midnight, and fell into a deep sleep.

CHAPTER 5

Rowanne woke up late Monday morning. Though she looked forward to being busy again, she had acknowledged the need to take a day off so that she could restore her tired mind and body. Eileen had thankfully understood and fully backed the idea, berating her for not having taken it sooner. Fortunately it had been a peaceful night, no nightmares.

Jumping into her leggings and t-shirt, Rowanne headed out for a run. The sun was shining in a clear blue sky and it was quite warm for an autumn day. She ran down to Westminster Bridge, and past the Houses of Parliament, easily keeping a fast pace right up until the next bridge, before turning back. She noticed the couples strolling along the river as sunlight glinted off the Thames.

Alexander walked along Westminster Bridge and, stopping briefly to look over the side, caught sight of Rowanne running below. He simply turned in the opposite direction and headed for the Eye.

Rowanne also stopped at Westminster Bridge, and climbed to the top for a brief respite, as she drank from her bottle. Shielding her eyes, she looked towards the river as the London Eye caught her attention. She smiled at the sight of the people in the pods; excited families, children crying who were most likely scared of heights, and couples, all of them looking out across the city.

Alexander's pod had reached the top. It was his first time on this attraction, and he had even gone as far as paying with their (human) currency, instead of making his own way up. He looked out at the magnificent city; affectionately referred to as his 'mortal home'. However, he laughed bitterly at what he had left behind, because from now on, this reality would take up most, if not all of his *mortal* life.

Buckingham Palace could be seen in the distance, Alexander had seen enough palaces to last a lifetime. After a while, they all seemed to blend together, and admittedly he had seen superior and more elaborate palaces that would dwarf this one.

His attention was drawn to one particular figure standing on the bridge: Rowanne. Luckily he was so high up that she could not possibly see him. His lustrous raven hair covered most of his face as it fell forward, not to mention the dark sunglasses that hid his eyes. He was about to turn his back, when...

Rowanne looked up at that exact moment, and caught her attention on the stranger in the top pod. Although, she could not see him very clearly, as his hair and sunglasses obscured his face. However, she still got the impression that he was looking straight at her, or in her general direction, and it baffled her.

Rowanne had caught him watching her, and slowly, casually, Alexander turned away as if something else had caught his eye. *I cannot believe she actually saw me in great detail, and from that distance...* A weary look came into his eyes, as he wondered what other side effects would arise from their blood exchange...

Rowanne shook her head, *I am becoming paranoid*! she thought, and, shrugging her shoulders, set off for home.

Arriving back tired, her face flushed, Rowanne took a nice long bath as she let the water gently knead her sore muscles back to life. She dressed in comfy jeans and an oversized jumper; her go-to clothes for when she felt like unwinding.

She made herself lunch and flopped down on the sofa, flicking through the music channels. *Finally I'm in luck*, she thought as her favourite band came on. Their music was an eclectic mix of rock and folk, which nobody seemed to understand except for her. *I mean what do these so-called purists know anyway*, she thought, quite smug in her knowledge of good music. Her favourite song was playing: a haunting melody with violins accompanying a song that spoke of a forgotten past.

Rowanne let herself be lost in the music, it made her feel nostalgic. *I haven't really kept in touch with my family. When was the last time I even called anybody outside of work?* and with a jolt she sat up straight as it hit her that she could not recall the last time. She felt miserable, her good mood gone.

Rowanne rang her grandmother, just to feel close to somebody who cared for her. She knew she was self-centred, but still, her motive was also love.

'Hello, Grandmother,' said Rowanne, her voice trembling at the uncertainty of the welcome she would receive.

'Hello, Rowanne. How are you?'

She needn't have worried as her grandmother's deep strong voice spoke in a loving and caring manner.

'I'm fine. I'm doing great actually.' Rowanne tried to keep her voice steady, fighting back the tears, whilst she unconsciously played with the amethyst pendant at her neck. 'I just wanted to hear your voice. I'm so sorry, I know it's been so long since I last called. Work has been hectic these past couple of years.' *What a sorry sounding excuse*, she thought. *How heartless must I sound to my grandmother? I mean, why couldn't I have just picked up the phone?* She felt tremendously ashamed and angry with herself.

'Rowanne, I understand that your work is very important to you, especially at your age, you want to be focused on your career. Your mother was the same, and in that respect you take after her.'

Rowanne could hear the admonishment in her grandmother's voice.

'You will always have work, but you must cherish your family. Phone once in a while! I just want to know that you're safe and happy,' said her grandmother with laughter in her voice, as she tried to lighten the sudden tension between them. 'By the way, is there anybody special in your life?'

'Seriously? You don't waste any time, do you?' asked Rowanne, secretly relieved at the change in topic.

'I believe the direct approach is best,' she replied trying to sound earnest, whilst trying not to laugh.

'No. Not at this moment in time.' She knew what was coming next, and tried to hold onto an affronted air, but could feel laughter bubble up inside of her.

'There is a lovely young man currently working at the British Library, perhaps I could arrange-'

It was very important at this juncture to interrupt her grandmother, who could talk on the subject of relationships, eventually coming to the importance of marriage, for a solid couple of hours.

'No, Grandmother,' Rowanne said in an exasperated voice, rolling her eyes heavenward. 'What I mean to say is, right now the editor is having me work on two major stories, so I'm afraid that most of my time will be taken up at the office,' she added in what she hoped was a sincere voice that would get her grandmother to leave the subject alone for now. She sighed, knowing that this particular topic would in all certainty be continued.

Rowanne's grandmother, Angelique Knight, was in her seventies. She'd seen much of the world, perhaps too much; there were some things, even a grandchild should not learn of. Old memories were threatening to break to the surface...

'How is Grandfather?'

Grandmother Angelique was snapped back sharply to the present by Rowanne's voice. 'He's abroad, working on a project. He'll be back in two months. You could come down, and keep me company?' she asked, amazed at how she kept her voice steady.

Rowanne felt guilty for being so neglectful for this long, especially as she heard the pleading note in her grandmother's voice, but instead she replied, 'I'll try and come over soon, alright? I've got to go now, my boss has just phoned in and is waiting impatiently on the other line. Give my love to Grandfather.'

'I love you, Rowanne. I'll see you soon then.' This time her voice quivered, but she could not help it. *Family is family at the end of the day, no matter how far they go from us. If only I could see her again,* she thought solemnly.

Keeping her voice light, so as not to further upset her grandmother, Rowanne replied, 'Me too,' and abruptly hung up.

Her grandmother on the other hand, kept the phone to her ear long after Rowanne had cut her off, and just sat listening to the static on the dead line, lost in her reverie.

Rowanne wiped her tired eyes and got out her laptop. She turned on the radio; *Classic FM* would be her background accompaniment while she got on with her work. Her editor really had sent her two stories to cover. The first was the normal kind, very mundane, but of "public interest" she wearily reminded herself, making air quotes.

Rowanne sucked in her breath as she looked at the second story: it was to do with Thomas, the missing security guard at her work. More than seventy-two hours had now passed, and combined with the evidence the police had of the altercation, it had now turned into a missing person's case. The police were treating it very seriously, and their appeal to the public had yielded positive results. A number of people had come forward with new evidence.

Eileen specifically wanted her to assist the police, as well as play detective on the side. Rowanne wondered how she could possibly find anything out without interrupting the police investigation. If she were to talk to the witnesses and get statements, and then publish them, it could be considered as a conflict of interest if it were to go to court. Despite that, she owed it to Thomas to find out what really happened.

If only I hadn't fallen asleep. If I had just heard something, then maybe I could have helped in some way. However, it was no use feeling sorry for herself, as positive action was needed now. *Don't worry, Thomas, I won't stop till I know what's happened to you.*

In the meantime, Eileen had come up with possible leads she wanted Rowanne to follow up on, and had also concocted possible scenarios as to what might have happened.

Rowanne looked through the list:

1. *Did an incident involving Thomas even take place?* (Rowanne did not like this question, but Eileen was right because it was no different to what the police did: they'd look at all the evidence logically, before making any assumptions).
2. *Was he involved in anything illegal?*
3. *Did he know the alleged perpetrators?*
4. *How did they get in?*
5. *Why wasn't the security alarm tripped?*

The list went on for a bit, but it was enough to get on with. Rowanne cross checked it with the one she had made earlier.

Eileen had told her that the CCTV footage from Thursday had been lost. The security team had informed her that it was completely damaged. Rowanne found this bit of news nerve-racking as she was hoping that the footage would show exactly what had happened within their office on Thursday evening, as well as the alleged incident outside.

In the afternoon, Rowanne got a call from the police station, requesting her attendance for an interview. *Oh great, just as I thought, I will be investigating the incident as well as being a possible witness. Definitely grounds for a conflict of interest there. Thank you, Eileen,* thought Rowanne sarcastically.

However, Rowanne spoke calmly to the police officer, although her heart was racing, and by the time she'd finished the call, her nerves were frayed.

As panic began to set in, she paced around the living room to try and expel the nervous energy. Outside it had grown very dark as thunder clouds loomed over the city. She walked towards the large windows and looked out at the ominous, electric blue sky, when suddenly it became very quiet.

The lights in the living room went out, plunging Rowanne into darkness. She started to inch towards the kitchen, but ended up banging into the sofa. Outside, the sky burst apart as flashes of lightning ripped the sky, and thunder clouds let out an unholy sound as if canons were being fired. She nearly jumped out of her skin and spun around at the sound.

There were sporadic bursts of light and dark as the storm raged on. Rowanne walked towards the window once more, caught by an idea... Lightning flashed momentarily, lighting the window, and Rowanne caught a brief glimpse of her pale terrified reflection.

Something, some memory, was trying to tug at the edges of her subconscious... It felt like déjà-vu, so familiar for some reason. Rowanne clutched her head as pain suddenly seemed to slice through it, and the more she stubbornly persisted in trying to remember; the more it grew in its intensity.

I will remember, no matter what, she thought, but screamed out loud as the pain became too much for her to keep inside any longer. Rowanne fell forward and blacked out as she banged her head on the window. Her body lay prone on the floor, and the storm ceased, bringing with it a false sense of calm.

Rowanne was back in her nightmare world, all around her was endless night. She was encroaching upon this place that had never known light, and even the pale moon was watered down to a fine gray.

The landscape seemed vast to her, as if it almost stretched into infinity. Well, it appeared that way to her tired eyes. *How do you measure the dark?* she wondered. There were no stars, or any real form of light that she could use to guide herself.

Gradually her senses started to adjust, and she could begin to make out what appeared to be tall structures in the far distance. They looked like huge monoliths. *There probably ancient. I can't think of a word to describe what I'm looking at,* she thought, with a mixture of fear and respect.

In documentaries they show the ancient world, and it is vast: palaces and temples being a city unto themselves, that's how grand the scale was, and yet this place dwarfed them, making them appear microscopic. *A place like this should not be able to exist, and I'm just this tiny insignificant being within it...* She felt that she could become lost within it, swallowed up and leaving behind no trace to suggest that she was ever there.

Alexander rushed to Rowanne's side, as he felt her distress. From his home, he used the demon paths as his most expedient method to reach her, and minutes later he was in her apartment.

There was a brief disturbance in the air, and then a portal opened, glowing impossibly red as if on fire with the urgency of its master's need fuelling it. Alexander stepped out and noticed nothing except Rowanne as he rushed to her side, blurring as he put on a burst of supernatural speed, almost impossible for the human eye to register. He began to lift Rowanne-

STOP.

Alexander froze mid way, and looked down sharply at Rowanne, but she was unconscious. However, he could have sworn that the voice had come from her. Nobody else besides the two of them were in the apartment, as far as he knew. He quickly scanned the apartment in less than a second. Satisfied that they were alone, he began to lift her once more.

I SAID STOP. NO MORE, in a menacing tone the voice issued from Rowanne with so much conviction behind it that Alexander immediately stopped.

PUT ME DOWN, she repeated in her sleep state.

The voice seemed to be telepathically shouting at a stunned Alexander.

He lowered her carefully down to the ground, amazed and slightly afraid himself at what was happening. He had not personally encountered something like this in his existence, although he had heard of it, and it made his blood run cold.

The body stirred and slowly Rowanne opened her eyes, but they were not her eyes; the green native to her had been replaced by a brilliant glowing violet. At first they were unfocused, but in the next instant they became determined and deadly as they immediately latched onto Alexander.

He took an involuntary step back, as Rowanne's head started to lift up off the floor, followed closely by her torso, and lastly the arms helped to push Rowanne's body into a sitting position. *It is grotesque*, he thought, referring to Rowanne as 'the body' because as far as he could tell, it was not Rowanne trying to get up: her essence seemed to be gone, replaced by that... thing. That monstrosity.

He started to back up, revolted by it. He felt uncertain of himself, and for the first time in his life, he was unable to decide how to proceed, how to handle this escalating situation. *This madness*, he thought. The flight or fight response in him was on high alert, but he did not want to risk hurting Rowanne, especially if he could not bring himself under control.

Slowly pushing her arms down and tucking her legs underneath her, Rowanne got up unsteadily, before finally standing. She wobbled on her legs as she began to lose her footing.

Alexander rushed forward to steady her, his fear momentarily forgotten. Abruptly, he went flying across the room, and was slammed into the wall by a tremendous force.

Standing before him, Rowanne said, 'No more. No more will I be weak. No more shall I rely solely on you to save me. It is abhorrent to us to be weak, cowardly and quaking in fear of the unknown. I shall not stand for it, Alexander of the Black Rose Clan,' her voice dripped ice, and the temperature of the room suddenly dropped to almost freezing. The lights went out, and an unearthly glow surrounded Rowanne. 'I have now awakened, and I know you.'

'Who are you?' Alexander asked, afraid.

'You will know soon enough...'

'Why have you come here and possessed this human?' Alexander didn't want to show that he had any interest in Rowanne just in case the entity, or whatever it was, should use it against him by harming her.

'Did you think that you could play with the laws of nature, break the Laws of *our* World, and actually expect to get away with it?! That is both arrogant and foolish. There are always consequences...' the voice shouted before whispering, 'no matter who you are...'

'But who are you?' reiterated Alexander, satisfied that his voice had come out steady. He was more interested than ever to find out the mystery behind who or what this being was. *Or had been*, he added as an afterthought.

'I am Rowanne Knight,' her voice was back to its acidic icy tone. 'Half human, half demon and half...' The entity laughed, before abruptly breaking off. 'I shall not recollect our conversations in my human form.' The entity began to weaken at its first attempt at possession, and suddenly it was too much to hold on to the body, and helplessly it slipped from its control. Rowanne's body slumped to the ground, like a puppet whose strings were abruptly cut.

Alexander rushed forward and caught Rowanne in his arms. He held her to him, feeling the other stronger presence gone for the moment. *Temporarily retreated*, he thought uneasily.

He carried her to the bedroom. Laying her gently down onto the bed, he moved her hair away from her face, tucking it behind her ears, and systematically checked whether she had hurt herself. Her breathing was even, but her mind when he reached for it felt disturbed. There were a few cuts and bruises, and an especially nasty one on her forehead, from when she'd hit the window and collapsed to the floor. *Lucky for you*, thought Alexander wearily, *the scatter cushions in front of the window took the rest of the impact.*

Alexander's eyes turned green as he lay his hand on her head. His energy flared into Rowanne as it made its way through her body; repairing any and all damage it had taken.

The yin yang tattoo started to reappear on Rowanne's left shoulder. Black and white energy emanated from the tattoo engulfing her body, as well as moving towards Alexander, and his body, too was briefly encased in this temporary cocoon of light.

Upon reaching Alexander, it seemed to suck the essence from him, as tendrils of energy passed back into Rowanne. The energy intensified to such an uncomfortable point that he grabbed a hold of Rowanne's hand, to steady himself. As he had done on that fateful night of their first encounter.

He could not believe that it had just been a couple of nights ago, four to be exact, since he'd saved this unknown woman from an attack by demons. Unfortunately for him, he'd been unsuccessful, distracted as he'd been by his own sense of importance and pride. Everyone knew what pride led to, and his had led to the death of the woman lying before him. *My penance or price*, as he thought disgustedly, *was losing my immortality.*

He'd have to live with it, but to come to terms with it would take a lifetime; *Would a human span do?* he wondered darkly, as his face was warped by vehemence, and his inner turmoil raged in his heart, in his very being. *The consequences of that night are far reaching, and even I can't predict what will happen,* he thought, as the energy slowly and painfully drained from his body, taking with it all the intense emotions that he had been feeling.

Exhausted, Alexander looked down at Rowanne; she seemed to be doing well. He released her hand carelessly, so that it flopped back down on the bed, laying still by her side. Standing up he squared his shoulders, his eyes hooded with an unnamed emotion, and he made his way out of her apartment.

CHAPTER 6

Rowanne woke in a daze and glanced at her clock worried, but thankfully it was only six am, so she did not have to worry about work just yet. Trying to gather her bearings, she tried to recollect the evening before.

Slowly it began to come back to her in stages. *There was a lightning storm, the lights in the apartment went out...* an uncomfortable feeling settled over her, as she pieced the events together. *I walked towards the window and tripped...* a memory of her laying sprawled out in front of the window flashed in her mind, and quickly she examined her face, but could not feel any bumps or cuts.

Rowanne went to the bathroom to make certain, and switching on the light, looked into the mirror. Her exhausted eyes looked back at her, dark circles underneath; *no doubt from my less than restful nights!* Other than that, there weren't any bruises on her face. She examined her body, which also seemed to be fine, nothing indicating that she had fallen at all. *This is really weird,* she thought uneasily.

How did I get to the bed, if I fell unconscious...? Rowanne did not like unanswered questions; especially when it concerned her. Her hands curled and uncurled in agitation.

Maybe after regaining consciousness, I dragged myself to bed before passing out again. Truth be told, she had her doubts. 'I can't explain this!' she shouted in frustration.

As she tried to recollect, pain suddenly flared through her mind. Screaming she clutched her head, and just about managed to sit down. *Think about something else, I have to try and think about something else.* As soon as Rowanne distracted her mind away from her quandary, the pain slowly and excruciatingly abated. *This is seriously annoying!* she thought, beyond exasperated with this painful amnesia, for lack of a better explanation. She considered visiting the doctor to try and get to the bottom of it.

She pushed her problems to the back of her mind and made her morning coffee. Flipping open her laptop she checked the day's mail, and then changed for work. She was just tucking her navy blue, silk shirt into her skinny trousers, when her phone rang.

'Hello?'

'Good morning, Ms Knight. I'm calling from Westminster Police Station.'

'How may I help you?' asked Rowanne. Despite feeling nervous she managed to keep her voice steady.

'I believe one of my colleagues phoned you yesterday regarding today's afternoon appointment?'

Rowanne's heart raced as if she were running a marathon. 'Yes, I believe the appointment was for four.'

'Unfortunately the time has been pushed back to six. I know this is rather late notice, and I am sorry for any inconvenience this may cause you, but the Detective Chief Inspector would appreciate it if you could come down in the evening.'

Rowanne considered this to be a godsend, as she really had to get down to the new offices this morning to sort out her work, and at least she'd have time to prepare. 'That's fine. I can rearrange some of the appointments that I have today. Please inform the Detective Chief Inspector to expect me at six.'

'Thank you, Ms Knight. Good day to you.'

Hanging up the phone, Rowanne took a few deep breaths to centre herself. *I know what I have to do*, and for the first time in days, she felt more like her confident self.

Brushing her hair, she pinned it up, and slipped into her ankle boots. She applied her makeup in the bathroom mirror. Looking back at her was a beautiful woman with sharp, clear green eyes lined in kohl, long lashes accentuated with mascara. She applied blusher, and finished with a lipstick in the shade of autumn leaves. *That's better*, she thought, and, grabbing her coat, went off to face an uncertain future.

In the lift, she quickly glanced over the work to be handed in; being a perfectionist, she could not help but go through it one last time. Finding everything to be in order, she slid it carefully back into her soft, leather satchel.

The sun glinted off the lift, illuminating the glassy interior, and Rowanne closed her eyes, feeling her spirits lift as the light played across her face, warming her within. She was excited at finally seeing the new offices, and being around people again.

Even the pending police appointment did not bother her as much as it had earlier. Rowanne felt the nip of the crisp, cold day as she stepped out of the lift, a reminder that November was only two days away. The day felt full of promise. *I can do this*, she chanted, and the last of her tension melted away.

Rowanne drove west on Westminster Bridge, and once over it turned right onto Victoria Embankment. She was happy that the traffic was good today, and smiling she tuned the radio to *Classic FM* as her mind sorted and catalogued the things that would need her attention for the day ahead.

In no time at all, she pulled up in front of her office building. The newspaper had been relocated to a grand building which had been renovated ten years ago into office space. Prior to this it had sat proudly amongst the other great names of the publishing world of Fleet Street. Other organizations shared the building alongside the newspaper, which held a respected position. She drove past the angel fountain covered in a layer of frost just as sunlight glanced off it creating the illusion that it was winking at her as it sparkled. She took it as an omen of good things to come.

Parking her car, she walked back past the angel fountain, oblivious of the fact that it had been disturbed by a stray gust of wind, causing ripples in the otherwise tranquil surface.

Rowanne was met with security outside the building.

'Good morning, Ms Knight.'

'Morning. I haven't seen you before.'

'I'm here as a temporary replacement. I'm to inform all employees of the paper that the offices have been relocated until the investigation is completed. If you just follow me, I'll escort you to the new location.' The guard checked Rowanne's name off against his list.

Following behind, Rowanne contemplated that the new guy was younger than Thomas, no more than twenty-five. He was tall, with black hair and brown eyes, and generally indiscriminate features. Maybe it was a requirement within security jobs that you simply look tough and fade into the background.

'Sorry, but I don't believe I caught your name?' she asked.

'John,' he replied over his shoulder, as he continued to lead the way through the building.

She was less than impressed by his surly demeanour. *Would it kill people to be decent now and again?*

They passed through the large, engraved wooden doors, and made their way to the lifts. Most of the original building had been preserved as the contract of sale had passed through English Heritage, who had stipulated that most of the original features were to be left untouched.

The entrance hall had a high ceiling with huge crystal chandeliers complementing the interior perfectly. The original stone bricks had been cleaned and restored to their original warm ivory tone. They passed the reception desk adjacent to the wide curved stone staircase; the centrepiece of the hall.

They went up in the glass lift, all the more to admire the interior. Looking up, Rowanne could make out the gargoyles and faces carved into the ceiling. *Breathtaking*, she thought. It afforded one the chance to really observe the features of the building which otherwise would have been lost to obscurity; from the ground it was difficult to appreciate their finer intricacies.

'John, I thought the offices were relocated to the ground floor?'

'They were, Ms Knight, but a burst pipe caused the offices to flood.'

'Where are they now?'

'The top floor. Or, one wing of the top floor, I should say.'

She was silent for the rest of the way up. She could finally go back to what she loved doing the most. She had *butterflies* in her stomach, and felt excited and scared, caught in the middle of these two polar emotions. *Get a grip, honestly!* She felt like a violin, whose strings were too finely tuned and if the pegs were tightened anymore, she might break.

Getting out of the lift, she briefly stopped to glance at her appearance in an office window. Her sparkling green eyes stared back, although dark rings encased her irises, a sign of all the stress she'd been feeling lately. Her smile was brittle. *Damn it, pull yourself together,* she thought.

Giving herself a stern rebuke did nothing for her nerves, but she managed not to channel manic into her appearance. At least that was something. Taking a couple of deep breaths she continued to follow the security guard down the hallway.

To Rowanne it felt like her first day at work again, her heart racing the closer she got. They walked along a corridor, and passed under arches; these small sections were open to the elements, although they did have a roof covering. She felt a slight breeze, as they were near the top of this massive building, and some of these courtyards linked corridors together. There were, however, glass doors at either end protecting the interior space from damage. The architecture was a marriage of the past with the present: old brick work seamlessly joined with glass.

Rowanne finally reached the new reception desk, and was given a pass by the receptionist. She smiled up at the woman in the black suit, realising that she too was new, and wondered how many more employees had joined their newspaper.

'Good morning. I'm Amanda.'

Rowanne thought that the woman was probably in her early twenties, if not twenty-two. She was tall, which was evident as she came around the desk to shake her hand, and her long straight blonde hair framed her heart shaped face.

'Nice to meet you. I'm Rowanne Knight.' She felt instantly at ease with this woman whom she had only just met. She didn't know whether it was her friendly demeanour or the way her smile reached her eyes, letting you know that she was actually happy to meet you, rather than a polite formality.

'Ms Knight, it's a pleasure to finally meet you. I have read all of your award winning articles. Eileen has been briefing me over the last two days, and speaks warmly of you-'

'I have to stop you right there,' said Rowanne shaking her head, and raising an eyebrow, 'she'd no more speak warmly of me than the rest of the team. You nearly had me there for a moment!'

With a slight blush, Amanda conceded to Rowanne's point. 'Well, the last two days have been a real eye opener, an education, one might say.' Her eyes held a look of amusement, while the rest of her face appeared serious.

'Now that, I can believe. So, welcome to the paper.' They laughed, having both gone through an initiation of sorts. 'What's the program for today? Is everyone coming in? And I assume there's still a paper to run?' asked Rowanne.

'The last time I checked, which by the way was five minutes ago, there still was. Unless a major catastrophe has occurred and David is suddenly in charge. Other than that, everyone has come in, and you are the last person, well minus one other that everyone has been eagerly awaiting. That's where you have to go,' Amanda indicated the last door in the corridor with an incline of her head. 'I'll take you there now, if you're ready?'

'I'm ready. It feels like aeons since I last saw the gang, but it must just have been a week ago. You know before...'

'Before the disappearance of Thomas?'

Rowanne saw compassion in the young woman's eyes, and liked her the more for it.

'Yes, that's right.' Rowanne felt as if she could not talk about him any further.

Amanda noticed how uncomfortable the subject was making her and moved on to other topics to distract her, while she led Rowanne down the corridor to the office.

The room had glass walls, and two large doors opened inwards. Rowanne's first impression was that she'd stepped into the past. There were high arches and columns she noticed as they passed a security area, walking past the rows of tables sectioned by glass cubicles. As they neared the back of the room, Rowanne noticed a huge mahogany boardroom table, enough to seat everyone twice over.

My goodness that's massive, and to top it off the chairs were all made from mahogany as well with wooden scrolled arm rests, and cushioned tapestries as back rests. Though by far, the best piece was the awe-inspiring chandelier that hung directly above the board table. It was in the replica of their historic building, and so precisely detailed, that one might assume a laser printer had created it, not to mention its immense size. It was more than beautiful, but she could not think of the word that would do it justice.

Continuing on through the office, Rowanne passed by computers that had the latest flat touch screens, replacing their old chunky desktops that frankly had belonged in a museum. She could not help but think about how much money must have been spent on the renovations of their offices as well as all this new up market tech. They'd certainly outdone themselves.

Rowanne approached her colleagues sitting at the board table; they looked as lost as she felt. *Maybe I'm projecting my own emotions onto them, I don't know.*

They looked up at Rowanne and smiled. She momentarily felt intimidated when they all approached her as a group.

Eileen came over and patted her on the shoulder, giving her a genuinely warm smile (as opposed to the formal ones, that were a polite but distant acknowledgement).

'Well, Eileen, what's brought on this sudden caring side of you?' asked Rowanne.

'Rowanne, I could easily have you fired,' replied Eileen sweetly with a look of slight annoyance. 'But on a serious note, you had me worried there for a bit. And we will talk more later,' she whispered, moving away to allow the others to have their chance.

'There's the Eileen I know and love,' replied Rowanne in an equally sincere manner.

Eileen raised an eyebrow, before making her way back to the head of the table.

'So, Rowanne, how have you been? Awfully sorry to hear about the business with the guard. But where have you been?' asked David.

David was a man in his early thirties, who had sparkling blue eyes and short blond hair. He behaved as a man far older, than himself; somewhat closer to the Victorian period.

Rowanne knew that she was being unfair and childish. He was actually a well spoken and smart man, who was genuinely decent.

However, his problem was that his efficiency coupled badly with his cheery demeanour; he was always ready to volunteer to pick up everyone else's slack, as well as requesting extra work, and this irked his colleagues. All of whom were equally hard working and dedicated, but rather more relaxed.

'Have there been any leads yet on Thomas's case?' asked Rowanne, completely veering off the topic.

David raised his eyebrows at Rowanne's blatant refusal to talk about her absence. *Smoothly done, Knight.* He did not let his slight irritation at having his question unanswered show; his expression calm.

'The paper has been helping the police with what little information it has. But to be frank, it's worth tuppence, nothing to point us in any real direction, apart from that alleged skirmish outside. No one else has come forward with anything new.'

'It is puzzling. And that reminds me, I'm due to go down to the police station later on today.' *Keep your face expressionless*, Rowanne told herself.

'That's right, *you* were the last one in the office Thursday night. I remember leaving before you. By the way, how did that story shape up then?'

'Just fine... Eileen liked it well enough.'

'I do beg your pardon. I was genuinely interested in knowing how it turned out. It *was* meant with the best of intentions,' said David, with an awkward smile.

Rowanne noticed that he suddenly had his hands clasped behind his back. *Oh no, he's got a weird expression on his face as if he's about to do something foolish.*

With a pained look of forced cheerfulness, David gave her shoulder a pat, and then proceeded to walk past her to the board table, where he took his seat.

Voila! just as I expected. What was that? She had thought that he would have come out with something on the lines of: 'There, there, dear,' or 'chin up,' or some other peculiar quip that she had come to associate with him. Rowanne was mildly amused, if somewhat puzzled.

Pushing the incident from her mind, she greeted the rest of the team. About ten minutes must have passed before Eileen indicated for everyone to take their seats, and they rapidly began to fill up. Eileen began the discussion on the direction that she would like to take the newspaper in.

There were papers piled in front of everyone, including a pile directly opposite Rowanne in front of a vacant seat. She wondered who they could be expecting. A guest maybe, or a new employee. Everyone else seemed to be accounted for as she looked around.

'First, I want to welcome everyone back. I'm glad you're all in one piece.' The staff responded with nervous laughter and coughing in the face of this slightly crass statement.

It was as if nothing could affect Eileen, she always gave off a wave of steely energy, Rowanne observed.

'Of course, we are deeply concerned with the disappearance of our most beloved security guard Thomas,' said Eileen, in the same formal manner with a neutral expression, belying no emotion whatsoever.

Eileen was one of the strongest women Rowanne knew, but even she thought the title of 'Ice Queen' was apt here. She had expected her to show genuine concern as she was close to Thomas and his family. He'd always escorted Eileen out when she was the last person to leave and lock up the office.

'As you know there is a police investigation going on into Thomas's disappearance. I would be extremely grateful if you could all assist the police with any information you think may be pertinent to the case. I will of course keep you all up to date.'

'When will we shift back to our old place?' asked a colleague.

'Well, I don't suppose you saw the police coverage... Been away have you?' asked Eileen in disgust of the fool who had apparently missed the recent events. 'The office is in no condition for us to work in right now. The wiring has been ripped out in certain places and it's a wreck. It's going to take some time to sort out. Time, I might remind each and every one of you, that we as a paper do not have the luxury of! I personally felt it was the right time to move into a better space. I am more than pleased with what we have been compensated with.'

'Yes, on this point, I'm slightly confused. How were we able to suddenly afford all of these new upgrades, not to mention this exclusive space?' asked Rowanne, more than curious to know where the money had come from. Even though they were one of the top newspapers, they'd had to make do for so long, partially to do with Eileen's frugality. It was bizarre to say the least, this move up for them. The journalist in her never slept.

'Well, I'm not at liberty to discuss the finer points of our new arrangements, but suffice to say it was a private benefactor,' replied Eileen.

This statement caused several conversations to break out as everyone began to speak at once, speculating as to the identity of their benevolent benefactor. There were murmurs of dissent, and one man went so far as to stand up and dramatically slam his fist into the table; talk about passion!

'Look, Eileen. I signed up to be a journalist, investigating and getting to the truth, not to work for some snotty rich bloke. Are we now to write what this new guy tells us to? Because, if that's the case, then I'll walk away today!' he said.

'Hold on.' Eileen put her hands out to stop the discussion from getting any more out of control than it already was. 'First of all, I made no reference to the gender of our benefactor. Secondly, the last time I checked, I am your manager, and you are answerable to me!'

Gruffly, the man acceded to her point and sat down. A slight blush highlighted his cheeks, as he thought of the folly of taking on Eileen; a fine manger and woman in her own right.

'Though we are indebted to this individual, we by no means have an obligation to them. Let me make it clear,' said Eileen, as she pointedly looked around the room, and continued, 'they have not asked for anything in return. When they approached me in a meeting, I clearly stipulated that they were more than welcome to make a generous donation, and that of course their name would be mentioned, and put on a plaque to honour them!'

The team broke out in laughter.

Eileen waited for them to quiet down, as she continued, 'But they wanted their anonymity. That was one of the demands that they made. So, I'm not at liberty to disclose further information with anyone in the office as to their identity. Moving back to our original subject, I'd like to remind you all that the offices on the first floor are out of bounds, and if there's anything you need, then tough. You'll just have to wait until the investigation is over, so unless it is urgent, I'd like to ask for your patience.'

Looking around, Eileen could tell that this news, had not gone down too well. If she could handle this slight hitch, then surely the rest of them could manage.

'I've highlighted the information I want you to focus on in each of your files, that should update all of you. Also, you may have noticed there's a vacant seat, reserved for our newest member of staff who will be joining our award winning team today!'

Conjecture immediately broke out as to who the new individual might be. There were helpful suggestions as to what the newcomer could do in terms of important tasks:

such as locating the photocopier, as well as the all important coffee machine.

'Newbie could start by bringing us all a welcome back coffee, followed by the elegant welcome back drink. I'm sure he or she will be happy to pay.'

'Yeah, they're probably just grateful to get this position!'

'Hey, Eileen, you're not firing one of us now, are you?'

Finally, Eileen brought everyone under control. 'Just give me a reason, any reason will do, and I'll be happy to oblige!' She looked at the team malignantly, then broke out in a genuine smile.

The atmosphere returned back to normal, and Rowanne got caught up in a conversation with her colleagues, and failed to notice that the seat directly across from her was now occupied.

The lights in the room briefly flickered and looking up Rowanne suddenly found herself captured in the gaze of the stranger opposite her. The room seemed to darken, and the only source of illumination that she could find was in the twin pools of sapphire fire that were his eyes. It was only for a moment, but it felt longer, and she felt slightly unnerved; it was like déjà vu. *Have I met him before? He's certainly not someone that I'd likely forget...* Only when the stranger released her gaze could she look away.

Finally, thought Alexander, *we meet at last in the formal sense.* He smiled with dark amusement, as he secretly congratulated Rowanne for her conscious state. She had now been a whole minute in his company and had not fainted or fallen, and had even managed to keep herself out of trouble.

Rowanne felt slightly flustered and chilled at the same time, and pointedly kept her eyes fixed on a point of the table which suddenly required her urgent attention as her heart re-entered her body.

'I want us all to welcome our newest member to our organisation, Mr Alexander Black.'

As everyone's attention turned to Alexander, Rowanne steeled herself for a second glance. This time however, she had no repeats of the incident, and put it down to fatigue.

Now that Rowanne was not directly in thrall to his eyes, *if I ever was*! she thought distractedly, she could make out more of his features. His age she put down to possibly around thirty years old. And as he stood up to say a few words, she realised he was tall and lithe, and there was more than a hint that he worked out; possibly every day. She thought of all this as dispassionately as a reporter gathering facts, with no hint of emotion attached. Although, she had to begrudgingly admit, that his face was all the more remarkable for those striking sapphire eyes.

Meanwhile, Alexander scanned the room, taking notice of everyone, and mentally filing away any information he could discern about them; after all, it could come in handy at just the right moment.

Eileen gathered the whole group for an informal get together, so that they could welcome Alexander for at least half an hour. This was considered quite generous by Eileen's standards, mused Rowanne.

Rowanne grabbed an orange juice from the nearest table as she decided to explore the new offices to try and get a feel for the new place. She was admiring one of the tapestries on the wall when she felt a hand on her shoulder.

Rowanne turned around, it was Eileen, who felt it her solemn duty to introduce one of her rising stars to the new guy. She'd expected there to be a long speech, but for once Eileen was succinct.

'Mr Alexander Black, let me introduce you to Ms Rowanne Knight,' with a look of satisfaction, she continued, 'I will leave the two of you to get acquainted,' and with that rather short and momentous speech (well, momentous probably in her mind) Eileen walked back to the gathering, grabbing a glass of red on the way.

Thanks, Eileen. Great, she had just dumped another new guy on her. *Am I supposed to be his babysitter or something?* Rowanne was less than amused to continuously find herself in these situations — courtesy of Eileen.

Bloody Hell, babysitter indeed! thought an irate Alexander. *I saved her miserable life countless times, granted she can't recall this, but you'd think there'd be some sense of gratitude or at least courtesy; sadly lacking in this century.*

Pulling himself together with an idiotic look of subtle puzzlement, he played the part of the new worker. *Great, I've sunk to new lows that I thought I couldn't possibly reach, but this woman seems to inadvertently find a plethora of ways to make my life wretched!* There was no dearth to what she could do... He was no longer the Great Alexander, but a bloody human. *If you only knew my real age...* he thought smugly, as a point in his favour.

'I apologise if I've interrupted you. Eileen took me by surprise, and voila! I find myself here in your charming company,' said Alexander.

Rowanne tried to keep the irritation out of her voice, and put on a pretence of actually caring about a word he said. *I'd rather bang my head on the wall. I cannot believe I am a mentor again!* 'Eileen can be quite direct, when she wants to be.'

'I can see that perhaps this is not a good time. I'll take your leave, Ms Knight.' He bowed courteously from the waist, and turned away, intending to walk back to the reception.

'Wait, Mr Black. Please forgive my rudeness. And you can call me Rowanne. Ms Knight sounds too formal for my liking, especially in the company of a fellow colleague.'

He walked back to Rowanne, and with a grave expression said, 'Please, call me Alexander,' and as he extended his hand, he broke out in his first genuine smile of the morning.

Rowanne knew it was stupid, but suddenly the thought of actually shaking his hand unnerved her. Smiling awkwardly, she slowly reached for his hand.

Alexander took one step towards her, and gently encased her smaller hand in his larger calloused one.

Rowanne was forced to look up as he was slightly taller than her. Again, an unpleasant sensation ran through her as soon as their hands and eyes met. She didn't quite trust the peculiar look that had come into his eyes, nor could she read his expression, and she quickly stepped back, forcing him to release her hand abruptly. He appeared mildly amused by it. *Damn you*, she thought contemptuously; she did not appreciate anyone making her feel this way.

'You're welcome,' he said, looking at her pointedly.

'I beg your pardon, did you just say something?' asked Rowanne.

Alexander shook his head in a perplexed manner.

'Alexander, have you ever worked for a newspaper before?' This was safer ground for her.

'I have not as such worked at a newspaper, but I have been involved in the field of investigation, you might say.'

Rowanne wondered why he was so cryptic about his previous job, and speculated as to what it might have been. 'Did you work for the police force?'

'No, I have not worked in an official capacity with the police.'

What about in an unofficial capacity? 'Hmm, you seem to be a man of mystery. Are you a spy then?!' laughed Rowanne.

Alexander smiled coldly. 'Do I look like a spy to you?'

Rowanne assessed his three-piece, very expensive looking, tailor made suit complete with brogues.

'How can you tell if someone's a spy? I mean apart from the badge that they'd wear on their apparel.'

'Touché, Rowanne. But no. I'm not a spy,' he said, liking this bizarre exchange less and less. Looking at her earnestly, he said with a hint of finality to his voice, '*Laisser seul*, Ms Rowanne.'

He obviously did not want her to pursue the topic further,

so Rowanne dropped the subject for now. *But mark my words, I will come back to it.* She was a journalist after all, and they were not exactly known for being timid, or letting things go. *'Laisser seul' indeed!* Rowanne looked at him with a painted on barely-there smile, seething underneath.

David walked over and smiled at Rowanne, oblivious to the now frosty atmosphere between the two. 'I see that you are getting acquainted with Mr Black.' He turned to Alexander, 'Well Well, Mr Black, I won't let you detain Ms Knight for the whole of the soirée.'

'Hardly a soirée, Jonathan,' said Rowanne, exasperated by his constant need to interfere in everyone's life.

Alexander turned to David nonplussed. 'I believe we have not yet been formally introduced.'

Alexander gave David the handshake of a lifetime (which he would be unlikely to forget anytime soon) looking at him intensely.

David stepped back suddenly, and Alexander casually released his hand at the same time. David proceeded to put his arm around Rowanne, and said quite loudly, 'I think Eileen wants a word with you,' and began to shepherd her back to the others.

Alexander laughed darkly as he watched the poor fool with his charge. *Well, that went well... probably best to tone it done a notch,* he thought as he tried to get his bearings. He had found the expression on Rowanne's face to be priceless.

Rowanne was fuming at David for herding her to safety. However, she could not do a thing about it as she did not want to make a scene, especially in front of all her colleagues. She spoke to them all, and politely removed herself from David's company.

As soon as Rowanne was alone, she had the time to think about the events that still lay ahead in the evening. The morning passed quickly, and she managed to collect and research as much as she could before it was finally time to head home. The new guy had left shortly after the reception, and she had not seen him since he left with Eileen, who was no doubt giving him the grand tour.

Rowanne looked around the office, everyone was at their desk furiously typing up assignments in time for the deadline. *Now for the hard part...* She could feel the giant knot in her stomach, twisting in every conceivable way. Her anxiety only increased as she put away the last of the work in her bag; she was absolutely dreading going down to the police station.

It was four o'clock, and in two hours time they would be questioning her. *What the hell am I going to say?* she wondered as she got into her car.

Looking in the mirror she was shocked to discover that she was heavily perspiring. *If I didn't give the game away before...* she thought, as she imagined herself walking into the police station with water running in rivulets down her face, and to complete this guilty ensemble: she'd be trembling. All this, even before she opened her mouth, would easily pronounce her guilty.

Driving home in a sombre mood, Rowanne tried to keep her mind on the road, but it kept careening of course and going around in circles, repeatedly returning to the police investigation. Somehow she managed to get home, and walking to the lift felt like a physical challenge; just trying to keep one foot going in front of the other.

Shaking, Rowanne finally managed to open her door, and with jittery legs she walked over to the couch and simply collapsed onto it. Feeling better, she had just decided to freshen up when the doorbell rang. 'Can't I even get five minutes to myself to just relax?' she asked irritably.

She strode up to the door as the person on the other side kept up their persistent tirade. *It's probably someone selling something,* she thought, but looking into the peephole made her already terrible mood worse. Trying to compose herself, she took a couple of breaths to ease her tension, rearranged her face into a suitable expression, and, smiling, opened the door to the new guy.

'Good evening, Rowanne. I hope I'm not disturbing you?' asked Alexander.

'Not at all. I was just finishing up on a couple of things before I headed down to the police station.' Then in an irritated manner she continued, 'I don't mean to seem less than hospitable, but I'm really busy and short on time.'

He could tell that she was annoyed. *She can't wait to get rid of me*, thought a rather perplexed Alexander, feeling put out. *Now how shall I go about this...* 'I'm going to drive down to the police station to check on the progress of the investigation, and Eileen asked me to stop by and offer you a lift. I mean,' and looking embarrassed at his faux-pas he continued, 'I'd like to drive you down, if you wouldn't mind?'

'Really?' asked Rowanne.

She did not seem pleased by his suggestion; in fact, the opposite of what he had been expecting. *What have I said...* wondered Alexander, and could feel his blood pressure rising at her smug look, and with a touch of annoyance he replied, 'Yes, of course.'

Rowanne looked at cool, collected Alexander, and was happy to see his facade slip to show the man beneath. *So, you are actually capable of showing emotion.* She waited a moment more, enjoying his discomfort, before replying, 'I have a car, and I am perfectly capable of driving myself to the police station.'

'Oh. Forgive me, I was unaware. Eileen left that small nugget out of our conversation.'

Alexander was embarrassed, and Rowanne realised that he had just wanted to be of help to his new colleagues. Ashamed at the way she had spoken to him, and remembering her own cringe worthy first few weeks at work, she set about clearing up the misunderstandings between them.

'Pardon my manners,' said Rowanne, apologetically.

Rowanne became more comfortable, Alexander observed, when she was not feeling so tense around him. 'I think, both of us have just had an encounter of the Eileen kind, which explains our temporary loss of sanity, and why my nerves are so frayed!' he added ruefully.

Laughing, Rowanne said, 'I think you could be right. Would you like to come in and have a drink?'

'Thank you. I don't know about you, but heading down to the police station is not my idea of a good time, but it comes with the job, I suppose,' he added.

'It's a perk alright,' she replied wryly nodding her head in agreement. 'Please, make yourself comfortable.' And once he had sat down, she asked, 'What can I get you?'

'I'd like something strong... Tea would be great, thank you.'

Alexander was content in just watching Rowanne, as she prepared the tea. And leaving the water to boil, she went into a room which he knew to be her bedroom. The same way he knew she had a car...

What shall I wear? she thought, closing the door and gently locking it behind her, not bothered in the least if she appeared rude. After all, he was a stranger, and what did she really know about him...

Searching through her wardrobe, Rowanne picked out a smart black dress and low heeled shoes. She tied her hair back into a ponytail. Looking back at her in the mirror was an effortlessly stylish woman, with nervous green eyes. *Great, now what?* shaking her head, she headed back out to the kitchen.

'Hey, you didn't have to do that,' said Rowanne, deeply mortified at finding Alexander pouring the tea into two bone china cups. The fact that he was her guest, and especially after the way she had just treated him, made her feel like a terrible host.

Alexander looked up at her, and smiled sheepishly. 'Honestly, it was no trouble at all. I have this innate problem of not being able to sit still, even for a few moments.'

'I could have sworn I just left the kettle to boil, and I don't remember getting the cups out, either...'

'You had everything laid out, it just slipped your mind. You seem to have a lot on your mind,' he said in a sympathetic tone of voice.

'Excuse me?' asked Rowanne angrily.

'I was just referring to the police investigation,' replied Alexander.

'Yes, right. Sorry, I didn't mean to snap.'

Taking a deep breath, she let her guard down once more. *I don't know why in the world I would with this stranger, let alone with anyone else. What is it about this man...*

'I've been under some stress lately. You see, I knew Thomas and his family. He was- I mean he *is* a genuinely nice man. I've been wondering about what might have happened to him, and also...' She had nearly blurted out the truth about Thursday night, but something at the last moment compelled her to keep her mouth shut.

'Sorry, you were saying?' asked Alexander kindly.

Rowanne looked at him cautiously before continuing, 'I was wondering... how his family were coping. Not to mention the several stories I'm dealing with at the moment,' she added lamely.

This is bad, thought Alexander. *If she continues like this up at the police station, then she's going to make life difficult for all of us. Damn it! She nearly blurted out the truth, or partial truth I should say. If she can't pass at the police station, if she should fail...*

Alexander put his rising panic under control, and clenched his fists a couple of times as he tried to ease the tension out of his body. He gently laid a hand on her shoulder, and led her to the couch. 'Please, sit down.' He brought over the steaming cups of tea from the kitchen, and placed one in her ice cold hands.

Rowanne seemed to stir from her reverie as she felt warm hands covering her own. She looked up into kind gentle eyes, and Alexander politely moved back to sit on the couch opposite her, and picked up his mug.

Alexander waited patiently, and then slowly began to coax the truth from her. 'Please, tell me more,' he recommenced gently.

'What are you talking about?' asked Rowanne.

'I think you know what I mean,' he replied assuredly.

'Anyway, there isn't anything more.'

'I just want to help you,' said Alexander.

'You certainly are no friend of mine. And what gives you the right to question me?' asked Rowanne contemptuously.

'No, and excuse my language, I bloody well am not. But I am the *only* one here!' he replied in an offended tone, but continued carefully, 'I could be, if...'

'If what?' Rowanne glowered at him.

'If you'll let me help you. I'll hear anything you have to say.'

Rowanne was fuming. Her shoulders shook, and her eyes shone with unshed tears threatening to spill over. She had finally had enough, and slammed her mug down onto the table causing the tea to spill. She scalded her hand in the process, but the pain only fuelled her anger.

'Oh, look what you've made me do! Who the hell are you? A complete stranger, barging into *my* home on the pretence,' and looking up at his hurt and shocked expression; which she vehemently chose to ignore, continued, 'yes, you heard right. On the pretence of being a helpful colleague, you then proceeded to interrogate me!' she said heatedly.

'Look, I think there's been a misunderstanding,' said Alexander, holding up his hands, hoping to appear less threatening.

'Get out! Before I...' shouted Rowanne at the top of her voice.

Alexander was barely able to control himself, let alone the escalating situation spiralling wildly out of his control. He too snapped and suddenly stood up to confront her.

'You'll what? Is this any way to treat a guest in your home?' he asked, equally peeved.

'I'm warning you, stay back,' said Rowanne, as Alexander cautiously approached her.

He wondered whether the entity was interfering with her mind as she appeared mentally unstable, and he feared that she might harm herself.

She got up, and slowly backed up into the kitchen until she felt the counter behind her. Turning around, she put her hands on the counter top and closed her eyes, breathing in and out a couple of times as she took deep shuddering breaths.

Her inner voice cautioned her not to give the game away, that there would be consequences in telling the truth. Bizarrely, her inner voice changed from being gentle to suddenly becoming sharp and commanding. Almost, as if it was taking control of her...

Stop! Listen to me.

Pardon? asked Rowanne, puzzled at where this voice was coming from. *Is it my mind talking to me? It certainly doesn't sound like me...* She felt afraid, yet strangely comforted at the same time.

Just do as I say, and I'll get you through this. All you have to do is smile, and repeat everything I tell you. Do you understand?

Yes, replied Rowanne to the voice in her mind.

Rowanne turned back and tried to focus on Alexander.

'Sorry, about that little outburst...' she said, slowly smiling at him. 'You see, I get these panic attacks sometimes.'

That's good. Stick near enough to the truth that it won't raise his suspicion, and he will be more inclined to believe it.

Alexander stopped in his tracks, a sceptical look on his face. Rowanne noticed that he was looking at her like she had a split personality. *He's not buying it. He knows I'm lying.* Her calm facade was in imminent danger of shattering.

You're doing fine, keep going, the voice in her mind encouraged her.

'I've recently gone through something and the memory of it brings on these panic attacks,' continued Rowanne bravely.

Alexander seemed less than impressed with what he had heard so far, and asked in a brusque manner, 'Right... And what exactly have you gone through, may I dare ask?'

'I don't feel the need to elaborate, or share my life story with a total stranger,' replied Rowanne pointedly looking at him.

Not in the least bit put off, he continued, 'Forgive my interference. I thought it might have had something to do with Thomas.'

'Well, you thought wrong!'

After a thoughtful pause, he asked, 'Are you taking anything for these panic attacks?'

Rowanne looked at him sweetly, and Alexander thought that she might actually give him an honest answer.

'In fact, as you've so politely asked, it's... none of your business! And it doesn't concern *you*.'

Alexander felt a metaphorical slap in his face. *The hell it doesn't,* he thought, furious with her. Holding up his hands and shaking his head in annoyance, he backed away and sat on the couch, counting to ten slowly to calm down. One of them would have to be the sane one in this situation. He then proceeded to methodically drink his tea.

Rowanne came to the table and wiped it clean. She sat down, and coughed to get his attention.

Alexander looked up at her, and thought manically, *She appears composed, but you can't always tell with her!*

Sighing, she asked, 'Do you still want to know what happened?'

Alexander continued to look at her with a stoic expression, not trusting himself to speak.

'Fine, though there isn't much to tell. I was working late that night, like I normally do. You know how it is with deadlines to meet etc... I was the last one in the office, and left just after nine.'

At this point in the story, Alexander sat up a little straighter, suddenly showing symptoms of actually being interested in her account.

Sorry, thought Rowanne, *there's nothing extraordinary coming your way*. 'I walked towards the car park, which I should point out is poorly lit.'

Alexander's heart began to pound as he waited, to see which way her story would unfold.

'Then I-'

'Yes?' he asked eagerly, as he mentally willed for her to go on; to put him out of his misery.

'Drove home, and the first I heard of this was on the news,' finished Rowanne.

'Judging by your earlier behaviour, I thought that there might have been more to it,' stated Alexander, looking confused.

Rowanne replied solemnly, 'There is... but, not in the way you imagine. Thomas is a friend, not just a colleague.'

Alexander continued inconsiderately, 'But you're a journalist, don't you deal with these types of stories every day?' and raised an eyebrow.

'How dare you belittle this! Yes, Sherlock, I deal with these 'types of stories', as you so crudely put it, almost every day.' Rowanne took a deep breath; for some reason this pompous excuse for a man seemed to rile her. She continued in a calmer tone, 'Isn't it always different, when it's someone you know?' she asked earnestly. *Insensitive jerk! He probably doesn't own a caring bone in his body, it's like he's not even human. Can you feel any emotion?* she wondered, finishing her mental tirade.

'No!' Alexander suddenly burst out, almost scaring the living daylights out of Rowanne.

'I beg your pardon?' asked a confused Rowanne, thinking that he had just read her mind, or worse: that she'd just said all of that, out loud.

'It is different, when it is someone you know...' he said contemplatively.

Rowanne didn't know how to respond to what he'd just said, so remained quiet.

After a while, she decided to approach cautiously, 'Forgive me for asking, but has something similar happened in your life?'

'No,' replied Alexander with a sense of finality to the word that broached no further enquiry on the topic.

Hmm, thought Rowanne, *it seems as if our resident 'Ice King' is hiding something... And why would he share it, with a complete stranger? Frankly, after my outburst at him to stay out of my business, I really don't have a leg to stand on, nor do I have any right to expect him to open up to me.*

'You don't!' he said sullenly.

'Excuse me?' asked a shocked Rowanne.

Alexander looked up, and continued with a completely sombre expression, 'You don't have any biscuits by any chance, do you? I haven't eaten anything since this morning, and I'm starving!'

'Right,' laughed Rowanne, as the tense atmosphere suddenly evaporated. She dutifully proceeded to the kitchen, and began to feel more relaxed in the company of this rather brusque and foolish man.

Oh that's just great! thought Alexander, *I've definitely made an impression on this woman. 'Alexander the Great' my foot,* he thought. *I'll be laughed out of existence, let alone the Court, if they could only see me now, reduced to this pitiful state. And if that was not enough,* he thought, looking fixedly at Rowanne's back, *she thinks, I'm foolish? Me!*

He had always thought of himself as a gentle man, the epitome of calm. *I can handle any situation thrown at me*, and looking despairingly at Rowanne, who was oblivious to all this, he finished lamely, *any situation that is, but this one!*

If I had to lose my soul, all that I am, could it not have been to a more noble, more refined woman? That said, he picked up a biscuit from the plate that Rowanne had just brought in, and began to munch through them methodically like a maniac. *I lost it all*, he thought mournfully, *to this woman?* and looked at her suspiciously as he continued to munch his way through half the plate.

Rowanne sat with a mug in her hand, and started to shake as she tried to suppress her laughter. *He really does look like some kind of crazy Cookie Monster*, she thought, as he devoured the whole plate. She got up and went to the kitchen to diligently refill it. Sometimes you just need a cup of tea and a biscuit, or biscuits in his case. Maybe he needed a sugar and caffeine hit; a deadly combo. *Poor thing, he's hungry, maybe he can handle it*. Rowanne was content to just sit there for a while.

All too soon the moment of calm had passed; it was time to face the storm. Rowanne reluctantly got up and grabbed her coat and bag. Alexander took the cue and put on his own coat. Together they walked out of the apartment.

They silently rode down in the lift, neither one saying a thing, each lost in their own thoughts. They walked to Alexander's car. Rowanne no longer wanted to argue the childish point and acceded to Alexander driving her.

He looked at her and asked cautiously, 'Look, I can drop you back as well, if you'd like?'

After some consideration, she replied thoughtfully, 'Let's just see how this turns out, alright? And thanks, I might very well take you up on your offer,' and gave him her first real smile.

Her legs were shaking, and she had a fine tremor running through her body; Alexander noticed all this as he walked beside her. He opened the passenger door to let her in. She sat quietly, as he got in and closed his door. He pulled out of the car park, and in no time at all, they were on the main road.

They drove in silence, Rowanne lost in her thoughts, and Alexander feeling at a loss for what to say; not trusting himself to speak. *The last thing we need, is for me to say something stupid, and have her feel even more tense than she is now, especially before the 'Police Interview,'* he thought ironically.

CHAPTER 7

In less than half an hour, they had made it to the police station. Rowanne quickly got out of the car as soon as it had stopped, and proceeded to walk sedately towards the stairs, not bothering to wait for Alexander.

Alexander could not immediately follow her because of the parking restrictions, and was therefore delayed and highly annoyed at not being by her side. He drove around the back looking for a place to park.

Keep walking, one foot in front of the other, you're a confident journalist. The most you have to do is answer a few questions. Relax, you'll do just fine. With that thought in mind, Rowanne finally looked behind her to see what was keeping Alexander. The sun rapidly began to set, and for a second Alexander was bathed in a fiery glow. Rowanne gasped: she could not see him clearly, he appeared as a silhouette against the infernal backdrop. Darkness descended with each step he took towards her.

Night was falling, dropping its veil over the sun, stealing its warmth. Rowanne shivered, and wrapped her arms around her bare shoulders to keep out the autumn cold. Alexander finally arrived, holding out her coat which she duly put on. In silence, she proceeded to walk to the building that now appeared to loom over her. Alexander kept pace with her as she entered the station.

She felt sick as she reached the reception desk, but knew that she had to keep herself together. *I am a journalist, am I not? This is what I do, damn it! I could do this much at least – I mean I will.*

Alexander resisted the urge to place his hand on her shoulder, to reassure her. He could feel his hand trembling with the effort not to, but he could not, especially here anyway. Leaning into her gently, he whispered by her ear, 'Rowanne, I can't come through with you, but I'll wait here. I've got some work on behalf of Eileen that needs to be done.' He gave her a warm reassuring smile; the only useful thing he could do for her.

Rowanne nodded her head, and turned away from him to talk to the officer on the reception desk. However, from the corner of her eye, she noticed Alexander walking away and began to feel his absence. She had to swallow before she could speak.

'Good evening,' Rowanne spoke confidently.

The young officer looked up, 'How may I help you?'

'I'm Ms Knight, and I'm here to see the Detective Chief Inspector for my interview.'

He checked through the records. 'Ms Knight, if you'd be so kind as to sign the visitor's book,' and as Rowanne hastily scribbled her name, he continued, 'please, follow me. The Chief Inspector can finally get started, he's been waiting for you.'

This sounded slightly ominous to Rowanne, but she mumbled a thank you and followed him down a long stretch of corridor, then through a set of double doors as they proceeded down a set of stairs. After what felt like a couple of flights down, they walked along yet another corridor. Finally, the officer left her waiting outside the interview room while he went in ahead of her. A minute later, he reappeared and ushered her in, then left abruptly, closing the door behind him.

Rowanne looked around the room nervously. It was poorly lit, most of the light seemed to centre around the middle section. She also spotted the two way mirror behind the table, where the detective occupied one of the two chairs.

He was a man in his mid twenties. His incredibly long legs were crossed in front of him. He had a toned physique, and his sleeves were rolled up above his elbows showing off his powerfully built arms. Rowanne had to suppress the urge not to stare as the detective had long red hair, and she wondered whether it was his natural colour, or whether he had dyed it.

He looked up at her, 'Good evening, Ms Knight. I am Detective Chief Inspector Driskell. Please, take a seat.'

'Thank you,' she replied, in what she hoped was a composed manner.

Alexander cloaked himself entirely, so that neither the humans nor demons would be able to detect him. What he had just seen through the two way mirror had sent shock waves through him, and a coldness encased his heart as he continued to watch the chilling scene unfold before his eyes. It was what he'd expected, but he'd hoped it would just stop at the interview stage, but apparently it was about to escalate.

Damn it! I can't even get into the room without revealing myself, and the blasted door has a magic seal on it. No human would be able to hear anything that went on in that particular interview room, let alone get into it. Once the doors had closed behind the human officer, that was it, they could not be opened from the outside.

Forcing himself to look back, Alexander noticed that the room had a fiery glow to it. It was in actual fact a vast chamber with a high ceiling, and the tiny room at the station only occupied the central space, or what was left of the original room. Surrounding the interview room were rows of long tables that were occupied by the law enforcement of his realm. His attention immediately centred on the one Noble surrounded by soldiers, all present as witnesses to the trial of Rowanne, or rather, he hoped, in potentia. He fervently hoped that it wouldn't go that far.

He damned the Shadows interest in her, because they, along with the incidents at the office, had no doubt attracted the attention of his people. He pondered as to how much they could know. If they knew everything, then it was all over. It finally sunk into Alexander that not only his life, but also Rowanne's, could come to a horrific end.

There were trials in his world for demons, as well as humans, especially in regards to a human finding out about Demon World. It was a million times worse if a demon actually revealed Demon World to a human of their own volition. The consequences for the latter were unspeakable. Not to mention that Rowanne's family, as well as his own, and anyone else who could be linked to them, were all in danger.

What have I done... thought Alexander, suddenly panic stricken. *What the hell have I done?* and he punched the solid concrete wall next to him so hard that it left an indentation. *I will have to fix that,* he thought distractedly.

A cold sweat began to run down his back, and a fine tremor ran through his body as the repercussions of his foolishness now struck him. He pulled himself sharply together. Now was not the time to fall apart. A deadly gray light entered his eyes, and his iris was encased in a blazing green circle. *I have to control myself for the both of us, or it's over right here!* thought Alexander. *I'm not ready to die. Not today. Let alone, this very moment!*

'Ms Knight, would you be so kind as to look at these documents for me?' asked the detective.

He has a slightly creepy smile, thought Rowanne.

Don't Look. Don't Look...

Before Rowanne's inner voice had the chance to save her, it was too late. She looked, and that was it. She felt as if she were falling forward, and she looked up into the detective's simmering green eyes and knowing smile once before losing consciousness.

Alexander cursed as he watched Rowanne being pulled into his world. It had all happened so fast that he had not had the time to react. He helplessly looked on at the now vacant interview room.

Damn it, I thought it was only an interview. They were supposed to start the initial proceeding in the manner of the human world, and then, and only then, escalate it to his world as a last resort. He wondered what had made them take this drastic step... What if they had found something linking Rowanne to him? Dark thoughts churned in Alexander's mind as his sapphire eyes started to bleed to a steely gray. He mentally prepared himself for an oncoming battle. *Always better to be prepared, after all.*

'Members of the realm, I present to you our next case involving a human, Ms Rowanne Knight who was allegedly present in the demon/human altercation that occurred at her office building. This case is delicate and extremely volatile as it involves a human law enforcer and demons coming to a confrontation, resulting in his possible disappearance. The media have unfortunately picked up on this news story, which we can all agree is not in the best interests of our world. More so, because the human police force are personally investigating it, and I will endeavour to ensure that no shred of evidence is left that could endanger our world by bringing it to the attention of the human world.'

All eyes in the room zeroed in on Rowanne, who suddenly became the centre of attention. Her fate was being debated while she slept.

Driskell continued, 'The whereabouts of the security guard are yet to be ascertained, but rest assured that I am personally taking on this case. It will only be a matter of time until I find him, or find what remains of him, and unravel this case.'

Rowanne awakened, and gradually the room came into focus. She rubbed her eyes, just to make sure, not quite believing what she saw. *I'm definitely not in the same room as before*, and looking around, she wondered in which part of the police station she had ended up in.

'I'm in a court...? How did I get here?'

The detective stepped forward and sat opposite her at the table. Rowanne's inner voice was strangely absent, and she felt alone for the first time. She was instantaneously mesmerised by the green eyes before her, and she sat a little straighter and smiled at the detective. It seemed silly that she had been afraid a minute ago. When she thought about it clearly, it all made perfect sense. *Not sure what the sense actually is...* she thought, as she shrugged her shoulders.

'Ms Knight, do you know why you are here?' asked the detective.

'No, but I expect I'm about to find out.'

'That you are,' he said in a stern voice, no longer smiling; the pretence over now that he was back in his own realm, and in his element.

'You have a nice smile,' said Rowanne, in her blissfully happy state.

'Really?' he asked, sarcasm dripping from his voice as he smiled at her, baring his perfectly polished teeth.

I wonder if he's got veneers fitted, it's like his teeth are made of porcelain. What kind of salary is he on? I'm definitely in the wrong profession!

She noticed something else that supported her theory: his expensive looking clothes. He was dressed in a designer suit, and wore a badge (some kind of insignia possibly, she could not quite tell) over the left side of his jacket, just where his heart might have been. He did not look like your everyday police detective, but someone higher up the ranks.

His black suit really set off his red hair to good effect, and his green eyes sparkled amid his cold pale skin, she observed. She could tell that he was not too pleased with her. *Uh-oh*, she thought.

'Yes,' she replied. 'When your face isn't all screwed up like that,' she continued sweetly, feeling slightly dopey as if she were drunk. She could gauge from the detective's severe gaze, combined with the glacial look that had come into his eyes, that he would definitely not go easy on her with the questioning.

Rowanne looked around again to try and get her bearings. The courtroom was vast with wood panelled walls and a high ceiling. There were benches staggered upwards all around her, filled with people, disconcertingly all watching her.

Every time she spoke, it seemed as if someone would make a note. She could not make out their features, for some reason they were a blur. It took a moment for the sensation to pass and suddenly panic set in.

As far as she knew, when a person went to the police station for an interview, they were not drugged and then immediately taken to a court to be interrogated whilst only just possessing half of their muddled faculties. She looked up sharply as the detective began to speak again.

Now was not the time for panic, she rebuked herself severely. Rowanne had no idea why she was brought to this place, or how far it was in relation to the police station in Westminster. *Is he really a detective?* she wondered suspiciously. She thanked God that whatever they had drugged her with had now worn off. All she had to do now was remain calm and act docile until she knew for certain what was going on.

Driskell specifically looked up at the people sitting on the top bench apologetically.

'Lady Enid, forgive me, but I think this one,' inclining

his head in Rowanne's direction, 'is going to take some time. She's a bit slow for a human.'

What a condescending git! thought Rowanne. *He does know my profession, right? Ow! That hurts,* she thought, moving uncomfortably in the chair without trying to draw attention to herself. Her grandmother's pendant hidden beneath her dress had given her a small shock.

It did the trick as her annoyance suddenly vanished. She reminded herself that not losing her head over her ego might just help her. She could use this situation to her advantage. Why had she let herself get worked up? The only explanation she could come up with was being in close proximity to this fool; she didn't suffer them well.

Rowanne looked towards the bench that the detective seemed to be addressing, and noticed the woman he had referred to as Lady Enid. She was wearing a long black dress as well as a black veil made of lace. Although it was hard to make out her features, the lace showed a glimpse of her gleaming blonde hair whenever it caught the light.

Rowanne assumed that Lady Enid must certainly be someone of importance, judging by the crown that she wore. It seemed to be made of silver with some sort of design that she could not really make out.

Lady Enid looked down upon Driskell as she addressed him. 'Carry on, Dewain. Take as long as is necessary. Demon World security is of paramount importance. And you would do well to remember that the House of Morning Star takes its duty and responsibility gravely.'

'Yes, my lady. Forgive me for my impertinence,' he said mockingly. 'But I could just move this case back into their world. That is, unless I find a reason for it to be otherwise. In this instance, I have the feeling it could be a false alarm.'

'There are no such things as 'false alarms', every case must be thoroughly checked. We must not become complacent, but be ever vigilant of the threat to our already precarious world. I want you to therefore proceed with your questioning.'

Driskell smiled malevolently and gave a low bow. 'As you wish, my lady.'

He turned around with a disgusted look that only Rowanne was privy to.

I think that I'm in for one hell of a ride here, and secretly smiling, she thought, *he doesn't look too pleased to be told his place, especially in front of other people. I wonder if anyone's spoken to him like that before.* Rowanne felt panic, but mostly at the idea that she might start laughing loudly. *What would he do? Would it be classed as a contempt of court?*

Breaking out of her train of thought, she watched as people began to leave, conferring in whispers. The only other person left in the court, apart from the detective and herself, was Lady Enid.

Driskell waited patiently for the room to empty, not wanting any distractions to his investigation. Looking up, he noticed Lady Enid coming down the stairs. Reaching the lower benches, she seated herself comfortably, and inclined her head that he should resume.

He needed no prompts, he was eager to get on with it. These days the job was the only thing that took precedence in his life. Many people would call him ruthless to the point of despair. Once you were investigated by Driskell, you entered willingly or not into his realm. And he did not let you leave of your own accord; his permission, nay, his pardon, was necessary.

Lady Enid sat quietly and shook her head in disgust behind Driskell's back. She had heard everything, he had thought: one of the perks of being born into the Morning Star Clan; one of many. *I agree with everything you've just said, you cold hearted parasite. Who but I can attest first hand to everything that everyone connects to your name. Demon Executioner, Judge and Jury, you call yourself. But still I think, my boy, that I hold some authority.*

A painful memory was evoked, and Lady Enid was nearly in trouble of drowning in her sorrows. However, with careful and painstaking precision, she pulled herself out of her pit of despair. She noticed the human woman being investigated, and felt an unexpected surge of pity for her. *Poor human, what did you do to end up here, of all realms?*

From time to time, humans ended up in one of their lesser courts, if it was an incident connected to Demon World through no fault of their own. This was usually the norm, but not always. If a human was found innocent, then their mind would be wiped of Demon World and false memories implanted; they were the lucky ones.

However, in cases in which humans out of their own free will chose to connect to Demon World, then the consequences for them were quite severe. There was no coming back for them. The smaller courts would be bypassed altogether, instead they'd be sent to the highest courts of the realm. The first court would judge their fate, as well as investigate anybody connected to them; their punishment would depend on how much they had learnt. This poor girl had ended up in one of the highest courts in the realm: the last one, before the Final Court, or Prima Stella as it was known.

The less said about Prima Stella, the better. Every demon in the land feared its very name. Anybody that was ever sentenced in that court never came back. There were never any details released, the outcome obscure. Nobody would dare to question the final judgement, as it was known. *We as demons know that there are worse things than death...* thought Lady Enid.

The Royal Court, otherwise referred to as the Noble Court, was equally as bad as the latter, but here the Nobles held sway upon matters concerning Demon World, and it was made up of members of the First Families. They only ever came to the proceedings if it was a particularly severe case, otherwise they left it to Lady Enid and their loyal servants. *Or servant, I should say,* thought Lady Enid, as she watched him towering over his next victim.

Driskell was about to continue with his questioning when he was interrupted by a nervous looking young man who had just entered the court.

'Sorry, to interrupt you, Sir, but you are urgently needed.'

Driskell looked as if he could murder the young man for daring to disrupt him.

'Needed urgently, you say? Tell them to wait. How dare you come in when I am in the middle of an investigation.' He said the last words in a quiet but barbed manner.

The poor man approached on trembling legs and whispered something to him. Driskell's expression remained the same: not giving anything away, nor did he feel the need to elaborate on what he had been told. The young man was duly sent out ahead of him.

Driskell turned around and bowed deeply to Lady Enid, a gravely apologetic look etched on his face.

'Forgive me, my lady, but I have to leave for a short duration as some urgent news has just reached me that requires my utmost attention. As you know, I take my duties very seriously and will never hesitate to fulfil them.' From a quiet and beseeching look, it had turned into one of ice cold arrogance. He looked deep into Lady Enid's eyes so that she could see plainly his cruelty. His look made his point and spoke volumes: things left unsaid, and better laid to rest...

Lady Enid suddenly became rigid, and Driskell smiled, relishing the fact that she understood what he had intended her to know. Turning swiftly around he strode out of the court, and the doors closed quietly on the turmoil that he had once more stirred up.

Lady Enid felt her violet eyes flare to green, but slowly and reluctantly, she reigned in her power. *I would have been content to unleash it on that evil piece of work.* However, after careful consideration, she realised that she would have a lot more questions that would need to be answered if she burnt the man to a pile of ash!

Not to mention, being tried in the Noble court. And these well meaning Nobles would feel it their obligation, and in the best interests of everyone in Demon World, to have a secure reign; not helped by an unbalanced Noble like herself. *They would send me straight to Prima Stella, and what a grand reunion that would be!*

Mentally shaking herself out of this downward spiral, Lady Enid slowed her breathing, and felt her eyes return to their natural violet. She sat quietly, watching the human woman.

Rowanne had been a silent spectator in the duel between the detective and Lady Enid. For some reason, she hated the detective with a passion, and not just because he had drugged her. *Which is completely ridiculous, since I've only just met him...* Being out of the detective's presence helped her mind become clearer.

Rowanne felt sorry for Lady Enid, and inexplicably wanted to comfort her. *What the hell is happening to me?* Where were these feelings coming from? They most certainly were not hers. Suddenly her necklace flared, and she pushed back her chair and stood up.

Lady Enid quickly took notice of the young woman. 'What are you doing? Sit down at once!'

Rowanne broke through the fog that was clouding her mind. 'It's not me. I'm not doing this!' she replied.

'What are you trying to say? Speak clearly!'

'Look, Lady Enid? I'm trying to tell you that I have no control over what my body is doing. And yes, I know that makes me sound like a crazy person.'

Lady Enid looked at the woman thoughtfully, and after careful consideration decided to help her. She had seen this type of thing before... The woman looked petrified as her body moved sporadically, as if something was trying to control it, but having difficulty in maintaining it. Could it be a case of possession, perhaps? The other possibility to consider was that there could be something wrong with the woman, medically.

'Come here, Ms Knight. Slowly. Slowly, that's right,' and at last Rowanne stood before her.

'Please, help me. I'm frightened. I don't understand what's happening to me,' and as soon as Rowanne reached for the hands of Lady Enid, she felt something crack open inside of her. Suddenly, her mind froze and something else took over. Rowanne felt her conscience propelled into a tiny corner of her mind. She tried to scream but it was silent, echoing back to her, as it bounced off the inner walls of her imprisoned mind. *Help me, help me*, she heard her own voice mocking her.

Rowanne looked up at Lady Enid, whose eyes blazed green as Rowanne's necklace started to burn against her.

I'm sorry, but Rowanne had to leave temporarily. You will now address me.

Lady Enid was shocked by the transformation. The entity, for lack of a better word, now stood in place of the petrified human. She could hear the voice of the entity within her mind. This new Rowanne seemed possessed of power, and more sure of herself, and there was also a touch of leadership about her. 'With whom am I speaking?' asked Lady Enid in an authoritative tone. She was by no means frightened, considering her ancestry; this entity would soon know its place, and that it was dealing with the wrong person.

For now, let that be a secret, Lady Enid of the Morning Star Clan. I am humbled to be in your presence, once more. It has been too long. The entity laughed, and for some reason it sent a shiver of recognition through Lady Enid, but before she could place where she had heard it before, it was gone, lost and fragmented.

'How do you know me? Answer at once.' Lady Enid wondered at how the entity knew of her status and clan name. Where could they have met before? It was obvious that whoever, and whatever, it had been did not exist anymore. It was a spectre long passed from the world of the living.

Look, I don't have much time, and this poor woman's body that I am possessing is emotionally on the verge of shattering. I dare not do this many more times, for a mind is a fragile thing, a glass ornament if you will. It has its filaments and sparks of life, but if you put too much pressure on it, it cracks. The filaments lose their connections and the spark dies out, or at the very least exist as a hollow empty replica of its former self, not yet living, but not quite dead.

Lady Enid was surprised at the entity's level of awareness and understanding. It was not malevolent, or it was not trying to be on purpose. And from what she could see so far, nor was it hurting Rowanne in any discernible way.

'Fine. For the moment, I am willing to give you the benefit of the doubt. I'll accept that you cannot tell me who you are,' although she'd find out eventually.

Thank you. I think in time, you will begin to see why it has to be this way. The entity extended Rowanne's hand toward Lady Enid. *I need you to trust in me enough to save this young woman's life. Do you think perhaps you could do that for her sake at least?*

Lady Enid found herself inexplicably warming to the young woman. She had a feeling that she could trust the woman, and perhaps even the entity. However, she was no fool; she knew perfectly well that entities could manipulate, and tell you exactly what you wanted to hear. Despite this, she extended her hand in courtesy to the entity.

Rowanne's face lit up in a smile, and her eyes held back the unshed tears threatening to spill over. It melted Lady Enid's heart, and when the young woman encased her hand in her own, she received a shock, like a current passing from the young woman's hand to her own.

It felt like déjà vu. Lady Enid almost recognised the power signature. It felt very familiar. It felt right. *What's this...* she wondered, awestruck, and for a second her heart soared with a nameless emotion. For a single moment, it had felt lighter.

I knew I could trust you. Believe me, your faith in me is warranted. I want us to work together in order to save her life.

After careful consideration, Lady Enid replied, 'I'm not sure why, but I will help you. And furthermore, you can most certainly put your trust in me, have no fear. However, we must act prudently and quickly before the detective's return.'

I perfectly comprehend your meaning, and he is most definitely not to be trusted. I feel his enmity, it radiates off him in waves.

Lady Enid nodded in accord. 'Yes, on that salient point we can agree.'

The entity looked at her thoughtfully. *Oh really? why is that?* the entity asked quietly.

Lady Enid could see the entity's tension reflected in Rowanne's face. It was almost as if her very answer was incredibly important. She did not know this woman, so why would it matter what she thought? However, after carefully weighing her words, she replied, 'There was an incident in my life that happened a very long time ago. I lost something very precious I can never get back, and have ever since reconciled in hating Driskell.' She looked curiously at the entity, and asked, 'Why do you not rejoice in the good detective's presence?'

Suffice to say that I too have had my fair share of run-ins with the dear, and spat the word contemptuously, *detective Driskell, and have come out the worst for it,* and gestured with her hands to emphasise her present lamentable state, and her plight; having to possess another's body. *This is all that remains of me. He is Dewain by name, as well as by nature.*

'I do not think that you belong to the human world. Your knowledge and manner of speaking makes me wonder if you were once a native of our world.'

You are correct, my lady, replied the entity smiling. There was a flicker of remembrance on the face.

'I have often wondered how it was possible for the demon's of our world to possess humans. But clearly, the evidence stands before me.'

The entity laughed bitterly as if at a private joke. However, sobering up, it replied, *Some questions, as I have already said, cannot be answered now. But I am surprised that you of all people would ask me this.*

Lady Enid hated it when they (entities) spoke in riddles, but let it go for now as they were running out of time. 'What exactly should we do to save this young woman's life?'

CHAPTER 8

'At precisely what time did the incident occur?' asked Driskell of the young soldier who had interrupted his investigation, as they stepped out of the portal, and back into the police station.

'Well, Sir, I was patrolling outside the interview room as you had instructed me earlier. I felt a disturbance outside of the room as well as inside it. I'm slightly confused,' he said vaguely, much to the disgust of Driskell.

'Your confusion does not help me in any way,' and taking a deep breath, he looked pointedly into the young man's eyes. 'Now, think clearly. Where. Exactly. Did. It. Happen?' he uttered the words slowly as if the man was dim.

The young man closed his eyes, and felt for any energy signatures that were out of the ordinary. He discounted everybody that should be in the building, including humans; they were not the problem here. Well, not today, anyway.

He walked back along the same corridor, and entered the interview room with Driskell following closely on his heels. Sighing, he tried to ignore the detective as much as was demonly possible, and instead focused himself wholly to the task ahead. 'There, Sir,' and pointed to the two way mirror in the room.

Driskell immediately ran to the room adjacent to the interview room and, flinging open the doors, found nothing, much to his chagrin.

The young soldier sedately walked in. 'Sorry, Sir. I didn't expect there would be anything to find, especially as there are no security cameras in this section.'

'Yes, well done for stating the obvious. But the station does have cameras placed throughout the building. And there is one I'm particularly interested in,' and looking heavenward in dismay at the stupidity of the man, he continued, 'in the reception area! Surely, it must have picked up something.'

Driskell and the young soldier made their way back to reception. Driskell knew that Ms Knight was not going anywhere in a hurry; not until he was finished with her. As for so-called Lady Enid, well she could just play minder to the human. He entered the backroom behind the reception desk.

The officer on duty saluted the detective before walking out of the room and leaving him to it. Driskell barely registered the man; after all, he expected no less. For the sake of appearances, for the human, he made a slight acknowledgement. *The things I have to do just to pass in the human world*, he thought despairingly as he turned on the cameras.

'Let's start with this evening, perhaps from just before six o'clock. That's when I was conducting the last interview of the day with Ms Knight. She might in some way be connected to this case.' His gut instinct was screaming at him that all was not quite right with that one. He was not sure why, but she was not all she appeared to be.

The brash way in which she had answered his questions had made him suspicious. People under his trance never broke out of it unless he wanted them to. He was the master of it after all. He felt that perhaps she had been feigning.

However, he was not a hundred percent certain on this point. After all, she could just turn out to be a normal human. Whatever the case may be, he would not let it go; she would be thoroughly cross examined when he got back.

He thought about bringing her back to the police station, out of the air of the Noble Court. He had his own reasons, after all, and would not be satisfied until he got what he needed; nay, what he wanted.

'Sir, I think you had better take a look at this,' said the young soldier.

'What is it?' Driskell asked sharply, mentally shaking himself out of his thoughts. 'My my. Look at what we have here. Is that who I think it is?' A decidedly dark look of amusement lit up his face.

'Yes, Sir. That is indeed Alexander Black.'

'What is *he* doing in London?' asked Driskell.

'He has been assigned to patrol this area.'

'That's all very well, but what is he doing escorting my interviewee, Ms Knight?'

Driskell was suddenly struck with a thought: *where have I heard that surname before?* For some reason it was on the edge of his subconscious, and he made a mental note to come back to it later; it was likely important. 'I think it's time that I had a talk with Mr Black and ascertain precisely why his presence was required here today.'

'The energy signature was definitely one of ours, Sir. I believe it to be a higher level, one of the Nobles perhaps, but it's hard to get a read on it. I would venture to say it's more than likely that it could belong to Mr Black. But then again, I cannot be a hundred percent certain.'

'Well done, lad. You have developed your skills well.' Driskell had an evil smile lighting up his face as he patted him on the back.

The young soldier looked up, but quickly decided that it was a mistake. He never wanted to get on the wrong side of the detective and his manic smile, which suggested that whatever he was contemplating was not good. He was glad that it was not directed towards him, and quickly looked back down.

Driskell turned on his mobile and slid open his contacts, scrolling through until he found who he was looking for, and made the call. 'Good evening, Alexander,' he said smoothly, knowing that he was going to enjoy this thoroughly.

Alexander received the shock of his life. He had been waiting in his car at the police station for Rowanne to come back. *If* she was going to come back... He had no notion of how long it was going to take. Unfortunately, he had not anticipated the added complication of her being taken to his world. But he had known that she might now attract interest from his world; frankly he should have known better.

He could not even risk going back to find out what was happening to her in case he alerted them (Demon World soldiers) to his presence, thereby putting her in further peril. Foolishly, he had been hoping that they would find nothing and just let her go. *How naive,* he thought.

Sometimes, he could be a complete idiot, or optimist as his friends and enemies alike constantly reprimanded him. *So what?* he thought. *Better an eternal optimist who fights and doesn't accept defeat, than some pessimistic dead guy.* Although, paradoxically his chances of living long were rapidly dwindling by the minute.

Things weren't looking so good with Driskell calling him. He was the Noble that Alexander had recognised at Rowanne's interview. He was of high rank, and could literally sit in judgement of any Demon World citizen. Even a Noble could not escape their fate at the Noble Court once they were charged, and especially if Driskell presided over the case.

Alexander started to break out in a cold sweat. Why would Driskell call him out of the blue? The chances of it being a coincidence were null and void, as far as he was concerned. He had obviously somehow connected Alexander to the police station, and it goes without saying that he probably linked him to Rowanne. *Damn! I should have been more careful. What the hell had I been thinking in escorting her into the police station?*

That's just great, I'm now a dead chivalric who has gotten his lady killed. He had to mentally shake himself out of his manic thoughts. He had to fix this, and fast. What was he going to do? He would have to proceed carefully if there was any chance that he could get the both of them out of this mess; otherwise known as his life. *Hold on Rowanne*, he thought. *I'm sorry. I seem to drag you further into my world each time I enter yours.* He slammed his fist into the steering wheel in frustration, but managed to hold off shattering it into pieces.

A feeling of doom pervaded Alexander as he tried to compose himself in order to calmly handle the Noble Dewain Driskell of the Dark Lake Clan. This was going to be a challenge. He had known Dewain since childhood, and they had both trained at the same academy to become the future law enforcers of Demon World.

They had both come from noble families with legacies of great defenders of their world, and so it had been natural for both young men to carry on this most noble of traditions. He remembered the Dewain who had been carefree, but at the same time a deadly expert in their field of combat. Not to mention being an excellent strategist; it did not come as much of a surprise then, that he rose to the prominent position of Enforcer to the Noble Court.

However, the days of their youth were long behind them, and each had taken a different path in life. Alexander knew that something intensely dark had occurred between Dewain and The First Family, but the details were lost in obscurity. Suffice to say, he was never the same after that, and had become the man all the Nobles feared today.

Alexander cleared his throat and answered the call. 'Good evening, Driskell,' he said in a cold voice, even as fear threatened to choke him. He did not fear for himself, but for the others that he might inadvertently end up dragging down with him. Mostly, he feared for her: Rowanne.

'Come come, dear friend. I can still hear the love that you have for me, even after all these years...' replied Driskell, laughing easily at his old friend's discomfort which he could sense coming at him in waves over the phone. Sometimes it was good having these abilities; unique to his family alone, as far as he knew.

'Of course, brother. I haven't forgotten about you... Though, it's been too long since we last spoke. Anyway, we work on the same side, the last time I checked.' Alexander was reassured by the fact that his voice now sounded calm.

'Yes, it has been *too* long. Conveniently long, some might say. Well, enough of the pleasantries. I need to see you.' Driskell's voice changed from wariness into something harsh and acidic that threatened to burn through anyone who dared to disobey him.

Alexander heard the change in his voice and had always expected that he would have a day of reckoning with his old friend. It had finally come, and not over 'the incident' as he had always thought, but over a woman of all things; and not just any woman - *a human*, he thought disgusted with himself. 'Really?' asked Alexander.

Driskell ignored the sarcasm dripping from Alexander's voice. 'Alexander, I warn you, I am not a man to be trifled with. You are to come immediately to The Salisbury pub. I am in need of your services,' he added quite politely.

'Fine, since you asked so graciously. Could you give me some time before I meet you? There are some things that need to be taken care of first,' asked Alexander; although he knew the answer.

Driskell considered for a moment, 'How about... right Now!'

Alexander heard the finality in the imbecile's voice, and had no choice but to accept his respective invitation; *order more like!* he thought angrily. Taking a deep breath, he replied sweetly, 'My dear Noble Lord Driskell of the Dark

Lake Clan, I, your humble servant of the Black Rose Clan, would be honoured to serve you in any way I can.' *That I see fit.* With that little insult, Alexander cut the call short. It was stupid of him, he knew. But if only for a moment, he got a sick satisfaction from imagining the indignation settling over his old friend.

Driskell counted to ten, not wanting to kill Alexander immediately. His blazing green eyes refused to calm. 'You will pay for your arrogance, 'Alexander The Great," he said sarcastically. *Damn Noble of the First Families, you think you are better than me? That little connection will only get you so far...* he thought, and he so loved chasing these Nobles like little pawns across a chess board. They were always surprised when he knocked them over, as if they had not seen him coming. Enough, now was not the time for this. He had a duty to perform, after all.

Driskell went back down to the interview room and locked it. He opened a portal back into Demon World, and flashed back into the Noble Court. He strode purposely along the corridor and threw open the doors with no more than a thought. He was furious, barely able to keep his power in check.

He found Rowanne sitting in the chair and looking down with a confused expression. He swiftly turned his attention to Lady Enid. 'My lady, forgive my lateness in returning. My sources turned out to be excellent, and I have discovered a new and rather interesting lead in this case.'

'Well done, Driskell. Let us not waste our time with this one any further then,' said Lady Enid inclining her head in Rowanne's direction.

Driskell observed the cold and calculated look in Lady Enid's eyes. *You would just love that, wouldn't you? However, I am not done...* 'My lady, as you went to painstaking lengths to remind me earlier that I should be most thorough in my investigation, and that each piece of evidence should not so easily be dismissed, it would therefore be remiss of me not to investigate my interviewee and cross examine her before releasing her. Would you not agree?' Driskell asked smoothly with a sick, satisfied look.

Lady Enid was annoyed at herself for appearing too eager to let the woman go, but she managed to remain somewhat calm. In an aggrieved voice she replied, 'That is still the case, Driskell. You mistook my meaning. I was merely thinking that if this human is not in any way relevant to the case, then we can dispense with her. Perhaps, continue the investigation back,' and Lady Enid looked disgustedly at Rowanne, 'in her world.'

This is going to plan, he thought, *and will work to the advantage of us all.* 'Lady Enid, what a fantastic idea. I was just thinking the same thing, but I see that your sharp mind has beaten me to it,' he smiled coldly, as he felt the waves of frustration rolling off her. He was sickened at the undue praise that he had been forced to heap on this woman, *but needs must,* he thought wearily. He may be a sycophant, but he enjoyed her discomfort. *You will feel helpless frustration, mark my words, if it's the last thing I ever do...*

Lady Enid looked Driskell dead in the eyes, a moment's confusion hovering over her features before once more being set in ice. 'Are you taking her back now?' she asked, her voice devoid of any emotion.

They call me *heartless,* he thought, *this woman would sooner sell her...* but no, now was not the time. There was always later. There would be a day of reckoning between them. He returned her measured look, even as he felt as if his heart was filled with shards of ice. 'No, not right at this very moment. As I said, I do have an urgent lead to follow up on. Later, I will be back for her, and then I will take her back with me to her world to continue questioning.'

Driskell turned his back to Lady Enid, and walked towards the doors.

'Driskell,' Lady Enid called his name in quiet anger.

He stopped in his tracks, and slowly turned around to face her. 'Yes, my lady. Was there anything else?' Driskell had a look of cold sincerity.

'The answer to your question is, yes,' she replied, and gave him a poignant look.

Driskell looked at her thoughtfully. *Now isn't that interesting...* and a wide smile broke out across his face. 'As you wish,' and bowing low and reverently to her, he swiftly turned back and strode out the doors, not bothering to close them after himself. All pretence at civility momentarily disregarded, as the lines were drawn, and the gauntlet thrown.

CHAPTER 9

Lady Enid waited a heartbeat for the moment she felt the portal close behind Driskell, then closed the doors to the courtroom. She came back and sat in the chair next to Rowanne.

'That was close,' said the entity, tilting Rowanne's head back so that she could look at Lady Enid.

'Entirely too close for my liking. Let us continue, we have to make it quick. I'm not sure how long we have,' said Lady Enid.

Lady Enid tried to figure out a plan of action to get Rowanne safely back without attracting any undue attention to the both of them.

'Hold on a moment, how is it now possible for you to actually speak through Rowanne? Before, I could only hear you communicate telepathically.' Lady Enid was bewildered by how much the entity seemed to be growing in power.

The entity looked confused, it was evident that this was also new for her as well. 'I thought that I was still speaking to you telepathically. I did not realise when the change occurred, and I spoke through her vocal cords. It seems to be a natural progression.'

'I think your possession of her is growing. Perhaps more so, because you are a demon.' Lady Enid feared for the young woman, whilst speculating how far this would continue, and ultimately meet its unforeseeable end.

The entity wondered in what other ways she would begin to merge with Rowanne. The fact that it had happened unconsciously on her part at least, was something to be anxious about. 'I don't like this, one single bit. This is not a good sign. It may appear that I am at an advantage here, but this bodes ill for both of us.'

'Is Rowanne's spirit growing weaker inside you?' asked Lady Enid, concerned for both Rowanne and the entity.

'No. She's still strong, but if we do not separate her from my spirit, I'm not sure what may happen. The human vessel should only ever hold its own essence, sharing it with another might weaken, or even destroy it. So far, her body has accepted me, but not her mind. Her mind knows that there is an intruder, and eventually it will do something...'

'There must be something we can do. How long do you think we have before Rowanne's body and mind begin to assail you?' Lady Enid's mind reeled with the thought of loss, all over again. She could barely find the strength within herself to go on. She alone knew how she had coped with her own loss.

'It's impossible to put a time frame on this situation, as it is more complex now that she is part demon. The other possibility is that nothing happens, and I stay merged, or 'trapped' as I call it, within her forever; this is an unacceptable scenario. I'm sorry, but I need to be freed. Please, do not feel sorrow on my behalf,' said the entity, at the horrified look on Lady Enid's face.

'You seem to take everything in your stride, my dear. But how can you willingly accept your demise?' Lady Enid spoke with sorrow in her voice. She was ashamed that she could not disguise it, when this entity had with good grace, chosen to do this noble deed. She was shocked when the entity held her hands in comfort and solidarity. It felt as if the entity was speaking to her soul, telling her that she was not alone in her grief. *This is madness. How can I feel so much in so short a time, for someone I have just met?*

'We are immortal, and yet we are not, do you not agree, Lady Enid?' The entity laughed wryly.

Lady Enid looked faraway, and all she could see was an eternal void. *What is an eternity without those you love?* she wondered sadly. 'It is both a gift and a curse that we choose for ourselves. Though, some of us have less choice than others.'

'Yes, that is true. And I assume, you allude to being both a daughter and matriarch of the First Family?' The entity wore a knowing look.

Just how much did she know of the First Families? And had she belonged to one of them? What had been the entity's position in Demon World? These questions churned inside Lady Enid's mind. 'It is true, my dear, that I have little choice in immortality since there are so few of us. Especially since I must carry the mantle until... Well, you know...'

'I understand,' the entity replied softly, perfectly comprehending the responsibility and burden of such a position. To forever toil, with no end in sight. The entity decided that they must for now put away their sorrows, and focus on Rowanne. 'We will come up with a solution to this, later. You know, you were a little too eager to have me sent back. I could sense him trying to read you, to figure out your motive,' said the entity, concerned.

'I admit that my common sense momentarily deserted me. You're right, I should have behaved differently. I got carried away in our *conversation* but at least he is taking you back. That is a positive outcome.'

'Perhaps. Or perhaps not, depending upon the way you look at the situation. If his angle is to rile you, then he might not make it easy. He will surely use Rowanne as a pawn against you.'

'That did actually cross my mind. I do not fear him, but for this young woman. It's foolish I know...'

The entity stayed quiet, contemplating, before replying, 'How do you intend to get us back to Earth?'

'Tell me one thing first: would it not be better to tell this human the truth? Perhaps the safest thing would be for her to know everything, "*Praemonitus Praemunitus.*" Forewarned is forearmed.' Lady Enid looked earnest.

'I don't think that she could handle it yet. Rowanne's mental state is very precarious at the moment. The slightest mishap causes her undue agitation. Though, I can't really blame her for that. I feel like her present state is a result of everything that's happened to her in so short a period; prior to this, she was a completely different person,' replied the entity sadly.

'Wait a moment, you said "not yet". So, is there a chance that we can eventually get through to her?' asked Lady Enid.

'There are some unexpected complications and I'm not sure, if I should even tell you...' The entity was afraid of revealing more.

Lady Enid took the entity's hands into her own, and smiled kindly. 'Look, my dear, do not be afraid of me. Had I wanted to turn you in, I would have by now. You asked for my trust and I gave it. Can you bring yourself to trust me further?'

The entity considered for a moment before replying. 'Lady Enid,' the entity proceeded cautiously, 'you belong to the First Family, and your position therefore demands that you uphold the law, is this not the case?'

'Yes,' Lady Enid replied baffled, wondering where this was leading to.

'Do you want to know about the laws that were broken?' The entity asked in a very matter-of-fact way, wanting to know precisely where she stood when it came to asking for Lady Enid's help.

Lady Enid thought very seriously on the matter, but finally came to a resolution; that had not entirely come as a surprise. Perhaps she had always known that she would reach this point after the first time. She breathed to ease the lump in her throat as she thought of her dark past. Some things you never get over, not really. They say that in time it becomes easier, that you learn to live with your past, you make a compromise. And for the rest of the world, it appears as if you have gotten over it, moved on, as they say, but only time does that, so ruthlessly; efficiently like clockwork.

The entity squeezed Lady Enid's hands, and spoke softly under her breath, "*Tempus Fugit*," and closed her eyes, as a single tear rolled down her ashen cheek. She understood all too well, the world had moved on without her.

Lady Enid looked up sharply, 'Did you say something?' For just a moment, she had felt the reassurance behind the words, light as the wind, and softer than a whisper, brushing gently by her. And she knew that she was not alone; the entity understood her.

The entity momentarily turned away to wipe away the offending evidence before replying, 'No, my lady.'

But Lady Enid had seen, and it weighed on her mind. She took out her handkerchief and dabbed at Rowanne's eyes as she gently tilted her head so that she could look at her. Just the very act of being able to care for someone again eased the pain in her heart. *It has been too long, after all.* She could see the inner turmoil playing behind the entity's very expressive green eyes. 'Let's continue, my dear. I take full responsibility for what you are about to say. I understand that rules may have been broken, and I will shoulder the burden with you.'

'No! You do not understand what it is that you are asking of me. I cannot let you!' said the entity anxiously.

'Let me deal with the repercussions. Do not worry on my behalf; I am not as fragile as I appear. I can rise to the occasion when required,' said Lady Enid pointedly.

'Fine. If you're willing, then I can do no less than share what I know. Rowanne is not alone in this situation, someone else is involved with her.'

'Who?' asked Lady Enid, her interest piqued.

'A demon no less, who resides in both worlds.' The entity proceeded cautiously, lest it backfire; then it would have been for nothing.

'A demon involved with a human? But how? You must tell me, it's very important.' Lady Enid was alarmed. *I did ask,* she reminded herself. Telling the truth was akin to the human game of Russian roulette; you would never quite know the outcome.

'Not in the way you might imagine. Only so far as carrying out his duty,' replied the entity.

'Who is *he* and what *duty* involved his coming into contact with Rowanne?'

She's more open-minded than people give her credit for, thought the entity. Taking a deep breath, she decided to trust Lady Enid. Whether it was a good idea or not remained to be seen, but she was the only person that she could truly talk to right now. Who else would entertain a spirit?

'My lady, it is none other than Alexander Black.' The entity waited a heartbeat to see how Lady Enid would react. However, she seemed to take it in her stride.

'I was wondering why I had not seen young Alexander at Court recently, it's been a couple of months at least. That at last explains it; volunteering for duties in the Human World. I am personally disgusted at the very idea. How did he cross paths with Rowanne?'

'I believe, my lady, that they met during the demon/ human altercation in the case that was presented before you,' *so far so good,* thought the entity.

'I think you had better start at the beginning,' said Lady Enid wearily.

'It happened about a week ago, last Thursday, I think. It's hard to sometimes follow the passage of time, when you are in another's body. Sometimes, my consciousness is pushed into a part of her mind where I am trapped. The only time I get to come out of my prison is when Rowanne is in danger. I think her mind grows slightly weaker at these moments, allowing me the chance to take over.'

'You do not consciously try to take over Rowanne's mind, do you?'

'No!' The entity looked shocked. The very idea that she would do that to another was abhorrent.

Lady Enid was satisfied, and had thought as much, but hearing it aloud gave her comfort. 'Forgive me, if I have offended you. It was not my meaning, I mean intention.'

The entity laughed at the way Lady Enid had phrased her answer. It was her secret joy, a nod to the past.

Lady Enid looked baffled, and failed to see what could be so amusing in their present situation.

The entity continued gravely, 'What roughly happens is that when her mind fears that the danger is too much for Rowanne, it propels me to the forefront and cushions Rowanne until the danger is passed. Then I reluctantly agree to be pushed back.'

'How do you tolerate it? Do you ever just want to take over completely?' and seeing the way in which the entity vehemently shook Rowanne's head, Lady Enid continued, 'I am sorry. Forgive me, for being so rude. What I meant was, with so little time at your disposal, and never really knowing the next time you will emerge, how do you accomplish anything?'

'My lady, I had to learn great patience in my short existence before it was so ruthlessly cut down. Imagine, if you will, a delicate flower in bloom cut before it could reach maturity.' The entity paused, Lady Enid had suddenly gone pale. 'My lady, are you well?'

Lady Enid clutched her chest as her heart beat wildly. The flood gates had risen dangerously close to the surface, and she felt she might shatter before the end, but courageously she pushed her feelings down. *The lake was still once more, though ripples disturbed it now and again...* 'Please, continue.'

The entity reluctantly let it go, but sensed that her words had caused Lady Enid distress; that had never been her intention. 'Do you know, you are the only person I can actually communicate with,' said the entity thoughtfully. 'As I have said, I only come into being at certain times, and it is extremely difficult to get anything done. I have to be careful, as I do not know whose presence I may be in, and sometimes even I am at a loss to do something if it is at the expense of both of us being revealed.'

Lady Enid nodded in agreement. 'How did you get past Demon World security? I'm impressed. I think you must once have been-' she quickly amended for fear of causing offence, 'and still are a powerful demon of our world.' She silently contemplated the entity's identity. Normal citizens of Demon World would not give off this much power, but the entity had mastery over it, which suggested to Lady Enid that the entity might once have belonged to a powerful family; perhaps to one of the First Families. She had a dawning realisation: *I wonder, could it be possible...*

The First Families were some of the most powerful demons in Demon World, and they jealously guarded their power. Often it was difficult to know what they were capable of; these were but a few of the reasons why it was so dangerous to go up against one of them, let alone the whole Court.

The entity pushed down the panic that had suddenly blossomed in her stomach. Well, in Rowanne's. *I have to proceed cautiously, or none of us will get out of this unscathed.* 'Lady Enid, you know that any demon can possess a human, it is hardly a speciality amongst our kind. However, it does take a lot of power to bypass our security, to pass through Demon World undetected. I could not reveal myself in Driskell's presence, or he would have detected my spirit in a heartbeat.' The entity left out the fact that she had revealed herself to Alexander, having decided that could wait for another time; it might create more problems than they needed right now. 'I need you to let go of any idea you might have of pursuing my former identity.' Looking at Lady Enid's indignant expression, she continued guardedly, 'My lady, I only say this for your safety, as well as that of Rowanne's, because I fear that once you know the whole truth, it will put all of us in great peril.' Silently, the entity willed and pleaded for Lady Enid to take it no further.

'Fine. I will not pursue this presently, and that is the only assurance I can honestly give you.'

'That's good enough for me. Thank you. Let me continue, and perhaps that will help you to understand everything that has led up to the present moment.' Taking a deep unnecessary breath; more an ingrained habit, since the entity did not really need to breathe, she continued, 'My second life began last Thursday, when Rowanne died.'

'I beg your pardon, but I'm not sure I heard you correctly, I thought you said she died?'

'You heard correctly. Are you really surprised? Think about it, Rowanne was attacked by Shadows outside of her workplace. Before you ask, I am not certain why they chose this human, it could very well have been a case of her stumbling accidentally upon their notice. They then proceeded to chase her, and I must say this woman has remarkable skills of evasion for a human.'

Lady Enid was interested in knowing more about this remarkable human. 'In what sense?'

'For one thing, she evaded the spears thrown at her back by intuitively moving her body. Perhaps, she also has a heightened sense of hearing. And lastly, she is quite fast, for a human. I sensed that the demons had to work hard just to keep up with her. It's quite baffling really, and if I was not in this predicament I'd want to know precisely what mettle she was made of.'

'I think we have underestimated humans in assuming that they are weaker than us. Perhaps we have become complacent, or maybe she is unique. It's worth investigating further...' Lady Enid had a faraway look in her eyes.

I have been careless, thought the entity uneasily; it had not been her intention to place Rowanne in further danger.

'Please, continue,' said Lady Enid, with an impartial look.

What are you thinking? wondered the entity. Lady Enid's expression could mean anything, or nothing.

'The Shadows had her cornered, and it might have been the end for this human, who knows?' said the entity.

'That's true, or perhaps Rowanne would have pulled out a trick or two, and somehow defeated them,' said Lady Enid laughing, growing fonder of a human of all people, the more she heard of her tale. *Rowanne is a brave woman*, she thought, *much like...* Lady Enid smiled, but it cost her dearly.

'I wish that was the case,' the entity said smiling sadly. 'However, she thought she had been rescued when a gentleman appeared to come to her aid.'

'What was her reaction?' Lady Enid began to build a picture in her mind of Rowanne's character. She thought she knew what the entity might say.

'She was annoyed with the insolence of the man, who just happened to step in-between her and the attackers.' The entity was uncertain of some parts of the scene that had unfolded, and did not want to create a false impression of the exchange between Rowanne and Alexander, as it could be very dangerous to them. 'I'll cut it short for now, time is not on our side,' and just as Lady Enid was about to object, she continued, 'I will save the rest for a later, more detailed account, and we will methodically go through it, you have my word.' She noted the reluctant acceptance on the part of Lady Enid. 'Rowanne was oblivious to the fact that she was in a den of demons, for lack of a better term. It appeared from her point of view that Alexander's attention was diverted, so she threw herself in front of the oncoming spear intended for him,' *which he could have deflected in his sleep,* thought the entity. 'She... passed instantly, her heart stopped at that precise moment.'

'You do not have to continue, if it's too painful,' said Lady Enid gently.

'No, I want to. It's important for the both of us. And it might help Rowanne in the long run, as her mind refuses to accept what happened to her. I also feel that there is magic at work preventing her from remembering. If I can get it all out, then she has a chance at recovering.'

Closing her eyes, the entity took a deep shuddering breath and plunged into their shared consciousness. She went back to the exact moment again, but this time to relive the parts that she was unable to speak of; that even Rowanne was unaware of...

It had begun with a purple haze enveloping her. She had come from a palace of pain and darkness. She was cocooned within, feeling trapped, but it was infinitely better than going back. Her life had been saved, or some semblance of it; maybe it was her soul, she didn't know.

She had not been able to feel her body. Did she have a body? Maybe she was incorporeal. Panicking, she had looked down to where she imagined her hands to be, but there was nothing. There is nothing more frightening than being aware that you are trapped in your mind: you see nothing, hear nothing, feel nothing, and for a moment you wonder if you are alive. Can you get back to yourself, to the world? For all intents and purposes you may appear dead, with no signs of life, but silently you scream: 'I am not gone.

I am here. Help me! Can anyone hear me?' And you wonder if you even have a voice. Your voice like the rest of you is trapped, unable to get out.

Time had seemed to the entity to pass slowly; a second became a minute, a minute an hour, an hour a year, and then infinity stretched out before her. She had thought that she was in purgatory, and wondered how long she'd have to wait there; what if it was forever? A scream that had steadily been building within her was finally released. She had not been able to stop. Not that it mattered much, for there had been no one to hear her.

Once more her mind had tried to shut down, but to no avail. She remembered being suddenly snatched from her asylum of hell, and plunged into consciousness. She had not known what world she was in, let alone the year. There had only been darkness at first, and she'd been confused with her surroundings. But she had suddenly been bombarded with so much new information that she had thought her head would split. Momentarily grateful to be free, she had come to the sickening realisation that she had swapped one prison for another; she now shared her awareness with another.

The entity remembered last Thursday: she had been pulled from a realm, or her world? Some parts were still a little hazy. The purple cocoon she had been enveloped in had given way to an explosive green spark that had shattered her prison and propelled her into Rowanne's body.

When Rowanne's mind, body and spirit were being put back together, somehow the entity too was incorporated as a natural additional part of the new Rowanne. Perhaps it was the demon part of her that had so readily accepted the entity. The body could not distinguish the entity as something foreign to Rowanne, so on a cellular level, or spiritual, who knows? Rowanne became three different combined essences: human, demon and spirit.

If it was a shock to Rowanne, then she didn't know. The entity's mind could not handle everything that had happened to it. The flood of information from her old life, and the pain was unbearable, she could not tolerate it. Her eyes had snapped open, blazing green fire.

Everything she looked at had exploded, as her demonic power was momentarily unleashed. The entity had seen flashes of her past playing before her eyes, on a loop that wouldn't stop. Things shattered in the room that she was in, and furniture had been destroyed. However, slowly and painfully she had come back to her senses, and reeled the incredible force back in.

The information from the past had stopped flooding in as Rowanne's life story began to unfold to the entity. It had helped to calm her down, and it had also protected Rowanne's heart from giving out. Sudden trauma and experiencing so much pain could not be good for the body, knew the entity. She viewed Rowanne's life, and for the next couple of hours she had all the knowledge that the young woman possessed of her life, and at the same time the entity assimilated information about the new world she now inhabited.

Once Rowanne's transformation was complete, the entity was at a much calmer stage, and was able to carefully construct an illusion to Rowanne's mind: that the room was intact. The entity would have liked to reverse the damage that had been caused but lacked the energy to do so. It had all gone into fuelling her rage, and then the last of the transformation had left her drained. Slowly the entity had felt itself being pulled back into Rowanne's mind to be tucked away in a corner, until it was needed.

That had been the only time the entity had screamed and shouted out, because it was being trapped once more. It had been futile and in vain, as Rowanne had unconsciously taken back control of her life. It was not a cold place; the entity now resided inside a being who was warm, and somehow familiar.

Rowanne had awoken to the illusion of a beautiful day, but the entity remembered the lamp smashing, and a surge of power being released as Rowanne had come precariously close to knowing the truth.

However, Alexander's magic was strong and had risen to the surface smashing the truth into smithereens, so that all that was left behind were shards. If Rowanne ever attempted to reach for those shards, then her mind would cause her pain, as if she had physically picked them up.

The entity knew that Alexander had placed barriers in Rowanne's mind, as much for her safety as his. The problem was that they were destroying Rowanne's mind. If she had any chance at recovery, then eventually she would have to face her trauma, no matter how painful, in order to overcome it. She sensed that now was not that moment: Rowanne was not ready to face the truth. But eventually, she would have to be forced to deal with it.

Perhaps, Alexander Black was the key to helping Rowanne, and the entity could also help in some way, being merged as she was with Rowanne's mind. They would have to take it extremely slow if Rowanne had any chance at becoming a whole person in mind as well as body, and she would have to deal with her new reality.

Rowanne would have to take a lot on board. It's not every day that a person realises that the world that they inhabit is infinitely more complex than the microcosm they call their life. Rowanne's world view must now include other realities, not to mention a whole new world existing alongside Earth; its dark counterpart, one might say.

The entity snapped back to the present, and suddenly panicked, wondering how long she had spent in her reverie. Lady Enid was looking at her strangely. The entity tried to recall the last point of their conversation. 'I do not remember much, only that Rowanne went home none the wiser that she left with an intruder in her mind,' said the entity self-deprecatingly.

'Do not speak of yourself in such a way. From all that you have told me, I have come to the realisation that you are not responsible for what has befallen you,' said Lady Enid.

'You think me the victim of fate, then?' asked the entity looking into the past.

'Do not speak to me of fate, I have had my fair share in its dealings. You have only to look at the foundations of our world... Anyway, I believe that we make our own destiny. We choose different paths, whether they be right or wrong. And we are always free to choose again, to create the life we want. It's never too late.'

The entity contemplated what Lady Enid had said, and silently laughed and cried at the twists life and death could bring. Was it never truly over?

It came upon the entity suddenly, as it always did, and took her by surprise again; she supposed that by now, she should be used to it. First it began with the light starting to fade, then the picture, as her reality started to fray around the edges. Then, a tremendous force began to reel her in. She was never quite free, but always tethered like a wild caged animal with only the illusion of freedom, until she was forced back into her cage.

'It's beginning... I feel cold,' said the entity.

Rowanne began to shake, and would have fallen out of the chair, had it not been for Lady Enid catching her. Rowanne's eyes closed. 'Wake up, my dear. What's happened to you?' She started to panic, she needed Rowanne to wake before Driskell's return. How would she even begin to explain all of this? Driskell's first question would probably be: 'Why are you holding her so tenderly?' Lady Enid splashed some water on Rowanne's face from a nearby cup. 'Rowanne?' she called hesitantly, as she did not know to whom she was addressing.

Slowly through the thick fog that was her mind, Rowanne clawed back to reality; albeit somewhat unconsciously. 'What happened to me?' and found herself being supported by Lady Enid.

'My dear, you seem to have passed out,' replied Lady Enid, still unable to ascertain whether it was Rowanne or the entity. She continued cautiously, 'What is the last thing that you can remember?'

'I remember feeling dizzy, and then nothing. I must have fainted.' Rowanne let Lady Enid help her back into the chair, and gratefully accepted the cup of water that she helped her to drink. Her hands felt shaky, and she had to remind herself how to hold a cup. It was unnerving that she had to relearn a skill that should have been as simple as walking. It was more than the fact that she had fainted, something within her felt off; she did not like it one single bit.

'How do you feel, has the dizziness passed?' Lady Enid asked anxiously.

'Thank you for your kindness. I feel a bit better. However, I am not the sort of person to have fainting spells. I think it's down to the long day that I've had.'

Lady Enid silently laughed at this courageous young human. She was quick to suppress her mirth at the pained expression on Rowanne's face.

'After all, it's not every day that you get drugged at a police station by a strange looking detective, who could possibly be a model, and then taken to a court of all places, to be interrogated in place of an interview. I should just mention that I willingly came down to the police station, and imagined events going differently. I think that about covers it.' Rowanne felt angry as it finally dawned on her what she had been put through.

'Incredible. I think you have covered everything. One thing eludes me; what is a model?'

Rowanne ignored the latter. 'All I know is that I think I will have to continue the interview with Driskell, am I right?'

'I'm afraid so. But where it will take place, I cannot say.' For Rowanne's sake, Lady Enid hoped and prayed that it would be back in her world at the police station, preferably in the presence of human police officers; in that sense Rowanne would have a modicum of safety.

'I don't quite understand what you're saying? Where exactly am I being held?' At least if she knew that, then it would be a start. Perhaps Lady Enid could explain how and why she came to be here.

'What I mean to say is, that you were brought down from the police station because the detective felt that you had an extra connection to the case. And for your own safety, you were moved to investigation headquarters, but I am not permitted to elaborate further on this at this juncture.'

Rowanne didn't believe it, there must have been more to it than that. She decided to confront Lady Enid head on, and wouldn't settle for anything less than the truth. 'Lady Enid, do you know what my profession is?'

'No.'

'I am a journalist, and as such it is my duty to find and present the truth. I'm well accustomed, you might say, to the subtle nuances of a person's character that tell me very clearly when they are being less than honest.'

Lady Enid was impressed with Rowanne, and had to admit that she would have made a fine enforcer in their world; had she been born a demon. What a loss to their world. She wondered how to tell Rowanne the truth without telling her the whole truth, and possibly shattering her fragile mind. Finally she decided upon subtly weaving the truth in a way that would be acceptable to her mind, for now, and eventually help her to accept the complete reality later on. 'Are you sure you're ready for what I have to say? Think about it. Once we begin, there is no going back for either of us,' she looked pointedly at Rowanne.

Rowanne thought about it, and sensed that she was

going to be told things that perhaps she might not be ready to hear, but she could no longer live in ignorance. She needed the facts to go forward, only then could she deal with the whole situation. 'I think it's best, that you tell me everything, before *he* comes back.' They both knew to whom she referred.

Lady Enid began, 'Do you know of the incident that occurred outside of your place of work?'

Rowanne swallowed before nodding, now was the time to stay calm. And how much did she really know of this Lady Enid? She could be working with Driskell. 'The police informed us that a security officer in our building had gone missing.'

'Were you well acquainted with the officer in question?' asked Lady Enid.

'Everybody in the office knew Thomas. He was a friendly man, always taking the time to get to know people.'

'Do you know what happened to him?' Lady Enid asked without judgement.

Rowanne wondered how much information she should reveal. More to the point, she did not actually know what had happened to Thomas. However, she suspected that she might be indirectly involved, because she had been in the office all night, but was still unable to recount anything from that period; it was a blur. 'The truth of the matter is, Lady Enid, that I worked late into the night on which Thomas went missing. I fell asleep, and cannot for the life of me recall anything else that may have occurred. That's about it, really.'

'I believe you, Rowanne. It strikes me as odd that you were brought down to this court for information that is hardly any use to the case.'

'That's why I could not understand why I came to be here. I'm sorry that I do not have anything further of any significance to add. I wish that I could have helped more.'

'I will pass on what you have said to detective Driskell. Hopefully, he will release you without further delay,' said Lady Enid.

'Do I stay here, or can I go to a waiting area?' Rowanne asked, feeling somewhat relieved, after giving her statement. *When they finally let me leave, I'll call up Alexander to come and get me. Funny, that he should enter my thoughts when he's the last man I'd accept help from.* Although, Rowanne began to think that she'd need all the allies she could get, if she were to escape this case unscathed. Something was definitely off about this investigation. The police had not released the full details, how much worse could it be? She needed help to get to the bottom of it; Alexander could prove useful, and of course, she would have to talk to Eileen at some point.

Lady Enid brought Rowanne back into the present. 'I'm afraid you will have to wait here until detective Driskell formally releases you.'

'Well, I hope this won't take long as I've got to get back to work,' *and see a doctor*, she thought.

There was more than a little wrong with her; since Thomas's disappearance, she had not really been sleeping well, and then there were the unexplained gaps in her memory.

Rowanne felt certain that something had occurred in that office, but she could not quite grasp it. The familiar headache began to rear its ugly volatile head. That was the other thing that concerned her: whenever she tried to recollect, she had to stop before the pain got out of control, in case it rendered her unconscious again. By now she knew what to look out for, and pulling her thoughts in a different direction felt exactly like the equivalent of walking over hot coals.

'I want you to keep acting docile - if Driskell thinks that you are harmless, then chances are he will let you go,' said Lady Enid.

'Was I that obvious? I thought I did a remarkably good job! Anyway, the first half was real enough.'

'Do not worry about it now. I too have the unique gift of reading people, which I fervently hope that our good detective does not also possess,' said Lady Enid solemnly.

'I won't be quick in dismissing the detective. He strikes me as being extremely intelligent, and he knows more than he lets on.' Rowanne felt that there was a mystery behind the man of ice, but she would rather not be the one to solve it. *To be in that man's world could be dangerous, and in the end prove fatal. Where the hell am I getting this from? I'm not the melodramatic type. Focus Rowanne,* she told herself.

The situation was bad: kidnapped of all things, by a supposed police detective. What kind of police station would allow this to happen? Maybe some kind of rogue operation was operating beneath their notice. Rowanne felt as if she was being held in some kind of closed court where the normal rules did not apply. What had she gotten herself mixed up in?

CHAPTER 10

My whole life is a complete mess, what the hell have I gotten into? thought Alexander as he started the car up and pulled out of the police station car park. Wearily he looked at the time illuminated on the dashboard: an hour left till midnight. The stars seemed to be at their most fierce, as if they too were gearing up for a battle - or so it appeared to him.

He hoped it would be more of the verbal nature, and that it would not become so desperate as to resort to swords. He needed to remain calm if he had any chance in hell of saving Rowanne.

Funny, I think about that woman a lot more these days, he thought in disgust. *She's like a thorn in my side; always ready to trip me up in both worlds, without even knowing it. If she ever regains her memory, then I will let her know exactly what she has done to me...* and he laughed rather unconvincingly.

In no time at all and with hardly any traffic to hold him up, Alexander soon found himself on the road leading to the pub. A thousand thoughts flew in his mind, like dark ravens flapping their wings heralding an omen. Though he could not grasp a single one. 'Rowanne, I'm coming...' his voice sounded ominous.

He would have liked more time to prepare, but this was not to be the case. He'd need his wits about him when confronting his old friend. For that was what they once were, and he'd have to keep that in mind when talking to the fool. He needed to keep his temper, and find out exactly where Rowanne was being kept. Somehow, he would get her back from Demon World.

He sensed that in this present moment, Rowanne was safe. There was also a nagging doubt that all was not right with her, but he could not pinpoint what it was. Maybe the entity was troubling her? Some, if not all, Nobles treated humans contemptuously, and he wondered which Nobles she'd had the misfortune of encountering. *Hold on,* he thought.

It had turned colder as he pulled into the side road next to The Salisbury pub. Alexander switched off the engine and sat in the darkness that followed, though his sapphire eyes burned brightly in the rear view mirror. He debated whether he should go in alone or get reinforcements. However, that would only draw more attention, as well as undermine his position.

Alexander squared his shoulders, and his eyes changed to gray with a ring of steel encasing his irises as he mentally and physically prepared for the confrontation. He once more became Alexander the fierce, the untouchable, as he went to meet his old friend and adversary; hard to decide between the two these days. *Somewhere, between love and hate, that is where our friendship lies.* He pushed open the door passing beneath the grace of the cherubs adoring the exterior of the pub. *Grace,* he thought sarcastically.

As soon as Alexander entered, he zoned in on his old friend Driskell, seated in the far back corner of the pub with glass partitions on either side. *Good,* at least it would afford them some privacy. Driskell was quietly finishing his pint, not bothering to look up and even acknowledge his presence.

Keep it together, do not let him ruffle your wings, thought Alexander as he walked with purpose, whilst trying to formulate a plan. He sullenly sat opposite Driskell, and put as much disdain into his expression as possible.

Driskell, on the other hand, finished his pint slowly, taunting Alexander. He found it highly amusing to witness the other man's discomfort. It had been an age since he'd had anything to laugh about. He could feel Alexander seething, and he oh so slowly raised his eyes to his old friend, using the term loosely to acknowledge his presence. And because he could not resist, he gave him a mock salute with his glass.

'Alexander, dear friend,' he said, not bothering to stand up and shake hands - he was not particularly in the mood to be civil, the pretence of it wore him down. Driskell's eyes sparkled roguishly, and his fiercely red hair was secured back by a leather tie. 'I didn't even notice that you had come in. I was absorbed in...' and indicated his glass with an incline of the head.

Alexander silently counted to ten, before answering, 'Is that so? Dear friend, a word of advice, do not be so engrossed in a thing as to have your attention diverted, even for a second. It could prove your undoing. Besides, what would you have done had I been the enemy?'

Driskell cocked his head to one side, studying Alexander through his glass, his reflection somewhat distorted. *Just like our friendship,* he thought. 'If *you* had been the enemy...' Driskell left it open, even though he didn't have the answer presently.

Alexander was at a loss for how to proceed, his friend's words weighing heavily. It was true that many people hated and feared Driskell. It was hard for him to accept this new Driskell, and reconcile him with the man he had been before. 'I think perhaps drinking does not sit well with you. It seems to impede your somewhat diminished powers. Wait a minute,' he added hastily, when Driskell raised his eyebrow in question as to where this suicidal dialogue would lead to. *I might as well fully test the waters,* thought a reckless

Alexander. 'I was actually being polite, because we all know that families after the First, have less than valuable 'gifts' to begin with... So, in concern for *you*, I thought it my rightful duty to help you maintain what little dwindling power you still possess,' Alexander added sweetly with a concerned smile on his face. He waited a heartbeat, and held his breath in anticipation. *I've probably signed my death warrant with my stupidity.* But what happened next scared the life out of him, and froze him to his core.

Driskell started to laugh heartily. He looked at Alexander, who seemed taken aback by it all, and who consequently was gearing up ready to fight if need be. He could almost read his thoughts, *he's probably wondering whether this is a precursor to a duel.* Alexander's eyes flashed from sapphire to gray, and this just made Driskell laugh harder. *The poor man doesn't know whether to remain calm, or fight.*

Driskell got up lightning fast in one fluid motion, knocking back his chair, and strode around to Alexander, pulling him up off his chair, forcing him to stand.

Alexander met Driskell head on, and was about to pull out his sword when he felt Driskell's arms going around him. Could it be that Driskell was hugging him, instead of pulling him apart piece by piece, as he had expected? He could go along with this, and raised his own arms up in an embrace of equal measure. After all, it didn't hurt to remind your enemy of your own strength, just in case.

'It has been too long. You're different, you're now more like your father than that brash youth at the academy,' said Driskell.

'I could say the same of you. You seem to have acquired titles, though I must admit, I wonder if they become you.'

Driskell smiled at him, 'Well, the titles help to keep people in check,' and with that, he sat back down.

Alexander took a gamble, 'Some of them are quite fearsome, are they not?' he asked, pushing Driskell, wanting to know how far he could trust his former friend. People changed, he knew that...

Driskell looked at Alexander with a sardonic look, 'I suppose, you mean: Dewain the Dark or Driskell the Ruthless... Have I missed any out? I'm sure I have. There are so many that it's hard to keep track, especially at the rate at which I'm acquiring them.'

'What about, Enforcer of the Noble Court?' asked Alexander, as he studied Driskell.

There was a slight twitch in the side of Driskell's face, and he stiffened momentarily, but in the next instant he behaved as if it had never happened. He composed himself with some difficulty which did not go unobserved by Alexander. *Curse him.* 'That's one of my favourites, and I take pride in that particular one,' he said in a light voice.

Alexander noticed Driskell's manic expression as he had uttered those words. *What the hell is going on?* he wondered. *I thought he'd be thrilled to destroy Nobles, especially those from the First Families;* which was why his name had become synonymous with death. The demons of his world feared the man sitting before him, there was a danger that seemed to permeate the very air he breathed.

This all went back, he feared, to the infamous case at the Noble Court which in itself was shrouded in mystery, and he wondered what might have happened back then. Alexander knew that it had not been an ordinary case, but 'The Case' that had made Driskell. So, why was his friend acting so strangely? *I think I will do some investigating of my own, and who knows what I may find...*

Driskell didn't like the way in which Alexander was studying him: as if he were plotting and planning. *I wish I had the power of the First Families, it would come in extremely useful right now.* He suspected that Lady Enid had a few hidden talents, one of which was telepathy. He too possessed this gift, but his was not nearly as strong as hers;

that was to be expected when you were a lesser Noble, and not a descendent of a First Family.

How much could Alexander do? he wondered. *Let it go. Some things are best laid to rest dear friend*, he thought. His eyes were a glacial emerald that could cut a person, if they dared to get close to him. *Unacceptable!* he thought violently.

'It seems as if we have come to an impasse,' laughed Alexander, trying to lighten the mood.

'I think it would be wise to move on, do you not agree? After all, let's not forget why we came to be here at this time,' said Driskell.

'Quite. And on that salient point, why am I here?'

Driskell had a cruel expression on his face. It made no difference to him, how this fool chose to interpret his command. 'Thank you for gracing me with your presence,' he said bitterly. *Somewhat too long, and too late,* he thought with a burning hatred.

The day of reckoning was not today: it could wait. His focus was Ms Knight. He found it remarkable how he could switch off his feelings like that; it scared him, how natural it had become. *Perhaps, I am truly the monster they say I have become.*

With a stern look, Driskell continued with his investigation. 'You are here, Mr Black, because I require your cooperation in an investigation I am conducting.' He looked pointedly at Alexander, but if his words had any effect on his friend, he could not immediately tell. *Give it time,* he thought. *He might still crack.*

Having to remain outwardly calm in front of Driskell was not without effort and it required intense concentration. 'How can I be of service to you?' asked Alexander.

Driskell waited a few moments, letting the unbearable silence stretch before he finally deigned to continue.

Alexander had felt each minute like nails being dragged down a chalkboard. *Imbecile, he's doing this on purpose.* If

Driskell didn't say something soon to fill the void, he thought he might break out in a sweat; tantamount to signing both his and Rowanne's death warrants.

Driskell continued at his leisurely pace, enjoying how smoothly everything was going. 'It involves the demon/human altercation that happened in central London. You may be aware of it. If I'm not mistaken, you were patrolling that immediate area last Thursday night, is this correct?'

Alexander watched Driskell's glacial eyes dance on the edge of danger. He felt as if he were playing with fire. He had no option but to tell a partial truth - if he lied outright, then Driskell would pick up on it. 'That's right, I have been assigned to London. Each night I am allocated the area with the highest demon activity. I'm sure, with you being so well informed, that you are probably aware of the others deployed here - after all, it's a big city! I'm not saying that I could not handle it on my own, what with me being Alexander the Great, but it's good to have backup. Occasionally.' He laughed, hoping to bring the tension down a notch.

Driskell smiled at Alexander's arrogance. He had never met a more conceited demon in his life. And he was reminded of why he had once liked, and perhaps still did, the man before him. Continuing to appear affable, Driskell asked, 'Were you within the area of the altercation? Perhaps, you were present at the incident?' he asked, still smiling.

CHAPTER 11

Rowanne was in a bad mood. Lady Enid pleaded with an earnest look that said keep calm and live if you want to find out what is happening.

Lady Enid knew that Rowanne was restless. She could not blame her, really, the young woman wanted to take up some action against what had been done to her. *She doesn't even know the half of it. If she did, then...*

'Lady Enid, is there something you wish to tell me?' asked Rowanne, who had noticed that for the past five minutes, she had been steadily looking at her. It was slightly unnerving to say the least.

'No, of course not. My mind wandered momentarily. I was considering what our next move should be.'

'Really? Like pawn to E6, that type of thing?' Rowanne had a demanding expression that pointedly asked for the truth.

Lady Enid was intrigued, 'Do you play chess?'

'When the mood strikes. I played a lot as a child with my grandmother.'

'Who taught you?' asked Lady Enid. She had played countless times with... *No*, she thought, stopping the memory in its tracks.

'My grandmother. She's quite the player, and if you ever fancy a challenge, then I suggest you play against her. She'd give you a run for your money.' Rowanne smiled fondly as she remembered the many opponents her grandmother had decimated who had dared to challenge her. Actually, truth be told, she encouraged people to try their luck; she was one wicked lady. In the best sense, of course.

'I like your grandmother. She seems like an interesting woman.' *Even though, sadly, I'll never meet her; it's actually a mercy to her.* For Lady Enid to meet a human outside of normal parameters was tantamount to a death sentence, possibly for the both of them. She decided not to dwell too much on this melancholy train of thought.

There was a loud knock on the door, that almost became the death of them as they jumped in their seats, unnerved as they already were. Looking at each other, they gathered their mettle, and metaphorically put on their venetian masks: they were ready for whatever would come next.

Sitting regally in her chair with her beautiful golden hair shimmering against the stark black of her lace veil which now concealed her face, Lady Enid commanded, 'Enter.'

That one word held such authority, and Rowanne looked on in wonder at the transformation of Lady Enid.

By the time the soldiers entered, Rowanne was looking down and acting docile again. They came into the court and surrounded her, moving into a half circle formation at her back, and to the side of her.

I wonder what the hell is going to happen next... Knowing my luck, it's going to be in this precise order: police station, kidnapped, drugged, and then probably death, most likely on this spot, she thought, as she looked out of the corner of her eyes and observed that the soldiers were armed with deadly weapons.

Weapons, she decided, was too vague a term: they would look quite at home in The British Museum, possibly the medieval period. Perhaps they predated even that...

The soldiers were even wearing metal armour, such as a knight would wear. Rowanne wondered whether they were part of an order that was obligated to dress in ceremonial clothing. It was undeniably becoming stranger by the minute.

'My lady, we have been ordered to escort the prisoner into detective Driskell's custody.'

The soldiers were composed and stoic, not that Rowanne had been expecting anything to the contrary. *I'm going crazy,* she thought. *Wait, what did they mean prisoner, have they found evidence against me?* Panic stirred in her stomach, coiled tight. If they had, she wondered if they'd be kind enough to share it with her. *Please illuminate me. I'm just as much in the proverbial dark, as you are. Just be calm,* she told herself, and took a deep breath to steady her nerves.

Lady Enid addressed herself to the soldier who had spoken, 'This is the first I've heard of these orders. I was told that this woman had been brought here for an interview owing to the detective's constraints on time. I believe she was to be taken back to the police station to continue questioning, and thereafter to be released for the time being.'

'My lady, the detective has been following up on leads, and therefore it will not be possible for him to return to the station presently. He has requested most humbly that you hand her over into our care, and we will escort her to the detective directly.'

Lady Enid's hands were tied. She could not even tele-pathically warn Rowanne; that would probably in all likeli-hood frighten her, and send her over the edge. *What can I do?* She considered her options: she could refuse, but she'd need a plausible reason as to why, otherwise she would arouse sus-picion, which would lead her straight to the top: *Prima Stella, here I come.* Dark thoughts ate away at her as she contemplat-ed their dire situation.

'Excuse me, my lady, if there isn't anything else, may I be permitted to take the prisoner now?'

Lady Enid looked at Rowanne as she spoke to the soldier, 'If the detective warrants this to be more than a routine session,' she paused briefly, as she rose out of her chair. She stood straight, forcing the soldiers to suddenly kneel before their Queen and pledge their allegiance. 'As daughter of the First Family of the Morning Star Clan, I will accompany the prisoner. I have a duty to see the developments that have taken this case beyond the ordinary, and if this has escalated, then I must be present to pass judgement at the courts. There is a protocol to follow, as I am sure you are well aware of gentlemen.'

The soldiers appeared unnerved by this speech. Maybe Lady Enid was more influential then she had initially given her credit for. What was a clan? Rowanne had never heard of 'Morning Star'. *What an unusual name*, she thought. Rowanne made a mental note of everything she'd seen and heard.

I wonder if Lady Enid is some kind of high court judge? She had not heard of her, but then again, how many judges did she know? Rowanne found the whole situation dubious - something was not quite right, but she could not put her finger on it.

As Rowanne stood up, she was handcuffed by a soldier to her considerable annoyance. *Do I look like some kind of hardened criminal? Honestly, this is going slightly overboard. And not to mention that I will be having the pleasure of seeing that red headed sociopath again. Maybe, if I'm very lucky, I'll watch Lady Enid cut him down to size.* She noticed Lady Enid's shoulders trembling. *I wonder what's gotten into her, this situation hardly warrants laughter.*

Lady Enid fought to stay in control; it was difficult to say in the least. Even in this alarming situation, the young woman never lost her good humour. She'd seen grown men break down at the prospect of having to face Driskell, but not Rowanne, who was valiant in her wit. *Sometimes, humour is all we have to get us through,* she thought.

The soldiers formed a circle around Rowanne, and Lady Enid preceded them to the doors. The lights turned off one by one the closer they got to the exit, and then the soldiers waited.

No sooner had Rowanne wondered why they had stopped when the doors swung open, and the room suddenly plunged into darkness, scaring the life out of her. Before her mind could register anything else, there was a flash of bright green, and everything quickly began to fade around the edges until finally she lost consciousness.

The soldier behind Rowanne caught her as she collapsed, then proceeded to carry her through the portal back to the Earth realm.

The court house fell away, blazing green momentarily, and the soldiers bathed in the green fire appeared at ease, having used this method many times before.

Lady Enid was bathed in a regal bluish green flame, like an immortal queen pulled from a dark fairytale. The police room started to come into focus, and runes flashed here and there as this new reality was taking shape and becoming solid by the minute. In no time at all, they were firmly back in the human world.

'My lady, please wait here while we arrange transport.'

The soldiers placed Rowanne in a chair. The two way mirror reflected a woman who was limp, looking pale and sickly with her hair plastered to her forehead. They left the room, closing the door behind them.

Lady Enid waited a moment and then knelt before Rowanne, tucking her hair behind her ears and helping her to sit straight. *Poor thing.* Travelling by portal was not the most comfortable method, especially if a person had never tried it before. It affected people differently: some could handle it, whereas others seemed to come out of it for the worse.

In Rowanne's case, magic had been used on her a couple of times already, and despite her iron constitution, she was now feeling the effects of it. Lady Enid hoped that it would soon be over. *Damn Dewain for putting her through all this instead of concluding this matter. But it was his way though*, Lady Enid thought bitterly, as he put demons and humans alike through hell in the name of investigation and upholding their laws. She sat back quickly and composed her face behind the veil as she sensed the soldiers approaching the door.

The door opened a second later, and the soldiers stepped through, having changed into human law enforcement uniforms. 'Sorry, my lady, for the delay. It took us longer than expected. If you'd like to come with us now?'

'Is the station secure?' asked Lady Enid.

'Yes, my lady. Only our people are in the building presently. We are good to go.'

Without further delay, two soldiers stood on either side of Rowanne, and, placing her arms around their shoulders, they gathered her up and carried her to the lift.

Lady Enid's mind worked overtime, trying to plan ahead, but so far, she had nothing. She followed the soldiers to a black car. They placed Rowanne in the backseat, strapped a seat belt across to secure her, and then sat on either side of her. Another soldier got into the front to drive.

'Lady Enid, if you would like to follow me. You will be taking this vehicle,' another said, and she proceeded to get into the back of the black BMW indicated as two soldiers got into the front. 'My lady, are you ready?' She nodded her head just once, and the vehicles pulled out of the police station car park.

There were three vehicles in total: Rowanne was in the first, Lady Enid in the second, and lastly followed by a black van, filled with Demon World's best soldiers, all armed to the teeth just in case their services were required; God help the mortal and demon alike who got between that van and Lady Enid.

The car had been driving for ten minutes when Rowanne began to wake from the induced sleep that she had been under to stop her learning of the portal and Demon World. It would be a lot to explain to a human, but more importantly, it was against their rules.

Where am I? Rowanne wondered. Her mind felt like a lead weight had pressed down upon it. She felt groggy as she started to come to her senses, and on the fourth attempt actually managed to keep her eyes open. She felt slightly nauseous but the feeling soon passed, and, sitting up straighter, she noticed the police officers on either side of her as they looked on dead ahead, impervious to her discomfort.

'Excuse me, but would you be so kind as to tell me what is happening?' Rowanne addressed the question to the officer in the front seat.

'Ah, I'm glad to see you are awake, Ms Knight. You seemed to have fallen asleep at the police station.'

Wait a minute, hold on. Did he say police station? As far as I can remember, I was at a court. Rowanne remembered talking to Lady Enid... Then realisation hit: *I can't believe they've tried the same thing on me, again! This is becoming a bloody nuisance.* How many more times were they going to drug and move her around?

'Where exactly are we going?' asked Rowanne, feigning confusion - not that it was that far from the truth.

'We are on our way to meet Chief Inspector Driskell. And we should be there soon.'

'Wasn't he supposed to be at the police station?'

'He got called away on an urgent matter. He apologises profusely for the delay, and thanks you for your cooperation. He realises that all of this may seem highly unusual.'

'I guess it's the life of a detective to never be in one place for very long, especially if he's involved in an investigation.'

'That's right, Ms Knight. He's like a bloodhound who doesn't stop, especially when he catches the scent, if you get my meaning.'

Rowanne didn't like the face reflected in the rear-view

mirror, it seemed almost demonic with a cruel smile. It had given her the creeps when he had described the detective in that way. What type of man was he? *Last I checked, you were supposed to put your faith in the police. They were the good guys, right?* Nobody could pay her enough to put her life in the hands of that red-haired madman.

Looking out the window, Rowanne could see the moon intermittently peep out behind the clouds. She requested the officer to open a window as it felt quite stuffy in the car, and he obliged. Cold air came flooding in, helping to clear her mind as well as honing it, so that she could prepare herself as best as possible for wherever they were actually heading.

They drove along the river down Victoria Embankment. Rowanne found it ironic that only a couple of nights ago, she had been running along this very river to avoid the police. Now look at her; same river, opposite side and in a police car. Sometimes, the very thing you want to avoid ultimately happens. Do we not have a choice in life? Is it all mapped out? If the answer was yes, then it was quite depressing. She stopped her morose musings, they were not going to be of any help.

I have to stay calm, that's what Alexander would tell me. I can't believe I just thought of that fool again. He is a pain in my side, but strangely, getting angry at him helped her to focus.

Where was the voice in her mind when she needed it, usually it would come up with something helpful. Rowanne felt a slight prickling sensation in her mind, almost as if a spider had crawled across her skin. She suddenly found herself becoming calm and amenable.

You called, I came. I see that you have gotten yourself into a bit of trouble here, again!

Rowanne sputtered, coughing violently which caused the soldier on the side of her to be alarmed.

'Ms Knight, are you alright, can I get you some water?'

'Thank you,' she replied, and gratefully accepted the bottle that was hastily placed into her hands.

Look, you might as well give the game away now. Can you be any more dramatic! the entity said in an irritated tone.

For a voice in my head that's supposed to comfort me, you are rather unpleasant! Rowanne replied in an equally peeved manner.

Have you never heard the expression, 'cruel to be kind'? Anyway, my job is not to be your friend, it's to keep you alive, you got that? The entity wanted to support Rowanne, but the best way to do that was to make her stronger, so that she would no longer need her. The entity had its job cut out for it.

Fine, then tell me, oh enlightened one, what should I do? Rowanne was willing to go along with the crazy scenario. *The voice in my head doesn't sound like me. It's official, I'm certifiable.*

First of all, let me make it clear, you are not crazy. But you can't act to save your life. If journalism doesn't work out, then don't let acting be your second choice, you will not win any awards! The public will pay not to see you! said the entity.

I beg your pardon, but what the hell has that got to do with anything? I'm doing the best I can here. Great, now I'm justifying myself to me, thought Rowanne.

Calm down, you need to do better frankly. Lucky for you, you have me.

I concede to the unfortunate truth of the earlier point. The dramatics were just for show, it takes a lot more to rile me. Now, if you've quite finished, how do you propose that we proceed? asked Rowanne.

The entity had to give Rowanne credit, maybe she had underestimated her. *There's still hope then, perhaps I can tell her the truth sooner than expected. I wonder why I was so hesitant to put the plan into action, maybe I'm projecting my own fears onto Rowanne. Maybe I'm the one that can't go forward.*

Hello? All I'm getting is radio silence, is anyone there? Can you hear me? Rowanne felt as if she was coaxing her mind, and found it quite bizarre. There was definitely something wrong with her.

Cut that out, I'm still here. Would you go completely off the rails if I said the voice in your head needed time to think. The entity held its breath; even though, the dead have no need to breathe.

On the weirdness meter, I'd say that's a category Freud. Psychologically, there is something not quite right with me, am I correct? asked Rowanne.

Do you want me to answer that? Think carefully before you ask, replied the entity.

You are me, but you don't sound like me, does that make any sense? asked Rowanne.

Completely! Right, here goes nothing, listen up. I am a part of you, but I am not you. I am not your voice in your mind, though I reside there, replied the entity.

That sounds like a riddle. I think it's something I will have to come back to later. For now, we should focus on the more pressing matter at hand. Rowanne could feel the edges of a migraine begin to appear, hence her hasty withdrawal from the topic at hand. She would eventually deal with it. Maybe she'd get professional help, it could not be ignored any longer.

Just like that, her mind shuts down anything it cannot explain. It's a shame. I placed too high an expectation on her, thought the entity, but strangely relieved at not having to explain everything at present.

I am about to tell you something, don't ponder on it too much, rather use the knowledge to your advantage, said the entity.

Fine, continue. Rowanne was impatient - the sooner this was over, the sooner she could get back home.

You are being taken to The Salisbury pub, there you will meet detective Driskell. But you will also encounter your colleague Mr Black. Now, Alexander will not be expecting you to turn up, as far as he is concerned, you are still at the police station. I can sense that you desperately have questions, but we do not have time on our hands, and we have nearly reached our destination. Detective Driskell has purposely arranged this meeting to observe the interaction between you and Mr Black. So, it is imperative that you act natural, and give out the least amount of information possible without arousing his suspicion. Believe me when I say that both your lives depend on this meeting going well, said the entity.

Looking out the window, Rowanne could see the sky had lightened to a dull yellowish tinge; dawn was only a couple of hours away.

The car suddenly came to an abrupt stop. The officer in the driver's seat lowered his window, and the officers on either side of Rowanne immediately became alert, like guard dogs awaiting their instructions. 'You two follow me. Ms Knight, pleased remain seated, this will only take a moment,' said the soldier in the driver's seat.

All three soldiers left, and Rowanne was alone in the car, but not for long as the door opened, and Lady Enid got into the seat next to her. 'Listen, Rowanne, I am afraid the plan's changed. I cannot accompany you to the pub, something's come up that needs my urgent attention, but fear not I will come back for you.' She could see the sudden panic set into Rowanne, who had been quietly confident, assuming that Lady Enid would be at her side. What would she do now? Grabbing Rowanne's shoulders, Lady Enid said, 'Look at me, Rowanne. Don't you dare break down on me now. You can do this, I have complete faith in you. You just have to trust yourself to get out of this situation.'

'You're right, this is embarrassing. I will try to be more level headed. I honestly think it's down to exhaustion. Please go, you shouldn't delay your business. However, promise me that you will come back, there are some things we need to discuss,' said Rowanne.

'I will, you have my word.' She wondered what Rowanne wanted to discuss, maybe she had remembered something. Taking Rowanne's hand she squeezed it, the only outward display of affection that she could get away with in a car that was surrounded by her men.

As soon as Lady Enid had left, the soldiers got back in and continued driving. Rowanne wondered whether they would question her as to what Lady Enid had said, but thankfully they remained silent.

In no time at all, they had reached the pub. As she got out, Rowanne felt a chill in the night air, but not just from the cold, and her stomach coiled uneasily. *This is it,* she thought.

She took a deep breath as an officer led her to the entrance. She had her head down, and her hair wisped around her like a dark halo as she passed beneath the cherubs, who judged all who passed before them. Cold, sightless eyes watched as she was about to enter. Rowanne had to pass the test, or the scales would unbalance, and the sword would literally plunge down.

CHAPTER 12

Alexander felt the waves of unease coming from the other side of the doors. He fervently hoped that Driskell was not an empath, otherwise the game was up. *Calm down, Rowanne. It will be alright,* he mentally willed for her to be at peace.

He sensed the moment she was about to enter. Unfortunately, so did Driskell, who looked at him poignantly before continuing, 'You did not answer my question.'

Alexander forced himself to tear his eyes away from the door, and instead face Driskell head on. It was proving harder than he had thought it would be. It was mentally draining him to have his mind split between the man before him and the woman at his back.

'You seem nervous, Alexander. What is it? Tell your old friend here all about it,' Driskell smiled condescendingly, taking delight in his friend's discomfort.

I can think of something better to call him than friend, he thought absurdly. *Focus Alexander, this is not helping. If I ever have the chance, I think I will settle some scores with my old beloved friend,* he thought disgustedly. Why was it so hard for him to focus? He saw the flash of green tinge Driskell's eyes, and he just knew he was being toyed with. *You manipulative piece of... How dare he try to use those cheap mind tricks on me.* Well, at least he'd gained the knowledge of another power that Driskell possessed.

Alexander's own eyes bled to green as his magic surfaced and wove a net around him shielding him from Driskell's power. Instantly, Alexander felt as if cool water had been poured on his head, and a gentle glacial breeze circled him, ready to cut down to size any ego lest it become too great.

Driskell nodded his appreciation at Alexander's ability. But also laughed coldly at how slow Alexander had been to understand that he was being manipulated. 'I was just getting started, as well. You've spoilt my entertainment.'

That was Driskell for you, he'd no sooner praise you than cut you down in the same breath. *Time to get myself back on track and stop acting like a complete fool,* thought Alexander wearily.

Alexander could not afford to waste any more time. His eyes returned to their normal sapphire tinged with grey, but they still blazed a not so subtle hint of violence towards Driskell, should it come to that.

Driskell's eyes burned equally fiercely in answer to the threat, and they too began to bleed to grey at the edges. He could not believe this blatant invitation to violence. *Drop the gauntlet, I beg you to you imbecile,* he was more than ready to kick Alexander's sorry behind.

However, there were still many hours in which to leisurely enjoy the outcome of the drama that was about to unfold, maybe even explode. No need to rush to the end just yet.

Driskell reigned in his power and smiled, cautiously assessing his friend. *Why do I keep calling him that? He is my... in fact, I'm not sure what he is to me.* He was caught off guard by Alexander's next words.

'I am ready to continue answering your questions. And if you don't mind, I want to proceed as quickly as possible. I do have many demands on my time, as you must be aware of, being a law enforcement officer yourself.'

Driskell raised his eyebrow in consternation at the situation that seemed to be going out of his control. What happened to the scared Alexander of a few moments ago? Why was he now so eager to answer his questions, when before he had seemed unwilling. There was definitely something going on, and he wondered as to what it might be.

Glad to see the smirk wiped off Driskell's face, Alexander sat straighter in his chair, using his height to intimidate his opponent, which in Driskell's case was pointless as nothing much riled him.

Alexander stuck to the truth as much as possible, so when Driskell would undoubtedly cross-check all he had to say, he would not be 'found wanting.'

He began his linear truth; 'I was in London last Thursday, you can check that with the Noble Court. They sent me to patrol the Westminster area, because there were energy signatures of rogue demons on the loose.'

Driskell had his hands steepled together and nodded for Alexander to continue, whilst making a mental note of everything he said.

'I was on the trail of Shadow men, who attacked me as soon as I was within their vicinity. I managed to overpower one of them. Unfortunately, and you know how I hate to admit this, but his friend gave me the slip.'

Driskell laughed at Alexander's inability in not being able to subdue more than one opponent. Noticing the glare Alexander was directing towards him only made him laugh harder.

'Where did the actual incident take place? No one has informed me yet on the finer details, there is much I don't know about this incident. However, maybe we can piece together what actually happened if we both work on this case.' Alexander tried to look both professional and sincere, hoping he could slowly try to gain Driskell's trust. Better to be on the side of the Devil, if only for show. It would buy him time, and direct attention away from him.

Driskell was taken aback with Alexander's declaration; he desperately wanted to believe in his old friend, but there was that nagging uncertainty in the back of his mind at this sudden turnaround. Still, if he worked with Alexander, then at least he could always keep an eye on him. And maybe he could be useful in solving this case... hopefully not to his detriment.

'Are you sure, Alexander? Think carefully. If you agree, then I take you at your word. But mark my words, there will be no going back. I will demand your full cooperation, and you *will* be answerable to me. Do I make myself clear?' he asked severely, putting the full force of his meaning into his eyes, as he looked unswervingly at Alexander.

Alexander knew that this would be an iron clad deal, he was almost giving away a piece of his soul. *Actually, I've already done that. How much more of myself, do I have to lose?* He wondered what Driskell would order him to do, and whether he'd be able to do it and live with himself. He gave the matter serious consideration. Driskell interrupted his macabre train of thought.

'Listen, do not give me your answer now, but think on it. I am a reasonable man, but let me make it clear, I will not wait forever. Either way, you will bear the consequences of your decision,' said Driskell.

If indeed it turned out that Alexander was involved, then nothing could save him. He would face the full might of Demon World law - and it would be headed by Driskell himself. This could mean the end for Alexander, especially if evidence was found against him. He would be sent straight to the Noble Court, and seldom did anyone return if they were found guilty.

This case worried Driskell. It might be more than he had first initially thought: from being a simple demon attack on a human, it could harbour something much worse. His intuition told him that not all was as it seemed. All of the players had yet to come onto the board and reveal their positions. No, for now, they watched as the pawns made their move before bringing out their elite arsenal.

Driskell did not enjoy being a pawn, pushed around at the beck and call of the Nobles. One of the reasons why he became Enforcer was to hold the Nobles to account; a momentous and thankless task. The First Families were akin to the Kings and Queens on the chess board, all other families of lesser nobility became their right hand men and women. *I wonder where I fit in...* he thought, and laughed darkly.

Alexander kept his face neutral as he thought, *I'd definitely place you as the dark knight. Perhaps, dark horse would be more appropriate.* Driskell definitely had a chip on his shoulder, growing bigger by the day.

The more that he observed of his friend, the more he questioned his true nature. Was he the monster that everybody painted him out to be? He was hiding something: his personality seemed to hover between camaraderie and enmity when it came to Alexander. Maybe he was biding his time, and in due course when the time was right, and he had gathered all the evidence, then he would probably make his move.

Driskell broke Alexander out of his thoughts. 'The incident took place at the former government building that is in Westminster, along the Victoria Embankment,' looking at Alexander's vacant expression, he continued indignantly, 'Whitehall Court.'

'I'm not familiar with the streets of London, though I understand that the borough of Westminster is no small area,' replied Alexander.

'I need you to be more accurate. Stop being vague, where exactly did you patrol? I want details!' Driskell pointedly looked at Alexander, hammering home the point that he would not settle for less.

On the contrary, Alexander understood perfectly and brought up an image of Westminster to mind so that he could account for his whereabouts. His mind quickly processed a map of the area.

'I was patrolling on the edge of St James Park, and I chased a demon across Birdcage Walk. I managed to subdue him down a side road, but cannot account for his friend who got away. Will this do, or do you require further details?' Alexander asked sarcastically, feigning boredom with the whole situation.

Driskell brought up his phone, and went online to bring up a map of the area to substantiate Alexander's story. Demon help him if he was lying. According to the map, Alexander would have been 0.6 miles away from the incident.

This placed him in a tricky situation, because Alexander had not been directly near Whitehall Court, however he had been within a short walking distance to it. He thought hard; the building was along the river, and Alexander would have been at the edge of the park, so he would not have known that a commotion had occurred. He also factored in that the building was actually hidden behind gardens. No, a person would have to be on the road directly before Whitehall Gardens, or one of the side roads on either side of the building, to have seen the incident.

'Alexander, I believe it is your lucky day, as I can see that your position places you outside of the incident area.' However, he was not inclined to dismiss him so easily.

Driskell did not let demons go easily, nor did he like loose ends. Only when he had thoroughly cross examined everything, and had the pure facts before him, would he deign to release poor Alexander, who judging by that contemptuous look, didn't seem to care either way.

Hmm, I wonder, innocent or guilty? Innocent or guilty... he imagined a sword swinging in a wide arc above Alexander: for now it hovered, but only time would tell if it would fell his old adversary.

Alexander remained outwardly calm, but internally he was in a panic, especially after the bizarre look that had come into Driskell's eyes. He didn't like the way his eyes moved from side to side, like some kind of macabre pendulum; once they came to a stop, they would spell doom on whomever they landed. Also, the fact that he had heard only some of Driskell's thoughts didn't help matters, but he had got the general idea.

Being telepathic was not straightforward. Alexander sometimes heard the whole part of what someone was thinking, but at other times he got a fragmented picture. The information he received all depended on the individual that he was probing. Humans, as a general rule, were the easiest, but you got the odd one, now and again, who could shield their thoughts; whether it be conscious, or unconscious.

Demons on the other hand, were in a completely different league, out of the exosphere as one might say. There was a hierarchy of demons, each with their own unique set of talents (powers) common to their group or family. Some of them even possessed a unique power as yet undefined, and not in the sphere of common knowledge. This was what made demons especially dangerous.

Alexander knew that he was not really safe; he may be out of the danger zone for now, but he was skating on thin ice. All Driskell needed was one link to chain Alexander to Rowanne, and that was it, The End...

Life for Alexander had once been carefree, but now he felt as if he walked along a cliff edge, never truly feeling safe. And he felt angrier these days, because he was so unsure of himself and others. He did not know who he could trust. Maybe it was not just a peril that demons felt, perhaps humans felt it too. After all, humans could lie just as well as demons.

The only thing he had in his world was loyalty: to his cause, and he wanted to trust those he had pledged fealty to, and it goes without saying to his world. *That is a joke*, he thought, *look at where I am now; at a crossroads, living between two worlds.*

He had to tone down his anger, otherwise it would shimmer in a haze around him. *Damn it,* he thought, *why am I so transparent with my emotions at the wrong time?* Perhaps it was a hazard of being in the Black Rose Clan; they felt things intensely, passionately, whether it be love or hate. His clan did not shy away from living to the fullest, nor were they quiet in their beliefs. They practised openly what they preached - no one would ever dare to call them hypocrites.

However, Alexander had to painfully pull away from what was so natural to him and shield like his life depended on it, which it did. He would deal with his errant emotions later. He did not blame himself, he just accepted what was, for now.

He could not afford to think of his new status. Driskell was the last person in Demon World who he wanted knowing about what had occurred between Rowanne and himself, leading to a change in their genetic makeup. *You're dead, dead,* his mind cried at him, echoing back like a forlorn ghost.

'Is that all? If so, I need to leave, with your permission, of course. I am a busy man, as you know,' he smiled sweetly at Driskell, while his treacherous heart beat a crescendo.

Driskell smiled broadly, 'Why the hurry, Alexander? There is someone very special that I want you to meet.' He studied Alexander carefully for any signs that he knew to whom he was referring.

Alexander looked at Driskell, his eyebrows raised questioningly. He did not seem unduly fazed by this, he was the epitome of calm.

This caused Driskell to pause, and reconsider the situation. It had all appeared to be going in his favour, but now he was not so sure of himself, and he felt some of his bravado slip. In his mind he had planned it to perfection. All the signs so far, together with the evidence he had collected, led directly to Alexander's involvement.

Though, Driskell had to admit that Alexander did have an explanation for his being in Westminster last Thursday. Now, if it turned out that Alexander had no connection to Ms Knight, then he was truly in danger of losing two of his main leads in the case. He would have to completely start afresh. He could not afford the indignation of the Noble Court; how they'd laugh him out of his position.

Driskell belonged to the Dark Lake Clan, which ranked below the First Families. This meant that he had no one powerful to back him, should he come to any difficulty within Demon World. He damned those Nobles and their archaic rules that gave the First Families so much power over the rest of them; the unfortunates, that belonged to lesser clans.

One of the reasons he hated Alexander was that he outranked him because he was born to a Noble Family, not just any, but to the clan of First Families: those who made Demon World what it was today. They had forged the rules that every citizen must abide by, whether they liked it or not.

It was not unheard of for a Noble to have a friend in a lesser clan, though most of the First Families would describe a connection with a lesser clan as an acquaintance. They knew that those clans would appreciate them for even deigning to talk to them; they bestowed their benevolence by acknowledging their very presence.

No wonder Driskell loved to hunt them and cut them down to size. He considered himself a champion of the lesser clans, daring them to break the rules, to see if by some miracle they could go undetected beneath his radar. He would dearly love to confer his own benevolence onto them in the Noble Court, or if he was a really good demon, in Prima Stella: the court of courts. The last one, where no other judgment but guilt and death would be pronounced. *A demon could dream...* he thought malevolently.

Alexander could see a dark aura pervade Driskell, whose eyes turned midnight black, and he could have sworn he could see stars shining in them like daggers glinting in moonlight. It frankly scared the life out of Alexander, who felt as if he had just aged by a decade. This was bad, what had gotten into him? He had been smiling only a minute ago.

Maybe Driskell's dangerous reputation was also partly to do with his split personality: affable one moment; psychotic the next, it was frightening just how quickly he switched. *I wonder which Driskell I'll be talking to.* Alexander could have kicked himself, because in the next instant that malevolent look was turned in his direction.

Driskell laughed maniacally at Alexander's weary expression. *He finally looks as if he's about to break, I was worried I was losing my touch there. That's better,* he thought, and the moment that he had been waiting for had arrived. 'Alexander, our guest is just outside. Should I invite *her* in?' He knew his emphasis was not lost, and swiping open his phone, he made the call, 'Bring the prisoner in.'

The officer placed a restraining hand on Rowanne, just as she was about to push open the doors. 'Just wait a moment, please. The detective has kindly asked if you could give him a few minutes to finish up with what he is doing, and he apologises most profusely.'

Rowanne didn't mind as it gave her time to compose herself as she felt goosebumps all along her arms. She felt sick with anticipation for what was to come.

Maybe it was the fact that she knew that Alexander was right on the other side of the door. She felt nervous at the thought of seeing him again; he seemed to have that effect on her, every time. Even though technically she'd only met him twice, she felt as if she'd known him a lot longer. *Hmm... strange.* This was nothing compared to the fear and anger she felt at having to face detective Driskell again.

Here was one man who really got under her skin, and from the short period that she had been in his company, led her to form the opinion that he was one dangerous individual. He should in no way be called a police officer, not after what he did to her.

Moreover, there was the question of what Driskell may or may not have done to Lady Enid for her to have an aversion to him. It went beyond two colleagues not getting along. And that was the other point, they were also acquaintances; how far and to what degree, Rowanne did not as yet fully understand.

It was hard for Rowanne to know whom she could trust. She felt like her world view had been considerably altered this past week: no one appeared to be who they claimed.

However, she had to remind herself that the only comfort she got was from work; at least, she knew the people there, and had built up a good rapport with them.

There were so many unanswered questions, and she would meticulously go through them back at her apartment later. She needed knowledge on her side to work out what was happening.

The guard nodded for her to go in, 'I will wait here, Ms Knight.'

Rowanne squared her shoulders and, taking a deep breath, pushed open the doors. She stood in the poorly lit entrance like a dark phantom. For Rowanne though, it was perfect - being in the shadows gave her a great view of the pub.

Rowanne's heart sped up the moment she spied Alexander, sitting with his back to her at a table towards the back of the pub. She also noticed with dismay that detective Driskell unfortunately occupied the same table, and that he was facing the entrance. As soon as she stepped into the light, he'd instantly see her.

Alexander imperceptibly shivered the moment Rowanne had entered. He did not have to physically see her to know she was in his vicinity; they were linked now, after all. Her power sang to him, every time. Actually, more so when they were in close proximity to each other.

He could pick up on Rowanne's emotional state if she was in distress, and their link became stronger if either one of them was in danger. And now it vibrated violently - Alexander could almost feel the indigo sparks shooting in warning that they were in dire peril. Rowanne would probably feel anxious, but wouldn't know the cause of it; after all, the link worked both ways.

Rowanne walked sedately towards the back table, her head held high. The beginnings of a plan formed in her mind with each step she took towards the two men. One of whom she could tolerate, barely; the other she despised.

Thanks a lot, Rowanne, thought Alexander, *you put that beautifully.* Honestly, she never changed, she was considerate and unremitting in her abhorrence of him. *Or maybe I'm giving her too much credit, and it's the idiot before me she hates, in which case, I thoroughly applaud her good judgement.*

Driskell looked Rowanne straight in the eyes as soon as she stepped forward. He smiled sweetly up at her, taunting. 'Ms Knight, please join us here,' he asked, indicating the chair at the head of the table which would place her squarely between the two men.

Rowanne would not fall for it, she would not give into this man; she would play this game her way. She noticed that the pub was completely empty except for the bartender, who was discreetly polishing cups and putting bottles away. He had not acknowledged her as she had passed the bar. Maybe he too feared Driskell, and that's why he studiously avoided making eye contact, never mind the pleasantries.

Both men got up, but it was Driskell who felt it his solemn duty to make the introductions. 'Alexander, may I introduce you to Ms Knight, who works at Whitehall Court newspaper, and is here today at my special request to help answer questions regarding the investigation into the incident that took place at her office.'

Rowanne and Alexander made short eye contact as they

shook hands. She smiled at him and he returned a non committal nod of the head by way of a response. She then faced detective Driskell and shook his hand, whilst keeping her expression neutral.

'Chief Inspector Driskell, may I ask why Mr Black is here today?'

Rowanne finally permitted herself to smile sweetly up at him, and it only broadened at the look of utter astonishment and triumph that lit up the detective's face; he thought that she had just slipped up. She pulled back the chair and sat down, waiting patiently for the men to join her.

After Alexander had recovered from the shock, he quickly rearranged his features into a firm expression. 'Ms Knight, I thought you'd be at home working on the next assignment.' He would leave it up to Rowanne, and trust and support her judgment in handling Driskell. The best he could do was match her confidence, and hopefully somehow they'd pull through.

'That was the plan. But I forgot to mention that I did have an appointment at the police station,' and Rowanne paused at detective Driskell's perplexed expression. She pulled out a seat, indicating he should join them at the table (instead of foolishly standing). Driskell sullenly accepted and sat down. Rowanne continued, 'Where was I? Oh yes, after which I was supposed to report back to my editor Eileen. However, it's far too late for that now,' she said accusingly in Driskell's direction.

'For that I am sincerely sorry, Ms Knight. I know that half of your day has been wasted.' Driskell tried to appear earnest, he had to change tactics fast, if he was to get anywhere. Ms Knight was more formidable than he had at first thought.

He would not be deterred from his questions, he must have the answers at any cost. 'In what capacity do you know Mr Black?' asked Driskell.

The table at which they sat had a light directly above, not to mention the Victorian lights on the glass panels, this meant it was so well lit as to almost be blinding, so there was nowhere to hide. Squinting slightly, Rowanne answered smoothly, 'He is a colleague of mine from work.' She didn't feel the need to elaborate, which she could tell caused a fair amount of annoyance to Driskell. *That's all you'll get, you conniving piece of work.*

Well done, Rowanne, thought Alexander, nearly sputtering at her last admission. He had to keep his face in check, when really all he wanted to do was laugh out loud. It had never even occurred to him that *Rowanne* would take on Driskell.

When he had imagined this scenario, Alexander had seen it unfolding quite differently. Never in his darkest joy had he expected for her to be so bold. He was quietly proud of her.

Rowanne had diligently avoided making eye contact with Alexander unless it was necessary: she did not want him to be the undoing of her, or vice versa. However, with Driskell's attention diverted to his phone, it afforded Rowanne the chance to silently communicate with Alexander. She looked him dead in the eyes, pleading for him to trust in her, that she would not let them down this time, there were to be no more repeats of the apartment. Rowanne felt more in control of herself, for now, and would not succumb to useless emotions, but rather accept them and deal with them at her own pace; privately, and not in public.

Alexander heard every word, and his admiration for her grew even more. *Not useless,* he thought. Emotions were never that, you needed to feel something as a human, as a demon, whatever you were, otherwise, what was the point? Alexander softened his features minutely, only for a second, before returning to his facade.

Rowanne could not put into words what it had meant to her, for Alexander to acknowledge and support her. She was grateful he had completely understood, and she had not even known that he had this softer side to him. *I wonder how long it will last?* And she could have sworn that just now, someone had whispered, 'not useless' in her mind. She was probably just imagining it.

Alexander rolled his eyes and snorted, which caused Driskell and Rowanne to look up sharply in his direction. *Honestly*, thought Alexander, and just shrugged his shoulders and shook his head dismissively. He thought that he understood Rowanne well, but in the next instant she would fling an insult at him, disproving his ludicrous theory! It was disconcerting to say the least, as he wearily looked at her.

Driskell looked up from his phone and noticed the disgusted look on Alexander's face as he looked at Rowanne. *This is promising – if he doesn't like this woman as much as I detest her, then I have a chance of making my case stronger and getting this blockhead to actually side with me, leading to Ms Knight's fall.*

You wish, you pompous pretender, as if I would side with you now. Perhaps once I would have, that and much more... But you have changed old friend.

Rowanne sensed that each man was caught up in his own world, but she didn't have the time to wait around; she needed to have this interview end quickly. 'I really must insist that you speed this up a bit, if you wouldn't mind, as I do have a lot of work pending.' This caused Driskell's eyebrow to rise up, and he looked questioningly at Alexander.

It was all Alexander could do not to laugh. He just nodded his head in approval, and smiled. *You haven't seen the half of it...* he thought, bemused.

Driskell looked bewildered at Rowanne for a moment, before continuing with his questions, 'Well, in that case, Ms Knight, let's by all means, continue. Do you have evidence that proves Mr Black works with you?' and turning towards Alexander, he said, 'Mr Black, I will need someone to substantiate this–'

The doors banged open, startling everyone. Driskell was the fastest to react, and got up. He noticed a tall woman with raven black hair, in a grey dress that matched the steel of her eyes, who came striding in, and, he bemusedly noticed, had one of his soldiers practically hanging off her arm as he tried in vain to stop her.

'Excuse me, madam, but I must insist that you stop right there,' said Driskell commandingly. All of which was lost on the woman, he noticed, as she looked disdainfully in his direction.

Rowanne was speechless, Eileen looked like an Amazonian goddess, who would not be deterred from her mission, especially by a mere man. *This is fantastic. But how had she known that I would be here?*

Women seemed to band together like warriors whenever they supported each other, observed Alexander. Unfortunately for Driskell it could not have come at a worse time, as he pitifully asserted his somewhat limited authority. *I had thought that Rowanne was bad enough, I guess I need to get to know Eileen better...* laughed Alexander silently.

Watching Alexander admire Eileen brought on a strange feeling in Rowanne: *It's probably disgust or loathing.* Were all men the same, she wondered.

From behind Eileen stepped out Amanda, who intrinsically peeled off, finger by finger, the officer's grip on her manager's arm. 'Excuse me, but you would do well to mind your manners. May I also remind you, as you have failed to grasp my earlier meaning, that if there is the slightest scratch on Ms Melville's arm, then I will personally sue you on her behalf, for excessive force.'

Driskell felt it his intrinsic duty to step in and salvage this altogether peculiar situation that was starting to get out of hand. One human he could deal with, but three were problematic: he could not afford to even attempt to control their minds. The good old fashioned form of communication was called for here.

Putting on his most charming smile, he walked towards the woman next to... What had her name been? Ah, Eileen.

He coolly noticed her tall frame and shocking mane of golden hair that framed her steely dark blue eyes. This woman gave of the vibe of being perilous, but what was it about her, that he was not seeing…?

Amanda looked distastefully at the oaf who was looking her over. *Please! Never in a million years would I look in your direction.* She really wished that he would stop staring.

Driskell caught himself looking too long at the woman, and brusquely got on with finding out who the hell she was. 'Madam, I would appreciate it if you would unhand my officer.'

Amanda looked at her perfectly manicured talons for a second before deigning to release him, which caused the guard to lose his balance and stumble before the two women, so that he ended up on his hands and knees. He managed to stop himself from falling completely flat on his face (thereby, humiliatingly prostrating himself before them).

Alexander and Rowanne burst out laughing, no longer able to hide their delight at the whole circus that was unfolding. They looked sharply at each other, and this just caused them to laugh harder, and Rowanne unconsciously grabbed Alexander's arm in camaraderie.

Alexander took a quick intake of breath, as he hastily removed her hand from his arm, but this was all lost on Rowanne. He separated them in time, just as Driskell turned around to face them angrily at having his investigation turn into a shamble.

Looking Alexander in the eye, he silently mouthed, 'I will deal with you two personally, later.'

Damn, thought Alexander, *just when I thought things were beginning to look up! What was that I said about emotions earlier on…* he thought ironically, as the smile faded from his face.

Driskell turned back towards the woman who had dared to attack his guard, thereby embarrassing him also. A slight red tinged his cheeks, and his eyes were practically shooting sparks as he glared at her.

Amanda noticed his demeanour change from mild to manic in under a minute. His shocking red hair, she absently noticed, matched the blush that now spread across his cheeks, making his green eyes, that were presently locked onto her, all the more vibrant.

It was her turn to be slightly uncomfortable as she looked down at the poor man on the ground. She lent him a hand, which he grudgingly accepted. No doubt he would probably have slapped it away, had his boss and other people not been around.

Nevertheless, she put it aside and helped him up, and there was a moment of shock on the officer's face as she easily lifted him in one go, not even breaking a sweat. He continued to steadily look at her with suspicion. *Crap*, thought Amanda, she forgot how strong she was sometimes.

Driskell had noticed this, as well as everyone else in the room.

Rowanne quickly got up and walked towards Amanda. She stood shoulder to shoulder with her, sensing that she now needed someone to rescue her.

'Chief Inspector Driskell, may I introduce you to my fellow colleague and gym buddy, Amanda Eghan.'

Amanda gave Rowanne a grateful look before turning back and putting her hand forward to shake Driskell's.

Driskell grudgingly shook her hand, which was soft to the touch, and her eyes were steadily trained on him. *What does she think I'm going to do? She's like a coiled cat, waiting to pounce.* He'd thought that he was the most neurotic person he knew; she made him look like a relatively sane person - and that was hard to do!

'Ah-hum, if you don't mind, I would like my hand back now...' Amanda thought it her duty to wake up *Sleeping Beauty* here. *God, how long is he going to stand there and stare*, she wondered, finding it slightly disconcerting.

He just looked at her uncomprehendingly, *what did she*

say? He looked down, he was still holding on, somewhat forcefully, to the woman's hand. Dawning comprehension came upon him very slowly, and just as he was about to release it, the woman beat him to it by pulling her hand out sharply from his grasp.

Driskell felt completely humiliated, again! Three times in one night, that had to be a record. Women! They were definitely bad for his reputation, and they paved the descent into hell for him, he thought half-heartedly. Still, he smiled broadly at her, enjoying her dismay. He was Driskell, after all (plus he felt like a total idiot).

Seriously! thought Amanda, nursing her hand. The man's grip was like a vice.

'Sorry, I do beg your pardon,' said Driskell in his most sincere voice.

'I just bet you are!' said Amanda quietly under her breath.

'Pardon?' asked Driskell, having heard her quite clearly, to his amusement.

Amanda was about to reply with a smart quip, but was saved by Eileen cutting in, who had been watching the spectacle like a match at Wimbledon. 'As much as this exchange is enlightening to say the least, it does waste everybody's precious time,' she was mainly referring to herself. 'If you don't mind, I'd like to know exactly what is going on here?' she asked sharply. She was used to ordering people about, and expected immediate answers to her questions.

Driskell composed himself, when what he would ideally like to do was to strangle every incompetent person around him; everyone in the room, in fact.

'Ms Melville? I have asked Ms Knight to come down here this evening to answer questions regarding the investigation of your former office.'

'That is all very well, but it's way past midnight now. And I find it rather disturbing that you have detained her for several hours, and judging by her appearance, it seems as if she may not be in the best state to continue with your questioning.'

Eileen looked at Driskell evenly, demanding an answer, her grey eyes positively glacial. *I'm really glad that I am not on her bad side, I wonder how Driskell will handle this?* Rowanne thought curiously.

Thank you for coming to my rescue, she thought. Who would ever have thought it, *Eileen you total legend, you let him have it!*

'Ms Melville, as you know quite well, investigations tend to take long. We are the law enforcement and sometimes regrettably, we may be called away in the middle of an interview, but that is something that cannot be helped. It was imperative that I finished my questioning of Ms Knight.'

'Why didn't you just decide to rearrange the interview at a time more convenient to the both of you?' She asked in an exasperated voice, clearly incensed at the lack of common sense in the supposed detective before her.

Driskell felt as if he was beginning to lose his composure with the woman before him. In an aggrieved voice he said, 'Ms Melville, like I stated earlier, I did not expect when I was called away from the interview that it would take me that long to resolve the issue. I thought that I would be back within the hour, but events otherwise got the better of me!' He sounded harsher than he had intended.

Eileen smiled at the loss of control in detective Driskell. *Do all men just lose it like that, or is it just my fate to encounter these obstinate fools?* It was hard enough being editor at the paper: put into the mix that she was a female, and leading a mostly male team, who would occasionally need reminding who they were answerable to, and you get the general picture...

'Chief Inspector Driskell, I can perfectly comprehend what you are saying. But would you not agree that in this case, it would be more prudent to continue questioning Rowanne at a later date?'

Rowanne held her breath, as everybody in the room silently watched and waited to see what the detective would do next.

Alexander thought, *She has you there, old friend. Give in you stubborn fool.*

Driskell considered his limited options - he needed to salvage what he could out of this whole debacle. Reluctantly, he turned towards Rowanne and in a weary voice said, 'Ms Knight, I will be in touch shortly to rearrange the interview. Again, accept my apologies for the trouble that I may have unnecessarily caused you today.'

Driskell turned to Alexander, and then back to the ladies, acknowledging them all, 'I will ask you to excuse me now as I must be going.' He pointedly looked at the guard quivering in the corner, who hastily got the doors for him, and they left without ceremony. Driskell's back was ramrod straight, a sign of his frustration.

The room suddenly came back to life after a moment of silence, as they all began to speak at once. They made a lively group.

Eileen spoke up, 'Quiet! he could still be on the other side of those doors,' this brought everyone back to their senses. She turned to Rowanne, 'How are you?' she asked gently, her eyes showing concern for her wellbeing.

Rowanne smiled awkwardly, 'I was actually doing quite well there, before you two barged in!' she said in mock anger. When she saw the consternation come into Amanda and Eileen's eyes, she added hastily, 'I was glad for the backup. I wasn't sure how long he was going to continue for, probably until we all fell asleep listening to his endless droning.'

'I see that I didn't really have anything to worry about. When you left for the interview, Alexander phoned to update me about your situation. I thought you'd take an hour if that, two at the max, and then you'd call me about the assignment.'

Rowanne noticed Amanda rolling her eyes in exasperation at Eileen, and imperceptibly nodded to acknowledge that there was nothing to be done about their editor.

'Rowanne, I'll let you off this one time, as I can see this situation didn't go quite to plan. But I expect that piece on my desk by midday tomorrow,' and with that she left. That was Eileen for you, she didn't stand on ceremony. She had one hand on the door, and turned around looking annoyed, 'Well? Why are you just standing there? Go and bring the car around for me,' she threw the keys to Amanda who caught them easily.

Amanda patted Rowanne on the shoulder, and with a nod to Alexander, she quickly strode out by Eileen.

Rowanne quickly ran outside after Eileen, with a burning question that needed to be answered, 'Eileen, wait!' she called, catching up to her.

'What is it, Rowanne?'

'I was just wondering how you knew to find me here, instead of at the police station?'

'Oh that, Amanda told me. Alexander must have phoned her. If you don't mind, I really need to get going, first stop back to the offices. Well, you know how it's like, our work is never done.' Eileen got into the back of the car that Amanda had finally brought around to the entrance. They drove off quickly, needless to say; Eileen was probably yelling at Amanda to get a move on and step on it.

Rowanne nearly jumped out of her skin as she felt a tap on her back, and, spinning around, she tripped. She closed her eyes and put her hands out in anticipation of the impact with the ground.

However, when that didn't happen, she cautiously opened her eyes, and looked up at a less than pleased Alexander who had caught her in his arms.

Why the hell in Demon World am I the only man saddled with this ungainly woman? This is really becoming a bad habit, and he less than gently helped her to stand.

Rowanne hastily extracted herself, and looked at him sharply, 'How many times have I fallen on you before?' There was a slight blush burning her cheeks, and she hated that she could not control it.

'I beg your pardon?' asked Alexander, shocked that she had just read his mind, and he wisely chose to continue as if he had actually spoken aloud.

He shrugged noncommittally with a bemused look, as his mouth turned up slightly in a smile or a frown, Rowanne could not tell.

'That's what I thought,' she said before walking away aimlessly.

'Wait, Rowanne,' called Alexander hurriedly, 'where do you think you're going?'

She didn't stop, but instead increased her speed, and spoke over her shoulder, 'Home. Not that it's any of your business.' Head down, she wrapped her arms around her frozen body. It was a really cold night, or early morning rather, and she could hear the birds singing in the nearby trees.

Alexander caught up to her in no time, especially with his long stride, and stood in front of her.

Rowanne could tell that he was frustrated and seemed on the verge of boiling over. 'What is your problem? Get out of my way,' she said tersely.

Alexander quickly stepped to the side and looked around to see whether they had attracted any unwanted attention. 'I was just going to offer you a lift. Or, have you completely forgotten this afternoon at your apartment.'

Rowanne's cheeks only burned brighter in shame as she recalled her earlier breakdown in front of Alexander. God, was she ever going to get it together? *What's wrong with me?* she thought.

Rowanne never broke down, especially in front of other people, she was the most together person she knew. *I'm not the nervous breakdown type,* but this sounded hollow even to her.

More like Jekyll and Hyde, thought Alexander, feeling put out. All he had been trying to do was help this maniac, who had a propensity to fall, or was it just his bad luck that it was only in his company.

Rowanne knew that she must come across as crazy, and reluctantly pulled herself together. 'Sorry, Alexander. You just have the knack for catching me off guard. I assure you, I am not like this with anyone else.'

She was trying to come across as reasonable, but Alexander noticed that she sounded peeved. Counting to ten silently to control his own flaring emotions, he wondered what he had done to deserve this woman. *I'd say karma,* any demon would agree with him there.

'Let's go,' he said gruffly, and stormed towards his car, not bothering to look back to see if she would follow.

Rowanne reluctantly trudged after. She would rather have walked, even though that was childish, but it would not have been feasible, and she had left her purse at home, and she would be damned if she was going to ask him for change.

Alexander parked his car in front, and said, 'Get in,' in a less than pleased voice, opening the passenger door in the front.

Rowanne would have taken her time walking leisurely to it, but the cold was just too much, and she quickly scrambled into the front seat next to him.

Alexander smirked at her petulance and started the car. They drove half of the way in silence, each too annoyed with the other to even attempt to start a conversation.

Rowanne stared listlessly out the window; the sky had turned that auburn yellow colour with flecks of pink, letting you know that dawn was just around the corner. She let out a yawn - no wonder with the day she'd had, she was dead tired.

Slowly Rowanne's eyes began to close, and her head would have hit the window if it had not been for Alexander's quick reflexes. He gently turned her head, shifting her weight, and positioned her head gently against his shoulder.

She looks peaceful when she sleeps, he thought dubiously. To his amusement and consternation, she began to snore quite loudly, and he just focused on the road ahead. His shoulders twitched slightly at his suppressed mirth. *Yes, that's Rowanne for you.*

He drove along the Victoria Embankment, enjoying the beautiful view of the city as it slowly began to wake, and there was virtually no traffic, only a few pedestrians. The London Eye gleamed in the early morning, and it seemed to wink at him from across the river. Everything had a golden tinge, or maybe it was just his mood that was better.

In no time at all he reached Westminster Bridge, and turned in the direction of Rowanne's home. They reached her apartment quickly, making good time on the roads.

He pulled into the underground car park, and parked quite close to the glass lift. Turning in his seat to face her, he said, 'Rowanne, wake up, we're here,' and gently shook her.

Rowanne was groggy, having had no sleep, and was not in the best of moods, when she slapped his hands away.

'Hey, do you mind!' Alexander quickly scooted back in his seat to avoid her flailing hands.

'What? Oh sorry, Alexander.' She rubbed the sleep from her eyes - it didn't help that they were still blurry. Slowly, she started to sit up in her seat, and tried to stretch her arms out, only to have them hit the car roof. 'Ouch! You could have warned me!' she said indignantly.

'I thought it best for my safety if I kept quiet. And you did attack me when I tried to wake you.'

Rowanne guessed that he was right, judging from the way he was pressed right up against his door. 'Well, that's what you get for waking me,' she replied sheepishly. 'Let's go,' she said to Alexander's less than pleased expression. 'I'll make you a pot of coffee. I don't just make it for anyone, you know.' She got out of the car grabbing her bag, and managed to bang her head on the way out. 'I assure you, I'm not usually this clumsy. Put it down to sleep deprivation,' she said, rubbing her head. Alexander stood to the side, looking as if he had somewhere better to be than in her company. *Great, I must come across as a complete idiot*, thought Rowanne, annoyed at herself, and at him slightly, for making her feel inept.

They got into the lift together, though Alexander preferred to stay on his side. He looked out at the view as the sun started to rise above the city, bringing with it some much needed warmth after the chill of the night before. The river sparkled, reflecting the spectacle on either side as people filled the empty streets, and cars took the monopoly of the roads. You had to love this city, it didn't stay still for long.

Rowanne observed Alexander as he admired the city, not realising he was being watched. He seemed younger than his thirty years, not that you could tell he was; he looked mid to late twenties. *Good genes*, she thought wryly.

Alexander felt her eyes bore into his back and stiffened, his easy manner instantly gone; he didn't like being caught off guard.

This didn't go unnoticed by Rowanne, who quickly turned to face the lift doors just as he turned sharply towards her.

The doors slid open as they reached the top floor, and Rowanne quickly walked to her apartment. She wedged her key in and opened the door, then stood to one side as Alexander brushed past her to get in. *Charming*, she thought, and, closing the door behind her, hung her coat and bag in the hallway.

Looking in the mirror, she nearly screamed at her ragged appearance: her hair was in knots and her mascara had run. *Damn it, I should have just used waterproof.*

'Alexander, please make yourself comfortable, I'll only be a minute,' with that said, she hastily left him to his own devices and headed into the bathroom. She quickly removed her makeup and splashed cold water on her face to wake up. Quickly combing her long hair, she gathered it into a bun on top of her head. *Great, now I look like a teenager,* and shook her head in dismay. After all, Alexander was not the only one to look younger than their years; she, too, was frequently mistaken for a twenty-five year old.

She walked into the open plan living room and found Alexander asleep on her couch, his long legs stretched before him. She smiled, glad to see that he was human after all. However, she had to sternly remind herself that he had been helping her since yesterday, and had not once complained. Reconsidering, she thought, *Not to my face anyway, and that's practically the same thing.*

She went into her bedroom, and opened the blinds, letting the sunlight flood in. She grabbed a throw from her bed and went back into the living room, placing it over Alexander, who seemed to have bags under his eyes.

In the kitchen, she filled the kettle with water and left it to boil. In the meantime, she rummaged around looking for mugs and coffee. She warmed milk on the hob, and poured the water over the coffee, and added sugar to her mug. She didn't know how he liked his yet, so left it plain. She added the hot milk to her cup, poured the rest in a small jug, and, grabbing a tray, she brought the whole lot into the living room and placed it quietly on the table.

I'll let him sleep for a bit, she thought, as she sat next to him on the couch. She tucked her feet underneath her, whilst she nursed the steaming mug in her cold hands. That first sip was good, warmth instantly spread through her, and she snuggled into the couch, letting her mind drift as she looked out of the windows.

CHAPTER 13

Alexander awoke and, in the process of stretching his arms above his head, knocked off the blanket covering him. *Wonder how that got there?* He felt a heavy weight leaning against him, and noticed that Rowanne had fallen asleep, and yet again, her preferred position was next to him. *Lucky I didn't hit her head,* he thought, smiling down at her. However, it was instantly replaced by annoyance as he felt a pain in his side from where she had jabbed her elbow. He gently got up and laid her on the couch with her head resting on the edge, and covered her with the blanket.

He aimed a surly look at the cold coffee. *She could have woken me, maybe I would have liked a cup,* but noticing the extra mug, he took it back. He took the tray into the kitchen, dumping the whole lot next to the sink, and switched on the kettle to make himself a fresh cup.

He looked at his watch; it was ten o'clock. Well, at least they still had the rest of the day to figure things out. He felt hungry, and he could not work on an empty stomach, so he proceeded to rummage around in her fridge and grab a couple of eggs. He placed bread in the toaster while he scrambled the eggs in a frying pan. He loaded their breakfast onto a tray and took it through. He placed the mugs of tea on the table, then laid out their plates with cutlery neatly placed; sometimes he liked things orderly as it gave him a sense of control. He placed the cream and sugar to one side, then it was perfect.

How serene she looks when she's not annoying me. And she appears a lot younger without makeup hiding her face. I don't know why women hide their natural beauty. It suits her, he thought considerately, just before he called her name, 'Rowanne. Rowanne.'

Rowanne bolted upright in less than a second, wondering where the fire was. 'What? What is it?' she asked, still half asleep.

'I just wanted to let you know that breakfast is ready,' he smiled darkly at the colour rising in her cheeks, and the anger that emanated from her green eyes.

Rowanne held up a hand to stop Alexander, 'In future, it would be wise, and I'm only thinking of your wellbeing, when I say,' and she paused before continuing, 'let me bloody sleep!' She uncurled her legs, stretching them out beneath the table.

Alexander just watched her silently as she grabbed her plate and ate her breakfast. Not one to stand on ceremony, he grabbed his own and tucked in vigorously.

Rowanne almost laughed at the way Alexander ate, as if he was always hungry. *Poor guy, I'll take him to an all you can eat buffet as a sign of my gratitude.*

Alexander raised an eyebrow, 'Thank you for bestowing your hospitality, but I am quite capable,' and at her uncomprehending look, he indicated the breakfast.

Rowanne had no idea what he was talking about. 'You're welcome. Honestly, it was nothing.' *Guess, he must have really liked the coffee.*

Alexander chose to ignore her inane comment and continued to eat.

'Listen, if you don't mind hurrying up, we have to sort out the Driskell situation.' Rowanne carried the things away to the sink to wash up, she was a busy woman, after all. *He hasn't even the courtesy to at least clean the mugs,* she huffed.

She was about to turn around and get his dishes when she nearly collided into him. *God, I didn't even hear him come up behind me.*

'Can you not sneak up on people like that, you nearly gave me a fright.'

Alexander chose not to get into a pointless argument, and instead went back into the living room to wait for her.

Rowanne's mobile rang, 'Can you get that for me, please?' she asked Alexander.

He came into the kitchen and held it next to her ear, as her hands were wet.

Rowanne felt a little disturbed by how close he was standing behind her, *Honestly, has he never heard of personal space?*

Alexander laughed quietly behind her, 'Just take the call, Rowanne.'

'Good morning, Ms Knight. I'm glad you're awake after the long night you had.'

Rowanne's shoulders stiffened. 'Who is it?' hissed Alexander.

She turned her head slightly to look at him, mouthed, 'Driskell,' and put her ear to the phone once more.

'Good morning, Chief Inspector. I'm not one for wasting the day away,' she heard Alexander snort derisively behind her. She looked at him sharply, but he gestured for her to continue.

'Good to hear it. In that case, you will be pleased to know that I have fixed a new time for your interview. If it's convenient to you, could you come down this afternoon at three o'clock? I hope to conclude without further disruption from unwanted guests.'

'That's fine, Chief Inspector. I'll see you then.' Alexander shut off her phone.

Rowanne dried her hands, sat on the sofa, and didn't move for a solid ten minutes. Well, it appeared that way to Alexander.

'Rowanne, hello, anyone there?' Alexander thought about gently shaking her, but then he reconsidered; he liked his hands intact. She had a rabid look about her that he didn't quite trust.

Suddenly, Rowanne got up. She had finally come up with a plan of action that she was satisfied with, and it didn't require Mr Black!

She stalked towards Alexander, who had his hands up before him in mock terror. She grabbed him by the forearms, and hurled him up into a standing position.

'Rowanne, what on earth do you think you're doing?' He was perplexed at her irrational behaviour, but also impressed that she could haul a man his size and weight so effortlessly.

I wonder if she just works out a lot, or if it's being a half demon that's given her this new ability. Already she was hearing his thoughts easily and replying back naturally, even if it was unconsciously. *The truth might only scare her, let her figure it out for herself, that's probably the best way*, he thought.

Yes, I agree with you there, Mr Alexander Black. Ha-ha-ha...

Alexander nearly jumped back in surprise, but Rowanne's tight grip kept him locked in place, as he helplessly watched her green eyes flash with an unearthly violet light.

'You!' he said angrily. 'What did you mean by that statement?' He had been wondering why the entity that seemed to possess Rowanne had been quiet lately. He assumed it would have come out when she had been forcefully taken to Demon world.

For your information, that would have defeated the purpose. For had I shown myself, it would have led her straight to the Noble Court, no further need for questioning. She'd be executed! The entity said in a trembling violent voice.

Alexander had recovered himself enough to continue, 'Point taken. You know a lot about our world. I think my first estimation of you is proving correct. I just don't know who you are, care to enlighten me?' he asked wishfully.

I am not presently at liberty to answer that particular question, replied the entity earnestly.

Alexander got the hint. 'Fine, but why do you possess her?'

Believe it or not, it wasn't my choice. I have the two of you to thank for that!

'Last I checked, I did not summon you. How could I have, when I don't even know your name. I'd need that much at least,' said Alexander, incredulous at the accusation being levelled against him.

Well, in principle you don't, but that's neither here nor there. My point is, Alexander, think about what happened, break it down.

'You seem to know everything, is it worth me even going on?' Judging by the look of annoyance that quickly flashed over Rowanne's features, he guessed he should just continue. 'Let's see, Rowanne died. No need to look at me like that, I know it's my fault, alright.' Alexander wondered how far he could trust the entity, but he was at a loss as to what else he could do. The entity probably knew everything that had happened to Rowanne already, so it made lying redundant.

He felt as if he was under a test of sorts: if he passed, he presumed that the entity would allow him to stay and support Rowanne. But if he should fail...

Please, just get on with it, we haven't got all day! said the entity.

'Why, is there somewhere else you have to be?' asked Alexander tersely. He could not help it, he felt a little powerless before this being, and hated even admitting that.

That was uncalled for, said the entity, annoyed at his childishness.

Alexander untangled himself from Rowanne's grip, and, stepping back, he extended his right arm with his hand resting on his abdomen, while his left arm extended to his side and lowered his head, bowing deeply from the waist in a pious act of contrition.

The entity bent down and looked at him, her eyes swirling an angry shade of indigo. Alexander didn't feel quite so smug now. In the next instant, he was proved right by being thrown in the air, and instead of falling back down, the entity walked underneath him, and smiled dubiously while he spun around continuously, like meat cooking on a spit.

Not one to accept defeat so quickly, Alexander used the opportunity to stretch his legs out, and placed his hands under his head, thereby adjusting to the situation to make it more comfortable for himself.

Immediately he was spun around so that he was now facing the entity. He arrogantly winked at her, a broad smile lighting up his face.

Why, Alexander, you look a little green there. What, no more grand gestures for your lady fair? asked the entity, pretending to swish an imaginary skirt, and then performed a solemn curtsy of her own.

Alexander hit the ground; it was lucky he'd had his hands extended out, otherwise he'd have smashed his head.

This wiped the smirk right of his pretentious face, the entity was happy to note.

Though the entity's head was still lowered, and from his angle, Alexander could still make out the cruel laughter that danced behind the veil of her eyes.

Do you want to know a secret? and looking at his pale face, the entity winked and asked, 'Is it me, or Rowanne? Rowanne, or me...'

Alexander froze at the new development: evidently, the entity's power had grown considerably since their last showdown in this very apartment.

Rowanne stood up. 'Alexander, please get up and stop lounging about down there,' she said as she extended a hand to him, which he reluctantly accepted and got up. She then turned him in the direction of the door, and pushed his back, forcing him to walk forward. She opened the door and stood to one side, 'Well, thank you for everything you've done today, but I really must be getting on with all the work I've neglected.'

Alexander just shook his head, angry at how ungrateful she was, but more so from his encounter with the entity.

'I will see you later,' he said making it sound like a solemn promise. He had a lot to think over.

'We shall see,' said Rowanne, flashing him an uncertain smile, but as Alexander was about to turn away, he saw a quick flash of violet wink at him, reminding him that just under the surface, the entity lurked and could come out at any time it chose. Well, he hoped it didn't yet have that ability, otherwise Rowanne was in trouble.

He had to think of a way to help her and fast. He needed the expertise of someone who was experienced in the field of possession.

He turned, and just before the door slammed shut behind him, he heard the entity, or Rowanne whisper, 'So, call a priest!'

He could hear strange laughter from the other side of the door, almost, as if two voices overlapped each other, and it unnerved him.

Rowanne stood on the other side of the door, leaning against it for support. She had heard the weird laughter coming out of her mouth. No wait, she had heard two voices, hers and another...

Rowanne had felt the bizarre exchange; it had been like she was present, but at the same time she had lost control of herself. She had wanted Alexander to stay, but felt compelled to get rid of him, because of his, his... She didn't know why he had to leave.

It would sound crazy if she said it aloud, but for one unholy moment, she could have sworn that Alexander was levitating. These increasingly unexplainable incidents were beginning to weigh her down.

She would be a fool to ignore them; to put it down to being tired, or her eyes playing tricks on her. Especially when other people's actions, like that of Driskell, and that Court place that she had been in, seemed to corroborate her suspicions.

Rowanne kept her mind as blank as possible while sending a quick text, praying that he'd pick up, and that he was not put off by her split personality, or so it appeared to Rowanne these days.

Alexander was in the lift, and it had just reached the bottom when he received Rowanne's text. The message read: 'Help me, please!' Even when the extraordinary happened, Rowanne managed to keep her head. *Don't worry, I'm not scared away that easily.* His world, after all, was the supernatural.

Alexander walked towards his black Lamborghini, *not the most inconspicuous car,* he thought, but then he liked its speed; Demons loved speed. Plus, it would get him to the one person who could help Rowanne, and time was not a luxury either one of them could afford. Getting in, Alexander reversed and sped away.

Rowanne decided to prioritise what to deal with first, and, grabbing a notepad and pen, she began:

1. Hand in assignment
2. Make a doctor's appointment
3. Finish dreaded and somewhat annoying interview with flamed haired Driskell.

She emailed her work to a pleased Eileen, who considerately sent over three more pieces with various deadlines.

Rowanne was unable to get through to the doctors, and waited at least an hour before she was through, finally booking herself for a complete check up.

By the time she completed everything, she looked at the kitchen clock and realised she had an hour to get down to the police station.

She quickly showered and got changed into a suit, completing the look with high heels. She put on her protective make up which consisted of a dark eyeliner and a smokey eye paired with a pale pink lipstick. Now she was ready to take on the world, and Driskell was just a man, after all; he didn't even stand a chance.

Driskell thought way too much of himself, like someone else she knew, but at least *he* had some manners; Driskell, on the other hand, was a bully. *I wonder if he's been like that since he was a child, he probably terrorized anybody he came into contact with.* She decided to go on the offensive. Well, if he tried anything then... Actually she didn't know what she'd do.

She draped her long black coat over her shoulders and grabbed her bag. Looking in the mirror, she saw a woman on the edge, someone who was not to be toyed with. She looked confident, and that was what mattered the most, especially in this unpleasant situation.

Closing her door, she walked into the lift and tapped her nails on the rail as she looked out at the city. Gray clouds had come in now, marring the beautiful day, and there was an electric atmosphere highly charged, just waiting for that one tiny spark.

Rowanne got into her Pegaso, and drove out of the car park, speeding off towards the main road.

Driving along the river, she didn't have the time to spare a glance at the churning waters that looked ominous as they repeatedly dashed against the river bank.

Rowanne's mood was off as she pulled up in front of the police station, before realising she could not park there. *Damn it,* and instead drove round back into the car park which was practically empty except for two cars. *Busy day I expect*, she thought.

She climbed the stairs, stopped just before the doors to take a deep breath, and then entered.

'Good afternoon, Ms Knight. If you'd like to sign here, please. Thank you. I'll escort you to the Chief Inspector,' said the officer on reception, whom she recognized from before.

Rowanne followed him down the stairs, and finally arrived at the now familiar interview room. 'Please, go through,' he said, and then turned and left.

Rowanne squared her shoulders; she was ready to take on this conceited nasty piece of work head on. She rapped her knuckles forcefully on the door, and waited.

To Rowanne's surprise, Driskell opened the door himself. She had been expecting him to call for her to come in.

'Ms Knight, if you'd like to take a seat, please.'

She looked at him squarely before sitting down.

It was as much as he had expected: Rowanne didn't quite know how to take his seemingly genuine smile, especially from him of all people.

He's up to something... He's trying to lull me into a false sense of calm, thought Rowanne.

Driskell looked at Rowanne, really looked at her for the first time, and noticed the formidable woman before him. He would reserve judgment.

Coughing to clear his voice, he said, 'Let me begin by apologising deeply for what occurred last time. I am sorry that you were detained for so long without proper notice as to why you were being held.'

He appeared sincere in what he was saying, but he did happen to conveniently leave out the part about her being drugged and moved to some secret closed court. *What was it called? Noble something or other.*

Driskell had expected her to relax somewhat after his explanation. But she still seemed to be holding a grievance against him. All she should remember was waiting at the police station, and then ending up at the pub...

'Ms Knight, you will think this an odd question,' he leaned towards her as his green eyes sparkled with an hypnotic aura, 'but what is the last thing you remember of our interview?'

Rowanne saw the way his eyes changed, and considered that he might be trying to hypnotise her. *Maybe the last time I was in his company I wasn't drugged, after all; he most likely messed with my mind then, as well.*

He was watching her carefully, waiting for her reaction before going on. Hell no, she was not going to play into his hands. What he was doing was illegal, not that anybody would be able to prove it.

'The last thing I remember is waiting an inconsiderably long time, and then instead of any explanation, or even having the courtesy to cancel and reschedule the interview, I am told to make my way down to a pub, of all places!' Rowanne gave off just the right amount of indignation; judging by the look of satisfaction that came onto Driskell's face and wait... could it be relief?

'I won't waste your time any further, let's continue where we left off,' said Driskell, as he settled back and opened his laptop, ready to take down her statement.

Driskell cringed inwardly when he recalled their last meeting at The Salisbury pub. He would dearly love to question that rather annoying and obstinate blond, who seemed to have incredible strength. He smiled inwardly at the rather amusing moment when his guard had been heaved off the floor in one momentous movement by the Amazonian looking woman. Putting the memory away, his features once more became solemn.

His moment of quiet reflection was not lost on Rowanne, who saw the way that his mood lifted and how his features softened, if only for a moment. *Is this the same man?* she pondered abstractly.

She could not afford to be thrown off by his mood swings, and continued valiantly, 'What is it precisely that you'd like to know, Chief Inspector?' Rowanne forced herself not to cross her legs or arms: she wanted to give of the air of being relaxed and open. *Trust me. I have nothing to hide,* she thought, and mentally willed for him to believe her.

Driskell didn't seem to care, one way or the other, instead looking up from his computer, he asked, 'Where were you last Thursday evening?'

Rowanne answered calmly, 'Let me see,' she paused as if considering, before continuing, 'I would have been at the offices, most definitely working hard to complete my work.'

'At what time did you leave?'

Rowanne gazed upward in contemplation, 'It would have been between seven thirty and eight o'clock in the evening when I finally managed to leave.' She didn't tremble once through this blatant lie, and carried on smoothly.

'Ms Knight, was there anybody else in the office with you that could verify the time you left?' Driskell had a penetrating look as he finished typing up her last response, and tried to gauge her body language as she answered this crucial question.

Not in the least bit disturbed, and feeling herself gain courage with the confidence she was building within her, Rowanne answered, 'Well, Eileen would have been the last to leave, but she had an appointment, so unfortunately there's no one to verify the time that I left.' She looked at him steadily, not giving anything away; much to his chagrin, she noted.

'Did you happen to talk to the security guard in the evening? I mean,' and looking somewhat embarrassed, he hastily added, 'Mr Thomas Dillian.'

Driskell appeared to be absorbed in typing up notes, but in actual fact, he was trying to get a feel for the situation:

how much did Ms Knight know? He'd have to have that answered before he could go forward and judge her fate. He was pleased, so far. She was doing well, *keep it up, Ms Knight*.

Rowanne answered truthfully, 'I last saw Thomas at the reception desk in the evening, when I left the office to grab a bite to eat. He was just starting his shift, and that would have been around, let me think... roughly five o'clock, I'd say.'

'And when was the last time you saw him?' His eyebrow was raised as he looked at her quizzically.

'That was the last time I remember seeing him, because I went back to the office afterwards, not leaving again until I finished. When I left, the reception desk was deserted which isn't really of any note, because I assumed he was doing the rounds of the building.'

'Where did you go after you left work?' Driskell had stopped typing, and instead had his long legs stretched out under the table, and his arms crossed, as he looked at her inquiringly.

Though his exterior gave nothing away, it still unnerved Rowanne, who didn't want to show the first signs of cracking.

'I drove home, Chief Inspector. It had been a typically long day, and once I arrived back home, I completed my work, then went straight to sleep. That is the extent of what I did last Thursday.' She watched him cautiously, wondering if he had believed her.

Driskell typed furiously, head bent in concentration, and looked up two minutes later - the longest two minutes of her life. Driskell was smiling at her, why was he doing that?

Damn it, I've blown it. He knows I've been lying through my teeth, and he'll probably read out my rights before handcuffing me. Then I'll end up...

Rowanne was brought out of her thoughts as Driskell announced without fanfare that she was free to go. And just like that, she felt light and free as if a huge burden had been lifted. Well, partially, because even though she had passed the interview, she was still no nearer to finding out what actually happened, and if she had played a part in it. It was a hollow victory of sorts, but she reminded herself to be grateful for each success.

'Well, Ms Knight, all that's left to say is that we have your details, and we will contact you in due course if we require anything further. Thank you for your assistance. My colleague is just outside, and will escort you out,' concluded Driskell.

Rowanne got up and left.

Finally, she was outside the confines of the police station, and the sun was shining, and even though it had started to rain, it could not dampen her mood as she made her way to her car.

I can actually make it on my own. I do not need that six foot ice king to help me out every time. Hang on, how many times has he helped me out, so far... wondered Rowanne, *twice, right...*

Her vision began to fray around the edges, and a migraine threatened whenever she thought of Alexander and the inexplicable.

This time however a curious thing happened; the headache disappeared as quickly as it had come on, and her vision was brought back into sharp focus by what felt like a mental slap in the face by something, some force. *Ow! that hurts*, she thought anxiously.

You deserved that! said the entity.

Rowanne had a surreal moment: the voice in her mind had just berated her. The situation was bizarre, to say the least.

'I thought that the voice in my head should at least be comforting,' and reconsidering, added, 'well, at least some of the time,' said Rowanne.

I was merely performing my civic duty by waking you out of your old patterns. Consider this: have they actually served you for your wellbeing?

'Now that you mention it-'

Quiet! You look like a lunatic speaking to yourself in front of the police station in the pouring rain. Trust me, get into your car as quickly as possible. You don't want Driskell catching you like this, he'll haul you back in no time. Now move! said the entity.

Rowanne did not need to be told twice, one mention of the detective was all it took, and she practically ran to her car.

Paranoia may just serve you this time.

Rowanne heard the voice echo in her mind as she got into her car, slamming the door shut behind her. Once her breathing came under control, she wanted to test her theory. 'Hello, are you there?'

Yes, replied the voice wearily.

'I need answers, now!' said Rowanne shakily.

Alright. But is this really the best place to get them? Take my advice when I say go home and then have a long chat with yourself! Afterwards, call the men in the white coats, ha-ha.

Rowanne's mood instantly sobered, annoyed at her own audacity.

'That's not funny. I have actually been considering for a while now that I may have had a nervous breakdown, but I didn't know why, which is frustrating as hell! I should go straight to a doctor,' said Rowanne.

Don't do that. Trust me, you're not crazy. And going to the doctors, telling them about all of this would be a monumentally stupid and hazardous idea! warned the entity.

'In what way is it hazardous? That sounds slightly melodramatic,' said Rowanne shaking her head.

It is not only a danger to you, but also to anybody else you tell, including your doctor. Think on it, but if anything untoward were to happen, then on your head be it. I've said my piece. And God knows, I would have liked someone to help me...

The voice in Rowanne's mind trembled, and she could have sworn that she heard crying. For some reason this pierced her heart, and she felt a deep sadness. She also found it a little spooky.

Rowanne wisely switched off and focused solely on driving; she dare not think of anything else...

The rain had become heavier, and the sun was imprisoned behind the steel grey clouds as violet lightning slashed down upon the city as she drove. It was an incredible sight; she'd never seen such a vibrant violet colour in her life, and it looked very unnatural and out of place.

The river accompanied her drive by obligingly churning and creating huge waves that smashed everything in its path. The heart of the city seemed blanketed by a strange electric atmosphere the closer she got to her home.

Rowanne parked her car, and as she got out, felt a piercing coldness accompanied by the scent of frozen lilies crushed underfoot. Shaking her head, she rubbed her arms to feel warm again. She got into the lift, and the doors closed behind her with a finality - or so it seemed to her.

Leaning against the glass wall, she closed her eyes briefly. When she opened them, she could have sworn that she saw violet eyes reflected back at her mournfully in place of her own green ones. She rubbed her eyes, and this time when she looked again, thankfully, only her own reflected back. *I am really tired,* she yawned. Where had all her energy gone... She had been more alive after the interview had concluded.

The doors swished open breaking her reverie, and she shuffled to her door, but just as she was about to put the key in, it opened inwards of its own accord. Rowanne jumped back in surprise.

Has someone broken in? she thought, reluctant to enter. Cautiously she approached, holding her bag loosely from the strap to use, if the need should arise; ready to swing it in the face of an intruder who might come running out.

She poked her head around the door and pushed it back to keep the path clear, *Always keep your exit point open*, she thought.

She was not about to stupidly call inside and alert whoever it was to her arrival, and instead tiptoed in. *Here goes,* she thought, and on the count of three, walked into the living room. Rowanne let out the breath that she had been holding as she surveyed her empty room and kitchen.

She had two more stops to make: first, she went into her bedroom, and checked under the bed, and behind the curtains. Finally, she went to the bathroom, and opened the door slowly, nearly jumping out of her skin when it creaked ominously.

Damn it! thought Rowanne clutching her heart. *I've been meaning to fix that,* but as the door opened, she saw that it too was empty. The shower curtain was open, *Thank God,* and her legs trembled in relief at not having to recreate a certain famous Hollywood scene.

Rowanne felt shaken and nearly screamed when upon shutting the door she saw Alexander standing in her hallway. Her frail nerves could not take it and her eyes felt teary, and angrily she swiped at them, hating to be caught in an emotional state every time *he* happened to be near. *God, I really hate him right now.*

'What the hell are you doing here?' she asked Alexander angrily.

'Give me a second,' he replied, before stepping back, 'right, go ahead,' he leaned against the closed lift in a relaxed manner.

'What are you doing? You look stupid, do you realise that? And far be it for me not to laugh if those doors open,' she said, somewhat frazzled by his calm demeanour.

'Well, I thought I'd keep my distance and prepare myself mentally for the onslaught. And by the way,' moving away from the lifts, he stood before her, his arms crossed, 'I am not quite sure what I have done this time.'

'Just don't. And you can take that look of your face,' she said at his incredulity. She grabbed his arm and dragged him into her apartment before leaving him in the living room.

She went back to her front door, and noticed that the lock was intact, and opening the door once more, she realised the front of the door did not look as if it was forced open, and was somewhat puzzled as she shut it.

Alexander looked at her questioningly as she came back.

'Well, what's happened?' he asked patiently.

Rowanne was taken aback by the sincerity that she heard in his voice, instead of the angry retort she'd been expecting at her ludicrous behaviour. She deflated somewhat and began to feel calm. She indicated for him to take a seat, and sat opposite him, hunched with her hands resting in her lap.

Rowanne took her time before answering, and when she looked up noticed the glass of water before her on the table that separated them.

'Where did that come from? I didn't even see you get up...' said Rowanne, surprised by his kindness, and yet at same time, somewhat baffled.

Alexander brushed her concerns away by focusing her mind on the matter at hand, which required their urgent attention.

'You're right,' replied Rowanne, agreeing with him. 'I think I may need your help,' she said slowly, watching his reaction.

Alexander felt his heart ache to see her in this state. He'd been on his way to see someone who could have helped Rowanne, when he was interrupted by the entity going out of control around her. He'd rushed back, inflaming the pathways with his supernatural speed.

The sound and lightshow of the storm had accompanied his every step. This was not normal weather; it was unearthly, and he had a feeling that one of his own was responsible for it.

He had felt emotions lash out at him, even on the pathways as time seemed to slow down. He had run through a transparent ghostly London, which had a violet aurora above it that seemed to shimmer and sizzle at alternate points. The rain had shot down, soaking his body so that he felt the chill begin to freeze his heart. Lightning had forked down, purposely trying to skewer him in place, thereby slowing him down so that he wouldn't have been able to reach Rowanne in time.

His own anger had thawed his heart and propelled him forward, so that the rain had barely touched him. His sapphire eyes had glowed emerald as a barrier encased and thereby protected him, and he had finally burst through the portal, setting it on fire. Thankfully, Rowanne had come out a second later, narrowly missing this incredible sight.

For all intents and purposes, she had seen him standing there bone dry, as if he had just driven to her apartment. Appearances and assumptions were important, especially where he came from; serving their Lords and Ladies well.

Rowanne looked at Alexander. 'I came home just now to find the apartment door wide open. I thought that perhaps someone had broken in.'

'Why the hell would you go in to take a look, why not call building security to come up and check?' Alexander was disgusted by her foolishness. Had she not watched horror films, there were certain things you didn't do...

Rowanne could tell that Alexander was upset on her behalf. She too would be angry if someone she knew did something so reckless. 'I appreciate your concern for me,' and looking at Alexander's less than pleased expression, she amended, 'I meant as a fellow colleague, you were worried for me,' she finished, exasperated that he could have mistaken her meaning. He really did have a high opinion of himself; *As if I'd even consider him in that way.*

Alexander started smiling widely, *As if she thought for one moment that I'd look at her in that way! What's more, I don't think of myself any more than the average man does...*

Rowanne really hated his smile, it was making her feel uncomfortable. *Arrogant git, he's not even my type – David, on the other hand, is looking a lot more appealing now,* it made her laugh.

That took the smirk right off Alexander's face to be replaced by a pained expression. *Really? David of all people, that fool. She truly has a questionable taste in men.*

'How's Eileen keeping?' asked Alexander lightly.

Rowanne abruptly stopped laughing, wondering why he was asking about her editor.

'Last time I called her, she was knee deep in work, other than that she's fine. Anyway, I would have thought you'd have her number already...'

Alexander watched her neutral facade.

'No. I didn't have time at the reception, and then it completely slipped our minds later on.'

Rowanne was puzzled; what did he mean by 'later on'? She remembered them walking off together, and where they had gone was anyone's guess. *Well, it's nothing to do with me.*

'Listen, I'll give you her direct line, that way you can ask her yourself,' she said, smiling sweetly.

Alexander thought that an excellent idea, but decided that could keep for another time.

'Is anything missing? Have you checked that all's in order?' he asked, whilst looking around at the same time, but as far as he could tell, in these two rooms at least, everything seemed in place, nothing disturbed in any way.

'I've checked everywhere, and I don't think I've been broken into. It's more likely that my damn lock is broken, or that I didn't shut it properly before going down to the police station. My mind was on other things, so...'

'Do you mind if I have a quick look around?' asked Alexander, clearly restless until he did his own inspection; only then would he be satisfied to leave her.

'Go right ahead,' replied Rowanne, who just wanted him to get on with it so he could leave her in peace.

Alexander got up, and muttered, 'Ungrateful,' under his breath as he went to her bedroom.

Rowanne was incensed at his rudeness: she had not actually asked him to come to her home and personally look around on her behalf, she was quite capable without a man, thank you very much! 'Idiot!' she whispered angrily.

Alexander's shoulders stiffened just before he entered her room. *Damn it! I wonder if she actually heard me?* and coloured slightly.

He walked into her bedroom and looked around. He could not believe that her hearing had grown so sensitive; he had the grace to look embarrassed before shaking it off and continuing his inspection.

He walked back out a few moments later, satisfied that there was nothing to be worried about. Where had the supernatural occurrence come from? That was the only thing that puzzled him, and he suspected that it must have emanated from Rowanne.

'I told you, everything is fine. And before you waste a trip to the bathroom, there's nothing there as well. I am confused by one thing, though: Why have you come here? I didn't mean that to sound rude,' said Rowanne.

Alexander smiled, taking it in his stride. 'I was just wondering how your meeting with Driskell went?'

Rowanne sat down and Alexander joined her, much to her annoyance: why was he sitting so close? But continued, 'As a matter of fact, it went great. It's now over, unless they need me, which I doubt very much as I don't have anything to add to my statement.'

Alexander felt a huge weight lift from his chest; he could finally breathe easy in the knowledge that, for now at least, they wouldn't be killed. In the future it could be a different matter if they were ever found out, but today at least, he felt optimistic.

Rowanne was pleased to see Alexander looking more relaxed than he did before. *It suits him; he appears more human when he smiles, and less intimidating.*

You've no idea, Rowanne, that's an understatement! he thought.

'Did Driskell mention anything else?'

He had used his name so casually, almost as if he knew the detective in another capacity... Rowanne did not like being out of the loop.

'Sorry, I meant detective Driskell,' he amended, at the suspicious look that had just come into Rowanne's eyes.

'No, he didn't say anything else,' she replied.

'Well, I'm glad it's all over... for now. I'd better be going,' he got up and started to walk towards the front door.

'Alexander, wait!' called Rowanne.

He turned around to find her standing behind him.

'Thanks for everything. I do appreciate you coming over to check up on me. You can report back to Eileen that I'm doing alright. And I'll get started on some of those deadlines now,' she said cheerily.

'I didn't come on behalf of Eileen,' he said indignantly.

'Oh,' said Rowanne, confused.

'I came,' he took a step towards her, bringing himself very much into her personal space. Rowanne politely took a step back. 'Because, I wanted to see for myself that my friend,' and shortening the distance by coming a touch closer, he finished sincerely, 'was doing well, and that the stress of the interview had not taken too much of a toll on you.' She was about to berate him, but he put up a hand to stop her. 'I remember you telling me that this case was hard on you because it involved not only a colleague but someone you considered a friend, Thomas.'

Rowanne looked at him with watery eyes, nodding her head in agreement. She accepted the embroidered handkerchief he gave her, and went about awkwardly drying her eyes without smearing her makeup.

'No, you keep it,' he said, when she tried to hand it back to him. She crumpled it tight in her fist.

'Well, I'll go now?' he made it sound like a question. Rowanne nodded her head, and he walked back to the door and opened it.

Suddenly, Alexander felt hands on his back, and he was pushed with such force that he was propelled out of the apartment, and only came to a stop as he collided with a wall. On his way out, he heard Rowanne's piercing scream just before the door slammed shut behind him.

Alexander quickly got up and beat his fist against the door to get her attention. 'Rowanne, open up!' he shouted, ignoring the pain in his knuckles as he continued to pound the door uselessly; he was not even making a dent, and this worried him exceedingly since he could pretty much punch through a brick wall, should the need arise.

CHAPTER 14

Rowanne screamed as she watched Alexander thrown out of her apartment head first and sickeningly collide with the wall opposite, before her front door shut of its own accord.

The sky had darkened, and lightning lashed intermittently, the rain formed a solid barrier outside her windows as it pounded down. She could hear the loud boom of the thunder like a gunshot to her heart.

Suddenly the power gave out, but just before it did, every door in her apartment slammed shut. She screamed, her heart almost giving out in fright. She blindly ran in the direction of the hallway and managed to reach the front door, and began pounding it with her fists, uncaring that her hands started to bleed.

The pain was nothing compared to how frightened she had felt at watching Alexander's body slam into the wall with a thud. Rowanne wondered if he was conscious. He would definitely need medical treatment, and it didn't help that they were caught up in some kind of supernatural event.

Most situations had a reasonable explanation as to why they happened; but this was not one of those, her panicked mind could not find the explanation behind it. She continued screaming for Alexander, as pathetic as it may sound to him, she thought.

'Alexander! Alexander, are you ok?' she shouted, hoping in vain that he could hear her.

'Hold on, Rowanne. I'm going to try and force my way in, stand back!' he shouted from the other side of the door.

Oh my God, thought Rowanne. *I can't believe he's already up and trying to save me after the knock he's just taken.* She felt relieved that perhaps she had misjudged how hard he had actually hit the wall. *I'm just glad that big oaf has a thick head, literally!*

Alexander paused in his pounding, *Is she really going to insult me, again?! She must not need my help that bad, she seems to be doing fine mentally!* he thought, disgusted.

Pull yourself together, thought Rowanne. This was no time for her to lose her head, so she ceased with the useless banging, and instead started to follow the hallway to the kitchen by feeling her way along in the pitch black.

Rowanne stopped and slapped her forehead, realising how stupid she'd been — it was the twenty-first century for heaven's sake. She had a mobile. *I'm saved,* she thought, in mini triumph. She slid it out of her pocket and fiddled about with it as she tried to remember which button turned the blasted torch on.

Damn it! She'd never had any reason to use it before, and after various failed attempts, found the right one. *Ow!* she had ended up shining the torch in her eyes. Great, now she had light spots dancing in front of her eyes, temporarily blinding herself, as well as losing whatever minuscule night vision she'd had to begin with!

She waited a few moments for her vision to return to normal, and in the meantime could hear Alexander progress from uselessly pounding the door to the equally futile act of trying to kick it in. *Come on, seriously!* Her front door was made of a strong wood, it could not be broken into that easily.

She turned the beam in the direction of the kitchen, and started to shuffle towards the draws.

'Don't worry, Rowanne. I'll find a way in, hold on!' She heard Alexander's inane shouting.

'Uh-huh, whatever you say,' muttered Rowanne under her breath, rolling her eyes heavenward.

Alexander was nervous because he had not heard anything for a few minutes after that small yelp. He hoped she was alright, and had not done something stupid to make the situation worse. There was only so much a demon could take.

Rowanne rummaged around in her drawer and managed to prick her finger on a fork. *'Damn it!'* However, she continued and managed to find a hammer in the bottom cupboard. 'Yes! this should do nicely,' and made her way back through the hallway to the front door.

Rowanne looked at the lock and raised the hammer, and shouted for Alexander to step back, before finally bringing it down in one go and smashing the metal pieces into smithereens with her sheer force.

Alexander heard something break on the other side, thereby completely missing what Rowanne had just said, and instead thought about charging the door using his supernatural energy. His eyes bled to green and a steel grey colour encased them, as magic and strength combined. He took a few steps back, and went charging in...

Rowanne had just managed to open the door, and was pleased with her work, when she saw Alexander hurtling towards her. 'What the hell?' she closed her eyes, and placed her hands uselessly in front of her body to protect herself from the impact, there was no way to avoid the inevitable.

Alexander was going too fast to stop in time, and instead, as he charged at Rowanne, who was petrified at the sight of him, he decided to change tactics. The unstoppable momentum carried him forward, and he effortlessly scooped her into his arms as they knocked into the sofa and fell, rolling on the floor, thankfully avoiding getting cut into pieces by her glass coffee table.

The magic finally ceased as Alexander rolled one last time and came to a stop with Rowanne on top of him. He looked up to check if she had been hurt in the maelstrom, and was met with contempt. *What is this? I wasn't expecting a thank you, but what's that look for?*

'Do you mind letting me go, now?' she pounded on his chest in frustration.

Alexander realised that he still had his arms around her, and released her so that she rolled off him and landed on the floor. He permitted himself a slightly gleeful smile before getting up.

Rowanne managed to quickly get to a sitting position, and looking up she saw his hand extended down towards her, but she just glared at him and slapped it away hard. *I hope that hurt!* she thought.

She got up in an undignified manner, much to Alexander's amusement, who had sat down on the edge of her sofa to watch the spectacle.

Rowanne stepped towards him, not exactly towering over him, but at least she was in control of herself. 'What do you think you were doing?' she asked him furiously.

Alexander got up suddenly, angry at her grating tone. His nerves felt raw every time he was around her; he felt emotionally exhausted. Suddenly, he was the one towering over her as he looked down at her.

Rowanne refused to step back and give him the satisfaction, and chose instead to stand her ground, ready to have it out with him.

'I was trying to break the door down when I heard you screaming. I thought perhaps we had both missed the person who'd broken in, and that they had pushed me out, and then attacked you.'

'I was doing perfectly well on my own,' and she flourished her hands in an animated manner towards the door, which lay on its side with the now useless missing lock.

Rowanne was pleased to see Alexander look at a loss for words, as he stared transfixed at the door.

Looking at Rowanne with astonishment and open admiration, he asked brusquely, 'How on earth did you manage that? I was kicking that door in for quite some time, but it didn't budge an inch!' He started to see Rowanne in a new light.

It was obvious that she was changing rapidly: within the past week alone, he had noticed the changes to her body that had begun the night he had saved her, thereby unwittingly making her part demon. *I wonder what other powers she'll acquire...* he thought, deep in contemplation.

Rowanne broke him out of his trance, 'Demon World to Alexander, hello?' she waved her hands in front of his face to get his attention.

'Stop that, it's very annoying,' he said as he grabbed both her hands, encasing them in his own. 'What did you just say?' he could have sworn that she had just mentioned Demon World...

'I said,' and ripping her hands from his grasp, she continued, 'it doesn't matter. I was trying to tell you how I opened the door, and saved us!'

'Really?' Alexander asked drolly, one eyebrow raised in disbelief, and gesturing with his hand, he said, 'Please carry on. I can't wait to hear.'

Rowanne felt a little light headed, but managed to make it to the sofa and sat down.

Alexander swivelled around and sat opposite, waiting for her. He knew she wouldn't appreciate him helping her to sit. He was worried that she might have gotten a concussion. It was an effort sometimes to not help someone when they were clearly in need of it.

Rowanne rubbed her eyes, and wondered, when the lights had come back on. She had been wondering why she could suddenly see everything clearly.

'I managed to find a hammer, and the lock they say is history!' this elicited a small smile from Alexander, who thought she had a terrible sense of humour.

'You must really work out...' said Alexander teasingly, trying to get a rise out of her.

'Pardon?' asked Rowanne, who was clearly at a loss as to what he was referring to.

'You smashed that lock as if it was made out of clay rather than reinforced metal... What type of workout do you do? You can probably put the men to shame,' he laughed heartily.

'Shut up!' said Rowanne, annoyed at his clearly sexist remark. But from his expression, she knew he did not mean it. And he did look good when he smiled; it softened some of his harsh features, especially as he constantly scowled at her.

Half the time she could not help but feel responsible for something she had not done when she was in Alexander's company. She felt guilty as if she should apologize, but for what? *Maybe he has that effect on anyone that he comes into contact with*, she thought. He was a bit of a hopeless case.

Looks weren't everything, especially with a personality like his, and it was a mystery as to how anybody could stay sane in his company. He was glowering at her again with those blazing sapphire eyes. *This is exactly what I mean*, she thought, exasperated with him.

Alexander did not value her scrutiny of him, and felt exactly the same way about her; *I can't relax around you, either.* When had he ever asked her to apologise? Though, she should; for the numerous occasions when she had unwittingly insulted him!

He admitted that at times he felt a burning anger buried deep within him at the injustice of last Thursday. He could be forgiven for his callous behaviour towards her, now and again. *I lost my immortality for demons sake! I didn't ask for a reward, but rewarded I was - in the form of a punishment!* He looked heavenward, *Thank you, God*, he silently screamed in his mind.

Outside lightning struck the living room windows, lashing at them in a futile attempt to get to the wayward son, who dared to defy heaven with his impertinence; or so it seemed to Alexander, as he wearily tried to leash his unbound emotions.

Rowanne studied him quietly; he seemed like a man who was broken and lost as a myriad of emotions passed over his face. *I wonder what he's thinking about... What's happened in his past to cast a shadow over his future?*

She often got the feeling that he hid behind a mask, that there was more to Alexander than he wanted people to know.

Alexander settled himself, and wondered as to how he should approach the topic of what had just occurred, but he needn't have worried, as Rowanne beat him to it.

'Listen, Alexander, I need to tell you something, and it's going to sound strange... You'll probably want to have me locked up!'

Alexander just looked at her, feeling slightly on edge, but wisely stayed quiet as he let her initiate it.

Rowanne breathed in deeply, letting the air out slowly, knowing she probably looked like a right fool. *Here goes,* she thought, taking the plunge. '*I* didn't push you out the door...'

'I never assumed you did. That was one hell of a shove, though. And looking at you it's hard to imagine,' said Alexander, and smiled contemptuously.

'What do you mean by that remark? I'd have no trouble tossing you out of here right now, if I felt so inclined.' Rowanne felt affronted by his poor estimation of her abilities, maybe it was not solely limited to her, perhaps he had that opinion of women in general.

'You're getting ahead of yourself there,' he said, angry at that sweeping statement of him. Had he not just a few seconds ago praised her strength. Humans! They could be exceedingly infuriating, *And now, I'm going to be a chauvinist; especially the women!*

207

The women in Demon World were also quick in making assumptions on opinions that he neither proclaimed or held. And in that respect, Rowanne was no exception, she was equally as cutting. He had an idea that was extremely amusing: Rowanne could easily have passed for a native of his world.

Rowanne held up her hands as a sign to put this little misunderstanding (generally on his part) behind them.

Alexander agreed to the first part, but was in discord with her as to the latter.

'Something... pushed you, and before you ask, no, I didn't see who or what it was. I felt this incredible force push past me and knock you off your feet,' said Rowanne.

So far so good, thought Rowanne, even if he was looking at her sceptically. *I can't blame him, really. If it were me, I'd probably wait for the person to talk about ghosts and goblins next, before politely asking them to leave, and magnanimously directing them to their nearest health centre.*

How generous indeed, thought Alexander. *I am glad that the shoe is on the other foot. I'll 'help' you alright...*

She didn't like the gleeful look that had suddenly come into Alexander's eye. *I swear he's just read my mind...* and as she thought this, his response was to smile wickedly at her. *Nice smile... Stop that, focus Rowanne!* she thought sternly.

Really? thought Alexander. *I can have some fun with this...*

'I should probably save you the trouble, and have myself certified now. Why, you might ask, because you're going to love the second part!'

Alexander just motioned for her to carry on, completely fascinated with her story.

'Just before the lights went out in the apartment, every single door in here slammed shut of its own accord. There, what do you have to say to that?' asked Rowanne, challenging him to come up with a rational explanation.

'I would say... that you are a deeply troubled woman, who has had a moment of psychosis,' he said solemnly.

'Shut up, you jerk,' said Rowanne, and, grabbing a pillow, she threw it at his thick head, but it was a futile attempt as he just batted it away.

'I actually agree with you,' he said, his mood now serious.

This actually made it worse for Rowanne as it was a confirmation: everything that had just happened was real. She was not imagining it. She felt her eyes go watery, and quickly walked away from him to stand before the window. She looked out at the city that was now warmly lit in the evening as the rain lightly tapped the windows.

Rowanne stiffened as she felt Alexander come up behind her. He offered her a tissue which she gratefully accepted. She dabbed at her eyes, embarrassed to be caught out like this - it was becoming a bad habit. *I am not weak*, she thought.

Alexander leaned on the window next to her, and, looking out at the drenched city, he said casually, 'I have always thought that it takes great strength to live your emotions openly, instead of hiding behind false masks like everybody else.'

Rowanne leaned into Alexander, who didn't move away, but instead put his arm around her in support and comfort. Silently they stood there watching the world pass them by as the rain gently soothed their minds.

Rowanne felt slightly self conscious; she did not want to give Alexander a false impression of how she felt about him, and, straightening up, she went back to the sofa.

To her dismay, Alexander sat down next to her, too close for her liking.

Alexander was oblivious of her discomfort, and turning to her he asked, 'What is the plan? Do you want to stay here tonight?' He looked at her seriously, his sapphire eyes waiting patiently.

Rowanne was caught off guard, wrapped up in her own emotions. 'I beg your pardon? What are you implying?' Her cheeks were inflamed, coloured to the darkest rose: anything could set her off, especially anger. She hated the fact that she had no control over it.

Alexander looked at her bewildered, 'What do *you* think I am insinuating here, Rowanne?' he asked her sharply.

He scooted closer to hear her out, and unthinkingly brushed his leg against her knee which caused her to shoot off the sofa like she had sat on a pin.

Idiot! He'd done that on purpose, she was sure of it. She stood her ground and crossed her arms, glaring at him.

'Rowanne, are you feeling ok? What is it that I am supposed to have done this time? Please, do me the courtesy of explaining so that I may have a chance of defending myself.'

'Look, maybe I gave you the wrong impression just now... But I don't think of you in *that* way,' she said.

Alexander took half a millisecond to process what all this was about, and found it highly amusing. It really was time to have fun... It was always nice to live up to people's expectations of him.

Alexander stood up suddenly, and looked at Rowanne questioningly. 'What 'impression' is that, Rowanne?' he accentuated her name, and took a step toward her. 'In what way, *do* you think of me?' he asked, smiling roguishly. 'I have only come here to help a friend, I hope you understand that,' he said solemnly. A hooded look came into his eyes, unnerving her. He took another step, saying piously, 'Friends sometimes need someone to lean on...'

Rowanne got the impression that he was playing with her. *Oh! I've definitely walked into this one,* she thought resignedly.

'Yes, you have,' replied Alexander quietly.

'Pardon?' Rowanne could have sworn he'd just replied to her thought.

'I said, it's good to have a friend to rely on. What do you think of the one before you...?' he asked. He stood still, waiting for her ludicrous response, which he knew was heading his way.

Rowanne really hated him right now; *I wish I had the power to blast green fire and wipe that smirk of his sanctimonious face.* Where the hell had that thought come from?

Alexander appreciated the fact that her knowledge of his world was growing, even though it was unconscious. *I'll add you to the list of people that want to burn me, you can go second after Driskell,* he laughed silently.

'I guess we can't choose our acquaintances any more than we can our family,' she said disparagingly, putting the topic to rest.

Alexander felt a metaphorical slap to his face, and his response was to smile darkly; it was not over as far as he was concerned. 'Oh, Rowanne!' he said theatrically, taking the last step that brought him face to face with her. He put his hands on her shoulders calculatedly and looked at her with smouldering devil-may-care eyes, and waited a heartbeat...

Rowanne was now almost level with him, he was only slightly taller than her. She tilted her head back to look up at him, feeling his hands scald her as her traitorous heart began to beat fast.

Alexander captured her gaze as their eyes locked. He leaned down, satisfied with what he saw there, 'Don't be so hard on yourself... You are not a bad colleague to work with. I even deign to- sorry, I mean, I even consider you to be a friend,' he said conceitedly, and his face took on a cruel expression as his eyes blazed furiously before he stepped back.

He returned to the sofa, and, stretching his legs out, he put his hands behind his head while he waited impatiently for her to calm down and put an end to this nonsense.

As if he would ever think of her in that way. *She thinks too highly of herself.* But as he reflected on his behaviour... *Even as a friend, I get it wrong!* he thought miserably, and sat up shamefacedly.

Rowanne stood for a few seconds while she willed for her heart to slow down, but she was barely in control. Her face was inflamed, she felt humiliated. *Conceited idiot! He thinks he's God's gift to women. I would never in a million years look at him in that way, even if he was the last human, no wait, demon, in the world!*

She walked back and purposely sat opposite him, letting her face unwittingly convey how incensed she was to be in his company. She wanted to say: 'Get the hell out of my house and don't let the door slam you in the face on the way out!'

It was painfully obvious to both where they stood in each other's estimation. There would be no more misunderstandings now, and the atmosphere was frosty to say the least.

Alexander was thinking he'd gone too far. If his mother had heard him, she would probably have rebuked him severely for his discourteous behaviour towards a woman; she'd brought him up better than this. In his defence, it was only this particular woman who made him forget himself and act recklessly.

'Rowanne, please look at me,' he said softly.

She just ignored him, and turned to the side. Much to her chagrin, he came around the table to her side, and sat close to her. He then had the audacity to take her hand into his. Rowanne wanted to pull her hand away and was about to, when he suddenly bowed his head down, so that it lightly rested on her hand; it was a bizarre act of humility to say the least.

Alexander looked up at her, and said, 'I beg your forgiveness, dear lady, for my insolent conduct.'

Rowanne took her hand back, 'Fine, on one condition. Sit over there.' He obliged her request.

He gets stranger by the minute, and the longer I'm in his company, the crazier I get. Rowanne didn't know if he was genuinely trying to apologise, or if he was mocking her by merely acting the gentleman.

Alexander ground his teeth - she really made it hard for him! *Please, stop talking,* he thought miserably. Suddenly he noticed that Rowanne's knuckles were grazed and bleeding, and leaning across the table, he gently held her hands to examine them.

'What do you think you're doing?' asked Rowanne wearily.

'You do realise that your hand is bleeding?! When did this happen?' he asked, appalled at himself for not having noticed, and angry at her carelessness.

Rowanne tried to extricate her hands but to no avail. His grip was surprisingly gentle yet firm; she was not going anywhere, and besides, she'd rather not damage her hands more than they already were.

'Stay here,' he said, and went to her bathroom.

Rowanne was having none of it. She was perfectly capable of taking care of herself, thank you very much; especially, after his awful behaviour.

Alexander turned around from rummaging around in the cabinet to find a very annoyed looking Rowanne standing in the doorway.

'I thought I'd told you to stay put. I'm trying to find a first aid kit.'

'Alexander, I am not your pet to command. And secondly, I am averse to follow orders,' and shoving past him, she knelt down to open the bottom cupboard, and took out the first aid box, then stood up and waved it in front of his petulant face.

Alexander snapped, and grabbed the box from her, placing it on the counter to open it.

Turning around, he said, 'Thank you, that helps,' he was not amused. Grabbing her by the shoulders, he directed her towards the edge of the bathtub and sat her down none too gently.

'Do you mind?' she asked angrily.

Alexander just looked at her steadily, and replied, 'Why of course not. I'd be more than happy to help. I'm glad you finally asked!'

'That's not what I meant, and you know it,' she said, getting up.

Alexander pushed her back down ignoring her protests, as he began to wipe the blood away gently with a wet cloth.

Rowanne reluctantly subjugated herself to his unwanted administrations.

She settled for glaring at him, which Alexander heartily accepted as he ripped open an antiseptic wipe and began to gently dab it across her knuckles.

Rowanne involuntarily hissed as it stung, and chose to look in any direction, but his; she didn't need his sympathy.

Instead, she got something unexpected, as he said, 'That's what you get for being oblivious, you should really take more care.' He sounded so reasonable and matter of fact that it grated on her nerves.

'Listen, how mindful can you be when you're trapped and trying to get out? It doesn't register in the moment of panic that you're hurting yourself. The situation was so intense that I wasn't exactly thinking of the pain. And I didn't ask you to unduly trouble yourself by helping me,' but silently, she thought, *it sounded suspiciously like he cared.*

He ignored her while he applied a bandage to each hand. 'There, done,' and finally releasing her hands, he went back to the living room.

Rowanne found him sitting on the sofa, looking at his phone; there went her theory that he actually cared. She sat on the opposite side to him, and decided to get on with trying to understand what had occurred earlier. 'Alexander, what do you think I should do?'

'You're essentially saying that your apartment is haunted,' stated Alexander, as he looked up.

'That about sums it up, Sherlock. That's what I have been

trying to tell you for the past- I don't know how long it's been.' Sometimes, Rowanne could not recall a time when Alexander was not around. He seemed to show up at the most unfortunate moments; it was maddening to say the least.

I don't particularly like spending time with you either but I have to bloody save you against my will. Try being me for a change! he thought churlishly.

'Are you going to remain in this ghost house today? Or, do you have somewhere else you can stay?' asked Alexander.

Rowanne thought that her choices were very limited: it would have been better if she'd had friends as well as acquaintances, but she'd been so busy working, that she never really formed any attachments outside of work.

She could not very well show up at her grandmother's home, either, and could just picture the disaster waiting to happen: 'Hello, remember me? Your only granddaughter, the one that rarely phones and hasn't seen you in years. Do you mind if I stay at your place tonight? I can't go home because I'm having an exorcism: it's like a party with an uninvited guest! Only the priest shows up, and even the host stays away until the big finale is over! Ta-da. So, what do you think?'

Rowanne could imagine her grandmother's response: she'd be thrown out so fast, that her head would spin — no pun intended. And as well as having her locked up, her grandmother would also take out a restraining order against her!

Alexander turned around and started laughing. *She's even more wretched than I thought!*

'Alexander, please turn around. I am pretty much at a loss as to what to do,' said Rowanne, wondering at his strange bout of lunacy.

Wiping his eyes, and trying to look solemn, he said wisely, 'So book yourself into a hotel until this,' gesturing at the apartment, 'settles down.'

'What if it follows me? I've seen those films where the ghost doesn't just haunt a place but a person as well, latching onto them.'

'Possibly, like superglue. Or an ex, as an example,' he laughed.

'Alexander! It would actually help if you could come up with a sensible suggestion!' she laid into him, letting him feel the full force of her anger. She did not find the situation funny; especially since it was happening to her.

'Is there someone you can call?' asked Alexander, curious as to whom she would name.

'No!' *My God, I sound lame and completely pathetic.* Trying to save herself, Rowanne amended rather desolately, 'What I meant was, that there is no one presently that I can call. They would be at work until very late, and I'd hate to imposition them.'

Alexander looked at her drolly. He came up with a solution that he was sure they'd equally hate. She was about to imposition the heck out of him; it would be all his own doing, though. *I am the master of my own hell,* he thought wretchedly.

He was munificent; lent a hand to those in need. He could do this.

'Rowanne, I have this piece I've been working on at home. It's my first assignment for Eileen, and the deadline is just around the corner. I was wondering... if you wouldn't mind giving it the seal of approval, before I turn it in. I can appreciate that you have a lot going on, but I really do need the help. Trust me, it's not easy for me to ask,' Alexander hoped he sounded sincere; this act was starting to grate on him.

Rowanne jumped at the change in conversation; *Thank God, something I can actually get my head around, and a way to prove myself useful.*

'Get the piece out then. I'll have a look at it now,' said Rowanne eagerly.

'The thing is, I have it on my laptop at home...'

'I was going to suggest emailing it to me, but judging by that look, I'd say that would be a problem too, right?' asked Rowanne perceptively.

'Perhaps you wouldn't mind coming to my home to look at it... I'll drop you back afterwards.' Alexander knew that this could go in any direction; including blowing up in his face, if she got the wrong end of the stick - again!

Rowanne looked at him steadily, and after considering her options, decided to agree. *At least if the ghost decides to attack again, then I can use him as a human shield. I am nothing if not fair towards my fellow man,* she thought, applying it distastefully to Alexander.

To his commendation, he kept a civil facade while internally frustrated with her.

'Let me grab some things, and I'll be with you in a minute.' Rowanne left Alexander waiting in the living room while she dashed into her bedroom to change. She grabbed items, shoving them into a bag.

She walked past Alexander to her bathroom to get the essentials. It didn't take long to change into her comfy jeggings and cotton plaid shirt, and after throwing a soft cashmere jumper on, she put on her trainers. She combed her hair putting it into a high ponytail. She could care less about makeup, it was only Alexander after all.

Rowanne came back out, and was surprised to find a repairman fixing her lock. 'When did you do this?' she asked Alexander.

He came towards her with her coat. Standing before her, he draped it over her shoulders. He really needed to learn what was and wasn't acceptable.

'I hope you don't mind, but I took the liberty of phoning reception, and they sent this gentleman to repair your door.' *She's telling me what's acceptable! She should lead by example; I'm not the one who changes in front of a guest so easily. She hates my guts, yet has no problem with me waiting while she dresses. I wonder if she is aware that she's entirely too comfortable in my company...*

On second thought, best not to mention it, she'd probably become self conscious. Rowanne seemed to be a person who liked to be in control. If she was slightly liberal with some things, so much the better! He laughed darkly, causing her to look at him questioningly. He shrugged his shoulders, leaving it up to her to make of it what she would.

'Thank you,' she said, 'let's go. I need to get back and finish my work before the night is out.' Rowanne could put up with his random inane smiles; God alone knew what went on in that disturbed mind.

They took the lift down in silence, and she followed him to his car. Alexander was amazed she didn't challenge him and insist on taking her own car. He wisely left her to get the door for herself; she'd only be peeved with him if he acted the gentleman.

It was really hard practising chivalry in this century; half the time you annoyed the hell out of women by being considerate. Even when you helped someone, they'd look at you dubiously as if you had an agenda. He could not win, it was a minefield, but it was hard to change your nature; he'd been brought up to be respectful.

Getting into his car, Rowanne thought, *Respectful my foot; I'd hate to see what his bad side would look like.*

Alexander strapped his seatbelt in, and asked, 'You would, would you?' his eyes glinted devilishly, and for a moment it seemed to Rowanne as if he had winked at her.

'Did you say something?' she asked in an irritated voice.

'I was just saying that you should leave your bag on the back seat, it might be more comfortable than holding it in your lap the whole way,' and he pointedly fixed his gaze over his left shoulder, as he reversed out of the parking space. He noticed that her mood was as sour as ever. She leaned towards him as she stretched behind to place the bag on the back seat.

Rowanne turned her head around the same time as Alexander, and froze at the close proximity to him, but he just looked at her coolly and smiled slowly before looking straight ahead.

Rowanne leaned back sedately; well, she hoped it appeared that way. She really detested him right now, he was such a Casanova. Did he have no inhibitions, she wondered. She made it a point to ignore him and looked out of her window; that way her cheeks could return to their normal hue.

The last thing on Alexander's mind was romance! He enjoyed provoking her, just to see the expression of sheer loathing on her face. Actually, he was not at all inhibited; his family were free spirits! If only the old adage could prove true; that men and women could just be friends! Was it really so hard? Why the complications?

He drove out of her building and turned onto the main road. Rowanne wondered what type of home Alexander lived in. Would it be a small place or somewhere upmarket? Especially if his clothes and car were anything to go by.

It was lashing down with rain, and she heard thunder, but even so it felt stuffy in the car, so she rolled down the window.

Alexander watched Rowanne close her eyes and relax as the rain wet her face. She seemed to be soothed by it, and slowly a smile spread across her face. *Fascinating, the moments that bring a person joy.* He quickly turned his attention back to the road, just as she spun around sharply to look at him, having felt his eyes on her.

'So, how far are we from your home?' she asked curiously, trying to break the tension between them.

'Actually, I am based- I mean live just two miles from you,' he hastily amended - he'd slipped up. He had to be cautious in what he said, especially to a journalist.

'That's not very far at all. So, are you 'based' in central London?' asked Rowanne, looking at him archly.

Alexander laughed, 'Well, you could say I live in the heart of the capital, so to speak.'

Rowanne's interest was piqued, and she was intrigued to know more. She swivelled in her seat to study him better, but all she saw was a stranger; there was something unfathomable about him. Alexander appeared transient, though, he was human when it counted, but at other times... she felt scared.

Alexander switched off the internal chatter to focus on driving safely in the harsh weather. He could see lightning bounce off the tall buildings as they got closer to their destination. It had taken longer than he would have liked as traffic had started to build up with people leaving work to get home. Rowanne remained strangely quiet, although he could occasionally hear her tapping away on her tablet. 'How's it going?' he asked, to kill time until they got moving again.

Rowanne looked at him tersely, hating to be interrupted. 'Alexander, do you think you could give me a few moments, I'm in the middle of something here.' She cast her eyes back down and began to type furiously. 'There, finished,' she said triumphantly. 'Forgive me for being rude. I've just emailed Eileen my completed piece.'

Alexander nodded his head in acknowledgment. It was remarkable what you could do these days: you didn't even need to sit in front of a computer to work, you could just do everything with a phone! He was fascinated with the advances in technology on Earth.

He kept himself updated on all the latest technology, and made use of what this world had to offer; not that he really needed it. He could relatively get by without it, just by using the ways of his world. However, he liked the convenience of Earth's gadgets: they saved time, and a lot of the Earth based demons used mobiles to keep in touch.

He even liked using public transport, finding it highly amusing. Occasionally, he was forced to use it for the sake of appearance, as well as adopting other Earth customs. The demon's who were sent to Earth were those who had been brought up on its knowledge, on how it worked, and they were the ones that could pass effortlessly as humans.

The demons didn't really integrate that much in society, keeping on its outskirts whilst wielding power internally, and always monitoring the situation between both worlds from their sometimes prominent, sometimes low positions; whatever suited them best — the key point was to gather information, that was where the real power lay.

Alexander held a finger to his lips, and a look of incredulity passed over Rowanne's face at being cut short; it gave him a warm feeling inside.

Alexander clipped a wireless headphone to his ear, and switched it on just as the traffic began to crawl forward. 'Call, Venus,' he spoke to the car system, and it dialled the number.

Rowanne had wanted to get one of these systems built into her own car, but she feared it could not be done to a classic like her 1955 Pegaso. She'd find a way, though.

'Good evening, it's Alexander. Yes,' he said, briefly looking in Rowanne's direction. 'No, I can't. Can we reschedule? Great. Forgive the late notice, I'll be in touch,' Alexander said before switching off.

Rowanne found it cryptic. 'Look, Alexander. You should have told me if you had plans, I wouldn't have come,' she could not believe his rudeness at cancelling a prior engagement.

He looked at her steadily, and replied, 'It wasn't important, it can keep for another day.'

The rain by this time had let up, so that Rowanne was able to observe the city lit up around them, especially the skyscrapers shining like beacons in the horrendous weather, unfazed each time that lightning struck them. Even the steel grey clouds could not hide the neon blues and reds.

Rowanne thought that she had never really seen the city like this; it was beautiful, a modern fairytale kingdom of steel and glass cast into spectacular structures that twisted and turned their way up, fighting to rise above the ancient city, taking it into the future.

After fifteen more minutes, Alexander turned onto St Thomas Street, and there before them was a colossal building. Rowanne thought, *We can't possibly be heading there... We'll probably drive by it.* She gazed in wonder as lightning struck the top of the glass behemoth, lighting it up momentarily as a supernatural wonder. The Shard was truly impressive, she thought.

Alexander slowed down and took the entrance to the underground car park, leaving Rowanne in no doubt, and she could not have been more astonished at learning that this was where he actually lived. He parked in his reserved spot, and facing her said, 'Well, this is where I call home. Come on, let's get out of the cold.'

CHAPTER 15

Rowanne sat dumbfounded until she heard a tapping on her passenger window - it was Alexander, and clearly he was annoyed with her.

He opened her door, wondering why she was behaving in this absurd manner. 'Rowanne, are you going to sit here all day, or will you do me the courtesy of coming up?'

She nodded mutely, and got out, shutting the door behind her, and following him to the lift. She looked confused as she asked, 'Don't we take the lift on the other side to go up?'

Alexander looked at her patiently. If she was so easily impressed by this building (he was bored of her admiration) then the next part would literally blow her mind. He smiled charmingly.

'No. I take this lift to get to my apartment.'

'But it only has one floor!'

'I know. It is my home,' he said.

'But that's the top floor!' said Rowanne, her jaw almost touching the ground.

'Yes, well if you don't mind, I really want to get a move on. I'd rather not stand here all night,' he ushered her into the lift and pressed the only button available (apart from the alarm, that is). His thumb was scanned a second time by the building's security as he placed it on the glass panel: the first had been outside the lift. The doors closed, and the lift began to rise up.

A disembodied voice spoke through the speakers, 'Good evening, Mr Black. I hope that you received your delivery expediently? Is there anything that you require?'

'Good evening. I was pleased with your efficiency,' as Alexander recalled having phoned his staff to have his car delivered to Rowanne's address. He continued thoughtfully, 'Nothing presently but I will let you know in due course,' he spoke like a person in power; used to having people obey him.

Rowanne looked at him, and speculated as to how he was able to afford one of the hottest properties in London that a person would have to part with a small fortune for. *Who are you, Alexander Black...* she wondered.

'The person who's inviting you into his home.'

'I beg your pardon?' Rowanne was having one of those moments again, she could have sworn that she had not just spoken aloud. She felt momentarily puzzled and mortified to be caught out thinking about him. *What must he think of me?* she wondered, and resolved to be more cautious in the future.

In no time at all they had reached the top floor. Alexander stepped to the side gallantly to allow Rowanne to leave first.

Stepping out of the lift, the first thing Rowanne noticed were the double doors made of mahogany with inlaid metal scroll work. There appeared to be initials elegantly written in calligraphy overlapping each other, but she could not discern the individual letters.

Alexander stood behind, amused at Rowanne trying to decipher the mystery of the door. If she calmed her mind, then the initials would stand out to her, although not what they stood for. He was perfectly safe, and not breaking any laws with his little indulgences.

He walked a fine line between life and death, and here stood one such testament: a clue to his world, and decipherable unto death, should anyone be foolish enough to solve it. He moved forward and stood shoulder to shoulder with Rowanne as he took out his key and touched it to the monitor adjacent to the door.

It opened before them, and he gestured for Rowanne to go through and the interior was just as spectacular as the exterior; she could not believe that people actually lived like this.

She stepped into the high ceilinged room, and to say that it was open plan did not do it justice. It was so beautiful and ephemeral. It was airy to say the least, as the windows almost gave you a three hundred and sixty degree view - depending on where you stood, of course. Turning to Alexander, she asked, 'Don't you mind not having any privacy? I know you're so high up that you veritably look down on everything, but still,' and gesturing with her hands all around them, she continued, 'I'm not sure, how I'd feel living in a glass house.'

'Rowanne, it might surprise you to know that I too value my privacy. Looking around, you wouldn't think so. But the beauty of this particular glass is that I can look out, but no can look in. We are virtually invisible,' he said with a flourish of his hands, and a strange look came into his eyes that unnerved Rowanne.

I don't know if I like being up here, so far from humanity, and hidden from view with only him for company, she shook her head to clear it of absurd thoughts. Alexander was silhouetted against the window, and a sudden burst of lightning behind him changed his appearance momentarily - he had appeared to be bathed in blue light, a black winged shadow with blazing eyes.

He gazed at her darkly with a knowing look, and Rowanne fought the urge to step back, turn around and run into the lift. He smiled, but this did nothing to ease the anxiety that she had felt ever since she had stepped into his home.

Coughing more out of embarrassment than anything else, Rowanne said, 'Well, let's get started, shall we? I need to finish this as soon as possible so I can get back.' She wanted to fill the uncomfortable silence that had started to build between them.

Alexander walked towards her, and just as he passed her, he whispered, 'Now that's a shame. I was hoping we could burn the midnight oil...' He picked up a tablet next to the front door, and suddenly the living room flooded with light.

Rowanne didn't even want to hazard a guess as to what he was implying and chose to ignore it. Instead, turning to him, she said sarcastically, 'I'm amazed that you could not just give a verbal command and have the lights come on. Everything else about this glass tower seemed so sophisticated and hi-tech!'

Alexander liked the challenge, and standing by the door, he replied piously, 'Lights off!'

Rowanne was suddenly plunged into darkness, and the room appeared much larger than it actually was, and she could see the city outside glittering in the night. Suddenly a shadow stepped in front of her, and her heart was in her mouth as the lights came back on quickly.

Alexander stood close to her, his dark eye's swirled an unearthly sapphire burning with a dark green corona. Funny, she'd never really noticed that before. Her eyes travelled down to the arrogant turn of his mouth, as he smiled at her tauntingly, and hastily she looked back up to his eyes.

Rowanne stepped back almost tripping, but Alexander's arm shot out encircling her waist, keeping her in place. She glared at him, letting him know in no uncertain terms that she'd rather have fallen than be rescued by him.

'Rowanne, you do seem to have the propensity to fall... a lot. A simple 'thank you' would have sufficed. And I hope your original question has been answered by my modest display,' he laughed darkly. Looking deep into her eyes, he said, 'I occasionally enjoy exerting some energy by switching on a light in the traditional way! I am not a slave to-' he paused, letting go of her and opening his arms wide to encompass the grandeur that was his home, he finished, 'all this!'

He walked away from Rowanne, speaking over his shoulder, 'Please, follow me this way, and make yourself comfortable,' gesturing towards the large sofa. She walked over and sat on the very edge of it. 'Can I get you a drink?' he asked, standing before her, forcing her to tilt her head up just to look at him.

Rowanne had a permanent look of disgust pasted onto her face, much to his delight. 'Do you have anything that will keep us awake long enough to go through your assignment?'

Alexander considered his options before replying mysteriously, 'I've got something...' he left her, and went into the kitchen.

He returned a few minutes later with a silver trolley with what appeared to be a mini stove on it. Rowanne was fascinated despite herself.

'Observe the sacred art of making tea,' said Alexander solemnly, as he looked at Rowanne steadily to ascertain that he had her complete and undivided attention.

He rolled up his shirt sleeves, and began by boiling water in a copper pan. To her questioning look, he replied, 'I picked it up on my travels through India.'

Rowanne was impressed, he appeared to be well travelled. She wondered what India was like...

'As soon as the water heats up, add the tea. I generally like to give it a kick, so to speak, by adding these,' and paused as he proceeded to add the spices from the glass jars that she had only just noticed sitting on the trolley. He held up each spice for her before adding it to the water. 'Cardamom,' he continued, holding a green pod, 'is best crushed or split,' he tore it apart, and black seeds floated down to sit on the water. Next, he added saffron, which to Rowanne looked like thin red threads. 'The most expensive spice in the world, worth its weight in gold. Now, we'll wait for it to infuse.' The flames licked the copper pot as the water simmered gently.

Rowanne was amazed at the level of concentration he devoted to what she would have called before the simple act of making tea. Apparently not; there was more to it! She would have just thrown a tea bag in a cup and added boiling water from a kettle, complementing it with cold milk and a lump of sugar to finish.

There was definitely more to Alexander than meets the eye – he was a dark horse waiting in the wings to take the time to enlighten her as to the finer intricacies of life, and the beauty that could infuse them. She was grateful that he of all people would take the time for her. Rowanne was puzzled, because she had been convinced that he disliked her... She laughed awkwardly.

Alexander raised an eyebrow and looked at her accusingly for breaking his concentration, and only resumed once she'd finished. 'Next, we add a pinch of fennel seeds, and a small stick of cinnamon,' he then took a mortar and pestle, and crushed black peppercorns and cloves before adding them to the water.

Rowanne leaned forward, resting her head on her hands, completely immersed in what he was doing, and forgot where she was. She felt completely at ease, and actually interested in something for once; a feat for her, as she was usually engrossed in work.

Alexander smiled as he sensed Rowanne was at peace; for the moment at least, he amended, and thinking better, he shook his head – it was a temporary state for her.

'Come here,' he said, and as Rowanne obligingly came to stand next to him, he proceeded to gently wave his hand over the pot.

It hit Rowanne in heady waves. The aroma alone invigorated her senses, and, closing her eyes she inhaled, smiling joyfully.

Alexander was amused at her child-like wonder, as it reminded him of his own childhood, spent travelling through various countries and experiencing things for the first time. Demons were not that different from humans; in many respects, they too had their fair share of joy and melancholy.

Rowanne opened her eyes to see Alexander holding a jug. 'Do you take milk?' She nodded her head, and he poured it into a small saucepan letting it heat up. 'You can do the honours, by the way,' and he gestured for her to add the milk.

Rowanne looked at him straight-faced, and asked, 'Are you sure you trust me? I might ruin it.'

Alexander looked at her wickedly with a mischievous glint in his eyes, 'I trust that you will do your best, or...'

She rolled her eyes at his pathetic attempt at intimidation, took the pot off the stove and poured the milk into the Chai tea.

Alexander waited a bit before finally turning off the gas. 'Please, take a seat.' He strained the tea, pouring it into two jewel coloured, glass tea cups. He set down the tray on the glass table, and placed a cup before her. 'Do you take sugar?' he asked. Rowanne nodded her head, and he brought back a small glass bowl of brown sugar. He sat next to her waiting patiently for her to take the sugar, before adding a spoonful to his own.

She held her cup in both hands for warmth and inhaled deeply. The taste of the individual spices danced on her tongue before converging into the whole. She felt rejuvenated and suddenly alert: it was akin to having a shot of espresso, but more complex and with a subtle fire that warmed the body.

Alexander was pleased to see her eyes sparkle with the intensity of the tea. 'I'm glad that it meets with your satisfaction.'

Rowanne looked sheepishly at Alexander, feeling embarrassed to be caught in such abandon over tea, of all things. 'Thanks, you've certainly delivered on your promise.'

'I'd hate to see what state you'd be in if you were intoxicated,' he said rather innocently.

Rowanne chose to not be goaded by him or play into his hands. 'I don't know about you, but I feel so alert as to be able to finish a dozen assignments before work.'

'Is that the tea or your ego speaking?' he asked unrepentantly.

'A bit of both,' replied Rowanne and laughed it off.

'I'll just get my laptop,' said Alexander, and went into a room that Rowanne assumed might be his office.

Rowanne used the opportunity to take a look around, and getting off the sofa, cup in hand, she walked towards the large glass doors. Despite the rain coming down in a fine shower, she had a strong urge to go out onto the balcony. After all, she might not come back here again. So, what excuse could she use?

She abruptly turned around at the sound of Alexander coughing. She had not even heard him come in, and he'd already started to set up his laptop.

'For your information, people don't usually find an excuse to visit a friend,' he said, busily trying to find the correct assignment. 'Just say, "Alexander, I'm coming over!"'

Rowanne coloured slightly having been caught out yet again talking to herself, about him. 'I was just admiring the view from the doors...'

Alexander was focused on the screen, and asked, 'Why don't you go out there? The view's better observed from the balcony instead of just standing there.'

Rowanne didn't mind getting some fresh air, especially, away from him, even if it was for a few precious moments. Opening the doors wide, she stepped out into the damp night.

There was no accounting for some people's taste; *She could not wait to get away from me*, thought Alexander, somewhat vexed.

He finally managed to locate the assignment that he wanted her to look at. He was about to call her in when he spotted her standing at the edge of the balcony looking up. Fascinated, he left his laptop, and walked towards her but stopped short of going out, and instead leaned against the door post.

Rowanne closed her eyes - she was drenched but she didn't care. The view was worth every penny this apartment cost, it could be sold for that alone. It was so beautiful, and she had thought that being on the London Eye was amazing, but that dwarfed in comparison to what she was looking at now.

She could see the London Eye, and the river Thames meandering away into the distance. The city was lit up in reds and yellows, a permanent shower of colour every evening as the sun set, and the city came out to play.

Rowanne felt the cold begin to seep in, and jumped when she saw Alexander watching her from the door, and wondered how long he'd stood there. He walked back inside, shaking his head. *What's wrong with him?* she mused.

He came back out a minute later to find her still engrossed in the city. He stood behind her as he draped his coat over her shivering shoulders.

Rowanne nearly had the fright of her life, he was too quiet, and turning angrily towards him, she asked, 'Are you some kind of jungle cat? Make a noise for the love of God, some indication that you are there,' she clutched her heart.

Leaning on the railing next to her, unfazed by the rain and cold, he looked out thoughtfully, and said, 'I haven't quite decided which view I prefer the best... It depends on the time of day, and of course the direction,' he was relaxed.

Rowanne studied his profile as the water dripped down his face and ran into his eyes, though it didn't seem to bother him at all. His shirt had become soaked, she noted absently. *He'll catch a cold.*

'Rowanne, it's rude to stare. And I could say the same for you!' he added, in response to her concern for him, as he turned to her.

Rowanne felt slightly stupid, soaking to death and freezing cold. It was November, what had she been thinking?

'No doubt you were enamoured with how good I look in the rain...' he replied archly.

Rowanne was taken aback, and for a second stood mute before coming to her senses, and thanked God, that the darkness and rain hid her blushes. '*Nǐ hěn mírén*,'[1] she replied mockingly, before haughtily turning away from him. She permitted herself a small smile, and was just about to step inside when his words stopped her in her tracks.

Alexander smiled darkly, two could play this game, and he replied softly, '*Nǐ hěn piàoliang*.'[2]

Rowanne's eyes blazed - of course, he spoke Mandarin, was there anything he could not do? Water dripped all over the floor as she walked back inside. She felt the cold even through Alexander's long coat, and felt guilty as she saw the label; it was an expensive coat.

Alexander came in and stood before her, and said arrogantly, 'No need to worry. I've got a dozen of those,' and taking her hand, he led her.

Rowanne found it absurd that he should be so presumptuous as to assume that he could do whatever he felt like. She was about to tell him so, when he interrupted.

'Look, before you start, I would just like to point out that you were standing there like a statue, dripping water all over my floor. I thought the most expedient thing would be to direct you here,' and opening the door, Rowanne realised that they had ended up at the bathroom.

Pulling her hand out of his grasp, she stepped inside and, turning around with her hands on her hip, she said irritably, 'I think I can take it from here,' and slammed the door shut in his conceited face.

Alexander was amused, *She has everything she needs. Well, she won't need me then,* and went back into the living room.

Rowanne's teeth chattered as she locked the door. She was awed by the immense bathroom; her own was tiny in

---

1   Mandarin for 'You are very charming.'

2   Mandarin for 'You are very pretty.'

comparison. The high ceiling was cone like, echoing the exterior of the building. A chandelier hung from a beam that ran across. Beneath it sat a huge bathtub on ornamental legs.

The floor was white marble with lashings of lightning shaped slashes interspersed. She spotted a Jacuzzi in the furthest corner, sitting in front of a floor to ceiling window. *I bet the view from there is stunning.*

There were glass doors at the other end, and not being able to douse her curiosity, she went to explore. Opening them, she was met with the sight of an indoor pool, which had a glass ceiling above it.

The room was exquisite, periodically lined with white marble columns: roses on vines were carved into them, and they seemed life-like, as if they had frozen in winter, yet retained their beauty ever to be immortalized. Rowanne was lost in her thoughts, and once more could smell the scent of lilies accompanied by a breeze that momentarily chilled her heart.

She froze, locked into place as her eyes glazed over, and could not move even if she had wanted to. She tried calling out to Alexander, but could not seem to make her voice work.

From across the pool a scene started to unfold before her. Mist gathered and formed into a human like shape, and the more that she focused, the more distinct it became until it took on the semblance of a woman hovering above the water.

The woman appeared wraithlike and transparent, and was looking directly at Rowanne. She started to glide above the water towards her, and stepped onto the floor extending her arms out in greeting, perhaps. Rowanne wanted to step back and run, but her muscles were locked into place: adrenalin flooded her body, and worked against her this time.

The woman's mouth opened and closed, as if she were trying to say something, but no sound came out. Rowanne wanted to scream that she could not understand her, but they were both silent. The language of the dead; to speak silence and to be unheard and unseen.

Each step the ghostly woman took towards Rowanne caused her necklace to glow brighter, so that the woman seemed to have a violet aura surrounding her. And finally, she stood before Rowanne.

She was a young woman, maybe in her early twenties, possibly younger, and she had the most violet eyes that Rowanne had ever seen. They were beautiful and mesmerising. Rowanne stood transfixed, and observed the woman's eyes darkening from deep purple to dark sapphire, and her face receded to be replaced by Alexander, who now stood before her with a curious look on his face.

Rowanne had not noticed him gliding towards her. 'You know, it's rude to snoop around a person's home,' he said.

She snapped out of her reverie, and looked at him blankly. 'Where did you come from? I locked the door...' Her mind was slowly waking up.

Alexander indicated with an incline of his head that he had come from the opposite side. 'This place has the good fortune of allowing you into rooms by numerous ways,' he said enigmatically. 'At any rate, I thought you might want these,' and he passed her some of his clothes.

'Thank you,' said Rowanne, feeling slightly stupid; what did she think she was going to get changed into, once she took off her wet clothes.

'By the way, there are fresh towels in there as well. And feel free to use anything else you might need, have a look in the cupboard adjacent to the bath.'

Rowanne nodded her head at him, and turning on her heels walked back into the bathroom, and this time, drew the silk curtains closed over the glass doors, as well as locking both of them.

Alexander worried that Rowanne might have gotten pneumonia, or maybe it was the shock of what happened in her apartment. How could he delicately approach the subject with her: 'Rowanne, you know the supernatural event that occurred? Well, it was all you,' No, definitely not the best idea that he'd ever had - he shelved it.

He strongly suspected it to be the entity inside her. It had definitely become stronger each time that he had encountered it. Why did it behave unpredictably? What danger was she in? *The entity knows I'd never hurt Rowanne... well, not intentionally, anyway.*

He was worried, and really needed to speak to his advisor soon. In the meantime, he'd keep watch, see if the entity became unstable and lost control - it could inadvertently end up hurting the very person it wanted to protect. He made a phone call.

Rowanne didn't trust herself to move. She slowed her breathing and her rapidly beating heart; she had remembered everything about the ghost girl. She had felt such relief on seeing Alexander, and had been frightened out of her wits, but strangely though she'd also felt a great sadness emanating from the ghost.

Rowanne felt a connection to her that she could not name. And could it be that she actually missed her...? *Stop it Rowanne. Do not think about it now*, she told herself sternly. She shook her head and went to the bath, only to find it filled with hot water. She could have sworn that it had been empty just a moment ago...

She found lavender bubble bath, poured a generous amount into the tub, and watched as the pearly liquid created swirls as it mixed in the water. She gratefully sunk into the deep tub, and holding her breath, immersed herself. She rested her head on the edge of the tub, finally being able to relax, but coloured fiercely as she realised that she was in Alexander's home of all places, having a bath!

After half an hour, she decided that she could not put it off any longer; she'd have to go out there and face one hell of an awkward situation. Getting out of the tub, she reached for the big fluffy towel, and quickly got changed.

Standing in front of his mirror, Rowanne scrutinised his choice of clothes: she was wearing jogging bottoms and a black t-shirt. She grabbed the bathrobe and put it on for warmth, noticing it had a distinct smell: slightly earthy and sweet. It reminded her of walking in a garden at night just after it rains, with the smell of jasmine permeating the air. In a roundabout way, it perfectly summed up the man whose robe it was. Alexander gave off the edge of danger, but at times he could be gentle; it was a heady mix, much like the deadly combination of his spices.

However, it did not in any way make up for his lack of social skills and borderline madness. Feeling fortified in her good judgment, she opened the door, wet clothes in hand.

Alexander was over by the trolley, no doubt brewing another cup of spice tea. He saw her and waved her over. 'Where can I put these?' she asked him.

'Just leave them on the edge of the tub, and come here. I've got something for you.'

She felt slightly guilty about leaving the clothes, but headed back out into the living room. Rowanne noticed that Alexander had gotten changed as well, but unlike her, he was not in anything that she'd consider as casual wear. *I mean, does the man only wear designer, even at home, even on his day off!* He was wearing black trousers and a black shirt with a silk tie; as well as being completely oblivious of her musings.

Actually, he did own casual wear but liked to dress up occasionally. This was what he called comfort wear. All she ever did was reprimand him; it was ever her way, though. *What do I do about a pain in the heart named Rowanne?* The possibilities were endless...

Rowanne sat on the edge of the sofa liking the distance; it afforded her the chance of not having to sit right next to him.

Alexander, unperturbed by her lunatic ramblings, decided not to indulge her and sat smack bang in the centre of the sofa: not too close for comfort, but not on the other side of the world, either.

Rowanne huffed in exasperation, but gratefully accepted the tea he was offering. Inhaling the scent, she realised it was camomile with a hint of ginger and honey; did he ever make regular tea?

'That's boring. Live a little by putting in the effort!'

'I beg your pardon?' sputtered Rowanne, shocked.

'I said, I hope you like the tea, it makes you feel alive.'

Rowanne wisely accepted this as, these days, she could not differentiate between what she thought and what she said out loud. *I'm slowly and methodically losing it...*

Alexander decided to have some fun as well as slowly opening her mind to other possibilities. 'Be in my company and good graces long enough, and you most certainly will,' he replied, wickedly.

Rowanne was being proven right. Why had she never noticed... *It is you! I need to get some distance,* she thought.

'Why is that, Rowanne?' he asked, scooting closer.

Rowanne decided to maintain a sedate appearance, whilst trying valiantly to ignore the fact that he was sitting shoulder to shoulder with her. She turned to him, and this brought her even closer to him, practically in his face. 'Let's have a look at this file then,' she said, pointedly fixing her gaze to the laptop.

Alexander smiled, and located it in under a second. *Wow, he's fast,* thought Rowanne suspiciously. *Why does he need my help...*

'Skim through it, and let me know what I can change, as well as what looks good.'

Putting her mug down, she began the odious task of reading the damn thing. *Newbies. Why me? I always get them,* she lamented.

This wiped the smirk of Alexander's face, but Rowanne was too engrossed in her task to notice. *Well, at least when she puts her mind to something, she does so with determination and dedication*; he admired these attractive qualities.

At long last, Rowanne finished. Stretching her arms above her head, she let out a yawn. 'Sorry. I didn't realise how tired I am.' She noticed Alexander turned towards her. Had he been watching her all this time... For once, thankfully her cheeks did not let her down.

Alexander had his arms crossed over, and casually lounged on the sofa.

'You know that you really didn't have to help,' he said.

'It was nothing, although... I must admit that there was a lot to edit.' Rowanne studied him, wondering how on earth he'd ever gotten a job in this line of work. He had a long way to go, and the editors would have a field day with him; he was their worst nightmare realised in the flesh.

Alexander's eyebrow shot up in consternation, 'Really? A lot to edit, was there?' he asked acerbically.

'Wait a minute. I didn't mean to offend you,' replied Rowanne, taking a sip of her now cold tea, and finished it in one go not wanting to insult her host any further. 'Anyway, may I remind you that you were the one that asked me to check it. I don't remember approaching you. So, you can get off your high horse, and accept constructive criticism. Especially as it was meant to help you.'

She was pleased to see that he was stunned by her remark, and he looked like a goldfish, opening and closing his mouth.

Alexander did not trust himself to speak, and slowly counted to ten. He could feel sparks shooting from his eyes.

'So, sue me instead of incinerating me. I hope that was a joke, by the way,' she looked daggers at him.

'You... heard me?' asked Alexander quietly.

'Generally when a thing is said aloud, there is usually the possibility of it being heard.' Rowanne noticed a mysterious green light within the depths of his eyes, and felt an uneasiness within her. It looked menacing, and she wondered how they could just change colour... She got up quickly, and looking down at an astonished Alexander, she said, 'I'm leaving,' and started to hastily gather her belongings, when she felt Alexander tap her on the shoulder.

He turned her to face him, seeming genuinely apologetic. 'Look, I'm sorry, Rowanne. I really didn't mean it. What man doesn't like to hear that they are incompetent, and as for the eyes, that's genetic; everyone in my family has this condition,' he answered smoothly. He had noticed the look of fear and confusion in her as his power had revealed itself. Thankfully, his eyes had now returned to their normal colour.

Rowanne felt ashamed at her reaction. Putting a hand on his shoulder, she said, 'I am sorry about... And you actually have great potential, just work on the piece a bit more. It was highly original, by the way. I can see you as one of the top elite in the future.'

She began to walk towards the bathroom to grab her wet clothes, but Alexander got there ahead of her, and stood in the doorway blocking her access.

'You do realise that it's quite late. It's after one in the morning.'

'What?! Where has the time gone?' she asked accusingly. She had not meant it to come out that way, and she saw Alexander looking regretful, as if he should never have wasted her time.

'It's ok, I'm going to call a taxi. I can see that you are in no condition to drive,' said Rowanne.

'Or, plan B... stay here tonight. I have many guest rooms, just pick one and make yourself at home,' he said innocently, though his eyes were beguiling, telling another story.

'I wouldn't want to bother you,' said Rowanne, trying to edge past him into the bathroom, but the man was like stone, there was no budging him. She had hoped that this would bring the conversation to a close so she could get back to her own comfortable cosy room.

Alexander refused to accept her protestations. 'Please, allow me to extend my courtesy to you, after everything you've done for me,' he said sincerely.

Not wanting him to be in her debt, she reluctantly accepted with a nod of her head. 'I'll leave early in the morning, so as not to disturb you. And the couch will do just fine.' *He had bloody well not put me on that uncomfortable sofa;* it just gave the appearance of comfort without actually providing any.

'Fantastic,' said Alexander, and before she could open her mouth, he grabbed her hand and walked through a set of doors, then led her down a glass corridor that veered off into several rooms. They ended up at the last door in the centre. 'For you, my lady,' he said, opening the door, and standing aside to let her pass.

Rowanne admired the room if a posh hotel room was what you were going for. It was a decent size, more like a master bedroom.

Alexander interrupted her train of thought. 'Well, if there's nothing else... I'll leave you to it.'

'Wait,' called Rowanne, to his retreating back and he turned back to face her. 'Thank you, for letting me stay here tonight.' He waved away her thanks, and left.

I guess he must be tired. I know I am. She closed the door and placed her bag on the bed. Time to explore. She wandered around, going to the cupboard: it contained towels and a bathrobe. Opening the door adjacent to the bed led into a walk-in bathroom. *Very nice,* thought Rowanne. It was marble and had gilded mirrors, not to mention the beautiful tub.

The interior of this apartment must have cost a lot; what else had she expected? She went to the sink and splashed water on her face. Looking back at her from the gold oval mirror was a tired looking woman with red rimmed eyes.

She decided to leave the rest of the work until tomorrow. Getting under the duvet, she switched on the nightlight, shutting off the glaring bright chandelier.

Her mind buzzed with the events of the last twenty four hours. Sometimes, it seemed to her that her life had been turned upside-down. She felt like Alice but not in a good way; hers was a land more of horror and less of wonder.

She could not believe that detective Driskell had behaved so reasonably. On the contrary, she'd been expecting a complete and utter psycho, especially when being alone with him. But he'd behaved decently. *Still, I wouldn't let my guard down with him though.*

Then there was the moment that had overshadowed this, and she'd thought that nothing could: the supernatural. She'd never been one to believe in ghosts. And until recently, she'd never even seen one! Occasionally she'd watched those reality shows that searched for evidence of the paranormal. So maybe she was a little interested.

I wonder what they'd say if I told them that I'd had poltergeist activity in my home. I could probably kiss my job goodbye as well as my reputation, never mind the ghost story. I would become the centre of attention. On second thoughts, best keep it to myself.

Rowanne's phone started to ring; it was Lady Enid. She didn't remember giving her number to her, but maybe she had, and was too tired to recall. 'Hello, Lady Enid. How are you?'

'Good evening, Rowanne. I realise that this is probably considered a late time to call. If I've disturbed you, then I sincerely apologise and I'll ring back-'

'Not at all. I was just wondering when I'd next have the chance to meet you,' said Rowanne.

'Unfortunately, I've been busy with work. And I'm going away for a bit. I'm afraid I'll have to postpone my visit. How are you, my dear?'

'Well, believe it or not, I've had my interview with detective Driskell. And before you ask, it went extremely well. I've given my statement, and from what he told me, it seems to be the end of it, for now,' replied Rowanne.

'I think, he in all likelihood must have treated you dreadfully during the interview, am I right in assuming?'

'Actually, he behaved courteously, for a change. I was taken aback by it, and could not believe that it was the same man.'

'I am glad that it went well. However, I will caution you to never drop your guard around *that* man,' she said vehemently.

'Lady Enid, it might be impertinent of me to ask, but I would like to talk to you one day about detective Driskell, and what type of man he really is. Perhaps, you could enlighten me as to your history with him.' This was met with silence, and Rowanne feared that she had said too much. 'Lady Enid, I apologise if I've stepped over the line.'

'...No, Rowanne, you have not. I was just thinking... let me get back to you on that.'

'Sure. How are you?'

'I'm keeping well, thank you. I find my life becoming busier the older I get. My job sometimes takes a lot out of me, not just physically but emotionally as well,' replied Lady Enid honestly; though, possibly more honest than she had intended.

Rowanne considered Lady Enid's line of work. She'd been present at the court, and had been the senior official, and her position exceeded detective Driskell's. Perhaps she was a judge.

'You could call me a judge, but I have a jury to answer to. And above me there are others of a higher authority, that even I stand powerless before...' and she laughed darkly.

Rowanne got goosebumps along her arm. For a moment, her mind conjured up an image of a place of unimaginable torment that even God had forsaken. She started to shiver uncontrollably.

Now it's happening with other people. What's wrong with me, why can't I distinguish between my thoughts and what I've spoken aloud? Rowanne found it extremely uncomfortable and nerve-racking.

Lady Enid could sense in palpable waves the fear that emanated from Rowanne. What could she do to help? Rowanne must face the truth and soon, if she wanted to retain her sanity.

Taking a deep breath, Lady Enid continued, 'I've always found its best to consider a problem from every angle, and then leave it alone - a solution will surely follow. I'm sorry to say, I have to go now. Good night, dear.'

Lady Enid had ended the conversation before Rowanne had a chance to respond to the cryptic message. She needed to help herself. Feeling sorry for her present state had got her nowhere. Practical solutions were what she needed.

Though, Lady Enid was right; Rowanne had problems, plural. It was not as easy as focusing on a single issue. Taking a deep breath, she thought of the things that were bothering her. She needed to share them with someone, yet she had no one. She loved her grandmother very much, but the point was, they never shared any real concerns between them.

It was partly her fault for never phoning, always being stuck on one assignment or another. Then there was the fact that her grandparents travelled a lot. How she envied them their almost carefree life of adventure, never being tied down to one place.

Thinking more on it, Rowanne realised that the reason she had become a journalist was to travel; admittedly though, she had not travelled very far. But the stories were different, it was what made her job so interesting.

Getting back on track, she realised that she needed to acquaint herself with more people, and actually start to build lasting relationships on a deeper level; friendship, to name but one. She needed to cultivate trust, not only in herself but in others.

Why could she not trust people? She got on well with others, but beyond that she'd never really let her guard down, or let herself become vulnerable. Now in the space of almost two weeks, there were people who wanted to help her, and who were seemingly kind and reliable; but could she trust them? Each of them knew a truth about her, but even then, she'd held back from being completely honest with them.

Alexander had the potential of being someone whom she could trust and lean on. And Lady Enid seemed like the type of person to help someone in need; though mainly Rowanne was thinking of herself, she admitted ruefully.

Rowanne thought it best to articulate her thoughts by committing them to paper, and proceeded to make a list.

1. What happened to Thomas?
2. Who is Alexander Black?
3. Who is Lady Enid?
4. How do Alexander and Driskell know each other?
5. How do Driskell and Lady Enid know each other? Other than as work colleagues.

'I'd like to stop you right there!'

'Who said that?' asked Rowanne startled. 'Is anyone here?'

'Ah, I see. I thought you'd recognise me. But I guess the fact that I'm not speaking in your mind has spooked you.'

'Alexander, if this is a joke, it's not funny. You sick-' said Rowanne angrily.

'Tut-tut, mind your manners, Rowanne. And no, it's not him.'

'Stop it! Come out and face me. I've had a really crappy day and this is the last straw, I'm warning you!' she said irritably to thin air.

'Fine. If you are adamant, but don't say I didn't warn you...'

Rowanne was beginning to regret her poor choice of words, particularly as the room's temperature dropped to freezing. *Oh no...* she thought dazed.

'Rowanne, walk to the full length mirror,' commanded the entity.

Rowanne felt herself drawn towards her reflection and could not help but walk towards it; she felt like she was on cloud nine.

'Ok. Now stop!' said the entity.

Rowanne stood just before the mirror.

'Now look into my eyes...'

Rowanne obeyed. *You mean, my eyes,* she thought absently. She looked deep into her violet eyes; *But my eyes are green...* On closer inspection, she could see long waist length blonde hair - she was absolutely not a blonde!

Rowanne stepped forward, fascinated with the person before her, and reached out a hand towards the mirror and froze — her reflection didn't mirror her, let alone look like her. The reflection smiled and walked towards the mirror, and tapped it. This alone nearly stopped Rowanne's heart. It spoke to her again.

'Hello, Rowanne. Nice to finally be acquainted with you. I was going crazy being trapped in here,' said the entity, tapping her temple.

'Where-where were you trapped?' stuttered Rowanne, as her lips became numb.

'In you, of course. Or, to be more precise, your psyche. Surely, you have to admit the truth of what I'm saying. Did you never wonder about the very helpful voice in your mind?' The young woman in the mirror laughed, and it was like musical notes hanging in the air.

'My mind...' Rowanne felt as if she were slow in comprehending what the ghost, for all intents and purposes, was saying.

'Come on, Rowanne. I know you're brighter than this. Think logically, this is not the first time that we've met now, is it?' asked the entity gently.

Rowanne thought hard, and came to the dawning realisation that she had in fact communicated with this ghost on more than one occasion, and on each of those occasions, it had been when she was in trouble.

Well, if this ghost had helped her before, then surely it wouldn't harm her...

'So, you're like Casper then?' she asked tentatively.

'I don't understand your meaning. But do not address me as 'ghost' - it's not as if I address you as 'human'! Though, technically I could...' she chimed in laughter.

'You were once a human. Sorry, I didn't mean for it to come out like that. What is your name?' asked Rowanne.

'Lily,' she replied. It seemed as if it was hard for her to get her name out. She was frowning and there was tension between her eyes, observed Rowanne.

Rowanne took a deep breath to steady herself, as she asked the all important question, 'Why are you haunting me? Now that I think back to it, I assume you caused that little scene at my apartment?'

'Yes, that was me. But in my defence, all I can say is that I don't always have control over my actions. And it is extremely exhausting,' replied Lily.

'Exhausting, indeed! Do you realise you scared the life out of me?'

Lily walked back and forth in the mirror in an agitated state. 'Yes, well... you seemed to handle it really well, after the first few seconds of your meltdown, that is.'

'I seriously hope that wasn't a compliment,' said Rowanne, who was now feeling angry at the blasé way in which Lily had condensed her moment of horror into a joke.

'Look, I'm in no mood for frivolity. I'm stuck here, of all places. What do *I* have to look forward to?' asked Lily, glaring at Rowanne.

'I think we both need to calm down,' said Rowanne, and sat on the bed to get her equilibrium back in a world that was rapidly losing it. 'Do you have something against Alexander?'

'What do you mean?' asked Lily.

'The way you hurled him out of the apartment, and slammed him into the wall! It doesn't exactly indicate that you are fond of him,' replied Rowanne, angry afresh at the memory of his suffering.

'Why the concern about Mr Black? Is he your other half?' asked Lily sassily, as she leaned against the mirror, her arms folded.

Rowanne would not be swayed, and replied smartly, 'Please, don't change the subject. I see that you are good at skirting the uncomfortable.'

Lily looked at Rowanne for a long time, before answering. 'So, it's good that I ended up like this, is it?' she asked, tears in her eyes as her voice threatened to choke on her pain that was insurmountable.

Rowanne wondered about what might have happened to Lily, and could feel the sorrow that radiated from her. The more she thought about it, the warmer she felt. *Hang on, why would I feel like that?!*

'Um, Rowanne. I'm not sure if you've noticed, but you're glowing. I don't mean that in the positive sense, either. There is literally a purple glow just below your throat. Is there something you'd like to share with me?'

Rowanne looked down, and sure enough there was a glowing violet light under her t-shirt. 'It's not me. Let me show you,' and pulling out her chain, she held her glowing amethyst pendant. 'As far as I know, this necklace has never done this before,' she replied to the sceptical look on Lily's face.

'Would you mind if I have a look at that? There seems to be writing on the silver rim that's holding the stone.'

'You have really good eyesight, most people wouldn't have noticed. It won't do you any good, though, as it's in a language that I've never seen before.'

'Rowanne, that is impressive. Are you acquainted with every single language on this planet?' asked Lily drolly.

Rowanne chose to rise above it, and went to the mirror and held it up for Lily's inspection.

Instead of a smart remark, what she got instead was one pale ghost — if a ghost could go a degree paler, that is. She started to feel fear at Lily's reaction. Panicking, she fiddled with the clasp.

'What are you doing, Rowanne?' asked Lily, frightened at Rowanne's hasty movements. If she should damage that stone... 'Stop!' she shouted.

Rowanne looked up at Lily. If a ghost feared this, then she was most certainly not going to carry it around. *It's probably cursed or something. No way am I keeping it.*

'Don't worry, Lily. I know what I'm doing. I'll destroy it.' There was a wild look in Rowanne's eyes that Lily didn't trust. *Oh my God, she means it,* she thought desperately. *How do I stop her? Foolish human.*

'Rowanne, you have to listen to me. Please, stop for a second. Didn't you say that your grandmother gave it to you?'

Rowanne paused before the mirror with the pendant in hand having finally managed to free it from her neck. 'How could you possibly know that... I've never told anyone,' she said shakily.

'I um... Look, I was in your mind, remember? I picked up one or two things there. It can get quite tedious occupying a single cell of a person's mind; it seems to shrink every second, whilst remaining the same,' said Lily, exasperated with Rowanne for not understanding what it was like for her, imprisoned as she was.

'I can't think about that right now. I want this all to stop,' said Rowanne. A steely look came into her eyes, her mind was made up. She angled her arm back to throw the pendant toward the mirror.

'No, Rowanne!' screamed Lily. But it was too late, as Rowanne let the pendant fly. All she could do was watch powerlessly as it flew towards her.

Lily calmed herself in that moment, accepting what was to come, and dealt with it by calling on her ancestry. The moment seemed to freeze, the trajectory still on course for the collision, but the speed slowed down.

Rowanne closed her eyes and covered her face, expecting an explosion of glass, but nothing happened. She opened her eyes to the incredible sight of time being slowed down. *What's happening...* she wondered, fascinated and puzzled at the same time.

'No. You. Don't,' she said to Lily, and began to wade her way through the river of time to reach the pendant before Lily could get to it.

'I'm sorry, Rowanne, but there's no other choice. I'm doing this for both our sakes. It may not appear so now, but in the future you'll thank me for rescuing you from your moment of stupidity.'

'Don't count me out just yet,' said Rowanne, as she got closer to the pendant, almost within her grasp. She'd just find some other way to destroy it... But first she had to get out of there.

Lily started to break into a sweat as she felt herself losing consciousness at the amount of concentrated energy it took just for this one small feat; *In the old days, this would have been nothing,* she lamented. The past echoed with the misery of others; uncaring, stretching back, or so it seemed to Lily who was alone in that empty space.

Lily had a reason to hope when the pendant hovered before the mirror. She felt herself fading, and looked at the triumphant grin on Rowanne's face. *I'm not finished just yet,* she thought, and gave Rowanne a wink as she thrust her hand forward with her last remaining strength.

Rowanne could see what was about to happen, and pushed her arm through some kind of barrier to grasp the pendant. But unfortunately, her hand went through Lily's, so that it was like they each held the pendant as one hand overlapped the other.

Rowanne and Lily looked at one another, shocked at the strength and magnitude that the other possessed. They quickly looked down as the stone started to vibrate, gently at first, then violently.

'Let go, Rowanne. Get back!' shouted Lily.

Rowanne looked at her hand, and then at Lily. 'It's no use, I can't move it. I'm locked in place. What's happening? I really don't like the look of it,' she said, panic stricken, and not just because a ghostly hand had popped out of the mirror and she was touching it.

'That's your fault. I told you to stop and stay back, but you insist on doing the opposite, every time,' said Lily irately. She had no idea what was going to happen, or why she had reached for the stone; some unnamed compulsion inside of her had urged her not to let it be destroyed.

The pendant by now was a blinding flash of indigo. It was too bright, and Rowanne was forced to close her eyes. She could feel it doing something, tugging at her.

'Before you ask, I'm not the one pulling it from your grasp. In fact, I'm getting the exact same sensation. I too feel like something's pulling me, and it's spinning really fast, like a tornado. Rowanne, call for help quickly before it's too late. I can't save you this time. Hurry,' said Lily, desperate to save both Rowanne and herself.

Rowanne looked at Lily, their gazes locked, the cerulean fire reflected in their eyes. Time stopped altogether and silence descended as the pendant pulsed, each vibration greater than the last, until finally it shattered, just as Rowanne asked Lily, 'You saved me before-'

The explosion was huge and shattered the mirror, causing each of them to be flung in opposite directions. Lily was flung towards the mirror's edge, and glimpsed Rowanne hitting the back wall hard before falling unconscious to the floor.

'Rowanne!' screamed Lily silently, before she too surrendered to the chaos...

CHAPTER 16

Rowanne opened her eyes. It was dark and silent. *Where am I…?* she wondered, rubbing her eyes. *Why am I on the ground?* She got up and walked slowly, each step bringing clarity, until at last the haze receded and she was fully awake.

She gazed up at the sky, and thought it looked beautiful, the stars strewn about forming constellations that she didn't recognise, but were nevertheless majestic, and she spied the moon hidden behind clouds that pulsed with the reflected light.

Rowanne could just make out a stone path, and followed it as it wound its way through the woods. Eventually she came out into a clearing, and before her stood a magnificent palace. She sighed, 'Finally, home.'

She passed under an archway and to either side of it, there were soldiers standing guard. They kneeled, heads bowed before her as she passed. She inclined her regal head, and walked to the courtyard.

Looking up, she could see the citadel rising in the centre of the palace, adjoining bridges connecting it to each of the four quadrants of the building: each with their own defence, yet working in concert.

The courtyard was paved in a pale stone that reflected the warmth of the moon. She went and sat by the fountain and looked into its depths, smiling at her reflection: a tall willowy young woman with penetrating violet eyes, long blonde hair hanging freely down her back. She admired the mid length white dress that showed off her long legs.

Someone came up behind her casting a shadow over her reflection, and blocked out the light. Looking up, she smiled as she recognised who it was. 'I thought you'd still be training with Alexander?'

The young man with flaming red hair tied behind smiled as perspiration glistened on his forehead. 'I'll go back in a minute. He's definitely one to watch out for, not to mention, he's fierce in his determination to succeed.'

'Only matched by yours, of course,' she replied laughing.

'Well, we both want to join the Queen's guard one day. I get better each time I go up against his stubborn fortitude. Even when he's bleeding and down, he refuses to be broken and springs right back up like a tiger, minus the claws.' He had a warm feeling in his heart as he thought of his partner and best friend, Alexander.

He was broken out of his thoughts by shouting. 'Are you coming back in?' called Alexander from the huge wooden door.

She turned to Alexander, who was in his training gear with a sword resting along his shoulders.

'Ah, I see it's the beautiful Lillian, iridescently annoying! If you care to let me have my partner back, then we can both finish before we become old men,' said Alexander.

Turning back to her, Driskell said, 'Ignore him, he's just envious. I'm here in your fine company and he's... well, he's Alexander for you.' And turning back to Alexander, he stated, 'The only old man I see is you. I'll give you time to recuperate my dear elder!'

'Come back in and I'll show you what this old man is made of!' said Alexander, smiling wickedly.

'I'd better get back in or he'll... anyway, it will be to my detriment,' he said with a shake of his head. Driskell was the very image of a penitent man, until he looked at her fiercely and, bending down, he placed a chaste kiss upon her hand.

'Very amusing. Now get going, or you'll really be in trouble,' said Lillian.

'I know, but a man can try, right?' he asked wistfully.

'When you're a man, ask me then,' she replied playfully, a sly glint in her eyes. She got up, leaving him speechless, with the sound of Alexander laughing raucously in the background.

Lily walked past the out buildings, oblivious of the shadow that lurked there, watching her every movement like a snake watching its prey, biding its time patiently just waiting for the right moment to strike. It withdrew - now was not the night, but some day...

'Hey, Lillian. Over here,' shouted a voice from above, and looking up, Lillian waved to her friend in the top window.

'I'm coming up. Is my mother with you?' asked Lillian.

'Yes, and you better hurry, she has a lot to discuss with you. I know it's a year away, but still, a person isn't crowned princess and heir apparent every day. So, move it you royal pain.' Her friend laughed mirthlessly having watched the little performance with Alexander and Driskell. Honestly, the three of them were as thick as thieves.

Lillian ran through the doorway and up the stairs, ignoring the bowing guards as she hastened to meet her mother. She finally reached the top, panting and out of breath, only to be met with the sight of a pair of steely eyes narrowed in frustration. 'Mother?' she asked apprehensively, expecting the worst. Before she could walk towards her, she felt herself being tugged. A vortex picked her up and threw her back, causing everything around her to fade to nothing. And suddenly, there was nothing as she closed her eyes, losing her mother all over again...

Rowanne experienced a splitting headache, the pain making her feel nauseated. She could hear a buzzing sound around her that was irritating to say the least. She felt a warm glow behind her eyelids, and was not yet ready to open them. Why was she being shaken from side to side? *Stop that!* she thought.

Slowly the buzzing receded to be replaced by a more cohesive sound; that of someone calling her name. *Ah, so that's what they're saying: 'Rowanne, Rowanne.'*

'Rowanne? Leave her alone for demon's sake! Look at what you're doing to her!' It was hard for Rowanne to place the voice but it sounded male.

Again the shaking started, and she felt warmth on her face from someone's laboured breathing. And now other sensations started to come back to her; that of a sharp pain in her back. She realised she was resting on someone's knees, no wonder she was in pain.

This time Rowanne made a concentrated effort to open her eyes, and slowly she did, blinking at first from the bright light. The room came into focus in stages and finally looking up, she was met with a look of concern clouding Alexander's face.

'Thank God you've come around. I've been calling your name for the past half hour,' said Alexander accusingly, his eyes two glacial pools of controlled fury. She was unnerved by him, so much so that she looked elsewhere while she regained her composure.

To her dismay, she found herself resting on the floor on Alexander's knees, he was supporting her weight, and his arms were around her to keep her from sliding off. She felt herself go crimson. *Why am I in this awkward position...?*

As if sensing her question, he responded, 'I heard a loud explosion, and came running to your room, with no doubt you'd probably gotten yourself into another fix. And it was the same as before, I could not get in as the door was blocked.'

'It was probably the resident ghost,' Rowanne said archly.

'I think so. It's followed you here, so your theory wasn't completely ludicrous.' He'd meant it as a compliment.

Rowanne looked at him drolly. 'My head's spinning.'

'Are you alright?' asked Alexander, concerned.

'I couldn't get over your compliment, plus my head is really spinning. Try not to move so much.'

Alexander looked at her stoically, and replied, 'I never hold back praise where it's due...'

Rowanne wondered how dense a person could be, and ignored his inane comment; he had actually meant it. She forcefully threw herself forward to get out of his grasp not realising that his arms were like steel, and consequently she bounced back and hit her head on his knees. 'OW!' *What an oaf!*

Alexander looked at her patiently, and in a puzzled tone asked, 'What is it precisely that you are trying to accomplish?' and held up his hand before she could reply, continuing, 'If, it's to knock yourself out again, then by all means, go ahead.' He was not amused.

'And if you'd care to release me, then I can finally get up,' said Rowanne, pointedly looking at his arms locked around her. He withdrew his arms accordingly.

Finally free, Rowanne got up and managed to stand. She looked at Alexander triumphantly, and froze as the colour drained from her face.

'Oh,' said Alexander. 'So, you've finally noticed...'

Rowanne looked from Alexander to the mirror behind him; it was in one piece. In fact, it reflected a room that looked remarkably more intact than the ruin she'd left behind; there was no broken glass or bits of wood, everything was normal. Except...

The mirror reflected a new addition to the room. 'Do you see it?' she asked Alexander, looking intensely at the mirror.

'Yes,' he replied calmly.

'It's behind you... Turn around slowly,' she said, needing him to acknowledge the horror, to prove to herself and him that she was not crazy.

Alexander looked at her steadily, 'You're mistaken, Rowanne. It's, or I should say rather, she's actually behind you.'

Rowanne wanted to scream but held it in, and instead tried to move toward Alexander, but she felt light headed as she had moved too quickly, and nearly lost consciousness again. Alexander moved fast and caught her in his arms. She let him hold her, and rested against him until it subsided.

Finally, she disentangled herself, feeling stronger, and turning to Alexander, mouthed a silent, 'Thank you.'

Rowanne faced the girl sitting on the bed. She was tall, and her shimmering blonde hair was tied back into a chignon. But instead of a dress, she had on a white trouser suit. She looked like the twenty-first century version of the medieval looking girl from her dream.

'Rowanne, nice to finally be able to meet you in the flesh... Well, you know what I mean.' She leaned on the bed, studying Rowanne, in whose mind she had been briefly imprisoned. It was not the poor human's fault, who stood before her bewildered.

'Alexander, it's been too long. What do you think of my new look, very fit for this world, is it not?' she asked, and winked at him.

Alexander's response was to bend down on one knee and bow his head. 'Forgive me, my lady. I did not recognise you,' he replied.

Rowanne looked from Alexander kneeling down preposterously to the arrogant ghost girl. She would not bow to someone that she didn't acknowledge as her superior in any way, form, or shape. At least, she had not to date. So, why start now?

'Alexander, what are you doing? Get up!' said Rowanne angrily.

'Stop addressing me as 'ghost girl.' I'm Lily.'

Rowanne responded bemused, 'Fine. Lillian.'

This stopped the girl in her tracks, and she reappraised

Rowanne as a sharp woman who was not afraid of anything — even, a demon. 'How do you know my real name?' asked Lillian.

'That, doesn't matter for now,' replied Rowanne, not wanting to give away too much, as she wanted to understand the situation first.

Feeling bold, Rowanne walked right up to Lillian, forcing her to look up, for once. 'How do you know Alexander?'

Lillian liked Rowanne's audacity. She was so used to commanding others that she had never really had to look up to anyone. Well, besides her parents and...

Lillian got up, and her long silk coat opened to reveal a silk shirt. She was, in fact, taller than Rowanne, and looked her straight in the eyes. 'Thank you for releasing me. I admit that this state is not desirable, but it is infinitely better than the narrow confines of your mind. No offence meant.'

'None taken,' said Rowanne stoically, fascinated with the woman before her.

'There is one matter of great importance that I'd like to address to the both of you. For the present, keep my identity to yourselves. This is a matter of life and death, not just for me, but for you as well. I hope you understand what I'm trying to tell you,' said Lillian.

Alexander raised his head and stood up, facing Lillian. 'I understand. We have to speak about...' He felt uncomfortable asking her of her passing. But he had to know and suspected that it was hardly natural. Not to mention the fact that he had not seen Lillian in more than half a century.

Lillian went to Alexander and patted him on the shoulder with great affection. She was not only the confident woman who stood before him today, but also the vulnerable girl with a strong spirit that he had known many years ago... Well, before her disappearance and the inevitable cover up.

Nobody in Demon World truly knew what had occurred, though, there were rumours and the Court was naturally rife with speculation. Alexander suspected that Driskell had been involved in Lillian's disappearance, but he was not certain.

Lillian leaned into him, and whispered, 'We will talk later.'

'Come and sit on the bed. We three have a lot to discuss between us,' and she held out her hand. Rowanne took it. Well, almost, as her hand passed straight through. And it took all of her willpower not to pull it back.

There was a sad expression on Lillian's face, and Rowanne sat down beside her.

Lillian looked at Rowanne, weariness etched her face. 'The crystal has at least freed me,' she said softly. Alexander cocked his head to the side to try and hear. She looked at Rowanne pointedly, purple and green energy flashed in Lillian's eyes, and once more, time froze.

'What did you do?' Rowanne asked in amazement, looking at Alexander frozen into position, a questioning look on his face.

'I simply froze him, for a moment. I need to tell you something which Alexander for the present must not know, it's a delicate matter. I don't feel safe telling you, even here... Let's go out,' and she passed through the door.

Rowanne ran after Lillian down the corridor, into the living room, and watched her glide through the glass door onto the balcony. She quickly followed behind, and finally leaned on the railing, a little out of breath, which was unusual for her.

The rain had stopped, or more precisely frozen into place: raindrops were suspended at different stages, hung like crystals in the air. It was a beautifully mesmerising sight. Rowanne stood transfixed until Lillian snapped her fingers in annoyance and brought her back.

'Sorry. I got lost there for a bit. But it's not every day that you see the laws of the universe suspended literally before you! You did this, didn't you? How?' Rowanne asked in wonder.

'Oh, this? It's nothing. I'm still testing the boundaries, and the realm of possibilities that this new incarnation can afford me,' Lillian said wistfully, with sadness colouring her aura. 'Are you afraid of me?'

Rowanne thought long and hard, before replying, 'Well, now that you are no longer in my head, I find I can think more clearly. I used to walk around in a daze, frightened and not really knowing my mind, but I feel differently now, good. I'm sorry...'

'What are you sorry for?' asked Lillian, looking steadily at Rowanne, trying to understand her.

'About you being trapped. I don't know how it happened. I feel like I should know, but there's a block. When I try to recall the week before, it's obscure. There are gaps in my memory... Care to enlighten me?' asked Rowanne shrewdly; the woman before her might have some of the answers, at least.

'Rowanne, do you really want to know? Think carefully before answering. What I say cannot be taken back. You might find a life of ignorance to be infinitely more desirable than the shadow you are about to cast on it. And mark my words, you will not like it.' Lillian held her gaze, willing her to be strong and brave, and believed that Rowanne could accept the truth, after all.

'I feel cold. And if I'm to face the truth, I think I'd rather be in a place of warmth, just to soften the blow, you know.'

'Very well, let us go inside,' and as soon as Rowanne was through the door, Lillian clicked her fingers and the rain began to fall once more, and passed through her; luckily, she was a spirit, she didn't feel the cold anymore than she did the rain. But she missed the sensation of feeling, of touching another being...

Rowanne huddled into Alexander's giant sofa as she watched anxiously, a knot of fear coiled in her stomach. But she was Rowanne Knight, she would not turn away; she'd stay and face whatever life had in store for her.

Lillian sat, well, hovered in a sitting position, next to her on the sofa. It was as much of a mystery to her as to why she didn't pass through the sofa, but she suspected that it had to do with concentrating really hard on what it was that she wanted.

'Why didn't you want Alexander knowing about this?' Rowanne asked, as she pulled the pendant out of her t-shirt.

'You guessed correctly. This pedant that you so casually hold is actually a family heirloom of mine. No, keep it on,' she said to Rowanne, who tried to take it off.

'I'm sorry. I didn't know that this belonged to you. It was actually my grandmother's, who gave it to me on my-'

'Eighteenth birthday,' finished Lillian, much to Rowanne's surprise.

'How do you know that?' asked Rowanne.

'My mother passed that very necklace to me when I was eighteen. It's a family legacy and how in the world it ended up here, is a mystery.' What Lillian had actually wanted to say was: 'on Earth,' but she was not quite ready to reveal Demon World to Rowanne just yet.

'Do you think by any chance you could be related to my family? How long ago did you receive the necklace?' asked Rowanne.

'It's been a very long time; more than half a century, if my calculations are right,' replied Lillian and laughed mirthlessly.

Rowanne quickly did the math and guessed that Lillian must have passed...

'When I was twenty, if you were wondering. You'll never ask, but to satisfy your curiosity: no, I didn't pass by natural causes. My family is more resilient than that, I hope,' stated Lillian.

Rowanne felt taken aback, and looked slowly up at Lillian, who wore a stoic expression.

'Don't worry, you're too polite. Yes, some ghosts can read minds, sometimes using it negatively against a person.'

Rowanne looked worried, *Well, at least I know I didn't say those things aloud.*

'I have another question: sometimes I think something, only to have a person reply back to me, as if I've spoken it aloud. How can this be possible?' Rowanne was dying to know, it had been bothering her for quite some time.

'Have you ever considered that you may be telepathic? And that you're a natural medium since you can clearly communicate with me; not to mention, you're probably psychic...' said Lillian to Rowanne, who paled at the idea of her new unwanted and unwelcome abilities. 'Those gifts, yes, you heard me correctly, could help you in the future, if you're willing to develop them, but I'll leave that to your discretion.' Lillian had to remain calm, when really she wanted to shake the uncomprehending human.

Demons revered all gifts bestowed on them, and made the most of what they were given; especially since in Lillian's world it was one's identity, a part of who they were, and could potentially save their life.

'Two weeks ago, I was a perfectly normal human being in a normal job that I worked hard to excel at. I did not have any supernatural gifts or experiences! So, what the hell has happened to change it?' demanded Rowanne, and looked pointedly at Lillian.

'Rowanne, take a deep breath. You are most definitely looking at the wrong person to blame,' replied Lillian calmly. 'Anyway, I thought you wanted to know more about the necklace...'

'Fine,' said Rowanne reluctantly. Though, she would come back to the topic. 'What is your surname?'

Lillian thought long and hard, before replying wisely, 'Knight.'

Rowanne got excited at the prospect that they might

actually be related. 'We both seem to have the same family tradition, as well as sharing the same surname, this looks promising. I should ask my grandmother about her family. Oh, but...' Rowanne looked crestfallen as she came to a realisation.

'What's that look for? I'd love to meet your grandmother, but I don't think she'd receive me very well... Why are you reluctant to ask her?' asked Lillian.

'We could still try and research our family ancestry with the little knowledge that we have between us. But my grandmother wouldn't really be able to give us any solid information,' replied Rowanne.

'Surely, she can provide us with the details of her parents and grandparents, at least. That would be a start,' said Lillian.

'My grandmother was adopted at birth, and doesn't know who her biological parents are. She's tried over the years to gather information on them but has been unsuccessful, so far. Even, her adoptive parents weren't given any details when she was left with them as a baby.'

Lillian felt sorry for Rowanne's grandmother - it must have been hard for her not knowing where she came from, or who her parents were.

'Don't worry, we may yet find information that could shed light on your ancestors. It would be in your best interest... But let us get back to the task at hand, from which we are digressing,' said Lillian.

Lillian was intensely fixated on the pendant. 'What can you tell me of this necklace?' asked Rowanne, intrigued. She was not a fool, she knew it was infinitely more than what it appeared to be.

'You're right, but its potential is more than you can fathom... That little display earlier, though magnificent, barely even scratches the surface of the infinite possibilities that this little stone is capable of,' replied Lillian.

'So, is it like a philosopher's stone or is it more like Aladdin's lamp in that it grants your heart's desire?' asked Rowanne.

'People rarely wish for what they actually need, rather, they wish for what they *think* they need. With time, they'd wish that they had not received what they asked for - it did not fulfil them as they had hoped,' replied Lillian cryptically.

'What can this purple stone do?' asked Rowanne.

'Well, for starters, it finally separated me from you. And even though I am still a ghost, I'm free. That is what I call progress.'

'Does it have the power to bring you back to life?' Rowanne asked. After all, she had seen firsthand the power it contained.

'I don't think so. But you could say that it saved my life, or a semblance of it. Not that I was aware of it at the time...'

'Who did this to you?' asked Rowanne tentatively, thinking that perhaps Lillian had come back to solve the mystery of her death, to get justice.

'I've been wondering the same thing myself,' said Lillian and smiled at Rowanne, who didn't flinch in response to her reading her mind; in fact, she was becoming a natural at this. There was so much more to Rowanne, though, she was the only one who could not see it.

'If, by some miracle, we can uncover the mystery of my demise, then perhaps I can move on but even then...' *Where do demons go, after they die...* she speculated.

'What are you afraid of?' asked Rowanne gently, and placed her hand above Lillian's in an unconscious gesture of kindness and solidarity.

'I'm afraid I don't have the answer to where demons go after they pass. Do we go back...? Are we redeemed...? Perhaps, we simply cease to be... I'm just tired and exhausted. It's taken a lot out of me, all this,' Lillian gestured around herself, trying to encompass everything.

Rowanne nodded her head, she too had a lot to wrap her mind around. *I'm talking calmly to a ghost — who would ever have imagined that!* 'I'm sure if we tell Alexander, he'd be able to help us.'

'We will consult Alexander, have no fear on that front. But the necklace is sacred and we bestow this arcane knowledge as a blessing upon the women of our family. It has only ever been passed down the line of women. No man has yet, to my knowledge, known of this crystal,' said Lillian, and tried to gently touch the pendant but her hand passed straight through it.

Rowanne really looked at the pendant for the first time, examined it, and was curious to know what the writing inscribed into the silver rim actually said. 'What does the tiny writing say?' she asked, pointing to the silver casing.

'You'll have to discover that on your own, I'm afraid. All I can say is, find out where you came from and trace your ancestors, and decipher this language.'

Rowanne had a deeply unsettling feeling that Lillian knew exactly what was written, as well as where it came from. But for some reason, she didn't want to share the knowledge with her at this stage. *Well, I can find out for myself, and I don't think it's beyond me.* 'I'd better take care of this thing, then,' she said half-heartedly. Realising that it was more than just a piece of jewellery, and it felt as if it weighed a ton; maybe it was just the knowledge that she had received that weighed heavily upon her mind.

Rowanne was snapped out of her thoughts by a crashing sound coming from the corridor.

'Alexander's grown powerful since last I saw him. Impressive. I don't think we have long to talk,' said Lillian.

Alexander felt the instant that he was caught in the gelatinous sphere, encased within it. Each time he moved forward so did the substance, it was like wading through dense water. His movements were slow and clumsy - it took an effort just to sync his mind and body.

Alexander wondered how much of the truth his old friend had disclosed to Rowanne, thereby putting her life in danger. Should Lillian disclose about Demon World, then it was almost certain death as punishment for Rowanne.

Hold on Rowanne. I'll get to you, thought Alexander. Lillian was nothing like the girl he had once known. Lillian and Driskell were younger than him, Driskell being closest in age to her. What had happened in Demon World... he needed to have those answers badly.

There was pain in Alexander's heart at the knowledge that Lillian had in fact passed away; he was never told, but it seemed as if his so-called friend Driskell had known. *Why didn't he ever tell me?* he thought bitterly. And was this then the reason behind his friends complete transformation, for the anger that was often directed towards him. *I didn't know!* thought Alexander pathetically, trying to justify himself. But there was no one to listen to him pleading.

Alexander silenced his mind and focused solely on the task at hand. His eyes began to pulse green and the fire built within him, which he released in a series of short sharp attacks to the sphere, weakening it successfully with each hit.

Lillian felt herself weakening, and began to fade in front of Rowanne's horrified face.

'Lillian. Lillian, come back! You wanted to tell me something.'

'I can feel myself going, Rowanne. I don't know how to stabilise myself. But just don't forget to keep the secret of the pendant, no man or anyone else must know of it, especially Lady Enid!'

'Why not? Can I not trust her? And who is she to you?' asked Rowanne.

'I can only say for now that you can trust her with your life... take my word for it,' replied Lillian. Though the irony was not lost on her as she looked at the disbelief on Rowanne's face. 'It is best for now. And please, trust me on this, you must not show her the pendant. It would cause her great sadness and possibly even break her. For now, please...' pleaded Lillian, willing Rowanne to understand.

Rowanne decided to trust Lillian, for now. She had to think more on it, instead of acting recklessly; she had a responsibility and must act accordingly. 'Alright. I won't tell her. And as much as it pains me, you'll have to tell me the secret you've been keeping from me.'

Rowanne's face paled. She didn't want to hear it, and her senses were screaming at her to avoid the subject, but she knew it was ultimately important to her wellbeing to find out the truth.

'If you're ready?' asked Lillian, not wanting to waste any more time. She didn't know how long she had left, and whether she'd come back next time with energy to restore her; after all, Rowanne had been her unwitting power supply, but she had not realised that she had been sapping her energy. Lillian felt extremely ashamed; ignorance was no excuse, she should have realised the toil it had taken on Rowanne.

'Rowanne, I think we should discuss some other matters, when you have time. I have much to make amends for in your regard. I am feeling guilty about what I did to you, when I was in your mind.' Lillian looked straight at Rowanne, ready to face whatever punishment she would think fit for her.

Rowanne suspected what Lillian was trying to say: after all, she'd been acting like she had a split personality these past two weeks, Alexander could testify to that. The poor man didn't know where he stood with her - polite one moment and psycho the next.

Rowanne looked at Lillian thoughtfully, 'It's nice to finally find out that I am not in fact certifiable. I was wondering what was happening to me. I thought perhaps that I'd had a nervous breakdown. I feel more like myself now. And believe it or not, I am not really the type to be easily frightened, and I do not go around fainting and hurting myself easily. If I fall,

I can rely on myself to get back up. I'm sure you understand my meaning,' and she smiled gently at Lillian, trying to reassure her that she did not blame her and she understood on a deeper level that it was beyond the control of them both.

'Thank you for your compassion, it means a lot to me. I always suspected there was more to you than I gave credit for; that was my misjudgement of you. I thought I'd gained a greater clarity on life in death, but I've just proven that I can be just as ignorant in death. In fact, I'm learning more of life now. And I have as long as I am here for,' said Lillian sadly, but also thinking that it would be a blessing to be freed, finally.

'What happens... after we pass?' asked Rowanne nervously, wanting to know and yet at the same time dreading the answer before her.

'I really wish I could answer that, but I don't think you'd understand if I said that it would be different for someone like me... especially due to the unusual circumstances of my passing,' replied Lillian guardedly.

Though Rowanne could not fully grasp what Lillian had said, she did suspect that the answer would be infinitely more complex than she could ever imagine. The next thing that Lillian said nearly stopped her heart.

'Perhaps, you could tell me how it's like... for your kind?' Lillian looked steadily at Rowanne, waiting for her to react to the horrendous news.

Rowanne felt sick, as if someone had walked over her grave. She felt unsteady and her palms began to feel clammy, and it didn't help that the room was getting warmer suddenly.

The door burst open. 'That is enough, Lillian. I beg you, do not speak another word, for all that is good!' said Alexander angrily, his fury barely in check.

Lillian floated closer to Rowanne and gently encased her hand, and looked at her, 'We have to go, there's no time to waste,' she said.

Rowanne took the hint and hid the necklace discreetly.

Lillian whispered in Rowanne's ear, 'This is going to briefly disorient you, and you'll have more questions than I care to answer. But no matter what, just hold on.'

'What, what are you going to do? Please don't hurt Alexander, again,' pleaded Rowanne, and she looked at him questioningly.

'Rowanne, you need to come over here, right now. Just walk towards me,' his eyes spoke volumes.

But Rowanne could not afford to let herself waver.

'Do not listen to anything she has to say,' and he slowly took a step towards them.

'Sorry, old friend. But it's time she learnt the truth,' said Lillian apologetically, though she knew that it was the right thing to do.

'No!' shouted Alexander, running towards Rowanne.

Lillian passed through Rowanne one last time before she could fade, and took possession of the crystal, setting her intention; it sparked a furious purple fire in response, the flames cocooning them.

Rowanne watched as Alexander tried to get through the unearthly barrier, but it was no use, this was full on poltergeist activity. She looked at him, and said, 'I have to go. I'm sorry. I know all of this doesn't make sense to you, but for my life and what little sanity I can hold onto, I need to know the truth.' She worried for him, how would he take all this?

'You really don't,' said Alexander, betraying himself as he burned on the pyre of truth. He saw the shock spread over Rowanne's face be replaced by hurt and anger that he had kept something important from her.

'I can't believe I ever trusted you. You're a liar!' shouted Rowanne, the flames reflected in her eyes; her pain radiated outwards, changing the supernatural fire into a violent crimson. 'Whatever it is, you should have told me. Especially when you could see it was destroying me, and changing and moulding me into someone I didn't recognise.'

'I'm sorry, Rowanne. I did it for our own good- Wait that's not what I meant,' said Alexander, as mistrust suddenly clouded her face.

'So, *you're* the reason, I'm like this?!' said Rowanne furiously, throwing behind it all the anger and resentment that had been building up inside of her whenever she was in his presence. 'Do you have any comprehension of how you've made me feel?' Rowanne felt sick; she needed to get rid of all the negativity that had built up inside of her.

'How *you* feel,' said Alexander quietly, not trusting himself to speak. He looked at Lillian, who shook her head at him. His breathing became laboured, and he tried unsuccessfully to steady himself. After all, he too felt a deep seated bitterness at the unjustness of everything he had gone through with her, because of her. *No wait*, he thought. *I don't blame her, she is not to blame for my decision. My decision*, he thought wearily.

'Let's go. I need to get out of here before I do something we'll all regret,' she said to Lillian. 'Good bye, Alexander. I hope we never have the misfortune to meet again.' Rowanne turned away from him, and went to Lillian, who was waiting patiently for her. The fire burned the brightest one last time before going out, and taking the two women with it.

CHAPTER 17

Alexander dropped to his knees and landed heavily, heedless of the pain that shot up his legs. His hands passed through the last remnants of the vortex as it snuffed out of existence. He sat there feeling a sharp pain; one that encased his heart and consumed him. It took a lot to bring him down, and he never thought that it would be a woman — especially, not a human woman. Head bent and eyes closed, he let the pain of all he felt, of his loss, wash over and through him. He cursed the warm liquid trailing down his face.

Alexander the proud, the fierce... broken, forsaken. He pounded his fists into the floor, and they became bloody, but he didn't care.

He felt a presence behind him and froze.

'Now that's hardly going to help, is it?' The voice came from behind him.

Alexander got up in one swift move to face the intruder.

'Lady Enid!' said Alexander, surprised.

'Well, you did call to arrange this meeting, or have you forgotten? Anyway, let us get you cleaned up,' she said gently.

'It's nothing. I'll deal with it later,' said Alexander stubbornly.

'Evidently. It seems you both have that in common,' said Lady Enid. Alexander felt as if he'd just been insulted.

Taking Alexander's hand, Lady Enid led him to the sofa where he reluctantly sat. She was about to tackle the blood, but he suddenly snatched his hands back and wrapped them in a handkerchief, tying one around each hand, uncaring of the blood soaking through.

Lady Enid knew that it took a lot to damage a demon. Alexander must not have cared as he pounded the marble floor not stopping, even as his fist went through and cracked it in half. *What happened?* she wondered fearfully, to make Alexander, who was one of the most level headed demons, that she knew, completely lose control like this.

'At least permit me to do this much for you,' said Lady Enid. Her eyes bled to emerald green as the power called forth from within her duly did her bidding; in a few moments, the floor once more became smooth as it repaired itself, with no sign of the destructive force that had rendered it asunder.

Alexander looked at her, his face devoid of emotion, although his eyes were eloquent in their reflection of his pain. It was more than the misunderstanding that Rowanne was under, he feared what her reaction would be once she learnt the truth.

He was yet to be truthful about the consequences of his decision to save a mortal. How was he to tell his family that he now only had a few short years to live compared to the eternity that the rest of them had chosen and would live. To a demon, a human lifespan was nothing, over in a mere blink of an eye, compared to an eternity.

No parent would want to outlive their child, and demons in that respect were no different than mortals. He had ripped their happiness apart, though not intentionally. Would they forgive him?

More to the point, how would they cope with the knowledge of his death? Sharp pain ripped through him afresh, and he fell forward, and would have smashed his head on the table had Lady Enid not caught him at the last moment with her incredible speed and strength.

She held him close and felt him submit, finally giving up the struggle; just grateful to be held, to not be alone.

'Don't you dare do anything stupid. I'm warning you, Alexander. You do not understand the horror a parent goes through, as well as the guilt and pain, when losing their child. Your parents are my dearest friends and I've always held them in high regard; one of the best families in our world, in my opinion. Don't you dare tell any of the other Nobles; they'd use this knowledge to further their ambition at our expense.'

Though Alexander felt cold and numb, he had nevertheless heard every word she had said clearly. He coughed to clear his throat, and said gruffly, 'Don't you mean life.' Lady Enid nodded her head in agreement to this truth.

Carefully detangling himself, he tried to bend down on his knee to pay the respect due to his Queen, but before he could even reach the ground, he felt himself being hoisted back onto the sofa by her Ladyship.

Alexander smiled ruefully at her for his momentary loss of control, but he needn't have feared, as she dismissed it.

'I do not stand on ceremony when it is not necessary. This is not the Court, it is your home. And there are no Nobles to enforce the proper conduct and obeisance due to the First Families.'

Alexander raised an eyebrow in astonishment and amusement at what Lady Enid thought of the pompous circus, otherwise known as the Nobles. Especially those of the First Families who got a tad murderous if they thought that they had not received the proper respect due to them as befitted their status.

'Alexander, may I remind you that we both belong to that elite 'circus' as you so eloquently put it. And in future, guard your thoughts well, my dear boy.'

'I knew there was a reason I liked you,' he quipped.

'Let us get back to the task at hand. I have made a special request to an ally of ours, who I am certain you will be pleased to see again after so long.' Lady Enid's eyes sparkled, as she fondly had a certain person in mind.

'I see,' said Alexander. 'And when can I expect her?' he smiled slowly at Lady Enid, finally receiving some good news for a change.

'She will come down tomorrow. And I want you to brief her on the newspaper. She will be well placed there to help us guard Rowanne, as well as helping us with the investigation. She was very keen to help. Well, you know her nature.'

'You hold a high opinion of her. I agree with you, she has been such a blessing to your family...' Alexander approached the subject cautiously not wanting to offend this bravest of women.

Lady Enid patted Alexander on the shoulder and looked at him with weary eyes, barely managing to keep her own emotions in check. 'Yes... Well, that was a long time ago, and she was truly a blessing, I would have broken, otherwise,' she admitted honestly; not easy for a person in her position. Especially as she was surrounded by vultures who'd love to pick at her wounds, rather than have an ounce of sympathy.

No, she could never afford to break down in front of the Nobles. She must portray and play the part of the steely Queen of the First Family; heartless, no emotion and ruling with her head (instead of in conjunction with her heart). *I played my part well*, she thought bitterly. *Too well*. She'd viciously encased her heart in steel, so that she could be of some use to these two young people.

Alexander held her hand gently, just sitting quietly. He could not even begin to imagine how she still functioned after all she'd been through.

Lady Enid smiled, as she thought of the extrovert way in which the Black Rose Clan conducted themselves; and Alexander was no exception. *Good luck to you Rowanne. He's a handful; you'll definitely need it, once the smoke clears...*

'Well, she's managed to get herself into another fine mess. I see that doesn't surprise you,' said Alexander.

'I suspected that Rowanne would encounter some hurdles...' said Lady Enid kindly in response.

Alexander rose to his feet. 'Can I offer you some tea, my lady?'

'Yes, thank you. We have much to discuss and plan for.'

Alexander went to the kitchen and quickly prepared a strong spice tea to keep them awake and energised. He needed his brain to function at the optimal level. He brought in the two cups and placed them on the table.

Lady Enid took the cup between her hands and felt grateful for the warmth. 'What happened, then?' she asked, getting straight to the point. 'I have to get back soon, many engagements on my time, as you know,' she finished solemnly.

'Driskell?' asked Alexander.

'Amongst others,' replied Lady Enid disgustedly.

'I really thought that I was getting somewhere with Rowanne.' *Gaining her trust bit by slow agonising bit!* 'She was finally opening up to me. And believe it or not, she wasn't intimidated in the slightest on seeing a ghost-'

'Ghost?' asked Lady Enid, and wondered whether he was referring to the entity who haunted Rowanne and resided within her.

Alexander studied Lady Enid - she didn't appear to be surprised by his news. He continued cautiously, 'Rowanne was haunted by a spirit, and my last encounter with it was violent. It has been growing powerful, and has now managed to break free.'

Lady Enid calmly drank her tea. 'But how is that possible? And how is Rowanne?' she asked uneasily.

Alexander got the answer that he had suspected all along. 'When did you encounter the entity?' he asked seriously, his demeanour changing.

'I see I have no choice but to tell you the truth considering how much you already know. It was when I first encountered Rowanne at the Noble Court. Driskell had brought her in for questioning.' Lady Enid knew that sharing this information was dangerous, but she felt that she was on the same side as the young demon before her.

It said a lot for him, that he gave up his eternity for a human span of time. There were a select few whom Lady Enid trusted: Alexander was amongst them.

Honesty was needed, if they hoped to get Rowanne back from the entity's grasp. 'I'll tell you everything I know, and I expect the same courtesy in return,' said Lady Enid.

Alexander nodded in agreement, with a look of determination.

'From my encounters with the entity, whom I strongly suspect as coming from our world, I had no reason to think that it posed a threat to Rowanne. On the contrary, the entity had stepped in whenever it perceived a threat to her.'

'That is the same pattern of behaviour that I have observed. The entity thought that I was a threat and dealt with me accordingly. I managed to ward off most of the attacks, but it was not without effort on my part. I fear the power it's now amassed without the confines of a host to keep it in check,' said Alexander.

'We are in trouble if the spirit was once a member of a First Family; there is no knowing the power it can wield. But do not lose heart, it has not harmed her thus far. Please continue with your account.'

'The entity separated itself from Rowanne and...' How could even he begin to approach the subject with Lady Enid, it would destroy her.

'Why have you gone quiet? What is it that you cannot tell me?' she asked angrily, not liking the look of sympathy on his face.

'It's L... L... L...' Alexander felt a sharp force take over his mind and control his tongue, so that he could not utter the entity's name without his teeth clamming down sharply on his tongue, and blood welled up as he tried valiantly, but to no avail.

'Alexander, stop. This is dark magic, do not utter its name for it may well be the last thing you ever say. This proves beyond doubt that it's one of us. Now we just have to narrow the field a bit. I will find out who it is, I swear on my honour.'

Alexander gratefully accepted the tissue she handed to him, and wiped his mouth, the blood smeared across his pale cheek. He tested his mouth and began again gingerly, 'The entity wished to tell Rowanne the truth of that night. I tried to stop her, but she took Rowanne with her, and the portal closed. I could not go after them, it was aligned to their frequency alone.'

'In a way, it would be good for Rowanne to finally know everything. I do not think she'd blame you, if that is what weighs on your mind. On the contrary, I think she'd be grateful,' said Lady Enid.

'To be a half demon, to have her world changed beyond recognition with a truth she must now bear... I'm not so sure. I know she's strong, but this may be beyond her.'

'I think you lack faith more in yourself than you do in her. And before you start protesting,' she said, holding up a hand, 'I have seen what she is capable of as you like to put it, and she has in my opinion, passed. Give her time to come to terms with the truth, she may need to be alone for a while. Focus on the investigation, that is the best way in which you can help her.'

Alexander reluctantly agreed with Lady Enid. If this was all he could offer, so be it. 'Just send me the details of where to pick her up, and I'll brief her on the way to work. Though, I am surprised that she actually left Demon World to come and perform this menial duty. No offence intended, my lady.'

Lady Enid laughed as she acknowledged what he alluded to. 'I was taken aback myself. I did not ever picture her as leaving our world, even for a short duration. But then, she has always been the reliable sort; in the best sense, of course,' she spoke with pride.

Lady Enid's phone rang, and she replied with a swift text before looking at Alexander.

'I'm afraid they need me back there. So, I will be going, take care. I'll be in touch and let you know if I come up with any ideas as to how to help Rowanne. And I still feel that we should not fear the worst.' Lady Enid opened a portal behind her, and she waved once to Alexander before stepping through. It closed abruptly behind her.

Alexander had much to do. He went to the bathroom and opened the first aid box, cleaned his wounds, and wrapped a fresh bandage around each hand. He could not summon up demon energy at this juncture to heal himself, later, perhaps. He was bone weary, and his soul felt bruised and battered.

Switching off the lights, he went into his bedroom. He looked into the ornately carved, black mahogany mirror, and his tired gaze reflected back at him. He undid the top three buttons of his shirt, and felt as if he could now breathe. He threw himself onto his bed, and flipped a master switch immediately plunging the whole apartment into darkness, before succumbing to the sleep of the dead himself.

CHAPTER 18

The vortex spewed Rowanne out, and she landed in a bedroom. Though she was disorientated, she nevertheless managed to catch herself on the four poster bed, subsequently having a cushy landing.

'Where am I?' asked Rowanne, looking around at the palatial surroundings; this room would not have looked out of place in Buckingham Palace, it oozed opulence.

'It's not bad, is it? This, my dear Rowanne, is my bedroom.' Lillian gestured at the long damask gold curtains and the golden gilded mirror on the wall, as well as the other lavish furnishings.

'All this is yours? Who were you, royalty of some sort?' asked Rowanne quickly without taking a breath.

'You ask a lot of questions,' said Lillian, finding them extremely tedious. 'Yes. You could say that my family is The Royal Family.'

'So, you are related to the Queen... But I've never heard of you,' said Rowanne excitedly. She could not believe her luck to have been possessed all this time by a royal - this was definitely a story to tell the kids one day. Well, when she eventually had kids. Perhaps Lillian had decided to keep a low profile by staying out of the media spotlight.

Lillian floated onto the bed sedately, and regally propped herself against the pillows with Rowanne resting by her feet.

Rowanne took one look at where she was sitting and quickly scooted up the bed to sit beside Lillian, who was gesturing to the space beside her. *I am not beneath anyone —
I am their equal,* thought Rowanne.

'I am glad to see you finally know where you belong!' laughed Lillian, and nodded in approval.

'You know... you're a lot nicer outside my head than you were within!' said Rowanne derisively.

Lillian turned towards her, leaning on one elbow, a thoughtful look on her face. 'Well, I was confined to a cell, no pun intended, within your mind. I got a little cranky. It's bad enough not having space enough to form my own thoughts, let alone listening to yours, day in and day out.'

Rowanne blushed furiously. 'You heard all my thoughts...?! Can you stop doing that, it's very disconcerting; half of what I think I don't take seriously, and it's mostly nonsense, anyway.' Rowanne was dismayed to think that Lillian probably knew her whole life story at this point - not that it was particularly interesting. The poor thing was probably bored.

'I was bored to tears, actually. Why haven't you done anything interesting with your life, like gone on some wild adventures or fallen in love? If your life were a film, and please don't take any offence to what I'm about to say, I'd skip it, or watch it as a cure for insomnia,' and she looked at Rowanne with a pained expression.

'I can really hate you, sometimes,' said Rowanne, annoyed with Lillian. *It's not like I asked her to share my mind, anyway. Why couldn't she have possessed a celebrity, instead; then she'd be living the high life!* After a moment, she asked, 'I suppose your life was filled with excitement?'

'As a matter of fact, I am glad you asked. It was almost a fairytale; there was romance and sword fighting-' she paused at Rowanne's dubious look, and continued, 'I was referring to my hobby. All of the women and men are trained in various fighting styles. It's common practice where I come from, and it forms an integral part of our upbringing.'

Rowanne found it fascinating, if a little vague; but it was up to Lillian to give a fuller account, whenever she was ready. 'It seems like an interesting place, perhaps you could tell me more about it. For instance, where did you study?'

'You wouldn't have heard of it, the DW Academic Institute of The First Family, most people know it as the Morning Star Academy. It's one of the finest and unrivalled, as far as I'm concerned. There are lesser institutions, but think of it in this way, if you had a choice between Oxford and Cambridge University and... which one would you choose?' asked Lillian archly.

'You're a bit of a snob. I didn't go to either of those universities, and I am pleased to say that it had no adverse effect on me. And before you ask, I am not going to tell you where I studied, it doesn't define me in any way,' replied Rowanne.

'I suppose I am a snob; it comes with the territory...' she agreed unashamedly. 'All of the children belonging to the First Families are spoiled rotten. I am a picnic compared to some of the others, but I'll let you find that out on your own... if you ever have the misfortune of meeting them,' Lillian said sweetly, not in the least offended. 'I suspect your university wasn't too shabby, it's probably world renowned...' she was amused by Rowanne's transparent expression.

Rowanne smiled broadly, shaking her head in mock disgust. Lillian was just being herself; she didn't mean any malice. And strangely, she felt a kinship with her.

'I knew, Ms Knight, that you'd eventually come around to my way of thinking. One of the *adverse effects* of being in my company, for too long,' mocked Lillian.

'I think you'll find that I *choose* to put up with you,' retorted Rowanne.

Lillian got up and walked around the bedroom of her childhood; revisiting the past in each corner that held bittersweet memories for her. Her mood dampened, and she became sombre as she observed that the room had not been changed at all since she was last here.

Rowanne came up behind Lillian. 'It's being here, again... It's bringing back the past,' she said astutely.

Lillian turned to Rowanne, her expression crestfallen. 'Nothing has been changed. Almost like it's been frozen in time; a monument to the person I used to be.'

Rowanne didn't know what to say, and wisely chose to listen instead.

'Do you know, the last time I saw this bedroom was the last night of my life,' Lillian had been about to say 'immortal' but caught herself at the last second.

'One thing puzzles me: I have heard of supernatural activity where the entity has been able to hurl heavy things as if they weigh nothing more than a feather-' Rowanne paused, and realised that she might inadvertently have caused offence to Lillian, whose eyebrow shot up as she looked at her drolly. *Oh, she thinks I'm talking about Alexander. But that hadn't even crossed my mind.* 'Sorry. But I really wasn't thinking of you,' she said sheepishly. 'What I'm trying to say is, that I have never heard of an account where the ghost could transport a person to another location...' said Rowanne pointedly as she steadily watched Lillian, wondering what explanation she'd give.

'Rowanne, I barely knew what I was capable of when I was alive, let alone what my possibilities are as one of the dead. Believe me when I say that I am just as in the dark as you are. You're one of the bravest humans I've ever met,' she said, smiling affectionately.

Rowanne didn't know whether to believe it, there was still a lingering doubt in her mind; Lillian was holding something back, she was sure of it. Something monumental, and for some reason Lillian felt that she could not trust her, yet. *I'm not sure if I want to know*, thought Rowanne apprehensively, but maintained an air of calm.

Lillian studied Rowanne closely. *You have to accept the truth one day. How long can any of us run away? No. Sometimes, we have to stand and face what we fear.*

'Are you sure we can be here?' asked Rowanne, hastily changing the subject.

'I brought you here because this is the last place they'd think to look. They're probably on their way to your apartment.'

'Who are *they*?' asked Rowanne, thinking of the only person it could be.

'Alexander and company, of course,' replied Lillian, looking sharply at Rowanne.

'You can be vague, sometimes.' *If not most of the time.* 'Can't you elaborate? Do you have an aversion to sharing what you know?' asked Rowanne.

Lillian smiled mischievously, and chose to reply in Rowanne's mind, *Let me share with you what I picked up in a certain impertinent human's mind, one day while I languished. Or, killed time to be more precise.*

Rowanne's expression paled considerably as her bravado slipped. She knew what was coming...

'I think perhaps, on second thoughts, I *should* share this with the rightful recipient: Alexander would find this information to be advantageous to your detriment,' said Lillian considerately.

A crimson blush spread furiously across Rowanne's cheeks. 'Don't you dare say anything of what you've learnt. Or, Ghost or not, you'll see the worst side of this 'human' as you so politely put it,' she looked at her wrathfully, daring Lillian to carry out her threat.

'Calm down. The colour actually puts some life back into you, it becomes you. I would not sink to such depths as spreading gossip, even if it's the truth,' she said knowingly, and smiled broadly at the look of disgust that marred Rowanne's face.

Rowanne turned away to suddenly occupy herself by looking around the room. After all, she needed to calm down. She was absentmindedly wandering about when a golden mirror caught her notice. She had barely glanced at it the first time around, but on closer inspection recognized the intricate carvings; the same demons and angels. Turning to Lillian, she said, 'I have got the exact copy of this mirror in my apartment except mine is made of wood. Where did you get yours from?'

'This mirror is very old; a family heirloom. It's been here ever since I can remember. The gothic intricacy is beautiful, is it not? If the gothic style could be encapsulated in a mirror, it would look something like this. Anyway, this is nothing compared to the rest of the house. Though unfortunately, I fear it wouldn't be safe to step outside these walls,' said Lillian.

Rowanne wondered if there was a company that specialised in making these beautiful creations.

'No, there is not. It's a speciality of my people,' replied Lillian.

Rowanne had actually gotten used to the fact that Lillian could read her mind. Besides, there was nothing she could do about it, anyway. 'I'd probably be arrested if I were to leave, right?' asked Rowanne.

'That, and much more you wouldn't want to face unnecessarily. Take my word for it.'

Rowanne looked around the room. It was clean as if someone regularly and lovingly maintained it; a testament of their love for Lillian.

'Speaking of the past, isn't it time that you finally laid some ghosts to rest?' asked Lillian. Rowanne's shoulders tensed and then slumped, as if she was resigned to the fact that she could not escape the truth any longer.

Rowanne went back to the bed and sat on the edge, her head down. 'Tell me. Tell me the truth. I'm so tired of running away, but I'm scared...'

Lillian sat beside Rowanne, and placed a ghostly arm around her shoulder. Rowanne looked up as she felt the air displaced around her, a gentle energy behind her neck.

Lillian took a deep breath. 'Have you ever wondered why it is that Mr Black is so very helpful towards you...?'

'Alexander is the type of man to help out anyone in need,' replied Rowanne magnanimously, even though she was deeply hurt that he had kept things from her.

'You are quick to defend the one who has been lying to you all this time,' said Lillian.

'I admit, when you first told me that Alexander had lied to me, I was very upset. And I still am,' said Rowanne.

'Need I remind you that was only a few minutes ago. How have you forgiven him so quickly?' asked Lillian, and wondered if there might not be something a little off with Rowanne rapidly switching between her emotions.

Rowanne noticed the look of confusion pass over Lillian, who probably thought that she was crazy, but wearily she began, 'Look, I didn't say that I had forgiven him. It's just that I'm still working through it. He has helped me a lot.' Rowanne held up a hand to stop Lillian from interrupting, 'I know what you're going to say: that he only helped me because he felt guilty at hiding whatever it is from me. I am not a complete fool, contrary to what you may think.' Rowanne gathered her courage and asked, 'It's really bad, isn't it? I don't think I want to know what you're going to tell me...'

Lillian sighed, heavy with the knowledge that she'd have to pass on to Rowanne. 'It's true, Alexander helped you for his own selfish reasons and to ease his own burden. Where do I begin...'

'I find it helps to start at the beginning and to end with a bombshell.' Rowanne tried to lighten the sombre mood that hung in the air.

'How can you joke at a time like this?!' exclaimed Lillian, incredulous at the sheer tenacity that was Rowanne.

'It's better than the alternative,' said Rowanne, who didn't feel nearly as nonchalant as she pretended to be.

'Well, let's get on with it. Do you remember what happened last Thursday?' asked Lillian gravely, carefully studying Rowanne at each juncture of the truth that she would reveal to her.

'I worked late into the night last Thursday. I fell asleep and woke up in the early hours of Friday morning,' replied Rowanne.

'Can you remember anything else, did anything unusual happen? Do you have any lapses in memory?' asked Lillian, and watched with unease as a green light slowly began to encircle Rowanne's head; though she was far from being aware that it was passing before her face. Humans could not perceive the subtle nuances of magic, and why would they?

Rowanne felt the familiar feeling of sick dread that sat in the pit of her stomach, always waiting for the opportunity to get out and decimate her with a mind splitting migraine that would come on slowly, and continue to build should she try to recall things better left forgotten.

'I don't think it's a good idea for me to even attempt to remember,' said Rowanne.

'Trust me. Nothing will happen to you. You have to get past the block in your mind, however painful it may be. You are not alone in your suffering this time, I'm here and I've got you.' Lillian smiled encouragingly at Rowanne, and concentrated hard so that she could hold her hand in support.

Rowanne looked up in shock, 'How is it even possible that I can actually feel the weight of your hand in mine?'

'It's difficult...' *and I'm sure I'll pay for it dearly, later on.* Each time that Lillian exerted power, she became weaker and tended to fade away far more quickly, as well as not being able to hold onto her form for long. 'But not impossible,' she finished.

Rowanne decided that if Lillian could bear discomfort on her behalf, then she could do no less than face her own. She reached far back into her mind to the events of last Thursday evening, and closed her eyes to help block out her surroundings to zero in completely to what she had been missing.

In her mind, she saw herself working late. She remembered thinking that the weather looked bad as if it would rain... What about it?

'Say it aloud, then I can walk this journey with you. I can help to prompt your mind, at the very least.' Lillian looked at the stubborn determination in the set of Rowanne's shoulders and the way her face was all screwed up as she tried furiously to recall her lost memories. She was proud of her.

'I remember finishing work and grabbing my coat and bag to leave-'

'Wait, hold on a minute. You said that you fell asleep at work. So, how could you have left? What's the true memory?' asked Lillian.

Rowanne was momentarily stunned with this insight. In her mind, she saw two scenes: the first was of her asleep at work. But when she peeled back the layer, she saw that it was superimposed onto a second; that of her leaving work, running down the stairs, and opening the doors to the cool night... it had been raining.

Lillian watched as the green light encasing Rowanne grew a shade darker and began to spin faster around her. Rowanne screamed, and fell back onto the bed.

'Rowanne, wake up. Wake up. What happened, what did you see?' Lillian asked, her voice was high pitched in terror. *What have I done to her...* she wondered.

Rowanne's head felt as if it had split apart: the migraine had exploded the moment she recalled leaving her work. It was if the pain were actually shielding her mind from delving any deeper into her blocked memories; it would only do more harm to her than good. Be that as it may, she needed to continue through the red haze.

'I'm standing outside of my place of work,' continued Rowanne, much to the admiration and sadness of Lillian, who could not understand how a human being could carry on through such debilitating pain.

Damn you, Alexander, for causing this poor woman so much suffering to hide the fact that you made a mistake. Was that what she really thought? Her conscience kicked in. After all, she too knew what it was like to break the rules and do the unforgivable; *I am undeniably lifeless proof of what happens as punishment.* At least they can live to regret, she thought hollowly.

'Lillian, are you there?' asked Rowanne faintly. 'I was worried when I couldn't feel you with me and thought perhaps you had gone.'

Lillian was snapped back to the present, and felt ashamed at being dragged back into her own tumultuous past, when before her was a living breathing person who needed her to be strong. *Rowanne was actually worried about me when she's in pain*, this brought a tear to her eye - a ghostly tear that evaporated within a matter of a second. She squeezed Rowanne's hand in encouragement to continue.

'I remember my grandmother's necklace glowing. Glowing?' she repeated to herself. Why had it done that? Maybe it had been a trick of the light, or... She had seen firsthand back at the apartment the power it contained, and shuddered.

'Anyway, I felt uneasy, as if someone were watching me. You know, that gut feeling you get that something's not quite right, but you can't put your finger on it.'

Lillian wondered yet again, if perhaps Rowanne was psychic, or ultra intuitive. *Human beings should not be so readily dismissed in our world*, thought Lillian.

Rowanne's breathing sped up as she remembered being chased in the rain by two men. 'Lillian. Lillian, there were men after me...! What is it that I can't recall?' and she began to hyperventilate.

'Calm down, Rowanne. Just breathe,' said Lillian, as she tried soothing Rowanne's mind. She had to use more of her power to bring Rowanne back to the present, so she could calmly revisit the past; not that she would find any peace there. Lillian felt anxious as her hands slipped in and out of focus. *So, it's beginning again...* But she was determined not to let on to Rowanne.

Rowanne felt herself being rocked back and forth, and slowly her panic became manageable to the point at which she could continue with the memory.

'It is pouring down with rain, and men are throwing things at me — spears! Can you believe that?' asked Rowanne, incredulous at what she was witnessing. 'Can this be right, or is my mind making this up?' she asked hopefully; fully in denial.

'You tell me, Rowanne. It's your mind, after all. You should know it better than anybody else!' said Lillian, trying to get her to face the inevitable.

Rowanne felt peeved at the useless response, but the anger took away from the fear. *Guess I should be grateful for her scorn.* She remembered running in the dark towards the car park, thinking that if she could just get to her car, then she'd have a chance.

'Lillian, why can't you just read my mind, like before? Instead of me repeating everything,' *and living through it twice,* she thought sombrely.

What could Lillian say to that? She could have read Rowanne's mind, but that would require more effort, and that meant using more of her energy; she was already fading. 'Rowanne, I am truly sorry. I don't know what I was thinking. Go ahead, I will see what you see.'

Rowanne relaxed at the thought of viewing her ordeal once; that was enough for anyone, especially if they wanted to remain sane.

Rowanne felt a warm and tingling sensation, and then unbelievably, Lillian appeared right beside her in the memory, which was frozen into place. Turning to her, Rowanne asked in astonishment, 'How is this even possible? I can now walk around my memory and observe it from any angle without it hurting me. Look, even those men are frozen. Remarkable.'

Rowanne walked to the two men who had frozen in mid run. Though their faces were blurry, the spears that they had thrown however, stood out in stark, sharp intricate detail. She could not believe how long they were. The wood glistened, and she could see the intricate metal work with the strange carvings that she could not understand. She noticed the water drops frozen on the sharp edge of the spear point — this was a weapon designed to kill fast and efficiently, when wielded in the right hands. Even though she could not see their faces to judge their expression, there was no doubt in her mind they had intended to kill her - but why? She didn't have the answer to that yet.

Lillian on the other hand, saw the scene for what it truly was. She could help Rowanne remember to a certain degree, so that she would know roughly what had happened to her, but all traces of Demon World were tied down in a strong magic. She could not believe how powerful Alexander was. She had always arrogantly presumed that her family were the deadliest and most powerful demons there ever were; she had been proven wrong with deadly consequences.

Now, yet again, she was being proven wrong by a demon who almost equalled her in his ability to intricately weave strong magic that was unbreakable at a deeper level. *I've only scratched the surface...* she thought, dismayed. She could not seem to get through any further than the superficial barrier.

Lillian walked around the Shadows and judging by their expressions, they appeared to be enjoying the hunt. The scent of fear only encouraged these lower level demons. Had they stumbled upon Rowanne by chance, or was it planned? If the latter, then it had to be a demon higher up in the ranks with the expertise and power to pull off this attack.

Why target Rowanne? What was it about her? wondered Lillian. Admittedly, Rowanne was no ordinary human; she had her ancestral necklace. How on earth had it ended up in Rowanne's family? Or, more precisely, in her grandmother's hands - that was the mystery. And it could be the clue that they so desperately needed, but the fact that she was adopted and had no recollection of her parents proved problematic.

Rowanne wanted to understand her memories but could they hurt her physically? Bravely, she touched the man before her expecting to make contact, but her hand passed straight through him. She was relieved to find that the memory was like a dream; she could not actually feel anything.

'Rowanne, I think we should make progress, I'll wind it forward for you,' said Lillian.

'Will I be observing it from the outside, or will I actually feel like the one being chased?' Rowanne felt nervous to continue, her stomach weighed her down with all the tension that it held there.

'Unfortunately if you experience it from the outside, then you will not have a complete memory. You won't know how you felt - it becomes stronger when you use all of your senses, helping you to remember. Don't forget, I'll be there right beside you. You will see me in the background, but I don't want to interfere with how you interact with it. However, I will give you the gift of freezing it, any time it becomes too much to face. I know this is bad enough! If you're ready, shall we continue?'

Rowanne shuddered and took a deep breath. The sooner she continued, the sooner it would all be over; damn the consequences! 'I'm ready,' she replied in a steady voice, despite not feeling the same confidence internally.

Slowly the scene began to play, and once more, she found herself running. Her heart was pounding as she ran beneath the rubbish streetlights that barely stayed on. Finally, the car park was in sight, and she tried to make a mad dash for it, only to find herself cornered at the angel fountain.

Where was Lillian when she needed her? Rowanne saw a ghostly figure behind the men; not that it gave her any courage. *They're going to kill me, what should I do?* She could hear the fountain roaring behind her. Suddenly, all sound ceased as the street lights started flashing on and off intermittently. Each time the lights came on they brought the attackers that much closer, and then they'd disappear in the darkness as the lights went out, concealing them, to her utter terror.

'Lillian. Lillian!' her mind started to freeze, her body wanted to shut down. Rowanne's mind became a blood-red haze of pain as the migraine began to splice her in half. She felt physically sick, and her legs were about to give out at any moment. She counted the number of times that the light went out, and the distance between her and them. She braced herself for the onslaught. *Not this time!* she thought defiantly. The pain increased with her stubborn refusal to back down, her vision started to go, and she didn't know how long she could hold on for.

The men were before her, murderous intent in their eyes, and she could not plead with them to let her go. There was not a shred of mercy in them.

Rowanne held up her arms to protect herself as the darkness closed in. The situation appeared dire, but strangely, help came from the last person she would have expected...

So, he was there... I'm not sure how I feel about this. Alexander pushed her behind him, and confronted her attackers with a broadsword. What the hell was he doing with a sword? He looked as though he had just come straight from an historical re-enactment, judging by his strange attire. Why was he dressed as a soldier?

'Lillian,' she called, but there was no answer, and there was so much that she wanted to ask her. Finally she spotted her in the distance, but she was fading in and out. *Oh my God, she's losing her power. What do I do if she completely fades, leaving me stuck in this nightmare?* Rowanne breathed heavily as she tried to move away from Alexander and the men, wanting to put distance between them. If she made it to her car, then she could possibly stop this memory and escape. Well, that was the plan.

I didn't even think about the cost to Lillian, how selfish can I be? Hold on Lillian, I'm coming for you, thought Rowanne, and took one step back, only to be blocked by Alexander's giant arm encircling her.

He turned his head around to look at her, 'Do you mind staying in one place? I'm trying to help you here.'

'I don't recall asking you to save me. I was doing very well on my own, I'll have you know.' *Who does he think he is?* She was in no way intimidated by him - though maybe of the weapon, she was not stupid.

He looked at her archly. 'Where's your weapon, then? How do you intend to fight them?' he asked scornfully.

'Sorry, but I think I left my *Chakram* in my other bag,' she replied sarcastically.

'What are you talking about?' he asked perplexed, clearly not getting the reference.

Rowanne looked at him steadily, and asked, 'Shouldn't you keep your eyes on those two?' indicating the men who had started to approach them, in no way fazed by Alexander.

He swiftly turned back to them, and replied over his shoulder, 'I'm more than a match for them.'

'Okay, Hercules,' this man was in another world, altogether. The men weren't backing down because there were two of them; plural. *What a moron.*

He surprised her then, by saying, 'Hercules is a myth — I'm the real thing. I wouldn't be so easily fooled by the gods. Now watch out for the man approaching you on the right, Xena,' sarcasm dripped from his voice. She missed the smile that unexpectedly crossed his face.

Rowanne didn't share Alexander's confidence, but at least she didn't feel alone; strength in numbers. 'Watch out!' she shouted, as both men rushed them at once, their swords aimed at them with deadly precision.

'Hold on,' whispered Alexander.

Rowanne missed what he had just said. Suddenly, Alexander grabbed her and spun around so fast that it made her head spin, and momentarily darkness enveloped her. Instinctively, she held onto him; as the only solid thing there was. She didn't want to faint, that was not going to help them in this situation in any way. She felt nauseous as she found herself on the ground sitting behind him.

What had just happened? Her memory was slightly fragmented. Rowanne looked around for Lillian, wanting to freeze the memory, but she was nowhere to be seen. More bizarrely was the fact that the two men were still in the exact same position, as if they had never moved.

Alexander helped her to her feet, and once more, pushed her behind him.

'Those men were running straight towards us... I thought we were about to be attacked. What's going on?' she asked.

'They haven't moved. You fainted and I caught you,' he stated matter-of-factly.

Rowanne didn't completely believe that this was the truth, judging by the looks of consternation on the men's faces. Not to mention they were panting as if they had exerted themselves. She knew that there was more going on than what she was being told.

How was it possible that she had been transported to another place? This was no mere ghostly activity, there was a bigger picture here, and more to the world than she had initially thought possible. Her familiar head splitting migraine came on, causing her knees to buckle, and as she quickly threw up her arms protectively in front of her face, miraculously the scene froze, but she still hit the ground and the pain in her knees felt real enough. *How is this possible? This isn't even real, it's already in the past. How can a recollection hurt me physically, just by reliving it?*

Rowanne clutched her head, and saw the image of Lillian freeze intermittently. She was trying to say something, but it was lost in the haze of pain that engulfed Rowanne's mind.

Rowanne's heart hammered as she saw a green flash in the distance. Then chillingly the memory started to unfreeze, or so it appeared, as Alexander began to move, slowly at first, inch by slow inch. *Oh my God... he's turning towards me*, thought Rowanne.

'Lillian!' screamed Rowanne, as she scooted away from him.

'Rowanne. I'm sorry...' she heard Lillian whisper, the second before she felt her presence leave. *Oh no.* She didn't know how long it would be before Lillian could gather enough energy to get back to her.

Rowanne tried to freeze the scene but it sped up, and at any moment Alexander would reach her. It was a battle of wills, and she was failing. Alexander had by this time completely turned around. He was saying something, but it was muffled, almost as if she had cotton wool in her ears.

Rowanne closed her eyes and balled her fists in an effort to retain control of her own mind. She shut herself off from her surroundings to the point that she missed the sound of footsteps approaching her...

'What do you think you're doing?' asked an angry male voice.

Rowanne's heart skipped a beat as she froze. But slowly she opened her eyes to be met with the sight of two blazing sapphire eyes, glaring down at her with deadly intent.

'This isn't supposed to happen like this... You should not have been able to do that...' mumbled Rowanne, sounding crazy to her own ears.

Alexander looked at her steadily, and, stifling a yawn, offered her his hand. 'Look, I don't know what you're talking about, but we should really get back over there,' pointing his sword in the direction of the two frozen men, as if the memory would only continue once she got back into her original position.

Rowanne knocked his hand back and quickly got up and pointed at him accusingly. 'Who, or what the hell are you?' she asked angrily, petrified at the same time.

Alexander looked towards the men, and then slowly back at her, smiling, as he replied, 'Well, for one thing, I'm animate... What did you do to them?' he asked, looking at her admiringly as he took one step towards her.

'Just wait right there! Don't you dare come any closer, I'm warning you.' Rowanne took an involuntary step back to maintain a distance between them.

Alexander looked perplexed, and shrugging his shoulders, put his sword away in the scabbard on his back. He took another step closer, completely ignoring her warning, and shook her hand. 'Nice to meet you. Alexander Black at your service, and you are?'

Rowanne looked at him dumbfounded; this fake Alexander of her memory was just as annoying as the real one. For now, at least, it appeared as if he didn't mean her any harm.

'Do I look like some kind of crazy man to you?' asked Alexander, aggravated.

I don't know, you tell me, she thought. Maybe he really was unhinged; he had gone from polite to peculiar in less than a minute.

'Look here, Rowanne. I am not the sort of man to harm a woman. And I take great offence to the fact that you briefly entertained the idea.'

Rowanne was shocked, 'How did you know that, and how do you know my name?'

She took another step back while keeping her eyes firmly on him, waiting to see what his next move would be.

'You are broadcasting your thoughts loud enough. And in answer to your original question: this is your mind, you can do whatever you like here. I suspect you didn't want me to be like them... What is it that you want to know?' he asked, appearing earnest. He began to walk around her, his eyes never leaving her.

Rowanne was forced to move; she didn't want him where she could not see him, but managed to back up to the fountain, where she had a perfectly good view of him.

He approached slowly and stood a little away, sensing that she didn't want him too close. 'Look, your subconscious is trying to tell you something... You've just got to ask the right questions,' said Alexander, his eyes blazing with an emerald fire.

Weirdly, Rowanne noticed that his clothing had changed from a soldier's outfit to a more casual look: jeans and a jumper — it's crazy what the mind can conceive of at the most random moments, she thought.

Looking down, he smiled, 'I don't mind the clothes, are they more to your liking?'

'That wasn't me,' she replied weakly, not knowing what was real. But it had not escaped her notice that he still wore the sword at his back; why would her mind not change that tiny detail? It was her mind after all, right...?

'Rowanne, you're fighting your own mind, not me. Why are you making it so difficult for yourself?' asked Alexander.

'I don't know,' she admitted resignedly. 'But I'm not doing this on purpose, and I'm only being shown half of the truth, not the entirety.' Rowanne watched Alexander's expression carefully. Something felt off with him, as well, for no matter how much she tried to freeze him into place, it didn't work. He seemed to be the only thing in her mind that she could not control, which made her suspicious. How was it possible that he was here right now…? Her world as she knew it was carefully dismantling piece by piece.

Alexander smiled broadly and looked at her with a strange expression that made her nervous.

'There's nothing funny about this situation,' said Rowanne.

'I was just thinking, you've come a long way since I first met you,' he mocked her by encompassing the immediate area.

'How do you know that — wait, don't answer. You'll just say something like: "I am a part of your memory, of course I'd know", am I right?' she asked wearily.

'Well done, you're finally getting it. When do you want to continue?' he asked light heartedly. But there was an intensity to his eyes that didn't quite match the tone of his voice.

'I want to continue, but I'm afraid that my mind will block certain parts of this memory, even if I get to the end, which is looking further away each time.'

Alexander became solemn, and sat down and moved closer to her, encouraged by her not moving away. Building up his courage, he asked, 'Do you really want to know the truth? I promise that if you do, I'll support you, and... you will no longer suffer any pain, you have my word on that. And I'm a man who will never break his word,' he appeared tense as he awaited her answer.

Rowanne really looked at him, and took her time to observe him. *I think this really is Alexander!* As crazy as it sounded to her. He felt different from the other two, who behaved as if they were on a loop, like a film that continually plays the same scene, whereas Alexander was actually interacting with her, saying things that she was fairly certain her mind had not made up. She decided to keep this nugget to herself.

After all, Lillian had said that Alexander was keeping something from her... How had he known about her headaches? It was like he was apologizing for them. *What could be so bad that he doesn't want me to know? And more to the point, how has he been blocking my memories?* That was one thing she could not forgive him for, if her theory proved correct.

Squaring her shoulders and crossing her arms, she turned to Alexander and asked the monumental question, 'Was it you all along that stopped me from remembering the events of last Thursday?' She looked at him solemnly.

Green flames flickered dangerously in Alexander's eyes as he looked at her intensely. His mouth was set in a grim line, as he replied, 'Yes... Only because I believed that it was for your highest good.'

Rowanne was furious, and gripped him by the arms. 'Who are you to decide what I should or should not remember? How dare you interfere with my mind like this!' she said, as she shook him by the shoulders.

Alexander gabbed her hands and carefully held them in his own. 'Calm down, Rowanne. I'll explain everything.' She took a deep breath. Strangely, she did not move her hands away; maybe she needed the comfort as much as he did. 'All your questions will be answered, but you will have to relive the whole of the memory without stopping. And this time, *you will* remember everything...' he made it sound like a promise and a threat. 'If you are sure, I'll start the memory. Do not fear, you will be aware at every stage. I'm warning you that you will find it uncomfortable and there will not be a thing you can do about it. You will feel the pain, but the migraine will not save you, this time. Yes, you heard correctly,' he said, at the dawning comprehension in her eyes. 'I thought that I was helping you when I placed the blocks in your mind,' he waited for her reply.

'What are you, a hypnotist?'

'If I replied in the affirmative, then that would be a lie. You have to be willing to see the truth for yourself. And are you sure you want to know what I really am? Presently, you have a comfortable world view, do you really want to venture into the unknown?' asked Alexander. There was a finality to the question.

Rowanne knew what he was asking of her, but she no longer cared to live in ignorance, no matter how peaceful a state it appeared to be - it was an illusion, after all. And why had she become a journalist if not to venture into the unknown and find the truth?

'I too shall go into the abyss and wade through chaos under eternal night, the space between heaven and hell,' said Rowanne cryptically. Her necklace glowed warmly beneath her clothes in response to this truth which it upheld. Something stirred within her, as if similar words had been uttered before... Was she remembering something? Maybe - this felt like an echo of the past, but not her past.

Alexander studied Rowanne coolly. Her eyes had changed to a combination of green and a strange silvery metallic violet which he had never before seen in a demon's eyes. Rowanne was changing in ways he could never have imagined; it frightened him, and he was a man who didn't frighten easily. What had he done to her... Her eyes returned to their normal green and the strange aura around her dissipated as quickly as it had come.

Rowanne looked at him questioningly, 'What are you so worried about? I'm the one who's about to step into the unknown.'

'*Paradise Lost*?' he asked wryly, a smile tugging at his mouth.

'Yes. I like Milton,' replied Rowanne awkwardly, thinking that she must have said something stupid; her mind had been in a daze.

'Good book,' he mused.

'I'm ready,' said Rowanne. *I have probably just signed my sanity away,* she thought unrepentantly, but she was determined now. And the fact that she would not suffer any more painful headaches fortified her. It was time; there was no turning back.

Alexander took her hands in his. 'Close your eyes,' he said softly, and as soon as she complied, his eyes bled to green, and the aura around him encompassed Rowanne. The green mist enveloped them both, and they disappeared from view.

Rowanne's heart hammered in her chest; she was aware of everything. The darkness receded and she found herself once more behind Alexander. His broad shoulders blocked her view. She felt the cold sensation of the rain that had started to fall. It was dark and only the streetlamps offered a measly light. Taking a deep breath, she faced what her mind had refused to accept the first time around.

Stepping around Alexander, Rowanne tensed and clamped her mouth shut as she stifled a scream. Before her were not men - the light revealed them to be monsters born of shadow; they were a macabre imitation of men.

Rowanne shuddered, her heart beating fast. No wonder Alexander had wanted to block this image from her mind. And it was only going to get worse... If they were shadows, then how were they able to hold the spears that they so expertly wielded? Surely they should drop through? Her mind tried to distract her from the horror show.

No, what I need now is not to be shielded. And why was it that Alexander did not seem in the least bit frightened? *I bet he really didn't come from a medieval fair.* Her doubts from before were amplified, and not to mention the fact that he carried a sword. She had been right to be suspicious of him.

What in the world was going on? She kept a wary eye on the two 'Shadow men' as she now referred to them. She felt her necklace glow beneath her clothes; it felt hot to the touch, and seemed to heat up when she got too close to them

- it was like a warning device. *I have to ask Grandmother Angelique about this, and when and if I get back, we are going to have a very long chat; excluding all talk of men!*

She watched Alexander engage with the nearest Shadow man. He seemed unfazed by their situation, as he remarkably wielded the sword as if he actually knew what he was doing. Dare she say, he even appeared to be enjoying it. *What a complete and utter lunatic. If I had my way, I'd be in my car by now and speeding away.* As it was, she was stuck with this oaf who fancied himself a warrior.

Alexander briefly turned to her in mid battle and winked before turning back, and raising his sword in a block, just as the Shadow man's spear came down hard; they were much stronger than their wispy appearance would initially suggest.

Suddenly, Rowanne spied the second Shadow man sneaking up on Alexander. She wanted to shout: 'watch out' but it was too late - he had already hurled the spear straight for the back of an unsuspecting Alexander.

Rowanne didn't even take a second to decide as she hurled herself in front of the spear's trajectory. She gasped as she felt the momentary sensation of pain all over again. And as she fell, the darkness claimed her long before she hit the icy water of the fountain.

Rowanne screamed in her mind. Despite being able to see everything, she was powerless to do anything, firmly entrenched in the memory. She was numb. *So, that's what happened... I died.*

Why would Alexander stop me from remembering? A million thoughts fluttered in her mind, but she could not hold onto a single one.

Rowanne fully expected to wake from the memory; it was the end, after all. But she was proven wrong as it continued.

In her mind's eye, she saw Alexander's shock at seeing her floating dead in the fountain. She watched the rain pound down on them both, washing away the tears that fell down his face. A lump formed in her throat; she didn't know whether she was crying for him, or for her passing.

Very gently, Alexander bent down and lifted her body from the fountain, taking incredible care as he carried her. *How did he know where I worked?* she wondered, as he strode through her office. She was still in awe of the doors opening remarkably of their own volition before him. There was definitely more to Alexander than she could have imagined, and she had a feeling that she was going to find out a great deal more before the night was out.

She felt herself being laid gently onto the couch. But in the next instant it became really strange, as Alexander pulled out a knife with unusual writing inscribed along the length of its side. She silently screamed, as he cut his palm, and then did the same with her right palm. He joined their bleeding hands, and whispered words she could not fully make out.

All that she could essentially understand from it was of Alexander losing something very important because he had saved her. She had looked away when he had pulled the spear out of her; some things were better not witnessed, the pain was real enough.

The overall impression she got was of Alexander's infinite kindness and care towards her as he treated her injuries. She should be dead, that much was evident. And how she was still alive was a mystery; but it was thanks to Alexander that she was still here.

He had performed a ritual that had tied her to him. He had somehow used his life force to bring her back from the netherworld and she had felt her spirit being pulled back. Rowanne could not recall for the life of her where her spirit had been before coming back — that was a mystery. Also, her life had not flashed before her eyes, but she did remember surrendering to an infinite darkness.

It was slightly disconcerting to Rowanne, the way that Alexander had looked at her for the longest time before leaving. She was not only reliving her memory first hand, but also observing it as an outsider. She saw her body paradoxically being cocooned in energy made up of light and dark. And bizarrely a strange tattoo glowed near her heart before fading away.

Finally, she observed herself waking up in the early hours of the next morning, as her body had fully recuperated and healed itself. Abruptly the memory ended, and her eyes snapped open as she found herself laying on Lillian's bed.

A thin sheen of perspiration coated Rowanne's face and her hands felt clammy. She tried to speak but her throat felt a little hoarse. 'Lillian. Lillian, are you there?' but there was no reply.

Rowanne felt disoriented and sick. *Where am I, really?* she panicked. It would have been nice to believe the story of her being magically transported to another place, but everything she had witnessed suggested otherwise.

Gingerly she tried to get up, but fell back. Her body felt sore, as if she really had been battered and bruised. And she felt a deep pain within her heart, as if her mind and body mourned for her. She had to remind herself that she was alive. But at what cost... She needed to speak with Alexander, however hard it may be for him; after all, he alone knew the truth.

How did she feel about what he had done? She could not answer that yet. However, when she assessed her feelings, she got the strong sense that she didn't blame him. She felt that perhaps Alexander blamed himself. *Oh my God, he must have been carrying this burden ever since the night of the attack.*

Rowanne was indebted to him for saving her life, and felt great sorrow for what he too had gone through; it went a long way towards explaining why he behaved the way he did with her — she did not excuse his behaviour, but rather, understood it better.

Rowanne knew that Alexander was concealing a great deal more from her. *I want to know who he really is. And what were those creatures, and how have they come into the world?* Perhaps the world had always been this way and she had simply been sleepwalking through it, blindly following and never truly questioning, but then, she had never had a reason to wonder if it was other than what she perceived it to be.

Rowanne held herself completely still as she suddenly heard footsteps coming down the corridor. *I need to get out of here,* she thought. There was a sudden flash to her side which startled her, but thankfully it was Lillian, who kept flickering in and out.

'Rowanne, I am truly sorry for everything. I can't keep myself together,' said Lillian.

The instant that Lillian reappeared, Rowanne quickly replied, 'Never mind that now. Someone's coming, what shall we do?' The footsteps were getting closer, and whoever it was would soon be right outside the door.

'The wardrobe, hurry.' Lillian disappeared.

With no time to spare, Rowanne wrenched open the door and flung herself into the giant mahogany wardrobe and managed to close it behind herself just as someone walked into the room. She held her breath, her heart hammering. If anything should happen this time, it would be permanent. This was not a memory she could wake up from - this was real life!

She nearly jumped when she felt a tap on her shoulder.

'Shhh, it's me. Don't make a sound. I'll get you out of here as soon as I am able.' Lillian stood close to Rowanne, and together they strained to hear what was happening on the other side of the thick doors.

'Ah, my dear, I find you here? I was looking all over for you. Are you packed?'

'Yes, Lady Enid. I've almost got everything ready, and I'll come over as soon as I've finished up. I thought I would check to see that everything is in order before I depart.'

'When was the last time you went over?' asked Lady Enid.

'It's been a while... You know that my time is more valued here than in that other world!' she said distastefully.

'Alexander will be pleased to see you again,' said Lady Enid.

Rowanne turned to Lillian, and mouthed silently, 'It's Lady Enid on the other side. I'm sure she could help us.'

'Don't even think about going out there if you value your life. I can't quite make out who the other person is, although she sounds very familiar.'

Rowanne looked perplexed as she asked, 'The lady spoke of the 'other world', what is she talking about? And she seems to know Alexander.' Lillian was hiding things from her, again. All the new people she had encountered over the past two weeks all knew each other. Either the world was a small place, or...

'Look, I'll explain everything when we get back. Just listen for now.'

Rowanne didn't like it. But neither could she expect a full blown confession in a wardrobe of all places; not to mention the fact that they were not alone.

Rowanne had a strong urge to open the door slightly, to see what was happening with her own eyes.

'Don't be stupid!' said Lillian, angrily.

'I was not really going to open the door,' replied Rowanne in a pained voice.

'Let us go. I've booked you a hotel. I know, the things we have to put up with on the other side,' said Lady Enid.

Rowanne heard them leave, as well as the distinct sound of a trolley being wheeled. Finally, the door shut behind them. She took a deep breath and let it out slowly, and waited a moment before she built up the nerve to step outside of the wardrobe.

'That was close. Come on, let's get out of here,' said Rowanne.

'Give me a minute. I'm completely depleted, it's going to take a while for me to recharge,' said Lillian.

'What if they come back?' Rowanne had visions of herself being caught and of the possible consequences.

Lillian was in her own world. Rowanne watched her trying to build the violet light vortex. *Best not to disturb her, then.* She wandered over to the window, pulling aside the heavy drapery before peeking out.

She got the shock of her life when she realised that she was in fact in the same place that she had dreamt of: there was the familiar fountain in the courtyard, she vividly remembered Lillian sitting there when she had been alive, talking to Driskell. The web they were all in was getting decidedly tighter. And Rowanne could almost feel the silken cords tighten around her neck; she was being pulled deeper and deeper into the mystery.

Thankfully, there was no one outside. It was midnight here, as well, and a million stars seemed to light the night sky, but she could not enjoy the view as she was suddenly pulled roughly back from the window.

'What do you think you're doing? Do you have a death wish? You could have been seen!' said Lillian, angry at Rowanne's lack of self preservation.

'Do you mind! There was no one there. I was perfectly safe,' said Rowanne, annoyed at being wrenched back.

'I can tell you for a fact that we have soldiers guarding this palace twenty four hours a day. And that if you'd been there a moment more, you'd have been spotted. And it's best you not know how that would end.'

The colour drained from Rowanne's face, and she sat on the edge of the bed.

'Come here, I think I'm ready,' said Lillian.

Rowanne stepped through the purple flames that now surrounded Lillian, and held on, her head rested against Lillian's shoulder. She closed her eyes as Lillian waved her hand to close the circle.

The vortex began to spin faster and faster, and Rowanne was sure that any moment now, they'd vanish and get back to her apartment, or Alexander's - she didn't quite know how it all worked.

After a couple of moments of nothing happening, Rowanne opened her eyes. The vortex had lost speed and was slowly coming to a halt. 'What's happening? I thought we'd have left by now,' said Rowanne.

'You're taking everything remarkably well for a human who's just had her world turned upside down...'

Rowanne looked at her sardonically. 'Well, I guess you could say that. This is my life now. I have to get used to it and fast. Why isn't your magic show working?'

'That's not funny. When you're being strung up in the dungeon, that smirk will leave you fast enough. And besides, I'm out of juice. I have no more of an idea of what to do than you.'

Suddenly, the door slammed open, causing Rowanne to jump back in fear, her heart nearly giving out as she stood guiltily with Lillian, who moved protectively in front of her.

'What are *you* doing here?' asked Rowanne. She had not been expecting him, especially here of all places. Perhaps she shouldn't be surprised anymore when it came to him.

'Nice to see *you* too,' replied Alexander, closing the door behind him, and leaning against it. 'I see I've reached you just in time to save you — again!' Alexander thanked Demon World that he had made it in time; though evidently, he was the last person in the world that she wanted to see. It's not like he enjoyed this, either.

'I find it incredibly annoying when you say that. I think I must have heard it a dozen times already. Let me make it quite clear: I am in no way a damsel in distress!'

Alexander laughed, replying caustically, 'That remains to be seen. Do you intend to spend the whole night here, or would you be willing to accept some assistance?' he asked in a sickly sweet voice that he was pleased to see irked Rowanne to no end.

Arrogant, conceited... thought Rowanne. 'For your information, *we* have the situation well in hand. Lillian is going to zap us back at any moment. So, you can go on your merry way.' Rowanne returned his measured look, but for some reason Alexander seemed to find it highly amusing as he turned to leave.

'Alexander?' Lillian spoke to his back, just as he held the doorknob.

He didn't turn around but stood still.

'Lillian, just let him go, we'll be fine,' said Rowanne, but her cheeks reddened at the pained expression on Lillian's face. And comprehension slowly and painfully dawned on her; they'd be forced to accept his help.

'Rowanne, quiet!' snapped Lillian. 'Alexander, I have no more energy to transport her tonight, let alone hold onto this form. I humbly request your help in getting her back home.'

He turned around smugly. 'I would love nothing more than to help Ms Knight to return to where she belongs,' he said bitingly. His eyes lit up as he focused his sole attention on the highly offended human before him.

'Let's just get this over with. Wait a minute,' and looking at Lillian, Rowanne asked, 'why can't you come with us? Especially if Alexander is helping.'

Alexander momentarily looked at Rowanne in surprise at her deigning to praise him. He reconsidered the fact in the same instance, as she made it a point to ignore him.

'Rowanne, I cannot come at this very moment, and who knows how long it will be before I can come back there. You do not have the luxury of time as the dead do, you have a life to get back to, and people you answer to.' Lillian held up her hand to stop the argument. Turning to Alexander, she reiterated, 'Take her back, for me. We'll talk later.'

Alexander nodded once in acceptance, and watched Lillian whisper into Rowanne's ear before floating through the door.

'I can't believe she just left,' said Rowanne, looking at the door. She turned back to Alexander, with a worried look on her face. 'Do you think she'll be safe here? Can't you get her to go with us? I'm sure she'd listen to you.'

Alexander looked at Rowanne, a pained expression on his face, 'Lillian is more than capable of looking after herself. And she would find it highly offensive if I offered to help her; she is my superior, after all.'

Rowanne was disgusted with him, he had not even attempted to try and persuade Lillian. She headed towards the door, intending to stop her. Sometimes the only person you could rely on was yourself.

'Where on earth do you think you're going?' asked Alexander severely.

'Well, if you aren't willing to stop her, then I will.' Rowanne was about to turn the door handle when Alexander's hand shot out, holding the door in place. She twisted the handle but to no avail - he was an enormous brute and the door held. She looked up at him crossly but was met with a look of boredom, as if all this was beneath him.

'Kindly move your hand,' she said politely, her teeth bared in a smile.

Alexander just laughed. 'No. Look, you're wasting my time as much as your own. Trust me when I say that this course of action is pointless. And you will certainly end up causing Lillian trouble.'

Rowanne grabbed his arm and was about to pull, when Lillian poked her head through the door and looked sternly at her. 'For the love of everything that is holy, will you just go with him? I don't need you needlessly risking your life when I've explicitly told you that I will come back as soon as I am able. There are some matters that need to be taken care of here.' She didn't wait for a reply as she ducked back out.

Rowanne was fuming, and glared at the obstinate fool who stood before her smirking. *How childish.* She pulled herself together. *Just move past this humiliation*, she thought. Lillian definitely reminded her of Grandmother Angelique, who was sweet, but could also reduce an adult to size. Why was it that parents and grandparents alike had the ability to turn people into quivering children?

'I did-' replied Alexander, but was cut off.

'Shut up, don't even think of finishing that sentence!' said Rowanne.

Alexander glowered at Rowanne, who had the ability to drive him crazy. She was more like Lillian than she knew; that same acerbic demeanour. *The women of this world, honestly!* and Rowanne being the latest addition was definitely no improvement.

Rowanne got a bizarre image of an Amazon chasing poor Alexander, it was such a ridiculous vision that she burst out laughing.

'What's so amusing?' asked Alexander dryly, not in the least bit fazed by her sudden bout of lunacy.

Rowanne sobered up as Alexander stood before her with his arms open, a mad look in his eyes. She took a step back. 'What the hell do you think you're doing?' she asked, giving him a sympathetic look; perhaps he really had lost it. *He thinks he likes me; how delusional can the poor man get.*

Oh, for the love of Demon World, not again! She really needs to stop believing that she's God's gift to demons. Alexander composed himself and smiling wickedly, replied, 'I think that should be obvious...' and took another step towards her, forcing her to turn with him so that she had her back to the door. He continued recklessly as he placed his hands on either side of her, against the door, trapping her. He looked at her steadily as his eyes began to change colour to green.

The impossible was happening right before her eyes. Lillian had done the same thing, but her eyes had also glowed violet. What was happening? Lillian was a ghost, so Rowanne assumed she'd have supernatural powers. But Alexander was a hundred percent human... Then how was it possible that he was doing this?

Rowanne ducked underneath his arms, and quickly turned around to face him. He laughed wickedly as he turned and leaned against the door, with his arms resting innocently behind him. She noticed that his eyes had returned to their normal sapphire.

'What were you doing?' Rowanne held her arm out, warning him to keep his distance.

But Alexander made no move to go towards her. 'I was trying to get us back,' he said, the very epitome of innocence.

Yeah right! He may look like an angel, but he's the devil in disguise. I wouldn't trust him with my life... Oh fine, she admitted begrudgingly he had saved her in the past, but still, she could not fully trust him.

'Lillian is a ghost; what are you? You're just a human, right?' Rowanne heard herself pleading and cringed internally.

Alexander looked at her as if she really were a child he had to explain it to patiently. 'Lillian is a ghost now, but she was not a *human* before... She's the same as me. Don't worry, I am alive. I'm a...' he paused at Rowanne's expression, which was one of disbelief. *Oh well,* he thought, and narrowing his eyes at her, he changed his eye colour, going through the three spectrums as her eyes widened.

Rowanne stared in amazement and disquiet as he vanished before her — actually vanished! Was this some kind of magic trick? She was unnerved by it, and suddenly felt the air displaced behind her as a cold breeze drifted across her neck. She stood completely still.

'Demon,' whispered Alexander by her ear, and watched as she jumped with fright, and then ran towards the door, flinging it open. She was so fast that he was momentarily taken aback.

Rowanne's mind had a hundred crazy ideas floating

about, each competing with the other for the most logical explanation, but sadly, all fell short of victory. *I need to get away from that psycho;* that was definitely the top priority.

Rowanne felt the door open behind her. A whirling wind seemed to be chasing at her heels, almost like a mini tornado, and when it had passed ahead of her, it dissipated, revealing Alexander stood before her in all his demonic glory.

He looked incensed, 'You could at least have come up with something original.'

'Stay right there, I'm warning you,' said Rowanne.

'This is becoming mind numbingly tedious. You asked what I was, and now you're not happy with the answer I provided. For the love of Demon World, what am I supposed to do with you...'

'Demon World? Where's that? Have I died and gone to hell?' asked Rowanne, bewildered.

'Not here. Get back in there!' Alexander said agitatedly. He had not meant it to sound like an order. He walked towards Rowanne, and was relieved when she started backing away; well, at least she was heading in the right direction. *Lunatic! She really does have a death wish.* He kept an ear open in case they had attracted unwanted attention; he'd be fine, but his wild half demon would face the death sentence.

Rowanne glared at him whilst walking back slowly, not wanting to turn her back to him. She felt the door knob behind her and turned it, opening the door, and once more she was back in Lillian's bedroom. She went straight to the back wall, and leaned against it, her arms crossed defensively before her. She watched Alexander with hawk eyes - he could in no way sneak up behind her now; but it was cold comfort. She'd probably seen it all now. Ghosts, she could deal with, if Lillian was any example to go by, but demons — she was out of her depth there; as she thought of the Shadow men, and now Alexander.

Alexander felt like gouging his eyes out just to have

something interesting to do, rather than deal with Rowanne. He sat on the bed, he didn't care now if it made her nervous. They had to leave and soon. And at least if she should attempt to jump out of the window, he could catch her, or...

Rowanne had the image of herself hurling out of the window flash in her mind: it was like the words painted an image, and she was sure it was Alexander projecting his thoughts. *Weird, maybe it's a side effect of dying — I get superpowers!*

'I'm not completely stupid, nor do I have a death wish,' she said to Alexander, her anger fortifying her in dealing with him; it was better than being scared out of her wits.

'Could have fooled me,' he said tiredly, rubbing his scalp. He looked at her angrily, 'We haven't got time for this, we have to go.'

'I've got questions that need to be answered first!' she said defiantly.

'Rowanne, if you persist in delaying, you may as well sign our death warrants, and that includes Lillian's. You may not care for my life, but I suspect you do care what happens to her.'

Rowanne thought carefully, taking into consideration the fact that they were not exactly in the safest place to have a lengthy conversation. 'You are extremely annoying for a demon. Are all demons like this, or does the accolade solely apply to you?' she asked earnestly, just to spite him, and smiled as she hit her target. Alexander gave her a glacial look.

Do not kill her. Do not kill the spiteful human; clearly deficient in manners. Looking at her murderously, he replied grimly, 'You tell me.'

Maybe it's not a good idea to antagonise a demon, thought Rowanne. *What the hell was he talking about?* she wondered, the smugness leaving her. 'How would I know? I'm human.'

She said it as if it were a badge of honour that she wore, something to be proud of, he noted. *Oh, how the mighty fall!* Alexander looked at her calculatingly, and replied bluntly,

'Only half, my love. The other side of you is like me,' he smiled maliciously.

'You complete and utter-'

'Now now, Rowanne, such language does not become a fine *human*, such as yourself,' he cut her off before she could finish.

They heard shouting down below followed by hurried footsteps coming up the stairs.

'Intruder alert! All guards to the Princess's Room.'

'Fantastic, I knew this would happen. Well done. Care to waste any more time? Perhaps you'd care to explain to the guards exactly what you were doing in this room of all places, in the palace and home of the First Family.'

There it was again, the same reference - who were the First Family? *Princess's room?* she wondered, feeling slow witted. Well, Lillian had told her that she belonged to a royal family. 'Look, Alexander, you have a lot of explaining to do once we get back. Do not for one moment think that you are going to get away with what you've done to me.' Her eyes were two glacial pools of ice with a fire raging just below the surface.

Wonderful, thought Alexander. *Get into line behind the others.* He'd deal with it later. 'Perfect, as you wish. But can you get up and come here?' He felt the last of his patience slipping, and held his arms open, looking at her with the very devil in his eye; he was fuming. If she didn't get up in the next instant...

Rowanne got up quickly, and not just because of the weird look that had come into his eyes — the guards helped to spur her on. She stood before him just outside the vicinity of his arms. Glaring at him, she asked, 'What am I supposed to do now?' She crossed her arms, and refused point blank to step into his.

Demon help me, I have never met a more stubborn person. 'Rowanne. Get. Here. Now!' he said each word slowly and deliberately, his voice threatening her with unmentionable consequences if she continued to stand there woodenly.

They heard footsteps on the other side of the door, where they came to a stop, and watched as the door handle turned. Rowanne's heart was in her mouth and perspiration beaded on her forehead. Finding the door to be locked, they started banging on it. 'Open up, in the name of our Lady of the Morning Star Clan. I repeat, open up now! Or you will face the death penalty without trial!' the guard's voice thundered and barked on the other side; it sounded like it belonged to someone who did not suffer fools well.

I think I'd lose my head as well as my jester's hat explaining my presence here, thought Rowanne. After all, this was not her world. Slowly the dawning magnitude of where she was began to sink in, instantly sobering her up. *No wonder he looks as if he wants to kill me; I'm putting more than my own life at risk,* and slapping herself metaphorically in the head at her callous behaviour, she didn't waste any more time.

'Well, shall we go?' asked Alexander quietly. Rowanne saw the firestorm rage in his eyes as they changed from sapphire to the darkest green.

Rowanne stepped forward, needing no further encouragement. Well, almost; there was still that last step between them. She looked him dead in the eyes, but would have preferred to look elsewhere - this was a bit too close for her liking. But in the next instant it went up a notch to an altogether uncomfortable degree.

Alexander waved his hand, and green fire leapt from it to settle over the door, ensuring that it would not open until after they left. With that problem sorted, he turned the full power of his gaze onto Rowanne; who squirmed beneath his attention.

'I think you will find this more comfortable if you take the last step and put your arms around me,' he said matter-of-factly. He didn't want her to misunderstand him in any way: they didn't have time. A demon greater than himself could come along at any moment and obliterate the door into smithereens; and then slowly torture them.

Rowanne realised that he was genuine in what he was saying and didn't have an ulterior motive. She turned off her internal chatter and took the last step. Closing her eyes, she put her arms around Alexander, and locked her hands together behind his back.

She still had the memory of coming with Lillian to this world: it had been hard, and taken a toil; she'd felt sick. She was not taking any chances this time, and if that meant a slight discomfort, so be it.

Alexander began to weave his hands and speak in a language that Rowanne could not understand. Bright green fire encircled them both, but most disturbing to Alexander were the violet flames that started to emanate from Rowanne. This unexpected power started to weave itself amongst his magic, and he didn't like the look of it one single bit; especially, as it started to mix and entwine the power of Rowanne and himself together.

He looked suspiciously at Rowanne, but she was completely unaware, as her forehead rested lightly on his chest. He could feel her arms locked around his waist as if she were holding on for dear life.

'Have we left yet?' she asked sarcastically, hearing the soldiers on the other side bashing the door trying to break it open, she continued, 'What's taking so long? Lillian would have had us out in a flash,' her voice rife with irritation. Rowanne felt brave, especially with her eyes shut tight so that she didn't have to look at Alexander's actual expression. She imagined the annoyance that would probably settle over his features, and enjoyed the fact that she could infuriate him. She knew it was childish but he was really easy to rile; besides, she could not count the number of times the shoe had been on the other foot.

'Hold on,' said Alexander patiently, as he brought the

flames into a burning frenzy, the cyclone of fire spinning faster and faster until they were hidden within its core. The fabric of the room began to waver, like a mirage in the desert. One moment they were standing before the bed, and the next, they had vanished into a portal that sealed closed behind them.

CHAPTER 19

Rowanne felt the ground beneath her feet fall away; they were rising up. She held tighter to Alexander, not wanting to fall. *Oh my God! this is worse than the first time;* it had seemed instantaneous then. So why did it feel like it was taking longer this time? She felt each agonizing moment.

Alexander lowered his arms, putting them around Rowanne, his hands interlocked lightly at her back; this way she'd feel more comfortable, and not have the frightening sensation of feeling as if she were falling. He was used to not having the ground beneath his feet when he travelled this way from Demon World to Earth, but for a human it could be petrifying. He admired the fact that Rowanne was maintaining an outward manner of calm.

It was a new sensation for him, carrying another being with him. He had travelled alone for so long, being sent wherever his duty took him, and he had not really stayed in one place too long when visiting Earth.

He revelled in the experience, which surprised him. Slowly the cyclone turned as they began to near their destination. Flashes of light pulsed around them as the fabric of space opened, and they slowly moved towards Earth. Alexander could not really see outside of the cyclone. There was only Rowanne and him, and it almost appeared as if they twirled within, as green and purple light flashed intermittently to play across their faces. He too closed his eyes briefly as they continued to dance their way across space and time. Alexander was close enough to Rowanne to feel her heart rate speed up, and smiled.

Alexander opened his eyes to find Rowanne and himself surrounded by a beautiful warm light, as if they both burned within the eternal flames. The fire raged around them, but in the heart of it they were still, their image frozen; a woman gently embraced in the arms of a man.

Slowly the cyclone descended, and in a matter of minutes they landed gently on a path. The fire dissipated, taking the portal with it. Alexander stood straight, supporting most of Rowanne's weight. He tried to gently extricate his arms from Rowanne, but she stubbornly refused to let him go, clinging to his coat.

Though he was exasperated, he said gently, 'Rowanne, we are safe. Open your eyes.'

Rowanne was embarrassed to find herself holding onto Alexander so tightly. It was like hugging a rock; honestly, there was nothing remotely gentle about the man before her.

The experience she had was needless to say not a pleasant one, and she was in no hurry to repeat it unless it was with Lillian; it seemed easier with her. Alexander on the other hand, had no concept of personal space.

She tilted her head up and tentatively looked around, wondering where they'd ended up. The first thing she saw was the aggravated expression on Alexander's face. *He doesn't look too pleased,* she thought, and looked away from him.

'Rowanne!' said Alexander impatiently.

She turned her attention back to him, 'Yes?'

'Would you mind releasing me now?' He looked at her archly, his eyebrow raised.

Rowanne released him fast, and stepped back. She willed her face into a dispassionate look.

Alexander looked out for signs of a meltdown, wondering how she would take this new experience.

It was Rowanne's turn to look at him disparagingly. 'Can't you censor your thoughts? I'm not some fragile china doll, I don't break down at every little thing. But mind you, this is new!' and laughed at the look of surprise that came onto his face. She turned away from him to take in their new surroundings; she knew where they were but she had not seen it in this light before.

They were in the heart of London, and it was beautiful and slightly mysterious at the same time, not to mention the fact that they were standing on a ghostly road which pulsed with supernatural energy. There were scores of these roads, and they seemed to criss-cross each other, heading into infinite directions. One only had to know the destination, and they'd get there pretty fast, she suspected. How did she know this? She could not answer; it was simply a knowing.

Rowanne had a sense of déjà vu; she'd seen these roads before. The necklace pulsed beneath her shirt and she kept her back to Alexander, not wanting him to see it. After all, she'd promised that no man would see it, and intended to honour that.

Rowanne faced Alexander, her eyes sparkling in wonder at discovering that her small world had grown in immeasurable ways that she could never have understood.

She walked up to Alexander, and asked, 'What are these purple roads called, and why is it that I've never seen or heard of them before?'

Alexander smiled. He was taken aback that she had actually handled it so well; so far, he added darkly. *You could never rest a hundred percent in this woman's company*, he thought unashamedly.

Feeling bold, he put his hands on her shoulders, and spun her outward, so she could face the roads before her. 'These are known as pathways in our world; you would most commonly know them as ley lines, but to us, they are infinitely much more than just grids of energy. A human might see a few if they are lucky, but to a demon's eye, we see all of the paths in their true light. And we can harness their energy to get from point A to B in a flash, if we choose. It depends entirely on the demon who's using it and their ability to bend the energy to their will. Of course, some journeys take longer than others, and it depends on how far you intend to travel; only within Earth, or the least travelled road - from Earth to Demon World.' Looking ruefully at her, he continued, 'Technically, I shouldn't be telling you all of this; humans are forbidden to have this knowledge!'

'I completely understand. Imagine what we'd be able to do with that kind of power...'

'That is partially a reason. Not that a human could actually have access to these paths, they don't have the power to harness its energy. And not being able to see them in the first place sort of defeats the purpose,' said Alexander.

'So, the fact that I am a half demon means that I can use these paths. Fantastic. Goodbye exorbitant rail fares and fuel costs! Ha! Watch me now...' Rowanne momentarily forgot herself as she did a little happy dance on the road.

Alexander started to laugh which brought a halt to Rowanne's momentary lapse of judgment, and her cheeks were red, but not just from dancing... she looked in every direction but his. This just made him laugh harder, and he could not remember the last time he'd felt as light-hearted as he did now.

Rowanne could not believe that the king of ice had actually melted. *Well, I'm glad that at least one of us is finding this amusing. What a fool. I can't believe, I did that — ME! and in front of him of all people; he probably thinks I'm a complete nutter.*

'Certifiable would be the term you're looking for,' he said.

Alexander had by this time sobered up, but there was still a suspicious twitch at the corner of his mouth which Rowanne suspected meant that he could go again at any moment.

'By the way, what were you doing? And if you tell me it's a primitive form of dance, I will not believe you,' said Alexander.

Rowanne feigned nonchalance, and trying to keep a straight face, replied, 'It's what us *human's* commonly refer to as 'the glee dance' or you can call me 'the smug dancer'. It's all the rage, not that you'd know anything about it!' she said haughtily with her head held high.

Alexander raised an eyebrow, 'Really? I know dancing. We have the finest dancers on Demon World, and not one of them would be impressed with that attempt.' He thought he was being quite polite despite her lack of ability and having no sense of rhythm.

He was a complete and utter idiot; Rowanne could not believe what she was hearing! She jabbed a finger at his chest in mock anger. 'Show me *your* moves, Fred Astaire. You have a lot to say but can you walk the walk?'

'I am in no way going to preen like some kind of peacock. I am more than satisfied with my ability, and do not feel the need to debase myself in order to prove a point.'

Rowanne laughed wickedly as the smug look dropped from his face, and he glared at her in consternation. 'It's okay, you can't dance, that's nothing to be ashamed of...' said Rowanne, relentlessly goading him.

'Don't push me, Rowanne. I have my limits... you've been warned!' he said menacingly.

Rowanne looked at him as if he had just grown two heads. 'Alexander the Great — now there was a man who could dance!' she said unrepentantly. She waited a heartbeat or two, and watched Alexander's face harden, and his eyes blazed fervently as their sole attention rested on her.

Alexander stepped towards her, an unearthly aura blazed around him. 'You asked for it,' he said quietly, and quickly closed the distance between them. He pulled her closer, with his right hand resting on her back. Rowanne placed her left hand on his right shoulder. Finally, Alexander clasped her free hand near his left shoulder. He began to twirl with her, around and around, spinning faster and faster, forcing Rowanne to keep pace. And much to his surprise and chagrin, she matched him, and smiled at his dismay upon learning that she could actually dance.

He slowed down and finally spun her out, keeping a hold of her hand, and then twirled her back in, so that she stood before him, her hand coming to rest on his chest.

Rowanne breathed heavily, and looked at him, unable to read his expression. A quiet storm brewed in Alexander's eyes which she didn't like the look of one single bit, and she stepped back, grateful to him for releasing her - if a tad slowly to her utter mortification.

She didn't like the knowing look that now lit his eyes, and that devil-may-care smile.

'I stand corrected, you can dance...' she said contritely.

'The same goes for you, Ms Rogers.'

Rowanne laughed quietly, wondering exactly how he passed his spare time - probably watching TV. *'Assimilate information on humans.' I make him sound like an alien!* This caused her to laugh harder.

'If you've quite finished with your one woman comedy show, then can I suggest we make a move? Otherwise, we are highly likely to bump into the others... Trust me, that is the last thing you'd want to happen.'

Rowanne knew their situation was dire, but could not help herself as she asked, 'Are you always this lively, or is it just being in my company?'

Alexander had walked on ahead of her, but he turned around and waited for her to catch up. 'Where do you want to go? I'll drop you off.' He looked tired.

Rowanne felt exhausted suddenly and yawned. And no wonder, it had been one hell of a day. 'Just take me home. Otherwise, I'm liable to fall asleep right here.'

'Your home it is then. If you grab my hand, I can get you there faster than the snail's pace we're travelling at,' he said accusingly.

Normally she'd have gotten annoyed, but was past that point, and just stepped closer, taking his hand. She liked the look of surprise on Alexander's face; she seemed to be doing that a lot today.

Alexander didn't waste any more time. His eyes blazed green, as he said, 'One, two, three!' On the count of three, they started to run at an incredibly fast pace.

Rowanne watched the road before them blaze. Everything became a blur, and at one point she could have sworn that they ran across the Thames; well, it did have the paths crossing directly above the river like phantom bridges.

She looked down and could see the river straight through the path, though how they didn't just fall through was a mystery - it was the weirdest sensation. The bridge at least felt sturdy, even though it was seemingly made from nothing more than light and air.

Alexander laughed at her petrified and slightly green expression. 'Keep going, Rowanne. That's it, we're nearly there.'

She looked at Alexander, but he was facing ahead again. 'Easy for you to say. I keep expecting these paths to collapse beneath us like clouds — they look insubstantial!'

'It depends on your point of view... If you close your eyes,' Rowanne obliged him, 'that's right, and walk on them, then they feel solid enough, right?' he asked.

'I suppose,' she agreed reluctantly.

Suddenly one of the paths led to a tunnel, which they ran through. It began to spin fast as energy pulsed out of it, and a portal started to open up. She could see her living room at the other end of it. *Oh my God, that's amazing!* she thought.

Alexander and Rowanne burst through the portal, coming to a halt in her apartment. She turned her head to look behind, and was just in time to see the portal getting smaller and smaller until it vanished with an inaudible pop.

She was panting as if she'd just run a race, and walked over to her sofa, collapsing onto it in an undignified heap. After all, who cared, it was only Alexander.

Charming, he thought. *She seems to switch from being elegant to the complete opposite in a blink of an eye. I wonder, if all humans are like this...*

Rowanne tried to sit up after hearing his inane comment, and cringed as he raised an eyebrow at her mockingly.

'Now now, Rowanne. Don't get up on my behalf. You lay there, relax. It's not like there's anyone to worry about here...' he said, amused by her.

Rowanne's face flamed, and grabbing the nearest pillow, she threw it at his head. Alexander laughed as he caught it.

'On a more serious note, would you like something to drink? Your body could go into shock as you've used a lot of energy travelling between worlds, as well as using the pathways. You need to refuel your body. I don't know what the consequences will be in the long term...'

Rowanne struggled to get up into a sitting position - it did feel as if her body were made of lead. Alexander went to her, and helped her to get comfortable.

'Thanks. And I should be the one offering you something,' said Rowanne apologetically, but he waved away the formality. She liked him better in that moment, and realised that he would always help her. 'I'll just have tea. Thank you,' she smiled up at him warmly, and Alexander relaxed as he went into the kitchen.

She looked at the clock; it was still quite early in the morning, and there were only a few hours left until she'd have to be at work. She didn't have the energy to start an assignment, let alone complete it.

She must have dozed off for a few moments, and slowly came awake as Alexander placed two steaming cups of tea onto the table.

She shakily held up her cup, inhaling the scent, which was enhanced by a slice of lemon. 'Hmmm, is it Earl Grey?'

Alexander nodded. 'Drink it slowly. Careful, it's hot!' He took a sip from his mug, before continuing, 'Rowanne, I really need to get back. I'm expecting an important visitor tomorrow, and I need to get some preparations done.'

'I understand. And thanks again, for coming back to get me. I know I'm not the easiest person to be around...'

Alexander looked at her thoughtfully, and broke out in a smile, 'Don't mention it. I know you have a lot of questions, and if I had the time, I'd tell you everything now, but I fear we have to put it off for now. This is going to be as much of a learning process for me as it will be for you.'

Rowanne looked at him questioningly, 'In what sense?'

'Well, for one thing, as a half demon, you are developing in exciting ways... just a little something to keep track of.'

It sounded ominous to Rowanne. 'Will I grow horns or turn into something resembling a monster?' she shuddered as she remembered the Shadow men. She could not handle it if she turned into one of them, and her heart began to beat fast.

Alexander placed a comforting hand on her arm. 'Don't think of them, you will definitely not change to that extreme. I think it's more than likely that you'll find yourself acquiring extra abilities. And I resent that last bit! Do I look like a monster to you? Or should I say, have I behaved monstrously towards you? After all, what constitutes a monster?'

Rowanne smiled sheepishly as she replied, 'Only when you have that extremely peeved look on your face! You're right, of course, human beings are capable of becoming monsters. I guess it's not about whether you're a demon or a human, but rather the way in which you choose to behave that's important,' she added solemnly.

Alexander put his cup down. 'I really have to go now. Will you be okay by yourself?' he asked seriously.

'I'll be fine, it's nothing that a little sleep can't fix. Good-night,' replied Rowanne. *Wait, I meant morning,* she thought tiredly.

Alexander squeezed her hand affectionately before opening a portal. 'Goodnight,' he replied before stepping through.

Rowanne watched the portal close out of existence, then dragged herself to the bathroom and washed her face and brushed her teeth; it brought her a sense of calm. She headed straight for her bedroom, and lay down on her bed, intending to close her eyes for a few minutes, but ended up falling asleep.

Her mind was filled with a chaotic dream comprised of all she had experienced. She tossed and turned before finally settling into blissful oblivion.

CHAPTER 20

Thursday morning came sooner than Rowanne would have liked as she angrily grappled with her phone, trying to turn the alarm off, and in the process sent it crashing to the floor. *Oh, that's just great!* Picking it up, she realised the time was seven am, and it had only been a few hours since Alexander had left her with a profound truth.

Her world had been changed, turned on its head. And not forgetting the significant part — she was now a half demon. A demon! As much as she'd love to spend the time trying to work it all out in her mind, she didn't have the luxury, she'd have to go into work today.

She headed straight to the bathroom for a quick shower, and then went into the bedroom with her head wrapped in a towel. Grabbing her laptop, she flicked it open and started to look through the various deadlines, and, when she was satisfied that all was in hand, she got ready for work.

After drying her hair straight, she looked in her wardrobe and decided to go for a smart trouser suit in black, with a fitted waist coat, and completed the look with a white shirt.

She walked barefoot into the kitchen turning on the coffee machine, as well as shoving a slice of bread into the toaster. Grabbing her breakfast when it was ready, she went back into the bedroom and placed it on her bed, then made the necessary changes to her assignment.

She felt ravenous. Maybe it was due to the events of the previous evening; her body just needed food to keep going, never mind her mental state.

One thing was becoming apparent though: she'd have to take time off work to actually consider all that she had gone through, and to figure out where her life was going. She thought she knew the direction her life was taking, and had been happy to be busy all the time; but at what cost...

Rowanne didn't really have any friends. She liked her work colleagues well enough, but she'd never really made any of them her confidantes. She occasionally went out as a treat — a treat!

Before Alexander and Lady Enid, Rowanne had never really considered how alone she'd been. The two of them had changed her life, especially Alexander - who had literally transformed her into something else.

She didn't know how becoming a demon would affect her in the long term, but she also wondered what effect it could have had on Alexander. One day she'd build up the courage and ask him, no matter how difficult a subject it would be for the both of them.

Then there was the question of the necklace. She'd spend her time off by visiting Grandmother Angelique to try to get to the bottom of the mystery, if it was at all possible.

She left her dishes in the kitchen and went back into her bedroom to apply her makeup. She lined her eyes with kohl to bring out the intensity of the green, and they seemed to sparkle with a new kind of vivacity.

It was strange, she didn't feel at all drained. She had assumed she'd feel like one of the walking dead today, but instead, Rowanne felt alive and buzzing for once. She looked towards the kitchen and shrugged; maybe it was the new brand of coffee! She added a subtle pink lipstick and voila, she was ready. She stepped into her high heels, and put on her heavy winter coat - she'd definitely need it, the grey weather confirming her suspicions.

She closed the front door behind her and headed into the glass lift, taking it down to the car park. Rowanne felt slightly on edge at the idea of going into work and seeing Alexander; it made her anxious, even though it had only been a couple of hours since she'd last seen him.

Putting her fears to one side, she got into her car and turned on the radio to ease her anxiety. There it was, again; the knot in her stomach. She noticed something wink at her, and a moment later her necklace became warm. She knew it was glowing, and hastily shoved it under her shirt with one hand on the steering wheel.

It always boded ill when her necklace did that, and combined with the way she was feeling, it made her think that something was going to happen today, something bad. She had faith in herself now, and listened to her gut feeling. Everybody had a sixth sense, or whatever they called it, that made them aware of danger, even if they could not quite put their finger on it.

She drove past the river that had swollen overnight - it must have rained heavily. Not that she'd have known, being in another dimension or world — whatever it was! It didn't make any sense. And no one would ever believe her; not that she had a wish to tell anyone, they'd definitely lock her up and throw away the key.

I'm dealing with demons, thought Rowanne. It was so far outside the scope of her imagination. And she wondered how she could identify who a demon was. *I'm one to talk; but then again, I know I'm not evil.* Rowanne rebuked herself: being a demon did not automatically make them evil.

She thought about Alexander and suddenly felt ashamed for having this train of thought: he was most definitely not evil, even if he was not human! The people who worked with Alexander, could they be demons as well...? Rowanne began to check people off her list: Lady Enid could be, as well as Driskell, and he could for all intents and purposes be a monster. Especially in the way in which he treated people, as if they were worth nothing, and beneath him.

Even though Driskell had been polite in their last meeting, she still could not bring herself to trust him. And she didn't particularly want to meet him again, but it would probably be more his choice than hers.

Rowanne pulled up into the car park, parked in a bay, and noticed the other cars. *Damn, they've all come in before me,* she thought, panicking.

As soon as she got out of the car, she was hit by how intensely cold it was as her breath fogged. Looking around, she noticed that all the trees had lost their leaves as they stood there ominously lined up together at the back of the car park. Shaking her head, she cleared it of morbid thoughts as she headed towards the fountain.

She looked up as dark clouds raced by, promising the retribution of a heavy downpour later on. The air seemed to sizzle with an invisible current as if it had suddenly come to life.

She reached the angel fountain and stood before it as it loomed over her in more ways than she could count. *So, this is where it happened...* she could not bring herself quite yet to say the word, although she congratulated herself for not falling apart and having a panic attack before it.

The angel statue was sinister in the sense that it was a being of pure goodness frozen in the act of violence: its sword raised above a monstrous creature, who cowered beneath its wings. Rowanne pitied the creature - who was to say that it was evil? Both beings, as she could clearly see, had wings, so what made the one beneath the angel evil?

Strange thoughts churned in her mind, and she felt her necklace glow in empathy with her. It took a lot of strength to walk away, but she wanted to put it behind her for now. Later, when she was ready, she would examine how she felt, but for now she was alright and that was enough.

Rowanne walked quickly towards her office building - the sooner she was immersed in her work the better.

She nodded at the security guard as she walked past reception, and headed straight for the stairs, briskly going up to the first floor. She went down the corridor to the office.

She was still smiling as she stepped through the police cordon that gave way before her, as she entered her former ruined offices. She started walking towards her old desk, but stopped dead as she finally realised where she had ended up. *Oh my God! How did I get here?*

She spun around to the door in time to see it close. Where a moment before it had been bright with the overhead lights, now it started to get dark, and the room seemed to be closing in on her.

The lights flickered precariously, threatening to permanently go out at any second. The hairs on her arm raised up. Rowanne felt a coldness in the air as the temperature dramatically plunged. *What the hell is going on here?*

She quickly went back to the doors whilst she could still see them, but upon testing them, found them to be jammed. She tried to nudge them open with her shoulder but to no avail. Where was her super strength when she really needed it?

'Lillian, is that you?' asked Rowanne. Perhaps she was trying to get her attention - but there was no reply. *At this rate, I'm going to be late for work even though I'm at work!* It was extremely annoying, to say the least.

Rowanne decided to look for another way out. But the moment she went further in, she saw a flashing light, and a purplish glow started to emanate from it, and wisely she stepped back slowly. After all, she had no intention of staying to find out the cause, but to her dismay the flash encompassed everything around it in seconds. She threw up her arms to block out the light.

Rowanne blinked a couple of times as light flashes danced before her eyes. She rubbed her eyes and ever so slowly the room began to come back in soft focus.

She stood dumbfounded as Thomas walked through the locked doors. Well, a ghostly looking Thomas, as his image stuttered, flashing in and out of existence.

'Thomas!' yelled Rowanne hopelessly, trying to get his attention. And on reflection, it was pointless; after all, he was not really there.

He proceeded forward, not even pausing when she called to him. The ghostly room as far as she could see was empty. She had a flashback to last Friday: she would have been outside in the car park at this time, so Thomas must have come in just after she had left.

She observed him making the rounds, travelling up and down the office, checking that all was in order. The most disturbing part was when he walked towards her, and she quickly backed up, not wanting him to get close to her. But to her utter horror, he walked straight through her, eliciting a small gasp of terror from her.

Rowanne turned around just as he walked through the doors that were now open. She wasted no time in getting out of the room and following him. She wanted to know what had become of him; seeing the ghostly image of him did not bode well...

She was just in time to see him walk down the corridor. She ran after him, not wanting him out of her sight. And as he descended the stairs, she ran faster, heedless of her heels; they could not slow down this journalist once she had her mind set on something.

Rowanne collided with a woman walking up the stairs. The woman thankfully didn't fall back, but Rowanne on the other hand twisted her ankle, and would have fallen straight down the marble stairs, most likely to her death, if the woman had not suddenly grabbed her, thereby saving her.

Rowanne sat on the stairs nursing her sore ankle. She looked up and noticed that the woman had been trying to get her attention.

'Are you alright?' asked the woman, sitting next to her.

Rowanne had not noticed her at first. *Oh! I must have been blind,* she thought absently. Before her sat a goddess of a woman: she was statuesque and strikingly beautiful with long black hair and midnight blue eyes. She appeared to be in her early twenties.

And right now those mesmerising eyes were trained on Rowanne with concern. 'Can you hear me?' she asked in a soft voice.

'Yes,' replied Rowanne slowly, as she tried to get up, but fell back down as a sharp pain bit into her ankle. *Great, I've probably injured it. Stupid heels! I knew they'd be the death of me one day.*

The young woman had a smile on her face that seemed to get broader, as if she were about to laugh.

'Let me help you up. Take my arm, just put your weight on it,' and seeing the dubious look on Rowanne's face, she continued, 'trust me, I'm stronger than I look.'

Rowanne managed to get up with the aid of the woman, who put her arm around her. She seemed to be holding her up effortlessly, supporting most of her weight. Together they hobbled, or that is to say that Rowanne did, to the lift. The woman stopped abruptly.

'I'm sorry, I was going to the top floor, and didn't even ask where you wanted to go.'

'That's okay. I'm also heading there. Thank you,' said Rowanne, as the woman called the lift.

The woman was slightly taller than Rowanne, more Alexander's height. An awkward silence lay between them as the lift climbed speedily to the top floor.

Blessedly the doors opened and they stepped out. 'If you can just help me to the office there, then I'll be fine.'

'No problem,' said the woman, as she helped Rowanne to her desk.

'Rowanne, what happened?' asked Amanda, who came

rushing to her aid, taking the weight of her from the woman, and helping her to sit.

'It's my fault. I didn't look where I was going and twisted my ankle, nearly pushing this poor woman down the stairs,' and looking up at her, Rowanne said with concern, 'I'm sorry, and I didn't ask whether you were hurt, forgive me.'

'Nothing to forgive,' she replied, smiling and waving away the incident. Her cheeks were red as if she didn't like all the attention focused on her.

Amanda shook the woman's hand profusely in gratitude.

Eileen walked up to them, coming from her office. 'What's all the commotion about? Rowanne, I expected you to be here early... Oh! Well,' and looking down at Rowanne nursing her ankle, she smiled and with a shake of her head at finding Rowanne in yet another predicament continued sweetly, 'when you have the time, I want you to come to my office and discuss the first assignment.' *That was Eileen for you; a no-nonsense person,* thought Rowanne as she watched her walk away.

'My goodness, how rude! Is she always like this?' asked the woman, astounded by the appalling behaviour of the manager.

'No! No,' replied Rowanne, coming easily to Eileen's defence. 'She doesn't mean any harm by it. And in fact, she's one of the nicest people I know.' The woman looked at her dubiously as if she really didn't believe it.

Rowanne was surprised as Alexander hurried into the office, his face red as if he had been racing to get here. She had never really seen him out of breath before, or looking so frazzled. He took a deep breath, and looking in her direction he calmed, once again appearing composed.

He strode towards them at a leisurely pace, noticed all eyes were trained on him, so gave them his most charming smile.

'Hello, how are we this morning?' and turning in Rowanne's direction, he said, 'I was looking for you everywhere. I thought we were supposed to meet last night, or early this morning at the very least,' he appeared annoyed.

Rowanne was baffled, she didn't know what he was talking about, and turned to Amanda, who just smiled knowingly at her. *Oh, for goodness sake!* thought Rowanne, warning her with a look. She didn't want there to be any misunderstanding regarding her friendship with Alexander; they were only colleagues, after all.

Amanda's smile broadened.

Rowanne cleared her voice and said to Alexander, 'Were we-'

Rowanne was cut off abruptly by the woman next to her, who stepped forward and walked up to Alexander, her shoulders set. *What's going on here?* she wondered.

'Alexander, I am not accustomed to waiting. We set a time, did we not?' she held up her hand before he could give his explanation. 'I expect you to be there exactly on the dot, if not earlier, in anticipation of my arrival.' The woman was clearly angry with Alexander, but her calm voice belied this, thought Rowanne. She was puzzled by the woman who'd spoken so rudely to Alexander. How did she know him?

Rowanne was about to come to Alexander's defence when she heard a clear voice in her mind that stopped her in her tracks.

Rowanne, do not interrupt! Alexander said sharply.

She felt stung by his words. *What a complete and utter idiot! That's the last time I come to his defence,* she thought churlishly.

The woman looked sharply at her, studying her intently, but for what purpose she could not say. Rowanne just looked at her and smiled, in no way intimidated by the two of them. Maybe I've passed that particular threshold; what's left to fear when you've died?

The woman looked impatiently at Alexander.

Alexander recovered quickly. 'Ah yes, forgive me,' he said, and taking the woman's hand, he continued, 'let me introduce you to Evelyn Blaze.' Turning to Evelyn, he said, 'This is Amanda Eghan,' whose fiery blue eyes were carefully focused on the woman before her as she stood close to Rowanne protectively.

Amanda put on her best smile and her eyes sparkled with feigned mirth as she formally shook hands with Evelyn, again.

Rowanne didn't wait for Alexander, instead hopping up, she gingerly hobbled forward. And though her ankle was in agony, she ignored the pain and stood determinedly, shaking Evelyn's hand.

'Nice to finally know the name of the woman who saved me,' and smiling warmly, she continued, 'I'm Rowanne Knight. Thank you, again.'

'WHAT?' said Alexander, momentarily forgetting whose company he was in, 'What happened, Ms Knight?' he appeared disinterested, as if he was asking out of politeness, rather than any real concern.

Rowanne wondered why he was behaving so formally with her, and acting as if he couldn't care less, but wisely she stayed quiet and went along with it.

'Are you alright, Ms Knight?' asked Evelyn coldly.

Rowanne deliberately turned to Alexander and replied, 'As you can see, it's nothing a pack of ice and a painkiller can't fix.'

Alexander smiled conspiratorially at her behind Evelyn's back. Rowanne kept her face carefully neutral as she looked at Evelyn.

'Ms Blaze, what brings you to our offices?' asked Rowanne.

Eileen walked towards them. 'Ah, I see you've met our newest member. She's temporarily here from Mr Blacks firm to collaborate on an assignment he's working on.' Turning to Evelyn, Eileen continued, 'Ms Blaze, if you'd like to come with me then I'll get you started,' and without waiting for Evelyn, she went into an office at the back of the room.

Evelyn silently counted to ten to stay calm: she had at least expected Eileen to have the courtesy of waiting for her. She turned back and smiled at the rest of the group, 'I should probably get myself acquainted with the work. Rowanne, is there anything else I can do for you before I go?' she asked sincerely.

Rowanne didn't know what to make of Evelyn: she was helpful one moment, rude the next. Maybe it was down to nerves; after all, it can be a bit overwhelming on the first day at a new workplace, and so she decided to give her the benefit of the doubt.

'Thank you, but I'm okay. And should you need anything, then please don't hesitate to ask,' replied Rowanne.

'Thank you,' said Evelyn, and turning to Alexander, she said curtly, 'let's go,' and together they went to his office.

'If he's a new employee, how is it that he has his own office? Whilst you, who's worked here longer- Erm, how long?' asked Amanda.

'Three years,' replied Rowanne, dismayed at where this was going.

'Exactly! Why didn't Eileen give you your own office in preference to Mr Black?' she asked sheepishly. Amanda didn't know what Rowanne's response would be, she was still getting to know her.

Rowanne allayed her fear by replying, 'I know. That's Eileen for you,' they both laughed. 'Amanda,' said Rowanne slowly, weighing her words carefully, 'I must say you are quite... strong... I think I'd like to train with you in the gym sometime.'

Amanda looked coolly at Rowanne, a sly expression on her face, 'Anytime, Rowanne,' she replied.

Ever since Alexander's revelation, Rowanne had begun to view the world differently, and kept her reservations close to her heart for the present.

Amanda looked at Rowanne as if seeing her in a new light, but could not put her finger on what it was. Though Rowanne appeared to be more confident, a shadow hung over her; Amanda got the strong impression that she was hiding something.

Amanda had always been good at reading situations and people, and she liked Rowanne, felt a kinship with her, which did not surprise her in the least.

Rowanne got up and hobbled over to Eileen's office, knocking twice before entering.

'Come in, Rowanne,' said Eileen. She went in, and gratefully accepted the chair that Eileen pulled out for her.

'So, what do you think of it?' she asked Eileen, who was studiously checking her work.

After a few moments Eileen looked up from her laptop, 'Good work. How are the other two assignments coming along?' Eileen didn't waste time overly praising people's work; after all, she had a paper to run.

'I've started them... they're a work in progress at the moment. But there's something else that I'd like to discuss with you.'

Eileen paused to look at Rowanne, her tone of voice serious. 'What is it you wish to discuss? And if it's about a pay rise, forget it!' she said, trying to lighten the suddenly heavy mood.

'I need to take an extended leave of absence for... personal reasons. I love working here, and before you ask, I can handle the workload! You know that I work best under pressure.'

Eileen nodded her head, waiting for her to go on.

'This is not easy for me to ask. I love to keep busy, and I find great fulfilment from working here. This has been the best three years of my life,' said Rowanne fondly.

'And long may it continue. I had high hopes for you. You're very ambitious and driven - you remind me of myself, when I first started out in journalism. I can still see you succeeding in this field.' Eileen steepled her fingers together and looked at Rowanne in quiet contemplation.

Rowanne sighed, 'I'm not saying that I'm permanently going. I do actually intend to come back at some point, then we can discuss the overdue pay rise!' and smiled warmly. 'A lot has happened, believe it or not, recently in my personal life, and I really need the time to deal with it,' she finished quietly.

'I can't pretend that I'm overjoyed at losing one of my top journalists. But I've been in this business a long time, and can understand the need for a break. Just don't take too long a leave of absence, or you'll find that David has taken your position!' said Eileen with a straight face. Rowanne was secretly amused but looked at her in disgust.

'That never gets old, the more you threaten us with him. One of these days, he's going to catch onto what you've been doing, and I'd dearly love to be a fly on the wall on that day!'

'Really?' asked Eileen, as she smiled knowingly at her.

'Getting back to the point, I've filled out all of the relevant forms for you,' said Rowanne, as she took the signed copies out of her satchel and handed them over to Eileen.

'I'll look over these this evening, and email you if there's anything further that I require. But I think that this is goodbye for now,' said Eileen.

Rowanne got up, though she knew that Eileen was not one to stand on ceremony, the emotional side of life was not really for her, so she simply shook her hand.

Eileen looked at her sternly, 'Take care of yourself and keep in touch.' She gently laid a hand on Rowanne's shoulder, and coughing to clear her throat, she continued, 'Rowanne, I'll see you soon. You've kept me long enough, and goodness knows how many meetings I've missed.'

That was Eileen for you, though she'd miss her. Rowanne

walked to the door, and gave her a wave before leaving.

Rowanne started to clear her desk of her possessions. The process was slightly unsettling, and a lump formed in her throat. *Oh for goodness sake! It's only a workplace, so why am I choking up...?*

Amanda came over from reception once the coast was clear, and had a surreptitious glance to confirm that Eileen was safely in her office.

'You know, she's going to fire you if you keep leaving the reception desk unattended!' said Rowanne.

'I'll risk it for you, not to mention that it gets really boring just standing there. This is my escape when it's not so busy,' said Amanda deviously. 'What are you up to, and why are you spring cleaning your desk?'

Rowanne explained patiently, 'I'm actually going on a leave of absence,' and added archly, 'taking time off to relax and enjoy life!'

'From what I hear from anyone who knows you, that is complete and utter claptrap! Rowanne Knight needing a break from work? Oh come on! What's the real reason?'

'It's true. I'm taking the time to figure things out,' replied Rowanne, as she finished packing the last of her things into the brown boxes that she had brought with her.

'I'll help you carry them to your car,' said Amanda.

'It's nice of you to offer, but I can manage, and I don't think that Eileen would be too pleased.'

'Give me a second, wait right there!' said Amanda, and dashed across the office to Eileen.

Rowanne watched them; there was much waving of arms, and it seemed as if they were talking intensely, and she felt bad that she was the cause of it. Finally, Eileen nodded her head - well that was positive, at least. And she watched poor David traipse over to reception a moment later, presumably to take over from Amanda. She almost laughed at his glum expression, she didn't know why he put up with it.

A moment later Amanda came running back to Rowanne. 'All set. Let's go, just one more thing,' and she ran over to David and whispered in his ear, causing him to go red and laugh out loud.

Rowanne found it bizarre to say the least: David was always so composed and serious, she'd never once seen him laugh like that. *Amanda's able to bring out the best in people,* she thought and smiled affectionately.

'What's that look for?' asked Amanda, slightly out of breath from running around.

'Nothing. Let's go. Here, you can take this one,' and she handed a box to Amanda, keeping the heavy one for herself; much to her chagrin. Amanda just looked at her in exasperation and came around the desk to take the box from her, effectively carrying both boxes much to Rowanne's mortification.

'Take that ridiculous look off your face and follow me. If you want, you can treat me to a coffee?' asked Amanda, and proceeded to walk effortlessly, the boxes in no way hampering her.

Rowanne shook her head and slowly followed after her; remarkably the pain in her ankle did not bother her as much as burdening another person. She took one last look around hoping to catch a glimpse of Alexander before she left. She'd been planning on telling him but didn't think it was appropriate in front of their new colleague.

She saw Amanda waiting by the door and this spurred her on - she didn't want her carrying that much weight for too long. She reached the door just as Amanda proceeded to the lift.

Rowanne felt hands on her shoulder, and turned around to face their owner.

'I've managed to get you alone, at last!' said Alexander, looking back over his shoulder to the office, he appeared nervous.

'Alexander! What do you think you're doing?' asked Rowanne, annoyed at him for taking her by surprise.

'I won't pretend that I'm not offended at you trying to secretly leave without telling any of us. I thought you'd at least tell *me*!' he said darkly, his eyes conveying his deep displeasure at being kept in the dark.

'I was actually planning on telling everyone... present company included, but the right moment didn't come up,' she finished lamely.

'You and I are going to talk later...' he promised, before adding, 'take care of yourself for both our sakes,' and abruptly he left her standing there. *No doubt, he's rushing back to the side of his new colleague,* thought Rowanne churlishly.

'Rowanne, if you've finished romancing for the day, then can we get a move on?' asked Amanda slyly, and laughed at the expression of disgust that instantly bloomed on Rowanne's face.

'I'm not dignifying that with a response,' said Rowanne, and walked straight past her into the lift. Amanda followed in behind. Rowanne pressed the button for the ground floor, and they were away as the lift speedily descended.

They had just walked past their former offices when Amanda stopped and put a restraining hand on Rowanne's arm. How the boxes didn't fall when they were so precariously balanced was a feat only Amanda could pull off.

'Rowanne, I always get a weird vibe whenever I'm walking past here. Looking at them ruined like this, it's a bit unnerving.'

Having no more wish to stand around the haunted office, Rowanne tugged on Amanda's arm, and they continued swiftly past them, heading for the stairs. 'I get the same feeling,' said Rowanne, relieved at reaching the exit. She held the door open for Amanda to pass through.

They walked in silence to Rowanne's car. Amanda helped to load the boxes into the boot, before getting into the front passenger seat.

Rowanne put on her seat belt and started the car, pulling out of the car park and then proceeded to drive onto the main road along the River Thames.

'You have to admit that we have the best work location. I just love being near the river, walking along it when I have a chance, and watching the world go by,' said Amanda, breaking the silence. 'If you're not in a hurry, then I know a good place where we can grab an early lunch from,' and looked at Rowanne eagerly.

'That sounds good. I have, after all, got time on my hands now,' she said mournfully.

'Pull up on the left, here,' said Amanda and pointed to the street food vendor. Great! She'd finally have a chance today, usually everything went quickly as she arrived late most days.

Rowanne obligingly drove the car down a side road and parked. They got out and walked back towards the line of people, and joined the queue at the very end in the biting cold. The sky overhead had lightened up and the sun peeked through.

'Thanks for this,' said Amanda.

'Don't mention it. I'm curious about the food, it had better be as good as you make it sound.'

'Wait and see,' said Amanda mysteriously.

They finally reached the front of the queue after ten minutes. 'What do you want, Rowanne?' asked Amanda.

The variety of Japanese dishes on offer looked delicious. 'Hello. I'll have the Miso Soba Noodle soup, please, and my friend here will have?' Rowanne turned and looked at Amanda.

'The Vegetable Yakisoba and Miso soup, please.' Amanda loved food, she was always hungry; maybe it was from all the workouts she did.

Rowanne rubbed her hands together to try and bring the feeling back into them. Looking at Amanda, you'd think they were in the middle of summer; she had not even brought a coat with her, and appeared quite comfortable in her short blue dress that complemented her striking blue eyes.

Collecting their order, they made their way across the road and sat on the first bench they came across.

Rowanne was quiet as she looked out across the river, watching it churn. The waves slammed against the side of the embankments; Rowanne's mood was no better, and she wondered if she had made a mistake by taking time off.

She would have no excuse now but to face everything she'd been putting off. At least work would have provided a distraction normally... but she reasoned with herself that she could not go on as she had been.

She would have to get used to being a demon - or a half demon as Alexander put it. *I wonder if I am a danger to others...* But so far, she had not done anything to put others at risk.

She was also keen to go to Grandmother Angelique's if it was at all possible today - it depended on whether she was in the country.

Amanda scrutinised Rowanne, who appeared troubled. She wished that she would confide in her, but truth be told, she had not been entirely honest with Rowanne either.

It was not that she didn't trust Rowanne, it was more a case of finding the right time. Amanda suspected that Rowanne knew there was more to her, especially after the incident with the guard...

She knew all about Rowanne's trouble with Driskell, who was zealously perceptive; that made him a dangerous man to be around. *He probably has his suspicions about me, I'll have to tread carefully there*, thought Amanda.

Amanda was frustrated. What was she supposed to say? Not to mention the fact that she had not yet been given clearance from the others to proceed. She would keep an eye on Rowanne, even if it was from a distance.

She felt sorry for Rowanne, so many people had kept her in the dark for her own good. *I wonder whether she'll see it quite in the same light as we all do...*

'Rowanne,' said Amanda, bringing her back to reality and out of her troubled mind. Rowanne blinked a couple of times and looked at her questioningly, a small smile on her face. 'I was just wondering how the case with Driskell was going?'

'Oh, that! Thankfully, I haven't been called to the police station again, and nor has the detective called me since,' replied Rowanne, with a calculated look. 'Now you tell me, Amanda, has Driskell called you...?'

Amanda looked baffled, 'Why would he contact me? I've nothing to do with the case.'

Rowanne smiled broadly, 'With the way you both seemed to hit it off, I'd have thought he might have phoned you... Perhaps, the both of you have gone on a-'

Amanda held up a hand to stop Rowanne. 'Get that ludicrous idea out of your mind. I found him disturbing, not to mention the weird vibes I was getting from him.'

Rowanne laughed, 'Is that what you call it these days? I would have said it's chemistry!'

She ducked as Amanda threw a vegetable towards her head.

'I'm just joking! I know that he's a man who's not to be trusted,' replied Rowanne, as she thought grimly of the flame haired detective. Rowanne was solemn once more as she thought of her spooky experience in her former offices. 'Do you believe in the supernatural?' she asked casually, dreading inside that Amanda would think her crazy.

Amanda looked thoughtful, and replied, 'You'll probably think I'm crazy for saying this, but I've had a strange knowing sensation, ever since I can remember. Even as a child, I felt the hairs on the back of my neck rise, and got goosebumps in the middle of summer whenever I was in an old building, or if I walked past a site or even a person.'

'You're not crazy,' said Rowanne, relieved to have another person to share her feelings and ideas with. She looked curiously at Amanda as she asked, 'What is a knowing sensation and where does it come from? And how does it work for you?' she finished breathlessly.

'Whoa, hold on there. I'm not Yoda! All your answers, I can answer not,' replied Amanda, as she put on her most pious look.

Rowanne laughed, 'That was completely rubbish! Great, I'm talking with a *Star Wars* fan!'

Amanda looked offended, 'I am actually a devotee, I'll have you know,' she sniffed, and continued, 'getting back to the main point, I think it's like a sixth sense, and that everyone has it to some degree. It's like a muscle – the more you use it, the stronger it becomes.'

'You definitely are a gym freak! Not that I'm one to talk, I'm obsessed with running!' said Rowanne.

'Speaking of freaks, you felt a little something yourself didn't you, back at the old offices? And that's why you could not wait to get out of there. Admit it!' Amanda looked at her challengingly, daring her to confess.

Rowanne felt comfortable in Amanda's company. After all, when you're with someone as open and seemingly honest as Amanda, you can't help but open up; besides, her gut instinct was telling her that she could be trusted.

'Fine, my turn to sound crazy. I absentmindedly went straight into the ruined offices...' and she began to recap the event, concluding with, 'and I saw Thomas walk straight through the locked doors!'

Amanda's expression had not changed, it was not giving anything away. 'So, you're saying that you saw a ghost?'

'I don't know, it was all very confusing. I ran after him, because it was as if he wanted me to follow him, but I was thwarted by my damn heels!' replied Rowanne.

'But they are a very nice pair of heels,' said Amanda admiringly. For her, the supernatural was the everyday, it wasn't unusual or frightening; but for someone like Rowanne, it must appear extraordinary.

Rowanne took off her shoes, resting her feet against the cold concrete pavement. 'What do you think?' she asked, hoping to get some solid answers. Maybe it was just the journalist in her; never satisfied, always wanting to know more.

'Inquisitive cats never fare well, but there's always an exception...' replied Amanda pointedly. Rowanne looked baffled. 'Have you not considered that perhaps you were looking at a scene on a permanent loop.'

'I don't understand. What do you mean?' asked Rowanne.

'If Thomas has...' Amanda tried to find a delicate way of putting it, 'sometimes when a person passes over, what's left behind is the person's energy. It's like a mini film of them, it keeps repeating their last moments of life. If they don't realise that they are no longer of this world, then they might hover in the place they've passed, and carry on doing everything they did when they were alive. You see, to them it's normal.'

'That's why you asked me whether it was specifically to get my notice. Now I'm more confused than ever, but one thing you said could help me. If I follow him this time to the end, then perhaps I can figure out what happened.' Rowanne felt sick to her stomach at the thought of it, but knew steadfastly that she owed it to Thomas to find out the truth.

'You are not going alone,' said Amanda, putting up her hand before Rowanne could protest, and continued, 'you can't change my mind. You've shared this with me and at some level you trust me. Can you trust this friend to see it through with you?' Amanda squeezed Rowanne's arm affectionately.

Rowanne considered her options: it would be better to have two people to go back there. At least if she lost his trail there'd be another person to take over, thereby greatly increasing their chances. But she didn't want to put Amanda in harm's way.

'I think it's best if I go alone, just in case he doesn't show up if there's the two of us. Spooky things are more likely to occur when you're alone,' she finished unconvincingly.

'That's ridiculous! Since we've both experienced something to some degree. I think it's more a matter of timing, and I don't like the idea of you going alone, it's best we go together. Strength in numbers you know,' said Amanda decisively.

Rowanne reluctantly acceded to her point. 'What time do you think we should go back?' she asked wearily; but she already knew the answer.

'The witching hour, of course!' replied Amanda in her spookiest voice.

Rowanne rolled her eyes - at least she was not going to be bored, not with Amanda in tow. 'How do you propose we get into a locked office?' The logistics of the situation were only now dawning on her.

Amanda finished her cold soup, while she thought of possible solutions. Suddenly, she gave Rowanne a sly look.

'Don't even mention it! It's not even a possibility that I would consider.'

'And if the occasion demand-' laughed Amanda.

'Next suggestion, please!' interrupted Rowanne, exasperated. He was the last person that she'd ever ask for help from. *Damn it, now I'm thinking of him!*

'That was all your own doing. And anyway, he's an employee, he can sneak us in tonight after everyone's left.'

'I think it's best we limit this to ourselves for now, just in case nothing turns up,' replied Rowanne. Speaking of nothing turning up, where was Lillian? She metaphorically slapped herself in the head. *Of course! I should have asked Lillian to help. She might be able to speak with Thomas, and get the answers that might be out of my reach.*

Rowanne would wait until this evening to try and contact Lillian. Every time she called her it took its toll on her. She had not seen Lillian since the last time they spoke, and she wondered if she was back from Demon World.

'Earth to Rowanne. Hellooo.' Rowanne looked at her guiltily. 'Where did you go?' asked Amanda.

'I was just going over the plan in my head,' Rowanne answered smoothly.

Amanda's phone started to ring shrilly. She swiped it open, and a look of dismay came over her, but she answered brightly if a little reluctantly, 'Yes, boss. I realise that... I do... Ten minutes. Goodbye.'

'I take it Eileen isn't too pleased!' Rowanne smiled gleefully.

'Apparently this is now my lunch break! Hello long hours and no break: my reward! David at least will be happy to see me.' Amanda laughed it off. She knew full well that she was at fault.

'I'll drive you back. I'm sorry.'

'Hey! I'm the one that offered. And I distinctly remember dragging you to the food stall. But I will accept your offer, thanks!' she smiled sheepishly.

They walked back to the car, and in no time at all reached the office. Amanda insisted on being dropped off on the main road.

'After all, you've just left. It's silly to go back, and it's not a long walk. Now don't forget, we'll meet here around eleven, eleven thirtyish,' with that she waved once before skipping back to work; well, it appeared that way with that boundless energy of hers.

Rowanne watched her approach the offices before making a U-turn in the road and heading back in the direction of Westminster Bridge.

The drive back was quick with no traffic to impede her. The sky seemed to darken as the clouds gathered together and blocked out the sun. The city seemed leeched of colour, everywhere she looked was sombre and grey.

She reached her apartment and drove down the ramp that led to the underground car park. She parked in her usual spot and got into the lift, carrying both boxes awkwardly. How Amanda had managed it, she had no idea.

She stabbed a finger blindly at the panel - thankfully it was the right button and the doors closed as the lift whooshed up to the top floor. Getting out, Rowanne walked unsteadily to her door, and put the boxes down to jab the key into the lock.

She stumbled into her apartment, quickly put the boxes down, feeling the life slowly come back into her arms.

She walked into her living room and flopped down onto the sofa. *Oh my God, I can't believe I actually did that!* It still felt surreal that she was jobless, even if it was of her own volition.

She got up and went into the kitchen. She had time now and might as well put it to good use. She tried to remember what Alexander had taught her, as she attempted to make Chai tea. She boiled water and added the Chai Tea bags followed by a pinch of mixed spices and sugar. She left it to boil while she got changed.

Rowanne came back out in her favourite jeans and soft jumper. The tea by now had started to boil. Judging it, she decided to add milk to give it a creamy consistency.

Turning off the gas, she poured the tea through a strainer into her favourite silly mug and brought it into the living room. She took a sip to fortify herself - she was ready now to make the all important phone call to her grandmother.

Grandmother Angelique picked up on the third ring, 'It must be my lucky day, two phone calls within the space of a few days!'

Rowanne cringed - she deserved that. Now, how to delicately bring up the next situation? 'Hello, Grandmother. How are you?'

'I'm doing well. Your Grandfather is still away, travelling. I miss him, and this big house feels so empty without him...'

'I think I can help you there! I was wondering if it would be at all possible for me to come down and visit today?' asked Rowanne, holding her breath in anticipation.

She needn't have worried, as her grandmother replied, 'Finally, my dear, it's about time! How about you come over now?' Her grandmother's voice was full of surprise and happiness at finally seeing her granddaughter again after so many years. 'We have a lot to catch up on. I can't wait to see you!'

Rowanne felt her face go red in shame, she felt so bad. *How could I have left it for so long?* She made a promise to herself to stay in contact more often.

'Rowanne dear, I'll let you go, there's someone at the door. What time do you think you'll be here by?'

'I'll be there by two o'clock and I'll text you when I'm near. Take care, Grandmother, and I can't wait to see you, too.'

'Goodbye, dear,' her grandmother replied and put down the phone.

Taking a deep breath, she finished the rest of her tea and contemplated her next move. She suddenly realised that her grandmother had moved since last she saw her. *Damn it! I'm sure I have the address somewhere around here.*

Getting up quickly, Rowanne ran into her bedroom and found her diary, rummaging through it until she found the address, and adding it into her phone.

She went to the kitchen and quickly prepared a lunch of whole wheat pasta with a salad. Whilst she ate, she contemplated asking her grandmother about her past, in the hopes of getting answers to whatever this *thing* was around her neck.

The necklace radiated warmth, as if acknowledging the fact that she was even thinking of it. Rowanne had the disconcerting idea that perhaps it contained an intelligence within it. She had to stop watching so many sci-fi shows, they were beginning to rot her mind.

Then there was the fact that she had decided to go back to work to chase a ghost of all things! She didn't know what she had been thinking, but hopefully tonight would put an end to the mystery, or perhaps she might be able to gather some clues anyway.

Lately she had been getting the feeling that she was being watched, ever since she had first dreamt about Lillian. She remembered vividly that Lillian had also been stalked by something or someone in the dream, but she had been unaware of it.

I should have told Alexander, but with everything happening so quickly, I just didn't have the chance to mention it. But I will talk to Lillian about it. She had a strong feeling that Lillian would know.

Her attention was brought back by the lightning storm that had now gathered over the city, and she hoped that it would not affect the GPS in the car on the way to her grandmother's house. Looking out of the window, she watched as the rain pounded the streets.

Rowanne gathered her things and left the dishes in the sink for later. She put on her heavy winter coat and grabbed her bag. She pulled on her knee high boots, and was now ready to brave the weather.

She opened the door to her car and threw everything in, fiddling with the sat nav as she put in the address. And after two frustrating attempts met with 'address not recognised', she finally succeeded.

She emerged into a downpour, as the heavens showered the city in its displeasure. She rolled down the window slightly, as she was feeling stuffy and uncomfortable. The flecks of cool rain that occasionally hit her face helped to calm and clear her mind.

She drove across Westminster Bridge and turned onto Victoria Embankment, driving parallel to the river. The windscreen wipers were really being put to the test. *It's almost like someone doesn't want me to make it to grandmother's house...* thought Rowanne, and laughed nervously.

She turned left onto Northumberland Ave, and was met with traffic that was painfully slow going. Thoughts of her grandmother filled her mind, the 'elusive adventuress' - maybe that was part of the reason why she had not really kept in touch as much.

Ever since she was a child, she remembered her grandmother rarely showing up for family occasions, but when they really needed her, she was there in a flash. *Even though she loves us, I wonder why she chooses to stay away so often. Maybe I'll ask her...*

Grandmother Angelique was the mystery woman of the family. This would also be a wonderful opportunity to find out how her grandfather was doing. He too, was a man of mystery, and wherever her grandmother went, he followed like her shadow; consequently, he had not been around much, either.

CHAPTER 21

Rowanne found herself at long last outside of Gloucester Gate in the Regents Park area. She pulled up in front of the beautiful, white, stucco terrace houses. The buildings looked old; possibly dating back to the 1800's.

Excitement built within her as she walked up to the front door and rang the doorbell. She heard footsteps rushing down the stairs, and a moment later the front door opened.

Grandmother Angelique stood grandly, her beautiful golden hair swept up in a sophisticated updo. The women in her family had good genes, one of which was that their hair colour did not fade with time but rather aged beautifully to a deeper shade; her mother was definitely a testament to that.

Remarkably, there was hardly a wrinkle on her face, and she could easily have been mistaken for a lady twenty years younger, Rowanne wondered what her secret was. Her eyes captured everyone's attention, for they were the most beautiful shade of deep violet. Her grandmother was tall and graceful, and radiated an ethereal aura.

Grandmother Angelique coughed to get Rowanne's attention, a bemused look on her face. 'Well, are you going to stand there all day, or will you do me the honour of coming in?' She opened her arms wide, and Rowanne obligingly stepped forward and hugged her grandmother tightly, who appeared fragile. She was afraid of hurting her, and not to mention she felt awkward, as if she were not used to being hugged.

Her grandmother didn't seem to notice as she shut the door behind them and guided Rowanne into the living room, not letting go of her, as if she would run away. The room had a high ceiling from which hung a glass lantern above the marble floor.

Grandmother Angelique invited Rowanne to sit on the chaise lounge next to her. 'You know, I can't quite believe that you're here. I have to pinch myself.'

Rowanne hung her head in shame, 'I am sorry, I've been so neglectful-' her grandmother cut her off.

'There's to be no talk of apologising while you are in my house, put it behind you. You are here and that's all that matters to me,' she said kindly, still holding on to Rowanne's hands gently.

Rowanne began to feel more comfortable, and could not believe that she'd missed out on getting to know her family. Work had always seemed more important, but she wondered if secretly she was trying to avoid her own insecurities.

In the last week, Rowanne had begun to enjoy the wonder of getting to really know people, not just as colleagues, and consequently, her world had opened up in more ways than one. She shyly squeezed her grandmother's hand warmly, feeling better inside herself.

'Would you like tea, or is it coffee you'd prefer?' asked her grandmother.

'Tea would be lovely, thank you,' replied Rowanne. Her grandmother went into the hallway, no doubt going to the kitchen.

Rowanne got up and wandered about the living room, looking at the various antiques her grandparents had collected on their travels. *Amazing, some of these items probably belong in a museum.*

There were antique books in the glass cabinet that appeared very old and fragile. Some of them were written in languages that she could not recognize.

There was a door slightly ajar and Rowanne could not help but take a peek inside. It proved to be the study: there was a deep mahogany buttoned leather sofa on one side, and adjacent to it, facing the door, was a desk in a beautiful burnt autumnal shade.

Cabinets lined either side, filled with the most curious artefacts she'd seen in a while. *What are they?* she wondered, as she looked at the monstrous creatures: some were winged, and had faces, whereas, others had faces missing. They were made in various materials: gold, silver, and wood, as well as burnt wood that appeared almost ivory white or silver.

Rowanne was delighted, and next time she'd insist that they take her on their next adventure, as she was curious to see what they'd turn up with next. Thankfully she had not received any of these as gifts. She would not know where to put them; never mind the fact that any of these would give her sleepless nights.

'I see you have discovered my dark secret!' said Grandmother Angelique in a theatrical voice, scaring the living daylights out of Rowanne, who spun around guiltily to face her. 'That look on your face is priceless,' she laughed.

Rowanne put a hand on her heart, 'I must say, Grandmother, you have a rather *remarkable* choice of collections.'

Grandmother Angelique walked into the room. 'They are rather beautiful and ghoulish at the same time,' she replied, wryly.

'This must have taken you years to build up?' Rowanne gestured towards the cabinets.

'This is but a trifle, you should explore the rest of the house, not to mention, what we have held in storage,' she smiled broadly at the look of astonishment that passed over Rowanne's face. 'Come on, let us have tea.' She went back into the living room with Rowanne following closely behind.

They sat sedately on the lounge, drinking tea. 'So, how is Grandfather doing?'

'He's back in china visiting family.'

'Next time, I think I'll go with him.'

'That would be wonderful. We haven't really gone on holiday together before,' replied her grandmother.

'Grandmother, speaking of family, I have a few questions of my own that I hope you won't mind answering,' said Rowanne, suddenly feeling like a child again.

Rowanne knew that it was a sensitive subject, and twisted her hands together nervously in anticipation of her grandmother's reaction.

'It's alright, Rowanne. I am not suddenly going to break down. I've lived with this my whole life, and time has offered me some perspective.'

She gently held Rowanne's hand, immediately feeling the tension drain out of her granddaughters shoulders as she began to relax.

Grandmother Angelique had a faraway look in her eyes as if recounting troubling memories. She gathered her courage and said, 'I remember it being a cold day, and the rain lightly tickled my cheek. Somebody carried me, perhaps my mother, I don't know... I like to think it was, even though... it was the last time.' She began to choke up, and her grip unconsciously tightened on Rowanne's hand.

'Grandmother, if it's too much then we should stop-' she was interrupted by her grandmother, fervently shaking her head.

'I want to remember. I was left in front of a big beautiful white house. The person who'd carried me had bent down for one last look, but I can't now recall how she'd looked, I wish I could. I remember the sound of a doorbell and her footfalls as she ran away.'

'What happened next?' asked Rowanne gently. She could feel the sorrow emanating in waves from her grandmother, who held her head in her hands as she tried to revisit her memories from seventy years ago. How on earth she'd remembered these small details was remarkable in itself.

Grandmother Angelique turned to Rowanne. 'You know, I often wonder, did she hide somewhere close by and wait to see if I was safely taken inside? Or, did she simply run away never to look back?' She didn't add the fact that she often wondered whether she was loved and wanted, and why she'd been abandoned. She smiled at Rowanne, though her eyes betrayed the turmoil she felt.

'Do you know why Great-Grandmother chose that particular house to leave you at, was there perhaps a family connection?' asked Rowanne.

'I had asked them many questions in my youth, when I was trying to track down my mother and father, but to no avail. And as far as I know, there is no family connection. I was brought up in a large family, amongst my brothers and sisters, and they were all wonderful. The Knights are like kindred spirits to me, and if I could choose a family, it would be them.'

Rowanne watched her grandmother's face light up at the mere thought of her adoptive family. The second part was going to prove trickier, as no one in Rowanne's immediate family had ever met any of Grandmother Angelique's adoptive family. It had always been the elephant in the room that no one acknowledged, out of great respect to her.

Rowanne had often wanted to ask but was always shut down by her parents, who'd insisted she respect her grandmother's privacy, and that when the time was right, she'd bring it up herself. They knew that grandmother had a close relationship with her adoptive family.

Rowanne looked at her grandmother awkwardly, 'Erm... can you tell me about your family?' she asked hesitantly.

Grandmother Angelique looked at her knowingly, 'What is it in particular that you want to know?' she asked.

'Why did you decide to keep your maiden name after marriage?' That was the other hot topic that ran in their family, and she'd often wondered whether or not she herself would change her surname after marriage.

'The Knight family have loved me as one of their own, and the surname is more than just a name to me; I've embraced it as my identity, and it's special to me. Your grandfather understood. And he has met my family,' she added quickly, nervously glancing at Rowanne beneath her long lashes.

Rowanne thought long and hard before she replied, 'Well, I'm glad he met them, and how did it go?'

Feeling relieved that Rowanne had not pursued it further, her grandmother continued, 'Actually, they got on really well. Your grandfather comes from a noble background and he's really down to earth. I've never known a kinder man or one more admirable.'

Rowanne had only met her grandfather Hou on a handful of occasions, and she was ashamed to say that she didn't really know much about where he came from. Part of the reason was that he was a private man who preferred to listen to others rather than speak about himself.

Rowanne admired the way her grandfather's eyes lit up every time her grandmother entered a room, it was like everything and everyone else melted into the background. She secretly wished to find someone like him, someone that made her feel treasured.

'Is he really descended from Chinese royalty?' asked Rowanne, deciding that this was the perfect time to find out as much as she could - why it had not crossed her mind before puzzled her. Every time she had thought of her grandmother in the past, the mere thought of just meeting her would cause her mind to drift, and as a result she had always felt like an absentminded granddaughter. But now, she wondered if there was another reason behind that...

'Your grandfather's ancestors ruled in Zhangjiajie, in the north western part of the Hunan Province.'

Rowanne knew that there was a beautiful national park there, and she would dearly love to visit her grandfather's homeland to learn more about her ancestors.

'Describe it to me?' asked Rowanne.

'It's like stepping into an enchanted world: it is a land of mountains shrouded in mist, the peaks stand magnificently, like sentinels guarding the land.'

Rowanne was mesmerised by the pictures that were conjured up in her mind from her grandmother's description.

'Grandmother, I have to ask, were there any papers left with you? A letter perhaps, from your mother?'

'There was nothing, only the clothes on my back and the blanket I was wrapped in, as well as...' Grandmother Angelique tapered off, wondering how much she should reveal to Rowanne. Was it safe? There was a reason why she had kept her distance from the family all these years...

'Please, Grandmother, you have to continue. Does it have anything to do with the necklace you gave me? You said it was ancestral?'

Grandmother Angelique let out the breath she had not realised she'd been holding. She'd have to proceed cautiously. 'That was the only item in the blanket that my family found, or I should say, my adoptive mother found. We thought my mother must have left it for me, but it didn't point to any clues as to who she was or where she came from. It is priceless, that much I do know. I'm sure you've had the same feeling of wanting to protect it and not let it out of your sight... For me it was the last connection to my mother...' Grandmother Angelique dabbed at the corner of her eye as a tear slid down.

Rowanne looked down guiltily, her cheeks aflame. 'I understand what you're saying. I wore it at first because it was a connection to you, a symbol of your love. But later on I began to build a connection to the necklace itself... Grandmother, did anything out of the ordinary ever happen with the necklace while it was in your care?' *She probably thinks I'm a nut case. I can imagine being thrown out with an antique flying at my head*, thought Rowanne.

Grandmother Angelique studied Rowanne for a long time, who squirmed under her inspection, but at last she said carefully, 'For as long as the necklace was in my possession, it never once to my knowledge behaved in any other way other than as an inanimate object. But I am rather curious to know of your experience with it...' she said in an amused tone, trying to keep it light. But at the same time, she felt herself begin to tense.

Rowanne watched her grandmother carefully as she wondered if she should tell her the truth. She desperately wanted to, but there would be consequences; it would put her grandmother in danger. *What would Alexander do?* she thought.

'Rowanne, sorry to interrupt your thoughts, but you're beginning to worry me a little. What is it precisely that you feel you cannot share with me?' Her grandmother was puzzled, and began in earnest to scrutinise her. There was something amiss with Rowanne; she was hiding something, but what could it be?

Rowanne looked at her, helpless to say anything. But her grandmother was not being entirely truthful, either: she felt it in the way she only gave brief answers, never truly giving anything away.

What was so terrible that her grandmother felt she had to lie? If she had attempted to tell her, then she might have understood, even if there was nothing she could have done. Rowanne was suspicious of the adoptive family: what if they really weren't as decent as her grandmother portrayed them to be?

Grandmother Angelique realised she'd have to make a decision as to whether to keep Rowanne in the dark, or to come clean. Telling her the truth was forbidden, and would put her in danger. She twisted her hands in agitation.

The family would forbid it, as it would put them all in great peril. Not just her adoptive family, but her own, and that included her granddaughter. She felt her mouth go dry in fear.

'Rowanne, I'll be back in a moment,' she left her and went to the kitchen. Her hands shook as she turned on the tap and poured cold water into a cup, drinking it slowly, finding it hard to swallow.

Someone placed their hands on her shoulders, and smiling, she turned around. 'You shouldn't be here! I've told Rowanne that you are in China visiting relatives.' She looked at her husband; she always got butterflies in her stomach whenever she was with him.

Ju-Long was a handsome man with dark brown hair, so dark it could have almost passed for black. His green eyes sparkled as he looked at his beloved wife. His heart always fluttered in excitement whenever he was with her, he could never stay away too long. If his duties didn't call him back so often, then he'd have rather preferred to stay in England, the land of abysmal weather.

His smile lit up his eyes, 'It seems I have come back at the right moment.' She walked into his arms and he held her close, brushing a kiss on top of her silky head.

'We've got problems!' stated Angelique, as she stepped back to lean against the kitchen sink.

Ju-Long closed the door with his foot, giving them privacy as well as advance warning, should their granddaughter walk in. 'I just heard the last part. Our granddaughter is now a half demon!' he proclaimed proudly, one eyebrow arched quizzically.

'Don't look to me for answers, I'm just as baffled as you are. I didn't even realise that she knew of our world. And all these years, I've sheltered them from and kept them out of the notice of Demon World by maintaining minimal contact,' said Angelique broken heartedly.

Ju-Long was instantly beside her and held her hand in comfort. 'I know how hard it was for you,' he said, looking her deep in the eyes with love and understanding. 'All these years almost being separated from them, not even being in our daughter's life that much, let alone in Rowanne's.'

'Do you know, she blames herself. The poor child thinks that she is the one in the wrong, as if she had a choice in keeping in contact with us...' said Angelique.

Ju-Long looked at her fiercely, 'We decided together when we got married that if we had children, and they turned out to be human, then we'd keep them under the radar of Demon World Authority, that it would be the safest thing for them. And if it meant that we could not see our children as much...'

'Hush, dear, we cannot blame ourselves for making that decision. We will always do that which is in their highest interest. And you know what? They never blamed us!' said Angelique.

'We've raised them well, and I'm proud of them, but,' he said wearily, suddenly feeling the years, 'I have missed them, and if there had been any other way, then I'd never...'

She hugged her husband tightly, resting her head on his chest; she could hear his heart beating erratically, giving away his emotions even as he appeared outwardly calm. 'I know, my love, but what should we do about Rowanne?'

'Now that she has been awakened into our world, we must be the ones to initiate her safely into it. We can no longer leave her in the darkness of ignorance, and if she is to navigate *our* world and *live,* then we must also be her guides,' replied Ju-Long.

'Let's go back in,' said Angelique.

Hand in hand, they went into the living room to the utter astonishment of Rowanne, who quickly got up and went to her grandfather.

'Grandfather, when did you get back? I thought you were in China!' Rowanne shook his hand eagerly, eliciting a warm smile from him.

Her grandparents gestured towards the couch, and Rowanne sat down and looked at them expectantly. How lucky that her grandfather should come back now.

Grandmother Angelique looked at her husband, who nodded his head in encouragement that she should tell her the truth. 'I'm afraid, Rowanne, that I haven't been entirely honest with you-'

'That should be *we*. I also take the blame,' he smiled at his wife before turning back to Rowanne.

What the hell is going on here? Rowanne felt a shiver run up her spine - she sensed that something momentous was about to happen, and looked at them steadily, giving them the time to elaborate.

The rain began to fall hard outside, and Rowanne was lulled by the sound as it struck the windows rhythmically. She looked out of the window briefly and noticed that the sky had suddenly gone dark as the clouds blocked out the light. It was as if she were cocooned in a dark blanket; but it was only a false sense of calm.

Grandfather Hou walked towards the light switch, instantly flooding the room in a soft glow that pooled the light in the centre, leaving the edges of the room in shadows.

Grandmother Angelique waited for him to sit down before continuing. 'When I said I didn't know who my parents were, that was the truth. But there was a very good reason why my mother, if indeed it was her, left me with the Knight family.'

Rowanne remained quiet, not wishing to interrupt, and waited patiently.

'She knew that she had to leave me with a family who'd understand my predicament... Someone who'd not hand me over to the authorities, once they learned the truth.' She took a deep breath, 'Even as a child, I knew I was different... I knew that my mother was like me. I grew up in this world that had few of my kind...'

Though Rowanne found it all very cryptic, she did, however, feel a warm glow as the necklace responded to the truth of the words, and perhaps also to being in the company of its former owner.

'You see, Rowanne, I don't actually belong to this world.' said her grandmother.

Rowanne's eyes widened as it slowly dawned on her what her grandmother was trying to convey to her.

Grandfather Hou nodded at Rowanne, 'I see you are just as sharp as your grandmother. You know, don't you?' he asked, looking at her steadily.

Rowanne laughed in disbelief. Here she was worried about sounding crazy to her grandparents, when it turned out, they had a little secret of their own! She ran a trembling hand through her hair, and her maniacal laughter subdued as the enormity of the situation finally dawned on her.

Rowanne stood up and began to pace the room. 'I can't believe this! I want to hear it from your lips,' she demanded, finally coming to a standstill before her grandparents. She looked at them with hurt and anger shining in her eyes.

'Sit down, please, Rowanne,' asked her grandfather gently, realising how hurt his granddaughter must be.

Rowanne sat quietly, but there was a questioning look in her eyes.

Slowly her grandmother began again, 'My mother was a demon, and she brought me over from Demon World to Earth. I don't know why she did this. But she placed me in a family of humans who knew all about my world. They never once questioned why I was left on their doorstep, they took me in and raised me. They filled in the blanks of how my world worked, the rules and regulations that governed it.'

Rowanne listened intently, but was puzzled by what she heard. 'Hold on a minute, Grandmother, you said the people that raised you were human. But then how could they possibly know of the existence of Demon World? I mean, I've never even heard of there being an alternate world to Earth, am I missing something here?'

Her grandmother nodded, 'The Knight family is made up of humans and... half demons.'

Rowanne tried to get her head around it for a moment. She eventually asked slowly, 'So, the people that are half demons, did they all die as well?'

Her grandparents looked at her in shock and confusion not comprehending what she had just said.

'Why would you assume that a human has to die to become a half demon?' asked Grandfather Hou sitting forward, suddenly alert.

'Well, am I correct in assuming that you know what I am?' The secret was out, she thought.

'As soon as I opened the door and saw you, I realised that you had become a half demon. I wasn't sure though, how it had happened. And I suspect you have a lot to tell us, as well,' replied Grandmother Angelique.

'Grandmother, how are half demons formed?' asked Rowanne slowly.

'You mean, born,' corrected Grandfather Hou. 'When a demon has a child with a human, it can, but not always, result in a half demon being born.'

'No wonder you were surprised with my question! So, is there no other way that a human can be converted into a half demon?' asked Rowanne, and held her breath as she wondered what they'd make of her situation. She felt nervous and sick to her stomach.

'There are other ways...' replied Grandfather Hou, 'but they are forbidden, as are half demons. A relationship between a demon and a human is strictly against the law!'

'But then, how is it possible for the Knight family to still be free, and why has no Demon World law stopped *them*?!' asked Rowanne.

'Now, we get down to it! The Knight family stretches back countless generations. They were the first, and as far as I know the last, humans to ever be made aware of the existence of Demon World,' replied Grandmother Angelique.

'I thought that humans were not to know of the existence of Demon World, so why was there an exception made for this family, and what was so special about them?' Rowanne was intrigued by her grandmother's adoptive family. And she felt that she had finally found a place where she might belong, and people to whom she could talk to about her experiences. She had a lot of questions, and if anyone had the answers then it would be them - also her grandparents, who were a fount of knowledge themselves.

Her grandmother answered, 'The Knight family, as Ju Long and any other demon knows, were especially invited at the behest of the First Family, who are the highest authority in the land, second only to the Courts, of course.'

'I've heard that term before... who are the First Family?' asked Rowanne, recalling Lady Enid mentioning them.

Her grandparents exchanged long looks, 'How do you know about them, and who have you been associating with? It is very important that you tell us, as for a human to know of these things could result in the death sentence, or at best a complete memory wipe.'

Rowanne broke out in a sweat; she didn't want to endanger Alexander. 'Let me start from the beginning...'

An hour later, Rowanne's grandparents were now seated on either side of her with tears in their eyes after having heard the ordeal she'd been through. Her grandfather looked as if he had aged a decade, his eyes gaunt.

'Rowanne, you have met some of the most prominent members of our world, and how you are still alive is a miracle! These Noble families cannot always be trusted... I will have to make arrangements to meet with Lady Enid, she is after all the ruler of Demon World, not to mention the fact that she belongs to *the* First Family. I must find out what her intentions are towards you,' said her grandfather.

'Wait, Grandfather, are you sure it's safe? Lady Enid does not know of your connection with me, it might complicate matters.'

'What could be worse than losing your granddaughter and not knowing what happened to you!' said her grandmother, distraught, her hands shaking. 'This is *my* fault. If I had kept in contact more, then I would have known! I thought I was doing the best for you and your mother by keeping you both out of our world.' Sobbing, she shook Rowanne by the shoulders, trying to make her understand just how hard it had been for her, and at the same time trying to convey how sorry she was for all of it.

Rowanne had spent almost two weeks in the world of demons: so much had changed, and she'd also gone through so much. Not just her, but Alexander also. And no wonder her grandparents had wanted to keep her safe; well, as safe as anyone can be in the world of humans. She now understood why her grandparents had distanced themselves. It was akin to what Alexander had done to her, but she didn't like it, not one single bit; no one would. Having her memory tampered with felt like a violation, although she knew that at the same time, they had done it for her own good, to keep her safe. And it must not have been easy for them; it had cost them, as well.

Rowanne hugged this strong woman who'd been separated from her family for so long... how alone they must have felt. She turned her tear streaked face to her grandfather, who patted her head awkwardly. He was never one to show emotion or displays of affection towards his family easily — only with her grandmother could he be so carefree.

'Why do you omit the name of the demon who saved your life? I would like to meet him, make him aware that you are not alone, that you have supporters from Demon World behind you!' said Grandfather Hou, strategising his next moves, and planning for Rowanne's safety to ensure that she had a future to look forward to.

'You also spoke of a ghost, Rowanne? You said it belonged to Demon World. Can you summon it here? Your grandfather and I would like to talk to this entity. We could find out what its purpose is and ask it why it possessed you,' said Grandmother Angelique.

Rowanne did not want Lillian to be harmed. She had omitted a fair share of the truth in respect to the people involved; they had only been trying to help her. After all, some of the secrets were not hers to share, and some of the events were beyond anyone's control.

'I'm not sure that would work here,' said Rowanne, remembering Lillian expressly asking that her name not be mentioned to anybody else, and she was sure that there must be a valid reason behind it.

'You are already displaying loyalty to these people, I see you fitting in perfectly with Demon World. But beware, it is very easy to be caught up in their power struggles and games. Make sure that you do not become a pawn to these people, being pushed around until you are no longer of use to them,' warned her Grandfather starkly, who was at his wits end as to what he should do with his granddaughter, who had so embroiled herself in their World; possibly to her detriment.

Rowanne breathed slowly. She could not blame them for being upset and angry with her; that was their right. And even though they were worried for her, she was nevertheless powerless to tell them everything that they wanted to know.

'Grandmother, have you ever been back to Demon World? And Grandfather, were you born on Earth, or do you come from Demon World? Sorry, I know I'm asking a lot of questions, I'm just very confused. It's like you said earlier, if I'm to navigate Demon World safely, then I need to arm myself with knowledge.' Rowanne did not realise what she had just revealed, as she said it in a matter of fact way.

Grandmother Angelique looked at her husband and spoke to him telepathically, *Do you realise she's been reading our thoughts all this time as if we had spoken them aloud?*

She isn't even aware that she's doing it, and she hasn't picked up on everything we've said. If she was actually doing it on purpose, we'd know! Well, she has started to develop as a demon, replied Grandfather Hou, as he purposely kept his face neutral.

We have to keep an eye on her. I wonder what else she is capable of, and I don't think she even realises the strength she now possesses, said Grandmother Angelique.

An untrained half demon could be a danger... said Grandfather Hou, coming to the slow realisation that he was in fact talking about his own granddaughter. She'd have to be taught eventually to control her powers; to keep not only herself, but others safe as well. He looked at his wife, who with an imperceptible nod of her head, made a silent pact with him to ensure their granddaughter's safety.

Grandmother Angelique turned to Rowanne, and replied, 'I have not been back to Demon World, even though I am a fully fledged Demon. The Knight family and I agree that there must have been an important reason why my mother chose to leave me on Earth instead of raising me on Demon World. We feel it would be unwise and not safe for me to return.'

'I am also a fully fledged Demon, and I do belong to Demon World. I have homes there, as well as here on Earth, in several locations.' Ju-Long looked at his wife as he continued, 'It took a long time for your grandmother to build her trust in me, let alone in other people,' and turning back to Rowanne, he said, 'I do not choose to live by the strict code of conduct demanded by Demon World. Their penalties are severe and cruel, especially when it comes to maintaining its secrecy, and all interactions with Earth.'

Grandmother Angelique looked lovingly at her husband as she addressed Rowanne, 'One day, I'll tell you the story of how we met. Your grandfather is actually a Noble, and his family belongs to the First Families! Thankfully, he isn't a bit like the others... from what he tells me, anyway,' she winked at Rowanne. 'Why he chose *me* is a mystery, since I don't even know my lineage. What you have to understand is that in Demon World, people marry not for love necessarily, but rather to form powerful alliances and political relationships to advance their status and family name.'

'Even humans do that, it's called an arranged marriage or a marriage of convenience,' stated Rowanne, as she wondered about the minefield that she had walked into; namely, Demon World politics.

Grandfather Hou spoke, 'To me, it matters little where a person has come from. Not all demons from the First Families agree to the law against associating with humans and half demons. However, we do all understand the importance of keeping our world a secret, and it is as much for our safety as it is for the humans.'

Grandmother Angelique looked at Rowanne in earnest, 'Imagine, if you will, what would happen if our two worlds were ever to collide. Imagine the far reaching consequences, the unimaginable loss of life on both sides; even demons, being powerful as they are, do not easily dismiss humans. They realise the threat that humans could pose to Demon World and its citizens.'

Rowanne had never had the knowledge before to consider all of this, she'd been too caught up in her own world, her own experiences. 'Grandfather, do they know you are married?'

'They know that my wife is a demon, that is good enough for them. They do not question me openly as to why they have never met her, and even if that day comes, they would not be able to uncover much. And your grandmother and I are not unduly worried about this.'

'Earlier on, you said the Knight family were the last humans invited to Demon World, can you tell me more about them?' Rowanne wondered how it would be like to visit another world, one inhabited by demons! She thought of the Knight family as explorers.

'You could call them that! Lady Enid's family are the Morning Star Clan and the First Family. They invited them at the behest of the highest authority of Demon World because of their special skills, and knowledge of ancient weaponry. They were masters of their profession. It's a mystery as to how they obtained the knowledge they did... The Knight family accepted the invitation, and were made aware of the knowledge of Demon World, and its laws. They knew the consequences of breaking them,' said her Grandfather.

'I'm assuming that something went wrong if they were the only humans... The experiment didn't work, did it?' asked Rowanne.

'That's an understatement!' replied her grandmother. 'However, I am not that well informed on the topic,' and turning to Ju-Long, she gestured for him to continue.

'You have to understand, Rowanne, that this scandal occurred more than seventy years ago, and the precise details are shrouded in mystery. All we do know is that it involved the First Family. Specifically, the heiress to the throne.'

Rowanne wondered what happened. After all, the First Family were protected by their status, so what could they possibly fear?

Her grandfather answered smoothly, 'All citizens of Demon World are subject to the law of the two Courts: the First is the Noble Court, this is where the initial investigations are carried out for misconduct of demons in their own realm, as well as investigations into possible demon and human altercations and interactions. The Nobles of the First Families preside over these Courts represented by the heads of each clan.'

'What are clans?' asked Rowanne, as she connected the pieces of the puzzle to form a complete picture of the inner workings of Demon World.

'Each family is known as a clan, and this conveys their status and power within Demon World. And obviously, The

First Families have the most power. Therefore the power passes through Lady Enid's family, and the Morning Star Clan are the only demons that are allowed to rule our world. The next heir would have been her daughter, the Princess.'

There was something puzzling Rowanne, 'So, you're saying that no other First Family are potential heirs, but what if there was no Morning Star Clan?'

Grandfather Hou answered, 'First of all, as far back as any of us can remember, they have always been the ultimate rulers of our world, and this is stretching back thousands of years.'

'How can it be possible for the same family to rule for such an unimaginable span of time? The Morning Star Clan must be made up of so many people.' Rowanne's imagination ran wild, just picturing it.

'Actually, it doesn't quite work that way. In Demon World, families do not produce many children, we are not quite sure why this is the case. You might be interested to know that one of the perks of being a full demon is immortality...' Grandfather Hou waited for Rowanne to digest this, and watched her eyes go wide as she coughed and sputtered in surprise.

She raised an eyebrow in consternation, not quite believing what she had heard, 'You really expect me to believe that?! Now I know you're making things up. If, as you said, 'full demons are immortal' then why have you both-' Rowanne was too embarrassed to continue.

Her grandparents smiled, bemused. Grandmother Angelique answered, 'Demons view immortality as both a gift and a curse,' she looked at her husband, who readily nodded his head in complete accord with her, and smiled as a knowing look passed between them. 'Imagine what it would truly be like, to live forever, especially, as you watch loved ones pass from both worlds, and how barren a place it becomes as the world changes. It becomes a curse, as you slowly lose the will to live. And the things that once gave you great happiness lose their meaning over time. You die inside, even though outwardly you can have the youth and exuberance of a twenty year old, and you might eventually feel as if you have become a living corpse.'

'Not everyone views eternity in that way, of course! There are whole demon families that choose immortality, as it gives them great comfort to know that they will never die, and a lot of families have consolidated power in this way,' said Grandfather Hou, thinking of his own family as being lasting rulers.

'So, you have the choice, then; you can age normally or become an immortal? That's incredible.' Rowanne didn't ask why her grandparents had turned their back on immortality; it was private, between the two of them.

'The First Family are the only ones that do not have a choice in this matter. As rulers, they have responsibilities that must be upheld by each member, forever. Now can you see how it is a curse to be born into that noble family? The power can only pass down through their line, as such there must always be someone to carry on the authority and legacy. You asked me before what would happen if there was no Morning Star Clan; there would be one of the biggest power struggles and bloodiest battles, the likes of which Demon World and Earth has yet to see - and I hope that dark day never comes. The Morning Star Clan are more than rulers, they keep the peace in Demon World as well as ensuring the safety of this one,' said Grandfather Hou.

Rowanne imagined hundreds of faceless demons made of shadow, descending on people. She envisioned the world being covered in a smothering dark blanket snuffing out humanity, and when the darkness cleared, what would remain of their world…?

'They are the only ones to keep the hordes of demons in check, although not every Noble family agrees with them. If any of the others ever came to power, then I'm afraid it would mean the very fabric of this world changing. There would be cruel laws to govern the whole of humanity, and punishment beyond your worst nightmares. We would become their prisoners,' finished Grandfather Hou.

'But then, if something has happened to the Princess, is that the reason why Lady Enid continues to lead?' asked Rowanne, wondering how she bore the weight of two worlds on her shoulders, as well as living with whatever happened to her child. 'And is there no other heir to carry on the family name, was she an only child?'

'That's right,' answered Grandfather Hou, pleased to see how sharp his granddaughter was at gathering all the facts and quickly putting them together. Rowanne would make one tough half demon, someone who would hopefully become a force to be reckoned with, especially if she took after the warrior side of his family! 'Lady Enid is a strong and wise ruler, but she also has no choice but to rule indefinitely, unless...'

'Unless what?' asked Rowanne, wondering what the alternative could be. She respected and greatly admired Lady Enid as a courageous person to look up to.

Grandfather Hou replied, 'She can pass on the power to another demon not of her family, as long as they belong to the First Families. This has never been done before in the history of Demon World. Again, the consequences of this could be catastrophic for *this* world, depending upon whom she passes the mantle to, and whether they looked favourably on humans. Demon World citizens and the Nobles would have to abide by this decision. This is the least terrible scenario that I can think of; though truthfully, it doesn't bode well for the humans.'

'Surely, Lady Enid must have support?' asked Rowanne.

Her grandparents exchanged weary looks before Grandmother Angelique answered, 'The Nobles are more likely to hinder you and stab you in the back than help you. It is all a game of chess played by pretenders who long for the ultimate throne.'

Grandfather Hou laughed darkly, and outside thunder cracked ominously, causing the lights inside to flicker and go out, so that momentarily they were plunged into darkness before the lights reluctantly came back to life. 'Well, perhaps not the ultimate throne! There's not a demon yet that would be that fool hardy, unless they have a death wish!' his green eyes glowed in fear at the thought even being voiced aloud; even to utter such things was not without peril...

Her grandmother nodded her head vehemently, sending up a silent prayer that they not be heard.

Rowanne's spine tingled and the hairs on the back of her arms and neck rose. Goosebumps broke out, and she felt ice lodge and settle in her heart. She had the strong feeling of someone walking over her grave. Ever so slowly the temperature in the room began to rise after it had suddenly plunged.

Rowanne felt the burning heat as sweat trickled down her forehead. 'Perhaps, we should move onto another topic,' she said, and smiled weakly at them.

Her grandparents held their breath, and once they felt the danger pass, the tension drained out of their weary bodies.

'What happened to the Princess?' asked Rowanne.

'She was accused of breaking the law but no one knows the exact details. And because it was a Noble of a First Family that made the accusation, she was investigated at the First Court. This created a great scandal for the Morning Star Clan, and Lady Enid barely survived it. Judgement was passed onto their daughter, and she was taken to Prima Stella,' answered Grandfather Hou.

'That's the highest court in Demon World, right?' asked Rowanne. Lady Enid had spoken of it with her.

Her grandparents worried about the level of knowledge that she already possessed, and hoped for her sake that the demons who had helped her were really on her side. When the time comes, would they choose her life over theirs? It seemed highly unlikely. If only they knew who these demons were, then they could manoeuvre themselves into a better position in order to protect her.

Rowanne caught the looks that passed between her grandparents. 'You have to have faith in me. I am a good judge of character, and I trust the demons who have helped me. They had no need to do what they did for me, especially as it was at great danger to themselves, but nevertheless, they shielded me, and came to my aid unbidden,' she looked at them unwaveringly with her strong green eyes. She sat straight as a tower, emanating a gentle power of her own; unbeknown to her. Was she scared? Yes, but she refused to be beaten down by fear. She'd face it, and come to a better understanding of herself because of it.

Rowanne thought of all the people that helped her, and if she could, she hoped to help them someday; once she knew more of how Demon World worked. She desperately wanted to help Lady Enid, and didn't like the idea of her being alone amongst the wolves. The Nobles were like scavengers, vultures just waiting for the opportunity to pounce on Lady Enid; and it would be when she least suspected it.

Rowanne's blood boiled, and the room flashed as lightning repeatedly struck the road outside. The ominous clouds gathered together, beginning to swirl unnaturally; this was not normal weather.

Rowanne was suddenly shook out of her dark reverie by her frantic grandparents, who worried for her, for what she was becoming...

She looked at them, oblivious of what had just occurred. 'Sorry, where were we?' she asked her grandparents, who sat on the lounge opposite her with strange looks passing between them.

Her grandfather coughed, clearing his throat that had swelled due to the fear she had invoked in them for her safety. If she continued like this, then she'd be on the Demon World radar in no time.

'The Princess did not return, and it nearly tore apart Lady Enid. From that day on, she rarely appeared in public, and when she did, it was behind a black veil. And still to this day she wears the mourning clothes. Her daughter was her light, her life resided in her,' said her grandfather.

Rowanne felt her heart become heavy, weighed down with sadness for this great woman, for all she had endured and still did for the greater good. She felt a connection with Lady Enid, and now understood what she had gone through, even if she could not fully realise her pain.

'Who was the Noble that raised the complaint against the Princess in the first place?'

'That information has never been revealed, but it made her prosecutor the most feared and hated demon in the land.'

My God! he makes Driskell seem like a walk in the park, thought Rowanne, and out of curiosity she asked who it was.

'Dewain Driskell of the Dark Lake Clan,' replied Grandfather Hou, and watched as the colour drained from Rowanne's face to be replaced by anger that flashed in her eyes.

'I knew that man was evil, but I didn't know what he was truly capable of.' It all began to make sense, why Lady Enid hated him so much, and why he feared her fury. But why did *he* hate her?

Rowanne knew now why Lady Enid had helped her: maybe, she was trying to reconcile with the past that had so cruelly taken her daughter from her, whilst, she had been powerless to stop it because of her title. Lady Enid above all others must be seen to uphold the law of Demon World, especially if she was to continue to be seen as the rightful ruler.

Everyone had told her that Demon World politics was akin to playing a deadly game of chess, and even Lady Enid was a piece on the board who had to manoeuvre herself safely through the minefield that was her world in order to consolidate her power.

Rowanne could imagine that there was no end to the Nobles who'd usurp the throne in a heartbeat, if they could. They were like jackals licking at Lady Enid's heels, maintaining only an outward show of respect for her power. In the end it was all an illusion; how fragile everything suddenly seemed to her.

Rowanne was alarmed at the knowledge pouring into her... Was this normal? She was processing everything quickly, her mind barely tired. Where was this all coming from, and were they even her thoughts? She could almost imagine her brain sparking as new connections were rapidly being made. She felt dizzy, and closing her eyes, sat back.

She must have passed out, because the next thing she saw was her grandmother lightly throwing water in her face to wake her.

'What happened?' asked Rowanne, groggily. Her head still felt like it was spinning, but she was getting used to its pace.

'Here, drink this. I think your body is going through some *adjustments*, shall we say. I've seen it happen at a slower pace for half demons that are born. But with the way you were transformed... I can't say. I suspect it's happening at a faster pace, and it is dangerous to have so much knowledge in one go, as it is too much for a person to handle, but thankfully your demon side is taking the brunt of it,' replied her grandmother.

Rowanne looked at her watch, and could not believe that so much time had passed - it was already late into the evening. She was due to meet Amanda at her offices soon. She smiled at her grandparents, 'I'm afraid I have to make a move. There are some pressing matters that I need to attend to,' she said, and started to gather her belongings.

'Wait, Rowanne, there is so much that you do not know! And there is still much to discuss,' said her grandfather, exchanging a worried glance with his wife.

Rowanne took a deep breath to centre herself. 'Don't worry, I'll visit again soon, I promise. I don't feel alone anymore. And I know now that if I have any questions, and I'm sure there'll be many, that I have family whom I trust and love that I can turn to.'

This didn't ease their tension, but they also knew that they'd have to eventually let her go. Rowanne was, after all, a grown woman, and they could shield her only so much; after that it came down to her instincts and her own sound knowledge. They were proud of her, and they would do all in their power to keep her safe.

Rowanne got up and hugged her grandmother fiercely; her grandfather shook her hand warmly, and gave her a meaningful look, and in her mind she could have sworn that he asked her to take great care of herself, for their sake.

Rowanne's grandparents walked her to the front door, and waved her off. They didn't go back inside until they saw her car pull out of the road.

CHAPTER 22

Dark thoughts swirled in Rowanne's mind, and she was now a different person than the one that had first stepped into her grandparent's house. Turns out, she was now an unofficial member of Demon World; but she didn't know how she felt about it. Did she even want to go to Demon World? Maybe... not that she'd be allowed, she'd probably be executed on sight!

She tried to focus on the road ahead; there was a lot of traffic, and by now it was dark, but thankfully it had stopped raining, and slowly she inched closer to home.

Rowanne was still trying to make her mind accept the fact that her grandparents were actually demons! She would never in a million years have believed them if she had not encountered it herself.

To think, my ancestry stretches back into another world... How could people not have realised that another world exists right alongside our own? Surely, scientists would have known by now? Where in the universe is Demon World? she wondered.

The world as she knew it had changed, and as much as she'd like to go back and erase everything, she could not disregard the knowledge she now possessed. How should she view the world? She could have been speaking to demons all along without even realising it, as they passed themselves off as humans in society. Would she now have to think twice before speaking to a person?

Rowanne's head hurt with the amount of things that she'd have to get her head around eventually. Some of her questions were still unanswered, including the precise nature of the incident involving the Knight Family and the Princess - it was still a mystery. It didn't seem as if her grandparents actually knew the finer details; it was all just speculation, not to mention the fact that the First Family would have covered it up.

The Knight Family would surely know the reason why their ancestors were expelled from Demon World, including Grandmother Angelique? *She grew up in that family, they must have told her; especially with her being a demon,* thought Rowanne.

If this was the case, then why would her grandmother not discuss it with her? Rowanne knew that the Knight family were extremely private, they guarded their secrets well; after all, they had survived Demon World.

How had the Knight Family survived unscathed, whereas the Princess it seemed had faced the full judgment and was (from all that she had heard and witnessed) executed? It was such an ugly word and her spine tingled with the horror associated with it.

She didn't even want to think about what a demon, let alone a human, faced when the death sentence was passed. Maybe it was the fact that she was dancing with death, her newly acquired knowledge putting her at risk of discovery from Demon World. And if they ever found out just how much she knew, then everybody she cared about would also be put in danger.

No wonder Alexander was always uncomfortable in her company. He must have always been wondering if she'd accidentally tell the wrong person about Demon World, and consequently how fast they would find not just her, but the demon responsible for her knowledge. How exactly would she explain being turned into a half demon...?

Her grandparents had known at once that she was a half demon, so how was it possible that Driskell (the most feared demon in the land) had failed to pick up on this vital knowledge... she had an uneasy feeling in the pit of her stomach. She had thought that she was free from Driskell, but now she could not help but wonder if that was really the case at all.

Driskell had discovered the truth about the Princess and then disclosed it. Unfortunately, her status and family name had not been enough to save her; *Who the hell am I in comparison, and what hope do I really have of keeping out of his clutches?* wondered Rowanne.

She was beginning to think it was just a matter of sheer dumb luck and helpful people that had kept her beneath his notice. Perhaps there was more to come. She was at the centre of a sinister game, and didn't know who all the players were, so how could she possibly know when they'd make their move? She had a feeling that a nasty surprise was in store for her.

Rowanne's necklace pulsed in warning. She wished the damn thing could actually communicate with her: what good was a warning on its own, without the details!

'That's what I'm here for! Hello, Rowanne, it's been too long...'

Rowanne swerved her car, and narrowly avoided the oncoming traffic in the adjacent lane.

'You scared the life out of me! You can't just show up unannounced like this, especially when I'm driving!' said Rowanne angrily to the beautiful girl in the passenger seat.

'Nice to see you, too!' said Lillian, irritated. After all she had done for the ungrateful human, she'd at least have expected a thank you. After all, she had been the one left behind in Demon World, whilst madam here had run off in the arms of her Romeo.

'That is not exactly true. If you remember, I was the one who'd insisted you not be left behind. But *you* told me to go!'

384

said Rowanne, mortified by what she was hearing. 'And another thing, escaping from the guards hardly constitutes romance! Alexander was merely helping me...'

'How quickly you come to his defence. Not so long ago, you were both at each other's throats!' scoffed Lillian.

Rowanne thought it best that they change the topic quickly: she didn't want to venture into those murky depths, especially with Lillian of all people. 'When did you get back? I tried to reach you.'

'It's getting harder now to come back each time.' Lillian didn't add that revisiting Rowanne's memories to unlock the truth for her, as well as taking her to Demon World, had taken its toll. She had used up a lot of energy in the human world; energy that was slowly trickling back to her, though there was less of it each time. And she didn't want to worry Rowanne by burdening her with this information.

'It's because we're separate, you are no longer a part of me. I think the necklace and my life force were what kept you going,' stated Rowanne matter-of-factly, not a hint of recrimination in her voice.

Lillian smiled, that was Rowanne for you! And she was beginning to sound more like her every day: that same, precise, no-nonsense attitude to life. Rowanne was looking at her with a funny puzzled expression.

'What is it, have I suddenly grown horns?' asked Lillian.

'For a second there, you reminded me of someone familiar... it's the expression on your face... I can't quite place it, but it will come to me eventually.' Rowanne observed the way the light seemed to catch Lillian's hair, and her eyes had a weariness to them of someone who has been in the world a long time; too long perhaps, and seen too much.

'Let's get back to business. And take that ridiculously morose expression off your face! I'm still here, and I don't plan on going anywhere until I have my answers!' and silently Lillian added, *and settled my scores...*

Rowanne's necklace glowed in anticipation of the trouble that was brewing ahead. It suddenly flared up, and produced a blinding violet flash that temporarily blinded her, so that she ended up slamming on the brakes. Thankfully, there had not been a car in front or behind her, otherwise...

'Lillian! You have to keep calm or very soon, I'll end up joining you!' said Rowanne, frustrated beyond belief; that was the third time today that she had nearly had an accident! And she remembered the superstitious belief that bad things always come in three. Well, she'd fulfilled her quota, what more could possibly happen...?

'I'm... sorry. I just got so angry. It's that necklace of ours! It amplifies everything, from your emotions to your powers! You must have noticed by now, that if you're really frightened or angry, then strange and inexplicable things start to happen around you.'

'Does it by any chance, and this is going to sound really stupid, effect the weather?' Rowanne waited with bated breath for Lillian to laugh at her. She started the car and once more began the slow shuffle home.

'Naturally. Though, it's probably *you* more so than it is the necklace. A higher level demon's mood could affect the weather, but most demons are trained, so that they don't let their emotions trickle out into their power. You have much to learn, my girl.' *Not that I'm any example to go by. I'm becoming a rank amateur!* she thought mournfully.

Lillian came across as a school teacher explaining basic concepts to an unruly child; or so it appeared to Rowanne. Lillian had the ability to rile people instinctively.

'I got back a couple of hours ago and have been looking for you ever since. I was trying to avoid using my abilities as much as possible. What's happened since we last met?' asked Lillian.

Rowanne was not sure how much she should reveal, especially concerning her grandparents. 'I've just come back from meeting my grandmother, but she could not help to shed any light on her family background, and said that she had inherited the necklace.' That was as close to the truth as she could get without revealing more. She felt a strange uneasiness at keeping the truth from Lillian, who was looking at her with a sad expression; it was as if she was more than disappointed with what she had heard.

'Are you sure there isn't anything else? She didn't mention any names?' This time Lillian looked at her with a fierce determination that unsettled Rowanne. She had not intended to make her uneasy, but she desperately needed answers of her own. There was more at stake than Rowanne's life; many more people were now consequently in danger, but unaware of it.

Rowanne bit her lip unconsciously, drawing blood. Looking straight ahead, she answered, 'No... I wish I could tell you more... but that is all there is.'

Rowanne failed to notice that Lillian's expression had changed, her eyes blazing an unearthly violet as a strange faraway look came into them. She sat in a trance unbeknown to Rowanne, who continued to drive. Finally, Lillian came back to herself, peace settled in her heart for the first time in a very long time. She knew what she had to do... She smiled at the necklace that glowed warmly in its former owner's presence. *Thank you, dear friend,* she thought.

Rowanne neared the Thames and stopped at a crossroads: she could either continue home, or go to the offices. The dashboard clock showed her that she had an hour to go, and making her mind up, she drove towards her offices.

'I must say that you are looking better than the last time I saw you. There's a calm about you, it suits you. Why are you going to your former place of work, I thought you had left?'

Rowanne whipped her head around fast, facing Lillian, 'How could you possibly know that? No one outside of work knows that I have left. I haven't even told my family!'

'Rowanne, it's *me*. Of course I'd know!' stated Lillian, by way of an explanation.

Rowanne drove up Victoria Embankment - she was nearly there. 'I have a lot to tell you! First, I nearly died chasing the ghost of the missing security guard, Thomas! Secondly, I plan on following him to the end tonight!' she finished quickly, without pausing for a breath. She let Lillian digest the information.

'Fantastic! this whole mystery might be wrapped up by tonight, what a splendid plan. I'm really impressed right now!' Sarcasm and disdain dripped heavily from Lillian. *What on Demon World is this human thinking? Of all the stupid schemes!*

'I'm glad you're so thrilled. Please, keep your enthusiasm in check,' said Rowanne resignedly. Lillian was like an annoying relative that you could not quite shake off. She pulled up into the empty car park and switched off the lights as soon as she had parked.

Rowanne sat in the dark, unable to see Lillian beside her; it was a little creepy but she sensed her presence.

'Well, who else is involved in this, Alexander by any chance? Maybe Lady Enid will pop up!' said Lillian, fuming.

'Do I look completely stupid to you? No, don't answer that!' She quickly amended, as she saw the eagerness with which Lillian was about to reply. 'I would never endanger Lady Enid or anyone else for that matter, but...' Rowanne looked at her remorsefully, 'Amanda, from work, has agreed to come with me...'

'How could you be so stupid as to invite another human into this mess? *You* are putting her in more danger than you realise, and I'm not talking about the harmless ghost, he's the least of our problems. What if not only you, but also your friend, came under the notice of Demon World? You're probably already on their radar,' said Lillian wearily.

'What do you mean by that last part?' Rowanne's heart began to beat fast, though she had been suspecting the same thing herself for a while now, just not wanting to acknowledge it.

'Then you *aren't* completely dim witted! We both suspect that the attack on you originally might not have been by random demons,' said Lillian.

'Why do you think I was targeted?' asked Rowanne.

'I suspect someone, most likely a demon, recognised the necklace for what it was. Not many people outside of my world know what that necklace represents, but they can smell power a mile away! A demon would do anything for power, and I don't have to tell you what power can do in the wrong hands. You don't need to look at *my world* as an example of that...' stated Lillian.

Rowanne received a text, 'Amanda's asking of my whereabouts. Hold on, give me a second.' Rowanne messaged back and instantly got a reply, 'She's told me to come to the back door, she's already in the building. She must have parked down one of the side roads to look less suspicious.'

'I like your friend. Thank God one of you possesses a brain!' said Lillian cuttingly.

Rowanne chose to ignore her and counted to ten in her mind before grabbing her phone, and leaving the car. She walked briskly to the entrance, while Lillian quietly followed her - this, however, did nothing to alleviate her fears. In no time at all, she had reached the back door, which was ajar, and she saw Amanda huddled on the threshold, nervously looking around.

'Thank God! You've finally arrived. Get in here quick, it's freezing!' Amanda rubbed her hands together furiously to keep warm - after all, December was not far off.

Rowanne felt the cold penetrate her heavy coat, and her breath misted in the air. The building was pitch black, not a single light was on. She quickly followed Amanda through the door, before closing it behind her.

Amanda stood beside the stairs waiting for her.

'Sorry. It took me forever to get here. I came straight from my grandmother's house,' said Rowanne, her teeth chattering.

Amanda looked at her steadily, 'How did it go?'

'Well, I guess it went better than I expected,' she answered vaguely, not wishing to go into any details just yet. 'Let's go to the office first and get some coffee, I have a feeling I'll need some just to stay awake,' she said, as she followed Amanda up the stairs.

She felt a tap on her back, a little reminder that she was not alone! *Great, that's all I need, Casper the Friendly Ghost!*

Rowanne stumbled forward, but managed to catch herself.

'Are you okay?' asked Amanda.

'Go ahead, I just lost my balance.' Rowanne waited for Amanda to continue before angrily turning behind her to confront Lillian, who wore an amused expression. Rowanne turned her back on her, but could hear ghostly laughter in her mind. Finally, she reached the first floor lifts, Amanda already waiting inside, and as soon as she stepped in, the doors closed behind, taking them to the top floor.

Stepping out, Rowanne followed Amanda through the office doors to the staff lounge.

'Sit down, you look like a human icicle!' said Amanda, turning on the coffee machine.

Rowanne gratefully sank into the sofa as Amanda brought over two steaming mugs, settling them onto the table. She gratefully held her mug, warming herself.

Amanda sat beside her, and asked, 'So, what's the plan? I'm going on faith here. You don't realise how difficult it was to set this whole thing up! I've switched off certain cameras, so we're safe on that front. The security guard is asleep, so there'll be no trouble from that end, either.' She drank her coffee, grateful to feel the warmth spreading through her.

Rowanne looked at Amanda with admiration, 'How on earth did you manage all that? I won't ask why the guard is sleeping... I'll take your word on that! I assume you *tweaked* the security system, otherwise we'd have guards running up here,' said Rowanne astutely.

Amanda had a rueful look on her face that didn't quite match the fierce delight that sparkled in her dark blue eyes, 'Yes, I like that word. I 'tweaked' the system, so that certain cameras will run on a loop,' she said, with great poise.

'I haven't got a solid plan, it's as basic as following Thomas, and beyond that we will have to see what happens.' Looking at her watch, Rowanne realised that they had half an hour to go, and putting her hand on Amanda's shoulder, she said sincerely, 'Thanks again, for coming. I know none of this makes any sense to you.'

'Hey, no problem. I'm always up for a ghost hunt. And I always wondered what the people on TV actually saw and felt when investigating haunted places,' replied Amanda.

Rowanne smiled, 'I guess we're about to find out.'

They sat, quietly counting down the minutes. The atmosphere became tense when they proceeded to make their way back down to the first floor. The lift doors opened and they stood in the corridor waiting.

'Are you ready for this?' asked Amanda, who felt the excitement like a current running through her.

Rowanne looked wearily to the office, and replied, 'As ready as I'll ever be. Let's go,' and slowly she edged closer, not wanting to make a noise — not that the ghost would notice, anyway.

They stood just before the door, just as the needle of her watch reached twelve o'clock exactly, and the show began without further delay.

The room started to glow an unearthly shade of blue. 'I'm debating whether we should go in, or just wait here for him. Listen, you go down the stairs and wait for him there, just in case I miss him,' said Rowanne.

Amanda didn't look happy with the plan, 'Are you sure that's a good idea? What if something goes wrong? I won't be there to help you.'

Rowanne looked at her steadily while keeping watch for the resident ghost, 'Look, the worst that can happen is that he doesn't show up tonight, and I miss the chance to find out what happened. Don't worry, I'm still in one piece from my last encounter with him. It's like you said before, he's reliving his last moments on a loop. Therefore, I don't think he'll interact with us,' said Rowanne, with a conviction she didn't feel - but it was enough as she watched Amanda head to the stairs.

Amanda turned towards her, and mouthed a silent, 'Good luck,' before heading down.

I can do this! thought Rowanne, as she entered the room. The overhead lights flickered on and off. She decided to go to the back of the room to get a better view of the whole office, and to be ready for his arrival; she would not be caught off guard, again!

Her necklace began to pulse, and glowed a shade of violet under her coat; it was one of the reasons she'd sent Amanda downstairs. She could not come up with a good excuse as to why her necklace did this. Well, an excuse that would sound plausible, at least.

This time the scene unfolded differently, or maybe she had somehow missed what had happened prior to Thomas entering the office. She jumped as she heard the doors to the offices slam shut, and had a feeling that they'd be locked, even if she were to try and open them.

Blue light appeared suddenly in the centre of the room in the form of a sphere that seemed suspended in mid air. Rowanne had a bad feeling about this...

It exploded outwards, and she quickly threw her arms up to shield her eyes, not noticing the blue light covering every inch of the office and bathing her too.

Slowly, Rowanne opened her eyes, light spots dancing in front of her, and she waited patiently until her vision returned, and finally noticed. Everything appeared sinister, her necklace glowing fiercely keeping the shadows at bay.

The light from her necklace reached out until it mingled with the blue light, then something strange happened...

Another memory was unlocked, despite Alexander's best efforts.

The room plunged into darkness, but Rowanne held her nerve. She was not about to run away, not this time. She waited a second as the lights turned on, and this time the room was bathed in a hazy white light, giving the now miraculously restored room a dreamlike quality.

Oh, this is how the room looked before it was ruined. It was empty, as if everyone had just left. Rowanne was mesmerised as ghostly doors were flung open and at the threshold stood Alexander. She stifled a scream as she saw a dead woman in his arms, only to realise... it was her! *Well, he did tell me that I had died,* she rebuked herself sternly; but to see it before her was another matter. Why was she being shown this again, now...?

The scene seemed to skip forward quickly, but she didn't miss the care and tenderness with which he had attended her. Rowanne felt tears run down her face as she watched him perform the ceremony to turn her into a half demon; her question was finally answered.

There was an ultimate price to pay for a demon wishing to bring a human back to life, and Alexander had not even paused to consider the ramifications: he had in his quiet grace, given her half of his life! Her grandfather had said that demons were immortal, and here was Alexander knowingly sacrificing his immortality so that she would live.

Why did he do that? Why did he save someone he had just met a moment ago? It didn't make any sense to her, but she felt the full weight of the responsibility that now fell heavily on her shoulders with this knowledge.

How on earth am I ever to repay such selflessness... thought Rowanne, feeling ashamed with how she had treated him. It made sense now, why he'd helped her instead of leaving her: they were in danger because of his decision. Rowanne knew it was permanent — Alexander was now mortal. Even if he wanted to live forever, he no longer had that option.

Rowanne did not know how she would be able to face him again, or how she should behave around him... And would he know the truth just by looking into her eyes? She didn't have much time to ponder as the scene faded, bringing her back to the ruined room. The light once more turned blue, and she felt perspiration dripping down her face, and her heart began to beat fast.

The lights in the room began to flash like crazy to herald Thomas's arrival. Ice seemed to form within Rowanne as the room's temperature plunged, her breath coming out as a cold cloud.

She watched Thomas make the rounds, and at one point he walked past the place where she had crouched down. But heedless of her presence, he just followed his eternally fixed course. She let out the breath she had been holding, and quickly scooted off the floor to follow him.

Thomas was fast, he had a measured walk; he knew what he had to do, and was unswerving as he went out the door. Rowanne was almost at his heels, but maintained a short distance between them. She followed him down the stairs, and called out softly, 'Amanda, get ready, here we come!' she didn't hear a reply, but was not unduly worried.

He had reached the bottom, and Rowanne looked around frantically for any sign of Amanda, but there was none. *I hope she hasn't run into the security guard...* thought Rowanne, and determinedly followed Thomas out the front doors. After all, there was every chance that she could be outside.

'Don't worry, you have me,' whispered Lillian.

'Where were you? I thought you'd be in the room with me,' said Rowanne, quietly.

'I was barred from going into the room! All I could do was pace outside until you came. There was strong magic concentrated in that room, and I didn't have the energy to force my way in,' replied Lillian.

'Don't worry about that now. I don't want him out of our sight. By the way, did you happen to see where Amanda went? She was supposed to be waiting at the bottom of the stairs,' said Rowanne, hoping that she was okay.

'I heard a commotion downstairs, but I could not risk leaving you to investigate,' said Lillian, hoping that Rowanne's human friend had not gotten into any trouble.

Rowanne felt a knot of fear curl in her stomach, as she thought, *Amanda, what's happened to you?* 'Listen, I know you won't agree, but I want you to go back and look for her. I'll continue to follow Thomas.'

'Are you out of your mind? Do you think for one moment that I'll just allow you to walk headlong into danger without me?' hissed Lillian, glaring at Rowanne. She looked frightening to Rowanne with the full force of her power trained on her.

'Lillian, you have to trust me at some point. I will be fine. And besides, this is not the first time I've had to follow someone! You'd be surprised at what I've done for my profession. I won't take any unnecessary risks, and I'll stay a good distance back. Now go and help someone who might really be in need of your help,' she looked pointedly at Lillian, whilst keeping Thomas in her sight.

Lillian thought it a stupid idea, and didn't like it, but realised that she was wasting time by arguing. She'd have to eventually let Rowanne go at some point, and had to have faith that she could survive without her intervention all the time. She looked at Rowanne disgustedly, before gruffly nodding her head and quickly headed back to look for Amanda.

Rowanne tried to make up the distance she had lost while speaking with Lillian, and was just in time to see Thomas turn a corner. She shot forward at a dead run.

She rounded the corner in time to see Thomas being attacked by two Shadow men. One of them knocked him out by hitting something against the side of his face, causing him to bleed and collapse; the second Shadow man caught him before he could hit the ground, and a portal opened behind them.

Rowanne had not expected this when she was going through all the possible scenarios! She stood where she was; it was safer than going forward. The surrounding street lights turned off, as if a power failure had occurred, and it extended to the surrounding buildings until the whole area was plunged into darkness.

In the centre of the portal stood a tall shadowy figure - it was hard to make out the finer details from where she stood. And the two men seemed to answer to that person, as they duly carried Thomas through the portal that closed behind them.

She had a small fleeting hope that Thomas could still be alive, but then why this whole elaborate display of him appearing in a ghostly form? And where exactly was he taken... to Demon World, or was he still here, somewhere on Earth? She had a sinking feeling... *It's a trap you fool,* her mind screamed at her, and her necklace had also been flashing wildly: she had felt an invisible pull to go back, but she'd been heedless of its warning, immersed as she was in what was going on before her.

Why would they take Thomas? It just didn't make any sense. Rowanne realised that she might very well have to go to Demon World to find out, if there was no other option.

Just as she was turning back to find out where on earth Amanda had got to, she received a sharp blow to the head.

CHAPTER 23

Rowanne heard a strange buzzing sound in her ear, and it took her a moment to get her bearings. She realised it was Alexander, trying to get through to her. She held her head in her hands, willing the sharp pain to go away, and closed her eyes to block everything out.

Slowly the pain receded to a dull ache, and she could now make out Alexander's concerned expression as he knelt beside her. 'Sorry, what were you saying?' her voice sounded unsteady.

'Are you alright? Do you want to lie down?' asked Alexander, with his attention trained on her. She didn't seem to be unduly concerned by the fact that someone had attacked her, and could still be close by.

'Well, apart from having one hell of a headache, I'm fine. Did you happen to see who attacked me?' asked Rowanne, as she tried getting up but felt a wave of nausea hit her, and collapsed back down.

'Perhaps I should take you to the hospital, you could have a concussion,' said Alexander, helping Rowanne up, who actually took his support without complaining for once! *Well, it seems there is a first time for everything*, he mused.

'I have to find Amanda first, she was here with me. I'm worried about her,' said Rowanne as she tried to walk back to the office building, practically dragging Alexander along with her.

'Walk slowly, otherwise you might collapse again. And then I will have no choice but to carry you into the hospital myself!' He looked at her with a disgusted expression, for the lack of care with which she looked after herself.

Lillian appeared before them so suddenly that Rowanne ended up walking straight through her, and spun around in shock.

'You have to stop doing that! Every time I get the sensation of someone walking over my grave,' said Rowanne, shivering.

'Well, that's the thanks I get for coming to warn you that our dear Driskell is just around the corner with Amanda! He doesn't look too pleased... Call me if you need me,' and with that, she vanished into thin air.

However angry she may be, Rowanne could still feel Lillian's presence; she was close by, and Rowanne found it extremely reassuring. She looked at Alexander's tense expression - she didn't want him to feel like that anymore. And she *would* try not just for herself, but for him, to become stronger to be able to face their problems. It was *her* turn to keep everyone safe, and she'd do whatever it entailed; damn the consequences to herself!

'We've got this, just follow my lead,' said Rowanne, with a confidence she only half felt.

She smiled at his look of astonishment. She stood straight, gently unclasped her hand from his arm, and after two wobbly attempts managed to walk forward with grace and poise, while he kept pace with her.

Rowanne stopped and turned to him, 'Look, I think perhaps it would be better if I faced Driskell alone. His suspicions will be aroused if he sees us together.'

'I don't think that's a good idea. You can barely walk as it is, and I'm amazed you haven't fallen flat on your face yet. Maybe I could be of some use to your friend, if she's in trouble,' said Alexander wryly.

'I haven't got the time to argue with you. It's important I

get to Amanda, who by the way is clearly capable of taking care of herself, and-'

'Taking care of the good detective as well. I remember,' added Alexander, under his breath.

'I don't know what you're mumbling about. But trust me, we can take care of Driskell, rest assured on that front,' said Rowanne, and looked at him steadily, hoping he'd get the hint.

'Finally! You're talking sense. Let's go,' he said, smiling brightly.

Rowanne coughed, and said awkwardly, 'I was actually referring to Amanda and I.' She was exasperated with him, but was pleased to see the smirk wiped off his face, replaced by a disparaging smile.

Alexander held up his hands, 'Fine. But I will be close by if you need me, and I will not wait for your permission,' with that bleak warning, he left.

He'll probably be close by watching my every move, thought Rowanne. *Now I have two sets of eyes on me.* How did he manage to turn it around to his favour, every time... perhaps the man was beyond help! *Don't count me out just yet...* she thought.

Rowanne rounded the corner, and found Amanda leaning against the wall, talking furiously with Driskell. Well, she had not expected that. What on earth was going on?

'Ms Knight, I was wondering when you'd join us,' said Driskell mirthlessly. 'Perhaps you can persuade your friend here to accede to my humble request,' he smiled audaciously at Amanda.

Rowanne looked at Amanda's awkward expression; she could have cut the tension with a knife. Amanda seemed to be the devil-may-care type, so what could have incensed her? But, then again, looking at Driskell, it all made sense.

Rowanne realised slowly that Driskell was not here for her, but for Amanda. He seemed to be fixated with her, and she didn't envy her that position. Driskell seemed to barely register Rowanne's presence.

'And what request would that be?' asked Rowanne, trying to figure out a way to intervene, if it was at all possible.

Amanda's eyes flashed dangerously; she was losing patience fast, as she quickly answered, 'I was just informing the Chief Inspector-'

'Please, call me Dewain,' insisted Driskell, he had on his most charming smile as he flashed his teeth; he was in an unusually good mood.

'Like I said, I've just been explaining to Chief Inspector *Driskell*, that you've been helping me with research on a piece I'm working on,' she paused, as Driskell's smile was replaced by a more contemplative look. He didn't seem to be the type of man to handle rejection well, and she doubted anyone had ever said 'No' to him before.

'I was just suggesting to Miss Eghan that perhaps I could help her with... research,' added Driskell quickly.

Amanda looked at him sharply; only moments before, he had asked her out for dinner tomorrow night. Why was he suddenly so reluctant to reveal this? She waited for him to speak, but he just looked at her with a death stare. Suddenly, she felt very cold, and it started to spread through her until her mind became murky.

Driskell took the momentary distraction to take Amanda's arm and loop it through his own. 'I'm so glad you've changed your mind. Let me walk you to your car,' and he was about to walk away when he was stopped in his tracks by Rowanne.

'I don't think she wants to go with you,' she said confidently, confused at the bizarre exchange between them. Rowanne looked at Amanda, 'Do you want to go with the Chief Inspector?'

Amanda thought it over carefully, and though her mind was confused, one thing was crystal clear — she did not want to go with him. But the look in those merciless eyes spelled trouble for Rowanne; that was the strong feeling she was getting from him. After all, she had promised the family to watch out for Rowanne, and she *would* do her part, even if it meant angering Rowanne.

Amanda put on her brightest smile; she hoped it was not too brittle, and she absolutely loathed what she was about to do... But diligently, she went through with it, and turning to Driskell, she replied, 'I could use your help.' Turning back to Rowanne with a yawn, she said, 'Look, Rowanne, it's been a long night, and I'm feeling lightheaded. I'm going to head back home. I'll catch up later to see what else we have to finalise on the piece, just send me the draft.' Amanda hoped Rowanne would understand, and she was curious to know what she had learnt of Thomas.

Rowanne took the hint - she was not in a good position to help Amanda, who wanted to keep her distance from her for now. She knew that Amanda would explain everything later.

Rowanne was becoming more adept everyday at reading people and their intentions; it was very subtle, like a watercolour painting slowly unfolding before her eyes. The different colours imbued their emotions, and then the story would unfold. However, it was harder to read some people; especially if they chose to shield themselves.

'I'll see you tomorrow, Amanda. Goodnight, Chief Inspector.' Rowanne watched them walk away towards Amanda's car.

'Is she still watching us?' asked Driskell, his voice low.

'Yes,' replied Amanda. She hated leaning on him, but her only other option was to fall, thereby giving the game away to Rowanne.

'Only a few more steps,' said Driskell. He held on tight, but he didn't know whether it was to keep her from falling, or running away - either way his grip tightened.

'Get in,' he said coldly, as soon as they had reached her car. Amanda reluctantly obliged and got into the passenger side, while he got into the driver's side and held out his hand for her key. He started the engine, reversed out of the car park and began to drive. He didn't speak again until they got onto the main road.

Amanda's brain began to clear as the fog receded fast, and, turning to Driskell, she asked sharply, 'Why are you kidnapping me, Chief Inspector Driskell?'

'I told you, call me Dewain,' he said, exasperated with the fact that she had deliberately chosen to ignore his reasonable request. He could not remember the last time that he had actually asked anyone for anything; he usually gave an order and that was it.

'So, I should be flattered that you're lavishing such attention on me?' she asked, mockingly.

'I see the headache is gone,' he said, by way of making conversation.

'A lot more will go in a second,' she said sweetly, pointedly glaring in his direction.

He laughed, and contemptuously replied, 'I think you're referring to my guard!' and gave her a quick derisive look, before turning his attention back to the road.

'Yes... the guard.' *I was referring to you! Pretentious idiot.* 'My patience is wearing thin, Chief Inspector. If you have something to say, then now would be the time. Otherwise, I insist you pull over to the side, and make your own way home.' Amanda crossed her arms. She didn't know whether it was to keep her distance from Driskell, or to stop herself from tearing him limb from limb.

'I find that amusing, if a little unreasonable! After all, I am only driving. Do you usually feel the same about anyone who gives you a lift?' asked Driskell charmingly.

Amanda wanted to wipe the arrogant look off his face, but she also had an instinct for self preservation. She knew of his reputation, and was not about to bring the wrath of the law upon her head just yet.

'I see my reputation precedes me,' said Driskell pretentiously; much to Amanda's chagrin. He pulled the car up to a deserted spot along the Thames.

Amanda calmed her breathing and steadied herself in case her life depended on it.

'You needn't look so worried. You shouldn't believe everything you hear about me. No, leave the light off, we can't risk being seen.' He watched her hand pull back as she backed up to the passenger door, putting as much distance between them as possible. *Not far enough,* he mused darkly.

'Speak fast, Chief Inspector. I don't intend to spend all night here,' she looked at him steadily, on the lookout for any sudden movements.

'Let's cut the nonsense, shall we? Which clan do you belong to?' asked Driskell, his voice sounded weary.

'How long have you known?' asked Amanda, as she carefully considered her next move — after all, it could very well be her last.

'It was blindingly obvious with that little *show* of yours at the pub,' he sounded highly amused. He looked at her squarely as he crossed his arms and relaxed back in his seat. 'Did you really think you could hide it from *me* of all people? You are sadly delusional as to your abilities,' he said disdainfully.

'And you are a narcissist!' stated Amanda.

Driskell was unfazed and nodded encouragingly. 'Well, naturally,' he said wryly, by way of a reply. 'Now let's get back to which clan you belong to...' and he tapped his fingers on the dashboard, as his other arm now rested behind her head rest.

'What right do you have to question me?' asked Amanda calmly. 'I haven't broken any laws.'

'You're a demon, but your power radiates a delicate complexity... and you seem to have an empathy with humans.

What's the connection, Miss Eghan? What am I missing?' he asked as he looked at her, head cocked to one side, continuing to drum out a rhythmic beat. Driskell enjoyed the look of annoyance that briefly flashed across her face. He could tell that she was trying to evade his questions - so much the better for him, he got to keep her company for longer.

'Having empathy with humans isn't against the law,' replied Amanda decisively.

'Which *law* would that be?' he asked, and continued to toy with her.

'Not coming from a Noble clan is nothing to be ashamed of,' said Amanda quietly but distinctly.

'What did you say? Are you trying to be impertinent?' Driskell suddenly became tense, like a cat on a leash threatening to let loose. He didn't appreciate any slander against his family, or on the reputation he had so diligently built, despite not being born into a First Family and having all that went with it! They seemed to radiate a golden aura, as if they were better than everyone else. He was cut short by Amanda, who had been trying to get his attention for the past minute.

'Finally! Before you went off on your little tirade, I was trying to say-'

'Measure what you say carefully. I am also a man with limited patience,' said Driskell, cutting her off. But to his deep vexation, she had the audacity to roll her eyes at him. She didn't even have the sense to be afraid! What was wrong with this woman? Well, apart from her mixed demon heritage: half of which, he was almost a hundred percent positive, was human; it had that essence to it.

Driskell felt he was well within his rights to have her carted off to the Noble Court for that fact alone. But he was being remarkably charitable by not even really deigning to pursue the truth beyond this car.

'You really do have an inflated sense of importance,' said Amanda, and before he could respond, she held up a hand to stop him. 'You might be interested to know that I was talking of myself!' There, he finally got it; she watched him deflate as all the anger drained from his body.

Driskell looked at her awkwardly. He did not appreciate anyone, least of all the woman before him, making him feel this way: uncertain and insecure. He glared at her, challenging her to explain herself to him.

Amanda didn't feel the need to elaborate; truth be told, she could not. She didn't trust the man before her, and she had people to protect. She watched his growing annoyance as the minutes passed, and she remained silent.

Driskell did not like to accede to anyone, but wisely chose to let it go for now. He would find out the truth eventually; he always did. It was his gift, or curse, depending on the situation, and who was involved. He watched as Amanda furrowed her brow, bringing her eyes close together in concentration as she tried to analyse him. What was she looking for? he wondered, and why did he care…?

He feigned boredom as his eyes casually slid to hers. Amanda's blue eyes suddenly dilated as she looked directly into his penetrating gaze — she'd been caught off guard, looked a little too long...

Oh for the love of Demon World, she thought, suddenly finding a spot in the car that needed her urgent attention.

Driskell smiled broadly. *Well well...* he thought darkly.

'We seem to finally have something in common...' he said brightly, bringing her up short in surprise.

'What do you mean by that?' asked Amanda, feigning nonchalance, and hoping that he was not encouraged in his delusions by her momentary digression. She had only wanted to figure out his motive, his plan, but to no avail. The man was like a fortress; she doubted whether anyone could get by his defences.

'Why our families, of course,' he said mirthlessly. 'What else is there?' he asked, raising an eyebrow questioningly as an iniquitous look played across his face, and he began to play a joyfully fast staccato on the dashboard.

Amanda straightened in her seat. 'Well, if there's nothing else then I think I'll be going, Chief Inspector,' and she made as if to grab for the door handle.

She paused, as Driskell said casually, 'Well, there is the small matter of Rowanne retracing the deceased's steps...'

Amanda froze. *Think fast,* her mind screamed at her. She heard the insidious laughter of Driskell behind her. And close by her ear, she heard the words, 'Check and mate,' whispered.

Damn! she thought. And flinging open the door, she ran across the road, but his laughter seemed to follow her.

'Please, don't make this any more interesting than it already is,' said Driskell, right behind her.

Amanda didn't hesitate, and performed a spinning kick which unfortunately for her, Driskell intercepted, as he held her leg securely under his elbow. He didn't look too pleased; more downright confused.

'Well, that was hardly the reaction I was expecting! You should be careful, you could have hurt someone,' he said conceitedly, as a slow smile spread across his face.

Funny, he seems less terrifying when he smiles, thought Amanda, as she tried to quickly work out a strategy to get out of this situation and back to Rowanne as soon as humanly possible. But first, she just had to deal with the dangerous moron before her.

Amanda struggled to pull her leg out. The man was built of stone, completely unmovable.

'Can't we just talk like normal people?' asked Driskell. Her response to this was to twist her body and leg downwards, throwing him off balance. Driskell let go, and watched her spin away into a run down the steps towards the river.

He watched her run across the demon path. He judged it, and suddenly let loose with his own preternatural speed, blocking her halfway across the River Thames.

Amanda was brought up short with Driskell suddenly appearing before her, and below her the river raged. *That's new. Damn it!* she thought, frustrated. *Why does he turn up like a bad penny?*

The path under Driskell seemed to burn: his speed alone had created its own path. Technically it should be impossible, but then again, demons had their quirks...

Amanda did a roundhouse kick, intending to strike the side of his head to knock him out, but he easily deflected her kicks with his arms, not even breaking a sweat. The problem was that he was in control of the situation, of his power; whereas her only thought was getting back to warn Rowanne.

'I could do this all night, and I wonder which one of us will tire first... Fine, if you want to tango then by all means go ahead,' he said, whilst deflecting strikes that were aimed for his face; it was as if she wanted to destroy his looks. Gently he pushed her back.

Amanda was tiring. She glared at him as perspiration glistened on her forehead. She straightened up and, taking a deep breath, centred herself and gathered her power before charging towards him.

Unsurprisingly, Driskell chose that exact moment to step to the side, but he grabbed her hand before she could lose her balance, and spun her in towards him, holding her close.

'Look, if you wanted to dance, you could have at least waited until our date tomorrow night,' he whispered against her hair.

Amanda was incensed, 'You conceited piece of work,' she replied, and duly proceeded to stomp and twist her high heel into his foot; he released her abruptly. She turned and watched as a dark expression settled on his face, the smile gone.

She was about to laugh, but was cut off as she was blasted off her feet. She had a look of surprise as she flew off the pathway and fell into the inky river below; it closed over her head...

Driskell dusted himself off. He controlled the panic in his stomach, and forced his breathing to slow down. His green eyes turned a shade darker, and his mask came down, so that when he took the hand that was proffered to him, he had a wickedly dark smile pasted onto his face.

'When did you get here?' he casually asked the beautifully tall woman before him, who lifted him easily to his feet.

She straightened her hair so that it fell in a cascade over one shoulder, and adjusted her dress as her midnight blue eyes mercilessly looked over it for any damage; there would be hell to pay if there was. And finally, she deigned to look at Driskell. She ignored his question, much to his consternation, and instead stated audaciously, 'Looks like you were having some trouble there. Good thing I came when I did.'

'Yes, Lady Blaze, how fortuitous of you...' replied Driskell dryly. This earned him a sharp look from her.

Evelyn walked to the edge of the dark path and looked down into the river for any signs that the hybrid could have survived. *It's disgusting, what they allow to live these days,* she thought distastefully of all the lower rank demons. Satisfied that the *thing* was dead, she went to Driskell.

Smiling brightly, she said, 'It won't be bothering us again. And by the way, I'm looking for Alexander, have you seen him?' her bright eyes stared piously into his. *The very picture of insincerity,* he thought.

'No, I haven't, Evelyn. You could try him at home,' replied Driskell.

Evelyn stepped closer to him and put her hand gently on his arm. 'Come by later, and give me the update on the investigation,' she gave him a genuine smile before walking off into the distance.

He could almost hear her heels strike the wispy path as she vanished into a distant portal.

Driskell waited impatiently and when he was sure enough time had passed, he ran over to the edge. Calling on the power within him, he raised a giant glass sphere to the surface of the river. Water cascaded off it as it continued to rise, and finally it hovered before him. He clicked his fingers and vanished through a portal with the sphere in tow.

Rowanne stood transfixed looking at the road, wondering if she really had done the right thing by letting Amanda drive off with Driskell.

'I think I should have stopped her,' she said to Alexander, who had suddenly materialised beside her.

'It would have aroused his suspicions had you tried to interfere. I was surprised at his causal and dismissive behaviour towards you,' said Alexander.

'I don't trust him. How can I suddenly be off his list? It doesn't make sense. Something is definitely going on with him.'

'He seemed to play the part of a love struck suitor a little too well. I think it's a ruse,' said Alexander. Rowanne shivered in the cold as their breath mingled. 'Permit me to give you a lift home, it's too cold for us to be out here,' he waited for the rebuke that would certainly come, but she surprised him with her equanimity.

'Thanks, but I can give you a lift back, if you want? Or you can come along to my apartment? I do have a lot to discuss with you,' and without waiting for his reply, she made her way back to her car. Her teeth were chattering by the time she opened her door and stiffly got in. Alexander got into the passenger seat.

'Your home it is then,' he replied, as he shut the door. He turned on the heater, for which Rowanne was grateful, as she managed to get the feeling back painfully into her ice cold hands.

She gave him a smile as she pulled out of the car park and drove back along the river towards her apartment.

They were silent, lost in their own thoughts. Rowanne had a knot in her stomach; she could not stop thinking about Amanda.

As she drove, she noticed forked lightning above the Thames that looked ominous. But finally, if a little anxiously, she arrived home.

Alexander got into the lift after Rowanne. He could feel waves of tension rolling off her; he too was concerned for her friend. Rowanne had a knack for attracting demons to her, and it was blindingly obvious that she had yet to work out that Amanda was a half demon.

He had not confronted Amanda about it; he thought the secret was hers to keep. And she'd disclose the truth to Rowanne when and if she saw fit. He would not interfere unless it put Rowanne directly in the path of danger. From what he had observed in the short time of being in her company, Amanda appeared to be a lovely girl, headstrong and clearly capable of taking care of herself, as well as others. He liked her more due to her choosing to keep Rowanne's company.

Rowanne got out of the lift feeling the weariness in her bones. When was the last time she had gotten any proper sleep, without something going wrong? She looked at Alexander, 'I feel like I haven't slept a wink since you entered my life,' she said, rubbing her tired eyes.

'I know the feeling...' he said amicably, to the sound of her derisive laughter.

Rowanne opened the door, and held it for Alexander, who walked past her. She kicked it closed behind her. Walking into the living room, she found Alexander resting on one of her sofas, and continued on into her bedroom.

She came out a moment later, dressed in jeans and her comfy jumper with her hair tied up in a knot. 'You don't possess the ability to sit still for even a moment, do you?' she asked accusingly, joining Alexander in the kitchen, where she found him making camomile tea.

She grabbed a bottle of milk from the fridge and handed it to him, leant against the counter, and rested her head against her hand, content to just watch him.

Alexander momentarily turned his head towards her and smiling warmly, replied, 'You should know me by now, I can in no way function properly with that less than perfect concoction you brew up and have the audacity to call tea.'

Rowanne punched him playfully on the arm, and snorted indignantly. 'Here, let me help you with that,' she said, and took the mugs through to the living room.

Alexander joined Rowanne on the couch, and grabbed a mug from the table. 'Tell me, what happened tonight?' he asked, looking less than pleased.

He looks infuriated, thought Rowanne.

'Well, are you going to tell me what you were doing in the middle of the night with an ill conceived plan involving your colleague?' Alexander was understandably worked up as, yet again, Rowanne had endangered her life and didn't even have the decency to involve him.

Rowanne's cheeks coloured; it didn't help that Alexander bombarded her with images and words to convey the depth of his displeasure. And normally, she would have got angry, and hurled harsh words at him, but she was beginning to comprehend herself, and him, better. He had every right to feel the way he did.

Rowanne took a deep breath to clear her frazzled mind, and decided to continue calmly. Alexander seemed to have the unwanted effect of making her into a crazy woman whenever she was in his company.

I can do this, rise above it! Rowanne smiled tentatively, 'You should rethink your choice of drink... I have just witnessed its shocking effects on your emotions.' She knew she was stalling.

'Rowanne...' he said quietly, trying to hold onto the last shreds of his sanity. She had a death wish it seemed, coupled with a horrendous sense of humour.

Rowanne held up her hands defensively, 'I was there to try and find out what happened to Thomas. Following his spirit seemed like the best bet.' She waited for him to explode, but was pleasantly surprised instead.

All he said was, 'Next time, include me in any plan you have. It's never a bad idea to have people with you. Not that you couldn't handle it alone,' he added quickly, as her eyes flashed at him. 'Just that, if something should go wrong, you'd have help.'

Rowanne considered his words carefully, and remembered the many times Alexander had risked his life for hers, but wisely kept this to herself.

'What did you learn, was it a demon attack? If it was, then it is my duty to track down the rogue demons and find out exactly what happened to the security guard,' he put his cup down and crossed his legs, rested his arm along the edge of the sofa as he waited intently for her reply.

Rowanne turned to him and started to recount the events of the night. 'And so you see, he might still be alive if they dragged him through a portal - possibly to Demon World?' she finished with a note of uncertainty in her voice.

'I won't tell you how dangerous that was. After all, you've seen firsthand what spirits are capable of-'

Rowanne found it absolutely necessary to interrupt him, 'I've learnt a thing or two by living with Lillian... And the first time I encountered Thomas's ghost nothing happened, therefore I had no reason to believe otherwise this time.'

Alexander was baffled, 'How did you know the exact time to be in the office?'

'I sort of just knew... And I suspect this is going to sound stupid, but I felt as if he was waiting just for me. I could have gone any time and possibly have got the same results. But there's less to explain after hours!'

'I think it could have been a trap to make it appear as if he's a ghost to lure you to a quiet spot, and then...' he left it open.

'That thought only occurred to me when I saw him being pulled through the portal. Someone wants me to go to

Demon World, but I don't think it's to uncover the truth of what became of Thomas,' said Rowanne.

'I think it's the work of an intelligent demon, and not the Shadows that have an interest in you. Probably someone with great power, and the demons are just working for whomever it may be. I have suspected for some time that the attack on you was not random. I think you're a pawn caught up in an elaborate scheme of a Noble.'

'Do you think it's Driskell, is it something he'd do?' asked Rowanne.

Alexander was well aware of Driskell's thirst for power and could not rule him out entirely. 'Maybe, but it could be someone higher up in the ranks. But why would they have a vested interest in a human? No offence meant.'

'None taken. They might take an interest if the human in question has a... demon heritage.' Rowanne wanted to be completely honest with Alexander. She knew she could trust him with more than just her life. She waited for him to digest her revelation, not knowing how he would take it.

Alexander's eyes widened in surprise as emotions flashed across his face. She could tell that he was rapidly processing this bombshell, probably wondering to which family she belonged.

Alexander grabbed Rowanne by the shoulders unthinkingly, and his eyes went dark; he appeared to be livid with her. He forced himself to calm down, and not to jump to conclusions. Then he asked in a quiet voice, that disturbed Rowanne more than if he had just shouted, 'You weren't by any chance concealing your heritage from me?' Alexander kept a light hold on her shoulders, but his eyes bore into hers, demanding the truth.

A hurt expression passed over Rowanne's features briefly. She tried to sit straight but it was awkward, to say the least. Cooling her anger, she wearily replied, 'Look, it was just as big of a shock to me as it is to you. Do you have any idea how I felt when I found out just a couple of hours ago?' Finally, Alexander released her, and she sat back to give them both space.

'Which family do you belong to?' he asked, with a calm he didn't truly possess. Everything had changed... It had made what he had done ten times worse. This could potentially put them in even more danger.

'On my grandmother's side, I don't know. She was adopted and the identity of her parents is a mystery. But my grandfather on the other hand, is Ju-Long Hou of the-'

'Dark Fire Clan,' finished Alexander in wonder. He looked at Rowanne in a new light, his head tilted to one side, his sapphire eyes sparkling as he tried unsuccessfully to work out the mystery that she was.

Rowanne felt uncomfortable with the way Alexander was making her feel. She wished he would stop staring at her; his eyes were practically trying to bore into her mind, if not her soul. To break the tension, Rowanne asked, 'So, you've heard of my grandfather? That's good, perhaps you could enlighten me?' This provoked a strong reaction from Alexander, who smiled broadly as his shoulders shook suspiciously, as if he were trying not to laugh.

'Heard of him? Everyone in Demon World knows who *he* is! He's a great warrior, not to mention that he is a Noble from a First family. Well, Rowanne, you've proven to be a dark horse...' he tapped his fingers rhythmically on his knee, his head rested in his other hand.

Rowanne thought that he looked entirely too comfortable; he'd been in her apartment so often that he appeared to have become a part of the furniture. *When did that happen? And how has he so immersed himself in my life that I notice when he isn't here...?*

'What does that mean?' asked Rowanne, and immediately regretted asking, dreading the answer.

'It means that you are now no ordinary human. Or half demon, I should say. You are, Rowanne, for better or worse, a player in the big leagues of Demon World society. You do realise that, right? You have powerful people backing you in the form of your grandfather and his clan! The question is, does whomever orchestrated the attack on you also know of this?'

'One other thing - I didn't mention to my grandparents that it was you who saved me, and...' said Rowanne.

'Changed you,' finished Alexander gently, sensing how difficult it was for her to say it. Alexander took her hand gently in his and kissed it; a look of surprise came over Rowanne, and he smiled captivatingly.

Rowanne controlled her features so that she appeared indifferent, 'What was that for?' she asked quietly.

Alexander kept a hold of her hand to her great annoyance; and his amusement. Looking steadily into her eyes, he replied humbly, 'For thinking of *me*. For keeping me safe... thank you-'

Rowanne interrupted him by slowly pulling her hand back. He raised an inquisitive brow and smiled archly, which she pointedly chose to ignore, much to his satisfaction. 'It was nothing... It was to avoid any unnecessary questions. For now, they've accepted my decision to remain quiet,' she didn't add that she was worried for his safety, and that she hated lying to those that she loved. However, she kept reminding herself that it was in their best interests. She was carrying around so many secrets, some of which were not hers to tell. *Great! I'm like a guardian of secrets,* she thought wearily.

Rowanne may have casually dismissed his gratitude. But thankfully, she was not yet adept at shielding her thoughts, and Alexander was amused and touched as he listened to what was not verbalised.

'What did you discuss?' he was curious as to what she'd learnt.

'In a nutshell, the precarious world that is Demon World politics, and you'll appreciate that there's nothing new

I could inform *you* of in that regard. But my grandfather is thinking of approaching Lady Enid. He's worried that she knows too much about me. But I don't know whether this is the best course of action, as she doesn't know of my heritage, yet.'

'It's a risky move, but if you have a Noble who's hell bent on using you to their advantage, then it wouldn't be such a bad idea to get as many powerful Nobles as you can to back you. We have no idea what their next move is, especially if the worst should happen and we end up in the Noble Court. And then, Rowanne, we are going to need their support, otherwise it's Prima Stella for you and me. And that's if we're lucky enough to keep our families beneath their notice,' he said darkly, in a sombre mood.

I'm sorry, she wanted to say. *It's my fault you're in this predicament. If it wasn't for me, you'd be living an eternity,* thought Rowanne, with a heavy heart.

Taking the cups, Alexander got up and turned away from her, so that she would not see the pain in his eyes, or the sorrow that was etched into his face. In a quiet voice, he whispered, 'Perhaps, but it would've been lonely...' *I will live an eternity in a mortal existence,* he thought, and went to the kitchen to rinse the cups out.

A lump formed in Rowanne's throat; she'd heard his words, thanks to her improved hearing courtesy of her demon side. She watched as the rain pounded the windows in the early hours of the morning.

Rowanne got up and went to the kitchen, and Alexander stiffened at her approach. But she walked right up to him, and hugged him fiercely from behind. And slowly his wet hands covered hers, holding her to him. He could feel her head resting on his back, and no words were spoken.

They stood together for a moment, as everything they felt, from their sorrow to their concern for their families and friends, engulfed them. A tear slid down Rowanne's cheek;

was it for him, or herself, she honestly didn't know. She closed her eyes, content just to hear the rain hitting the windows.

Rowanne wiped her eyes, and went back to the living room, and Alexander followed behind. They sat in silence. Rowanne was bone weary, and after a while her eyes closed, and she fell sideways, her head coming to rest on Alexander's arm.

Alexander got up carefully and positioned Rowanne on the sofa so that she lay comfortably on it with her head resting on the edge. He went into her bedroom and a second later returned with a blanket which he covered her with, gently tucking her in.

He sat on the opposite sofa intending to keep watch. But perhaps the mortal side of him was just too tired, because suddenly his eyes closed of their own accord, and he, too fell asleep.

The lights in the apartment suddenly went out and Lillian materialised. She stood before Alexander and shook her head in disgust. *He calls himself a 'guardian' - indeed!* Rather, she'd watch over the pair of them!

Lillian walked over to the huge floor to ceiling window and sat before it, tucking her long legs beneath her. And as she leaned against it, she could almost feel the cold seeping in where her face touched the glass. Well, almost. Technically she could not feel a thing physically.

But it was nothing compared to what she felt emotionally; her inner turmoil. She'd learnt a lot in the last few hours - to say it was a small world was putting it mildly! She had wondered whether it was a coincidence that she had ended up possessing a human — a normal human with a normal life... if only. Sometimes the Fates could be cruel.

Truth be told, they were all a part of a giant web: the silken cords were slowly reeling each of them in and soon there would be nowhere to hide. What would happen as they confronted each other...?

Lillian could see as clear as day, a giant tree: the lines of ancestry of the various families running with life. Some of the branches were cut off and dripped with blood, as new shoots grew preparing to take over, but certain branches refused to take their designated path. Instead, they twisted, gnarling back in on themselves, and stood firmly, ready to usurp the others, and take control of their final destination.

Lillian realised that she had more to lose than she had initially thought. A great responsibility rested on her shoulders: she'd have to see through the obligations that she'd made more than seventy years ago.

'At least I don't look bad for an old lady,' she said, smiling intensely at the reflection of the young woman with old eyes; they looked back at her, waiting to tell her story. She watched as the sky began to gradually change colour. She'd wait patiently for the dawn to break, bringing her vigil to a close. After all, all she had now was time... endless, unbound time.

CHAPTER 24

Driskell stepped out of the portal and into his apartment. Turning, he manoeuvred the giant glass sphere, so that it gently lowered to the ground, coming to a rest on his wooden floor. He didn't quite know how to take the look of vengeance frozen on Amanda's face. Her eyes seemed to shoot invincible daggers at him. *No doubt aimed at my heart,* he thought, dispassionately.

Stepping back, he flicked the light switch on illuminating the dark room. He clicked his fingers, causing the glass sphere to disappear in the blink of an eye, so all that remained were sand particles, and in their midst Amanda, who was fuming.

'What the hell was that? Were you trying to kill me, is this your sick twisted fantasy?' asked Amanda, as she took a menacing step towards him.

Driskell held up his hands to show that he meant no harm. 'For your information, I was actually saving your miserable existence! Do you have any idea of the damage you've done with those knife-like shoes of yours?'

'I'M GLAD! So, you are actually capable of feeling something.' Amanda slowly advanced towards him. Driskell backed up slowly as if he was watching a dangerous animal that could pounce at any moment.

Driskell looked pained, 'I was referring to my shoes,' he said quietly.

That did it! The pompous idiot was actually more concerned with his shoes than the fact that he had nearly drowned her; maybe he really was a lunatic! She flung herself at him, intending to show him exactly what she would do to his precious shoes.

Driskell stepped to the side and circled Amanda, whose eyes widened, waiting for a chance to strike him. They slowly circled each other, though he was getting bored with the tedious and pointless violence.

'Look, Amanda, I'm trying to tell you something! But if you test my patience, I'll have no choice but to resort to unpleasantness, which could be avoided if you would do me the courtesy of sitting down whilst I explain a few things to you.' Driskell looked grim.

Amanda was not a fool - standing before her was a full demon from another world. Who knew how powerful he actually was? Maybe it would be better to bide her time, and find out what was going on. She realised she had been acting recklessly; but he seemed to have this effect on her. She counted to ten and sullenly sat on the sofa; to her great relief, he sat in the chair opposite to her.

She glared at him. *She doesn't like taking orders,* he thought. *She may also be slightly deranged... always fighting someone or other, every time I grace her with my presence.* This enlisted a snort from Amanda who looked at him contemptuously.

Who the hell does he think he is? Demon World's gift to women!? 'Well, why am I here?' She looked disdainfully at her surroundings - here was someone who liked to flaunt their wealth.

Driskell crossed his long legs and narrowed his eyes angrily at her disrespect. 'What is the last thing you can remember?' he asked gruffly.

Amanda thought hard. '*You* blasting me off the bridge! Almost drowning-'

'You almost drowned, the imperative word being 'almost', but survived thanks to *my* sphere. Which by the way, I sent as soon as Lady Blaze blasted you off your impertinent feet,' he said conceitedly and smiled.

'You complete and utter-' she stopped herself from finishing the sentence, and taking a deep breath, she continued, 'you're actually enjoying this?!'

'Well, the look on your face as you went head over heels - priceless. By the way, are you hurt?' he asked cautiously. Joking aside, he had seen the blast strike her, and how she was still alive was frankly a miracle.

'Don't tell me, the Great Dewain Driskell actually has a caring side?' she asked sarcastically.

'Do you know how expensive this floor is? I really don't want you dripping blood all over it,' he replied disdainfully.

Amanda sat forward and looked at her arm, realising only now that it had a great gash on it that was bleeding heavily. She remembered throwing her arms up in a futile attempt to protect herself as much as possible from the blast. Admittedly, it stung somewhat, but she had put the pain out of her mind as she had faced the dangerous idiot before her.

She waved her arm tauntingly in his pretentious face, and droplets of blood fell on the floor. She smiled blatantly at his horrified expression.

Driskell swept out of the room and returned in a blink of an eye. Amanda stiffened at his close proximity, ready to fight him if necessary. He was appalled with her. 'Follow me,' he said, as he wrapped a towel around her arm to stop the bleeding.

Amanda looked at him with mistrust, before reluctantly following him down the corridor. He stood before an open door, and as she got closer, she realised it was a bathroom, and walked past him as he stepped to one side.

Driskell opened a cabinet and took out an old worn first aid box. The contents in it seemed new. *How many times must he have used it...* wondered Amanda, her eyes widening in surprise; it should not actually have come as a revelation.

She considered his formidable reputation for hunting down rogue demons, no matter their rank, and dispensing his own style of justice.

He was about to rip open an antiseptic wipe, but Amanda stopped him.

'I've got this,' she said dismissively, taking the box from his hand. He laid the wipe down on the side of the sink.

He looked at her with detachment, and replied, 'As you wish. I'll just be in the living room,' with that, he turned around and left, closing the door behind him.

She heard his footsteps receding, and finally let out the breath she had been holding and with it some of the tension eased out of her body. She put down the box, and, turning the tap on, cleaned her wound, watching the black congealed muck falling away into the bath. She applied a gauze to it before wrapping a bandage around it; hopefully it would stop the bleeding. She'd deal with it later.

Amanda looked at herself in the mirror: her blonde hair was in disarray and her blue eyes were dull, as if the life had been taken from them. Splashing water on her face, she thought, *I can do this!* She wondered how Rowanne was, but thankfully, she had Alexander by her side. She smiled momentarily; perhaps it was the other way around.

Amanda carefully replaced the box in the cabinet before leaving the bathroom, and going back to the living room. She was pleasantly surprised to find that Driskell had brought her a glass of water. *He's just feigning, luring me in before he makes his move,* thought the cynical part of her.

'Thank you,' she said, before taking a sip of water.

Driskell looked severe, 'Well, as I can see that you are not about to bleed out on me, I think we should return back to the matter at hand - that of Ms Knight,' he finished coldly.

Amanda nodded her head, secretly relieved that he had returned to his normal self. 'What do you want to know?' she asked calmly; inside she was fighting not to panic. She could not let Rowanne down, let alone... She fought to keep her mind blank.

The perspiration gathering on her forehead was not lost on Driskell, who continued to gaze at her intently, as if he could bore the information straight out of her mind. He sat back casually, but his eyes began to flare an unearthly green colour, almost like an emerald set alight.

Amanda tensed. *Oh, no!* she thought. *Here it goes...* She called on her training and innate strength of will as she fought against being bespelled into revealing everything that she knew. Driskell's laughter created goosebumps along her arms.

'Look at me, Amanda... It's common courtesy to look at your host when they're talking to you.'

It was a battle of wills; they'd soon find out who the victor would be.

You arrogant, psychotic piece of work, thought Amanda. As she slowly raised her eyes to him tentatively, an evil smile lit up his face. Nevertheless, she looked directly into his eyes boldly; daring him to do his worst...

'To which clan do you belong?' he asked in a hypnotic voice. His eyes were mesmerising to look at.

'My name is Amanda, and I belong to the Eghan clan,' she answered brightly, and waited patiently to see what his next move would be.

'You know very well that it is not a clan of Demon World. You have given me a human name! I want your demon clan name,' he demanded.

Amanda watched him tapping his fingers, waiting for her answer.

'We can do this one of two ways; this is the more civilised approach. Do not presume to underestimate me, I fear you would not like the other way...' his eyes flashed dangerously at her, his face a mask of stone, cold and foreboding. He was giving her one last chance; which was more than he did for most of the people who found themselves inadvertently in his company.

Amanda felt certain that he would not do anything. After all, he had saved her, so far. And if he wanted her dead, she was in no doubt that she would not be sitting here now. She looked at him condescendingly; her first mistake. Her second was to walk away from him when he was in the middle of questioning her.

She walked around the room to buy herself some time to think. She looked at the many photographs on the wall. *So, they do know each other...* thought Amanda, as she looked at a photograph of Alexander and Driskell: they seemed to be standing next to a fountain. Driskell had his arm around Alexander, and they were both smiling cheerfully.

She never heard Driskell sneak up behind her. The hairs on the back of her neck rose, and she spun around. He was practically in her face, but she could not step back, there was nowhere to go. She could feel his power rising; she was in trouble. *Don't look at him,* she thought, desperately.

Amanda accidently knocked the picture off the wall, and it smashed as it hit the floor. Whatever Driskell had been about to say was lost as she swiftly bent down to pick up the pieces of glass. She was almost afraid to look up. *I've definitely done it this time... if he didn't want to kill me before, he will now,* she thought.

Driskell bent down to Amanda's level. He looked into her shocked expression, as he grabbed her hand before she could cut herself on the glass. 'Just leave it,' he said quietly. Her eyes narrowed as a look of frustration came upon her; much to his bewilderment. He could not fathom her reaction. After all, *she* had broken his picture; had he said anything? No. So why was she peeved? He dropped her hand, and continued to pick up the glass.

Amanda rubbed her hand on her dress as an uncomfortable look flashed across her face. Thankfully she managed to rearrange it into a scowl by the time Driskell looked up at her briefly. He took the glass away to the kitchen.

Amanda took the opportunity to pick up the photo. It felt thick, which she thought was strange, and turning it over she discovered a second photo had been glued to its back. On closer inspection, her anxiety grew as she recognised the man in the photo; although, she didn't know who the woman was. She was beautiful, and looked as if she belonged on the cover of a magazine.

She turned her attention back to the man, who was possibly twenty years old. He had beautiful soft brown hair, or so it appeared. And he wore a uniform of some kind... What fascinated her the most was the way his green eyes were longingly fixed on the woman beside him. If a picture was worth a thousand words; then, his look told of a passionate love story. She had never seen him like this before...

His picture hung in the hallway of her ancestors, it has been there for over half a century. And in that photo, he wore a suit, and even had the same smile; but his beautiful emerald eyes had an intensity to them, some might even have called them captivating. He certainly appeared more solemn there than he did in the picture before her.

'Great-grand-uncle?!' she gasped, too caught up in her thoughts of why his picture should be here of all places, to notice Driskell standing in the doorway looking pale, as if he'd seen a ghost.

Driskell strode forward and pulled Amanda to her feet. She had the presence of mind to hold onto the picture, which she clutched desperately. He looked at her severely as perspiration beaded on his brow. 'Repeat yourself immediately! Do. Not. Lie to me,' he said, a wild look in his eyes.

Amanda tried desperately to cover her tracks, realising that she'd made a fatal error; one that could come back and finish them all off. 'I don't know what you're talking about,' she replied, flipping over the photo to conceal what she'd discovered, knowing that it was futile. But she continued single-mindedly and pointing to the picture of Alexander and him, she remarked, 'I didn't know that both of you were so close... Best friends, perhaps?'

Driskell sighed; he was getting tired of this game of cat and mouse. His hand shot out fast and captured Amanda's face, tilting it gently towards him. And before she could lash out, he solemnly announced, 'Times up.'

Amanda looked at him blankly, and before she could ask him what he had meant, the room began to grow dark. Fear consumed her as his face slowly disappeared, and the last thing she saw were his disembodied eyes that grew intense and more luminous; drawing her in until there was nothing left, and then, mercifully, her brain shut down.

Driskell waited until he was satisfied that Amanda was under his enchantment. She fell straight into his waiting arms, and he caught her easily. He helped her to gently sit in a chair.

He pulled up a chair and sat before her. 'Amanda, wake up,' his voice was weary. Her eyes slowly opened and she looked about her in a confused manner. Slowly she focused on him, panic in her eyes. *Interesting... she's stronger than I gave her credit for,* thought Driskell.

Amanda could not break free from the trance he had weaved, or from his hypnotic eyes. He was trying to compel the information from her mind by his insincere smile and soft voice; she was not fooled by it, though.

'Amanda, I think you know what's happening. Nod your head if you can understand me,' she nodded. 'Good. Now who is the man in this picture, and what is your connection to him?' Driskell held up the photo he had taken from her, and pointed to the man standing next to the woman.

Amanda wanted to lie... *Do not think of the family,* she repeated to herself. 'I don't know who he is. I've never

426

seen him before,' she replied, trying to look the picture of innocence.

'Enlighten me as to who "the Family" are?' he asked, smiling radiantly as if he'd just won first prize.

I don't like that demented grin of his, thought Amanda. Her eyes travelled upwards absently, noticing that his long red hair had started to come loose from its braid, little bits of it sticking out at odd angles, generally adding to his manic look.

'I am pleased that you have finally noticed *me* and that I am to your liking. But we should really stick to the question at hand.'

Amanda glared at him, and then smiled sweetly, 'I was just contemplating what I'll do once this enthrallment ends. The good Chief Inspector, I think, is perhaps a little *delusional* himself and has overestimated his *abilities*.' She knew it was stupid to provoke him, but somebody had to knock him off that pedestal! *Who the hell does he think he is?*

Driskell suddenly went still, his eyes flashing dangerously before he burst out laughing. He could not remember the last time someone had challenged him; and from such a precarious position. 'Touché,' said Driskell, recalling his earlier demeaning remark.

'Well, it's good that you can acknowledge your mistakes, there may yet be help for you to become a decent person,' then again, she was being forced to answer his questions. Looking directly into his eyes, she said archly, 'On second thoughts, perhaps not.'

'How is it that you can compliment me and tear me down in a single breath?' he asked, looking at her with a wicked gleam in his eyes.

Amanda matched him with a saccharine look of her own, and replied, 'It's a gift, what can I say?'

'I haven't actually got the time to be playing these games with you, as much as I'd like to. So, one more time, who is this man, and who are "*the Family*"? If you choose not to cooperate, then I will be forced to bring in Ms Knight for questioning in relation to the missing security guard. I'm sure I can find evidence linking her to his disappearance. And once this information is released to the press, you will not be able to stop the story and investigation from gaining momentum; to Ms Knight's detriment.'

Amanda was enraged, 'You complete-'

'Now now, you know I don't like such language. Just answer the question. I do actually have other commitments, and I'm already running late.'

'Do you know what? I can't understand you. One minute you're trying to kill me, the next threatening the people closest to me, and then again, you save me... It's like you have a split personality.'

Driskell's eyes flashed in anger, his smile bitter, 'Don't presume to know me... or to think I actually have a soft spot for *you*; that would be a grave mistake on your part.'

Amanda wanted to scream her frustration. She would dearly like a rematch with this maniac.

Driskell raised an eyebrow at her remark, 'Don't worry, *we will*, later...' he replied softly, with a devious smile.

Amanda kicked out hard despite the magic, and for a second, Driskell looked alarmed. *Good. It's nice to know he's human in some respects.*

'Do not insult me by using that term, again,' he said contemptuously.

'Perhaps you should kill me, then! After all, I'm half human.' Amanda was desperate to hide her family's identity, including her great-grand-uncle.

Driskell got up sharply, pushing his chair back. He stood before her so that she was forced to look up at him; he could tell that she detested this. With a snap of his fingers, the magic vanished as quickly as it had appeared.

Amanda was confused. Suddenly she found that she could think clearly, and more importantly, move as well. She quickly stood up, facing the man before her, ready to fight for her life if need be.

'By the way, you are entirely too cavalier with your life; always ready to throw it away... And don't insult me by thinking that I care for demons or humans, either way. I do that which serves my interests, and for the moment, I need you close to me.'

Amanda looked at him with a disgusted expression, and asked, 'What am I to you, Chief Inspector?'

'Leverage. I'm sure there'll be some powerful people looking for you; so much the better for me if they find you, don't you agree?' he asked acerbically. There was a dark look in his eyes, 'Please, do me the courtesy of sitting down,' he gestured to the couch.

Amanda thought he really must be crazy, and wondered whether he ever tired from his mood swings; it was certainly wearing her out. If she stayed in his company for too long; she'd end up an emotional wreck. She finally settled into the couch, not too sure of where this was all leading to, and felt dread in the pit of her stomach.

She stiffened as Driskell sat next to her; she was on edge.

'This man is your great-grand-uncle,' he stated. Her eyes widened in horror of him reading her mind, realising she'd let slip vital information.

No! thought Amanda. *I'm dead... everyone's dead!* She never truly got emotional, but tears gathered at the edge of her eyes. She didn't want her traitorous tears to make her look weak; especially in front of her enemy.

Driskell unexpectedly produced a handkerchief of silk and passed it to her; much to her mistrust. He laughed softly, 'Is that what *we* are? Well, at least you think of me, that's something I suppose.'

Amanda wanted to turn her back to him to wipe away her tears, but you never turn your back on a snake. She sullenly dabbed at her eyes, never breaking contact with him, so that she was forced to look into the sparkling eyes of her adversary. He looked world weary, not that she cared, and some of his bravado had seemed to slip. He seemed like a man. Just a man. *Yeah right,* thought the cynical, and therefore the wisest, part of her. *Don't be fooled.*

Driskell thought that she was quite adept at coming up with adjectives to portray him. They were at opposite ends of the spectrum. It would do for a start, but he planned on bridging the distance... not that she'd like it.

Amanda wished that she could block out his thoughts as effectively as covering her ears would surely muffle his voice. To her mortification, he laughed as if he had heard her.

'What do you plan on doing with the information?' she asked sharply.

'So, Elisedd is *your great-grand-uncle!* Then... that makes you a Knight?!' asked Driskell in wonder, completely ignoring her question.

'Like Arthur, you mean?' asked Amanda, trying to deter him. He narrowed his eyes, and she could tell by the look on his face that he was hell-bent on getting the information out of her. With a sigh, she replied, 'Fine. Yes, I'm a Knight. But how do you know my great-grand-uncle?' she asked. After all, she had questions of her own.

Driskell's face lost some of its colour at her confirmation. He could not believe it... He felt like a man drowning on the ocean of his past. He knew one day he'd have to face his demons... *That's funny,* he thought, and started laughing hysterically.

Amanda worried that he had finally snapped. What was wrong with him? She ran to a room she assumed was the kitchen, and thankfully she was right. She brought back a cup of water for him, hating to be this close to his demented proximity; but she needed him somewhat coherent to find out exactly how much he knew.

Driskell abruptly stopped, and looked suspiciously at the cup before taking it, inadvertently touching her hand in the process. She jumped back in alarm, which amused him to no end. He kept his eyes on her while he drank.

That's just plain weird, she thought. *Although, I shouldn't have overreacted*. Even so, she dearly wanted to wipe her hand, and barely managed to refrain from doing so. *I'm acting a little nutty myself... what's wrong with me?*

'Don't worry, it's not poisoned. I leave that Machiavellian crap to you oh so special Nobles,' said Amanda blithely.

Driskell laughed so hard, he thought his sides would split. 'Where have you been all my life, my flaxen haired lady?' he asked archly.

Amanda regarded him coolly, 'For one thing, in your dreams,' *You complete nutter*, she thought sweetly. 'Secondly, does that line actually work? No, don't tell me, you alter it accordingly.'

He smiled broadly, 'Back to your great-grand-uncle,' he said abruptly.

Amanda nearly got whiplash from how fast he'd switched topics. 'What was he to you?' she asked sincerely.

'How long do you have?' he replied seriously.

'Well, I was about to leave but since you've asked so politely, I think I'll stay awhile longer.'

'Get comfortable. Where to start... So, you're a Knight. Remarkable,' he said, getting distracted again. Suddenly another piece of the puzzle fell into place for him with a loud resounding thud, like an echo long forgotten carried back on the winds of time. 'Knight!' he said sharply, causing Amanda to jump in alarm.

He could not believe he had been so dim-witted. All this time he'd had the answers right under his nose, but his mind had refused to join the dots. He had wondered why Rowanne's surname had stirred something within him; something dark and long buried, but never forgotten.

Amanda felt like she needed to be wearing a seat belt whenever she was around him; she could never be at ease in his presence. She felt on edge, especially since she knew what she had to do... *I may have to face the wrath of the courts, but so be it. If he knows too much, then I can't let him endanger us all...*

Driskell chose to pointedly ignore her childlike threats. After all, there was a line of people who would dearly love to finish him off. 'Is that why I always find you hovering at Ms Rowanne *Knight's*,' he emphasised; knowing his point wasn't lost on her, 'side? I thought it quite unfortunate that *you* always seemed to turn up at the wrong place and time...'

'That's your opinion. But I don't think Rowanne would see it in quite the same light.'

Driskell looked at her steadily, and came to another realisation - he was on top form tonight. 'I take it Ms Knight is unaware of your connection, or your true identity?' he asked rhetorically. 'Don't answer, that look is enough.' He had a lot to consider.

Amanda knew that the time was drawing near to end this, especially at the alarming rate at which he was gathering information; he'd have the complete picture before dawn broke.

Driskell gave her a look of mild annoyance; she seemed to be obsessed with the transience of his life.

Amanda looked at him steadily. *I have to. I can do this... What other choice do I have? If he lives, they die,* she thought. But then, why was she stalling if it was really the right thing to do...?

Driskell looked at her solemnly, having made his mind up. 'There's nothing for it, then, I suppose. There's really only one option left to me... The two of you will now be under my protection. Great, this is getting better and better,' he said in an aggravated tone, less than pleased with the task ahead.

Amanda's jaw dropped, flabbergasted. This was the last thing she'd expected him to say. She narrowed her eyes, disbelieving of what she had just heard.

She was about to question him further when a knock on the door made them both jump. He swivelled his head around quickly, and turning to Amanda, he placed a finger on his lips to indicate she shouldn't make a noise.

The knocking became louder, and deciding that it was too late to do anything else, he scooted closer to Amanda, who was about to protest loudly, but he quickly covered her mouth with his hand to mute her insults.

Driskell quickly whispered, 'Look, you need to go now. Trust me when I say, you do not want to go a second round with the lady on the other side of the door.'

So, it's her, Lady Blaze. Lady my foot. And actually I wouldn't mind going a second round; or a third for that matter. She won't find me quite so easy a target when I'm on guard and standing before her...

'If I remove my hand, you won't make a sound, right?' asked Driskell quietly, trying hard to keep a straight face. He was sure that this time, Amanda would emerge the victor. She nodded, and he tentatively removed his hand.

She was about to whisper that he certainly had a lot of explaining to do, when suddenly, he leaned in close and smiled wickedly, causing her mind to go blank. This close, she could see his eyes swirling a beautiful shade of malachite.

'See you later, my Scythian warrior,' whispered Driskell. Her eyes inflamed, and before she had time to react, he pulled her upright. Opening a portal, he quickly propelled her through it unceremoniously, and then closed it.

With a smile on his face and a spring in his step, he walked slowly for his amusement; much to the annoyance of the Noble he was about to entertain. He opened the door, 'Lady Blaze, you do me the honour of visiting my home.'

She looked at him condescendingly, 'I was expecting you at my place more than an hour ago. I do not like to be kept waiting. I thought I'd come pay you a visit, to find out exactly what was so important that it kept you from your duty,' she smiled beguilingly while her eyes studied everything carefully, not missing a single thing.

'You seem to be my lady Morning Star's companion these days,' said Driskell calculatedly. 'Please, this way my lady,' he said in his most charming voice. She obliged him by sitting on the couch, and then had the audacity to sneer at her surroundings. What was it with these women? Be they demon or half demon, and not forgetting the all important humans, they all had more in common then they'd care to admit; for one thing, they loathed his choice of furnishings. And secondly, and most importantly, they were united in their hatred of him. *I'm a giver, what can I say? Just doing my civic duty, just ask any Demon World citizen...* he thought, coldly. He felt a warm glow inside that left him hollow much like his existence.

'I'm merely helping her,' Evelyn replied. 'You know how hard it was for her when she lost Lillian.' She deliberately brought up the one topic designed to cause him pain as well as enrage him. She liked the look of pain he wore. Raw. Naked, for the whole world to see. She looked at him dispassionately, 'Are you okay, Driskell? You seem pale, what's the matter? Was it something I said...?' she added. She was vindictive, and she knew it. But so what? This was but one of her few pleasures in life.

'No, my lady.' How he hated these Nobles. The women were more vicious than the men; cold and merciless. *But then again, that's probably what they call me,* he laughed darkly, and saw the first twitch of annoyance on Lady Blaze's face.

There was a time when she was just Evelyn, and he, Dewain; two friends, no titles. He realised just how naive he had been growing up.

'Yes, you were the *one* that was *always* there for *her*.' The emphasis, he noted, was wasted on Evelyn.

'Yes, well, she had a lot to deal with... And I felt it only right that a fellow Noble be the one to help her. Who else could understand her predicament, especially as our families are so close.'

'Third in line,' *close, but not too close. Almost within reach, her fingertips brush The Crown.* She looked sharply in his direction, but it only added to his dark delight.

'I beg your pardon?' her voice was low and insidious.

'I was just saying how close the two of you have become.' He watched her eyes regard him like an insect that may need to be crushed; especially if he escaped her web.

'Lillian was my best friend... it killed me to lose her.' She showed signs of sadness as the tears painfully leaked out of the side of her sparkling eyes, and some even hung on her eyelashes; a beautiful testament to her loss.

Driskell came closer, 'I'm sorry. I didn't mean anything by it.' He felt remorse for having hurt her.

Evelyn sensed his feelings, 'We were friends once, before all of this,' she waved her hands to encompass her title, the ranks of their world, and lastly, the things that drew them apart. She looked around carefully.

'What is it, my lady?' asked Driskell. She appeared nervous, and hesitant to speak.

'Stop calling me, that! Leave it for the Courts of Demon World. Here, I'm just Evelyn to you. And you're just Dewain. Let's drop the pretence,' she said, and gave him a real smile. Tentative at first, but as she watched him relax, it broadened. Evelyn debated internally for a moment then became serious. 'I have long wanted to discuss a matter dear to both our hearts, but I was afraid to bring it up in case... I didn't have your support.' She looked at him wearily, less like a noble woman and more like the girl he had known long ago.

'You know, you could have told me anything. You can trust me now with whatever you have to say.' He sat opposite to her; as was proper, but she indicated that he should join her, and so he did, and she gently held his hand.

'I have always wanted to find the demon, be it Noble or lesser, who destroyed her. I get into a rage whenever I think about it. I shouldn't be saying this, but do you have any idea how many nights I put Lady Enid to sleep, only to find a wet pillow in the morning.' She crushed his hand at the painful memory.

Driskell patted her shoulder uneasily; he didn't know what to think, let alone believe. He had long formed his own theory as to who was responsible, but wisely he did not voice it.

'Lady Enid practically held her head in shame in the maelstrom that followed. Though the exact details of the incident were covered up, the Nobles had the audacity to demand her renunciation of the throne. And how she held herself together, and practically got those Nobles back under her control, is a testament to her leadership.'

Yes, what a remarkable woman she is... 'She did everything in her power to keep her family name intact. After all, the First Family could hardly step aside and allow another to rule in their place,' he said sarcastically.

'You're right. Lady Enid would do *anything* to keep the family in power. Their name could never be allowed to tarnish,' said Evelyn obscurely.

Amanda had heard enough. For some reason, the portal had not completely closed, there had been a tear in it. Perhaps his power was waning. *He isn't nearly as powerful as he likes to think he is,* and just as she was pondering this, the portal finally closed, flinging her sharply through it.

A few moments later, the portal opened above her car, and remarkably, she was gently deposited into the front seat — drivers side, of course. *Show off!* she thought. After all, she should not really expect anything less from him. Amanda had a lot to contemplate, but the first thing was getting to Rowanne as quickly as possible.

CHAPTER 25

Rowanne began to stir as light flooded through her windows, shining directly onto her face. She made an unintelligible sound of annoyance, and turning her head to block it out, she froze. Her head appeared to be under someone's elbow...

Rowanne's eyes flew open. To her embarrassment, she found herself lying on the couch with her head resting on Alexander's lap. He must have fallen asleep where he sat. She peered to the side to find his arm resting on her shoulder; this was not what she had expected to find this morning.

She was in the process of carefully removing his arm when he stirred. She froze and looked up quickly, but thankfully his eyes were still closed. She successfully removed his arm, and started to get up lifting her head an inch at a time, until she was almost in a sitting position.

Suddenly, to her great annoyance, his arm slammed back down taking her with it, so that she ended up in almost the exact same position that she had started in. He started to stir once more, which promoted her to redouble her efforts to untangle herself. Having at last succeeded, she moved to the opposite end of the couch and closed her eyes feigning sleep.

'Rowanne?' she heard her name being called softly.

She slowly and reluctantly peeled open her eyes only to find Alexander practically in her face, towering over her. Oh God, the man did not understand the concept of personal space! There was something iniquitous about the way he looked at her that she did not trust.

Alexander's mouth slowly curved up in a smile. 'Good morning. You're finally awake.'

Rowanne got up haphazardly, as he didn't even have the decency to give her any room by backing up. 'I'll put on some tea for us,' she said awkwardly.

He finally moved back and relaxed, stretching his long legs out before him. She cringed as he moved his arm around stiffly, and quickly turned her back to him, intending to head into the kitchen; but much to her chagrin, she was not fast enough to block out his idiotic remark.

'Thanks. And by the way, I hope *you* had a good night's sleep... My arm, on the other hand, seems to have fallen asleep, but my legs are just fine. Next time, I'll get you a cushion. Or maybe you were quite content with where you lay...'

Rowanne's shoulders stiffened, and his laughter seemed to follow her all the way to the kitchen. *What a complete moron! Comfortable my foot!* Her neck hurt. Ignoring it all, she put the kettle on.

Alexander watched Rowanne in the kitchen. He too was perplexed to find himself on her couch when he clearly remembered going to sleep on the opposite couch. Hopefully it was not anything to worry about. He heard ghostly laughter, but, shaking his head, he put it out of his mind. He felt good, rested.

Steeling herself, Rowanne finally turned around. 'The water's heating up, I'll be back in a moment.'

She went into the bathroom, locking the door behind her. *God! I'm a mess,* she thought, looking at her reflection in the mirror; her hair was knotted and tangled. *I must look like a cavewoman to him!* Taking a quick shower, she set about untangling and blow drying her hair. The funny thing was that her eyes seemed less tired, as if she had finally gotten a decent night's sleep.

Rowanne felt slightly self-conscious to head out in a bathrobe, hence she made a beeline for her bedroom, leaving Alexander to deal with the breakfast. She got ready quickly, and had a feeling that it was going to be another long day. She put on a light jumper over her tight fitting but extremely comfortable jeans, and pulled on her boots. Her hair was tied back in a clip and five minutes later, she was done.

She walked out to the aroma of tea, and was just in time as Alexander brought in the breakfast, laying it out on the living room table. She gave him a warm smile, at which he shrugged nonchalantly, and waited for her to join him.

Alexander bit into his toast. 'I'm really concerned about Amanda. She hasn't contacted you yet, has she?' he asked.

Rowanne looked at him, her stomach a tangle of nerves. 'I'm worried, too. I think she may be in some trouble. She was supposed to get back to me yesterday. I really hope that I'm wrong, but one possibility is that she may still be in Driskell's company.'

Alexander looked at her thoughtfully as he drank his tea. 'I was thinking along the same lines. I suggest you phone her now, find out if she's alright.'

Rowanne quickly dialled Amanda's number. She looked at Alexander, panic clearly etched on her face, as Amanda failed to pick up. 'This is not looking good,' she said, and hung up.

However, Alexander urged her to keep trying.

'Why did I ever allow her to leave with Driskell? If anything happens to her, I'll never forgive myself...' She needed to do something, but what?

'Let's get her,' said Alexander, lightly laying his hand on her shoulder in support. She smiled at him, vigorously nodding her head in agreement.

Rowanne was about to get up when there was a knock at the door. She looked at Alexander expectantly - maybe it was Amanda! She rushed to the door, and felt Alexander following closely at her heels. It was maddening to say the least, but he meant well by it.

And what about you?! Rowanne incensed him constantly, she had the ability to single handedly drive this demon into a crazy man! He snorted as he heard Rowanne correct him telepathically.

Caveman! Rowanne laughed. She could practically feel the wheels of Alexander's mind turn as he contemplated on what he'd dearly like to do... She blocked him out as she reached the front door.

Rowanne flung open the door to find Amanda looking dishevelled. *Oh my God! What happened to her...* She swept Amanda up in a hug, who responded by flinging her own arms around her.

'Good to see you too, Rowanne. You have no idea how much...'

Rowanne steered her into the apartment, while Alexander closed the door behind them, locking it for good measure. *Sometimes it's good to have another person around,* she thought, feeling reassured by his presence. She walked Amanda over to the sofa, and helped her to sit.

Alexander brought in a glass of water, as well as a cup of tea, and placed them on the table before Amanda, and sat opposite. 'How are you?' he asked gently.

'I was so worried when I couldn't get in touch with you,' added Rowanne, still feeling guilty.

Amanda squeezed her cousin's arm gently. She thought of Rowanne as more like the sister she had always wanted. Alexander gave her a long and piercing look. He smiled, and nodded imperceptibly. *He must know!* she thought. He is a fully fledged demon, after all. However, he had not revealed her identity to Rowanne, for which she was extremely grateful. She liked Alexander the better for it, and thought that Rowanne was extraordinarily lucky that he had come into her life.

The other way around, Alexander replied to Amanda. She looked sharply at him, a smile tugging at her lips.

'Amanda, are you okay? I think you're going into shock, you're smiling as if nothing has happened!' Rowanne was concerned about Amanda's mental state.

She looked at Rowanne, 'I just thought of something, it's not important. I could do with a nice cup of tea, though. Something to wake my fuddled mind up.'

Rowanne quickly handed the mug to Amanda, and watched the colour slowly returning to her pale face.

'This is good! Thanks, Rowanne.'

'Don't thank me, it's one of Alexander's concoctions,' she corrected, and reaching out, absentmindedly squeezed Alexander's arm in gratitude. And completely missed the smile that lit his face as his eyes sparkled in amusement.

Amanda was the silent spectator and found the whole situation hilarious. Rowanne certainly was blind! 'So, he's made tea for you before?' she asked innocently.

It was lost on Rowanne, though, who asked, 'How did you manage to escape Driskell?'

Amanda laughed aloud causing Rowanne and Alexander to look at her sharply for signs that she was losing it. *I wonder if they'd believe me if I told them that he let me go.*

Amanda debated on where to begin. The last part of the conversation between Lady Blaze and Driskell had been bizarre; she hadn't fully understood it. How much should she reveal to Rowanne was the question - without revealing Demon World.

'You look like you're lost in your thoughts, what happened? I'm getting really worried considering how long you've been away.' Rowanne was concerned that perhaps Driskell had hurt Amanda, and that she might be reluctant to talk of it.

'It started with Driskell taking me in for questioning,' said Amanda.

'I beg your pardon? But what does he have to question *you* for? After all, you joined the company after Thomas disappeared.' Rowanne looked at her for any clue, then something clicked. 'Wait, he took you in because of *me*, didn't he?' Rowanne grabbed Amanda's arm, trying to literally shake the truth out of her.

Amanda looked away - Rowanne was not supposed to know.

Rowanne gently turned Amanda's head to look at her, 'I'm so sorry... you've got pulled into this because of me.' *Do I end up endangering everyone I meet...* she wondered wretchedly. *First Alexander and now this young woman whom I consider a friend.*

'Rowanne, I chose to go with him, to try and find out what he was up to. I didn't like the way that he always seemed to be after you,' said Amanda.

'You know what?' Rowanne addressed them both, 'I was exceptionally naive to think that when he said he didn't need me for the investigation anymore, that it would actually end there. He's still suspicious of me and I probably head the list of suspects.' She turned to Amanda, 'Don't you dare do anything so reckless ever again! Otherwise, you'll have to face my wrath, and trust me, I make Driskell look like a picnic.'

Alexander's eyebrow was raised in mild amusement. *That's our Rowanne for you,* he thought, as Amanda began to laugh.

'Just don't,' said Rowanne.

'I didn't say anything,' replied Alexander, trying unsuccessfully to keep a straight face.

I'm morphing into the female version of him! I need to get away from him, or pretty soon it'll be hard to tell where he ends and I begin, thought Rowanne uneasily.

Don't be too hard on yourself, I'm just so damn alluring. I have that lasting effect on people, whispered Alexander through Rowanne's mind.

Rowanne's face turned crimson, and Amanda immediately turned to the culprit: Alexander, who had a wicked look on his face as his eyes sparkled teasingly.

I've never seen this side of you before, said Rowanne. *And he comes across like a charming gentleman...* she thought, amused.

You've only seen one side of me. Stay around long enough and you'll see that the rest of me is just as- what did you call me? Charming, replied Alexander. He laughed, as Rowanne shied away.

Amanda coughed politely to interrupt whatever was going on between the two of them; they could have their lovers tryst after she'd gone home. She held back laughter as she watched Alexander reluctantly break away, turning to face her. She could almost imagine him crying in frustration; whereas Rowanne was more subdued. Honestly, they were acting like a pair of squabbling teenagers; ideally, she would have loved to bang their heads together.

Amanda fretted on how much to reveal: if she revealed her truth, then Driskell could use it to his advantage against Rowanne. No, she could not risk that, instead she'd relay the conversation that she had overheard between Driskell and Lady Blaze.

Rowanne turned to Amanda, 'I guess we have to be weary of Driskell. Did you learn anything from him?'

'I heard a conversation between Lady Blaze and him. You remember the woman that helped you when you sprained your ankle?'

'Yes. She seemed... nice. But what was she doing at Driskell's place, and how does she know him?' Rowanne had an uncomfortable feeling in the pit of her stomach. She had at first liked the woman, before she had behaved rudely towards Alexander. There had been something off with her, but she had not been able to put her finger on what it might have been.

Alexander stiffened imperceptibly at hearing that name. It had not really come as much of a surprise that Evelyn

Blaze knew Driskell; after all, they had all grown up together at the palace, and had also trained together at the Academy.

Evelyn was a fully fledged Demon, and belonged to the Adara Clan: they were third in line to the throne, after his family. They all belonged to the First Families with the exception of Driskell; it was the bane of that man's life.

'What did they speak of?' asked Alexander, his eyes weary.

Rowanne studied Alexander - it was no mystery to her that he knew Driskell. When Evelyn had turned up at the office, it was obvious that she knew him. Rowanne dearly wanted to ask him of his relationship with Evelyn, and whether she was a person who could be trusted, but it sounded ludicrous to her ears. What business of hers was it? No, there was no polite way to bring this awkward conversation up. Rather, she'd have to leave it to Alexander to take the initiative. If he ever did...

'They spoke of Lady Enid? I'm guessing your friend walks in high circles. She must be someone important, then?' asked Amanda.

Rowanne suppressed a laugh. Leave it to Amanda to ask the delicate questions. *Maybe, if I'm lucky, I'll find out everything I need to know.*

Alexander arched an eyebrow in amusement, 'Before you continue, I'll just clarify,' and looking pointedly at Rowanne to her utter mortification, he said unashamedly, 'Evelyn is more of an acquaintance. Her family is close to mine, as well as to Lady Enid's,' he silently laughed, as the colour seeped into her cheeks.

Rowanne wondered for the first time just how powerful Alexander was in terms of Demon World hierarchy. She had never really questioned him about his family. Well, there was never a reason to, but now... She knew he was a demon and had accepted it. She had never bothered to find out the different types, but if his family were close to Lady Enid, then that meant he was more than just your average demon; there was so much that she didn't know about him.

Don't get a complex about me. If there's something you want to know, just ask! he whispered in her mind, causing her to look up at him sharply.

That's really annoying! replied Rowanne, frustrated. She didn't think it was possible to be any more embarrassed than she already was, and wished that a hole would open up and swallow her.

Alexander was at a loss - she truly aggravated him to the extremes. Taking a breath, he replied, *Learn to shield your thoughts, then!* She was practically flinging her thoughts at his face.

Rowanne tore her smouldering gaze away from Alexander. A fire had built within her, and she wanted to... never mind. 'Sorry, Amanda. You were saying?'

Amanda could have cut the tension with a scythe. 'Lady Blaze spoke of Lady Enid losing someone called Lillian-' she was interrupted by Rowanne.

'What did you just say?' asked Rowanne. She had the sensation of ice cold water being poured down her back, and her heart began to beat rapidly. She grabbed Amanda, shaking her by the shoulders. Alexander gently pulled her back and held her.

'Rowanne, what's wrong? You suddenly look pale, you're scaring me,' said Amanda, concerned.

Finally! thought Alexander. *Rowanne knows.* It was like a spell had broken, and he was now at liberty to talk of Lillian; whereas before she had cast magic to prevent him speaking of her. But thankfully, Amanda was not bound by any such constraint.

Rowanne was shaking, as she remembered all the times that she'd been possessed by Lillian, and not once had she told her that she was related to Lady Enid. The question was how?

Rowanne looked at Amanda, weighing her words carefully not wanting to endanger her by revealing too much. 'There was a time when Driskell took me away for questioning, and I happened to encounter Lady Enid. I think she's a colleague of his, but it didn't seem as if she really got along with him.'

'Did she happen to mention the name Lillian?' asked Amanda, wondering just how much she really knew.

'No, she didn't mention her, and I'm still not sure how they are connected,' replied Rowanne. She looked pointedly at Alexander, and said, *I think you could probably enlighten me as to what the connection is between them*. She didn't yet wish to discuss it in front of Amanda.

I think it best if you ask Lillian yourself. I don't think she'd take it too kindly if I revealed her truth. And you've already seen what she can do when she gets mad, he replied.

'What else did Lady Blaze mention?' asked Rowanne.

'I don't quite understand it, but I think that Lady Blaze was trying to get into the good graces of Lady Enid, who seems to really rely on her for support. Perhaps Lady Blaze is not as awful as she appears,' said Amanda.

Rowanne didn't like the idea one single bit, and felt her skin crawl at the idea of Lady Blaze clawing her way into Lady Enid's good books. She felt there was a whole other side to this woman that they could not even conceive of; especially because she belonged to a First Family, and was trying to cosy up to the queen...

'I think Driskell knows Lady Blaze quite well and may even be working with her,' said Amanda. Her phone went off and she briefly turned away to answer it - turning back she covered the mouthpiece, 'Look, I really have to go. Family thing. No, don't worry, I'm fine,' she said, at the look of dismay on Rowanne's face, who was about to protest. 'If I have any problems, I'll call you. But honestly, it's really important for me to go now. I'll stay in touch, though.'

She stood up, gave Rowanne a quick hug, and inclined her head at Alexander, who walked her to the front door.

Before leaving, she said in a quiet voice, 'Take good care of my cousin.' He gave her a warm smile.

Alexander closed the front door and joined Rowanne on the couch. He nodded his head that the coast was clear; she was safe to proceed.

'Lillian? Lillian get down here, I need to ask you something,' shouted Rowanne.

Lillian materialised on the opposite couch, looking less than pleased to be summoned, and looked at Rowanne archly. 'What is it? You don't have to shout.'

Rowanne wondered how she should bring up the delicate topic.

Lillian sat up straight crossing her legs, her arm rested along the top of the couch. 'So now you stand on ceremony. If you have something to ask, just ask for demon's sake!' She knew exactly what was on Rowanne's mind, having hovered close by and listened into the conversation in its entirety. But strangely for her, she was also at a loss as to how to begin. She would rather Rowanne just spit it out, so that they could discuss it and move on from it as quickly as possible.

Rowanne recounted what Amanda had just told them. 'And so I was wondering, is it true that you are related to Lady Enid's family?' She waited with bated breath, unsure of Lillian's response, who could become agitated and emotional; two things a person doesn't want an entity to feel, as it usually ended badly.

'Huh,' snorted Lillian, 'speak for yourself!' and took a couple of deep breaths before continuing, 'the time has come for me to step out of the shadows. Let me introduce myself properly. I am, or that is to say, I *was* Lady Lillian, daughter of The First Family of the Clan of Morning Star.' It felt bizarre to talk about herself after more than seventy years of silence; in a way it was freeing, she felt light.

'So, that makes you Lady Enid's... daughter?' asked Rowanne hesitantly, not wishing to offend her.

'The one and only, unfortunately,' replied Lillian painfully.

Rowanne scooted forward on the couch, and taking Lillian's hand in her own, she asked gently, 'What do you mean?'

Lillian looked at her in wonder, 'Do you know, I get surprised every time you do that?' When Rowanne touched her hand it became solid; it was unnerving to say the least — and that too from a spirit! It had to be the power of the amethyst pendant behind this phenomenon.

Courtesy of our little friend, replied Rowanne, echoing her sentiment. She smiled broadly at Lillian's look of surprise. Well, she was certainly embracing these 'gifts' of hers... She looked at her knowingly; neither of them eluded to the necklace in front of Alexander, knowing it was forbidden to talk of its existence to a man.

Lillian braced herself once more, so that she could speak of her painful past. 'With no other heir, it falls on my mother to continue as Queen indefinitely... therefore immortality has been forced onto her. Can you even conceive of the idea? Of how it must feel to rule forever? Frozen in age and never being free, bound by all those laws and customs of a Noble ruling over Demon World and its citizens.'

Rowanne remembered the conversation she'd had with her grandparents; they too, had spoken along the same lines. Her heart felt heavy for Lady Enid - she wanted to put her arms around her to comfort her. But how could she do that? They had never even spoken of her losing her daughter.

Frustration weighed heavily upon Rowanne. 'Is there no way that she can pass the power onto someone else? Forgive me if I have spoken out of turn.'

Lillian gazed fondly at Rowanne. She liked this generation very much; they didn't rest on their laurels, always eager to progress and challenge the status quo when it had become redundant. Unlike the demons of her world, who were sadly less inclined, unless the vultures saw an opportunity to get to the top.

'My mother,' it felt strange every time she uttered the word. A lump formed in her throat, but there was nothing else for it but to push on, so she continued, 'Could pass the leadership onto the next in line,' and she looked pointedly at Alexander.

He looked uncomfortable and loosened his tie - the room suddenly felt stuffy as if he could not get enough air.

Rowanne watched the bizarre exchange between the two of them, and wondered if it was possible for a demon to pass out, because Alexander looked like he was on the verge of a nervous breakdown.

'Alexander, what's wrong?' Rowanne released Lillian's hands, and placed a hand on his shoulder.

'I'm fine. Never better,' he replied evasively. 'What could possibly be wrong with me?'

'Oh, for the love of Demon World, we haven't got all day. Just spit it out! No? Okay.' Lillian turned to Rowanne, 'Alexander is a son of the Black Rose Clan, who are a First Family. Furthermore, he is also second in line to the throne, should my mother choose to relinquish it to *this* demon,' she said unenthusiastically and without any conviction; it spoke volumes. She thought of Alexander's poor prospects as a potentate.

These women are relentless! It was bad enough that he thought he was not fit to rule Demon World, he didn't need it reiterated by anyone else! Thankfully his family had never pushed him, they were happy with his position; however, others probably thought of them as foolish for not pushing their son in the ideal direction of the throne.

Frankly, he admired Lady Enid, and thought her the rightful ruler. Contrary to what they thought, he had actually taken the matter into serious consideration. He'd had his whole life to, after all. And if the day should come (and he fervently prayed that it would not) that Lady Enid wished to step down, only then, would he accept the position.

And only if Lady Enid herself asked him; he would not trust another Noble to speak on her behalf.

'Oh,' said Rowanne quietly, as the full magnitude of the situation hit her like a ton of bricks. *Well, I did want to know! I should have been careful; too much knowledge can be a burden. I can't believe the heir apparent to Demon World chose to forfeit his life on numerous occasions to save me.* She felt humbled by the man next to her. How could she even begin to thank him; or apologise?

'Rowanne, say something!' said Alexander, who felt decidedly uncomfortable with the way she was gawking at him. It was bad enough in Demon World, where the offers came in left, right and centre for marriage proposals; he hoped he had not created another love-struck admirer.

Rowanne turned calmly to Lillian, 'Do you mind if I...' and winked at her. 'I know he's the heir, but...' her mind sparkled in a tranquil state.

Alexander wondered where it was all leading, and smiled charmingly at Rowanne. *There are worse fates,* he thought, as he leaned closer to her, taking her smile as an encouragement. Her green eyes smouldered; no doubt for him. *I should've just told her at the beginning,* he thought, arrogantly.

'Be my guest. Though, you don't rightly need my permission,' replied Lillian, smiling savagely.

Alexander was pleased. Even Lillian was giving them her blessing; this day was getting better and better.

Rowanne pushed him back hard, and barely made a dent. He just looked at her nonplussed; as if she'd grown another head. 'How could you be so stupid as to risk your life?! You complete and utter...' she felt like tearing her hair out. 'Do you have any idea of how important you are?'

'Oh, Rowanne. I didn't know you cared, so much,' he said tauntingly.

'I was talking about Demon World.'

'As was I,' said Alexander churlishly.

'Lady Enid needs you as her second in command. Demon World needs you, and not to mention Earth! You are the last man I'd have ever envisaged as being a ruler,' said Rowanne thoughtfully.

'Thanks,' said Alexander coldly, feeling his mirth fly out the window.

Rowanne placed her hand on his chest, 'Hold on, I haven't finished. I was going to say that you're our best hope for peace between our worlds. I don't know what the other candidates are like but I can safely vouch for you.'

Alexander was pleasantly surprised; there'd been sincerity in her voice. He was humbled by her faith in him.

'You're only as strong as the people you surround yourself with,' said Lillian matter-of-factly. 'Believe me, I can attest firsthand to what happens when those closest to you betray you. You burn in hell, literally!' She felt angry when she thought of her death, and the lights in the room began to flicker threateningly in response to her emotions.

In fact, all of their emotions were heightened.

Rowanne tried to calm herself down, otherwise she'd be no good to the people in the room. 'Lillian, I know it's painful, but can you speak of it?' she asked carefully.

'Before I do, there's one thing both of you haven't considered,' said Lillian, glaring at them.

'What's that?' asked Rowanne, looking puzzled.

'Don't, Lillian! Now's not the right time...' pleaded Alexander, looking pained.

Rowanne observed them - it seemed to be a battle of wills, and she'd had enough of it! She had a sinking feeling that she was at the centre of whatever it was that Alexander dearly wanted to conceal.

'Just tell me, Lillian. I want to know,' said Rowanne wearily — Lillian would tell it to her straight; she counted on it.

'Alexander is next in line to the throne, right? Well, the throne exists on the mandatory principle that the ruler

451

must always be an immortal...' Lillian looked pointedly at Rowanne, hoping to hammer the point home, and briefly passed an annoyed glance in Alexander's direction.

'But that's not a problem because Alexander is immortal-' said Rowanne quickly, before the cold dawning realisation poured over her. 'Or, he was...' she turned to him with watery eyes, fighting against the tears. 'I mean you were... before you saved me.' How could she even begin to apologise for ruining not only his life, but the wider implications for saving this insignificant human. *Oh my God, what have I done...*

Rowanne wanted to put on her trainers and just run away to try and forget everything that had happened. But she could not do that, not now. Instead, she chose to face the consequences with Alexander; she'd be damned if she let him go through it alone.

Taking a deep breath to steady her nerves, she took Alexander's hand in her own. They'd face it together, bravely. She smiled at the look of astonishment on his face, and turned to Lillian, missing the intense look that had come into his eyes as he gazed at her.

'Right. What can we do, and is there any way to make him immortal again?' asked Rowanne with a confidence she didn't truly possess; she was scared, but she would not let it hinder her.

Lillian thought long and hard. She wanted to test this young woman's mettle; it was very important. Taking a deep breath, she said casually, 'Would you be willing to give up your demon half, and return it back to its rightful owner?'

'Yes. Let's do it now! Why waste time?' replied Rowanne, with conviction. She had not even hesitated in answering.

Lillian chose to pointedly ignore Alexander as she continued, 'Are you sure? There's no going back, once you agree. It will be an iron clad agreement!' she warned ominously.

'Rowanne, NO! Don't! You do not know what you are agreeing to...' Alexander angrily grabbed her off the couch, and pushed her behind him, so that he stood protectively in front of her, looking down at the demon who had not moved from her position. He'd face her if it became necessary.

'Alexander, need I remind you of who I am? You will address me as Lillian — not demon!' she said in a voice that dripped with ice.

He had the grace to look embarrassed - after all, she had not insisted on protocol, otherwise he'd be addressing her as 'my lady'. He gruffly nodded, acceding to her point. This was her being downright polite as a Noble...

'You've had the chance to get to know Rowanne. It is therefore inconceivable to me that you of all people would even suggest this,' he said despairingly.

Lillian looked up, 'Sit down,' she said, addressing them both. 'Alexander, you have my word on our friendship that I will in no way harm Rowanne, intentionally.'

He found Lillian's choice of words dubious, especially that last one; it had him worried. He'd have to be vigilant of Rowanne just in case; you never knew when the mood may strike these Nobles.

Rowanne pulled a reluctant Alexander back onto the couch, and gestured for him to sit back so that she could finally speak. 'What will happen when I hand back my demon half to Alexander?'

'Finally, you're asking questions instead of blindly walking into a situation unprepared. *If* you decide to give Alexander back his demon half, he will more than likely be able to reclaim his immortality...'

'Now tell me the part that you're reluctant to speak of?' Rowanne wasn't a fool; power came at a price, especially immortality. She had a sick feeling in her heart that she knew what was in store for her... Nevertheless, she wanted Lillian to confirm it - then at least she would be in a position to set her affairs in order, to say goodbye to her loved ones.

Lillian was more proud of Rowanne than she could say. Her throat had formed a lump but she pushed past it, and shielded herself from the pain she felt; after all, her family as rulers could not afford to be seen as weak or emotional. They had to appear detached and cold, ruling with an iron fist as they say — *she* had to be ruthlessly practical.

The situation they now found themselves in was volatile - it could blow up in their faces if it was not handled head on, and each of them had to take responsibility for it: to do whatever it took to set it right. It was no longer about themselves, a lot of lives were at risk. Potentially there could be a devastating war between the two worlds.

'Lillian, are you alright?' Rowanne asked, concerned as she watched Lillian flicker in and out of existence.

Lillian was snapped out of her bloody vision by Rowanne. 'Sorry, I was lost there for a moment. I was thinking of the wider implications... Anyway, back to your question, you would be giving up your life.' She had not meant to sound so coldly utilitarian.

'Well, I certainly asked! I'm still willing to do it, after I've had a chance to sort things out...' Rowanne's voice sounded like it was made of iron. She was resigned to her fate but would meet it with dignity.

Alexander was proud of Rowanne - she was more of a warrior than he'd ever be. She sounded like a leader, someone willing to give up their life in order to save billions of people, and demons, he should add.

'Rowanne, that is the stupidest plan you've had to date,' said Alexander, to her sardonic expression. 'If you think throwing your life away like it means nothing is magically going to bring peace to our worlds, then I am sorry to say you are sadly deluded.'

'Alexander!' said Rowanne angrily. She knew the reason behind his anger, but eventually she'd have to make him see that it was the only way.

'If you do not value yourself, and give away your life so easily for mine, then *I* should be the one to decide what to do with it, don't you agree?' He was not asking; it was an order plain and simple.

For the first time, Rowanne truly saw him as a demon of high rank, and could feel the power coming off him in waves. There was a look of disgust in his eyes for her actions, and she had felt his voice thunder out the command. If he ever does take on the crown, then Demon World would probably bow down before him; he had the potential to become a powerful leader.

However, that said, *she* was not one of his future citizens, and she had not bowed down to anyone in her life; and she most assuredly was not about to start taking orders now!

'I will decide what's best for me,' she said to Alexander in a cold voice that practically froze him in place. He could feel that Rowanne's power had grown tremendously; the funny thing was that she didn't realise how strong of a person and half demon she was.

'Let's agree to disagree on this point. And remember, there's always the chance that this might not work, so it would be a complete waste of your life,' said Alexander.

Rowanne didn't know whether she agreed with him, but it was sensible to come up with alternative plans. 'What else can we do, Lillian?'

'Have Alexander accept the proposal from the Adara Clan: thereby, agreeing to marry their daughter.'

Alexander tensed up.

Rowanne looked at him pointedly; he'd never mentioned any of this to her. He needed to do the right thing.

She turned to Lillian to get the answer's she needed, 'Who are the Adara Clan?'

Lillian finished her account by adding, '...And their daughter is-'

'Lady Evelyn Blaze,' interjected Alexander in a disgusted tone.

That explained the strange exchange between the two at the office. No wonder Evelyn had been frosty towards him. Rowanne suspected he'd probably rejected her family's proposal, thereby considerably hindering their chances of getting closer to the throne. After all, they didn't have the knowledge that Alexander had forfeited the chance of being second in line by becoming human. She thought her head might explode from all that she had learnt. She was deeply conscious of the fact that there was far more to it than this. How much more, though, and did she really want to know the answer...?

Everyone had repeatedly asked her at each junction whether she really wanted to know the truth. Lady Enid, Alexander and Lillian had all warned her that there'd be consequences; once she knew, there would be no going back to her beautifully ignorant state...

'I remember her. Do you think it's more than a coincidence that Evelyn went to Driskell's home? Alexander, I think you might be in a better position to give me an answer, right?' asked Rowanne.

'I can answer for the both of us,' replied Lillian. 'Evelyn was my best friend and one of my ladies-in-waiting. I can vouch for her, she went through everything with me, and was one of my supporters. The fact that she still helps my mother every night is a testament to our friendship, and the kind of warm hearted gentle woman that she is.'

'Evelyn warm hearted?!' asked Alexander incredulously.

'Watch what you say, Alexander. You grew up with her as well. You know her. A woman can be gentle and also firm when the need arises. If you think the two are mutually exclusive, then think again!' said Lillian.

Alexander hated it when these women presumed to think for him, and put words into his mouth that he had never uttered. For demon's sake! He respected women. He had only to look to his own mother, or Lady Enid for that matter, to know how wise a woman could be. They were formidable warriors in his heart, and at the same time they had the capacity for infinite kindness.

Rowanne looked at Alexander; some of what he had just thought had unwittingly drifted through her mind, and she smiled, amused, knowing that he'd hate it if he thought someone had just read his mind. He could be a mystery at times that incensed her, and yet, again, he could be transparent as glass, not afraid to show his emotions. Rowanne could almost hear him say: 'This is who I am and I make no apologies for it. Deal with it!'

To break the tension between the two, Rowanne intervened, 'Alexander, will they still accept you if they find out you're human? I don't quite know what to call you...'

Alexander broke his glare from Lillian, and turning to Rowanne, he said, 'Even though I have lost my immortality, I'm still technically a demon. I still have the powers of a full demon, except with a human life span. So far, thankfully, they haven't detected this pertinent fact.'

'It's not going to be good if they find out, right?' Rowanne didn't want to think about the inevitable consequences.

'It would be horrific, I won't sugar coat it for you,' answered Lillian starkly. She turned to Alexander and looked at him steadily, and said, 'Forgive me for saying this, but now is the time to lay out all the facts on the table. We can't afford to bury our heads in the sand and admit defeat. Well, *I* can't, anyway.'

'Fine. I would be executed,' said Alexander coldly. 'And that would not be the worst fate... I could accept that. But what would follow would be far more horrendous-'

'You're talking about our families. They'd investigate them and... deal with them accordingly.' Rowanne could not bring herself to say killed, wiped out of existence.

Rowanne felt physically sick, her heart ached, and she knew that Alexander was going through the same emotions. They had to find a way for the sake of their loved ones.

'So, operation proposal is out?' asked Rowanne.

'No one has rightly asked my opinion, not that I have ever really considered the proposal, but out of respect, I have spoken with Evelyn,' said Alexander, directing his answer to Lillian.

She snorted. *As if Evelyn would ever approach this fool,* she thought.

'Hold on a minute, if Alexander is out of the running, then that means — Evelyn is next in line?!' asked Rowanne.

Lillian answered smoothly, 'Well, naturally. That is the most likely scenario, if and when they find out. I love Evelyn, but I'm not so naive as to not know that, as Nobles, her family would push her to take the crown in a heartbeat.'

'But you just said you were best friends and that she is supportive of your family,' said Rowanne, though she had a feeling what Lillian's reply would be.

'Love and friendship has its own place. It's a system, Rowanne. It's just the way things work. If a ruler of our world steps aside, then naturally the next in line will be looked at as the successor. Power is extremely addictive, once you've tasted it, you want more. What's more enticing than the throne? Never forget that underneath their beautiful veneer, all of us Nobles are sharks just waiting to seize our prey.'

Rowanne was shocked at hearing these words come out of Lillian's mouth. She could not reconcile them as being true of the woman before her; least of all, with the few demons she had met who were so far removed from sharks in their candour and demeanour. She silently disagreed with Lillian, but thought it best not to argue the point.

'So, Evelyn taking the crown, and I mean no offence by this, Lillian, is a bad idea because of the consequences to Alexander and myself, not to mention our families.' Rowanne thought long and hard before hitting upon an idea, 'What if Alexander and I directly approach Lady Enid. I mean your mother. We could explain the situation and if it comes down to it, perhaps ask for her intervention?'

Lillian's eyes gleamed as she looked at Rowanne. 'I see what you're saying. My mother and Evelyn, as far as I know, get along and respect each other. When we take all of these factors into consideration, then we might have a chance.'

Alexander looked sceptical. Both of them, as far as he was concerned, were deluded. He could not think of Evelyn as someone to go out of her way to help others, even those she considered friends.

'Do you really believe that if we set up a meeting between Evelyn, Lady Enid and I, and give Evelyn leverage in the form of the knowledge that I have lost my immortality, and therefore, cannot legally ascend to the throne, that she'd happily agree to keep quiet about it, while taking the throne for herself?' asked Alexander derisively.

It sounded laughable to Rowanne's ears, now that she really thought about it. 'So, Evelyn will agree as long as you're willing to renounce your claim?' asked Rowanne, and turning to Lillian, she said, 'I mean no disrespect to your friend Evelyn, but what's to stop her from getting rid of Alexander, once she's the queen? She could easily expose his truth. There is also another thing you've both overlooked.'

'What's that?' asked Lillian, not liking the direction this was heading in.

'I was thinking the same thing myself...' said Alexander to Rowanne, before turning to Lillian, 'Rowanne is alluding to the quandary I now find myself in: if I formally renounce my claim to the throne, then Evelyn and the other Nobles will become suspicious, and will want to know why. It will only be a matter of time before they discover that I have lost my immortality. What explanation can I give that will satisfy them without involving Rowanne? After all, there's only a limited number of reasons why a demon loses their immortality. And if they should piece it together... Think about it, if you were in Evelyn's position, what would you do?'

'I hate to admit it, but you're right. Friend or not, I can't afford the possibility that at the last moment Evelyn or her family turn on us. I do not want to be deceived a second time by those I love and trust...' said Lillian cryptically.

'We need to think of another plan. We could still approach your mother, she knows the truth. Maybe she could have some idea as to how we can survive this situation unscathed, if at all possible,' said Rowanne.

'You're right, Rowanne,' said Lillian. 'I think the time has now come when we can no longer put off going back to Demon World.'

'You're both crazy. You'd be risking Rowanne's life, and if she were to be caught, then you know very well what that would mean for her. If I go back, then I'll have people I need to answer to as well. Let's not forget the fact that if a demon finds out my truth, then we will have lost before we've even started.'

'Be that as it may, we are left with very few options. The one thing that you both have going for you is that you have powerful families that could shelter you there, until we come up with a plan,' said Lillian.

'We have to get Lady Enid alone. How difficult is that going to be, Lillian?' asked Rowanne.

Alexander hated the plan, he thought it was beyond reckless to go into Demon World, not to mention the fact that they might be playing into the hands of whoever originally attacked Rowanne. One word was screaming in his mind, drowning out all thought.

'Hold on a minute, Lillian,' said Rowanne before she could answer. Turning to Alexander, she said, 'You're not the only one to think that going to Demon World could potentially be a trap. I too, believe that we haven't actually considered every angle, but despite that we still have to deal with the present situation. And we can't avoid the question of who'll be the next to rule.'

Alexander nodded his head in agreement. There was something bothering him that he could not put his finger on. He hoped he'd remember what it was before it became too late.

'We can rely on my family to shelter the both of us, or you could stay with your grandfather,' said Alexander to Rowanne. 'Incidentally, Lillian, did you know her grandfather is no other than Ju-Long Hou of the Dark Fire Clan?'

An uncomfortable expression quickly passed over Lillian's features.

She knows! thought Rowanne. Why would she hide this...? It made her suspicious. She wanted to slap her forehead, as she recalled Lillian's earlier words. How had she found out? Then it dawned on her slowly. *Lillian is always close by me, even when I can't sense her presence, so she probably overheard everything that was said in my grandparents house.* She could not shake the feeling now that Lillian was hiding something from them...

'Yes, I know who your grandfather is. He's a powerful demon of our world, and there's no one you could be more safe with than him. He would have a veritable army of demons to protect you,' said Lillian.

'I don't want any bloodshed over me. If we can avoid fighting, so much the better. I'm not naive, though, so perhaps it's better if we can keep as many people out of this as possible.' Rowanne thought that if they could not link her to her family, then they would be spared.

'I think you're right,' Alexander squeezed her hand in solidarity. 'Rowanne, I think I can find a place for us to stay in Demon World. I will try to make less frequent trips, if it can be helped, but they do call me up for work, which is unavoidable. Perhaps I could ask for a permanent transfer to Earth.'

'I find that idea to be entirely fanciful. It would work if you were a lesser demon. But First Families cannot reside

461

permanently in this world, it's against the rules, or have you forgotten everything of our World. Especially the fact that *you* are second in line!' said Lillian in a disparaging tone of voice.

Her voice alone could cut through glass, thought Rowanne. 'So that is the reason why my grandfather travels a lot.'

Alexander tore his hostile gaze away from Lillian, and turned back to Rowanne. 'Yes. It's to keep his cover and to protect all of you,' he said in a kinder voice.

Rowanne knew they'd need more information to help them. The time had come for Lillian to reveal what she knew. 'Lillian, I know you don't want to talk about it, but can you tell us what you remember of Demon World, when...' she knew that Lillian understood.

'Alright, but I don't see what relevance this has to our present situation, and I don't remember much, anyway.' Lillian dearly wanted to lay her hands on the individuals responsible for her demise, but knew in her heart that it would have to wait; if she ever got the chance at all. 'I was sent to Prima Stella to be judged, and was found guilty of treason against our World... and the rest is evident,' she said devoid of emotion.

Rowanne was shocked - there was definitely more to it than that. Lillian didn't seem the type of person, especially after spending time with her and Lady Enid, who would ever do something to jeopardise her life, let alone her family's.

'Can I ask you something?' said Alexander.

Lillian nodded reluctantly. He felt the icy chill of the tower she was trying to imprison herself in to avoid talking of her passing.

'Does this have anything to do with the infamous case that made Driskell the formidable demon he is today?' Alexander didn't know the exact details. The First Family had covered it up; but they could not shut down the rumours that had abounded in its wake.

The living room light started to flicker on and off. Rowanne could hear the rain as well as hailstones start to ricochet off the window. The room grew darker as outside a magnificent grey cloud blanketed the entire city.

'Lillian, you have to calm down, or never mind Demon World, they'll find us right here.' Rowanne went to Lillian and sat beside her, and gently turned her face away from the city, bringing her awareness back to the present, to the people around her.

Lillian shook her head, and the violet light that had smouldered dangerously in her eyes slowly diffused. The lights came back on, but the weather continued to lash outside, she could not help it. Had she not told Rowanne before of the dangers of demons who could not control their powers; yet here she was doing the exact same thing, again.

Lillian turned to Alexander, 'That man, whom we both used to call friend, is partly the reason behind my demise.' She squeezed Rowanne's hand instinctively, trying to reach out. She was tired and could not do it alone. 'It's hard to believe that we were once children, that time seems so long ago. I was eighteen, my birthday only a few months away, and was getting ready for my coronation for the following year. When a new ruler is crowned in our world, it is a momentous occasion, and you can just envision the sort of grand celebrations we would have had. My mother had ruled for a long period up to that point, and was glad to pass the mantle onto me.' She took a deep breath before continuing, 'I only reached the first initial ceremony of accepting my title as Princess and Lady of the Morning Star Clan. The following year I would have been crowned Queen of Demon World.' Lillian appeared quietly happy at the memory, almost as if she were reliving her past, her lost youth.

Rowanne could not even begin to imagine Lillian's life. The Queen and the royal family were her closest comparison.

'What happened?' asked Rowanne gently.

Lillian looked long and hard at the people before her - maybe they'd be luckier than her... She'd damn well make sure that they would have a chance at least. 'I was happy for almost two years, life seemed like one long celebration. What was it that Shakespeare said in one of his sonnets? "... *But thy eternal summer shall not fade...*" You see, when you are young, you think you're invincible, the world seems to be made for you. How wrong I was, dying at the tender age of twenty. Wait, I mean — my life was cut down and stolen at that age!'

Rowanne could feel waves of pain coming off Lillian, and her hand had become numb from her death grip, but she bore it quietly. Before her was one of the strongest women she had ever had the privilege to meet.

Rowanne looked at Alexander, who gave her a small smile. He too was enraptured by Lillian's story. Rowanne knew that there was some enmity between him and Driskell, but she had not been able to find out what it was, let alone ask about it; it was not her place.

'What did Driskell find out?' asked Alexander. His old friend had never fully gone into the details of what had happened. Nobody outside of the royal family knew - that he was aware of. He wondered whether Lillian had confided in the others within her inner circle, those closest to her who she trusted.

'You're very perceptive, Alexander. I was wrong about you. You merely play up to people's expectations of you. Beware of this one, Rowanne. He is a dark horse,' said Lillian, watching Alexander's carefully maintained neutral facade.

Rowanne looked steadily into his eyes, then quickly turned back to Lillian. He was not a danger to her, it was as simple as that.

Are you sure you aren't a little afraid of me? asked Alexander of Rowanne.

She arched an eyebrow, *Possibly of your manners. Were you born conceited?* He looked at her wickedly.

I get better with time, it gives me a chance to cultivate my natural talents, he replied sardonically, much to Rowanne's dismay.

Lillian smiled wistfully for a brief moment at the quarrelsome pair before her.

'Was Driskell the only other person outside of your family to know the exact details of what happened to you?' asked Alexander.

Lillian thought about it. 'I told only those closest to me initially. My mother knew. Definitely not my father, for painfully obvious reasons.' Alexander shuddered in response; most people thought of her father as intimidating. 'I told one other and that was–'

'Your best friend Lady Evelyn Blaze, of course,' supplied Rowanne confidently, confirming what her gut was telling her.

'Yes,' replied Lillian, smiling. 'You have to understand, Rowanne, that neither Alexander or Driskell knew the truth. Sometimes I get a little hazy on the finer details. I can't always fully remember the events.'

'So, your inner circle would have consisted of Alexander, Driskell, Evelyn and Lady Enid as the people you could implicitly trust?' asked Rowanne.

'Actually, that's not quite true... Tell her the rest. You know...' said Alexander.

'Alexander was the oldest in the group, and he had spent his time away from the rest of us developing his skills. He'd more than likely be found in Driskell's company; they were almost inseparable.'

'Well, what Lillian means to say is that we were both competitive,' said Alexander.

'In my eighteenth year something extraordinary happened... it was a first, as far as I know for Demon World,' said Lillian.

Alexander leaned forward eagerly.

'It was 1944 or maybe it was '45. Rowanne, you have to understand that it was unprecedented at the time: the first time a human was allowed to reside permanently in Demon World. The pilot programme started a few years back with specially chosen humans, who were temporarily allowed access to our world because of their unique skill set,' said Lillian.

'The exact details are murky. Lillian's mother probably knows more than she'll ever be allowed to divulge. The point is, they were so impressed with one family in particular, that they were officially invited to stay,' contributed Alexander.

Rowanne looked at Lillian's melancholy expression. 'Am I right in thinking that this is when the problems began?' She had only to think of her own situation to know that a demon involved with a human inevitably led to trouble.

'Sometimes trouble can be a good thing... it depends on your perspective,' said Lillian secretively, a whimsical smile lighting up her eyes.

'I don't understand. What do you mean?' asked Rowanne.

Oh, don't you? asked Lillian pointedly. She could feel Rowanne's discomfort, and could almost envision her squirming beneath her inspection. *Good. She's not completely dense, then.*

'Rowanne, she's referring to- now this stays strictly between us. Nobody outside of our circle knew that we had befriended the humans, especially their son. We had included him within our inner sanctum, as you might call it. I didn't know him all that well. I only ever met him personally on a few occasions, but I liked him well enough. He seemed to me to be a sterling man,' said Alexander.

It was Lillian's turn to feel discomfort, she was reluctant to bring up the next part. 'He was a good friend to us, even Driskell seemed to take a shine to him. Do you remember, Alexander, before he became the man he now is?'

He only nodded. He could see the Driskell of old in his mind's eye: that carefree young soldier. The more he thought on it, he recalled that Driskell had spent a lot of time with Lillian and the human.

'What was his name?' asked Rowanne. She was captivated by the dark tale, and wondered what it would be like to live in that world, to leave humanity behind and walk amongst the demons; the idea was as terrifying as it was thrilling. *Could I do that? Well, I guess that is exactly what I will be doing and soon.* Her stomach knotted in fear of the unknown.

Take care that in leaving humanity behind you don't also leave behind your humanity, said Lillian sombrely. Rowanne looked at her steadily, and nodded. The spell of Demon World momentarily broken.

Alexander was about to answer when Lillian interrupted. She wanted to be the only one to speak his name. 'Elisedd.'

'Nice name. Does it have a meaning?' asked Rowanne.

'It's Celtic and refers to one who is kind; he certainly lived up to his name.'

'People spoke well of his family, not just for the skills they brought, but for the way they conducted themselves with a quiet dignity,' said Alexander fondly.

'Would I be right in assuming that something went wrong, and that his family no longer resides in Demon world?' asked Rowanne.

'They were banished to earth, all except one...' said Alexander gravely.

Rowanne looked towards Lillian, who was hugging herself as if the very memory of that time had left behind a coldness in her.

Lillian looked at her with a steely expression, but her eyes gave her away; so full of despair and infinite sorrow. 'Alexander is referring to Elisedd...' A lump formed in her throat. She felt tears burn behind her eyelids. No! She would not break down, and could do this for her beloved.

Lillian's mind relentlessly pulled her back to her youth. Even now, she could picture him: a tall man with sparkling emerald green eyes, looking at her in their usual wicked way, complete with that devil-may-care smile of his; solely for her. If she concentrated really hard, then she could even hear the sound of his laughter... *No. Stop it! Stop it, Lillian,* she rebuked herself, and covered her face with her hands trying to block out the memories she so longed for; after all, they were the only thing left connecting her to him.

Rowanne gently pulled Lillian's hands down and hugged her. She felt the subtle shift in Lillian as she gave herself up temporarily to her care. Rowanne looked at Alexander and they exchanged uneasy glances, both deeply concerned for her wellbeing both physically and mentally.

Lillian straightened up. Calling on her power she wrapped her heart in an amethyst cocoon, and taking a deep breath she pulled herself together. She was not used to these public displays of emotion. It was hard.

'I formed a friendship with Elisedd, and in the second year of our relationship, somebody informed on us to the Noble Court.'

'It was only a friendship, that is not enough to be sent to the Noble Court for- Oh. I see...' said Alexander, finally realising the truth.

He could not believe he had been so blind, it was there right before him; but he had dismissed it as a friendship.

'It was Driskell, wasn't it? That man can see everything. He has to only look at you to know your innermost secrets,' said Alexander angrily, at the thought of his former friend and adversary.

'Yes, our *friend* Driskell,' replied Lillian bitterly, as an ice cold fury flowed from her to surround everyone in the room. It started to crystallise with jagged sharp points, insensible of whom they were aimed at.

'Lillian!' warned Alexander. She looked at him with cold piercing violet eyes that seemed to be changing into a steely grey, threatening violence for anyone who got in her way. However, she began to slowly and painfully reel her power in.

This was bad; they could not afford to have Lillian lose control, especially because of who she was, and the tremendous power she still wielded, even in death. Alexander looked uneasily at Rowanne's close proximity to her.

Rowanne studied the woman beside her, who was transformed by circumstances outside of her control. Before her very eyes, Lillian started to change into a monstrously beautiful but deadly entity. Yet, despite this she reached into the ice cold fire (it didn't burn her at all) and took a hold of her hand, much to Lillian's astonishment.

Rowanne's own power rose, a beautiful deep green that encircled Lillian's ice cold violet, until the two combined. Rowanne's necklace flared quietly under her jumper, its own power warmed Lillian, and reached for her heart, where it encountered an impenetrable barrier. So, instead it chose to encase her heart; the warmth would eventually sink in.

'Keep holding onto me, Rowanne. Just until I finish speaking of this,' it was hard for Lillian to ask for help, it was not something that came naturally to her. 'Driskell wasn't the only one, like I said earlier, but he did enforce the rules,' said Lillian. She wanted to tear him apart with her bare hands, and could feel her emotions violently trying to surface. Only Rowanne's power somehow kept her from becoming a destructive mindless force, hell bent on revenge. God help anyone if that should happen...

Thunder rumbled ominously before lightning started to lash out at the city. Lillian's power thrummed as shockwave after shockwave left her, attacking the city. The rain brought hailstones that pounded down upon the unsuspecting people caught outside.

Rowanne's forehead was beaded in perspiration from trying to calm Lillian. She reached for the energy of the crystal, and as she did so, her own eyes started to bleed to a deep amethyst hue. She was puzzled by Alexander's apprehensive look.

He watched in sheer wonder as Rowanne started to transform: her hair almost became lighter in tone, and her features became softer. There was something almost bewitching and ephemeral about her. Her very power had absorbed Lillian's so that a new ultra violet, almost indigo, energy encased them both.

Alexander had never seen anything like it before. The cerulean light shone fiercely in Rowanne's eyes; storm clouds seemed to gather in those twin pools. He watched Rowanne's power leave the room, shooting out and chasing the storm, finally leashing it, and soothing its nature. Though the gray clouds remained, the rain reluctantly subdued to a light drizzle.

Lillian looked steadily at Rowanne. *Who would ever have thought that a half demon could rival me?!* she thought, amused but not in the least surprised.

'It had to be someone you knew,' said Rowanne breathlessly. She felt tired and her heart weighed heavily, like she had just gone ten rounds in a boxing ring. Alexander seemed to have a ridiculously idiotic expression, and the weird smile just bothered her. There was nothing amusing about this situation; well, not to her, anyway. Lillian was trying to pour her heart out, and here he was smirking as if the whole thing was one big joke. Honestly, she didn't understand men sometimes.

'I think you could be right, but I honestly can't think of who it might have been. Any one of the Nobles or lesser demons could be responsible. Whoever it was seized their chance to advance. They used the knowledge wisely by going straight to the Enforcer. They probably worked with others as well, for all we know,' said Lillian.

'Didn't your title protect you? Your family is powerful, surely something could have been done to find these people and stop them before they did harm with the information that they possessed,' said Rowanne.

Lillian looked at Rowanne, who was in many ways sharp but could also be a little bit naive.

Alexander stepped in to answer, 'Rowanne, you have to understand that as powerful as we are and the titles we possess, we are nothing in the face of our law. If we are seen to not uphold the law and deliberately go against it, then we face harsh punishment. Getting rid of a member of the First Family would be seen as a triumph among many, especially those seeking to advance. And especially considering the fact that Lillian is an only child. Then with her out of the way, they would systematically get rid of the other heirs to achieve the ultimate goal of becoming ruler. It would be a lot harder, they would have to make compromises and form alliances to ensure that they had powerful allies to back them, all the while seemingly following the correct procedures.'

'But they'd need evidence, right? They could not just make an allegation that they could not back?' asked Rowanne.

'It's all a matter of strategy. They wouldn't dare face the backlash and severe penalty without solid proof,' replied Alexander.

'That's what bothers me. I was watched for almost two years, they would have systematically been gathering information until they could prove that I had formed a relationship with a human,' said Lillian.

'Relationship?' asked Rowanne surprised.

'There is a law against humans and demons forming relationships, especially because of the fact that half demons could be born of that union. Imagine the backlash at the court when they discovered their beloved princess had chosen a human above a demon as a partner,' said Lillian, her anger slowly simmering.

'The First Families and I, as well as the rest of Demon World, never knew the exact details, all that was released was the sad news of your untimely demise. There were rumours but never anything spoken aloud for fear of backlash,' said Alexander.

Alexander's hatred of Driskell grew; he could not believe that their former friend would have walked Lillian to her death. As Enforcer of the law, he would have ultimately acted as executioner. He wanted to kill Driskell if he ever got the chance, but unfortunately, none of them could do it outright, for fear of retribution from the Noble Court. But the day would surely come when they would not be able to protect him; then, he'd have his chance.

Lillian could almost read the dark thoughts that flittered over Alexander's face, not to mention the steely determination in his eyes. *Get in line*, she thought. If there's any justice in the world, then surely he will face his day of reckoning. *Watch out you traitor...*

Lillian looked at the pair of them, 'I was a princess who chose a human consort, and because I was also an heir, it was unacceptable to them. It was treason. They would never have accepted a human elevated to such a prominent position of power, especially not in Demon World. They would see it as an affront to their power and status. Two things that a demon does not easily forgive or forget. More than one rule was broken... When they found out, you cannot even conceive of the repercussions *we* faced...' a hunted look had come into her eyes.

'What was your family's response?' asked Rowanne shakily, terrified of the answer.

'Publicly I was disowned in the Noble Court, so that there would be no stain on the other members, and my mother, Lady Enid, could continue as Queen...' replied Lillian, the memory of it tearing through her, burning her, igniting her anger.

'Lady Enid would have stood by you. I cannot believe that she would have thrown you to the wolves,' said Rowanne fervently.

Lillian looked sadly at her, 'You must understand that it wasn't an easy choice, and that we, that is my mother and I, discussed it privately. *I* decided that my mother should make an outward show of renouncing me, so that the rest of my family wouldn't be implicated, and they'd be spared. Do you understand what I'm saying?' she asked, as she shook Rowanne, trying to get the point through to her.

Rowanne gently stopped her. She got it. *What would I have done, if I was in her position, to save my family?* It could not have been an easy decision for Lady Enid to come to terms with, let alone accept. Lillian had thought of others besides herself. She was a true leader and selfless. What had her crime really been? If it was falling in love with the 'wrong' person, then she was sure quite a few have been guilty of that, but it didn't warrant death. She could not get her head around the barbaric laws of Demon World.

'Elisedd and I accepted the punishment. The sentence, as you can see for yourself, was death; an inconceivably painful slow death. They all stood there watching us... as we burned...' said Lillian quietly, holding herself still. She refused to think on her words too deeply, because if she did, then she doubted whether Rowanne's apartment building would still be standing; she didn't need the deaths of innocent people on her head, as well.

The agony of watching each other die was something no one, demon or human, should ever have had to face. Above all, she had to block out the pain...

Rowanne thought she was going to be sick, and watched Alexander's face drain; he had become pale and deathlike from the shock of what he had just heard.

Alexander captured Rowanne's gaze, seeing his horror mirrored in her eyes. *I'm so sorry, Rowanne. What the hell have I gotten us into...* He didn't want to think about the implications should his truth be revealed. *I would rather die than let anyone lay a finger on Rowanne's head.* Noble Court be damned, he'd take on Prima Stella if it came down to it. He would risk a lot to save the valiant woman opposite him. He had not been able to save Lillian, but he'd be damned if he didn't save Rowanne.

Alexander's energy swirled dangerously around him, and consequently the winds outside began to respond in kind by coming together violently and starting to form a tornado. The sheer size of it was magnificent, and it would reduce the city to ruins, if he chose.

A dark fury took hold of Alexander and began to transform him into something else... Darkness seemed to leak out of him and swirled around him, almost obscuring him from view, until only his eyes, that burned with rage and an unholy fire, shone through.

Rowanne was terrified of and for Alexander; he was becoming in every sense the demon that she had read of in books and seen in horror films. 'Alexander!' she cried out desperately. However, she could not afford to leave Lillian, for fear that she might unleash her powers again.

Rowanne was literally caught between two extremely powerful demons, and didn't have a clue as to what to do.

Thankfully, Lillian stepped in, 'Alexander Black, you will cease immediately!' she said, walking towards him. Her power seemed to lash out at Alexander, almost as if he received a slap in the face. Slowly he came back to his senses - her energy was like ice cold water pouring over him, dampening, if not quite putting out his anger.

'Thanks. I needed that,' he said, smiling darkly at her - but his sapphire eyes held a storm of impenitence.

Rowanne had never seen him like this, he almost looked like the Shadow men who'd attacked her. *This is Alexander,* she reminded herself. *I know him...*

Alexander watched the uncertainty flicker in the depths of Rowanne's eyes. It dawned on him, finally, how he must appear to her in this state. He snapped his fingers, and once more became the man she knew. He gave her a penetrating look, uncertain of what he was searching for... hoping for.

'So, it appears you have anger management issues... I don't think a therapist could help you, especially when you go all *Hulk* on us,' said Rowanne.

He laughed, secretly relieved and amused by the film reference. 'An unfortunate side effect of our species...'

'That's nothing! You'd be petrified if you ever got on the wrong side of me!' teased Rowanne.

Lillian gave her a small grateful smile, before her features became grim again. 'Well, it seems the time has come for us to actually make a move. Rowanne, grab anything you might need. I'm not sure how long we will be gone.'

She knew they'd have to go to Demon World eventually, she just had not expected it to be right at this very moment. She felt nervous and sick. *But I'm not ready...* Alexander came towards her and pulled her gently to her feet in one go.

'Come on. I'll help you pack,' he said to Rowanne, and looked at Lillian, who gave him a quick nod of approval.

'Go ahead, Rowanne. I need time to open the portal, anyway,' said Lillian.

Alexander led the way holding Rowanne's hand. He could feel her reluctance but she didn't let go.

'I'll need a suitcase. Wait, will that be too heavy? I don't quite know how it works,' said Rowanne.

'Don't worry. I'll help you,' he said, as he grabbed her suitcase down from the top of the wardrobe and placed it open on her bed. He looked around her room contemplating what she'd need.

Rowanne was uncomfortable for obvious reasons to let Alexander pack for her. 'Um, would you mind waiting outside? I have a few things to do,' she said, hoping he'd understand her subtle meaning.

He smiled roguishly, 'As you wish. I'll be outside making arrangements, but I could have been a great asset to you...' he said slyly, hoping she'd understand his not so subtle meaning.

'I'm sure you could be,' said Rowanne under her breath. *In your dreams!* she thought.

Alexander looked at her piously, the very picture of innocence, but his smouldering sapphire eyes gave away his less than pious intentions. *Try as you might, you can't shield from me, can you?* he asked rather smugly, as a look of annoyance flashed across her face.

He revelled in Rowanne not being able to properly shield from him. After all, it only benefited him. Was he a cad? Maybe... He turned and left.

Rowanne was grateful to have him leave, and locked the door for good measure. She heard his male laughter. *Damn it!* He'd heard her turning the lock.

Her cheeks were inflamed, but she was grateful that he was not here to see her like this. God only knew what he'd think. She tried to put it out of her mind as she strode over to her wardrobe and opened the doors. What would she need? Sadly there was not an app on her phone that told her: 'In Demon World it is currently thirty degrees.'

She walked to the door, and called out, 'Alexander, what's the weather like over there?'

He smiled, and leaning against the other side of the door, he replied, 'It's cold right now. We are heading towards winter, so dress warmly. Let me in and I'll help you...' he said unrepentantly, and laughed as he felt her mortification at the idea.

Lillian faced Alexander with a disgusted look, 'Honestly, just cut it out and make the damn phone call. I'm trying to focus here, if you haven't noticed!'

Alexander became serious. Sitting on the sofa, he made the call to arrange for them to have a place to stay. While he spoke, he watched Lillian struggle a few times to open the portal. Each time she tried to begin, to create the force needed, it would sputter out of existence.

Putting in his Bluetooth headset, he made his way over to Lillian to see if he could be of any help. She looked at him gratefully. She must really need the help, if she was willing to use his energy as well. He held her hand, and together they focused on opening the portal. Their combined power opened a vortex, and finally it grew big enough to admit them entry.

Rowanne opened the door and stepped out. She'd packed the essentials, as well as shoving in her winter wardrobe. She was dressed in jeans and a jumper over which went her long indigo coat, finishing the ensemble with knee high boots. She was finally ready. Well, as ready as anyone can ever be going to a new place, or in her case, leaving the planet! It sounded farfetched and preposterous to her own ears.

Rowanne was shocked as she looked at her living room. She quickly ran across the room to draw the curtains. The portal was flashing with a bright ultraviolet light, and if anybody looked up, they'd think there was a party going on in her apartment.

Alexander looked at Rowanne quizzically, 'What are you doing? We are so high up that no one is going to notice anything, let alone look into this room! Hurry up, it's difficult to keep a portal open for long.'

Rowanne grabbed her suitcase, and quickly checked that her gas was off, and the front door locked. With one last desperate look around, she took a deep breath and quickly walked up to Alexander's outstretched hand, and as soon as she grabbed it, he pulled her in tight. She held onto him for dear life. The vortex closed, plunging the apartment into darkness.

CHAPTER 26

Rowanne felt herself being pulled through the portal, and found it disorienting, not to mention that it took longer this time. Lillian flickered in and out as she tried to hold onto her form. Rowanne would have grabbed her hand but Alexander shook his head.

'Wait, Rowanne. Lillian isn't stable at the moment, it would be dangerous to hold onto her. I know you want to help,' he said kindly, he could see the concern in her eyes.

Alexander held Rowanne to him, while he focused his attention on getting them to Demon World. Lillian smiled at him. The energy pulsed around them, it was like they were floating at the centre of a mini tornado, mysteriously being helped up. Rowanne turned her head towards him and closed her eyes. He could see that she looked a little green. Travelling through portals wreaked havoc with the body, if you weren't accustomed to it.

After what seemed like an eternity to Rowanne, the vortex began to spin slowly, and the energy gently dissipated around them. A portal opened before them and they stepped through. She almost stumbled in her haste to get out, but thankfully Alexander caught her, steadying her.

Rowanne quickly looked about her for Lillian, and the relief she felt at seeing her standing only a few feet away from them was quickly replaced by fear, as she vanished in a burst of brilliant light. All that remained was a green shimmer in the spot where she had stood only a moment ago.

'Nooo!' screamed Rowanne, and would have run towards the very spot if it had not been for Alexander holding her back. She turned towards him, confused. 'Did you see that? Tell me that wasn't normal? Lillian's lost her form before, but I've never seen anything like this. It's as if she was violently wrenched away.' Her heart was in her mouth. She knew Demon World was dangerous, it played by its own mysterious rules, and she had better learn fast, if she was to stand any chance at getting back in one piece.

Alexander looked at her with a pained expression, 'Precisely the reason why I don't think it's a good idea for you to go to that spot. There could still be traces of the magic, and it could just as easily pull you away as well. However, I can't honestly say whether this was Lillian's unstable power, or if there's an external force at work...'

He had felt the magic in the ether. Rowanne was right, something felt off. He sensed that in coming to Demon World, they had all sealed their fate.

'Rowanne, we should make a move. We shouldn't stay here.'

Alexander walked over to where Rowanne's suitcase lay discarded on its side in the furore. He held out his hand to her so he could lead the way.

Looking up, Rowanne was mesmerised by the sight of the night sky lit up by hundreds of burning stars lending it their radiance. She was grateful to have dressed warmly as the cold began to seep in. She took a step towards Alexander and linked her arm with his, absently noting that from the outside they appeared to look like a couple.

As if reading her mind, he answered practically, 'This way, we won't look too conspicuous. If you lug that thing around, and walk behind me a few paces, then I guarantee we are going to draw unwanted attention to ourselves. If we delay further, then whatever *that* was will be after us next,' said Alexander.

Rowanne acceded to his point. Looking around the forest, just in the distance she could make out an enormous citadel. *Oh my God*, she thought. *We're back where we started...*

'Why are we in the heart of Demon World? This is the palace, surely it's heavily fortified? How will we be able to get past the guards, and what if we run into someone you know? How will you explain my presence here?' asked Rowanne breathlessly, as she thought about the number of things that could possibly go wrong.

Alexander stopped walking and looked at her. 'The reason I opened a portal in the forest is because this is the safest place. They are less likely to track my energy signature out here in this wide open expanse, especially in view of the fact that you are with me. Imagine how easy a target we'd be if I'd portalled us into the heart of the castle, they'd be able to pin us down with precision. We are perfectly safe, you just have to trust me. I know what I'm doing. This is the last place they'll expect us to be. However, we do need to be within the castle, it's vital if we hope to obtain the information we need.'

The ground crunched beneath Rowanne's feet. She felt something wet land on her nose, and realised that it had started to snow. *Beautiful*, she thought, as she put out her hand to catch snowflakes. She felt a semblance of peace out here in the snow capped forest. There was an eternal silence here and she was cocooned within it, where nothing could touch her. *Are you sure about that?* her mind taunted cynically. After all, only less than a few moments ago, Lillian had vanished in this so-called safe haven.

He watched Rowanne's sense of wonder, finding it strangely endearing. She was wrong of course: they were no more safe out here, than inside. Wondrous places often hid unseen perils, though, this in no way diminished their beauty.

'Rowanne, I hate to be the voice of reason but if you've quite finished, we really have to get a move on,' reiterated Alexander brusquely.

Rowanne nodded, and they began to walk. 'You know, I think the odds were stacked against us from the beginning,' she said wryly, as she considered all that they had gone through so far. Now they had willingly embraced danger by walking head first straight into Demon World.

Alexander turned to her, a sardonic smile lighting up his face, 'We've faced worse, and *you* seem to come out of it quite well. In fact, with added perks, I should say, despite everything!' and he gave a little flourish of his hand to encompass their disastrous odds.

'Famous last words,' said Rowanne bleakly. Luck ran out, after all. What would they do then, when the situation was at its worst? More to the point, what would she be prepared to do, to sacrifice...

They finally reached the other side of the forest, and stepped out of the line of trees.

She was at once awed by the roaring fires in the citadel, and in each of the adjoining watchtowers. It was a magnificent sight to behold, not to mention the heavily armed demon guards stationed along the top in their fine regalia.

The snow had started to fall heavily by the time they had made their way across to the castle. They passed under an arch, and ended up in a courtyard. Rowanne was familiar with this place from sharing Lillian's memories. Her eyes widened in trepidation as a man stepped out of the shadows to stand before them.

'Alexander? Good, you've finally arrived,' said the tall man, with a billowing long coat buttoned up to just under his chin. Rowanne observed that his clothing looked military, especially the brass buttons with the strange insignia that winked in the dark. The bottom half of his face was covered by a scarf, so that only his eyes could be seen.

The man noticed Rowanne for the first time, and turning to Alexander, nodded. 'You can go up, everything's ready for you. We all wondered at what was keeping you so busy that you avoided Demon World. I see that it wasn't only duty...' he winked at Rowanne.

The man offered his hand to her, and she managed to shake his hand without trembling.

'Good evening, my lady. I'm Kieran Black, Alexander's cousin, at your service,' he gently bent his long frame at the waist to kiss her hand. Turning back to Alexander, he said, 'I can't wait until you introduce me to?' and turning to Rowanne, he said, 'I beg your pardon, but my cousin has sadly neglected to introduce us properly.'

'Rowanne,' she quickly supplied, and then slapped her head metaphorically at giving away her real name.

'Rowanne, follow me, please. I'll show you that not all demons are so ill mannered,' he said, pointedly looking at Alexander. 'Where was I? Oh, that's right. I'm sure the rest of our family will delight in your company. You're in for a treat,' he laughed wickedly.

She was about to protest that they were just acquaintances, when Alexander looked at her intensely, trying to convey a warning.

Alexander stepped forward smoothly, and unceremoniously dumped her suitcase on his cousin, much to his chagrin. He put his arm lightly around Rowanne's shoulders, and turned her briefly away from his cousin. Sparks were shooting out of her eyes at this indignity, but after a moment of him glaring right back at her, she turned around with her brightest smile, and mirrored him by placing her arm around his waist.

Kieran smiled dubiously at the pair, although they could not see his expression beneath his scarf. 'Follow me this way. Why you do not stay with the family is beyond me,' he spoke over his shoulder, as he led the way through the courtyard towards the back of the castle. 'Rowanne, you will soon see for yourself that my cousin dearest has his... quirks. And if they ever become too much,' and this time he turned around, 'I'll be happy to show you how a true gentleman treats a woman, especially a beautifully formidable one.' Kieran gave Rowanne a long penetrating look, and smiled smugly at her beaming smile, not to mention Alexander's expression. *If looks could kill...* he thought, enjoying himself, especially now that his fool of a cousin was back.

Don't encourage him like that... warned Alexander.

His cousin began walking again. Rowanne could feel Alexander desperately gripping her hand, as if he thought that she'd leave him and choose to walk on ahead with his cousin instead. *You know, your cousin is very charming, you could learn something from him*, she said sweetly.

Alexander chose to ignore the inane comment. He walked quietly with her, all the while keeping his cousin firmly within his sight.

Rowanne looked about her in wonder; it was like being in a gothic tale. Here and there the fires from the top of the watchtowers illuminated parts of the huge complex, so that the roof and windows, which were coated with a layer of frost, sparkled like diamonds.

She was not so mesmerised as to not notice that there was a very real sense of danger and foreboding that seemed to cling to this place; underneath its beautiful facade it concealed innumerable dark secrets...

It took a while to reach the buildings that were situated towards the back of the castle. Kieran opened a door that led to a staircase winding its way up. Alexander stood aside and let Rowanne pass before him, before following closely behind.

At the top, Kieran led the way along a corridor with several doors branching off. He chose the central one and opening it stood aside to let Rowanne and his cousin pass through, and quickly closed it behind them.

'Here's where I leave you, I'm afraid,' he said seriously, addressing Rowanne. 'Hopefully we will get to talk under more pleasant circumstances.' For a moment, the facade of the joyfully carefree young man slipped. Kieran Black knew that this was no social visit. He knew of the danger his cousin and the woman before him faced.

Alexander hugged his younger cousin fiercely; they both knew what was at stake. He nodded his head and watched his cousin walk away. After all, they had both decided to keep their families out of this, but he'd been forced to ask his cousin for help.

Alexander had needed someone on the inside to keep him informed of what was happening in the palace. Kieran was the perfect candidate: he knew the guard shift, and the precise time they needed to be at the castle gates in order to pass through unnoticed.

Rowanne felt a burden on her heart at the thought that Alexander had been forced to use a family member. She watched the door at the end of the corridor close behind Kieran as he left.

Alexander flicked a switch, flooding the large living quarters with much needed light.

Rowanne stood in the centre of the large room and slowly looked about. It was more like an apartment, she observed, with doors leading to separate rooms. It was lavishly furnished with beautifully gilded furniture and long ornate mirrors that hung on the walls, not to mention the massive chandelier that hung in the centre.

Rowanne turned to Alexander and asked, 'Is your cousin by any chance a guard in the palace?' He patted the seat next to him and she joined him on the chaise lounge.

'Kieran is five years younger than me. And yes, he works for Lady Enid. He is a part of the royal guard. His living quarters are close by,' he replied.

'Who's apartment is this?'

'This,' replied Alexander nonchalantly, 'is my place. Or more rightly it is reserved for my family's use when visiting the palace. Hence, the adjacent rooms along the corridor are for the rest of my family.' He watched her look about curiously.

'I wonder how the rest of the palace must look if these are simply the guest quarters,' she spun around at the sound of Alexander's laughter. *Damn it.* She had not realised that she had said it out loud.

'Where in Demon World do you live, Alexander?' asked Rowanne, genuinely intrigued. Did he live alone or with his family? She had a dozen questions she'd love to ask, but would not.

'I will take you there one day, after all of this has been settled,' he said sincerely, his sapphire eyes piercing her with their intensity of emotion.

'Sure, after we get out of this in one piece,' she said, punching him lightly in the arm. She looked away feeling confused.

The chaise lounge was as uncomfortable as it looked. What she would not give for her own sofa right now. She shivered, she could not seem to get warm.

Alexander looked at Rowanne; she looked cold and out of place in his world - he was sorry to have dragged her here. He walked to the fireplace and lit a fire, and as he stoked it, he called to her over his shoulder, 'Come here. I think this will help.'

Rowanne walked over and sat on the rug before the fireside, and taking off her gloves warmed her hands. Alexander finally sat back next to her, satisfied with his handiwork.

'Thank you,' she said, and could have sworn that she'd just seen her breath mist before her. This place was certainly draughty...

'The rooms are a little too ventilated,' he said ruefully. 'I'll make us tea, or would you prefer coffee?' asked Alexander. He looked serious like a man on a mission.

'Whatever you're having will be fine.'

Alexander disappeared through a side door which she assumed must lead to the kitchen. He reappeared shortly with an ornate gold trolley, and she was glad to see that not only did it have two steaming cups of tea that smelled slightly sweet, no doubt made from some kind of flower, but food, as well. She looked at it lovingly and thought, *I could kiss him*.

Alexander set the tray down on the glass table before them, and then turning to Rowanne, leaned towards her obligingly until he was level with her face.

What the hell was he thinking? Again, he invaded her personal space. However she refused to back away this time and looked him straight in the eyes, exasperated with him. 'What is it?'

Alexander pointed to his cheek, smiling sweetly at her. After all, he was not one to turn down a reward...

Rowanne reciprocated his smile and leaned forward. His eyes widened in surprise, this was not what he expected... but, oh well. She picked up the sandwich and took a huge bite of it, and laughed gleefully at Alexander, as she could almost hear him lament. Well, it served him right. *Keep out of my head!* she thought.

He sat back resignedly, taking a bite out of his sandwich, and thoughts of Rowanne slowly faded as he began to tuck in with gusto. *I can't believe how hungry I am. I have not overexerted myself beyond what I am normally capable of, or, have I?*

Rowanne studied him; he was a man that didn't do things by halves, but really went for it. She took a sip of tea, identifying it as rose. 'It's the human side of you, opening the portal drained you more than you thought.'

Alexander waved her explanation away as he mournfully started his second sandwich. *That's most likely the case. She inherits demon powers, becoming stronger, whereas, I on the other hand, gain old age and become weaker,* he shuddered.

'So, when are you going to answer my questions, old man?' she asked helpfully.

'Really?' asked Alexander, raising an eyebrow. 'Do not test my patience, Rowanne...' he said menacingly.

'Don't worry, I'll have Kieran bring in your walking stick,' said Rowanne considerately.

'Rowanne, you will regret those words. I will prove to you that I am in no way frail, just wait until this is all over...' promised Alexander, as he looked at her wickedly.

'Uh-huh...' replied Rowanne sarcastically. 'But only if you don't use up all of your energy before then, dealing with this mess,' she added sweetly. She dared not smile, it would only encourage him.

They finished the rest of the meal in companionable silence. Rowanne's thoughts ran in different directions, each vying for her attention; uppermost was Lillian.

'Lillian?' Rowanne waited a heartbeat but there was no reply. She turned to Alexander, 'I thought it was worth a try, anyway. She's powerful, and has been through worse. I thought there might still be a way for her to reach us.'

He patted her hand and looked at her solemnly. 'I feel that her energy is waning, but she has done remarkably well to hold on for this long. However, she's used up too much of her life force. It regenerated before but now it's slowing down to the point at which it will eventually cease, especially if she carries on at the rate at which she is going. Every time she uses extreme amounts of power, she loses more of herself, and there's no one to anchor her anymore... The other matter is that she could be held at this very moment by a higher level demon. If she is, then we are all in danger.'

Rowanne felt a tear slide down her cheek, she could not help it. She felt an incredibly strong connection to Lillian, but could not put a name to it. She didn't want to lose her, despite knowing that she had passed long ago, but her spirit was still here. Was she selfish in not wanting to let Lillian go...?

CHAPTER 27

Lillian found herself materialising outside of Lady Enid's room. *What's happening?* she thought, alarmed. Was she losing her ability to maintain her powers? If so, then this was not a good sign. There had been so much more that she had wanted to tell Rowanne before she had been ripped away from them.

It felt strange to be back here. She had not told Rowanne that she felt that this was really the last time for her. Deep down, she felt that time was running out.

She sensed danger, the very air was permeated with it.

She could hear her mother's heartbeat beyond the door. Maybe it was a good thing that she had ended up here after all, as she really needed to face her mother. She listened in, and her senses confirmed that she was alone in there. When had she come back? she wondered. She had not expected her to be back so soon, this didn't make any sense.

Lillian drifted through the door, and saw her mother, Lady Enid, resting in a chair, her eyes closed. She was about to walk towards her when someone stepped out of the shadows, blocking her path.

Lillian looked at her best friend, who stood tall and regal with her long hair framing her delicate features. Her blue eyes shone brightly as her mouth curved into a smile; it was more of a grimace, really, as if she'd seen something distasteful.

'Evelyn,' said Lillian wonderingly. 'It's me, Lillian. You remember, don't you?'

Evelyn's eye's blazed green as her magic saturated the room, cocooning Lillian within it. 'I was expecting you, old friend,' she replied sneeringly. 'I knew you'd show up one of these days. I just had to make sure that I was here to intercept- I mean welcome you.'

'I don't understand, how could you possibly know? What's wrong with you?' asked Lillian, clearly perplexed by the whole situation. This could not be the same girl that she had grown up with.

Lillian remembered a gentle girl who was good hearted and always ready to help. The cold calculated look that had come into the pitiless woman before her shook her to the core. She had a bad feeling about this; if she was not careful, then the situation could go completely out of her hands.

'I'm perfectly fine, Lillian. Everything is just as it should be now. It's all going to plan rather wonderfully. Though, I'll admit, you nearly ruined my plans with your meddling: helping that half breed of a girl, setting her up to stand in *my* way!' said Evelyn viciously.

'What happened to you, Evelyn? What's made you go against us? We were friends once.' She tried to buy herself time to come up with a plan. This was worse than she had thought: she had to try and warn her mother and Rowanne before it was too late.

She felt foolish for not seeing it before, but she was a trusting fool, apparently even in death. She'd inadvertently led them all into a trap.

'How did you manage to get me here?' asked Lillian, shocked by the strength of her friend.

'Why do you keep referring to me as your 'friend,' how naive can you be?! We belong to the First Families, but what does friendship have to do with it? My mother rightly pushed me into your circle because of your status. I had everything to gain. You were ever a means to an end for me. But really, in the end you brought this all on yourself. If you had just stayed within protocol and married a demon of a First Family, you would have been safe. I would not have been able to lay a finger on your credibility, had you not chosen to cavort with a human, thereby placing him above your duty. Don't look at me like that. You can't judge me for simply doing my duty, anybody else of high rank and nobility wouldn't have hesitated to do the same,' finished Evelyn, as if she were lecturing an unruly child.

You cold manipulative Noble, thought Lillian. She was seething, her anger spreading through her making her blood boil. She had never wanted to kill a demon before, but now... Oh, wait there was also Driskell. Her list seemed to have grown exponentially and where it would end, was anyone's guess. 'I thought I could trust you,' she said, her voice dripping with rage. 'Never in my wildest imagination would I have expected this from *you*. It was you, I now see, who reported Elisedd and I to the Noble Court,' said Lillian.

'Elisedd... I haven't heard that name mentioned in forever. That fool of a human who dared think he was good enough to court a princess, let alone have the presumption of thinking that demons would let him rule over them. Never!'

'You misjudged him, he didn't have any sort of intention. And do not say his name. You have no right to even utter it! Your problem is that you don't even know what goodness is, let alone recognise it, even if it were right before you. You think that the whole world is there for your taking, and that everyone has a plan and desire to get to the top regardless of the consequences,' said Lillian.

'I love that word *consequences*,' Evelyn mimicked Lillian, enraging her. 'What good,' she spat, 'came from joining hands with that pathetic human? He could not protect you in the end, or...' she smiled calculatingly.

Lillian felt as if the rug had been pulled from beneath her. *She couldn't possibly know… Could she?* Panic set in as her heart pounded in her ears.

Lillian decided to shift the focus, as they were heading into dangerous territory. 'I suppose Driskell must have been your accomplice in this?' asked Lillian in a disgusted tone.

'That must hardly have come as a surprise. Did you think that you had enthralled him completely? It was sickening, the way he always fawned over you, always ready to fulfil your every whim, Princess,' said Evelyn tauntingly.

'I was under the dual mistaken belief that he was my friend, and that he respected Elisedd. It appears I have been wrong on numerous levels, especially when it came to my inner sanctum,' said Lillian.

'I find it amusing that even with you belonging to the most powerful family in Demon World, you are still so susceptible to being manipulated by those around you. It sickens me. You disgust me. You did not even deserve to be born into that noble clan, it would have been better had I been born in place of you,' said Evelyn acerbically.

Lillian felt each of those words burn into her skin. She had not known that her friend was capable of such anger and resentment. Was it the fact that she had been born third in line? Had her family pushed her too far, or had she always been this perverse?

'Driskell, for all his faults, proved a valuable ally for me, and it didn't take much to persuade him to my way of thinking. The right way, I might add. He hates the Nobles; they treated him with distaste, even as they feared him once he became Enforcer. Oh, how quickly they outwardly showed deference to him. He agreed with me that it was not right that his beloved Lillian had aligned herself with a human. He could forgive many things but not this. It was only natural that he helped me to gather information over the two years, so that he could present his findings before the Noble Court,' said

Evelyn gleefully, as she remembered the hard work she had put in to get rid of the abhorrent woman before her.

Lillian wanted to get her hands on Evelyn and Driskell. She took a menacing step towards her but stopped as she raised a hand pointing to her mother, who was frozen in place.

'Don't you lay a finger on her!' Lillian warned.

'On the contrary, I have no such intention. What, do I look stupid to you? You think I'd risk Prima Stella? No, Lillian. I am more subtle... I follow the rules. I don't break them so heedlessly, and there is no trail that leads from me to your pathetic demise. I have loved your mother more than my own. What, you don't believe me?' she asked at Lillian's look of incredulity. 'I naturally love the woman who treats me like her own daughter,' she twisted the words like a knife straight into Lillian's heart. 'Especially as I have now successfully supplanted you. I'll have you know, I diligently attend to her every need. I'm quite conscientious in my work, and there's never been a need for her, since the day you *left*, to seek help elsewhere,' Evelyn smiled evilly.

I'm sure you are, thought Lillian, and wondered what else Evelyn had managed to accomplish during her absence.

'Don't look so shocked, time didn't stop with your passing. Did you think everything would be frozen, that nobody would move forward with their lives, just because you'd gone? Lady Enid worked damn hard to rebuild her life and reputation afterwards, or what there was left of it, thanks to you and your selfish ways,' Evelyn wagged her finger at Lillian, looking at her ashamed. 'I've had more than seventy years to earn your mother's trust, she would be nowhere without me. I made sure to defend her good name when those Nobles came like vultures to pick at her in the hopes of destroying her. I was quite vocal in the Noble Court, you can ask anyone, they'll tell you how I stood by your mother, incidentally where you should have been, instead of in the arms of that pathetic mortal. Your father has taken quite the shine to me, especially since I am against half breeds, we talk of how things should be. Demons hate the idea of them, it's repugnant. A half demon tainted with mortality — that's the price you pay with your offspring,' there was a zealous light to her.

Incredible, she actually believes the nonsense she's spouting, thought Lillian. Evelyn had completely lost the plot, but then again, half of Demon World probably agreed with her. No matter which realm you were in, you'd always find those that spread hatred; there would always be something a person could find that they disliked. *Are we incapable of peace? Maybe the very idea of it frightens us, so that we subconsciously sabotage it for ourselves.*

Of course, my father would listen to her. He'd always been a conservative demon, upholding the 'old ways' as they were known; these ancient traditions passed down without anyone ever daring to question them, for fear of the unknown, or Prima Stella. *Maybe I was born in the wrong era*, she thought mirthlessly.

Lady Enid did not always agree with everything her husband believed. There was the outward show for the rest of the clans, but her mother had stood by her to the end, despite not being fully aware of the truth. It made her sick to think that this revolting woman was anywhere near her mother, poisoning her day in and out with her insidious talk of how the realm should be run.

'For your information, I have never influenced your mother, one way or the other. I have stood by her like her shadow. It's not long now till the day I am rewarded, and your mother feels it's the right time to step aside and let another take her place.'

'You mean Alexander, I suppose?' asked Lillian.

'Well, naturally, one step at a time. But... now that won't work, will it, Lillian? Alexander can no longer be the next in line,' she smiled craftily at her.

'What are you implying?' asked Lillian innocently, her heart rate accelerated. She was being played for a fool. How stupid could she have been not to know how far this went back... Evelyn's eyes shone triumphantly as she looked into the eyes of her childhood friend and realised that Lillian had begun to work it out.

'Now, Lillian. Don't play dumb with me. I see that I have to spell it out for you...'

CHAPTER 28

Amanda looked down from the window as she tapped an agitated rhythm against the wooden frame. She didn't have a very clear view, though, as the snow had become heavier in the past couple of hours. She rubbed her hands up and down her arms in a futile attempt to get warm.

She turned away and pointedly glared at the man sitting on the chaise lounge, his long legs crossed in front of him, one arm carefully draped over his eyes. *I can't believe he's so relaxed about this that he's actually gone to sleep!*

She strode towards him and confronted him. 'Hey, wake up! You're the one that convinced me that I had to come here for Rowanne's sake. Now you have the audacity to sleep?!'

Driskell slowly moved his arm, causing his shocking red hair to fall carelessly about him, as he lazily opened one eye that fixed on her with a keen piercing look. He had a ridiculous smile on his face, and yawning, he stretched.

Amanda could not help but notice his physique; he was almost cat-like with his lithe muscular body, especially evident when he stretched. *So he works out... So what...*

Driskell raised a quizzical brow.

This only served to fluster her. 'What?' she asked impatiently, and hated that stupid knowing look on his face. He smiled broadly.

Driskell raised his hands in a gesture of peace, while he wondered what had come over her. But of course, he knew... He was a wicked man.

'I thought you might have bored a hole in the window. How long have you been sitting there?' He sat up straighter. 'Please, sit. You looking down at me like a mannequin isn't likely to bring them here any quicker.' He watched her huff and sit on the seat opposite to him with her arms crossed.

'Are you sure that they're heading here? This plan seems foolhardy to me. Why the hell would someone walk directly into a spider web? It's naive to think that the spider won't see you,' stated Amanda matter-of-factly.

Driskell laughed silently at her quirky way of phrasing things. *I don't think I'll ever be bored for a minute - not in her company,* he thought.

She didn't like the weird look that had come into his eyes. God! The man made her nervous, sometimes. *Nervous? Really?* taunted her mind. 'Well?' asked Amanda abruptly, hoping he'd hurry up and answer her questions.

'I was just thinking, we'd make a good team: my brains and your brawn,' he looked deadly serious.

'Shut up, you idiot!' Amanda could not help it, she burst out laughing rather loudly in an undignified manner. She should be offended, but the amorous fool had her spot on; her family could sadly attest to this fact.

Driskell looked at her suspiciously, his eyes widening in shock. Was she mentally stable? One look at him and she laughed harder. He gave up the facade and joined her; it was a nice feeling. He had not had a carefree moment like this ever since Lillian...

Amanda held her sides suddenly sobering. *What am I doing exchanging jokes with Driskell of all people?* She watched as sadness flitted through his eyes too fast to catch, even as he laughed. She'd never really seen him like this before; it was a bit of a revelation, to say the least.

What could he be thinking of to cause such raw pain to surface? She studied him, and smiled kindly.

Driskell caught Amanda's thoughtful expression. Damn, he had let himself become vulnerable. His eyes became a glacier green, that of nature gripped in the torrent of an eternal winter.

Amanda was no coward: she may not particularly like the man before her, but there was definitely more to him than he let people see. Building her courage, she went to him. He stiffened at her approach and sat back as if trying to maintain a distance between them. He reminded her of a wounded wild animal, one that had seen too much, experienced too much, to be able to trust anyone, let alone let anyone get close to them.

Amanda sat down slowly and turned to him, deciding to drop her own act just for the moment. 'Do you know that this is my first time here? It's laughable, right? A demon who's never been to the world she came from. To be fair, and this is strictly between the two of us, I'm finding it slightly overwhelming.'

Driskell gave her a sceptical look. 'I wouldn't expect a woman who would go barging up to a demon, threatening to kick the living daylights out of him, to be scared of anything,' he said bemusedly.

Amanda punched him in the arm playfully. 'You'd think that, right? But *you* I can handle. It's the rest of these Noble nutcases that have me faintly worried. I can take on some of them, but going up against a whole army might be...' she tapered off, trying to come up with a suitable adjective.

'Crazy, would be the word you're looking for, my Scythian warrior,' said Driskell, as she snorted at him in derision. *So, you think you can handle me? That opens up interesting possibilities...* He very much liked the idea. He gave her an unbalanced grin that matched the wicked gleam in his eyes.

Oh boy, it doesn't take much to set him off. He must be the Casanova of his world, she thought. She didn't appreciate the subtle way in which his body language had changed, as he now leaned in towards her with one arm artfully draped along the lounge stretching behind her.

Amanda subconsciously placed a hand on his chest intending to push him back, but carried on oblivious, much to Driskell's amusement. 'Actually, I was going to say 'challenging'. I quite like the idea of it,' she said fiercely, as her eyes lit up at the very thought of it.

'I know what you mean...' said Driskell with a sly smile, wondering how long it would take for her to realise that she had not moved her hand.

'I beg your pardon?' asked Amanda suspiciously, and looking down she dropped her hand as if she had just touched a hot coal, and scooted back an infinitesimal amount. She took a deep breath. Right, now how to approach the delicate subject of... everything with the man before her.

Driskell shook his head dismissively, 'Let's get back to the important reason for why I brought you here.'

'Before you do, I want to know — why are you helping Rowanne and I?' She recalled his words back at his apartment: 'the two of you will now be under my protection'. It was evident that he had meant for her to hear the conversation between him and Evelyn.

Later on, Driskell had called her to a coffee shop, where he had set about convincing her to go to Demon World, because it would be in the best interests of her cousin - but he'd been vague, not really answering her questions. God alone knew why she had agreed, and why she was trusting him to tell the truth.

Driskell looked thoughtful for a moment, 'Do you know how I came to acquire my reputation?'

Amanda thought of the rumours she'd heard, but decided she'd rather hear the truth from him, so she shook her head.

It was highly unlikely that the half demons of Earth would be well informed of what was happening in Demon World, thought Driskell. They didn't possess the ability to portal, only a full demon could do that, a half demon could meet their untimely demise should they attempt it and get it wrong.

'More than seventy years ago when I was a young demon, I had the good fortune to befriend one of the best men I've ever known, and also the brilliant woman who captured his heart,' said Driskell.

Amanda looked at him uncomprehendingly. Well, this was certainly news to her: Driskell had friends?

'I can tell by the look on your face that it's hard to believe. Anyway, I learnt a lot from your great-grand-uncle Elisedd.' Driskell let the implication of what he was saying reach through to her.

'So, you were friends? I'm sorry, but I find that hard to believe. When did this happen? I wouldn't have believed that my family had actually lived here, if it had not been for that photo in your apartment of great-grand-uncle Elisedd and the woman. By the way, who is she?' Amanda scooted closer, fascinated.

It was true her family knew of Demon World and demons in general, but they had never spoken of their time here, and nor was it recorded in her family history, either.

'You really have no idea as to who she is?' asked Driskell suspiciously. He could not help it; his inquisitive nature needed to know how much information the Knight family had of Demon World.

'Look, if I knew I'd hardly waste time asking pointless questions. We don't have much time, so enlighten me,' said Amanda.

'Like I said, I knew your great-grand-uncle from long ago. This was way before your time-' he paused.

He looks good for an old man - the perks of being a full demon, I guess.

'What is it?' asked Driskell gruffly, puzzled by her contemplative look when he had not even begun to get started.

Was he boring her already?

'I was thinking that you're really old,' replied Amanda helpfully.

'Thanks a lot, my dear,' he said disgustedly.

'Keep your hair on old man. I was going to add that you look younger than your age. I'm jealous of the gene that keeps you full bodied demons immortal. I mean you never have to worry about wrinkles again or gray hair for that matter,' sighed Amanda wistfully.

Driskell added solicitously, 'It's not as great as it sounds, there's a price to pay...'

'Sign me up. I'll pay whatever it is,' said Amanda half jokingly.

'That's what everyone says until they read the fine print... Believe me, even lawyers forgo reading the whole of a monotonous contract. Well, they can always argue their way out!' Driskell said, amused.

'It's easy for you to say, *you're* never going to die — unlike the rest of us,' said Amanda solemnly.

Driskell looked at her wryly as a look of pain washed through his eyes, like a wave dashed against the side of a cliff. How could she possibly understand? She was still so young and full of life. *Let her live a little, then by all means, she can tell me how wonderful life is,* he thought darkly.

Amanda was subdued by the knowing look on his face. She felt like a child. *I probably am being naive,* she thought sullenly. It was time to change the subject, for now.

'You were talking of my great-grand-uncle and the mysterious woman,' she prompted.

'It was 1944 in Demon World, in terms of your world history it would have been a year before the second World War ended.'

Amanda conjured up an image of her great-grand-uncle in a smart suit looking vaguely like the famous Australian actor Errol Flynn - like him, her great-grand-uncle had short wavy brown hair, but unlike him, he was clean shaven. He had classic features and a beautiful symmetry to his face as well as high cheekbones.

'The thing that really fascinated me about Elisedd was his warm hearted approach towards everyone he met,' said Driskell. Amanda looked at him oddly as if he'd just grown a second head. 'In a way, he was a lot like Alexander. They are open and honest; what you see is what you get.' Driskell scooted closer to Amanda, and poked her teasingly in the shoulder, 'On pain of death, you will not repeat to anyone, especially Alexander, what I have just said.'

Amanda batted his hand away casually, she could not believe what she was hearing, and felt slightly uncomfortable on hearing *him* talk of feelings. Who would ever have imagined that he could be so open; certainly not her.

'You have to understand that the demons in my world are shallow, power hungry beings, but this human man had a way of getting through to them, of making them listen to him. I wonder sometimes if perhaps he didn't have a little demon blood mixed in his genes somewhere,' said Driskell, amused as he fondly reminisced of his old friend.

'As far as I know, there are no full demons in the Knight family. The few of us that are demons are through marriage and consequently having a half demon child,' said Amanda.

'Ah, but you can't be a hundred percent certain, can you? You clearly don't know the whole of your family history, where demons are concerned. They haven't told you the truth about your great-grand-uncle Elisedd, or the fact that he was in love with...' Driskell tapered off. Amanda's eyes widened, an eager smile playing upon her lips as she rested her arm on the lounge, her hand gripping his arm. He smiled, shaking his head; what she didn't know could not hurt her.

'What are you saying? In one respect you're right; they didn't tell me of my great-grand-uncle Elisedd, but I don't think they did it intentionally. Maybe they were trying to protect me, or perhaps the truth of what happened to him has been lost in obscurity.'

'You are just as naive and entirely too trusting as your great-grand-uncle was...' She glared at him as her grip tightened on his arm in her agitation. 'I'm just saying it wouldn't hurt you to do some digging around. You might be surprised by what you find...' he said mysteriously.

'As much as I hate to admit it, you could be on to something. Even if the information about my family residing here is lost,' she said uncertainly. 'There is still the pressing question of how we came to know of your existence - demons I mean,' she amended.

Driskell rubbed his arm, having finally extracted it from her death like grip; losing the use of one's arm was in no way romantic.

'Shame. I was hoping you'd have the answer to that one. Demons in my world have long speculated as to why your family was allowed to reside here, and how you came to learn of our existence.' Driskell's eyes sparkled as he contemplated this great mystery.

'If I knew the answer to that one, then I think I'd find enlightenment,' she joked, putting her feet up and sitting cross legged.

'I wonder why they're really hiding it from you... I'll reiterate again, that it's worth looking into, at least you'll have that knowledge. You never know, it could come in handy one day,' said Driskell solemnly.

'Knowledge is power, that type of thing?' asked Amanda. Driskell reprimanded her with his eyes.

Whatever the case may be, her family had been right in one sense: not to tell her anything which could be used against them. This was the perfect example of why: in case of capture, the demons could not extract information from her which she did not possess.

On the other hand, if no one in her family had information about their origins, then that was hardly any better. Perhaps it was stored somewhere... *Why does my family train all of us so hard, and why do we live the way we do... Great, now he's creating an existential crisis within me.*

Amanda would not leave this topic alone. When this was all over, she was going to have a nice long chat with her family. She would also drag Rowanne along to meet them. It irked her to no end to keep admitting that Driskell was right: it had not done any of them any good to be kept in the dark, and separating Rowanne from her family had not been the right decision.

In the end, Rowanne had ended up in their world anyway; admittedly through the most unlikely of circumstances. Hmm, did she believe in coincidences? She had a lot of unanswered questions. Before she would have let it go for the greater good of the family, but now because of the man before her, she was daring to question them.

Amanda looked at him sharply, begrudging him a smile, 'Thanks,' she said gruffly.

Driskell looked at her questioningly, but she simply dismissed it with a wave of her hand. He decided to drop the subject of her family, reluctantly. He could not believe that for a woman who had mistrusted him at every turn, she had remarkably opened up. Then again, his rather callous behaviour had hardly been engendering of trust of any kind. 'As I was saying, I formed a firm friendship with Elisedd, and it never bothered him that I wasn't from a First Family-'

'That's stupid,' said Amanda, cutting him off.

Driskell counted to ten before jumping to conclusions. 'What do you mean?' he asked in a clipped voice.

Amanda stopped short of rolling her eyes. This man was entirely too sensitive when it came to the delicate subject of his family status. 'What I was trying to say rather inelegantly is that I, along with my great-grand-uncle

Elisedd, wouldn't think twice about where you came from, much less your family status. You get to know the person, not their standing in society. Would you still speak to me even if I didn't belong to a wealthy or well known family? What if I was just a normal working class almost-human gal?'

'What has that got to do with anything? I'd still approach a woman like you: hardworking, and clearly strong! Perhaps a little too headstrong. Beautiful inside and-' said Driskell, looking at her attentively, captivated by her words.

'Exactly the point I was making,' said Amanda, cutting him off. 'Wait, what?' She had clearly missed something, and he was looking at her oddly again.

'Never mind,' said Driskell, enjoying the moment. He may have lost one of his best friends, but in a way his friend had come back to him in the form of his descendant: the beautifully vibrant young woman who sat before him.

He may not have been able to save Elisedd, but he'd be damned if he didn't try to save Amanda, and Rowanne. The Knight family were turning out to be every bit as complex and secretive as Lillian's family, and demon knows they held the monopoly when it came to secrets that could make and break not just a kingdom, but the very foundation of Demon World.

There was more than one reason to hate the Nobles and First Families: he'd envied them their knowledge, maybe that was one of the reasons why he became an Enforcer. Driskell wanted to wheedle out their secrets one by one. Why was it that *they* wielded power over the rest of them...

'Driskell?' called Amanda, as she waved her hand before his face. Finally he came back to his senses. He had seemed to go into a trance there. She certainly had not liked the stone mask that had descended over his features, or the way his eyes had become a dark inky green, almost black, causing goosebumps to break out on her arms.

Driskell caught her hand, 'Sorry, too much on my mind...' he said distractedly, and laughed maniacally as she looked at him apprehensively.

Amanda thought it wise to let him continue - she'd get her hand back eventually, he obviously needed to hold onto someone. 'You mentioned great-grand-uncle Elisedd being in love with...?' she asked, gently steering him back onto the original topic from which he repeatedly deviated.

'He was in love with Lillian Morning Star of the First Family.'

'Who?' asked Amanda.

'She *was* the princess of our Royal Family...' Driskell replied casually, waiting for the information to sink in.

'Oh!' she replied, clearly taken aback by what she'd just learnt. She could not believe it, it was implausible. When she could finally speak, she asked excitedly, 'Was it reciprocal?' She knew what the answer would be, even before he nodded just once decisively. She grabbed him by the coat. 'But when did this happen, 1944 right? That's what you said,' she answered her own question. 'I got a bit carried away there...' she said ruefully, as she began to smooth his coat much to his amusement. She was clearly in a daze. 'This is incredible. I don't really know anything of great-grand-uncle Elisedd's past. Tell me more of his life with Lillian.'

'That's Lady Lillian, to you!' said Driskell. He wanted her to acknowledge Lillian with the respect due to her, as a daughter of the First Family.

'Alright!' said Amanda; clearly she'd put her foot in it politically. 'So, what happened? I'm guessing Demon World wouldn't have approved of such a match.'

'That's the understatement of the century! Let's start at the beginning. Your family had established themselves in Demon World, and everything was working out for a while, until-'

'Great-grand-uncle Elisedd came along, right?' supplied Amanda. 'The rebel of the family you might say...' but she went quiet at the look of annoyance that flashed across Driskell's face at her interruption. 'Sorry, please continue.'

'Yes,' said Driskell begrudgingly - he preferred to tell the story in his own way. 'When Elisedd came along the equilibrium shifted. For a while there, he behaved in accordance with the rules, but then he crossed the line... to the detriment of us all.'

'Just say "he fell in love!" It's not something that can be helped, and it happens to the lucky few of us fortunate enough to find it,' said Amanda, irritated with his long winded approach.

Driskell glared at her and continued, 'He noticed the Princess straight away, and began to develop a fondness for her. Though he appeared reserved, this was by no means the case, especially when it came to something he desired or was passionate about. Accordingly he made himself a part of our group. He got along well with all of us, though, admittedly Lady Blaze didn't give him the time of day. She doesn't associate with lesser demons or humans, and would probably put them all in the same category as half demons. No offence intended,' he added hastily, at Amanda's look of disgust.

'None taken.' God, she hated that woman. Everything she'd heard about Lady Blaze sickened her. *How she must have loathed pretending in front of us at the offices. She probably couldn't stand the sight of Rowanne and I,* thought Amanda.

'Elisedd told me that he had started to develop feelings for Lillian at her pre-coronation party. Incidentally that was the first time he properly spoke to her-'

'And the rest they say is history!'

Lillian was a beautiful woman, Amanda had seen that in the photo, so obviously he'd notice her, but the fact that her great-grand-uncle had been daring enough to approach a princess to start a relationship with out of all people, spoke volumes about him. *I wonder what Lillian had seen in him...* she mused.

'How does an immortal come to love an ordinary human?' asked Amanda.

Very easily... 'It's one of those great mysteries. I'm afraid I don't really have an answer. But she must have seen something in him that she liked. Lillian is not the type of person to allow a few pesky political rules to stop her. After all, she's a Noble and they're all stubborn. If they see something they want, they go for it, consequences be damned. It certainly makes my job easier, knowing their nature inside out,' he laughed darkly.

Of course it does, thought Amanda, disturbed. 'And how well do you presume to know me?' she asked boldly, looking him straight in the eyes. There was a dark intensity to his eyes as they fixed securely onto her, while he contemplated her unexpected question. She would not be the first to look away.

Leaning towards her only inches from her face, Driskell asked softly, 'Do you really want me to answer that? I'd be happy to oblige your request...'

Amanda sat back, still not breaking eye contact, and crossed her arms. 'Well, go ahead...'

'Frankly, I find you perplexing and infuriating to a large degree. Wilful. Shall I go on?' he asked with a small smile, thoroughly enjoying the shade of beetroot that now inflamed her cheeks. He could almost see the sparks fly like daggers - probably aimed at his heart. Honestly, she was so easy to rile, he mused.

Amanda thumped him in the arm in response to the idiotic remark.

'Do you feel better?' asked Driskell patiently.

'I'm getting there...' replied Amanda archly.

CHAPTER 29

'Thanks,' replied Rowanne, as she gratefully accepted the handkerchief and dabbed at her eyes. 'What should we do? We can't exactly go looking for her.' For the past half hour, she had tried focusing in on Lillian to call her back, but to no avail.

Alexander started to pace restlessly. A sense of trepidation hung in the air, though he could not place his finger on precisely what it could be. He did not want to worry Rowanne, but he had felt power resonate throughout the room, as if it was sent by a higher level demon searching for something... or someone.

Though, it was not the only thing that was bothering him: he had felt a headache come on the moment he had stepped back into Demon World with Rowanne. Although he had not mentioned it, putting it down to his human half, now it was becoming more and more relentless. The pain began to hammer at his mind, and he was finding it difficult for the first time to formulate his thoughts; he'd never encountered these problems as a full demon.

Rowanne watched Alexander's brow furrow in concentration, and didn't like the fact that he was on edge. It disturbed her the way his eyes would furtively look around the room. What was he searching for? 'Alexander, I have a weird feeling about this room. I think it's time we left.'

'I agree with you. Let's go now while we still can,' said Alexander. Concentrating on Rowanne's voice seemed to help him to focus.

She didn't need to think twice as she quickly buttoned up her coat and wrapped her scarf around the bottom half of her face so that only her eyes could be seen.

Alexander went to the door and, turning around, he motioned for Rowanne to stay where she was for the moment. Taking a quick peek, he found the corridor was empty, and urged her forward. 'Stay behind me,' he whispered.

'Where is the safest place for us to be right now?' asked Rowanne.

'Let's make our way towards the royal tomb, or I should say the Morning Star family's tomb. We will stay there for a couple of hours and try to formulate a plan,' he replied.

Suddenly he began to shake as his vision faded in and out. He jerkily turned around to her as her eyes widened in horror.

'Don't worry, it's noth-'

'Alexander!' screamed Rowanne, catching him as he fell. Thank God she had demon strength. He was a tall man; the human side of her might have buckled under his weight.

Rowanne pulled him back into the room and gently lowered him to the floor, then reaching up she closed and locked the door behind them.

'Alexander, can you hear me?' she asked in a panicked voice. Though there was no response, she was relieved by the reassuring rise and fall of his chest. Her heart had nearly stopped when he'd collapsed. She had thought he was having a heart attack, from the look of intense pain that had flashed across his face, and the way he'd seized up on the spot.

Perhaps he had pushed himself too far by portaling into this world as a half demon. God knows that she had found it extremely uncomfortable each time that she had stepped into a portal, especially when travelling to Demon World; that's when it really took a toll on her.

Rowanne felt his forehead - it was hot to the touch and covered in a thin sheen of perspiration. She went into a room she assumed would be the kitchen (it was) and finding a cloth, ran it under the tap and wrung it out before coming back to Alexander. She knelt on the floor beside him, gently dabbing at his forehead.

'Come on, get up. This is not the time to be sleeping,' she said, shaking him gently, hoping for a response. His eyes moved rapidly as if he really were dreaming. *I wonder what he's thinking of, it doesn't seem to be good...* His lips were curled into a snarl, as if whatever he saw had him on edge.

Come back, Alexander, thought Rowanne. *We have so much to do, and I can't do it alone. I won't. Not without you.* She did not even know where to begin, let alone how to navigate her way around the castle without walking straight into the first guard she'd undoubtedly stumble across. All she could do was wait patiently by his side.

Alexander began to thrash about, his arms flailing dangerously. Rowanne quickly scooted back on her heel out of harm's way. Suddenly he went stiff, and she observed a green mist form above his body coiling around him. It changed to a darker shade of green before turning a disturbing shade of black.

The net seemed to tighten around him until he was cocooned within the energy, then to Rowanne's dread it seeped into his body, leaving behind no trace to indicate that it had ever been there.

Heart pounding, Rowanne cautiously approached him. 'Alexander?' she called softly - for some reason she thought it best to whisper. The air in the room sizzled, and there was a deep quiet that she mistrusted; the calm before the storm...

Alexander slowly opened his eyes and blinked a couple of times before the room came back into focus, and the first thing he noticed was Rowanne's anxious face hovering above him.

'What happened?' he asked, dazed and confused. How had he ended up on the floor?

'Thank God you've come back to me... I mean you've come awake. You had me slightly worried there,' said Rowanne tenderly, her heart slowly calming.

Alexander tilted his head up and smiled as Rowanne scooted closer, and gently lifted his head resting it on her lap. 'Thanks. It's nice to know you were only *slightly* worried,' he said roguishly, and raised an eyebrow at her. He had not missed a single thing she'd said, even if his senses were only gradually coming back to him.

That's just great. I wonder exactly how much he heard... 'I told you that you had exerted yourself too much. You're a human now. Well half, anyway,' she amended, at his less than pleased expression. 'You need to rest more as well as eat more, especially with the amount of energy you use. If a human were to attempt even half of what you have done, they'd burn out. I'm amazed you didn't collapse sooner,' said Rowanne, gently chiding.

She really knows how to take care of a sick man, thought Alexander, amused by her ministrations. He attempted to get himself up, but fell back at the first attempt.

'Rowanne, I think I may need your help?' It was not easy asking for help, especially with a name like his! He had to at least attempt to live up to it.

'I thought you'd never ask,' replied Rowanne wryly.

She lifted Alexander up easily as he put an arm around her shoulders for support. She put her arm around his waist supporting his weight, and together they slowly made their way to the chaise lounge, where she helped him to sit.

'Can you get me some water, please?' he asked. His throat felt parched, and Rowanne obligingly went to the kitchen.

Alexander felt a spasm start within him as he began to convulse. A headache suddenly came on strongly, and slowly, painfully his mind began to shut itself down from the pain. In less than a minute it was over and his eyes closed.

Rowanne came back and discovered Alexander slumped on the lounge. She ran in and hastily placed the cup down, causing the water to slosh. She helped him to sit up as she supported him.

Alexander opened his eyes. They felt wrong... Something was off. He looked at Rowanne, there were tears in her eyes, but he could tell she was trying to be strong for him. 'I think it's what you humans call a migraine,' he said gruffly, his voice sounding strange to his own ears.

'I see you really are experiencing the side effects of being human,' said Rowanne, a brittle smile upon her face.

'I'm fifty percent certain that we will make it out of here, but you will have to help me to walk. Now don't look at me like that, we can't stay here either. Be practical,' said Alexander sternly.

Rowanne was taken aback with his harsh tone; it sounded nothing like him, but then, she reasoned, he had just collapsed twice. It would be enough to fray anyone's nerves; especially a proud man like Alexander.

She helped him to stand, and placed her arm around his waist; he in turn put his arm around her shoulders. Once she was satisfied that she could support his weight, they began to shuffle towards the door. It would be a miracle at this rate if they weren't caught.

Alexander unlocked the door with his free hand, and looked at the woman before him unsympathetically. Well, it was about time that she helped him; he could not count the number of times that he'd helped her. Too many.

Rowanne felt a cold shiver run down her spine, as she felt Alexander's cold merciless sapphire eyes bore into her. What was going on? She didn't like this one single bit, but nevertheless managed a warm smile in return which only seemed to compound the situation, as he grinned at her baring his teeth.

He looked menacing instead of sincere, and Rowanne's guard automatically went up. She could not afford to trust this world. After all, she'd been warned of the duplicitous nature of the demons here, especially the Nobles.

However, she could not bring herself to place Alexander into that category, even if he was a Noble. Whatever was going on with him, she'd put it down to temporary insanity brought on by stress, and the fact that he was becoming more human by the minute.

Alexander's eyes hurt as he felt a veil descend upon them. Rowanne was looking at him oddly. Had he said something inappropriate? He could not see her too clearly, and stopped smiling as it didn't seem to be helping the situation.

Rowanne's heart began to beat fast as she looked deep into his inky black eyes, which were ringed in a blackish green colour. She didn't have the heart to tell him that they had changed. There was no point in worrying him until she could understand what was happening to him.

'I think it's safe to proceed,' she said, after waiting a few moments and ascertaining that nobody else was around in this part of the building.

She proceeded cautiously along the corridor, her heart literally in her mouth. However, she pushed down her fear, or attempted to, by reminding herself that Alexander now depended on her; she had to keep a level head for both their sakes.

'I'm coming,' replied Alexander, as if Rowanne had just asked him a question.

'I beg your pardon?' asked Rowanne, still focused ahead.

'Nothing. I didn't say anything,' replied Alexander. He was confused, he didn't recognise where he was.

Rowanne listened intently at the final door, and edged it open slowly to reveal an empty stone staircase. The whole place felt cold to her, or maybe castles just gave off that feeling, being open, airy places in the worst sense; you'd freeze if you weren't careful.

'Listen, you stay here while I run down to check whether it's safe. Here, let me help you,' she said, helping him to sit on the top step.

Rowanne left him as she quickly descended the stairs. Taking a deep breath she was about to open the door when she felt a hand on her shoulder...

'Alexander?' she asked carefully. Technically he shouldn't be behind her, he could barely walk unaided.

'Well, that quite depends on who answers the door...' whispered the voice behind her insidiously.

Rowanne's blood ran cold as she spun around to face the threat, only to be met with Alexander's slumped figure on the top step as he looked at her questioningly.

'Were you just behind me?' she asked, watching carefully for his response.

'Rowanne, if I had managed to walk down the steps alone, then I would hardly need your help to walk, now would I? And for that matter, why the hell would I walk back up? Are you alright, you didn't bump your head by any chance?' asked Alexander, worried for her. She was behaving peculiarly.

He seemed to sound more like himself. *Maybe I'm imagining things... The sooner I get out of this hell hole the better.*

Rowanne slowly opened the last door that stood between them and the dangers of the palace. She took a cursory glance and was rewarded with a cold blast of wintery air that blew her hair back, and filled her mouth with snow for good measure. She struggled with the door barely managing to close it as the diabolical winds pushed back. She slumped against the door trying to catch her breath.

She trudged back up the stairs to Alexander and collapsed beside him as she tried to get her motivation back. Thankfully his eyes had returned to their normal colour. 'Listen, it will be hard going. The wind is going to pummel us, but since you insist that we should continue, I'm with you, against my better judgment. Don't worry, I think my little *side effect* will help,' she winked, smiling impishly.

Rowanne easily hoisted him to his feet. *I think I could carry him if I wanted to...* she mused. Focusing her mind seemed to make utilising her demon strength that much easier instead of pondering how to accomplish the task ahead.

Alexander smiled at the look of wonder on Rowanne's face. *See, being a half demon is not so bad,* he thought.

Rowanne cautiously descended the stairs with Alexander, who leaned against her for support, his other hand on the stone wall to steady himself.

'Ready?' she asked.

'As ready as we'll ever be, Knight,' replied Alexander cryptically.

Rowanne looked at him oddly before stepping out into the winter storm and closing the door behind them. 'Which way now?' she asked, for there were multiple avenues before them.

Knight... thought Alexander. *Why is that name so familiar? Oh, it belongs to you,* he thought, looking at the woman beside him. She was asking him something... He tried to focus on what she was saying, but the strange buzzing sound in his head was making it difficult, splitting his attention. *Focus.* Well, he was endeavouring to.

'Pardon? I could not quite make it out above the roar of the winds,' said Alexander. That sounded quite plausible to his ears. *Yes, it was an exceptional answer,* he thought manically, as he nodded and smiled at her.

Rowanne tried not to gasp as his eyes changed back to a blackish green colour. He looked wild and out of control. She didn't like the way he was smiling like a Cheshire cat and how he continually bobbed his head up and down like an automaton.

'Which way do we go?' shouted Rowanne this time. They were in no danger of being heard above this din.

'Just follow my lead,' he replied, and tugging on her arm, he guided her towards the back wall of the castle. 'We will follow this wall to the outskirts, and from there we will make our way over to the tombs.'

Rowanne and Alexander slowly made their way as the snow fell heavily, coating them in flakes that, while geometrically beautiful, were nonetheless damn cold as they melted into her coat weighing it down. She could barely breathe, and adjusted her scarf which constantly slipped, and once more her mouth was covered. She used her arm as a shield - after all, she needed to be able to see, even if her vision was limited.

They stubbornly trudged through the snow while mercilessly being pushed back by the winds. Alexander stumbled on a couple of occasions and would have fallen if Rowanne had not been there to steady him; by now she was supporting most of his weight. At times, he lost consciousness, and God alone knows how she dragged him forward, hoping against hope that they were going in the right direction.

It felt as if they had been walking for quite some time before Alexander abruptly pulled her towards a large building. It seemed quite grand from what she could tell, though it was hard to make out any distinguishing features. She looked to him for confirmation, and he nodded decisively.

He led her to the front door, and took a quick furtive look around, before ushering her in ahead of him.

It was dark inside, and Rowanne nearly jumped out of her skin as the door banged shut behind her. She quickly looked around, straining to hear whether they'd captured anyone's attention. 'Alexander, quietly,' she whispered furiously.

Alexander got out his phone and with a swipe of his finger, he had a torch which provided them with much needed light.

'Point it down, you're blinding me! I can't see anything. Thanks a lot! By the way, are you purposely trying to get us caught?' Rowanne gestured angrily at the large hall and staircase; anybody could be wondering those corridors.

'Relax, you worry too much. It's just through here,' he indicated a large set of metal gates adjacent to the door they had just come through.

It looked foreboding to Rowanne. There was a stone passageway behind the wrought iron gates that seemed to descend further on. Where did it lead? To a subterranean world...? *I really don't want to go down there*, she thought, as her Ancient Mythology lessons flashed through her mind. *Okay, now I'm really losing it.*

'Rowanne, we really need to move before one of the guards passes this way. Mark my words, we probably have less than a minute, if that,' said Alexander impatiently.

'I could not agree more. However, I don't know whether it's escaped your notice, but the gates are locked. So unless you can pull a Houdini, we are going to have to find a set of keys — and fast,' said Rowanne, equally annoyed; she was not stalling for fun.

They heard a sound coming from the back of the large hall, almost like a door closing. Rowanne looked at Alexander in alarm as he quickly put the light out and covered her mouth with his hand before she could speak.

'Listen carefully, you have to make your way towards the staircase. Be as quiet as possible, and wait for me at the top,' whispered Alexander against her ear. He felt her shaking her head in protest at leaving him alone, to face whoever was coming rapidly in their direction. He shook her angrily, 'We don't have any more time left. I will only slow you down. Now go!' he shoved her away from him.

Rowanne barely managed to keep her balance, and glared back at him. In her confusion, she made her way towards the footsteps instead of the staircase, and just as she came close to being revealed, she ducked down at the last moment, and waited to see what the person would do next.

The footsteps stopped close by. 'Give me a minute, sir.'

In the next instance the large hall was flooded with light. Rowanne found herself kneeling behind an ornate sofa, and quickly swivelled her head in Alexander's direction, fearing he'd be caught out in the open.

The guard walked towards the front doors.

A voice shouted from behind him, 'Well, what do you see?'

'Nothing. There's no one here. I told you it was a bloody waste of time. Who the hell would be suicidal enough to break in here of all places?' asked the guard, and this was met with gleeful laughter from his colleague.

How can that be? thought Rowanne, craning her head, she noticed that the spot where Alexander had stood was now empty. Relief flooded her as well as dread. Where could he have got to? She hated to think of him out there in the blizzard.

Finally the guard made his way back to the light switch. Rowanne held her breath and fervently prayed for him to leave, so she could look for Alexander. She was plunged into darkness once more as the guard switched off the light, his footsteps retreating down the corridor.

Rowanne waited for a moment, and when she thought it was safe, got up. She was about to make her way back towards the front door, when a sound from above caught her attention.

'Rowanne, up here,' Alexander said quietly.

How had he gotten up there so quickly, and without the guards noticing? *He would have had to go past me... and I didn't even hear him!* thought Rowanne. She quickly and quietly made her way up the staircase to the enigma that was Alexander.

'You look confused, but it's simple, really. I took a shortcut. These ancient buildings are riddled with passageways — you just have to know where to look,' said Alexander, as she reached the landing.

'What about the guards, surely they patrol those areas as well?' whispered Rowanne.

'This way,' he said, and with Rowanne's help he made his way along the corridor. 'Only the royal family know of them. Quick escape passages, if they ever needed them, not that they ever would, or have to my knowledge, anyway,' Alexander stated matter-of-factly.

Rowanne turned to him, 'Then, how do *you* know? I wouldn't have thought they'd share this information with anybody outside of their immediate family.'

'Now that is a good question...' he said, leaving it pointedly unanswered.

She didn't know whether Alexander was usually this mysterious, but he was behaving strangely.

'Hurry up, before we encounter another guard.'

Rowanne picked up the pace, and together they made their way towards the door at the very end of the passage. Fortunately, Alexander was relying less on her for support; maybe he was recovering.

He suddenly stopped before the door, and put his ear to it. His hair tie broke, and his long hair cascaded around his shoulders, half of it obscuring his face.

Alexander looked at her, and the one eye she could see was shining a brilliant green. It fixated on her and alternately to the door. His mouth curved into a macabre grin, before his hand suddenly shot out, grabbing hers.

'What are you doing, Alexander? What's wrong?' she was getting a bad feeling about this.

'What could be wrong, my dear? Everything is perfectly in order, just as it should be,' he answered, in a manner that was quite unlike him.

Rowanne began to tug on her hand but it was useless, he had her hand in an iron vice.

'Be reasonable, there is no point in struggling,' said Alexander.

CHAPTER 30

'I'm afraid I'm rather slow, I don't quite understand what it is that you are implying,' said Lillian.

Evelyn clucked her tongue, 'Now now, Lillian. Don't play the fool. I haven't got time for your games. Let me make it plain,' she suddenly smiled, and turned her head slightly as if she had heard something that pleased her a great deal.

Lillian didn't like the self satisfied smirk on Evelyn's face, how she would dearly love to wipe it off. *Patience,* she counselled herself, *All good things come to those who wait...* Demon alone knew how hot her vengeance burned, and in no way had it diminished after all these years. Now it had a target at long last, and she would satiate it.

Evelyn turned her head sharply towards Lillian, 'You're in for a treat, old friend. We will continue the rest of this enthralling saga after we invite a couple of our acquaintances in. After all, it's rude to leave guests standing at the door, and I'm quite the accommodating host. Before the night is out we will have a veritable party,' she said, and laughed maniacally in a high pitched tone; it hurt the ears just to be subjected to it. 'Come in, my dear,' called Evelyn. Lillian's look of apprehension satisfied her.

Alexander dragged Rowanne in as she struggled to be free of him.

'Let go of me, Alexander! What are you doing? What's gotten into-' Rowanne suddenly froze, as her eyes locked with Lillian, and then she finally noticed the others in the room.

Lady Enid was asleep (or so it appeared) on an ornate chair that looked uncomfortable and cold. But it was the woman before her, Ms Blaze, who captured her full attention.

Rowanne looked back at Lillian, who gave her a death stare. She got the point: keep their connection hidden. That was all fine and good, but she could not rely on Alexander not to speak. She could not believe that she had just thought this of him, but his behaviour only compounded this belief.

'Ms Blaze, how wonderful to meet you again. I see that you are taking excellent care of Lady Enid,' said Rowanne disdainfully.

'Rowanne, I like your direct and rather insolent approach. Lillian, you could learn a thing or two from her. She reminds me a great deal of you. Rowanne, there are some things I'd like to discuss openly with all of you. And as for,' she paused, to look behind her at Lady Enid fondly. This disgusted both Rowanne and Lillian, offending them to the core. 'Well, we will let her sleep for a bit. No need to wake her before... I mean, for any undue unpleasantness that may arise. And you can wipe those self-righteous looks off your faces.'

Rowanne turned towards Alexander, hoping to wake him from his stupor. 'Why am I here, Alexander?' she asked, looking him in the eyes.

Alexander threw his long hair back over his shoulders, he found the length to be irksome. He looked up as something came flying towards his face and caught it in his grip. 'Thank you, my lady,' he said to Evelyn, completely ignoring Rowanne.

He used the leather tie to bind his unruly hair, then gave Lillian a long and penetrating look, smiling broadly at her.

'You know, I think I'll cut it short as soon as I have the time. I always preferred it short,' he winked, startling Lillian.

Rowanne looked questioningly at Lillian, but she was equally puzzled; it was beyond her why he was talking to her in this peculiar way. After all, she didn't give a damn what he looked like.

'Alexander, refrain. It's not quite time... Behave yourself,' said Evelyn.

He made a slow bowing gesture with a sweep of his hands to either side.

'What have you done to him?' demanded Rowanne, as she angrily made her way towards Ms Blaze, but unfortunately she was intercepted by Alexander, who pulled her arms behind her back, effectively trapping them. She was temporarily stunned by his behaviour. She didn't know if she was more hurt by him or the pain in her wrists, and doubted whether he'd care, either way. Not this new Alexander.

'Don't even think of laying a finger on my lady. You will regret it, I promise you...' he said in a low threatening voice.

Evelyn beamed at Lillian, 'Look how good he is to me. Come here, my dear. Don't worry, that half breed isn't going anywhere.'

Alexander roughly let go of Rowanne, causing her to stumble and fall to her knees painfully. She inhaled sharply, suppressing the pain, and watched him as he left her there on the floor, and went to Ms Blaze, where he stood slightly behind her, placing his hand on her shoulder in an affectionate manner.

Rowanne could not believe what she was witnessing. Lillian had moved next to her, but didn't extend a hand to her. Rowanne understood that the less Ms Blaze knew of their ability the safer they'd be, and it could come in useful later on. No point in showing their hand just yet.

'Are you alright?' whispered Lillian.

Rowanne shook her head as she got up slowly, and deliberately stood shoulder to shoulder with her. She felt her energy engage with Lillian's and as it did so the woman beside her became more solid. Finally, at least something was going right.

Evelyn casually snapped her fingers, causing Lillian and Rowanne to step forward, as they felt a subtle push from the energy that had formed behind them. They spun around, and to their dismay were faced with a green wall of energy that barricaded the door; they were all trapped in the room.

'Why are you doing this, Ms Blaze? We, none of us, have ever harmed you to my knowledge in any way,' said Rowanne.

Alexander stepped forward menacingly, only to be stopped by Evelyn's restraining hand on his arm.

Rowanne wondered why he was treating her like a stranger.

'It's alright, my dear,' said Evelyn affectionately to Alexander. 'She is an ignorant half breed. Let me enlighten her as to how things work around here,' and turning to Rowanne, she said disgustedly, '*You* will address me as Lady Blaze, and never presume to use my first name, that is reserved solely for my close acquaintances, and then, only to those that are my equal. You are quite frankly in another *category* altogether.'

Rowanne found the whole scene appalling. She didn't like the way Alexander was fawning all over the woman before her, but she knew that he was being controlled in some way. She just had to figure it out, soon. Preferably before he killed them all on this psycho's orders.

Lillian turned to Rowanne, 'Let me introduce Evelyn Blaze, my former best friend and lady in waiting. Not to mention, her other titles: murderer, usurper... Shall I continue?' she asked, looking down on Evelyn, and was pleased to see how incensed she was upon hearing this.

'You would do well to mind your tongue, Lillian. I may not be able to touch you, but I can certainly kill *that*,' she said, gesturing to Rowanne.

Rowanne marched up to Evelyn. 'Who the hell do you think you are?' she asked angrily.

Evelyn simply clicked her fingers causing a powerful force to knock Rowanne off her feet, so that she crashed into the wall of energy behind her.

Rowanne threw her arms up in front of her as she smashed into the floor. Her elbows and legs took the brunt of the force, causing excruciating pain to shoot up and along her joints. She glared, and would have retorted if it had not been for Alexander. He stiffened, as pain flashed in his eyes, and for a second there was recognition there as he looked at her desperately.

Rowanne, called Alexander in her mind, his voice was full of pain. He was helpless.

Rowanne was heartened; somewhere in there, Alexander was trying hard to break out of whatever power had him in its grip. Even as she thought this, she watched the confusion disappear from him, as once again, the mask descended and he became Evelyn's puppet.

Evelyn looked sharply at Alexander, who smoothly brought her hand to his lips and placed a gentle kiss upon it, while looking at Lillian with hooded eyes.

Lillian felt her heart flutter in her chest. What was wrong with her? Could it be that she was actually feeling jealous... This was not like her at all.

Rowanne watched Lillian as a look of pain flashed across her face. She seemed to be torn between Alexander and her. She could not understand this bizarre reaction from Lillian. Was she missing something here...

Lillian looked at Rowanne, capturing her gaze, and she shook her head. She didn't have any answers yet; she was in the dark, as well.

Rowanne's stomach had recoiled at the sight of Alexander kissing Evelyn's hand. *Why do I feel like this... It doesn't matter to me one way or the other, who that idiot kisses. Or does it...* She felt a white hot anger deep inside. She was getting a little teed off with being pushed around and ordered about by people on a power trip.

Rowanne pushed her hands down and began to get up, when she felt the power slap her back down. She looked up at Evelyn.

'I don't recall giving you permission to stand, half breed. Stay down, the floor suits you better,' said Evelyn, laughing gleefully as her eyes sparkled in mirth.

'I. DON'T. THINK. SO!' said Rowanne furiously, enunciating each word coldly.

She pushed herself up, and fought off the power that tried to push her back down at each instance. It felt like the equivalent of a hundred hands trying to hold her down. God alone knew where she found the strength. She'd had enough. Sometimes you have to say, *No more. I'm not willing to accept this any longer.*

Rowanne finally stood in her own power. Even as Evelyn strode towards her, she didn't falter.

'What did you say, half breed?' she asked angrily, shouting in Rowanne's face.

'I have a name. Rowanne Knight. *You* will kindly address me properly,' replied Rowanne tauntingly, throwing the words back in Evelyn's face.

Evelyn's hand shot out, connecting with Rowanne's face, whipping it to the side. She breathed heavily as if it had taken more out of her than Rowanne.

She turned her face back slowly to Evelyn, wiping the blood from her nose. She smiled impudently. 'You definitely have this situation in hand...' said Rowanne sarcastically. 'Is that all you've got, *Evelyn*?' She was glad to see the annoying smile wiped off her face. She would be damned if she addressed her as 'my lady' anything.

Evelyn raised her hand intending to strike again, but Lillian suddenly stepped in front of Rowanne protectively.

'You need to back off, Evelyn. That is the last time that you lay a finger on her. Try it again, and I'll show you what *I* am capable of,' said Lillian, shaking with rage at the brutality that Rowanne was being subjected to.

Evelyn lowered her hands, apparently thinking better of it, before pushing her hands through Lillian, intending to push Rowanne back. Two things happened then...

Lillian realised that Evelyn's hands had passed straight through her. She didn't mind the mortification; what bothered her was that she was unable to help Rowanne.

Evelyn just laughed, looking condescendingly at her. 'I didn't think I had to fear a spirit, and my point is proven. So, stay quiet, shade,' she said brusquely.

The second thing that happened was that Rowanne grabbed both of Evelyn's hands in a death-like grip, taking her by surprise.

'What, did you think I'd lay aside and let you strike me a second time? You don't know me very well,' said Rowanne, who proceeded to fling Evelyn's hands out of Lillian, and in the process Evelyn lost her balance and would have fallen, had Alexander not caught her. *Where did that come from?* thought Rowanne, puzzled by the strength flowing through her body.

Evelyn glared at Rowanne, who could see the first sparks of fear in her eyes. *Is she frightened of me...? But she's a full demon, as she constantly reminds us.*

Evelyn whispered into Alexander's ears and handed him a metallic object. Striding towards Rowanne, he grabbed her roughly and shoved her into a chair, then proceeded to pull her arms behind her back, restraining them with a metal handcuff. He looked at her menacingly before resuming his place beside his lady.

Evelyn sat beside Lady Enid in the adjoining chair. 'Now now, step back, Lillian. I haven't harmed your mother, yet.' Lillian took a reluctant step back. 'You're probably wondering why I've brought you all to my little soirée. I won't keep you in suspense any longer.'

'Do get on with it! For someone who's dying to *reveal all*, you do have the propensity to waffle,' said Lillian.

Evelyn just smiled malevolently at her. Before this night was out, she'd wipe that smirk of her so-called friend's face. 'You think you're so smart, don't you, Lillian? You used this-human,' she was going to say 'half breed' but one look at Rowanne's face had her backtracking, and she continued, 'to try and stop me. When has a human ever been able to stop me? Or have you so quickly forgotten poor Elisedd,' she said, squeezing Alexander's hand.

'Since when have you taken a liking to Alexander?' asked Lillian, casually leaning back against the barrier of energy.

'Alexander? Oh, I could not give a damn about him. He's only useful to me as long as he can be of use to me,' replied Evelyn cryptically, as she looked lovingly up at him. He merely laughed upon hearing this.

Rowanne and Lillian exchanged long looks. Had Alexander lost his mind completely? Evelyn talked of his downfall, and his response had been to treat it as no more than a joke.

'I see that you are both confused, but it will all soon become clear...' Turning to Alexander, she asked, 'Can you leave us, my dear, for a moment? I'll call you in shortly. In the meantime, deal with our rat problem.'

'Shall I poison them?' asked Alexander, his voice devoid of emotion.

'No. Just bring them to the Great Hall. We will be over shortly anyway,' replied Evelyn, a knowing look on her face.

Lillian looked deathly pale - all of this was too familiar. Was history once again repeating itself? She would not allow Rowanne to become another victim; to become her.

Lillian looked at Rowanne determinedly and was pleased by the fierce look that she reciprocated. One thing was certain,

Rowanne would not go quietly. Not without a fight. *Maybe that's what I should have done... then perhaps my Elisedd would still be here.* She pushed back the white hot tears scalding her eyes. She would not cry, especially in front of this poor excuse for a demon.

Rowanne watched Alexander leave them, as he quietly closed the door behind him.

'I have to thank you, Rowanne. You did me a great favour,' said Evelyn.

Rowanne shifted, trying to get loose of the metal chains. Damn demon strength, it came and went of its own accord. When she really needed it, like now, it let her down. *Someone should really write the guide to being a demon,* she thought.

Rowanne looked up, annoyed, 'Unintentionally, perhaps. I don't make the same mistake twice,' she said, sarcasm dripping from her voice.

'You really are Lillian's prodigy. Or shall I say, imitation. Anyway, I was referring to the last night of your human existence,' when Rowanne failed to acknowledge this, she continued, 'last Thursday.'

Rowanne's heart beat fast. She understood perfectly. And it was Alexander who had said to her that he didn't think the attack on her had been random.

'So, it was *you* who orchestrated the attack on Rowanne, and ordered those Shadows to go after her,' said Lillian angrily, as she tried to walk towards Evelyn - but to no avail, she was in the grip of her power.

Evelyn smiled at Lillian's futile attempt to break free. Maybe she would have succeeded. Actually, it was more than likely she would have had she been alive; but death had rendered her powers useless.

'Well, yes. It made sense. Don't you see why I chose her?' asked Evelyn.

Rowanne and Lillian exchanged uneasy looks. How much did she know about Rowanne... and why specifically her?

Lillian prayed, despite being aware of the irony; a demon praying. She hoped fervently that Evelyn didn't know the whole of Rowanne's history. After all, she had deliberately kept some vital information from Rowanne for her wellbeing. She had learned much by being in Rowanne's mind, the missing pieces of the puzzle had all finally clicked into place for her. She tried hard now to shield her thoughts. All it would take would be one stray thought to lead to disaster...

'You are both either extremely dim or good actresses. Let me enlighten you to some of the changes that have happened in the last seventy odd years, that you most likely are unaware of, Lillian. Alexander now works as a high ranking soldier on behalf of Lady Enid on Earth, guarding against rogue demons that escape into that world.'

'Escape?!' asked Lillian incredulously.

'Actually, Rowanne, you wouldn't know this, but the demons from this world cannot enter your Earth easily, unless they are powerful enough to open a portal. Thankfully for you humans, most of them aren't. It takes a powerful demon to portal them through, that is the only way.'

'But why me, what did I ever do to you?' asked Rowanne, realising that Evelyn was to blame for the state she now found herself in. If not for her, she'd be living a normal human life. Well, as normal as life could be with demons for grandparents...

'Alexander was on patrol that night in your area. I had portalled into Earth with my men, looking for a potential victim. I saw you and thought, why the hell not?' said Evelyn in a cold calculated voice - she was very matter-of-fact about it.

'What did you intend to happen?' asked Rowanne smartly, not willing to give away any information to Evelyn, even accidentally.

Thank God she didn't blurt out everything there and then, thought Lillian, relieved. Rowanne was picking up the rules of their world quickly. She smiled ruefully at Rowanne, who gave her a firm look, as if to reprimand Lillian for thinking her so careless.

'I wanted to ambush Alexander while he was busy saving you. I wanted those idiot Shadows to kill him. However, my dear, instead of being my pawn, you became a thorn in my side,' replied Evelyn. 'I had no way of knowing that he'd save a pathetic human's life. Or that he'd turn you, *that* was quite unexpected. Nor did I account for your sheer stupidity in jumping in to save that proud man, and that's what did it, I'm sure. Alexander's family do not like to be indebted to anyone, certainly not a human. So, if you were under any illusions as to why he saved you, then let me make it plain, it was to clear his debt to you.'

Evelyn observed that Rowanne had not even flinched at her words, perhaps there really was nothing between the two of them. They probably worked together for their mutual benefit, and nothing more. This was something that she could understand, as it was common for demons to work together to get ahead, forge alliances; love and other such useless emotions didn't really come into play in their world.

She had been prepared to marry Alexander, if it meant that she was a step closer to the seat of power, but love him? No. He was beneath her notice, otherwise; only his position as a high ranking Noble and second in line to the throne rendered him a good match for her.

'I think you've underestimated… Humans are not as weak as you first thought,' said Lillian tauntingly.

'She was weak. Still is. Becoming a half demon has done her no favours,' replied Evelyn condescendingly, as she sneered at Rowanne. She turned back to Lillian, and continued, 'My plan wasn't completely ruined. In making Rowanne a half demon, he condemned himself. It all worked out rather well for me: he cannot ascend to the throne, for he is now a wretched half demon.'

'I thought you said that you adhered to the rules of Demon World? How then, do you justify murder, and involving yourself in an attack upon a human?' asked Lillian.

'Which human, and what murder?' asked Evelyn shrewdly.

'You attacked Thomas and I, not to mention Lillian and Alexander,' replied Rowanne calmly. She would not lose her head; now was the time to gather information.

'Yes, Evelyn. How will you explain all the charges laid against you, when you stand before the might of Prima Stella?' asked Lillian.

'Do I look in the least bit disturbed? You would have to first connect me personally to any of these so-called charges. Do you have any proof?' Evelyn looked conceitedly at the two women.

'You are going to regret all of your actions. Mark my word, you will pay *dearly* for what you have caused. That Lady to whom you sit next to is *my* mother, and I wonder what she'd do if she ever found out that you killed her only daughter...' said Lillian, her eyes swirling a dangerous violet and green light.

'You condemned yourself, Lillian. *You* broke the rules by choosing Elisedd, and signed both of your death warrants. There, that charge is on *your* head. I didn't force you to love a mortal. You could have acted selflessly by choosing to ignore his advances, and he'd have been sent back to Earth, and of course, his memory would be wiped, but at least you'd both still have been alive.'

Lillian's blood boiled at hearing this partial truth. She could not understand why loving a human was punishable by death. Even so, it was her backstabbing best friend who had turned them in, and for that, she was guilty in her eyes.

'I am guilty only of doing my duty, and that, my dear Lillian, does not amount to a death warrant. Next charge, please. As for Alexander, well the Shadows would naturally be blamed for his death. Did I force them to work with me? No, they chose it out of their own free will. I didn't personally lift a finger against dear Alexander...'

'But you were the mastermind behind it. They wouldn't have attacked, except on your orders,' said Rowanne, her mind spinning from all that she had heard.

'That's null and void, since he's alive, for now at least. Anyway, he hanged himself by making you a half demon. Did I put that idea into his head? No, that again was all his own doing. For you, either way you look at it, your death is assured. You survived the first time, but when Alexander stands before the Nobles with you as the evidence of his rogue behaviour, then it will be death for the both of you,' said Evelyn gleefully.

'I will expose you, and speak up on his behalf. I will let them know exactly what you did to Lillian!' said Rowanne defiantly. She was not feeling in the least bit scared; well, that was what she told herself, over and over.

'I hardly think they will take into account what a human has to say, especially to one who has been converted. Anything you say will be discounted as Alexander's influence over you. You will not be able to discredit me in any way. My word will always hold a higher value above yours. You who are nobody. Belonging to no clan, a despised half breed,' said Evelyn.

'What about Thomas, what did you do to him?' asked Rowanne, hoping to finally get answers as to his disappearance.

'What my Shadows do in their own time, is no concern of mine. Again, another useless charge laid before me,' replied Evelyn.

Rowanne did not trust her, especially her sly look, as she so easily dismissed Thomas. No, she definitely knew something, but she was not about to tell them.

Lillian wondered at how deranged her former friend had become: from having the audacity to sit next to her mother, who was the ruler of their world, to just confessing everything in a blasé manner. Did nothing frighten her? Apparently Prima Stella held no fear for her; it most certainly was not doing its job right.

'What are you smirking at? Your situation is becoming more dire by the moment!' said Evelyn, annoyed by Lillian's bravado. She still thought of herself as Princess — even in death!

'You're right, many things have changed over the years... Prima Stella is no longer a deterrent, I see,' replied Lillian ominously, as her eyes glowed ruby red. She was pleased by the fear that appeared in Evelyn's eyes. *She's not completely dim witted, then.* 'So you haven't forgotten who rules Prima Stella... Now we wouldn't want to go up against them, and at least you know to which noble family I belong to. I think Prima Stella might just want to know what became of their beloved daughter,' said Lillian, standing tall, her golden hair streaming behind her as her power began to flow around her.

Evelyn cowered against her chair, but in the next instance composed herself; no human or entity would get the better of her. Her mind games would not work. No, for all her bragging, Lillian would also not want to go against Prima Stella, no matter who her family were. This fortified her.

One thing was certain to Rowanne: as far as Evelyn was concerned, she was just a pawn in her rise to power, she didn't know anything of her family. Rowanne thanked God for small mercies.

Lillian too, was glad. After all, it turned out that Evelyn knew nothing of Elisedd and her illicit past, and she hoped that it would stay that way. She had too much to lose if the truth were ever to be revealed.

'It's time to join the others, we've wasted enough time on useless matters,' said Evelyn.

Focusing her energy, Evelyn temporarily snapped open one hand cuff, and forced Rowanne to stand, before snapping it closed again. She made her walk ahead of her, even as she pointlessly struggled. Evelyn was sure of her power; it definitely dwarfed that of a half demon.

'Let her go, you have nothing to gain by her. Your problem is with me,' said Lillian, approaching them. She was stopped as she felt herself encased in a gel like sphere, trapped; ironically, she had used something similar against Alexander.

Evelyn moved Lillian in position ahead of Rowanne, and marched them out of the room. They walked along the corridor, and descended the grand staircase. At the bottom they turned left, and then right, finally standing before two giant doors.

Rowanne swallowed, as she felt the first stirring of unease.

Lillian felt a mixture of intense rage and unending fear. This was exactly the same as before, except, then it had been her friend Driskell who had marched her down alongside her mother, who had been helpless to do anything.

Now the one person she had thought she could trust twisted the knife, and she felt the pain of it with each torturous step. There was nothing worse than watching those you loved hurt, and being powerless to do anything about it.

'Enough wasting time. I've waited more than seventy years for this moment,' said Evelyn, as her power burst forth, flinging open the heavy doors in her eagerness to begin.

CHAPTER 31

Rowanne entered a massive room with a high ceiling, and noticed the multitude of chandeliers all ornately shaped. There were floor to ceiling windows, some clear, others stained glass. The images in them were beautiful as well as terrifying: they seemed to tell the story of Demon World.

Oh my God, what have I stumbled into... thought Rowanne. Was this hell...? What precisely was Demon World? She looked at the depictions; some of them were of people walking into the darkness that consumed them. Others were of great fires with demons gathered around them, the flames reflected in their eyes. Those demons appeared crestfallen and lost, and some of them were looking up, but at what?

Rowanne had a bad feeling in the pit of her stomach; all of these pictures were stirring something deep within her, an awareness of knowledge greater than herself. She felt the doors of reason open within her. It was as if a light was shining in her mind, and minute by minute she was losing her fear. *What's happening to me...?* she wondered, feeling confused.

Soldiers waited just inside beside the doors, and marched her and Lillian towards the front of the hall to a naturally raised platform made of stone and marble. Looking down, Rowanne realised the lower level of the floor was completely made of marble, a whitish grey colour with streaks of black, almost like lighting. It was similar in appearance to a howlite crystal.

Rowanne was startled out of her observations by a soldier prodding a spear painfully into her back. She wanted to scream, but kept quiet as she felt the first trickle of blood run down her back. Her eyes flashed green as her power slowly awakened, though she was oblivious of it. Turning her head around, she glared at the guard, who responded by pointing the spear at her, ready to poke her again if necessary. She reluctantly turned back, and continued onward, and it was only now that she realised the hall was filled with smartly dressed people. She could not believe she had not noticed them before, who were they?

Rowanne followed Lillian, who was now free of the gelatinous sphere, as they ascended the stone steps to the platform. Apparently, Evelyn must have thought that they no longer posed a threat, especially now that they were surrounded by soldiers; they would not dare to attempt to escape, that would be suicidal. *She really doesn't know me very well,* thought Rowanne, as anger ignited within her.

She looked at the empty throne. Evelyn or someone else would soon be sitting there, condemning them to their fate, and passing judgment, and the chances of a fair trial were slim to none. This was Demon World, after all, and even Lillian who had been a princess had not been spared, so, what chance did she really have...

Rowanne's heart rate sped up as she spotted Alexander standing next to the throne, and before him kneeling on the floor with their hands tied behind their backs, were Driskell and Amanda.

'Amanda? Chief Inspector Driskell? What are you two doing here?' asked Rowanne, and made a move towards them, but she was pulled back painfully by a soldier.

Why were they here, together? wondered Rowanne, puzzled. They all mistrusted Driskell, or so she had been led to believe.

Had he tricked Amanda and brought her here under false pretences?

'We were betrayed. I came here for you, Rowanne,' said Amanda, looking her squarely in the eyes, hoping her cousin wouldn't misconstrue the situation, despite how it may appear.

Rowanne decided to give her the benefit of the doubt, she trusted her, after all; though the same could not be said of Driskell, and only time would tell. He was looking at her oddly, and as she met his eyes, he shook his head imperceptibly. What was he trying to tell her?

'You sold me out for power?! I would never have expected this of *you*, Alexander! But in the end you are all the same,' said Driskell bitterly.

He had been strategising with Amanda on how they could possibly help Rowanne, when the doors had been flung open, and before them had stood none other than Alexander. However, he had not unduly been worried, assuming that Alexander had come there on a misunderstanding to save Amanda, probably on Rowanne's explicit orders.

However, Driskell's relief had been short-lived, as Alexander had brought soldiers with him, who proceeded to arrest Amanda and him. He could not believe it, he was knocked for six. He didn't know who was more in shock: Amanda with her mouth hanging open in surprise, or himself.

Amanda too, recalled the exact moment Alexander had strode towards them, and instead of acknowledging them, he had declared them to be traitors of Demon World. She had tried to reason with him to find out what was wrong, and had challenged him on his cold behaviour, on treating them like strangers, but it had all fallen on deaf ears, and they had been brought to the Great Hall.

Rowanne was made to kneel, whereas Lillian stood her ground; nobody could make her do anything against her will. Especially being a former ruler, she would bow down to no one.

They all waited uneasily until finally the moment came when Lady Enid's arrival was announced. Rowanne turned her head behind her, and watched as scores of demons knelt down in acknowledgement and respect of their Queen.

The soldiers made Lillian and Rowanne stand to the side of the throne, and on the opposite side the same thing was being done to Amanda and Driskell, so that all four of them were partially facing the throne and the hall. The platform afforded Rowanne a better view of the hall: she had not fully realised its immense size, or most importantly that it was packed to the rafters with demons as far as the eye could see.

The front half of the hall was occupied by demons of higher rank, observed Rowanne, as they were guarded by soldiers.

They looked up at the newcomers with deadly intent, while some of them looked condescendingly down upon them.

I don't even know these people, who are they to judge me? thought Rowanne, who assumed a calm posture. Her eyes swept across the hall, and she met them head on. She would not look away, and noticed a few of the demons trying to come forward offended by her audacity.

The front line of guards was the only thing standing between Rowanne and a hall of demons.

Lady Enid came up the steps and briefly paused before Rowanne, who saw her twitch as her eyes fixed on the person beside her, and the knowledge hit her hard. Her eyes looked at long last on the face of her beloved daughter... the very daughter who had died seventy years ago.

'Lillian?' whispered Lady Enid, her voice hoarse and barely managing to get the words out past the lump in her throat. Though she was in a state of shock, she managed to hold back the hot tears threatening to break the floodgates. She could not afford to lose it now and break down; the lives of these children were in her hands. Oh, she knew they were adults, but in her mind they were children who had barely even lived. After all, what was seventy years to an immortal — nothing.

'Mother,' said Lillian, her voice also quiet. *Mother*, she had never thought to utter that word again. Now here she was before her, and there was so much that she wanted to say; but she dare not say any more. Of course, it didn't help that Evelyn stood beside her, and the fact that they were in a hall of demons with exceptional hearing. She would have to be smart and play it by ear.

'Come, Your Majesty, this way,' said Evelyn, escorting her to the throne.

Lady Enid stood before the demons, then regally took her rightful seat, her back straight. Her mind worked at a furious pace as to what she could legally do within the scope of the law to get them freed without a death sentence. At the moment it looked hopeless, but she would be damned if she let her daughter die a second time without lifting a finger.

Lady Enid knew her responsibilities towards her people, and could not do anything that would cause an uproar, and there was also Earth to consider. How she hated the fact that her hands were tied down in politics, but even so, there had to be another way. She was beyond anger, a fury that knew no bounds raged within her, as she realised that the woman next to her was the real traitor of Demon World. She looked at her standing there smugly, even having the nerve to smile at her knowingly.

Lady Enid realised that Evelyn knew exactly what she was doing, and was counting on the fact that she would behave as a ruler, not as a mother. She turned her gaze onto Driskell. *Ah, yes, the defiant demon who dared to pass the judgment of death upon my only child.* It was a small mercy that he was kneeling before her: passing her sentence of death upon him would be easy. He openly stared contemptuously at her with hatred. Well, at least now he had dropped all pretence.

Driskell loathed Lady Enid with a passion, and *she* was the one who was ultimately responsible for Lillian's death. He would bide his time before he challenged her. Suddenly, his heart skipped a beat as before him stood the very person that he had damned himself for — Lillian! A plethora of emotions ran through him, threatening to rend him apart. He smiled manically as he looked at her in wonder. He didn't know whether to laugh or cry. *Maybe I'm not damned, after all,* he thought. *She is before me, isn't she?*

Although he was uncertain of how she now perceived him, he still nevertheless held onto a sliver of hope for redemption. In a soft voice, he spoke hesitantly, 'Lillian? But how is this possible, how are you here?' asked Driskell.

'Don't even presume to talk to me. You are a worthless excuse for a demon,' replied Lillian menacingly. She rushed towards him, intending to rip him limb from limb, but was brought to a standstill by the sound of Rowanne recoiling silently in pain. She turned to the guard who dared to hurt Rowanne, and looked at him with deadly intent. To her satisfaction, he flinched and took a step back, finally realising who she was.

It was nice to see that they had not completely forgotten her. There had been a collective intake of breath as the demons realised that none other than Lillian Morning Star was being marched before them. They were shocked and confused by the arrival of their former princess long thought to be dead. They wondered how she had come back from Prima Stella, and consequently looked up at her in equal parts of fear and wonder. Lillian held back her laughter as she defiantly looked them in the eyes: at the people she had known long ago — her people.

Lillian could feel them wanting to kneel before her, but unsure of how they should proceed. They had probably assumed that they were walking into a straightforward case: that of a human hybrid, who would most likely be sentenced to death alongside her maker; the demon, who had dared to convert her. However, they had got a lot more, for before them stood the very people they had least expected, and on the wrong side of the law...

Amanda had no idea what was happening, but she recognised Evelyn - the evil vindictive woman who had blasted her off her feet in the hopes of killing her. She dearly wanted to go up against her, to show her that she was not so easily defeated.

'Driskell, I thought I had gotten rid of this half breed... It seems we are beset and overrun with them. This is a problem. You see, my lady, Earth is full of these... 'things' for lack of a better word,' said Evelyn.

Evelyn went to Alexander, who took the arm she proffered, and together they faced the hall. 'My dear Lords and Ladies, I present to you the scourge of our world. These half breeds born of the immoral union between demons and the loathed humans will prove a threat to our very existence,' said Evelyn.

Evelyn was pleased as she looked out upon her future; she would rule these demons. They would look to her to enforce the law. And enforce it she would, to the hilt. There was a look of hatred on the demons' faces as they shouted, 'Kill the half breeds.' The hall resonated with their death tones.

Alexander outwardly smiled, baring his teeth at the crowd of demons below. He leaned in close to Evelyn's ear, and whispered, 'I don't care what happens to this lot, but you promised *her* to me...'

Evelyn turned towards him, and saw the glacial green power swirl dangerously in his eyes; a fire raged internally within the dark depths of his soul. She needed to get rid of him, especially now that she was so close to her goal. If giving him her childhood friend was the price, then she was more than willing to pay. To hell with Lillian.

She looked at him, and nodded imperceptibly, and his smile widened. She turned her back to the demons and led him to Lillian.

Alexander stood before her. There were many things he wanted to say, but not here, not right now. 'Come, my love. It's been a while...' he smiled at her feverishly, as confusion and uncertainty chased across her delicate face.

'Alexander?' asked Lillian. She didn't like the manic way in which he stared at her; he seemed like a demon possessed.

'What's going on, Lillian? What's wrong with him?' asked Rowanne. She could clearly see that for Alexander, nobody else existed within this great hall except Lillian. There was a coldness in his eyes.

Lillian dared not take her eyes off the demented demon before her. 'I think it's Evelyn, she's done something to him.'

Evelyn laughed quietly, causing Rowanne and Lillian to swivel their heads in her direction.

'Let him go, right now!' demanded Rowanne.

Evelyn found the whole thing tedious, and looking out at the crowd of demons, she suddenly clicked her fingers, causing a green mist to descend upon the hall.

Rowanne watched in astonishment as Evelyn's eyes burned with a greenish black energy. She had frozen the entire hall. All of the demons including the guards were like statues. Bizarrely all of their eyes were closed, and their heads down; they looked like an army sleeping — a deadly one, that could attack as soon as the command was given.

'How is this possible?' asked Lillian. She could not believe how powerful a demon Evelyn had become; this by all accounts should be impossible.

Evelyn looked at her, and shrugged. 'So now you're impressed? Like I said, a lot has changed since your departure. I've changed...'

'Evelyn!' said Alexander impatiently, clenching his fists, trying to keep a grip on what little sanity he had left.

'Oh, *you*,' said Evelyn disdainfully to Alexander. 'Take her already,' completely oblivious of the look of shock on the people still standing on the stage.

Lady Enid was disgusted with the spectacle unfolding before her. Now that the demons were frozen, she was no longer bound by her duty. She walked up to Evelyn, and put the full force of her pain into the resounding slap that knocked Evelyn off her feet and sent her crashing to the floor.

'Who the hell do you think you are to give away *my daughter* as if she's worth nothing? *You*, my dear, are sadly in denial if you thought that you ever meant anything to me.'

Alexander didn't waste any more time as he realised that the situation was rapidly going out of his hands. 'I beg your pardon, Your Majesty.' Lady Enid was bewildered by his strange behaviour, and kept her eyes fixed on him.

'Get away from my daughter, Alexander!' ordered Lady Enid.

'Who is this 'Alexander' you keep referring to?' he asked contemptuously. Turning to Lillian, he said, 'You and I, my love, have unfinished business...' his eyes burned as they gazed obsessively into hers.

Lillian averted her eyes; if she had looked any longer, she might have drowned in the intensity of emotions that seemed to overwhelm him. To her utter astonishment, he had used her momentary distraction to snake his arm around her waist, and spun them straight out of the hall. The only thing left behind was a scorch mark on the floor to indicate that they had ever been there.

'Lillian!' shouted Rowanne. She had not been able to do anything as her hands were bound behind her back.

'Two down — the rest of you shall follow,' said Evelyn, dusting down her dress.

Lady Enid grabbed her by the neck and lifted her up in the air. 'Where did he take my daughter?' her voice was cold, and her energy flared a deadly violet; there was a promise of death in the electrically charged air.

'Release me and I will answer. Then perhaps we can discuss this like civilised demons. And before you get ahead of yourself, let me remind you that it won't take me two seconds to unfreeze them. Then, by all means, you can try to explain everything to them,' replied Evelyn arrogantly.

'You think they would not listen to their Queen?' asked Lady Enid.

Evelyn looked into her eyes, and replied with a question of her own, 'Do you really believe your position as Queen is as secure as you'd like to think it is?'

'What are you implying?' asked Lady Enid.

'I find the lack of oxygen to my brain makes me forget. Where is Lillian? It's all becoming a blur-' Evelyn was cut off, as Lady Enid let go of her. Her legs jarred as she landed painfully on her feet. She massaged her neck, her throat sore; she'd make her pay for that.

'Well, I'm waiting. Get on with it,' said Lady Enid.

While Evelyn was occupied with Lady Enid, Rowanne used the opportunity to slowly edge closer to Driskell and Amanda. Finally she stood back to back with Amanda, and quickly untied the rope that had been binding her. How she managed, she had no idea; it was like her hands suddenly knew what to do.

Amanda nursed her sore wrists - the rope had bitten into them, leaving behind angry red marks. She turned to Driskell, who looked defeated, as if he fully expected them to leave him where he was.

'Rowanne?' asked Amanda quietly.

'I'll leave it in your hands. It's *your* decision to make, after all...' she said solemnly. Rowanne realised that Driskell was starting to become Amanda's responsibility, and she had a faraway look in her eyes, as if she were suddenly privy to visions that others could not see.

Amanda watched in fascination as Rowanne's green eyes started to change to violet, and suddenly the cuffs snapped off of their own accord as they fell to the ground. *I can't believe I didn't realise it before... here I was worried that Rowanne shouldn't learn of Demon World and the Knight family legacy; turns out, cousin dearest is also a half demon just like me.*

Rowanne grabbed Amanda's hand and looked at her intently, observing the green fire deep within her eyes. She laughed, 'It seems like we have a lot to talk about, once this is through! Go help him... Cousin,' she smiled warmly as Amanda's eyes widened in surprise.

'Rowanne, how did you know, and what's happened to you?' asked Amanda. This had seriously thrown her off balance; there was more to Rowanne than she could ever have conceived of.

Driskell cleared his throat, bringing their attention back to him, 'We haven't got time for your family reunion. I could do with a bit of help over here,' he said dryly.

Amanda quickly set about helping him, and with one tug she managed to open the rope, as he winced from the force of it. 'What did you expect?' she asked irritably.

'Nothing more, nothing less,' he replied, smiling intriguingly at her. He liked his warrior woman's strength.

She hated the way he seemed to turn every situation to his benefit, and wanted to throttle him accordingly, as well as wipe the smirk of his face.

Driskell stepped closer to her, nursing his wrist. 'I make you nervous... I affect you more than you care to admit...' he whispered boldly. He especially appreciated her blue eyes smouldering dangerously at him.

Rowanne left them to it as she made her way back to Lady Enid, and stood beside her, secure in the knowledge that the two of them could work something out, and probably fight, if it came down to it.

Evelyn loathed the sight of Driskell smiling at that half breed of a girl, and summoned her soldiers to form behind them. She watched as the Shadows took on the form of people.

Rowanne didn't trust the dark look that had suddenly come into Evelyn's eyes, and quickly glanced back. Amanda and Driskell were oblivious to what was happening just behind them.

'Look out,' screamed Rowanne, just as the first soldier thrust his sword towards Amanda.

Driskell quickly turned, and managed to deflect the blade with his bare hand in the nick of time.

Amanda watched the blood trickle down his hand, as the demons began to form into a semi circle, intending to cut them down savagely.

Driskell grabbed Amanda with his good hand, and ran.

She tried unsuccessfully to pull her hand out of his, but it was no use as Driskell seemed to be focused with deadly precision on getting them out of the hall.

'Stop! What do you think you're doing? We can't just abandon them to those monsters. We have to stay and fight!' pleaded Amanda; but it fell on deaf ears.

Driskell replied gruffly, 'You can't help Rowanne if you're dead. Anyway, they're following *us*, we need to lead them away from her. Then you can let loose as much as you want to on them. I'll even help, if you permit me to!' he laughed madly.

'Great, I'm shackled to a mad man,' she said under her breath.

'It could have been worse...' he said. *I could have kissed you... and then where would we have ended up...?* he whispered audaciously in her mind, and winked at her. Before she could reply, he hurtled her unceremoniously through the large doors.

That was the last that Rowanne saw of them, being chased by a score of Shadow soldiers at their heels. She felt sick to her stomach as she pondered how to fight something insubstantial yet powerful enough to rip a person to shreds. She prayed that Amanda and Driskell would work together long enough to fight the demons off.

God only knew where Alexander had taken Lillian. They'd need Evelyn alive if there was any chance of discovering them, as well as freeing Alexander's mind out of her control.

Rowanne put a restraining hand on Lady Enid's arm, just as she was about to throw the full force of her power at Evelyn.

'We need her to find out where they are,' she said gently.

'So, I'm to be saved by a half breed of all things,' said Evelyn contemptuously.

'Rowanne is the only person keeping you alive. You cannot even conceive of what I have planned for the one who tortured and killed my child,' she said in a strong voice, as she beat her chest with her hand, no longer able to control the violent emotions that wanted to tear their way out of her heart.

'You speak like a mother should, or should that be a "so-called mother",' said Evelyn sarcastically.

'Don't you dare presume to think that you know me. You have no idea what your actions have cost me!' said Lady Enid bitterly.

'Don't make me laugh with that act! What kind of a mother stands by and watches while her daughter burns to death?' asked Evelyn triumphantly.

Rowanne wanted to defend Lady Enid, but sensed that perhaps the best way she could support her was by listening - maybe then, she'd find a way out of this. Evelyn might let slip something which they could use in this Noble Court they kept speaking of. In this way, they could finally bring Lillian the justice she so rightly deserved. Alexander was definitely rubbing off on her, as she could almost imagine him telling her to: 'Use your brain, Rowanne, and bide your time.'

Lady Enid stepped back as if she had been struck, as Rowanne stopped her from stumbling. She looked briefly with gratitude at the human woman beside her, who lent her strength by her very presence. Rowanne could have run away and saved herself, or even have gone after Alexander, but instead she had stayed back, not wanting to leave her alone. Lady Enid was more touched than Rowanne would ever know; in a way it was like having her daughter with her. Although it was bizarre that this thought should enter her mind.

'How pathetic. You need a human to support you. You are in no way fit to be a ruler. I admit, though, that I admired you for a while. Especially the way you let Lillian die, so that the clan of Morning Star could continue to rule.'

'You are very much mistaken, if you think I'd let my daughter die for the love of politics. I am in no way worthy of your false praise,' said Lady Enid disgustedly.

'Very well, lie to yourself if it helps you to sleep better at night... However, the truth is that we are more alike, than you'd care to admit. We both want power no matter the cost. What are other people's lives worth? Nothing. You wanted to remain queen, so, bon voyage daughter and good riddance!' Evelyn laughed cruelly, watching Lady Enid's power gather around her. She'd struck a nerve, but was she scared? No. After all, politics was not the domain of the timid.

'It was not like that...' said Lady Enid through gritted teeth.

'I've done the same thing myself; gotten rid of a few *nuisances*. What's a death now and again between colleagues?' she asked coldly. 'It's the world we inhabit. We play the great game that is life, and the rise to the top was always going to involve a few casualties. Unavoidable I'm afraid.'

'You are a monster,' said Rowanne, unable to keep quiet any longer. 'You were Lillian's friend, how could you do this to her?'

Rowanne felt something spark within her, some power long dormant. It started slowly as she felt something leave her, and shoot out into the crowd of frozen demons below the platform. Evelyn was too consumed in reliving her glorious rise to the top to notice, and Rowanne intended to keep it that way.

Lady Enid looked sharply in Rowanne's direction. She knew that Rowanne was a half demon, but even so, she should not have been able to do what she just did... She sensed the demons stirring awake, only their bodies were frozen, as a hundred minds snapped to attention. She dreaded what they'd do once they regained the use of their limbs...

After all, they weren't ordinary demons, but the crème de la crème of Demon World's high society. They may have been Nobles by birth, and Nobles by nature, but they lacked the intrinsic qualities that made one noble. Less righteous and more self-righteous. Self-serving.

'It's simple, really. I wanted to rule, but Lillian was in the way. The circumstances were to my advantage, and besides, no other Noble family has ever had the chance to rule Demon World. It was high time Lady Enid stepped down and allowed another more rightful ruler to be Queen,' said Evelyn.

'What makes you more worthy than any other Noble to rule? How did you have the audacity without consulting them to name yourself as the next Queen?' asked Rowanne in a firm, crystal clear voice that carried out into the audience.

The demons listened patiently, realising that they had been betrayed by the daughter of the Adara Clan. Blood was chiefly on their mind; that clan would be made to answer for treason.

Rowanne and Lady Enid could hear the deadly collective consciousness; it screamed, 'Prima Stella! Prima Stella!'

Rowanne knew that she should be afraid, but from the moment that she had untied Amanda, she had felt the awareness which she had first encountered in the hall growing steadily within her, and there were no signs of it stopping its momentum. She didn't know what was happening to her, but nevertheless accepted it with a quiet grace.

Lady Enid sensed a force of such magnitude and power forming in the atmosphere. Where was it coming from? she wondered, and felt an uneasiness deep within her core.

Rowanne knew the exact moment when the demons heads went up and their eyes snapped open. The demons wanted to unleash the full force of their power on Evelyn, she could feel it; ironically, Evelyn was the only one keeping it in check.

After giving it some serious consideration, Evelyn answered thoughtfully, 'It's not just me who thinks that the time for the Morning Star Clan to rule has passed.'

'And what do you mean by that impertinent remark?' asked Lady Enid, standing tall and graceful, in no way ready to step aside so easily to allow the conniving girl before her to ascend to her throne.

'There are many demons here who do not — and it might come as a bit of a surprise — like your way of ruling. You have become soft, and lenient to the point where you allow half demons to walk free. Don't even get me started on your debacle of allowing humans to reside here...' said Evelyn calmly.

Rowanne could sense a mixture of feelings, all of the demons in this world were outwardly obedient to their Queen, but she could feel the hatred they had for half demons and humans. The Queen was in danger from more than one direction. Evelyn was just the first to make an outward attack. This was a volatile situation, and it could just as easily go in Evelyn's favour; the Queen was not assured of loyalty here in this hall, anyway.

Lady Enid had been wondering the same thing; how many of her so-called supporters would dare to stand beside her...

'So, you're not so self assured now, are you? Whereas I know who I am and embrace all parts of myself. When I ascend the throne, eliminating half demons will be top priority. I will cut off all interaction between Earth and Demon World; no more interacting with humans. Thus minimising the number of half breeds.'

'You speak as if you're already Queen, that's presumptuous,' said Rowanne.

Rowanne felt the demons heads turn in her direction. They probably wanted to tear her to pieces as well; it was not only Evelyn that they wanted to punish. They were probably questioning the audacity of a human to stand as an equal beside their Queen, let alone talk to one of their Nobles.

Well, I can't let them down now, can I? thought Rowanne; she intended to continue the way she had started.

'I could say the same of you: how dare a half demon presume to lecture me. You are nothing in this game. No one. When all this is over, no one will remember you, Ms Rowanne Knight!' said Evelyn contemptuously.

How will I protect her now? thought Lady Enid, sadly. Rowanne's identity and status as a half demon were now laid out before the Noble Court.

CHAPTER 32

The portal flashed open, and Alexander pushed Lillian through it.

She turned around angrily, hell-bent on going right back through it, but she was too late as it snapped closed, taking with it her only means of escape.

'What the hell do you think you're doing, Alexander?' she asked, keeping her arms loosely by her side as she watched his every move intently; she was ready to fight, if need be.

'Why are you so tense, my *beloved* Lillian?' asked Alexander mockingly.

For the first time, she felt a cold dread take hold of her heart as she looked at where they had ended up.

'Do you like it? I thought it was the perfect spot for our long overdue reunion...' said Alexander. He wiped his hand along the wall. 'See, not a speck of dust. I've looked after it well, don't you agree?'

Lillian felt physically sick as she looked around the candle lit crypt. She wearily circled the stone table accommodating the two coffins. She had a bad feeling about this place, especially the coffins; they made her skin crawl...

Alexander had crept up behind her while she had momentarily been distracted by the sight before her.

Lillian snapped her attention back, but it was too late as Alexander encircled her from behind. She struggled in vain. How was it possible for him to even touch her? Only Rowanne had that ability.

'I thought you didn't fear anything, love, but your heartbeat tells me otherwise... Don't tell me you fear death, especially now?' he whispered against her ear.

'My heartbeat? That's laughable. It stopped seventy years ago,' she replied sarcastically.

Lillian heard him laughing bitterly behind her. His breathing had become shallow and he took a deep breath.

'I know...' Alexander said cryptically by way of a reply.

'It's common knowledge, I suppose,' said Lillian.

'No!' said Alexander forcefully.

She struggled against him, but it only made him hold on to her more tightly. It was like he was made of stone. She craned her head back to look at him, and was met by his beautifully glacial green eyes boring into her own, as his mouth slowly turned from a grimace into a smile; but there was a bitterness to him. She turned away from him.

Alexander let her go but kept a firm eye on her as she moved slowly around the table keeping a distance between them.

He smirked, 'Are you not in the least bit curious as to why I brought you here, of all places?' as he gestured at their macabre surroundings.

'If I had known of your grave obsession, then I'd have warned Rowanne to stay the hell away from you,' she replied tauntingly.

Alexander just laughed darkly, 'My only *obsession*, as you so eloquently put it, is *you*, love.'

'When did you develop this unhealthy attraction?' asked Lillian, as he slowly inched his way around the table towards her - but she matched him step for step. After all, she was a reluctant partner in this dance, it was best to keep her distance.

'How long do you propose to keep this up?' he asked sardonically.

'For as long as it takes to strike you down and get back to Rowanne,' replied Lillian, equally derisive.

'Tut tut, Lillian. What would Rowanne say if you destroyed *her* Alexander?' he asked, smiling evilly.

'I'm sure she'd understand. If you belong to Rowanne, then why am I here?' she asked, genuinely intrigued as to why he'd taken her instead.

Alexander paused at the foot of the coffins, and looking piercingly into her eyes, he replied, 'Now, that is a good question. Why did I choose *you*? Once, you really consider it will become painfully obvious, love.'

'*Stop* calling me that! I'm not *your* anything!' said Lillian irritated, as he began to stalk towards her again.

She was missing something here. What was it he had said earlier... 'What did you mean, when you said you knew of my death?' She breathed a sigh of relief as he paused.

Alexander smiled broadly, 'Now you're on the right track. Keep going.'

Truth be told, she was confused as to what he was referring to. She could tell that he was frustrated with her lack of understanding, as he restlessly tapped his foot against the floor.

Lillian began moving again as he advanced towards her. She backed up, not realising that the wall was behind her, and accidentally knocked a candle off. Shocked, she looked towards the floor, and then back up at Alexander, who was smiling broadly.

'Confused are we? You're probably wondering how it's possible for a ghost to knock things over when you are insubstantial, right?'

She was in a daze, not understanding what was happening to her, and this only compounded her frustration. *Hang on, if I can knock things down, then... it stands to reason, that I can hurt him!*

'You're welcome to try, love...' he said condescendingly.

Lillian felt the flames of anger burn within her; she'd wipe that smirk of his face. *Egotistical moron.*

'Are you sure it's *anger* that burns within you...?' he asked innocently, before suddenly rushing towards her. Grabbing her hand, he placed a gentle kiss upon it, and before she could grab him, he rushed back out of her reach, laughing heartlessly.

'Do you know how I died?' she asked, taking deep breaths to steady herself whilst looking for an opening to take him out.

'Well-' he began, momentarily distracted as he contemplated how much to reveal to her.

Lillian rushed him, intending to knock him off his feet, but he just went along with her attack, using her momentum against her. He lifted her up and brought her crashing down onto one of the coffins.

'You-' but she was cut off, as he covered her mouth with his hand.

He shook his head gravely. The eyes that looked down at her were now a blackish green. 'My dear, sweet, Lillian.'

She realised that it was not Alexander above her, but suspected she was looking into Evelyn's eyes instead; it even sounded like her. She had never imagined Evelyn to be this powerful, to be able to split her mind so effectively that she could be in many places at the same time.

However, it was not only Evelyn who occupied his mind; there was someone else making their home within Alexander.

Lillian kicked with all her strength, aiming the full force of her power against his larger frame, sending him crashing against the wall. She got up quickly and swung her legs over before gracefully jumping down to the floor. She was satisfied with her handiwork.

Alexander, breathing heavily, got onto his knees and looked up at her. His lip was split and bloody, and he had angry bruises blossoming on his forehead and cheek.

'Very good, love,' he wiped his mouth coming away with blood.

'Just tell me what you want me to know so I can get the hell out of here.' Lillian straightened her crumpled suit jacket. *Wait a minute...* She looked at him with a mixture of fear and wonder. How was it possible that she could actually feel her jacket? It felt silky. *No, this was not possible... was it?*

Alexander smiled up at her, 'It's wonderful to be able to feel after so long, is it not?' he asked, as he got up off the floor to lean casually against the wall; well, as casually as a man with death on his mind was able to. He laughed softly.

Great, it's my luck to be stuck with him in this small room, thought Lillian. *He is right though,* she admitted reluctantly; it was incredible to have the sense of touch back after being so long without it, however impermanent it may be.

'What's happening to me?' she asked wearily.

'I was there, when you died...' he said coldly.

Lillian stumbled back as she felt the force of those words strike like a knife directly to her heart.

'Hurts, doesn't it?' he asked maliciously.

She swallowed painfully a couple of times before forcing the words out of her mouth, 'Who are you?' she asked quietly, not trusting herself to speak. It was clear that the man before her could not be Alexander; who had not even been present at her trial, let alone know the gory details of what became of her.

'I was wondering how long it would take for you to figure out that I am not this idiot, Alexander, before you.'

'Were you one of the Nobles at my trial?' It had been a closed court in Prima Stella. There would have only been a few elite Nobles present, and they too, would have been sworn to secrecy on pain of death.

'Nobles,' he spat. 'No, I do not belong to *that* ignoble circus.'

Funny, he sounds like my mother, she thought, and mentally shook herself out of her manic state. *Great, it must be infectious; his state of lunacy is rubbing off on me.*

He strode towards the coffins, pausing briefly to look at her.

'No. Don't do it!' pleaded Lillian. She intrinsically knew that she didn't want to look at whatever lay in those coffins.

'I'm tired of waiting, love...' and holding her gaze, he mercilessly ripped the lids off the coffins.

The silence was deafening in the aftermath of the lids crashing to the floor.

Lillian refused to look down, and instead kept her gaze locked firmly with his. His eyes were a dark bottomless pit; there was no mercy to be found there. A cruel smile played on his lips.

'Eventually you'll look down... You won't be able to help it,' said Alexander, as his eyes changed to the colour of metallic green.

Lillian felt the full force of the combined power of Evelyn, and whoever the entity within Alexander was. She tried to fight against it but her energy was dwindling fast. If she should disappear now when Rowanne needed her the most, then what would happen?

Alexander's gaze captured hers, and slowly he began to look down, pulling her right along with him, so that she had no choice but to look into the coffins. She felt cold as the temperature in the room suddenly dropped, and her breath misted before her. She should not be surprised though; another thing that should be beyond the realms of possibility for what a ghost could or should be able to do.

Alexander watched the surprise and fear chase across her face. Finally the moment had come that he'd been patiently waiting for, for so long...

Lillian's heart almost stopped as she looked into the coffin before her. She looked back up at Alexander, but there was no comfort to be found there.

'What trick is this?' asked Lillian.

'What you see before you is the truth,' he replied calmly.

'No! I refuse to believe it!' said Lillian in denial, and started to back away when suddenly her knees gave out, and she collapsed.

Alexander walked around to her side and knelt down beside her. 'It's not that bad, really... It could have been worse,' he said bitterly.

'No. I remember exactly what happened; I died. That... that *thing* in there is not me, is it...?' she asked uncertainly, as her energy momentarily deserted her.

Confusion clouded her mind; she could not make sense of what happened all those years ago when she had died. Lillian covered her face to block out the images that were cascading down, visions of herself and Elisedd in the fire.

'Stop it. Stop it!' she screamed, but the echo of her own screams came back to haunt her...

Lillian felt someone rubbing her hands, bringing her back from the brink of eternal madness, and desperately she followed the sensation back and slowly opened her eyes.

'Alexander?' she asked her voice hoarse.

'No, I'm afraid not, love. Still *me* here,' said the entity possessing Alexander.

'Who are you?' she asked again, hoping to actually get a reply this time.

He stood up and offered her a hand. When she refused, he shrugged his shoulders, and watched her struggle up. She was unsteady on her feet and ironically leaned against the coffin for support.

'I'm glad you asked, but in order to answer your questions fully, I think I need to get rid of this dead weight.'

Lillian was more than ready to face the entity.

He took a step away from her and a green mist seemed to cocoon him, which pulsated with light. A shadow detached itself from Alexander, who would have fallen had not the shadow caught him, and turning to her, he said, 'Give me a moment, love.' The entity momentarily portalled out of the room but was back in less than a minute.

'What did you do with Alexander?' asked Lillian anxiously.

'Relax, I've set him outside. He's a bit dazed but that should soon pass. Alexander was never my target. I just needed him to get to you,' said the entity matter-of-factly.

'Why do you still persist in hiding? Stand before me as your true self!' said Lillian indignantly.

'Patience, love. That wish will come true in a second whether you like it or not... But first, have you not wondered why there are two coffins?'

'That thought had briefly crossed my mind. Am I right in assuming that the other is yours?' asked Lillian.

She could not quite get over what she had seen in the coffin; just this thought was enough to make her morbidly curious. Her feet seemed to move against her volition, shuffling slowly and inexorably until she was once more before the coffin.

'You see, you can't help it! It calls to you, drawing you in-' said the entity cut off suddenly.

Lillian looked sharply towards him; he seemed to be having an internal dilemma.

The entity looked with unseeing eyes straight through her, momentarily distracted by someone or something else; probably Evelyn. She watched in fascination as he held a one sided conversation.

'You promised that she would be mine. NO! I will most certainly not be taking orders from you anymore. You nearly damaged her with that stunt of yours. Do not ever presume to use my mind against me like that, ever again! I don't care who you are. I take my leave of you.'

Lillian tested a theory, 'I don't think Evelyn will take too kindly to that tone of voice. She does not accept rejection easily.'

The entity swung his head back in her direction, and smiled, 'I've had her in my mind for more than half a century...' he sounded pained.

'Though I can empathise with your situation, I find my emotions waning at your hands,' said Lillian firmly.

'Fair enough, but at least I don't have *her* in my mind anymore. You can't begin to fathom what it's like to share your mind with another. For one thing, there's never any privacy. Not to mention, I've been her puppet all this time...'

'Believe me, I know exactly what you mean,' said Lillian.

'Of course you do,' he said coldly.

'What do you mean by that?' she asked, as anger stirred within her.

'You know perfectly well to what I'm referring,' he said, emphasising his point in a cold, acerbic tone.

'I'm afraid I really don't,' said Lillian.

At least she didn't have to deal with Evelyn, and she could teach this shade a thing or two now that he had discarded Alexander's body as well.

'Really? I'd like to see you try. You would be mistaken if you think that this is my only form. I admit it; the other coffin *was* mine...'

Lillian swallowed, and looked down at the sleeping figure. How was it possible that it was her laying there? She could not dispute this, not with the evidence before her. She watched his ghostly hand stroking her hair lovingly.

'Get away from me, don't touch me!' said Lillian, as her hand passed through the entity's hand.

He stood before her coffin looking lovingly down into it, before meeting her fiery gaze, a thoughtful expression on his face, 'Well, at least you now accept that *this* is your body laying here.'

He began to disintegrate and then disappear before her eyes. This was an all too familiar sight to her. It was the effect of using too much energy; the entity could not hold onto its form.

Suddenly finding herself alone, she wondered how long he would be gone for. But Lillian had never been one to wallow, so set her mind to the more pressing task of actually getting out of the room. It was circular with a high ceiling and there were no obvious entrances... *Had the coffins been portalled in...* she wondered.

Lillian began to examine the stone walls in the hope of coming across a secret door. She hit the wall hard in frustration, and screamed as she felt the pain shoot through her hand. An idea began to form in her mind and once rooted it wouldn't let go, demanding she see it through to its conclusion.

She looked at herself in the coffin: her hair was long but how had it not lost its colour or lustre? It was still beautifully golden. She was taken aback to find herself wearing the white dress she had died in. How had it not burnt to ashes... she wondered. It looked fresh and in no way faded after all these long years.

Lillian looked at her hand in the coffin but it was turned in. Slowly and gingerly she reached in and turned it over; her theory proved correct, there was indeed blood on it. Anything that happened to her ghostly form also happened to her corpse. She was about to drop it out of fright, as her own hand slowly started to disappear before her.

She screamed and stepped back, and would have collapsed if it had not been for the strong arms suddenly supporting her. Someone was whispering by her ear.

'Just go with it. It's not so bad, after the first time. Breathe...'

Lillian didn't know who it was and frankly she didn't care; what mattered most was the horrifying vision of her missing hand with only the stump of her arm remaining. Her eyes were drawn towards the body in the coffin; the hand started to curl and uncurl, and strangely she could feel the sensation, as if she were connected to the body. *It must be me controlling it — it's my corpse, after all*, with that final thought, her eyes fluttered closed as she lost consciousness.

Lillian came to after a few moments, and slowly opened her eyes. She was lying on the floor with her head propped up on someone's legs.

'Finally! I was wondering how long I'd have to wait — it seems to be a speciality of yours,' said the voice derisively.

Lillian's eyes snapped open, and she tilted her head and looked up into the beautiful emerald eyes that she'd never thought to see again - not in this lifetime, anyway. She laughed, and it sounded unbalanced.

'Not really the reaction I was expecting after all this time, love,' he said.

She got up quickly, her mind still reeling from the person before her. She nearly stumbled but he caught her, and her hands came to rest on his arms.

'Elisedd?!' asked Lillian in disbelief, not trusting herself to hope that he too had survived the fire which had consumed them both.

'Well, I could say in the flesh, but that sounds a tad crass. Remember the empty coffin? Well, I couldn't very well spend my whole eternity in it, now could I?!' asked Elisedd sarcastically.

'But how is it even possible...? We died, so how did you come back?'

'The same way you did, when you decided to abandon *me*!' shouted Elisedd.

'I... I didn't even know that you had survived... If I did, I would have torn this world up looking for you!' she pleaded.

'Once, I believed in you... But you *left* as soon as you saw your chance at life. Left me, trapped here, alone... Evelyn revealed the truth to me when she saved me!' said Elisedd.

'Saved you?! More like she condemned us to death! Don't you know, she's the one behind our downfall. She orchestrated the whole thing!' said Lillian, shaking with rage. A fire burned deep within her core, and it had Evelyn's name written on it.

'More lies! I admit she is not my first preference for a companion, but she was the only one!' said Elisedd, his own eyes burning with his inner torment.

He gripped her arms, and he felt strong; he was alive. 'What exactly did Evelyn do to bring you back? After all, the dead can't rise again...' said Lillian doubtfully.

'Quite. That's one thing you've got right. The dead can't, but the living...'

'No. We died!' said Lillian, shaking uncontrollably.

'Are you certain...?' asked Elisedd seriously.

'But the pain... it was unbearable, I felt each moment. It's scarred into my psyche. How could it not, when... I watched the fire consume you...' she said quietly.

Looking deeply into her eyes, he said quietly, 'I know, love. I watched you die as well... You were the last thing I saw before... Well, you understand.'

'What- what happened after- afterwards?' stuttered Lillian, finding it difficult to speak past the constriction in her throat.

'You mean, after we died?' he asked gently, and as she slowly nodded, he continued, 'I was in the worst pain imaginable... my skin felt raw and bloody. I remember screaming, I was out of my mind. I could feel the last vestiges of my sanity slipping, when suddenly, a blinding violet-green energy ripped me from the fire just as it covered my entire body. By the way *that* was the last time I saw you... just as the fire burned you out of my view...' said Elisedd, frenzied.

She watched as he shivered and trembled at the horrendous memories, and his eyes held a glazed faraway look. She brought him back to the present by encouraging him to go on. 'Afterwards, what can you remember?' she asked cautiously, not wanting to cause him any undue harm.

Once more he focused on the woman before him, *My beloved*, he thought, mockingly. *I died for her and she left. Just left! with no more thought of me, and not once did she look back...*

'I awoke in this chamber!' he spat; his prison really. He had been locked up, and let out occasionally when it served

Evelyn, and even then only under her control. How he hated that woman with a passion. When the day finally came, and it would, that she stood before him, powerless to control him, then he would love to repay her in kind for saving him... he thought darkly, his eyes murderous.

Lillian ripped her arms out of Elisedd's grip as his hands painfully dug into her arms. She knew that if she were to look at her body in the coffin, then it too, would bear the same angry red marks that were on her arms.

Elisedd mentally shook himself out of his manic state. He tried to calm himself down but it was not without tremendous effort. He looked at her apologetically, 'Sorry, love. I was lost there for a moment.'

He looked as if he were ready to kill someone, she thought uneasily, as he walked determinedly to her coffin.

'Don't worry, love, it wasn't you I was thinking of,' he said quietly. A gentle look came into his eyes as he gazed tenderly down at her in the coffin. 'How does this feel?' he asked, over his shoulder.

Lillian was taken by surprise as a comfortably familiar sensation came back to her as she felt him gently massaging her arms where he had unintentionally hurt her. She closed her eyes hoping to block him out, but it proved in vain.

'Open your eyes, Lillian,' he said softly.

She felt a hot breath upon her face, and reluctantly opened her eyes. He was close, too close for her liking.

'Some memories don't fade with time but become more vivid...' said Elisedd, his eyes smouldering with an inner fire.

He looked at her wonderingly and took another step towards her, smiling knowingly. He was amused, when just as his hand would have caressed her cheek, she stepped back, so that he only brushed it with the tips of his fingers; but it was enough, as her eyes widened.

Lillian turned abruptly away from him. He was not making things easy for her...

'I'm not going anywhere, love. I have always been right where you left me...'

'I suppose Evelyn was here to greet you,' she said. Her emotions were fighting within her. She would not go to him, it was too late...

Elisedd huffed in exasperation behind her. Lillian was sorely mistaken if she thought that he'd intended to spend eternity alone. He felt her emotions as fragments of her thoughts beat at him; she was just as confused as him. Where did they now stand within each other's lives?

You are not a coward, she rebuked herself ruthlessly, as she forced herself to face the man she had once loved above all others. After all, they had died in each other's arms.

Elisedd's gaze locked with Lillian's; he could drown in those soulful violet eyes. 'I stood as a shade before Evelyn, and she showed me our bodies. How peaceful we looked lying side by side,' he said, indicating the coffins. 'At her behest, I got into my coffin, and sunk easily into my body, my soul returned to its earthly abode.'

'Your body accepted you back, but then what happened to me?' asked Lillian, wondering why she had not ended up here as well.

'You're getting ahead of yourself, love. Before I could awaken as a human once more, Evelyn performed a ritual while I was still trying to adjust to my body. I could not stop her!' said Elisedd angrily.

'What ritual, what did she do to you?' asked Lillian, stepping close to him and shaking him desperately by the shoulders.

You still care, love, even if you don't say it aloud, thought Elisedd in wonder.

'She transferred her blood by making a small incision in my hand, and then did the same with her own before finally joining our hands, and speaking words which I no longer recall.'

'You must have slept for a couple of hours while the conversion happened,' stated Lillian matter-of-factly.

'I suppose you would know, after all. I dreamt that I was lost in a midnight world without end, and I kept calling for you, but was met with silence. The only thing keeping me going and saving my sanity was that when I awoke, you would be before me. Alive. I never believed in miracles before... my Lillian, alive and unhurt with me. How stupid of me!' he said acerbically, his pain evident in his voice.

Lillian could tell him of her own nightmare world, but only if and when he was ready to listen, then she'd recount what she had been through.

'I awoke as a half demon but you were still asleep. I called your name and shook you but to no avail. Fear took a hold of me as I thought that Evelyn had not been able to save you. I asked her, grief stricken, what had gone wrong. She replied that you had not chosen to come back, and that your soul had decided on a different path,' said Elisedd coldly, reliving the pain and misery of it all over again.

'Contrary to what she told you, I in fact did not choose a path for myself — it was chosen *for me*, and by our great granddaughter of all people, even if it was an unconscious decision at the time. Admittedly, she was fighting for her own life then,' said Lillian, uncertain of how he'd react to this monumental revelation.

'What did you just say?' he asked in disbelief; after all, it could very well be another ruse on her part.

Lillian was silent as she waited for him to accept the truth. A truth she had carried alone for far too long.

'*Our* daughter?! Lived... still lives?' he asked tentatively, as it finally sunk in. This was more than he could ever have hoped for, but he was anxious of the answer that awaited him.

'She lives, and has a daughter, as well as a grandchild,' replied Lillian, as tears hung on her eyelashes.

Elisedd fell forward, the grief of being separated from his child and first love proving too much for him to handle. Lillian caught him, and they slowly sunk to the floor. He felt her arms around him, just holding him, as she waited patiently; it brought back bittersweet memories.

'What happened to you?' he asked, after they had spent some time in companionable silence. He gently disengaged from her and sat opposite.

She felt as if he were drawing away from her again, and hugged her cold body as a faraway look came into her eyes. 'I awoke in our great granddaughter's body; though I was unaware of her identity at the time. It's taken some time to piece the puzzle together. I had wondered why my soul had chosen a random human, and that too on Earth away from Demon World.'

'What became of our daughter?' asked Elisedd eagerly, shuffling closer.

'Seventy years ago I left Angelique with your family...'

'My family...' said Elisedd in wonder. 'Our treasured Angelique, I've often wondered through these long years of what might have become of her, and imagined the life she might have lived. I know you understand as I do, how it feels to never see our child again...' said Elisedd, with tears sliding down his face.

She leaned towards him, and wiped his tears away gently. Tears streaked down her face as she could no longer hold back the floodgates of her own grief. Elisedd was the one person she'd share this with, no one else.

Elisedd gently wiped Lillian's tears, reciprocating her kindness. She let him, and for that he was grateful. He would not have been able to bear it had she turned him away in his grief.

'Do you know of what became of my family?'

'I thought Evelyn would have told you,' she said, shocked.

'I have spent more than half a century shut up in here looking after you. Waiting for your soul to return...'

She wanted to look away but his intense gaze captured her. How must it have felt to be down here in this miserable existence... to be caged, and never having a chance at life; cut off from everyone and from the world.

Lillian grabbed his hands and held on for dear life; or so it felt to her. 'Nobody knew of what became of us. Everyone, including both our families, thought that we had died.'

He squeezed her hand painfully, 'Did we save them? Please, tell me we didn't die for nothing!' he pleaded with her. He would go mad if she told him otherwise, and he was barely managing to function as it was.

'We did,' she replied, and he sagged in relief.

'Show me everything that you have seen so far, that way I'll know the truth,' demanded Elisedd in a firm voice; he would not accept, 'no' for an answer.

'Close your eyes. Journey with me, merge your mind with mine...' she said wearily.

Elisedd obliged as he held her hands, and let his mind gently drift towards hers. He shared her memories, re-lived her horror. *No! it could not be.* Evelyn had lied to him. He wept for Lillian, who had been confined to their great granddaughter's mind. He saw her fight valiantly for Rowanne when her life had been in danger, only to be shoved back into her mind once it had passed. Finally he knew his great granddaughter's name!

'Who is this Alexander?' asked Elisedd.

'He is actually, or to be more precise, he was, the next heir to Demon World,' replied Lillian, amused by the thought that the Knight family seemed to have a penchant for royalty; demon royalty... And Rowanne was no exception, whether she knew it or not.

He continued to share her memories, and learnt that Alexander had given up everything for Rowanne.

'I like him, he is a perfect match for our great granddaughter,' said Elisedd. 'So, he's a half demon now, and will age after willingly given up his immortality. At least he can grow old with Rowanne,' he added as an afterthought.

'Elisedd, you're a half demon, so why haven't you aged?' Lillian wondered what had stopped his aging process; he still looked the same age as when he had died.

'You know, at first I thought it may have been because we had not really died. Evelyn had pulled our bodies out of the fire, and brought them down here, and sort of froze us in space and time.'

'What are you talking about? The pain was real enough!' reiterated Lillian, shocked at his revelation; she didn't know how to take it.

'Of course, you wouldn't have known! She separated our souls from our bodies, but there was still a small connection, just enough to keep them alive. But she kept our minds firmly locked within the fire — evil woman that she is. So that we would feel our death... she had to make it look convincing to us, as well as to the Court,' replied Elisedd.

'So, she didn't kill us... because she didn't want to face Prima Stella. That is where she would undoubtedly end up, if she actually killed *me*,' said Lillian. Evelyn would not dare kill a daughter of the First Family of the Morning Star clan, she thought. Well, not outright anyway... but there were always other ways, as she had so recently discovered.

'You're probably wondering why she kept *me* alive,' said Elisedd solemnly.

Lillian gave him an apologetic look.

'I was a human, so she could quite easily have let me die, safe in the knowledge that no consequences would occur. I think it was partly to do with her making me her slave.'

'The other part was probably keeping you alive in the knowledge that I'd died never knowing you survived. Or even if I survived in some form, I would wander about lost in my grief for you. Her sick sweet revenge,' said Lillian furiously.

'If I ever get my hands on her–' said Elisedd.

'When *we* get *our* hands on her,' amended Lillian.

Elisedd nodded his head, and squeezed her hand affectionately as she smiled wearily at him.

He could think more clearly without Evelyn in his mind, and said gravely, 'You know, that was not me that hurt you with the coffin... She had an iron control over my mind... but still, I am sorry to have hurt–'

Lillian covered his mouth with her hand, 'I know. You would never deliberately hurt me. When I looked in your eyes, it was Evelyn looking back,' she said gently.

Elisedd felt the knot in his stomach uncoil. How stupid he had been to ever doubt her love for him.

'I can't believe how far back her plotting and planning actually goes,' said Lillian. 'Though, we have one advantage over her,' she said smiling.

'And what's that?' asked Elisedd, his expression hopeful.

'Evelyn never knew about our child and our grandchildren. She thinks that I have no descendents.'

'Thank God for that. Wait, can a demon pray?' he asked.

'I don't see why not,' said Lillian.

'Lillian, there is one thing you must now do, you cannot put it off any longer...' Elisedd said, turning his head toward the coffin where her body lay sleeping, waiting for her return.

'I'm scared that it won't work, after all this time. When you came back, it was in the same instant. So, it makes sense that your body would accept you.'

With determination in his eyes, Elisedd got up and pulled Lillian to her feet. He held out his hand for her, and she took it, and he led her to the coffin.

'What do I do now?' asked Lillian, who was not quite sure how it worked. How would she make her soul return back to her body?

'Climb in and lie down, then close your eyes, and put the intention in your mind that you want to go deep within yourself. You'll know it's working as you begin to sink into your body as it finally accepts you,' replied Elisedd.

Lillian climbed in holding onto Elisedd's hand as she got onto the table. Taking a deep breath, she began to lie back above her body in the coffin.

'Nothing is happening, I'm just hovering above it,' she said in a disheartened voice.

'It is because you are fighting it. You do not trust yourself enough to let go. Think about why you are doing this...' said Elisedd patiently.

Lillian closed her eyes, and tried to focus on getting back, but that didn't work, either. She tried to clear her mind. *Silence*, she thought.

'Just breathe, love. That's it,' whispered Elisedd. He sounded calm, but secretly feared that it might not work, and looked on desperately as her soul stubbornly refused to sink in.

After about ten minutes, Lillian opened her eyes, frustrated, 'It's no good, this is not working!'

He felt riddled with dread. 'You need to give it time. We knew this was not going to be easy. Do not stop, keep trying... for me,' he added.

Lillian got up, and was dismayed to find herself sitting on top of her body. She stood up and hopped down from the coffin, much to Elisedd's annoyance.

'You are not even trying!' he said accusingly. *It's almost as if she doesn't want to return...* he thought resentfully, as his eyes became glacial.

Lillian went up to him and embraced him. Her head rested against his chest as she listened to the sound of his heart beating strongly; at least he was alive. She could accept her death as long as he lived. She closed her eyes, content to just stand there for a while.

CHAPTER 33

Rowanne just laughed in response as Lady Enid and Evelyn both looked at her as if she had truly lost her mind. *Perhaps I have...* she thought. Pressure built in her chest, and her head ached with the amount of knowledge that was pouring in at an alarming rate.

'Rowanne, are you alright?' asked Lady Enid, placing a hand on her shoulder.

Rowanne patted Lady Enid's hand. She turned to the crowd, 'My Lords and Ladies, you have just witnessed one of your Nobles state that half demons should be killed. Were you referring to me by any chance, Evelyn?' asked Rowanne boldly. There was a collective gasp and fierce whispering broke out; the demons were shocked at the nerve of the human to speak to Evelyn, especially being so informal and insolent as to address her by her first name.

Evelyn froze, slowly turning her head, realising that her power had worn off and that the demons in the room were now beginning to move about freely. There was a look of hatred on their faces; directed towards her.

How had the situation gotten out of hand? They were supposed to hate the bloody Queen, and shred Rowanne to pieces. This was not how it was supposed to unfold. *Think quickly,* thought Evelyn.

The first thing Evelyn did was to hastily remove the last of her magic that she had weaved over the crowd of demons.

Rowanne watched as the demons surged forward, but the soldiers kept them back; but, they too were torn between loyalty for their Queen, and the Noble families they served.

'STOP!' uttered Lady Enid, in a quiet command that carried throughout the Great Hall. All the demons stopped in their tracks. 'This is the Noble Court, where we will behave as civilised demons, and hear the evidence in its entirety before passing judgment. No demon has the right to carry out punishment out of their own volition, that will be decided and acted upon in Prima Stella.'

Rowanne watched as the demons became subdued with the threat of Prima Stella before them. They looked mercilessly at their Queen; their patience would not last forever.

Evelyn seethed with rage as the demons obeyed their Queen. 'Present your evidence, *my lady*!' she said mockingly.

Lady Enid smiled malevolently at Evelyn, who took a step back. *Good, at least she understands me...*

'Rowanne, please continue,' requested Lady Enid.

Evelyn faced the crowd as she piously pleaded her case, 'You can see for yourselves how our beloved Queen dares to allow a half breed to speak before us — as if what she says actually matters. The evidence of the half breed is clearly before you! Let us not waste any more of our valuable time, and declare death upon *it*!' said Evelyn passionately.

'Kill the half breed!' shouted a demon in the crowd. This chant was picked up by the rest of the hall, as they added, 'Death to half breeds!'

'My Lords and Ladies, we should extend this courtesy to all demons who dare to support humans and half breeds,' and turning towards the Queen, Evelyn looked her dead in the eyes as she continued, 'no matter their rank,' she finished triumphantly. There, she had played her ace.

The crowd chanted, their voices full of rage, and Rowanne suspected they would love any excuse to get rid of their monarch, to take her place.

Bravely, Rowanne stepped forward, even though the guards were barely able to keep the mass of demons away from the platform. 'My Lords and Ladies,' she said with great dignity. However, the crowd refused to listen, after all who was she? No one of any real significance or importance.

Rowanne's eyes blazed green as her power flared around her like a shimmering emerald cape. This captured their attention; they were frozen in place by this spectacle. They had arrogantly thought half demons to be beneath their notice. The demons watched the power swirl around Rowanne, who was completely oblivious of it.

'Thank you, for your consideration. Lady Evelyn Blaze of the Adara Clan has condemned all half demons, and in doing so has condemned herself,' said Rowanne in a crystal clear voice.

Evelyn strode towards her. 'Explain yourself? Do not presume to make false allegations they could prove fatal for you.'

'Lady Evelyn and I are more alike than she would care to admit,' stated Rowanne boldly. The demons laughed scathingly in their arrogance.

Evelyn smiled, and condescendingly stated, 'I am a Noble, as well as a daughter of a First Family. What precisely is your status?'

Rowanne smiled beautifully, replying, 'Don't you mean *our* status? You and I are half demons!'

Evelyn lost control, and shoved Rowanne to the floor.

'Hurting me will not change the truth,' said Rowanne, getting up and dusting herself off.

'You will desist, Evelyn,' said Lady Enid, stepping in front of Rowanne.

The situation seemed to be completely out of her control. Lady Enid felt torn: should she do the right thing and in doing so, possibly condemn an entire planet to death, all for Rowanne? She felt drained - sometimes she hated being the ruler. She could not afford to think of herself, to just be Enid.

'It's okay,' whispered Rowanne to Lady Enid. Rowanne's eyes never wavered; there was a determination within her to set things right.

Lady Enid turned to Evelyn, 'Is it true that you have become a half demon? If so, you have committed treason against our world by converting a human.'

The Nobles and other demons could not believe their ears, and a deadly silence descended upon the hall. It was unthinkable for a Noble of all demons, and that too from a member of a First Family. Now, instead of one execution, they would witness two; the second would be recorded in their history.

There were whispers and rumours concerning the scandal surrounding the Morning Star Clan; in particular, their former Princess Lillian. Now it seemed the Adara Clan were also suffering the same fate. The demons watched as misfortune struck the Noble families. The Nobles in the hall felt an uneasiness, it seemed as if for the first time, their titles meant nothing; they were not truly as invincible as they liked to think. Worse yet, they could hear the jeers coming from the lesser demons at the back of the hall.

Rowanne felt the tension in the hall rise. *They could break out in a fight...* she thought. *The Queen could very well be in danger, this was not what I wanted...*

The Queen stepped before Evelyn, and said, 'Give me your hand, and I will prove, as you claim, that you are not a half demon.'

'No. I do not trust a demon who spends her time in the company of half breeds. I want another independent demon to verify my status,' said Evelyn coldly.

'Very well, as you wish, my dear,' said Lady Enid, beckoning a royal guard to step forward.

Rowanne kept a straight face as she realised the guard coming onto the platform was none other than Alexander's cousin, Kieran of the Black Rose Clan.

Evelyn gave her hand to Kieran, and looked at him intently; there was a promise of death within her eyes, should he fail her.

No, Kieran, thought Rowanne. *Don't do it, don't risk your life.* He turned his head as if he had heard her, and gave her a quick look. *Oh no...* she thought. He was very much like Alexander; willing to do the right thing, even if it cost him his life.

Kieran's eyes sparkled with a green light as his power flowed over Evelyn, and revealed her new form as a half demon; they could see the immortal part of her gone, ripped out.

Kieran let go, and faced his Queen, 'Your Majesty, is it your wish that I detain Lady Evelyn?'

'You worthless demon, do not underestimate me. Approach me at your own peril...' warned Evelyn.

Evelyn called upon her power, and it began to fill her whole being. *They think they have got the best of me?! They think I'm weak, because I am a half demon. Useless demons, the lot of them. I'm worth more than all of them combined.* Her eyes changed from their natural blue to a blackish green colour.

'Guards, detain her at once!' commanded Lady Enid.

Rowanne watched, as half a dozen royal guards raced to Evelyn, securing her. Kieran used metal cuffs to secure her hands, as Evelyn looked contemptuously at him.

'This way, my lady,' said Kieran, as he slowly led her off the platform.

Evelyn watched Lady Enid smile at Rowanne. *Look at them rejoicing as if they have won.* She bowed her head and waited, noting that there were more guards in front of her, than at her back. The Queen had no protection at all; assuming the danger had passed. *Foolish, really.*

Evelyn judged the moment to be right, and let loose with an energy blast that threw the guards off the platform. She quickly picked up a sword that one of the guards had so conveniently dropped for her benefit.

Rowanne saw the murderous intent in Evelyn's eyes, and Lady Enid was momentarily distracted, appearing dazed after the blast. After all, she had been in closer proximity to it than Rowanne, and struggled to now stand.

Rowanne had also been thrown back. Remarkably though, the throne was untouched. Her demon blood had helped her to recover quickly from the shock, but even so, she too struggled to stand, and watched in slow motion as Evelyn ran towards the queen, raising the sword above her.

Evelyn gazed triumphantly down at the Queen, and could feel the royal guards cautiously approaching her from all sides. 'They'll be too late, my Queen,' she laughed. 'I have been at your side and have served you for seventy years! So, it is only right that *we* should die together. Don't you want to be with your daughter again?!'

Evelyn raised her blade high as the Queen looked at her defiantly; Lady Enid would look death in the eyes. Evelyn brought down the sword in one brutal blow, but to her horror the person it went through was not the Queen... She screamed in frustration.

The shock waves of what had just transpired reverberated through the hall. 'Get her!' shouted the demons from the Noble Families. 'Treason,' they yelled.

A single voice cut through the din, 'Rowanne!' screamed Alexander.

Alexander had found himself outside of the Morning Star Family's abode, and was out of his mind and in a daze. It had taken him a while to piece together that he had been possessed by a demonic entity.

Instinct had led him back towards the Noble Court. He had been forced to fight his way through the crowd of demons.

Then before his mind could make sense of the scene before him, it was over. He had been too late to prevent Rowanne from rushing with inhuman speed towards the Queen, and throwing her body over her just as Evelyn plunged the sword down, impaling Rowanne.

He made his way slowly towards Rowanne with a sharp pain in his heart that he could not identify. His breathing was shallow and the room seemed to waver before him. He walked up the steps towards her, pausing briefly as he noticed his cousin's body below; blood coated his forehead. Kieran lay amongst the other soldiers caught up in the blast. *He's not breathing...* thought Alexander dispassionately, as another piece of him broke from within.

The hall of demons was subdued in the wake of this tragedy. They could not believe what they had witnessed. Why would a half demon risk her life for one of them? Especially knowing that she would most certainly be facing the death penalty at Prima Stella.

Alexander walked towards Rowanne, noticed that remarkably she seemed to be breathing, and rushed to her side.

'Check Lady Enid first, help her,' said Rowanne weakly.

The royal guards converged around the bodies, unsure of how to proceed, not wanting to hurt their Queen. They listened in astonishment, amazed at the bravery of the human impaled on the sword; if this is what it means to be a half breed... they thought. Rowanne was challenging their established world view; one insignificant human...

'Move back, let me ascertain if the Queen is hurt,' said Alexander in a clear command. The soldiers stepped back as one, but stayed on high alert in case anything else should happen. 'Keep her back,' he said referring to Evelyn, who was hidden from view by the soldiers surrounding her.

The soldiers walked to the end of the platform away from their Queen, as a seemingly subdued Evelyn walked quietly amidst them.

Well, at last my work is done, thought Evelyn, and smirked as she thought of the poor fools trapped within the confines of her personal chamber. *Now at last you get to spend eternity alone Lillian, with your dead love...* She was sure that the sword had passed through the Queen as well. Her soldiers had taken care of Driskell and the half breed he was so intent in keeping from her notice.

Alexander crouched low to the ground and looked beneath Rowanne. There was a steady pool of blood dripping down, but not as much as he had thought there'd be. The sword had gone straight through, and extended out the other side. As for the Queen, she was not moving and there was blood on her clothes...

'Help me,' he called to one of the guards. He was shocked, as before him stood his cousin. 'I... I thought you were dead,' said Alexander breathlessly.

'I'm harder to get rid of than that, and you of all people should know it. I admit, I'm not looking my best right now,' said Kieran.

Kieran helped to gently lift Rowanne up just enough that Alexander could get under her to pull the Queen out without hurting either of them. Kieran knelt on the ground, supporting all of Rowanne's weight.

Alexander's heart broke as he looked at Rowanne's broken and limp form. *How can she still be smiling, trying to comfort me, when she is the one who needs help?* There was a helpless anger within him, and he did not feel stable right now. He was a demon on the edge; Rowanne was the only one keeping him sane, for now.

'Alexander, how is the Queen?' asked Kieran, gently reminding Alexander of his duty: first and foremost to their Queen.

Lady Enid stirred within his arms, and he laid her down gently onto the floor. 'My Lady Enid, are you hurt?' asked Alexander.

Lady Enid's eyes held a haunted look as she turned to Rowanne. A single tear slid down her cheek. 'Help me to sit up.' Alexander accordingly helped her, supporting her weight. 'Thank you, I am well, as unlikely as that is to believe. It is Rowanne who needs our urgent attention. The force of the attack caught me off guard, and this is not my blood,' she said, her voice coming out faintly.

'Get help for the Queen,' commanded Alexander. The royal guards hurried away to get the medical supplies.

'Oh, Rowanne, my dear, you saved me.' Lady Enid wanted to reach out and hold her hand, but she could not, especially, in the presence of all these demons.

Rowanne nodded her head in understanding; it was too painful to speak anymore. The demon blood was to thank for her not dying instantly, as well as the fact that the sword was stopping her blood from rushing out in one go. Once it was removed, she was fairly certain that she would not have long to live.

'Here, help the Queen,' said Alexander, as he passed her to a guard.

Lady Enid reluctantly let herself be led to the throne where she took her rightful place, but not where she longed to be: by Rowanne's side.

'Let me help you to carry her, Kieran?' asked Alexander, and between them, they started to carry Rowanne off the platform.

Evelyn's eyes flashed in malice. *The Queen lives?! No!* This was not allowed. *The audacity of that half breed, why could she not just have died?!* The soldiers faced outwards, assured that she was no longer a threat. *That is your downfall; when will they ever learn?*

Evelyn split her consciousness, focusing her intent, and suddenly the sword was violently pulled out of Rowanne's chest. She smiled wickedly as she heard Alexander shouting for her to be subdued. She watched as Rowanne bled to death

- they could not stop the rate at which the blood flowed out.

Just as the soldiers turned on Evelyn with their swords pointed at her head, she closed her eyes and collapsed to the floor, as she sent her spirit on its last leg to finally be rid of her old friend and adversary.

CHAPTER 34

Lillian pulled back from Elisedd and looked at him with dread.

'What is it, love?' he asked.

'Something's wrong... I can feel it. Something terrible has taken place in the Great Hall!' said Lillian, feeling uneasy.

'Who else was in the hall with you? I'm sorry, I did not recognise everyone on the platform.'

'Our great granddaughter was up there, along with my mother, and a half demon, and... Driskell.'

'Rowanne!' said Elisedd sharply. Only now realising from Lillian's memories that the woman with the long brown hair and green eyes who had spoken forcefully to him had in fact been his great granddaughter. *I did not even realise...* His sole focus had been on getting Lillian away.

'If they dare lay a finger on her...' said Elisedd, his eyes burning with a violet green flame.

Lillian looked with fascination at him. *How did I not notice that before...* she mused, as she took a step towards him and cupped his face between her hands. She looked deep into his eyes - there was something else mixed in with his demon blood, but what...?

Elisedd bent his head closer to her, just as a sword was thrust straight through his chest. He pushed Lillian back out of instinct. She screamed as she was thrown back into her coffin, and the force was enough to propel her soul back into her body. It had helped that her mind had been distracted, so that her body had accepted her back without resistance.

However, the timing was completely wrong as she lay trapped within her body, and looked out helplessly.

Elisedd staggered to her coffin, and leaning over, he brushed a bloody hand across her cheek. 'My love,' he said, barely able to speak.

He knew it would take time for Lillian to fully merge with her body. She would not be able to lift a finger until mind, body and spirit connected. Also, she would not be able to speak.

'At least I had a moment with you. I am lucky in many ways, I never thought I would see you again. At least now I can tell you how very much-' he coughed up blood and wiping it away, smiled tenderly at her. 'I-love-you-' he said, fighting to get each word out, before suddenly collapsing on top of her.

Lillian screamed within her mind. How was she going to live when she had just witnessed her love dying a second time? There was only so much a person could endure before they snapped. *Elisedd, Elisedd,* she called for him as tears slid down her face; what good were they to him, or to her?

Evelyn leaned over, 'Now really, you brought this onto yourself. If you had just let him go all those years back, and not encouraged his delusions, then he *would* have lived. You have all of eternity now to reflect and repent,' she said cruelly.

Lillian looked with unbridled fury at Evelyn; she would not allow such a reprehensible demon as her to live. She felt the power within her build. True, she could not use her limbs, but there were other ways... she was a demon, after all. Just as she was about to let loose, she was suddenly blinded by a flash of power.

The room was shrouded in a violet mist, as sparks of green energy flashed, bouncing off the walls. There was a scream, and Lillian could not see where Evelyn had disappeared to.

The room plunged into darkness as each and every candle was extinguished.

Elisedd, she screamed, and watched in horror as the magic descended upon them both. *Was this Evelyn's doing?* she wondered. She and Elisedd were covered in a shower of green and violet power. Her skin glowed and pulsed with the light. Meanwhile, a mass of white light began to build behind Elisedd. Lillian prepared herself for the next inevitable explosion of power, and her last thought was, *I'm sorry, my love...* and closed her eyes just as the light reached its pinnacle, and exploded.

CHAPTER 35

Alexander craned his neck and looked at Evelyn's collapsed body. 'Check on her, she may be feigning.'

He watched as the guards carefully checked Evelyn cautiously in case of another onslaught of power.

'Stand aside. I know how to deal with this,' said Lady Enid. The guards were reluctant to allow their Queen to go near such a dangerous demon, and an unpredictable one at that; nevertheless, they obeyed.

Lady Enid encased Evelyn's body within a silver sphere, then ordered the guards to take it to the prison reserved especially for their kind. She would like to see Evelyn break out of *that*!

Lady Enid addressed the demons, 'Remember what you have witnessed here today. It was one of our own that attacked your Queen and also dared to challenge the order of our ways. And, it was a *human* who saved me, and risked her life...' finished Lady Enid, as the weight of her words carried authority throughout the hall.

The demons were subdued for the moment.

Lady Enid went over to Alexander, 'We need to help her now,' and at the look of concern on his face, she replied, 'do not worry about them. I'm not overly concerned about what they think right now. I will not stand aside any longer and let those I care about die!' *This is for you, my Lillian*, thought Lady Enid.

Rowanne suddenly went limp in Alexander's hands as her eyes fluttered closed.

'Rowanne, wake up! Don't you dare give up on me,' said Alexander angrily.

A soft violet-white light started to emanate from within Rowanne, and began to lift her body, much to Alexander's surprise. The celestial yin yang tattoo on her left shoulder began to change and formed into a new avatar, changing with it Rowanne's very essence, transforming her.

The light started to build, becoming brighter, blinding everyone in the hall. 'Take cover, Your Majesty,' said Alexander. The soldiers hurriedly took her down the stairs, trying to get her as far away from the platform as possible. Alexander shouted to the rest of the demons below in the hall to take cover.

Alexander would not leave Rowanne's side, even if this was their last moment together in this existence. He smiled down at her and closed his eyes, just as the light from within her exploded...

The platform was bathed in a beautiful golden radiance. The light began to dim slowly, and it was easier to see what remained. Many of the demons still had light spots dancing before their eyes.

Lady Enid made her way carefully back up to the platform. She had been unaffected by the blast. The hall appeared undamaged, and the demons were unharmed; the only two casualties appeared to be Alexander and Rowanne.

She was frightened of what she might find as she took the last step, and upon reaching the platform, she stood still...

Lady Enid did not know what to make of the scene before her. There laying on the floor were Alexander and Rowanne. They seemed to be sleeping side by side as Rowanne's hand was encased in Alexander's; they seemed at peace.

The royal guards pushed the Queen back, but she demanded to be let through.

'Please, my Lady Enid. We are not sure how to proceed, and have not to my knowledge dealt with *this* type of situation before. It could be dangerous,' said Kieran.

'It is my duty as Queen to ascertain what exactly has occurred. You are permitted to stay by my side and act accordingly, if anything should happen. But for now, you will not obstruct me. Is that understood?' Lady Enid did not seek permission; after all, she was the Queen.

Lady Enid knelt down to look at the bodies. She took Alexander's pulse, then Rowanne's.

Turning her head to look up at Kieran, she said, 'They are alive, against all odds.'

'Where did the sword go? There is only a tear in her clothing to suggest it was ever there. She has stopped bleeding as well,' said Kieran, dumbfounded by what he was looking upon.

Lady Enid looked around the hall, and spied a stained glass window at the back. It had not shattered, but bizarrely the sword had gone partway through it to the other side. She pointed behind her, and Kieran looked in wonder.

The stained glass had an image of a demon and an angel with a human standing between them. The sword seemed to go through the human. There were fissures from where the blade had struck, but for now it refused to shatter.

'Do you think that is symbolic in some way?' asked Lady Enid; it was ironic to say the least.

'Looking at these two... it could well be,' said Kieran perplexed.

Rowanne began to twitch, her hand starting to move. Alexander began to stir too, slowly attempting to open his eyes, but it was still too bright for him.

'They are waking up,' said Lady Enid. 'Give them some room, everyone stand back. Now, form a line before them,' the soldiers stood like a wall facing out at the crowd of demons, giving the Queen the space and privacy she needed.

'Alexander, can you hear me?' she asked as she knelt beside him, while Kieran knelt beside Rowanne on the opposite side.

Alexander's eyes finally stayed open, and looked up at Lady Enid questioningly. He turned his head to look at who was holding his hand, and his breathing nearly stopped. 'Rowanne,' he said forlornly. Everything that had just happened came crashing down upon him. He struggled to sit up, and Lady Enid helped him, for which he was grateful.

He knelt beside the prone figure. 'Rowanne, wake up.' *You had better not have sent me back alone...* 'Wake up,' he repeated angrily, whilst shaking her gently by the shoulders, afraid of hurting her.

When she did not respond, Alexander's heart nearly gave out, but suddenly her eyelids fluttered. Slowly she began to come around, her eyes reluctantly opening. The first thing she saw was Alexander's severe expression, coupled with the storm that seemed to rage deep within his eyes, and as for his mouth? Well, it was more of a scowl than a smile really.

'Good to see you, too,' whispered Rowanne, and coughed to clear her throat. She looked down at the hand holding hers, and then back up at him. 'I wouldn't have come back if I knew that this is what I have to look forward to!' she smiled mockingly.

'How many times have I told you, not to play the lone hero!' he added gruffly.

'Fine. Help me up, I'm not feeling too heroic at the moment. My back is killing me, I feel burdened. One more thing, I seem to remember you holding me at my finest moment...' she said, her eyebrow raised. *Well, if exploding in a ball of light counts as a fine moment; more like my last moment!* She laughed as Alexander waved away her comment indignantly.

'Erm, Rowanne, there is something a little strange about you... Now, don't panic,' said Alexander.

Accordingly, she panicked, her heart racing. *Maybe I've been hurt in the explosion in some way... But I feel fine.* She wriggled her fingers and toes, and moved her arms and legs; everything was working perfectly. She felt her face; no, nothing hurt there, though as she touched it, she came away with dried blood. *Okay, not good, but still nothing to worry about.*

Turning to Alexander, she said, 'See, there's nothing wrong with me–' Rowanne was cut off as something huge wacked her in the face. She froze. Her panicked eyes locked with Alexander's, but strangely he was calm. *Why does he have a weird smile on his face?* she wondered.

Rowanne breathed deeply and whatever it was went away, but then it came right back a second later. 'Make it stop! What is it...?' she asked Alexander, as she gripped his arm.

'Rowanne, I must say you've *grown* in more than one way, besides the fact that you nearly ripped my arm out! This *thing* that keeps hitting you is... another appendage, or a pair, I should say, that you have gained,' said Alexander highly amused.

This time Rowanne grabbed it, bending it slightly, though if she tugged on it too much, it hurt her back. *Oh my God!* she thought. *I used to tease Alexander about growing horns as a demon; turns out I'm the one that's grown wings!*

Rowanne looked with a mixture of trepidation and awe at her wings. They were beautiful, with a long wingspan. The feathers were so soft and a brilliant white glow emanated from them.

'Your eyes have changed as well, my dear. They are no longer green but the violet inherent to our Royal family,' said Lady Enid. She felt a recognition within her that Rowanne belonged to her clan.

'What? But how could this have happened?' asked Rowanne, scared at what she'd see in the mirror, *Will I even recognise myself...* she wondered. She looked at Alexander, her eyes widening in surprise, 'Alexander, I'm sorry, but whatever that blast did to me, it also seems as if you didn't escape unchanged either...' she said, pointing to his back.

Alexander flexed his muscles, and a dark wing came flying at his face, but stopped short. He looked at Rowanne calmly, and said, 'I was wondering what that cumbersome thing upon my back was. But I put it out of mind, focused as I was on *you*...'

'How can you take this so well? I'm panicking at the thought of turning up to work with two wings protruding from my back! Not to mention I'll never be able to wear clothes properly again!' said Rowanne, knowing she sounded hysterical.

'Just breathe. It's not so bad, is it? We're both alive, it's just that...'

'What? Say it,' said Rowanne, expecting the worst.

Alexander looked at her solemnly, replying, 'The small matter of you turning us into... angels!' he laughed heartily. He wondered why Rowanne's wings were white whilst his were black... *One of those mysteries,* he thought.

Trust Alexander to laugh at the most inappropriate time. Rowanne felt angry, but this only served to make her wings flap up and down uncontrollably. She watched in annoyance as Alexander and Kieran fell to pieces laughing, and even Lady Enid was trying unsuccessfully to hide her mirth behind her hand.

That's it, if they don't want to help, I'll figure it out on my own. Rowanne did not care one iota, if the demons tried to stop her, she could put these wings to good use and swat them away!

Rowanne stood up as the anxiety and frustration built within her. Suddenly her mind went hazy; it had become too much for her, and she felt fear at the sight of her wings moving powerfully up and down.

'Alexander, what's happening to me?' she shouted, as she began to rise up. She flew above the guards and kept rising. Below her the hall of demons looked up in awe, their mouths hanging open in surprise.

Suddenly, Rowanne stopped rising, but thankfully her wings kept flapping, so that she hovered above them all. The power within her was feeding the necessary information to her mind, so that she could gain control of the wings. She slipped down a couple of times. *Keep your mind clear,* she thought. *Accept it.*

It was like a muscle she had never used before, that was the only way she could describe it. The process of questioning how it worked confused her mind, and once the link was lost, she'd start to waver and fall.

Alexander watched her - she was by no means safe. He had accepted the wings as being a natural part of him. Closing his eyes, he focused and steadied his breathing, and was up and away as a powerful updraft carried him to Rowanne.

He smiled at her bemusedly, 'Rowanne, you do seem to find yourself in the most awkward situations possible. As a demon, I thought I'd seen everything, but then *you* came along and turned my world upside down,' he said, winking at her.

'That's rich! I could say the same of you. I was a perfectly ordinary human, before you came along. Now look at me — I'm an angel!' Rowanne glared at him, and for good measure added, '*You* should come with a health warning!'

Alexander laughed darkly, 'Rowanne, look at where you are.'

Rowanne was amazed to find herself on the ground. Alexander had distracted her enough, that she had descended naturally without even thinking about it.

The guards stood before the Queen, with their spears held out towards Rowanne and Alexander.

'Put them away, these two do not pose a threat,' said Lady Enid.

Kieran gave the command to stand down, and duly the soldiers stood to either side of the Queen in a defensive formation.

'Rowanne, my dear, welcome to the family!' said Lady Enid. Rowanne went to her with Alexander by her side. Lady Enid turned to the Nobles in the court. 'My Lords and Ladies, may I present–'

'My great granddaughter,' said a voice from the side of the platform, cutting off Lady Enid.

Lady Enid froze and the soldiers converged into a protective stance before her, blocking her view. She heard footsteps approaching, coming to a stop before the soldiers.

'Now really, is this any way to treat your Princess?' asked Lillian boldly.

'Let her through,' said Lady Enid weakly, her heart still recovering from all that she had witnessed. The soldiers parted, and before her stood her daughter.

Lady Enid stepped forward hesitantly. Lillian appeared to be alive... She touched her daughter, and inhaled sharply; she felt solid. Wasting no more time, she fiercely hugged Lillian. She may not have understood how her daughter had come back, but she was just grateful that she had.

Lillian felt tears running down her face as she hugged her mother back, feeling her touch for the first time in seventy years.

'Lillian, are you really back?' asked Lady Enid hoarsely.

'It seems I am, and,' bending close to her mother's ear she whispered, 'I have Elisedd and Rowanne to thank for that,' as her mother looked at her curiously.

Lady Enid knew that Lillian would explain later when there were not so many inquisitive demons about.

'Let me speak with them, Mother,' said Lillian, and a single tear slid down her mother's cheek. Lillian could tell how deeply it had touched her.

'My Lords and Ladies, the rumours of my demise were sadly exaggerated. Furthermore, I am back to take my rightful place,' she looked out at the sea of demons; they were frightened and shocked, for before them stood their next

Queen. She was a ghost no longer, and had come back from death — resurrected; or, so it appeared to them.

Lillian gestured for Rowanne to stand before her.

'This full bodied demon before you has now ascended to our rightful form, our true form, that of an Angel. May I present, Ms Rowanne Knight, my great granddaughter, and the next heir of the Morning Star Clan.'

The full force of the words reverberated through the room, and a deathly silence descended. The demons found it difficult to digest the news, especially those of the Noble clans who began to realise the full magnitude of power that belonged to their Queen; and was now also painfully obvious in her descendents.

However, the demons owed their allegiance to the Queen, and now also to the Princesses. They all knelt as one, heads bowed and hands placed upon their hearts as they paid obeisance to the First Family of Demon World.

Rowanne turned her head and looked at Lillian, shocked. *No! What did she mean?* She turned to Alexander, who shook his head, indicating that this was not the right time to question her.

Rowanne noticed a tall man beside Lillian, who held her hand, and he too, had white wings. His green eyes were currently trained on her, and he gave her a warm smile. Rowanne quickly faced the crowd of demons. An unsettling feeling had come over her, for a moment it was as if she were looking at a relative, his features were so familiar...

'May I also present my consort, Lord Elisedd Knight, and to clarify for those of you who may question his status... He is also a full demon. Furthermore, the Royal family will cooperate fully with the Noble Court to ascertain our status, and accordingly a further meeting will be held to discuss the findings,' stated Lillian in a clear and confident voice, daring the Nobles to challenge her openly.

The Nobles all stood, as silence rang clearly in the hall. They looked on in trepidation and incredulity at the latest additions to the royal family, not quite trusting what they saw. However, their history was coming back to them in the form of the three angels that stood before them. Angels! They thought, after so long... What could this herald...?

Lillian bowed to the demons, and then turning to her family, she whispered, 'Let's get out of here while they are still in an accommodating mood!' No one needed to be told twice, as they gracefully, but rather quickly, made their exit from the Noble Court.

CHAPTER 36

Lillian assembled everyone in the Queen's quarters. Unfortunately, there was one unwelcome addition to their group. 'Are you sure you want him here?' Lillian asked Rowanne, glaring at Driskell, who sat on the sofa he shared with Amanda; to her consternation.

'I am in complete agreement with Lillian,' said Elisedd, who would like nothing better than to confront the man whom he'd had the misfortune to consider a friend.

The Queen was about to call in the guards to have Driskell escorted out, but Rowanne intervened.

'There has already been enough misunderstandings, we shouldn't make the mistake of adding another. I think we should do him the courtesy of allowing him to tell his side of the story,' said Rowanne.

Driskell looked suspiciously at Rowanne, causing Amanda to huff in exasperation as she nudged him in the side, but this only served to antagonise him further; he scowled at her.

'Just tell them! I'd rather not spend any more time here than I have to. I have people waiting for me back home,' said Amanda, equally peeved with Driskell.

Driskell felt a mixture of feelings; he was confused, hurt and angry at being so casually dismissed from Amanda's life,

595

and his face once more wore a mask of stone as he let the cold encase his heart.

'What is it that you want to know?' Driskell asked Lillian in a bitter voice.

Lillian counted to ten to calm herself down as anger raged within her. Why was he feigning ignorance? 'Why did *you* betray us? I considered you a dear friend...'

Elisedd shifted uneasily in his chair as his eyes seethed with unbridled rage.

'Why is it that people make so many unjustified assumptions when it comes to me?' asked Driskell blithely.

Amanda could tell it was taking a toll on him. The whole situation was volatile; it did not help that they were confined together in a small room, and they could very well end up hurting each other if they were not careful.

Amanda took a deep breath, and wondered, *Do I trust this man beside me?* All the evidence was against him, and there was no one willing to stand up for him; but then again, he had saved her life... She held his hand, and said, 'I think we all need to take a step back, and give him a chance. Rowanne is right, until we have all the facts, we should not condemn him.' Amanda was more than a little uncomfortable as she looked at everyone, and could tell they were confused by her unexpected gesture. Frankly, Rowanne was the only one not surprised, as she nodded in support. She thanked God she would always have her cousin's support.

Amanda turned to Driskell, and looked at him encouragingly. His eyes widened in surprise, and he gave her a strange look... It's probably disbelief, she thought, not wanting to dwell on it too much.

Driskell looked for a minute longer than was necessary, and to Amanda's mortification, he squeezed her hand before swiftly facing the room full of his potential executioners.

'Lillian, I never intended to go against you. And, Elisedd, you know how much I valued our friendship,' replied Driskell, and still did to this day.

'But you helped Evelyn anyway. So, our *friendship* as you put it, did not mean a damn thing in place of getting a promotion and becoming Enforcer to the Noble Court!' said Lillian coldly.

'Evelyn told me of your relationship with Elisedd. She was concerned with your welfare, and asked me to do a background check on him. I duly verified all the information for her, and told her there was nothing to be concerned about,' said Driskell.

'Why did you not come to me and tell me of this?' asked Lillian.

'She seemed satisfied with my findings, and never mentioned it to me again. I thought in all honesty that the matter had been dropped. I didn't realise how far she'd pursue it,' replied Driskell desperately.

'What about the rest of the information you gathered on our relationship solidly for almost two years, that you so conveniently gave to Evelyn to use against us in Prima Stella?' asked Lillian, the fury rife in her voice. She felt Elisedd's reassuring presence, and patted his hand; still trying to get used to having him around again. Elisedd looked at her in wonder, and Lillian remembered the moment he had almost died.

She had been trapped within her body in the coffin. She had been screaming in her mind, and her heart hurt as it broke a second time at the sight of Elisedd slumped over the coffin, bleeding to death. She remembered looking into his eyes, and then the explosion...

When Lillian had eventually regained consciousness, she had found herself on the floor, the coffins lying shattered beside her. The room was in semi darkness, most of the candles extinguished. Her heart had stopped beating at the sight of Elisedd lying on the floor against one side of the room - the wall seemed to have blown out behind him. Testing her legs and arms she found to her relief that she had finally regained

597

control of her body, and proceeded to make her way over the rubble towards him.

'Elisedd, can you hear me?' asked Lillian.

She looked in wonder, as spread out behind him were large beautiful white wings. She stroked them hesitantly.

Elisedd's eyes began to slowly open, and in a hoarse voice he replied, 'I think you are taking advantage of me, love, in my weakened state.'

She thumped him lightly in the arm, before resting her head on his chest, and hugged him fiercely.

Elisedd looked down at her as strong emotions chased across his face. Bending his head, he placed a gentle kiss on top of her head, and embraced her, wrapping his arms protectively around her.

They were content to just be for a few moments. Reluctantly, Lillian began to pull back, much to Elisedd's annoyance, causing her to break out in laughter.

Elisedd got up with Lillian's help, and together they surveyed the destruction around them. 'I see that you're back where you belong,' said Elisedd.

'I could not have done it without you, though your timing was appalling!' said Lillian with a glower.

'It's sort of hard to think, with a murderous demon trying to kill the love of my life. So, you can forgive a man for acting recklessly.'

'Where is she?' asked Lillian, looking at the empty room.

'I'm not too sure. After the explosion she disappeared. Either she was caught up in the explosion,' he smiled unrepentantly at the thought, 'or, it's more than likely she made a hasty exit once she was convinced of our demise,' said Elisedd, as anger flashed in his eyes.

Lillian stepped close, circling his waist with her arms, and Elisedd reciprocated, clasping his hands tightly behind her back, scared to death of losing her again. 'I am not going anywhere without you again!' said Lillian firmly.

Elisedd laughed darkly as a wicked look came into his eyes, 'As if you even had a choice...' he said, teasing her.

'Elisedd, I think you've been holding out on me... I thought you were a nice, normal human, turns out-' said Lillian.

'That I am a man of mystery, and more wonderful than you could ever have imagined,' he goaded, interrupting her.

Lillian gave him an aggrieved look. 'I'm serious, did you know about your heritage?'

Elisedd looked thoughtful, 'My family never told me that we had angel blood within us. It is as much of a mystery to me as it is to you. They will have much to explain to us when we return.'

Lillian was uncomfortable at the idea of returning back to the palace after so long. There was also the minor issue of being brought back to life... How would they be received... she wondered.

'You are not alone, we will be together when the time comes. Let us take it one step at a time. Speaking of which, it is time we leave this hell hole, and help our Rowanne, and your mother.'

'How could I have forgotten? Evelyn could be up there right now causing mayhem, and who knows what state we will find them in. Oh, and let us not forget the hall full of demons out for blood!' said Lillian.

'Hold on, love. I'll take us up,' said Elisedd. Lillian smiled at him warmly as she stepped completely into his arms. Elisedd spun and in the next instant a portal opened on the platform. They had arrived in the Noble Court.

'Lillian? Lillian, are you alright?' asked Rowanne anxiously, kneeling before her trying to get her attention.

Lillian was brought out of her reverie, 'Sorry, I was somewhere else...' she said, and patted her hand. Rowanne left her and sat beside Alexander. *She must have so many questions to ask me, but she sits quietly with infinite patience,* thought Lillian. Rowanne gave her a peeved look, destroying the effect.

'Lillian, I never collected any other evidence. I don't know what she told you, but it is a complete lie. Do you not remember the conversation we had?' asked Driskell.

'What are you talking about?' asked Lillian, clearly confused.

'You and Elisedd both came to me by the time it was too late, once you realised that a Noble had collected evidence against you. I went to the Noble Court and learnt that evidence had been presented before the committee,' replied Driskell.

'I cannot recall Lillian and I speaking to you about it,' said Elisedd, mistrusting Driskell.

'Neither do I! I would not have forgotten-' said Lillian.

'But you could have been *made* to forget,' interrupted Rowanne, as everyone's attention in the room turned sharply in her direction.

Alexander looked repentantly at Rowanne. She touched his arm lightly, and shook her head.

'Rowanne is right. She can attest to the fact that I did the same to her,' admitted Alexander. 'I thought I was saving her by suppressing her memories, and in doing so keeping her away from Demon World. After all, even if the Courts were to question her, they would not be able to get much information from her.'

Driskell gave Alexander a contemplative look. *So, that is partly the reason why I could not get any real information out of her,* he felt Amanda's eyes boring into him. She gave him a disgusted look as he turned to her, but he was not bothered in the slightest as he whispered dispassionately, 'Once a detective, always...' he trailed off.

Perhaps not everyone can be redeemed, thought Amanda, looking especially at Driskell. *Or could they...*

'You think that Evelyn tampered with our memories?' asked Lillian, really considering the idea for the first time.

'I think that could be a real possibility. Do you remember much of what happened around the time of...' Alexander tapered off uncomfortably, not wanting to bring up their painful past.

'It's alright,' said Lillian reassuringly. 'Actually, when I think back, I find it hazy. Initially, I thought that it was to do with my departing, that I would naturally forget things, but now I wonder... Elisedd, what do you remember?'

'I have a strong feeling that Driskell is behind everything,' replied Elisedd.

'Are you sure he actually did anything?' asked Rowanne, much to Driskell's surprise.

'No, now that you ask. I do not have a clear memory of him going against us. But I do have an intense feeling of rage and unease whenever I think of him,' replied Elisedd, less certain of the truth than before.

'It's the same with me,' said Lillian. 'There's a strong feeling within me that I should not trust Driskell, but when I try to reason it out, it eludes me. My memory has become less than reliable.'

'I think Evelyn used strong magic to imprison not only your minds...' Alexander said to Lillian and Elisedd, and turning to the Queen, he continued, 'forgive me for saying this, Lady Enid, but I believe she also influenced your mind. If you really give it some consideration, you will begin to see how you became more *amenable* to her wishes,' he added politely, not wanting to insult his Queen.

The Queen was silent. *It could be true...* she thought. Her memories were not as reliable as she wished them to be. She too had thought Driskell to be the executioner of her daughter, and her cold encounters with him, as he appeared to mock her at every turn, had only compounded her belief.

'Alexander, you might be onto something,' replied Lady Enid reluctantly. However, she still felt a deep-seated rage inside of herself whenever she looked at Driskell, and she found it hard to believe that he had not been an accomplice.

Driskell contemplated deeply on what he was hearing. The pieces were slowly falling into place for him, but even so, he could not bring himself to reconcile the Queen's actions which had led to her daughter's death; regardless of the reasons behind them.

'Who would ever have thought Evelyn capable of such treachery. I am sorry to say, my dear Lillian, that I allowed her to come close to me, but I would *never* have allowed her to take your place, that was all in her mind!' said Lady Enid sorrowfully, ashamed at having allowed herself to be deceived.

'We were all deceived, Mother. She orchestrated everything, taking care of every little detail. From gathering information, and then in all likelihood, having her soldiers present it stealthily to the Noble Court on her behalf, but without disclosing her name. No wonder we were sent straight to Prima Stella without having a proper trial!' said Lillian.

'Not to mention the fact she carefully planned our deaths - this part you may not have been aware of,' said Elisedd quietly.

'I want to know how it is that you survived?' asked Lady Enid. She held her daughter's hand, as Lillian recounted the events. 'I have never encountered such an evil and depraved mind,' she said afterwards.

'My immortality has been returned to me, and bizarrely Evelyn's blood exchange has had some unexpected effects on Elisedd. He is now partly an angel and a demon, and has gained an immortal existence...' said Lillian.

Elisedd smiled affectionately at Lillian, as he put his arm around her shoulders. 'I could not think of a better way to spend it than with you,' he said, looking deep into her eyes, taking the news in his stride.

The Queen gazed contentedly upon them, her heart felt light; it was as if a weight had been lifted.

'Hang on a minute,' said Rowanne, interrupting the moment. 'What about Alexander, has his immortality returned?' she asked hopefully.

'Rowanne,' said Alexander.

'Why are you all looking at me like that?' She saw mild amusement in Lady Enid's eyes. Lillian was giving her a disdainful look, as if she had not grasped the obvious. Though, the worse by far was Alexander, who was smiling roguishly at her with one of his famous idiotic knowing looks.

Alexander gave her a dismayed look, before replying, 'Yes, Rowanne, I'm an immortal again, but...'

'That's great! Thank God, for that,' she said, sighing with relief. Finally the knot within her loosened; she had been carrying the guilt of destroying his life, for so long. She wondered how she would ever be able to repay his kindness, but more than that...

'I haven't finished,' said Alexander exasperated with her, after hearing her thoughts. Holding her gently by the shoulders, he looked at her compassionately, 'Rowanne, you are also one of us now...' he said ruefully.

'I know. I'm a half demon and an angel,' she said resignedly.

Lillian gave her a disparaging look; what was she going to do with her great granddaughter. 'He's trying to tell you that *you* are also an immortal now!' said Lillian.

Rowanne laughed nervously. 'Uh-huh. Shouldn't I feel differently now? Come on, it's not true... How is it even possible?' She fully expected them to break out in laughter at any second, telling her that it was all a joke, but nobody did.

It was Elisedd who answered, as he walked over to her. 'Let me introduce myself, I am Elisedd Knight, your great grandfather.'

Rowanne looked up at him in surprise, and turned to look at Lillian behind him. 'Lillian, what's going on here?' she demanded angrily, feeling out of her depth, as if she were losing control of her emotions.

Lillian came to her side. 'It's true,' she replied. Looking at her mother, she continued, 'Seventy years ago, Elisedd and I had a child... We knew we could not keep her, so I travelled to Earth and left her in the care of Elisedd's family. I left strict instructions with them that the truth be hidden, as much for her safety as for theirs.'

'Wait, you said Knight,' she looked at Elisedd, 'are you by any chance referring to my grandmother Angelique?' asked Rowanne.

'Elisedd didn't know where I hid our baby. I didn't tell him, to keep her safe. Trust me, when I say that the hardest thing for any parent is saying goodbye to their child, knowing they'll never see them again in their lifetime...' said Lillian, as tears welled up in her eyes once more.

Rowanne held Lillian's hand comfortingly, 'You know, we have to tell my grandmother the truth. She thinks of you both,' she said, turning to look at Elisedd.

'You can rest assured that we will finally have a long overdue family reunion,' replied Elisedd, as his eyes glistened with tears.

'I think that perhaps it would be better if I prepare her for the news, and I'm not sure how she will take it...' said Rowanne, as she contemplated the best approach. 'I can't believe that you are my great grandfather,' said Rowanne to Elisedd. She could see the resemblance in the striking green eyes, and in the contours of his face. She'd ask him to share his story with her one day, so that she could finally learn more about the time he had spent in Demon World.

'I look forward to getting to know you as well,' said Elisedd kindly, still unable to take in the fact that he had descendents. He had much to learn of this new world; a lot had changed outside of the death chamber he'd inhabited. After all, time didn't stop for anyone.

'Great Grandfather Elisedd, may I introduce you to my cousin, Amanda Knight or Eghan as she is known,' said Rowanne, as she gestured for Amanda to come forward.

Amanda strode forward confidently, 'Hello, Great-Grand-Uncle, it's nice to meet the man behind the picture!' she smiled warmly at him, shaking his hand.

'Don't tell me I've been relegated to a spot on the infamous hall of ancestors,' he said amused. He wondered how they'd receive him in the flesh.

'I can't wait for you to meet them, it's going to be priceless,' she said. Leaning towards them, she whispered so that only Elisedd and Lillian would hear, 'He kept a picture of you, hidden all these years. Make of that what you will...' and gestured discreetly at Driskell.

They both looked at her sceptically; they would need time to think it over. They could not quite bring themselves to trust Driskell yet, understandably. They would need to go through their memories to sort out what was real from the illusions that Evelyn had planted in their minds.

Driskell looked suspiciously at Amanda's back, and wondered, *What on Demon World could she be up to now...* Did he trust her...? How much did he really know about her?

So, how does it feel to be an immortal? asked Alexander in Rowanne's mind.

I'm trying not to think about it. Give me a century or two! replied Rowanne. She had not brushed the issue aside, it was just that she was feeling overwhelmed with everything she was learning.

No wonder she had felt such a strong connection with Lillian; turns out, the annoying spirit was her great grandmother! It must have been the work of the pendant that had belonged to Lillian. A family heirloom passed down to each daughter when she turned eighteen. Lillian had left it in the care of Grandmother Angelique, who had then passed it down to Rowanne on her birthday.

It crossed Rowanne's mind that the pendant must have housed Lillian's soul all this time. When she had died the pendant had released Lillian's soul into her body, after she had been converted into a demon. *No wonder the pendant chose me as the most suitable guardian to entrust Lillian's soul to.* The amethyst pendant around her neck was as mysterious as

it was daunting. She wondered again about its origin and age...
I should give it back to Lillian, she thought determinedly.

No, Rowanne, don't you see, it's yours. You think your grandmother gave it to you because it was tradition, whereas in actual fact, she must have felt the crystal calling to her for a new owner. Don't you see, it chose you, said Lillian emphatically.

Chose me? thought Rowanne. She had always suspected that the crystal pendant had a mind of its own, but it was unnerving to have her suspicions confirmed. *I wonder how long it will decide to be in my company...*

When you have a child, and if it's a girl, then... laughed Lillian, as she felt Rowanne's discomfort.

Lillian, I know it's always passed down the female line, but sometimes even traditions may need to be changed, said Rowanne politely, as she wondered why a male could not also be worthy of it. Perhaps, it would choose a boy next time, she would leave it up to the crystal...

'Rowanne, are you alright? You seem to be burning up,' said Alexander with concern.

Rowanne felt deeply mortified, *Why did he have to be the one to ask?!* She looked sharply at Lillian, who had a sudden bout of uncontrollable coughing. Rowanne glared at her, certain she was trying to suppress her mirth.

Alexander looked between the two women, and wisely sat back; he had no intention to get involved in their business.

'And another thing,' said Rowanne, 'how can I possibly be the next heir?' Everyone turned in her direction, looking solemn.

'I'm no longer, automatically the next heir anymore. Lillian, you will take the crown. Then naturally in the future, Rowanne, it will be you who ascends to our throne,' answered Alexander.

'How do *you* feel about that?' Rowanne asked Alexander.

'I'm not sure,' he answered honestly. 'I have been trained from birth for this day, as have all the children who are potential heirs in the First Families. However, I can confidently say that with proper training, you will make a good leader. It's time we had a regent who can walk between both worlds, and you will bring your knowledge and experience of Earth, whilst being immersed in Demon World's various laws and customs,' he finished, smiling at Rowanne.

'I'm not sure if I'm ready to be a leader; to give up everything I've known so easily, to leave my home, and live here permanently...' Rowanne admitted, worried at the daunting challenge. *Right at this moment, I'm not ready.* She'd need time — a lot of it — to come to terms with her new life...

Lillian hugged her, 'Don't worry, Rowanne, take as long as you need to. I'm sorry I concealed so much from you. But don't forget, you are not alone in this, just look around you, this room is filled with people who want to help you,' though she looked dubiously at Driskell.

'Maybe even Mr Driskell. After all, he did help Amanda and me. I think we misjudged him to a degree,' said Rowanne.

'Thank you, for your mild consideration,' said Driskell, less than pleased to be included in the group before him.

'She's right, you're lucky we are even thinking of you at all. You helped us, but you also put us through hell...' said Amanda brusquely, with a piercing look.

Driskell held up his hands to ward off her hostility, thereby further antagonising her. It could not be helped, really; it amused him too much. He noticed Alexander's measured look, as he approached him.

'You never intended to hand Rowanne in, did you?' Alexander made it more of a statement than a question.

Driskell spread his hands enigmatically while giving Alexander an eloquent look, his mouth curving up into a sly smile.

Alexander wanted to wipe the smirk of his pretentious face; he was sure the fool had lived up to his reputation, but what a clever ruse.

Driskell leaned towards him and whispered, 'I find it's best to give people what they want... You cannot prove either way that I have not condemned a single soul, now can you?' he asked Alexander dangerously.

Alexander wanted desperately to believe in his old friend, but he was not completely naive either - he would keep his friend close.

Driskell sat back, just as Amanda joined him, choosing to sit next to him this time. He raised an eyebrow at her, as if to ask, *Are you sure, this is where you belong?*

Amanda looked at him perceptively with a wicked smile, 'I'm *choosing* to put up with you, strictly out of necessity of course, and only for the time being.'

'Am I right in presuming this is for Rowanne's benefit?' asked Driskell wryly.

'Naturally,' she replied pleasantly.

'What happens now?' asked Rowanne. She felt tired, but knew that her life no longer solely belonged to her.

'Security measures are going to have to be put in place, you cannot simply return to your home, Rowanne. I'm sorry to say you will have to stay in a safe house for now. You must cooperate, along with the rest of us with the Noble Court, while they assess each of our eligibility to the throne, as well as the right to stay in Demon World,' said Lillian.

'It's going to be a long process, right?' asked Rowanne wearily.

'I'm afraid so,' replied Alexander. 'And if you wouldn't mind, then I'd be pleased if you chose to stay with me while we try to straighten things out.'

Rowanne's cheeks coloured faintly - all the more noticeable with her porcelain complexion - and to compound the situation, everyone's eyes were now trained on her as they eagerly awaited her reply. She gave it some consideration, before asking, 'What about my grandparents? Perhaps, I could stay with them for a while. And I think it would be best if you, Lillian, along with Great Grandfather and Lady Enid, eventually join me there, after I've laid the groundwork of course,' finished Rowanne.

She smiled timidly at Alexander, as she said in his mind, *I am sorry, but I really think it's best for now that I help Grandmother Angelique. She needs me more at this time. Not to mention the fact that I have no idea what I will be able to tell my parents — they're human. Well, the last time I checked anyway.*

Alexander's dark sapphire eyes looked deeply into Rowanne's, as he replied with a hint of amusement, *I am a patient man... eventually you'll need someone to train you, and I could be that man*, he said benevolently.

I'm not too sure about that, I think Kieran might be a more appropriate choice... said Rowanne subtly, as his gaze bore into her. She could practically hear the wheels turning in his mind; he was up to something, she was sure of it. He would make it known in his own good time.

You know I will, replied Alexander innocently.

Rowanne ignored him and his childish threats.

However, he was unrepentant and diligent, as he continued, *It's a promise, and I do not make them lightly. I see them through...* said Alexander, leaving it up to her to interpret as she wished.

Rowanne tore her gaze away, 'One other thing, what am I going to do with these?' she asked, pointing to her wings. She could not fathom a life with them; they were as cumbersome as they were beautiful.

'I think Alexander can help you with that dilemma,' replied Lillian brightly, much to Rowanne's displeasure.

'I'm going,' said Driskell, and when no one stopped him, he got up and walked out of the room.

'Wait for me, you can drop me off,' called Amanda. 'After all, not all of us are immortal, and some of us can't portal, either,' she said wryly to the room. 'Rowanne, I'll talk to the family, as well as set a date for all of you to come over once this settles down,' she hugged her cousin, and took her leave of everyone.

'I'll talk to you soon, my dear,' said Elisedd, patting her on the shoulder.

Amanda walked out, closing the door behind her. Driskell was leaning against the wall waiting for her.

'Let's go,' he said.

He looked brooding; this she could deal with. At least he was not in one of his funny moods.

'Come here,' he said innocently, but his eyes lit up as she stepped into his arms. 'Hold on,' he was highly amused when she put her arms around his waist.

'Just don't say anything. I'm dead tired after the day I've had.' Amanda closed her eyes; she hated this method of travelling, it made her feel nauseous. Curiously she heard his heart beating fast as she leaned against him.

Driskell wisely kept quiet and opened a portal, and a moment later it closed after them.

The door opened and Rowanne stepped through with Alexander, who closed it behind them.

'I know there is still a lot to discuss, but we do have time on our hands now, it can wait for another day,' said Rowanne, yawning, and covering her mouth hastily.

'I want to take you somewhere,' he said mysteriously.

'Alexander, you promised to help me with these, and then just point me to any empty room so I can pass out!' said Rowanne.

'This won't take long, demon's honour,' he said solemnly.

Rowanne groaned in frustration as he grabbed her hand and led her down the corridor, eventually stopping by a door. He opened it to reveal a staircase that led up, and she trudged up, barely able to walk. He opened another door at the top, and suddenly she felt the cold night air drift in, instantly waking her up.

'Where in the world are you taking me now?' asked Rowanne, as her teeth chattered.

'Live a little,' he replied. 'Sorry, probably the wrong thing to say in your case,' he added unrepentantly.

Rowanne responded by gathering a handful of snow off the ground, and expertly wielding it so that it connected with his thick head. She smiled broadly, feeling immeasurably satisfied with the sound it made on impact.

Alexander stalked over to her with a less than pleased expression and a dangerous look in his eyes. He held onto her arms, and let his power flow over the both of them. He watched Rowanne's eyes grow luminous as her own power responded, mirroring him; though unconsciously. He focused and lifted them both off the ground as his wings spread out beautifully behind him.

Rowanne stifled a scream as she rose, leaving solid ground far below, and felt the power surge within her. She dug into Alexander's arms as panic took hold.

'Just breathe, Rowanne, that way you can enjoy this. Think of your wings as a precious gift,' his eyes captured her gaze.

She tried to still her chaotic mind, and as she did so, gradually she began to notice the finer details around her that she had missed, like the fact that it was snowing. She took the time to actually appreciate the intricacy and beauty of the snowflakes that gently fell on them. *How could something so beautiful have so short a span of existence...* she wondered. She looked thoughtfully at Alexander; it was thanks to him that she could view the world in ways she could never have imagined. Her vision was sharper and a hundred times better than what it had been when she had been a human.

'Should I be worried?' he asked, feigning terror.

Rowanne's hair and eyelashes were covered in snow. 'Not yet, but you should be...' she replied.

Alexander spun her around, and then hovered high above the castle. 'This is now all yours, Rowanne,' he said, encompassing the surrounding area.

Rowanne could see as far afield to the forest where they had portalled into. It looked beautiful, the trees covered in a sea of white. She looked down at the castle, and only now realised how large an area it covered. It began to dawn on her the enormity of what she would one day be taking on. Expected to take on; there was no choice now, after all.

Suddenly she felt overwhelmed by it all, and her natural instinct was to reach for Alexander as she rested her head on his chest. He gently descended with her, his arms wrapped around her.

'Thank you,' she said, as she opened her eyes and stepped out of his arms. 'Now, how do I deal with these?' pointing to her wings.

Alexander smiled unrepentantly at her - she'd definitely come to love flying, he was sure of it. Stepping back, he concentrated and his wings simply vanished.

'How did you do that?' asked Rowanne, as she walked behind him, looking at his back. She could not see any noticeable tear in his clothes. Where did they go? she wondered, and started to examine his back with her hands.

'Rowanne, what are you doing?' asked Alexander amused.

Having given up, she replied, 'I was trying to ascertain where your wings disappeared to.'

'Just hold the intention in your mind that you want them to retract, and they will. They will become a part of you once more, and will come out when you have need of them,' said Alexander patiently.

'But what happens to them when they disappear?' she asked.

'They have always been there, I suspect, long before you became a demon. I don't think you were entirely human to begin with...' he said contemplatively. 'You naturally have a lot of power within you, and they sleep within that realm. You effectively shape them, and give them life.'

Rowanne considered Alexander's words. 'The sooner I talk to my grandmother's family, the sooner I'll get the answers to the angel blood within us,' said Rowanne.

'With your permission, I would like to meet them?' asked Alexander, and held his breath in anticipation of her response.

'That's a given,' she replied, amused that he would think otherwise.

Alexander held her hands and looked at her pointedly, 'Now calm your breathing and centre yourself. That's it,' he said, as Rowanne followed his instructions.

Looking into his eyes brought a feeling of peace as her eyes changed to violet. She focused on what she wanted, and felt the magic surround her as her wings began to slowly fade away.

Rowanne opened her eyes, and looked at him jubilantly. 'They're gone!' she said, laughing and grabbing his hands, and added, 'We did it!'

'Was there ever any doubt?' he asked, raising an eyebrow as his mouth curved into a smile. 'Now let's get off here,' he tugged on Rowanne's hands, causing her to fall against him. She was about to protest as he held her close, when suddenly a portal opened. 'I just thought you might want to go home,' he said softly.

'But what about Lady Enid and Lillian? They were against the idea.'

'Rowanne, as the future Queen, I think you can afford to break a rule or two. Besides, they said you had to have security. I fit the role perfectly, do you not agree?' he smiled wickedly as his eyes glinted darkly.

Before she could answer, he pulled her into the portal, her eyes sparkling furiously.

Rowanne accepted reluctantly, 'You are to drop me off, and then be on your way!' she said sternly.

'Of course, I didn't think otherwise...' he said magnanimously.

The portal closed with a finality, and Alexander's expression spoke so eloquently that she closed her eyes to shut him out; it was a shame she could not do the same with his laughter.

EPILOGUE

It had been five months, since the night that Rowanne had discovered who she was, and who she would eventually become...

A lot had happened since then. Rowanne had sold her apartment, and had moved in with her grandparents. The day Alexander dropped her off at their home, well to say it was emotional was an understatement. She recounted to them of the events that had transpired in Demon World. Grandfather Hou and Grandmother Angelique had been furious to have been left out of the loop. Rowanne had promised on pain of death to include them in all future endeavours that she might pursue.

Grandmother Angelique would need time to come to terms with the truth; understandably she had been shocked by all that she had learned, so much so that Rowanne had been worried for her health.

However, she had not seen the point in delaying any further, having waited her whole life to meet her parents.

Lillian and Elisedd had come by themselves, while Lady Enid had stayed back to help the Nobles investigate her family. Rowanne had decided to stay away, and had given them time to get to know each other again. Grandmother Angelique had only been a baby when they had left her, so she had never really had the opportunity to form a bond with them; after all, it's hard to accept two strangers as your parents. However, as Great Grandfather Elisedd had kept pointing out to Rowanne, they have now got time.

However, Grandmother Angelique had chosen at present not to explore the angel blood within her. When Rowanne had asked her if she would ever consider immortality, her reply had been that it was something that she and Grandfather Hou had decided against; they wanted to live a human span of time, or however long the demon blood naturally extended their life to.

This had not been received well by Lillian or Elisedd, who thought they would have a long time to get to know their daughter. Grandmother Angelique had slowly built a relationship with them over the past couple of months, and had become quite fond of them. She had learnt so much about their life in so short a period of time.

Grandmother Angelique had also turned down Lady Enid's invitation to live in the palace in Demon World. She loved her home, and would not trade it in for the world. Furthermore, all her friends and acquaintances were on Earth. It was the world in which she had grown up in, the place she was most happiest and comfortable — in short, the place she called home!

Although, Grandmother Angelique had agreed to visit between both worlds, in order to form a relationship with her grandmother Enid; that had been another emotional rollercoaster for both women. Especially when Lillian introduced her daughter, Angelique, to Lady Enid. It goes without saying they had a lot to catch up on. Grandmother Angelique had enlightened Lady Enid to the wonders of Earth, but Rowanne could tell that visiting Earth had not really been her cup of tea — it had always felt a bit alien to her!

Rowanne had been called back to Demon World numerous times in the past couple of months, and had undergone tests along with Elisedd and Lillian, and lastly Alexander. The tests had gone well, and they had not been able to discredit the Morning Star Clan.

Rowanne found that the process had pushed her further into the world of demon politics, and consequently she had learned so much, but it would inevitably be an ongoing process. The demon blood had enabled her to process information at an incredible rate, even more so than when she had been human.

Rowanne knew the investigation would soon be over, but another had opened: investigating demons with angel blood and especially looking into the origins of this. It was a subject which had long been debated amongst the demons, not to mention, the legends and myths surrounding it.

Until that moment in the hall, when they had been presented with three demon-angels, the demons had not quite believed that such a thing was possible, especially in their world. Rowanne was interested herself, but she had not yet visited her grandmother's family, but she hoped to visit them soon. She had thought that they might be able to provide her with the answers she had been searching for.

Some of the Noble Families had suggested talking to the demons in Prima Stella: the oldest and highest court in Demon World. Truth be told, Rowanne had been reluctant to go there, even Lady Enid and Lillian had felt the same. Her grandfather Hou had suggested to her that it could in all likelihood be a suicide mission.

What exactly is Prima Stella, and who is really in charge of it? All Rowanne had been told was that it was the abode of the ancient demons. God alone knows how old they must be... It had brought back to mind a dream she had of an ancient place, forged in blood and fire... Did she really want to explore further? Would she even have a choice in the end?

After all, the time would come one day when Rowanne would have to rule Demon World. Alexander had often been found by her side in the past couple of months, sharing his knowledge with her. It had been a long process, and she still had a long way to go before she was ready.

Rowanne had been training to fight, but so far she had fallen well below par. She had found it heartening that Great Grandfather Elisedd had decided to help her, for they had both been in the same boat. Kieran and Alexander had both readily agreed to become their teachers.

Rowanne thought that Alexander had taken a twisted pleasure in teaching her; he had seemed to be in equal parts highly amused and incensed at her slow progress. She had reminded him that she had never been a trained fighter, and had never wielded a weapon in her life. His less than satisfactory reply had been that she needed to learn to defend herself before even attempting to use a weapon, as she might accidentally hurt herself! She had found it unbelievable, his arrogance had not reduced; on the contrary, he had become more annoying than ever.

Grandfather Hou had invited Rowanne to travel with him to China, to meet his family. She had been hoping to stay there awhile, and perhaps get him to train her in military strategy, as well as in different fighting styles. Then the next time she met Alexander, he would not be so self assured, especially when he would be looking up at her from the floor!

Driskell had been a tremendous help over the last couple of months by speaking with the Nobles on Rowanne's behalf. He was still well respected within Demon World, and continued to hold the position of Enforcer. He had managed to round up half of the demons involved with Evelyn; the others were still on the run.

Evelyn had received a severe punishment: life in imprisonment, which had been passed by the Noble Court. Lillian and Lady Enid had decided against sending her to Prima Stella, though, they were well within their rights to do so. They had known that the Adara Clan would have opposed the decision, and consequently, would in all likelihood have incited the other First Families into civil war against the Queen.

It goes without saying that not everyone had been pleased to have Lillian back; the demons were more enraged that Rowanne would become their future Queen after Lillian. It would take a lot for Rowanne to win any supporters at all; hence, security around her had been tightened.

The Queen had assigned a team of elite royal guards to Rowanne's security, in fact Kieran had offered to be head of the team, which she had reluctantly accepted, because of Alexander. He had said that it was best that she have people that she could trust around her. She had not liked the idea of anyone endangering themselves on her behalf, but as she was well aware, and Lillian had kept pointing out, these were volatile and uncertain times in the history of Demon World.

Evelyn had pointedly refused to tell anyone of what happened to Thomas; there had been no news of him from Earth, either. The demons working for Evelyn had remained loyal to her, and had kept quiet. Every day that had passed without any new leads to his whereabouts had been disheartening, and Rowanne had wondered if she would ever be able to give him the justice he deserved. But with Driskell working on the case, who knows what he may uncover. After all, he is called the Enforcer to the Noble Court, for a reason.

Evelyn had been guarded around the clock, as she had been classed as highly dangerous. Her cell had been shielded, so that she would not be able to use her abilities. Rowanne along with her family could attest to what happened when that psychotic woman had been free... She had heard troubling reports of her gaining support amongst the demons, especially those in favour of getting rid of humans and half demons.

Driskell had been working with Amanda covertly amongst the demons to find support for Rowanne from the half demons, and those outside of the Noble Clans. Unsurprisingly there were a lot of demons who had been less than satisfied with the way Demon World had been run: especially as they had been treated as second class citizens, and therefore considered beneath the notice of those higher up. Rowanne knew that all of them had a lot of ground work to do.

This had also been the reason why she had sadly decided to give up on her dream career. Grandmother Angelique had been against her decision, and had urged her to reconsider, reminding her of the hard work she had put in to get to the top in the first place.

Rowanne knew deep down, that she had made the right decision. As much as she had loved her job, she had not been completely content, if she were being honest. She had always felt that there could be something else out there for her. She had got what she had wanted: Demon World had found her, after all.

Rowanne would look at this period in her life as a chance to do something really meaningful, and to learn from the sacrifices her family had made. Whether Demon World wanted her or not, she was here to stay, and hopefully be of some service to it someday.

It was June 1st 2018 and Rowanne had the honour of attending Lillian and Elisedd's wedding - they wanted to make it official before the Nobles. Especially as, in December, Lady Enid planned to finally pass the crown to her daughter Lillian. She decided it should happen as soon as possible considering the current unstable climate of Demon World politics.

Lillian as Queen would most assuredly instil fear into the Nobles; she survived Prima Stella, after all, and this will ultimately strengthen her rule. The demons would be in for a rude awakening, and would rue the day that Lady Enid stepped down as their ruler, but the regency moved forward — and soon a new era would begin.

Rowanne heard knocking on her bedroom door. 'I'm coming, just give me a few more minutes.'

'It's not even your wedding, and you have been in there almost an hour. I think it's only right I come in there and help you,' said Alexander in his most pious voice, as he leaned against the other side of the door.

I'm sure you would love to, thought Rowanne. 'I can manage *alone*,' she replied pleasantly.

She heard Alexander lament as he walked away. She looked at herself in the black mahogany mirror - it was exactly the same as the one she had hanging in her room back at her grandparents home, with demons and angels carved into a frozen dance at its edge. Thankfully her eyes had returned to their normal green; she had not recognised herself with violet eyes, and her hair too had returned to its native deep brown. Her hair was braided into a series of elegant French braids that were pinned back into a messy side bun, and Lillian had insisted on the sparkling hair pins haphazardly placed to complete the look. Here was a bride who was not frightened of being upstaged. She had insisted that now Rowanne was a part of the royal family, she would have to dress the part, if only to appease the Nobles. The Morning Star Clan would appear their brightest tonight in all of their finest regalia; after all, they were making a statement.

Rowanne finished applying her soft summer makeup expertly, but her nerves on the other hand were in a knot for some inexplicable reason. Alexander was right, it was not even her wedding, so why did she feel on edge? Taking a deep breath, she opened the door and stepped out.

Alexander's eyes widened as Rowanne stood before him. He admired her beautiful emerald green dress which only served to complement her deep smouldering eyes that were currently trained on him. His eyes dropped to her delicate rosy lips as they curved into a tentative smile.

She had seen Alexander dressed smartly before, so why should the sight of him in a black tuxedo unnerve her now... He caught her lingering gaze, but try as she might, she could not avert her eyes from his, it was proving too difficult.

'Rowanne,' he said, and taking hold of her hand, he twirled her around, so he could admire her, before finally bringing her to a stop before him. 'You look-' and leaning in close, he watched her eyes widen in surprise, as he whispered softly, 'beautiful. I am enchanted by you.' He smirked, as she took a step back.

'*Que ferais-je sans toi?*'[1] she asked, in a daze. Sometimes it was easier to voice your feelings in another language.

Alexander took a step towards her, not liking the distance between them, especially after that declaration/question! 'You don't have to... *Je resterai à jamais à vos côtés,*'[2] he replied, with sincerity.

'Wait... No. I was just remembering the lines to a song. By the way you don't look half bad in that suit,' she added hastily, trying to distract him as her cheeks flamed. The spell was well and truly broken. *What was I thinking... You look decent, really? That's the best I could come up with.* Her traitorous mind mocked her with a Emily Dickinson quote, *"The heart wants what it wants-"*

"...Or else it does not care," supplied Alexander helpfully, and felt her cringe at him having heard her innermost thoughts.

Alexander laughed deeply with a satisfied expression. 'Quite... Now it's really time we head down.'

Rowanne had one of her déjà-vu moments: that laughter, she had heard it before... at The Caelum restaurant. *Was Alexander there that day?* She lost the thread of thought, but if

1   French for 'What will I do without you?'

2   French for 'I will stay by your side forever.'

she was brave, then one day she would have a long chat with the annoyingly smug man beside her.

She was feeling nonplussed but determinedly took the arm he proffered. Together they made their way outside, and descended the grand staircase which was strewn with white rose petals that delicately scented the air. Rowanne looked up at the velvet black sky as the stars winked coldly back.

Alexander and Rowanne observed the extra security that was now in place around the palace. 'I suppose it has to be this way...' said Rowanne, as they made their way along the courtyard towards the platform.

Alexander walked along the white carpet, wary of the demon guests that lined the route on either side; the palace was full of them. 'We don't know when Evelyn's supporters will make their move, it pays to be cautious.' He squeezed her arm tenderly.

Rowanne finally made it onto the platform, and along with Alexander, waited for Lillian's arrival. She politely acknowledged the royal family. *My family...* she thought, though she had not had the opportunity yet to meet them all. 'Is that Lillian's father over there beside Lady Enid?' whispered Rowanne to Alexander.

Alexander bent his head close to Rowanne, and whispered in her ear, 'Yes. He's been away for the last couple of months. He doesn't look too pleased...'

Rowanne did not quite trust Lillian's father, who wore a disgusted expression as he looked in their direction. Despite his contempt, she smiled amiably but her eyes widened, as he was about to walk towards her, only Lady Enid's restraining hand on his arm stopping him.

'Don't mind him. Anyway there's two of us he'll have to deal with,' said Alexander boldly, as he gave Lillian's father a calculated look; there was the promise of retribution in his eyes, should he even consider harming Rowanne.

Finally Lillian arrived, and ascended the stairs to the platform, accompanied by Elisedd. Rowanne's heart melted at the sight of them as they looked at each other with a love so profound.

Lady Enid's eyes welled up unexpectedly and her husband lovingly dabbed at them with a handkerchief. 'I am a husband as well as a ruler,' he whispered for her ears only, before once more resuming the stern facade that his people had come to expect from him.

Rowanne held onto Alexander's hand instinctively, lost as she was in the ceremony before her. She watched Lillian exchange vows with Elisedd; they looked so happy and content. They had literally fought death to reach this point.

They exchanged rings, and Lillian's eyes sparkled as Elisedd placed the ring on her finger.

Elisedd looked intensely into Lillian's eyes as he said his vows, 'You are my first, my last and my only love, and at long last I get to spend the rest of my existence with you, where I have always belonged.'

'I choose to spend my life with you, my beloved. My best friend, my husband. And it will damn well be for a long time,' stated Lillian, and began to laugh just as Elisedd bent his head towards her and stole a kiss. She closed her eyes as she put her arms around his neck, blissfully lost within the moment.

Finally they were announced as husband and wife, and everybody applauded the happy couple, and their future Queen. Rowanne looked out at the sea of demons. How many of them were actually happy... she wondered. She was broken out of her reverie by Alexander nudging her in the side.

She made her way with Alexander over to the reception area, and observed that the castle was indeed colossal. The whole of the wedding was held outside, and thankfully the weather was beautiful with a warm breeze in the air.

They made their way to the table reserved for the royal family, and took their seats. They watched Elisedd and Lillian as they cut into the wedding cake with members of the family feeding them. Finally the moment had come for the first dance. Rowanne contentedly watched Lillian and Elisedd as they danced to a slow waltz. The royal orchestra was magnificent, observed Rowanne, as they played beautifully; angelically some might say, even though they were demons.

Elisedd and Lillian seemed to be lost in each other, oblivious to the other demons that had begun to join them on the dance floor. Lillian laughed as Elisedd spun her around.

Rowanne felt the heat from the beautiful torches that lined the edge of the dance floor. She felt someone's eyes on her, and turned to find Alexander gazing at her, the fire reflected in his eyes that smouldered only for her...

Rowanne was about to turn her head away when Alexander gently held her hand, and led her to the dance floor. 'Alexander, I think I've forgotten how to dance.' She was definitely out of her comfort zone here, in more ways than one...

'Just follow my lead,' he whispered close to her, before straightening up and putting his arm around her waist, encasing her hand within his own.

Rowanne swallowed her nerves, and placed her free hand on his shoulder. She shut her eyes as Alexander began to lead her into a slow dance.

'Rowanne, this might be infinitely more enjoyable if you actually open your eyes,' said Alexander, admiring the fact that she could actually dance with her eyes closed.

Rowanne's eyes snapped open the moment she felt his hot breath on her face.

'There you are, don't hide those enticing eyes of yours,' *because, I plan on getting lost within them...* thought Alexander, as a deep crimson blush spread across Rowanne's cheeks.

She cringed, wishing she had not just read his mind. Alexander spun her to the edge of the dance floor where it was less crowded with people. The music changed to a beautifully haunting piece, and they slowed their pace.

Rowanne had her arms locked behind Alexander's neck as his hands rested on her waist. She was lost in her thoughts.

'What are you thinking about?' asked Alexander.

'I'm glad this evening has gone so well for Lillian. I was afraid the demons might try to sabotage it,' she replied.

'The palace has been fortified with a veritable army of elite royal guards. They would be foolish to attempt anything tonight,' said Alexander.

'Oh, she's finally arrived,' said Rowanne.

Alexander followed her line of sight, and spotted a less than pleased Driskell making his way over to them accompanied by Amanda, who also looked as if she would rather be anywhere else than here.

'I'm sorry that you couldn't be here for the wedding,' said Rowanne to Amanda, who had finally reached them.

'I knew it would be in the best interests of Lillian. She has had enough to face with trying to take her rightful place as Queen. The last thing she needed was for a half demon to attend her wedding, thereby further complicating matters,' said Amanda considerately.

'Lillian didn't actually say that, she wanted you up there with Rowanne!' said Driskell angrily on her behalf, knowing what it was like to be shunned aside, and looked down upon for not being a Noble belonging to the First Families.

Amanda held his hand reassuringly but could not help but frown at him. 'I told you that you should at least have been up there with the rest of the gang,' said Amanda.

'Anyway,' said Driskell moving on, 'we had a perfectly good vantage point.'

Alexander smiled ruefully at Driskell, who gave him a meaningful look of his own. They had spoken a lot over the past couple of months, each being pushed forward by Rowanne and Amanda respectively to resolve their differences.

'Are we ready to leave?' Amanda asked Rowanne and Alexander.

'Hey, you promised me one dance for not taking you to the wedding!' said Driskell unashamedly to Amanda's chagrin.

Alexander and Rowanne exchanged awkward but highly amused looks.

'We'll take our leave of the family, and meet you at the entrance,' said Alexander, as he hastily led Rowanne away from the less than happy pair.

Amanda petulantly allowed Driskell to pull her close for a dance. She thought she was safe as it was a waltz, but to her utter dismay it ended, and the tango took its place...

'You've got to be kidding me!' she said to Driskell, her blue eyes shooting sparks.

Driskell's eyes gazed full of meaning into hers, 'Amanda, are you under the illusion that *I* actually planned this? By the way, I like your dress,' his eyes swept over her short, royal red taffeta dress.

'Thanks,' she said suspiciously.

Driskell admired the way she had pinned her hair up for the wedding, with loose curls framing her face. He absentmindedly tucked an errant strand behind her ear, but not to her amusement.

'Are you sure it's a good idea to dance in front of *them*?' she asked, inclining her head at the Nobles.

A wicked look came into Driskell's eyes as his mouth curved up into a broad smile. 'Let's not disappoint them...' he replied enigmatically.

Taking her hand, he led her to the centre of the dance floor, and briefly paused to bow deeply to Lillian and Elisedd, who were now seated at the royal table.

Lillian gave him a knowing look, and laughed when Driskell winked at her; there was the old friend she had known...

'You really have a death wish, you know that right?' asked Amanda, as she felt the full weight of a hundred eyes centred on them. She noticed the centre of the dance floor clear as the Nobles edged away from them, and none too subtly, either. This only served to intensify her resolve. 'I'm with you. Let's give them a performance they're unlikely to forget,' she said, in a feisty mood, much to his delight.

Amanda placed her left hand lightly behind Driskell's shoulder and gave him her right hand. His arm went around her back as he placed his hand on her spine just below the shoulder blades, bringing them closer together. They exchanged intense looks as Driskell asked, *Do you trust me enough to give into me for this one dance?*

Amanda was a control freak, she did not like the feeling of handing over control to another.

The word you're looking for is trust. I swear, you will not regret it. Just entrust yourself into my care, said Driskell.

I... trust you, said Amanda. She could tell how much it meant to him, as he smiled at her; a genuine, honest smile.

Driskell took one step back with Amanda before stepping to the side, and then walked forwards two steps before gliding to the side. She followed his lead as he displaced her foot in a Sacada, and turned with him, moving her foot out of the way each time. They turned a few times before resuming their steps. He spun her out quickly before they embraced and glided to the side. They were caught up and consumed by the music as they continued to work their way around the now empty dance floor.

He paused and dramatically dipped her back, before pulling her up sharply, then walked her back slowly. She hooked her leg onto his as he held her close, their eyes locked as he quickly spun with her before coming to a stop.

They enjoyed the murderous glances occasionally thrown in their direction.

It's funny, thought Amanda, *but when I look at him, they all seem to fade into the background. There is only the two of us.* Driskell was so alive and exuberant with his fiery eyes. She never would have thought that he would be the type of man who would enjoy dancing.

On the contrary, I had yet to find the right partner, said Driskell, as Amanda looked at him archly.

Determined not to let him down, she matched him step for step as they intermittently quickened and slowed their pace.

'I didn't know you could dance,' said Driskell quietly.

'I'm just full of surprises. You'll discover more, if you plan on sticking around...' said Amanda mysteriously, as Driskell performed a Gancho; blocking her foot with his, and leaning her body back closer to him, she performed a series of quick sharp hooks and flicks, as their feet parried each other.

He smiled dangerously; he most definitely planned on 'sticking around,' as she so eloquently put it.

They finished with Driskell holding Amanda's weight as she leaned back into a dramatic pose. He pulled her back up and they bowed deeply to the royal couple before leaving the dance floor.

'Here they come now,' said Rowanne. 'Let's never tell them that we spied on their date. Sorry, I mean dance!'

'I never thought I'd see the day when *Driskell* would let loose,' mused Alexander.

'Shall we go?' asked Rowanne, trying to keep a straight face as Alexander nudged her in warning.

Amanda's cheeks were flushed. 'It's beginning to get cold out here, even your summers are just as unpredictable as ours back home.'

'Really? I think it's becoming rather warm...' said Driskell helpfully, as she gave him a despairing look. He found the whole situation entertaining.

Amanda watched Alexander opening a portal, and Rowanne waved at her before disappearing through. Now she was alone with Driskell. *Great, just my luck,* she thought resignedly.

Driskell opened a portal, and Amanda stepped through holding onto him. She would never get used to how claustrophobic it felt; it was such a small space, after all. The energy pulsed around them, and she watched the colours playing across Driskell's face.

Driskell gave her a brooding look, 'Are you sure it's alright for me to come with you? You can still reconsider...'

'No, it's fine. I told them you were coming, that I was bringing you with me,' she amended, giving him a slow smile.

'I'm sure they were delighted by that,' he said sardonically.

'Like you said, they've kept Rowanne and I in the dark for long enough, it's time they squirmed a bit.'

'Amanda, I think I've influenced you to your detriment.'

'Maybe... maybe not,' she replied, laughing.

The portal finally opened, and Amanda and Driskell stepped out. They spotted Alexander and Rowanne outside the house, waiting for them.

Amanda led them up the steps, and rang the doorbell that seemed to echo through the rather grand house. Just as the front door opened, she turned back to them, and said, 'Welcome to Knight Manor...'